Tiny Fractures

J. V. Reese

Artemis Publishing LLC
www.JVReeseAuthor.com

ISBN: 978-1-964739-01-4 (print)
ISBN: 978-1-964739-00-7 (e-book)

Cover, internal design, and formatting by Done-For-You Services

Editing and proofreading by Motif Edits – www.motifedits.com

Content Warning

This book is meant for mature audiences and contains content that may be triggering for some readers—including sex, alcohol, profanity, verbal and physical abuse, domestic and dating violence, as well as mentions of suicide.

If you or someone you know is contemplating suicide, please call or text the National Suicide Prevention Lifeline at 988 or go online to www.988lifeline.org.

If you're the victim of domestic or dating violence, please reach out to the National Domestic Violence Hotline at 1-800-799-SAFE (7233) or go online to www.thehotline.org.

For Thanos (not the finger-snap guy!)

breathe love into my lungs
let it take root
spreading through my veins
unhindered
until it suffocates the pain
until it consumes me
and everything that came before you

***

Saturday, April 17th

Cat

"Are you ready to hit the road, Kitty?" my mom asks. She stands in the doorway to my bedroom, leaning against the doorframe with a somber look on her face.

"I guess so," I sigh. I push myself off the edge of my bed, then take my backpack from the floor and sling it over my shoulder. I take a last look around the four walls of my small bedroom before I walk past my mom and meet my dad in the living room.

It's Saturday, which is normally my favorite day of the week. I would usually spend it with my best friend, Julie, especially when the weather is as perfect as it is today—cloudless, the temperatures in the mid-seventies, the sun shining and begging us to spend the day outside. But this isn't a normal Saturday. In fact, it's anything but normal. Today marks the beginning of a new life, a new me, as I prepare to leave the only home I've ever known to move from my small North

Carolina town—population just over 3,500—to a place that couldn't be more different: New York.

"Do you have everything you need?" my dad asks my mom and me, his voice thick. He's trying to be stoic, to act unaffected by the fact that his wife and his oldest daughter are leaving while he and my two younger siblings are staying behind, at least for now. I can tell this is as hard on him as it is on everyone else in my family, and guilt and shame once again wash through me. After all, I'm the reason my mom and I are making the ten-hour road trip to New York—where my parents are originally from—the reason why the last two months have been hell for my family, and I cannot begin to count the times I've wished I could go back in time and reverse every misstep that has led me to where I am today.

"Yes, I think we're all set," my mom tells my dad before she pulls first my little sister, Samantha, then my little brother, Benny, into her arms and then squeezes them. They're both teary-eyed, unwilling to let go of my mom, knowing it will be weeks—if not months—before they see her again. I feel ashamed for the millionth time.

"Kitty," my dad says, wrapping me into his arms. "Please be safe. Please," he urges. "I don't want—"

"I know, Dad," I say, my voice muffled as he holds me tightly against his chest. "I will, I promise."

I'm the oldest of three children, with a significant age gap between me and my two younger siblings. And I'm a daddy's girl. Always have been, spending the vast majority of my free time with my dad and Julie, going camping or fishing, playing T-ball—and, later, softball—and hanging out with him whenever he tinkered with his car.

I also think I'm what people would consider a "good girl," or maybe I'm no longer that? I don't know. Things kind of derailed a few months ago, and I guess I'm trying to find a way back to myself, to move past the shame, the embarrassment, the guilt. God, there is so much guilt.

"Do you have all your softball gear?" My dad releases me from his hold. "Because your new team is expecting you at practice on Monday."

"Yep, got it," I say, even though I'm nervous about a new school and playing on a new team in a city I've only ever visited on a random weekend or during school breaks to spend time with my grandparents.

"Okay," my dad says with a sigh. "Call me when you guys get there," he tells my mom, then kisses her deeply.

I stoop to hug my little sister and brother.

The decision for my mom and me to just up and move was a spur-of-the-moment idea by my parents, who only told me about the plan a week ago. I was upset and anxious, angry and confused. I didn't want to leave my home, my best friend, my family. I wanted to stay here. After all, I've never known anything different than my small bedroom with its large windows and baby blue curtains, the creaky hardwood in our kitchen, the tiny bathroom with its black-and-white checkered tile, and our beautiful front yard with the giant oak tree that provides ample shade during the summer months to just sit and read.

Ultimately, I knew it was the right decision because life here had become unbearable for me. Leaving North Carolina is supposed to give me a fresh start, and when I walk out of the house and climb into my mom's car—silently wondering if it will actually make the five-hundred-mile journey since she bought it used when I was only two—I promise to leave the old Cat behind.

I vow not to make the same mistakes I made these last six months that have resulted in so much stress and sacrifice for my family.

Ronan

Thirty minutes after arriving at Shane's beach house, I'm already three shots of tequila deep. It courses through my veins and steadily makes its way to my head.

It's pretty great, you know—that feeling when your thoughts start to blur. Nothing feels quite as sharp as when you're sober. Everything is just sort of *shrug shoulders*, I guess. But that was hours ago. As much as I enjoy a good buzz, I hate getting blackout drunk. Always have. I hate the idea of not being in control, especially of my own body. I like the lowered inhibition, sure, the way I'm more relaxed, but anything beyond that isn't up my alley. Today was a shit day, though, and I was so on edge when I finally got to Shane's after escaping my own home that the first thing I did when I arrived was throw back two shots, no chaser.

It's eleven o'clock, and I've been at Shane's for the past five hours, enjoying the mild spring night. Mid-April in New York City is hit or miss. Sometimes the weather is positively atrocious; other days, like today, it's perfect.

"Hey, Ran," Shane calls to me as he makes his way onto the large wraparound deck.

It's Shane's eighteenth birthday tomorrow, which, in typical Shane fashion, warrants an outrageous party with two hundred people—some of whom I know, most of whom I don't—at the beach house Shane's mom calls home.

That's not to say that Shane needs an excuse to throw epic parties. In fact, he regularly makes use of the beach house—and his mom's frequent absences—to get as much booze as he can conjure up and allow hundreds of people to have a great fucking time.

Not every weekend is a party, though. Most of the time it's just Shane, me, and our close group of friends, which consists of my brother Steve; his girlfriend, Vada; Vada's twin brother Zack—who also happens to be my brother's best friend—Zack's girlfriend Summer; and Shane's girlfriend, Tori. Sometimes we're joined by Summer's best friend Cheyenne, and Drew, the goalie of the varsity hockey team Shane, Steve, and I play on.

"What?" I say, nodding my head in Shane's direction. I'm lounging on the large rattan outdoor sectional sofa with one leg hitched up. My brother sits on the other end of the sofa, his girlfriend Vada's head in his lap while she chats with Tori and Summer. Zack is busy fiddling with his camera, a near-permanent extension of his body these past few years. He's always filming. *Always.*

"Did you see that petite brunette standing by the kitchen counter?" Shane asks me. He sits down next to Tori, draping his arm around her and pulling her toward him. "The one with the really nice... shirt," he says, a big fucking grin on his face.

Tori raises her eyebrows at him. "Boobs. You mean really nice boobs," she says, rolling her eyes.

"Whatever," Shane chuckles. "But, yeah, did you see her?"

"I don't know, maybe." I shrug. "Why?"

"Because I just overheard her telling her friend how hot you are," Shane says, still grinning at me. Shane has always been the best wingman. I'm the only one in our group of seven who isn't in a relationship.

"Oh yeah?" I look past Shane through the wall-to-ceiling glass windows that give a perfect view of the home's interior. It's huge—the driveway alone screams *money*, and Shane's family definitely has that. Though Shane is about as down-to-earth and unimpressed by his parents' money as they come; he understands full well that his parents worked hard to get where they are, that everything was earned and nothing was given.

A few people mingle in the modern, all-white, stainless-steel kitchen, and I spot the girl Shane's talking about.

"Yeah. Heads-up, though: her friend goes to school with us and was trying to tell her that you're a—and I quote—'man whore.'" Shane laughs. "She told her friend that you don't do girlfriends, only hookups. Ran, your reputation precedes you."

"She's not wrong," I say. "What did the brunette say in response?" I'm still checking her out through the window. She's attractive, short and petite. Her brown hair frames her face and skims her shoulders, which are covered by a tight-fitting V-neck shirt that leaves little to the imagination. A pair of curve-hugging jeans finishes off her outfit.

"She didn't seem to care what her friend had to say; she just kept ogling you through the window."

Sure enough, the brunette's eyes find mine as Shane is talking. A smile spreads across her face before she looks back to her friend.

"I'm going to grab another drink," I say, and get up off the sofa.

"See you in an hour," Zack says, grinning.

"Nah, thirty minutes max," I hear Shane say as I walk into the house.

I make my way into the kitchen to strike up a conversation with the brunette, whose name turns out to be Sunny.

I'm not really sure how to feel about all of this. I never meant to be the guy girls warn their friends about; I never meant to be the guy who just hooks up without any meaningful connection or relationship, but here I am. And honestly, it's better that way.

***

"Before we do this," I say when Sunny and I are in one of the guest bedrooms, "you need to know that I'm not going to call you after this. And you're not going to call me." It didn't take long for us to end up here. We chatted for ten minutes, but we both quickly got to the point and decided to find somewhere private, leaving her friend to walk out of the kitchen with a huff.

"That's what I figured," she says, already breathless, half-undressed, her bare chest fitfully rising and falling as she leans in for another kiss. Then she slips her right hand into my jeans and begins to stroke me.

I reach behind me and pull open the second dresser drawer where I know Shane has a stash of condoms. I always keep a pack in my car; I stopped carrying them around with me in my wallet when I heard that body heat may diminish their effectiveness. But when Shane repeatedly noticed me heading to my car to grab protection, he took it upon himself to keep each bathroom and guest bedroom of his mom's beach house well-stocked, telling me with a suggestive grin that he had my back.

"You're prepared," Sunny breathes against my lips, increasing the pressure with her hand.

"Uh-huh," I groan. I push her panties down her hips and back us up to the queen-sized bed. I don't fuck around without condoms, especially when I don't really know the girl I'm about to hook up with. Sex is great and all, but not great enough to risk getting a girl pregnant or catching a disease.

Sunny and I spend maybe thirty minutes in the room, each getting what we came here for, and after catching our breath we get dressed without much conversation.

"Well," she finally says with a content smile on her face as we're about to depart the bedroom, "I wouldn't mind a repeat of this some time, but I hear that's not really your style."

"Sorry, not really," I admit with a frown, feeling shitty. I mostly feel like crap after hookups. They obviously feel good in the moment, but they don't sustain me. I'm not even really sure why I do it other than to scratch the itch—and because I can, I guess. I don't know.

"Yeah," she says, and lets her gaze roam my body. "It felt freaking amazing, though. So thank you."

I walk her back out of the room and make sure she finds her friend. "I'll see you around, Sunny," I say.

She smiles sweetly. "I'd like that," she says, and hooks her arm under her friend's before walking away.

"Forty-seven minutes. Pay up!" Steve says to Shane and Zack the moment I rejoin my friends and sit my ass back on the sofa.

"What the hell are you guys doing?" I ask, looking around at my brother and friends.

"They had a bet on how long you'd be gone with her." Vada shakes her head. "Zack said an hour, Shane said thirty minutes, so Steve came in at the halfway point."

"Was she good?" Zack asks as he pulls a twenty out of his wallet and hands it to my brother.

"Forget it, man." Shane throws his balled-up twenty at Steve. "Ran doesn't kiss and tell."

He's right. I might have casual sex, but I don't take advantage of any girl. Ever. I'm not in it for the grandstanding or dick measuring. I don't keep track of my "conquests," and I definitely don't talk about the girls I've hooked up with. I've always hated it when guys talk about their sex lives, especially when it's derogatory or demeaning of the girl. I won't even go there. As far as I'm concerned, that shit is private.

Monday, April 19th

Cat

"I guess I can finally scratch 'being the new girl' off my bucket list," I mutter when my mom's car comes to a stop in the morning drop-off line in front of my brand-new-for-me high school.

My mom smiles empathetically. "It's going to be okay, Kitty." I reach behind me to the backseat and retrieve my backpack that, as of now, holds only the bare-minimum essentials: a five-subject notebook and some pens and pencils. "Do you want me to pick you up, or are you going to be okay walking home this afternoon?"

"I'll be fine walking, Mom. Don't worry about me." I stare out my window with some apprehension, my hand on the handle. I hesitate to actually open the door and step out onto the sidewalk to blend into the hundreds of high-schoolers making their way into the overwhelmingly large building with its brown brick façade.

This is going to be a change. My small North Carolina hometown had only two rival high schools with graduating classes of sixty-three and fifty-nine students, with just over two hundred students at each—not large by any means. From what I understand, my new high school has a student body of over a thousand and over three hundred kids in my junior class. But I consider this a good change, a chance to be a face in the crowd rather than *the* face in the crowd—the girl everyone knows, talks about, despises.

"Text me when you have your schedule," my mom says just as I shove open the passenger door. "And let me know if you happen to have Mr. Lawrence. He was your dad's and my physics teacher," she adds with a girlish giggle.

I smile. My mom and dad are high school sweethearts who met at this very school some twenty years ago. They eventually eloped to North Carolina right after graduating from high school and beginning their educations at Duke. "I doubt it, but sure," I tell her, then finally clamber out of the car, shut the door, and wave at her one last time.

She drives off, leaving me standing on the sidewalk, the shadow of the giant building just in front of me eclipsing the bright spring sunlight.

If the building seemed huge from the outside, it's downright giant inside. There are four stories with wide, locker-lined hallways crammed with students eager to get to their classrooms. I spot freshmen—still with their childlike faces and voices that go from pitchy to deep in the middle of a sentence—all the way up to seniors, who honestly look like full-blown adults. It's always fascinating to me what a difference four years make, especially in boys who turn into men between the ages of fourteen and eighteen.

I stand awkwardly for a moment as students push past me through the double front doors. I try to orient myself and find my way to the office.

A burly guy with the stature of a linebacker stops in front of me, his eyes skimming my entire body while he grins. "You look lost, gorgeous. Can I help you find something? The bathroom, maybe?"

Heat rises in my face. "Uh, where's the office?" I cross my arm over my chest to grab the strap of my backpack and cover myself in the process. My body tenses with the unwanted attention from what is very obviously a football player and jock.

"Down the hall and just to the left before the stairs." He smirks, pointing in that direction. "Want me to walk with you?" he adds with a low growl.

I swallow hard, shaking my head. "No, thanks. I'm good," I tell him, the volume in my voice diminishing despite my best efforts. I hate the way I react in these situations now.

"I'll see you around then, gorgeous." He leaves me standing there while he walks down the hallway, then takes a right up a wide staircase.

Jesus, I hope I don't have any classes with him—or any other football player, or baseball player, or whatever player, or preferably any guy at all. I'm perfectly aware that this last part is wishful, but one can dream.

I finally make my way to the office where I'm swiftly walked through the administrative onboarding process—including, to my utter dismay, having to take a picture for my plastic student ID badge. I'm supposed to wear it at all times while on campus. Then I'm given a map—who even knew I'd need a map to find my way around my new school?—and schedule.

I note with a grin that my first class is physics with Mr. Lawrence.

"Across the hall, up the stairs to the fourth floor, make a right, then a left down the second hallway, another right, and find room 407," the office clerk tells me, unimpressed by my newbie status.

I nod and hitch my backpack over my shoulder, then walk out of the office. The hallway is mostly empty now; the bell rang—more like buzzed—a couple of minutes ago, making me late to my first class on my very first day. Great.

It takes me another I-don't-even-know-how-many-minutes to trudge up the stairs and find my classroom. I've already forgotten the directions given to me by the disgruntled-looking office clerk and have to rely on the small black-and-white map in my hands.

I finally find room 407 and open the door slowly. I blush the second the door creaks and thirty-five heads, plus the teacher's, turn in my direction. The air is muted as I make my way into the classroom and to the teacher's desk.

Mr. Lawrence looks like he's in his mid- to late-sixties. His gray, shoulder-length hair is wispy and his back is slightly hunched, though his face is friendly and he appears energetic. I guess you have to be energetic to be teaching high school in your sixties.

"Ahh, yes, welcome, Miss..."—he studies my note for a second, his reading glasses low on his nose as he glances over their rim—"Stevenson," he finishes, and smiles at me. "Why don't you take a seat next to Miss Walker?" He motions toward the only open seat in the room. "And please don't hesitate to come and complain to me if Miss Walker is too chatty. She thinks I can't hear well, but she underestimates my near-supersonic hearing, and I know full well that she enjoys a good chat, which is the reason she's currently without a tablemate." Mr. Lawrence laughs, and a good number of the students join in.

"I would never," the girl Mr. Lawrence just talked about huffs, pressing her right palm to her chest as if offended, though her sly grin makes it clear that nothing Mr. Lawrence just said was a lie.

"Oh, you're right. I'm talking about innocence personified." Mr. Lawrence chuckles and nods for me to take a seat.

"That's correct. Please don't ever forget that Mr. Lawrence," the girl says, batting her long, dark eyelashes. I already appreciate her for how she takes the attention off me.

"I would never, Miss Walker. Okay, where were we? Oh yes, how to calculate the rate of decay of our lovely isotope." Mr. Lawrence chuckles and turns back to his smart board.

I make my way to my table and take the seat on the empty lab stool.

"Hi, I'm Vada," the girl says in a whisper. She smiles widely, holding her hand out for me to shake.

"I'm Cat," I whisper back, taking her hand.

"Like Catherine?"

I bite my bottom lip, shaking my head. "Nope, just Cat," I say like I have a million-billion-gazillion times in my life, because that's what everyone always asks me. "With a *C*, like the animal with whiskers and a tail and the ability to purr." I follow it up with a giggle.

"Holy shit, I love that!" Vada exclaims, loudly enough for Mr. Lawrence to turn around with his lips pressed together.

"Miss Walker! At least give your new friend an opportunity to get acclimated and maybe listen to the lecture for a few minutes," he warns Vada with a throaty chuckle.

"Sorry, Mr. Lawrence. It won't happen again," Vada says.

Mr. Lawrence doesn't look convinced. "Yes it will, and everyone here knows it," he says simply, and turns back to continue his demonstration of the proper formula to calculate the rate of decay of an isotope.

Mr. Lawrence is right. Vada doesn't stop talking to me—at me, whatever—for the remainder of the class, and I can't say I hate it. By the end of the lecture, I know that Vada is on the varsity softball team. She screeched with excitement, earning her another warning from Mr. Lawrence, when she realized I was the new teammate her coach had told the team about last week. I also learn that Vada has a twin brother, Zack, who is apparently way more "artsy" and less "science-y" than Vada, and that she has a "hot-ass boyfriend"—Steve, a senior—whom she's been dating for almost a year now. This, in turn, leads to Vada telling me that the varsity ice hockey team—on which her boyfriend is the first line left forward—brings home all the trophies and championships, whereas the football team can't ever seem to make it to playoffs season.

"What's your next period?" Vada asks after she pulls me out of the physics lab and brings me to a halt in the middle of the hallway, causing the onslaught of other students walking between classes to part like the Red Sea.

"Uhh, French with Miss Trudeaux." I pronounce the name slowly, looking at my schedule.

"Ew, okay, let me walk you there really quick," Vada offers sweetly, leading me to my third-floor classroom. "Okay, so it looks like we have the same lunch period—yay," Vada says, glancing at my schedule still securely clasped in my hand. "We don't eat in the cafeteria. We eat under the large oak tree in the courtyard when the weather is nice. You can't miss it. Grab your lunch—abstain from the chicken sandwich," she warns with a disgusted face, "and then meet us there."

I don't get a chance to ask her who "we" and "us" is before Vada whirls around and rushes away to whatever her next class is.

***

I make it through my next two classes okay, desperately attempting to fly under the radar. Then I head to the cafeteria where I get the egg salad sandwich and an apple. When I walk out to the courtyard, I see Vada was right: it's impossible to miss the large oak tree. Vada's already sitting cross-legged in the grass next to another girl, chatting animatedly.

"Hey!" Vada calls to me, waving me over the second she sees me approach.

I set my tray down on the grass, then sit cross-legged, facing her and the other girl whose big blue eyes are absolutely stunning, especially offset by her dark hair and tanned skin.

"Cat, this is Tori. Tori, Cat," Vada introduces us, and I shake Tori's hand.

"Hey, Cat," Tori greets me sweetly.

I notice movement in my periphery and turn my head in the direction of a guy who looks just like Vada but in male form.

"Hey, did you grab my water bottle this morning?" the guy asks Vada, not even acknowledging me as he unceremoniously sits down in the grass and pulls his backpack open.

"Uh, why the hell would I do that?" Vada asks him.

"Because I have yours," the guy says, pulling a light-green metal canteen out of his backpack.

"Oh, shit." Vada laughs and pulls open her own backpack, sheepishly retrieving a black metal canteen. "Whoops. Sorry about that." Vada nods toward me. "So, I made a new friend."

The guy's head turns in my direction. "I'm so sorry. Whatever my sister has already said or done to you... I'm so sorry." He reaches his hand out to me, and I laugh out loud while shaking it.

"Oh, shut up, Zack," Vada says with an exaggerated eye roll. "This is Cat. She's new, obviously, and being the charitable individual I am, I have immediately adopted her."

"I'm so, so sorry," Zack whispers to me, earning himself a swat on his shoulder from his sister.

"Cat, this is my twin brother, Zack. Some just refer to him as my stupider, uglier sibling, but you can call him Zack," Vada says.

Tori laughs while Zack grunts.

"Fuck off," Zack tells his sister. "I'm the better, hotter, smarter twin. And I'm three-and-a-half minutes older, so I'm also more experienced and obviously wiser," Zack tells me with a grin.

I notice the small GoPro camera in his left hand. I don't love cameras. I don't like having pictures or videos taken of me, especially if I didn't expressly consent to it.

"Are you filming?" I ask him, trying to keep my voice steady.

"Always," Zack says with pride.

"My brother thinks he's the next Steven Spielberg or one of the Coen brothers or Martin Scorsese or whatever, so he walks around with a camera all day every god damn day," Vada explains.

"Oh, okay," I say apprehensively. I don't know how to feel about someone capturing my every move, every angle.

Vada studies me. "Yeah, sorry. It's annoying as hell, but if you want to be friends with me—and you definitely want to be friends with me—this is one of the less fun parts, along with having to endure my brother's presence a lot of the time. But I promise you'll get used to it. The camera, at least. Not so much my brother's presence," Vada says with another eye roll, which is mirrored by Zack.

Tori and I laugh.

"You're so fucking funny," Zack says. "Look—Cat, is it? You might want to reconsider any intention of being friends with my sister. She's an asshole."

Vada waves him off. "Aww, you know you love me."

"Psh, the only reason I put up with you is because you're my best friend's girlfriend," Zack says.

"Not because she's your sister?" Tori asks him with a laugh.

"Nope," Zack says adamantly.

"Oh, wait, so your boyfriend Steve"—I point at Vada—"is your best friend?" I ask, moving my index finger to Zack.

Both he and Vada nod.

"Yep," Zack says. "But to be fair, Steve has been my best friend *way* longer than he's been Vada's boyfriend."

"And her boyfriend," Vada chimes in, pointing her own finger at Tori, "is my boyfriend's little brother's best friend. Well, Steve's brother is also one of my closest friends, but, yeah."

I knit my eyebrows together. "Hold on, your boyfriend's little brother is also one of your close friends, but he's Tori's boyfriend's best friend?"

All three nod at me.

"Yep, she'll do just fine," Zack decides with a slap on his knee before he takes a giant bite of his sandwich.

"Oof, okay," I sigh, hoping I'll remember all of this.

Tori laughs. "It's a lot easier once you see the dynamic."

"I imagine so," I nod. "So, where are your boyfriends?" I look around as if I know who the heck I'm even looking for.

"Oh, their lunch period is after ours," Vada gripes.

I have to admit that the idea of different lunch periods is new to me. At my old school in North Carolina everyone ate at the same time, but that's probably because it was much, much smaller.

"Oh, shit. Hey guys," I hear a male voice call.

Turning my head, I recognize the burly guy from this morning; he's accompanied by two others with similarly wide statures.

"Hey Drew," Tori says.

Drew veers in our direction while his two buddies stay back, and he comes to a stop next to Vada. He grins at me. "Ahh, so we meet again, gorgeous," he chuckles.

Vada raises her eyebrows, looking from me to Drew. "You've already met Cat?"

"Well, she looked lost this morning, so I offered to show her around." He leaves out the part where he asked if he could show me to the bathroom. "Your name is Cat?" he asks, and I nod. "I'm Drew." He holds his hand out, which I shake.

"Nice to meet you," I say, even though I'm uneasy. Drew has the stature, the face, the air of a guy I try to avoid now—self-assured, cocky, aggressive. A jock, in other words.

"Drew plays on the hockey team with Steve and Tori's boyfriend, Shane," Vada tells me.

"Oh, I thought you were a football player, maybe." I don't know why I say it.

He snorts. "Nah, those guys are losers. Hockey is where it's at."

Vada rolls her eyes.

"Dude, let's fucking go!" one of the other boys with Drew calls over to him.

"Alright, gotta go. But it was great seeing you again," he says with a wink and a smile at me. Then he turns with a quick wave to Tori, Vada, and Zack, and rejoins his buddies.

"So, that was Drew. He's the varsity hockey goalie," Tori says, noting my apparent consternation.

"Okay," I say simply, feeling Vada and Tori's eyes on me.

"Don't worry about him. He's like a chihuahua—all yap, not a ton of action," Zack mumbles, his mouth full.

"Sounds exactly like the way he plays hockey," Vada opines. "Did you hear about that own goal he scored at the playoffs against the Knights? Steve was so pissed," she adds with a giggle.

"Have I ever." Tori nods. "Shane couldn't stop talking about it. He gave Drew such a hard time for weeks afterwards."

The talk about hockey continues for a few minutes before the topic veers to other subjects. I enjoy sitting and eating lunch with my new friends, who are funny and down-to-earth, and I'm delighted to learn that I share two afternoon classes with Vada and Tori, and my last with Zack, who introduces me to his girlfriend, Summer.

***

When the bell rings, I head to the girls' locker room where I meet Vada and Tori to get ready for our softball practice this afternoon.

Practice goes well. Vada giddily introduces me to the rest of the team, and I'm happy to find that nobody really seems to care that I'm new. By the time practice is over and we return to the locker room to change, I have to admit that this first day went better than I could have ever hoped for.

"Hey Vada," one of our teammates calls from across the locker room, "is it true that Shane is throwing a party at the beach house for Steve's eighteenth birthday in a couple of weeks?"

"Yeah, are you planning to be there?" Vada calls back.

The girl pulls a hair tie out of her jet-black hair, which plummets all the way down her back, stopping at her waist. She nods, a gleam in her brown eyes. "Will Ronan be there?"

"Uh, duh. He's Stevie's brother, of course he'll be at the party," Vada says with a shrug.

The girl turns to her two girlfriends, all three of whom stick their heads together, giggling and whispering.

Vada just shakes her head at them, then resumes getting dressed.

"When is your boyfriend's birthday?" I ask Vada as I sit down on the bench to pull on my shoes.

"May second," Vada tells me, sitting down next to me.

Tori sits down on my other side. "Shane is throwing him a party on the first; it's a Saturday. You should come."

Nope. I don't do parties. Not anymore. Parties equal people, and alcohol, and sex, and all the things I'm trying to get away from. "Oh, I don't... I won't be able to make it, I think. We're having dinner with my grandparents that night." I desperately attempt to control my face, to stop the heat rising in my cheeks and giving me away.

"You could come afterwards," Vada suggests with a smile.

"Those dinners usually drag on all evening, and I haven't seen my grandparents in a while, so... maybe next time."

Vada and Tori nod.

"There'll be plenty opportunity to experience Shane's parties," Tori laughs. "He has them a lot."

Great. Apparently, I have a radar for people who are part of the in-crowd, are jocks, or who have friends who are jocks and throw parties. So much for getting away from my past. Just perfect.

Saturday, May 1st

Cat

"Alright, let me see what you got on. Legs!" Vada says, strolling into my bedroom at just before six this evening.

I spin around, startled. "How did you get in?" I ask, holding my hand over my frantic heart.

"Umm, your mom let me in," Vada tells me with an eye roll.

Tonight is Steve's eighteenth birthday party, which Tori's boyfriend Shane is throwing at his mom's beach house. And even though I was reluctant at first, I finally agreed to join my new friends. This will be the first party I've agreed to attend in months.

It took quite a bit of begging, whining, and convincing by Vada and Tori—mostly Vada—and nightly talks and reassurance by my mom to see beyond my past and trust myself and others enough to give in to Vada. She was adamant that I couldn't miss Steve's birthday bash.

What ultimately convinced me, though, was when Vada and Tori assured me this "party" would actually be a relaxed get-together. "Nothing crazy," Tori promised. Plus, I've enjoyed nothing more than hanging out with my new friends these past few weeks. There's no pressure, fairly little drama, and most everyone has been warm and welcoming.

From the second I met Vada, I knew she was one of the most extroverted people I've ever met. She has no problem making friends, and thank goodness for that. I'll forever be grateful that she immediately started chatting with me during physics and diverted the class's attention from me—the newcomer whose only wish was to remain invisible—to herself. Since meeting her, Vada has so naturally inserted herself into my life that I already don't know what I would do without her.

We hit it off and have been hanging out quite a bit. Aside from Tori and her brother, Zack, Vada has been slowly introducing me to her other close friends. There's Vada's boyfriend, Steve, whom I had the pleasure of meeting a few days after moving to New York. Steve is tall, with light-brown hair and cinnamon-brown eyes. You can tell that he, and most of the other guys in this group of friends, are athletes just by the way they're built—lean and muscular, the result of almost daily conditioning and training. I knew from Vada, even before meeting Steve, that he's on the high school hockey team. Well, *was* on the hockey team, I guess. Steve, along with Shane—Tori's boyfriend and another member of this tight-knit group—is about to graduate from high school.

Then there's Vada's twin brother, Zack. It's fascinating to see the two of them together: Zack really is Vada but in male form. He's taller than Vada but has the same shade of bronze-brown hair and brown eyes.

I quickly learned that Zack isn't an athlete, but he considers himself the documentarian of the group. He wasn't exaggerating when he told me he's always filming; he has either his cell phone or his GoPro running and documenting every part of life. When I asked him about it, he dove into his ambitions to attend school in California and ultimately direct movies. So, he explained, he's been vigilantly documenting and filming life with his friends.

I was extremely uncomfortable with the idea of Zack capturing my every move. Having pictures and videos taken of me didn't used to be an issue. It used to be fun, actually, until it wasn't anymore, and having a camera in my face all the time has taken some getting used to. But Zack is so nonintrusive about it, and the others assured me that soon I wouldn't even notice the camera anymore. They were right; after only a few weeks I don't even notice Zack's filming any longer.

"Can you please not call me 'Legs?'" I plead with Vada. "It makes me feel... freakish."

Vada laughs. "You're not a freak. You're gorgeous. I'd kill to look like you."

I blush violently. People call me beautiful. I have long legs and long, wavy blonde hair that, if left to its own devices, will quickly turn against me. At five feet nine inches, I'm fairly tall. Honestly, I consider myself kind of lanky.

Vada, on the other hand, is a bombshell. Though six inches shorter than me, she has a beautiful body and perfect curves. Her gorgeous brown hair, blunt-cropped at her shoulders, turns bronze when the sun hits it just right. It's no wonder her boyfriend, Steve, is crazy about her.

"Okay, okay, I'm sorry." Vada gives me a quick, appeasing squeeze before she meanders over to my floor-length mirror and briefly fusses with her hair.

"I like your shorts," I nod, noting Vada's cutoff jean shorts.

She grins. "I wore them especially for Stevie. He likes them on me."

"I'm sure you could be wearing a paper bag and Steve would still like what you're wearing," I snigger, and Vada smiles. She's crazy about Steve. The two have been dating for almost a year—which, let's face it, is an eternity in high school. Although Vada recently confided in me that she has no clue what will happen once Steve leaves to attend college in Boston this fall. Vada, on the other hand, has another year of high school ahead, which means either trying to weather a long-distance relationship or ending it amicably before hearts can get broken.

"And what are you wearing tonight?" Vada asks, taking a quick, disapproving glance at my faded jeans and baby blue t-shirt that flows over my torso and accentuates my humble curves.

I'm most comfortable in just jeans, a soft shirt, and my Converse. I don't really care about the latest fashions or hairstyles. In fact, ever since I moved away from North Carolina I try hard not to stand out or draw attention to myself. That's precisely what I wanted to get away from in the first place.

"Uh, this right here?" I say, looking down at myself.

Vada frowns. "Okay, so nothing different than what you usually wear to school. Got it," she says with mock exacerbation.

"Yep. What's wrong with it?"

"Cat, you are so beautiful. Seriously, so, *so* beautiful! Why do you feel like you need to hide?" she asks, scanning my body top to bottom.

"I'm not hiding. I just enjoy wearing this. It's comfy," I say, and Vada smiles. "By the way," I add, "I got my mom to extend my curfew to midnight tonight."

"Nice!" Vada smiles and looks at her watch. "Are you ready to go, then?"

I consider her for a minute, then make a split-second decision. I unbutton and pull down my jeans and exchange them for a pair of jean shorts.

Vada smiles triumphantly and pulls out some lip gloss. "You're so hot, Kitty Cat! You know it, I know it, and everyone else knows it. Here, put some of this on," she says, handing me the gloss.

I apply the sticky substance to my bottom lip and dab my lips together, feeling Vada's eyes on me. "What?" I ask, looking at her reflection in my mirror.

"I was just thinking that it's a shame you're single," she says slyly, but doesn't elaborate.

"I don't know about that." I close the little tube of gloss and hand it back to Vada.

Vada and I meander downstairs and toward the front door.

"Midnight, and not a minute later," my mom calls after me and Vada as we walk out of the house. "Please drive safely, Vada. And no drinking and driving!"

My parents have always been uber-protective, especially of my younger sister and me. My parents were originally from New York, and despite eloping at eighteen and having me when they were only twenty, my parents are actually quite strict, my dad even more so than my mom. And that certainly hasn't changed after everything that transpired over the past few months.

I can't blame them, I guess.

Ronan

"Rise and shine, princess!"

My brother's voice edges itself into my consciousness, and I blink my eyes open to the dim light in my room. The shades are drawn, blocking out the sun and heat. I'm lying on my bed, stomach-down, and I roll over to face Steve, who stands in the doorway between my room and the cramped Jack-and-Jill bathroom that adjoins our bedrooms.

"What time is it?" I mumble, my voice thick with sleep. I meant to take only a quick nap before the party, but I obviously passed out hard. I'm not even sure I shifted positions while I slept.

"Five thirty," Steve replies, looking at his watch. "You better get up and ready, because I'm leaving in ten minutes. Unless you want to drive your own car."

"Nah, I'm sure one of us will be drinking tonight. Safer to take only one car," I say, and Steve chuckles.

"So young, yet so wise," he teases me, and I flip him off.

Steve is my big brother, though he's not that much older—and definitely not much bigger—than me. We're exactly thirteen months apart to the day, and at six-four he's a measly two inches taller than me. We're about as close as brothers can be: we've played hockey together all our lives, and because we have the same circle of friends, we hang out together all the time. Nonetheless, there are some things I don't share with him, and some things that make us about as different from each other as humanly possible—and I don't mean just looks.

I sit up and put my feet on the ground, relishing the cool wood floor under my bare soles. It's only the beginning of May, but already the temperature is creeping up. Heat in New York can be miserable; most houses don't have adequate A/C, and my parents live in this old, two-story brownstone that's definitely not up to twenty-first-century standards. A few years ago my dad retrofitted the upstairs and downstairs with coolers, but they only help so much, and my mother hates them because they're noisy. So unless temperatures reach the mid-nineties—or, God forbid, triple digits like in July and August—the coolers are off and we're forced to rely on our ceiling fans. Steve and I have resorted to opening our windows and allowing the air to flow through our shared bathroom. This works great unless Vada is over, which, understandably and inevitably, results in Steve locking his doors.

I push up off my bed, then pull my damp shirt over my head and discard it on the floor while walking toward the bathroom.

"Are you alright?" Steve asks, watching me intently while stepping back and retreating into his own room.

"I'm fine," I say, barely looking at him. I'm afraid he'll be able to see in my face that I'm lying.

"Are you sure? You were out cold for a couple of hours. You feeling alright?"

"Yeah, just exhausted," I assure him. "Give me ten minutes to get ready and we can head out," I say, then ruthlessly shut his door to the bathroom and click the lock in place. I do the same with the door to my own bedroom. Then I turn on the shower and allow the hot water to steam up the mirror, but not before checking on the yellowing bruises on my upper back. After more than a week, they're barely visible now. I exhale with relief, drop my jeans and boxer briefs to the floor, and step under the scorching water, relishing the sting and allowing the heat to numb my skin. I let my head fall forward, feeling the water run down my neck and torso, wishing it would wash away more than just sweat and dirt—that it would wash away fear, and pain, and sin. But it doesn't; it never has.

***

I do perk up on the drive over to Shane's. I sit in the passenger seat of Steve's Challenger, windows down, music blasting, while Steve flies down the interstate at a speed that's definitely not legal. I close my eyes, feeling the wind while the music drowns out my thoughts.

When we get to the house, Shane yanks us outside and down to the beach. He's relieved to have an excuse to get away from the house and proceeds to complain about how his mom decided that a dinner soiree today for some of her closest friends and business acquaintances was a great idea, and how she invited all these people Shane doesn't even know.

Shane's parents are successful entrepreneurs, owning several Irish pubs around the city, including Murphy's, which is where both Shane and I work after school and on the weekends. The beach house has been Shane's mom's homestead ever since his parents separated a year ago—the demands of their businesses and the loss of their youngest son, Liam, too hard on their marriage. Ever since his parents' separation, Shane has ping-ponged between his dad's place and his mom's beach house. Though lately he's been spending the vast majority of his time at his dad's—which is also Shane's childhood home—and only spending his weekends at the beach house.

A few minutes after our arrival, the rest of our friends trickle in and make their way down to the dunes. I decide to start a fire with the dried driftwood and some lighter fluid.

Shane, Steve, Drew, and I talk about hockey. I've been playing with Steve and Shane since I was seven and Shane and Steve were eight. At first we only played club together, but once I started my sophomore year of high school after moving back from Montana a couple of years ago, I added varsity hockey to my extracurricular activities.

"As much as I'm going to miss playing," Shane says, "I have to admit that I'm looking forward to all the extra time I'll get to spend *not* at conditioning at the ass-crack of dawn."

"Lucky you," I chuckle.

"You're gonna miss me, huh?" Shane says, nudging me with his elbow.

"No, not really," I say dryly. "It'll be nice not having you yell at me all the damn time."

"Shut up. I never yelled at you!"

"Whatever you say," I say with a shrug.

"Actually, you did yell at Ran," Steve says, and Drew nods, taking a sip from his beer. "Remember when you were so pissed that we were losing to the Spartans and you kept yelling at Ran to just check everyone in sight?" Steve laughs. "Meanwhile Ran already had a black eye and had been in the penalty box like three times."

"Fine, I admit that wasn't my finest moment," Shane admits. "But I was just living up to my responsibilities as team captain."

"Speaking of which, I have a feeling you'll make captain now that Shane's gone," Steve says to me.

I shrug. "Maybe. I have no clue. Jayce has been on the team as long as I have, and he started playing club a lot earlier than me, so I wouldn't be surprised if he got picked instead of me."

"Yea, but Jayce isn't half as good as you are," Shane says. "He's third line and gets like two and a half minutes of ice time a game, dude. You're the god damn center forward, and unless you're hurt for some reason, you're always first line."

"I mean, I've been on the team just as long," Drew chimes in. "Who's to say I'm not going to make captain?" he adds with a shrug.

Shane chuckles. "Yeah. Nice try, man, but you've been slacking a bit lately. May I remind you of that embarrassing own goal you scored against the Knights last season? And you're the freaking goalie. You have no business scoring any goals at all, especially not against your own damn team."

"Yeah, man, the only reason we ended up winning that game was because Shane and Ran scored two goals in the last seven damn seconds," Steve adds with an approving nod.

"And you've missed a bunch of practice, too," Shane doubles down.

A scowl has slowly carved itself into Drew's face. "I had family stuff, man," he says through gritted teeth before taking another drink from his bottle.

"And that's fine, dude, I'm not knocking that. All I'm saying is that Ran is really fucking deserving of making captain," Shane says, and turns his attention back to me. "Seriously, Ran, after me you had the most points scored last season."

"You know I'm not the one you need to convince, right?" I laugh at Shane's passionate recital of my hockey accolades. "And maybe I don't even want to be captain."

"Shut the fuck up," Steve exclaims. "Of course, you want it."

"I'm not so sure," I say. "Maybe I should just quit now that you both are gone. I wouldn't mind not having to get up at the ass-crack of dawn either." I shrug, causing Shane's mouth to drop open.

"You know both Coach Belmont and Coach Fox would die of a heart attack, right?" Steve chuckles.

"Plus, man, think about the scholarships you would be giving up," Shane says. "You have a real shot at going a lot further with this."

"Okay, you can drop it, Shane. I'm not going to quit playing." I laugh at the disgruntled look on his face, enjoying the banter. After these last few days, it feels amazing to just hang out at the beach, surrounded by my brother and closest friends.

Cat

"Holy crap, looks like Mrs. O'Connor has her own thing going on and invited all of Long Island," Vada exclaims as we make our way up the stairs to Shane's mom's beach house, the sound of music and chatter wafting our way.

The house is incredible. It's modern and filled with light. The entire wall facing the deck and beach is made out of giant wall-to-ceiling glass panels that stack onto each other and open up the entire side. The floor is a light-gray wood tile that continues through the whole house, adorned here and there by large white area rugs. The furniture throughout the house is clean, white, and modern, and Shane's mom always manages to have the most beautiful fresh flowers in her home. Today, the white side table next to the sofa holds a beautiful crystal vase filled with light-pink hydrangeas. And to top it all off, the house is also ideally situated overlooking a narrow stretch of the beach, its large wraparound deck furnished with several lounge chairs, a rattan outdoor sectional sofa that looks even more comfortable than the sofa at my house, an outdoor bar area, and a hot tub that, though steaming invitingly, remains unoccupied for now.

"Do you see Steve anywhere?" Vada asks while she scans our surroundings.

I let my eyes roam the deck and the spacious house as we enter the kitchen. "Nope. Is he even here yet?" I ask, unable to spot a familiar face in the crowd of what are obviously friends and acquaintances of Shane's mom.

Vada pulls her phone out of her back pocket and types out a message to Steve. "Well, I guess we'll find out soon," she says, sliding her phone back into her pocket. "Hi Mrs. O'Connor!" Vada puts on her Sunday smile as Shane's mom walks into the kitchen.

Mrs. O'Connor is a short but slender woman in her mid-forties with stunning blue eyes and wavy copper hair framing her face. She's wearing a tight black cocktail dress and black Louboutin pumps that I'm certain would cause me to break both ankles at once were I to attempt walking in them.

"This is quite the party," Vada says a little too enthusiastically.

Shane's mom smiles, not picking up on Vada's sarcasm. "Oh, yeah, just a little something I threw together last minute. You look very nice, Vada! And who is this?" she continues, smiling at me.

"This is my friend Cat," Vada says.

"Nice to meet you, Mrs. O'Connor. Thank you for having me," I say, extending my hand.

"Please, girls, call me Nora," she says, taking my hand gently into hers. "Goodness, you are gorgeous. And tall. Do you model?" She gives me a skilled once-over.

"Oh, no," I say, shaking my head with conviction.

"Well, maybe you should," she says, smiling.

I keep shaking my head uncomfortably, and Vada picks up on the shift in my energy.

"So, where's Shane, Mrs. O'Connor? I don't see him anywhere." Vada pops her head up, trying to make out Shane or any of her friends in the crowd of adults who are drinking wine and eating hors d'oeuvres offered to them by a handful of young waiters roaming the large kitchen and sitting room.

"You know, I haven't seen him in about half an hour. That's just like him. Here I am wanting to show off my handsome boy and he goes and hides somewhere. Well, if you find him, tell him to make a showing, would you?" Mrs. O'Connor frowns. She spots someone or something in the adjacent room, turns around, and skillfully struts away from us, leaving us standing in the kitchen.

"Wow," I say, confounded. "Who are all these people?"

"I have no idea." Vada's phone beeps, and she reads her text message. "The boys are down by the beach. Let's go."

Vada takes my hand and leads me out to the back deck where a narrow staircase leads to an equally narrow sandy path and, finally, a private stretch of beach. Halfway down the stairs we're met by Steve making his way up toward us. His eyes find Vada, and his smile is instantaneous. Vada lets go of my hand and bounds toward Steve, planting a kiss on his lips while he lifts her in the air.

"Happy birthday, baby," Vada exclaims, her arms wrapped tightly around Steve's neck.

"Thank you, babe. I'm glad you're here," he says, then kisses her deeply before lowering her back to the ground.

"Me too," she says breathily, looking up at him with a love-struck expression, and I smile.

"Everyone is down by the beach," Steve explains, then picks up Vada and carries her piggyback as we walk down the remaining stairs and along the sandy beach path. "Shane wasn't feeling the vibe at the house, so we've just been hanging out by the water," he explains as I trudge behind him and Vada.

Walking down the beach, I spot Zack's girlfriend, Summer, and Summer's best friend, Cheyenne, sitting in the sand, and I wave to them.

Summer's name suits her well. She's pure sunshine—upbeat, good-natured, and always happy. She's pixie-like both in stature and personality.

Summer's best friend is Cheyenne—Summer's polar opposite. Where Summer is chatty, Cheyenne is quiet. But not quiet as in shy; she's calculating and analytical. I can tell she's smart, but I haven't received the warmest reception from her the few times we've interacted. Cheyenne's wavy hair is chin length and dyed bright red with black streaks. She has a small, sparkly stud in her right nostril and several ear piercings. She's beautiful but intimidating.

Drew's sitting in the sand next to them. He thankfully stopped calling me "gorgeous" after I eventually told him I didn't enjoy the nickname. I've come to learn that Drew has been playing on the varsity hockey team the past couple of years. He's shorter and burlier than Shane and Steve, which I guess is what makes him a pretty good goalie. He has buzzed black hair, brown eyes, and a thick Jersey accent. He talks loudly and laughs even louder. I hear Drew make some joke with a sexual innuendo, and both Summer and Cheyenne roll their eyes—hard.

Twenty feet farther down the beach, Zack and Shane stand by a still-small bonfire. Shane holds a bottle of beer in one hand while the other is draped around Tori's hip. Zack's holding his small GoPro—obviously memorializing the occasion—and I walk by a separate camera set up on a tripod. *Always filming the goings-on*, I think to myself, trying to avoid the camera's lens, though I know it's useless. As we approach Zack, Shane, and Tori, I feel as though someone is looking at me, and, sure enough, I notice a boy I haven't yet met but whose features look remarkably familiar. And, holy cow, he's gorgeous.

Ronan

"You look like you could use one. Or maybe you just need to get laid," Shane says with a chuckle as he holds a freshly-opened bottle of beer out to me. "I'm sure Cheyenne would be down for it," he adds and winks at me. I just grin at him while Zack and Tori laugh.

I made the mistake of hooking up with Cheyenne before. Twice. I'm an idiot for doing it because I know Cheyenne is looking for more than just casual sex. I, on the other hand, am just not interested. She's nice enough and certainly cute, but I don't want a relationship with her, or anyone for that matter. The idea of letting someone in scares the shit out of me. The less people know about my life, the better. But I also don't want to play games with Cheyenne. "I think I'll just stick with beer for tonight," I pronounce, laughing. I bring the bottle to my lips and tip it up to drink.

"Yeah, whatever. Let's see what you say four beers from now," Zack prods with a chuckle. "I'm sure some chick will end up dropping her panties for you tonight. This camera witnesses everything," he says, pointing at his GoPro. That damn thing is like a third hand to Zack. When he first started recording nonstop roughly a year and a half ago, it annoyed the hell out of everyone, but at this point we hardly even notice it anymore. "In fact, I bet Shane's mom would drop her—"

"Watch what you say, dude," Shane growls at Zack, who chuckles. "That's my mom you're talking about here."

"I'm just sayin'," Zack says, oblivious to Shane's darkening expression, "your mom definitely likes Ran the most out of all of us. Didn't you notice how long she hugged him the other day?"

"That's because she's known me since I was a kid," I say, desperate to defuse the rising tension.

"She's known me just as long, and she most definitely doesn't hug me like that—all sweet and inhaling me and stuff," Zack continues.

I shake my head at him, wishing he'd get the hint and stop this bullshit.

"I'm gonna tell you this one time, man," Shane growls. "I love you, but I'm not above violence. Knock it off."

"Alright, can you guys rein in your testosterone, please?" Tori finally chimes in, and gives Shane a soft kiss on his cheek. "And sorry, baby, but your mom definitely checks out Ran," she adds with a giggle.

Shane just grunts in response.

I look past Shane. In the distance I can make out my brother and Vada. They're not alone; with them is a girl I've never met before. I analyze every one of her moves as she follows Vada.

She has long, wavy blonde hair and slender features. Her long legs make her taller than Vada by at least five inches, and even from this distance, I can tell she's absolutely stunning. I can't take my eyes off her.

“Ran? Ran! Ronan!” Shane says, drawing my attention away from the girl. I turn toward him, confused. “You’re staring,” he says with a knowing grin.

“Who is that?” I ask, nodding my head in the new girl’s direction. Her hips sway left to right with each step, her jean shorts conform perfectly to her toned, long legs, and her shirt accentuates her curves without being overtly sexy. Her blonde hair falls past her delicate face and over her shoulders, moving softly with the breeze. God damn, I can feel my heart pounding in my chest.

“That’s Cat, Vada’s friend. She moved here a little while ago. She’s been hanging out with Vada and Tori a bunch, and they invited her tonight, so...” Shane pauses, scanning my face. “She’s cute, huh?”

I don’t answer, watching instead as Cat strolls down the beach next to Steve, who picked up Vada to give her a piggyback ride. I divert my eyes, really trying not to stare, fuck, I can't believe how damn perfect this girl is.

Cat

I nudge Steve to get his attention. "Hey, who is that?" I ask him quietly, nodding my head in the unknown boy's direction.

A grin breaks across Steve's lips. "That's right, you haven't met my little brother yet."

Vada hops off her boyfriend's back and eagerly bounds toward the group of four, coming to a stop right in front of Steve's brother with a simpering smile on her lips.

"Kitty Cat, this is Stevie's little brother Ronan. We call him Ran," she tells me quickly, then faces Ronan, her index finger pointed squarely at me. "Ran, this is Cat," Vada says giddily.

It’s bewildering how much Ronan looks like his older brother, yet how different they look at the same time. Ronan has tousled, dark-blond hair, strands of it falling onto his forehead while the sides fade into a tight crop. His eyes, unlike his brother's, are strikingly green. Ronan is almost as tall as Steve and equally well-built. His faded jeans hug his hips and he's wearing a dark-green hoodie, which somewhat surprises me—although it isn't particularly hot now that the sun is setting, it's nonetheless a comfortable temperature. It certainly isn't what I would consider cold. Still, I can't deny that the simple outfit looks incredible on him; the color of his hoodie emphasizes the green of Ronan's eyes. His strong jaw and handsome facial features resemble his brother's but aren't altogether the same.

"Nice to meet you," Ronan says to me, his baritone voice smooth in my ears, and I immediately feel myself relax as he shifts his body in my direction. He looks straight at me with those green eyes, and I notice his full lips and long, full eyelashes as he holds his hand out for me to shake.

I take it, noting the warmth and softness of his skin, a little tingle forming in my stomach. "It's nice to meet you, too," I say feebly, and he gives me a dazzling smile.

"So, uh, Shane?" Vada interrupts. "I saw amazing food in the kitchen and none down here. Why are we at the beach again?" she questions loudly, giving Shane and Steve a look of consternation.

"Um, have you seen how many people my mom invited? And I don't know seventy-five percent of them. I'm not going up there!" Shane protests, clearly frustrated, but that doesn't deter Vada, who is now on a mission.

"Fine, then we'll just grab some food and bring it back to the beach. I need some volunteer helpers, though. No way am I schlepping food for all of you down here by myself!" She looks around the circle of friends, stopping at Steve's face and raising her eyebrows at him.

"Alright, let's go grab some food," Steve relents with a deep sigh. He takes Vada's hand and begins to walk back up the small beach path toward the house. Zack joins them, then obviously convinces Summer, Cheyenne, and Drew to tag along, too, because all three get up and follow Zack toward the house. I'm left standing with Ronan, Tori, and Shane.

Shane is the epitome of an Irish boy. His shoulder-length strawberry blond hair is pulled back into a small bun that shows off his short undercut, a hairstyle that he has explained to me is very much disliked by his parents, who consider it unprofessional. He has light-blue eyes and fair skin that I would imagine probably burns easily without sunblock.

Tori, on the other hand, couldn't be more different from Shane. She has beautiful olive skin and dark-brown hair with big, strikingly blue eyes, the result of a Puerto Rican father and a French mother. I still remember meeting Tori and immediately noticing her stunning eyes and long lashes. Shane has his arm around Tori's waist and she's leaning into him, her own arm draped around his hip. At more than a head taller than Tori, Shane is easily able to kiss Tori on her head while she talks to us.

"You know, I'm thinking we should all get together again for July Fourth, and do it here at the beach rather than in the city," Tori suggests. She looks expectantly up at Shane, and he nods his head slightly.

"I really don't think that'll be an issue," Shane says. "Unless my mom has her own festivities planned." He nods his head up and in the direction of the house. "Then maybe we'll just do at it my apartment. I really can't handle my mom's parties."

"Oh, were you able to find a place?" I ask, interested. I had known that Shane was looking for a place of his own in the city.

"Yeah, I found a fairly affordable two-bedroom apartment in Queens. Just need to find a roommate to chip in half of the rent," he says, and throws a glance at Ronan.

"Are your parents coming to terms with you not wanting to go to college?" Ronan asks. I take the opportunity to study his profile, a curious little flutter expanding in my chest.

"My dad is cool with the idea. He knows I want to take over the business, but my mom isn't super excited about my plan. She wants me to go to college, be a lawyer or doctor or accountant." Shane makes a face and shakes his shoulders as if he just got the willies. "So, we just don't talk about it," he chuckles. "Honestly, I've never really been the academic type. Unlike our boy Ran here." Shane pushes Ronan's shoulder, still chuckling. "Cat, did Vada tell you that she's been competing with Ronan for the number one spot in your guys' class since the beginning of mankind?"

Ronan looks down, shaking his head ever so slightly. Apparently Ronan isn't one to brag about his academic accomplishments. I find myself analyzing his features and only stop when I notice Shane grinning at me. His eyes flit from me to Ronan and back again, obviously hinting at me checking out Ronan, and I blush. I've always hated that my face gives me away so easily.

"Stop," Ronan grumbles at Shane. "I have the homeschool advantage over Vada."

He was homeschooled? Seems like we might have that in common.

"How long were you homeschooled?" I ask, and blush again. I seriously have got to get this under control.

Ronan's face softens as he gives me a half smile. "Only about a year while we lived in Montana."

"Oh, I've always wanted to go to a ranch in Montana," I say, and Ronan's smile widens.

"They're not all they're cracked up to be," he chuckles. I raise my eyebrows at him and he continues, "My grandparents own a cattle ranch and host guests that feel like"—he makes air quotes with his index and middle fingers—"roughin' it."

"Do you get to visit them often?" I've traveled a bit with my parents and siblings, but Montana is on my wish list.

"Not as much as I'd like. I was born there, but then started moving around a bunch, mostly between New York and Montana, with really short stints in Tennessee, Virginia, and Georgia. And then about two years ago we moved back from Montana to New York again," he recites, and it sounds exhausting.

"Are your parents in the military?"

"My dad," he nods. "Air Force. But we never lived on base with him, so I'm not totally sure why we kept moving with him. He's been stationed in Virginia for the last two or three years. Occasionally he'll just make the decision to move us." Ronan makes a face, and I can tell he's exhausted by all this upheaval.

"Why?" I ask, truly curious.

He shrugs. "I think he believes he's making it easier on my mother." Ronan's expression changes for a moment. I can't quite decipher the emotion that just appeared in his eyes, and before I can pinpoint it, his expression has changed again.

"Sounds exhausting," I say out loud.

He nods, his eyes unfocused as if replaying the years of instability in his mind. But then he snaps back, and his cute half smile is back. "How about you? Shane said you just moved here not too long ago."

"Uh-huh. My mom and I moved here a couple of weeks ago from North Carolina, and Vada pretty much immediately took me under her wing."

"Yep, like an orphaned pigeon," Vada chimes in, laughing.

I hadn't noticed the others walking toward us, loaded with the goods. Vada's carrying a giant basket of what is obviously food while Steve and Zack heave heavy coolers, followed by Cheyenne carrying blankets while Drew's arms are full of firewood for the bonfire.

Ronan moves from my side and takes the heavy basket from Vada's hands. "Did you leave any food in the house?"

"Only the stuffed olives. Yuck," Vada says, sticking her tongue out.

"Good call," Ronan agrees, and easily sets the overfull basket in the soft sand.

***

Cheyenne and Summer set up the blankets around the bonfire, and Steve and Zack distribute drinks while everyone settles around the crackling fire as the sun sets. I grab some food and sit on a blanket with Vada and Tori on each side, chatting about finals in a few weeks, summer plans, and next year's softball season. The sun finally sets completely, replacing the humid heat with a cool ocean breeze.

It's certainly not on purpose or even voluntary, but I frequently find myself glancing at Ronan, who stands with Shane, Zack, Steve, and Drew. Drew dominates the conversation, which is clearly about hockey, and I notice three empty bottles of some alcoholic beverage in the sand next to him. Seems he gets even louder when he drinks, and I can tell Shane is getting annoyed.

Shane comes over to us, crouching next to Tori. "You guys feel like going for a quick dip in the water?"

Tori immediately jumps up. "Let's grab some towels," she urges Vada, who seems on the fence about the whole idea.

"Um, kinda cold, don't you guys think?" Vada says, and Shane laughs.

"I'm sure your birthday boy would be happy to warm you right back up," Shane says as Steve, Drew, and—my heart skips the smallest of beats—Ronan walk over to us.

"What am I happy to do?" Steve asks, and Shane shares his idea of a quick swim in the ocean.

Everyone is on board, except for Ronan, who shakes his head. "I'm gonna sit this one out," he says, and I must admit that I'm ever so slightly disappointed I won't get to see what he looks like under those clothes. I mentally slap myself; this is not what I need or what I should be thinking. What I need is not to feel any sort of attraction to anyone, especially someone as good-looking—god, so good-looking—as tall, as obviously athletic as Ronan. From what I know, guys like him are dangerous.

Vada and Tori retrieve a stack of towels from the house, then join the others, who are already in various stages of undress, in removing layers of clothes. In a matter of minutes, the boys are stripped down to their boxers while the girls are in bras and panties.

I laugh when Steve grabs Vada, slings her over his shoulder, and makes a beeline for the—what I imagine to be—frigid Atlantic water.

"Don't you dare," Tori screams in a high-pitched voice when Shane makes to follow Steve's lead. He pulls Tori into his arms, picks her up like a newly married couple, and jogs toward the shoreline with her.

"How about you, gorge... umm, Cat?" Drew says, his speech drawn out and slurred by alcohol. "Need a lift to the water?" He wiggles his eyebrows at me while running his tongue over his bottom lip and, for a second, he reminds me of a housefly.

I shake my head at him. "I'm good. Thank you, though."

"Are you sure you don't want to get out of those itchy clothes?" he asks again, taking a few steps toward me. His eyes roam my body, lingering on my chest.

Drew hasn't been shy about hitting on me from the second he saw me that first day at school. He's asked me on dates a couple times, and I've always politely declined. Drew is nice enough and certainly handsome, but he's also loud and gives off an aggressive vibe, which I know all too well. I'm really not attracted to him, physically or emotionally, and the last thing I need is someone else accusing me of leading them on.

"No, really, I'm fine right here." I plant myself more firmly in the sand, crossing my legs in front of me.

"Can't say I'm not disappointed," Drew replies, continuing to eye my body from top to bottom.

"Let it go, man," Ronan says, standing a few steps to Drew's left, and I notice the edge to his voice as well as what I can only describe as a protective posture. His brow is serious, eyes slightly narrowed as they lock on Drew with a wordless warning.

Drew gives Ronan a derisive look before he turns and makes his way into the water.

"Sorry about him," Ronan says to me, his voice soft. "Are you alright with me sitting down with you?" he asks, as if he can sense my apprehension, the tension rising within me at Drew's not-so-subtle attempt to hit on me.

"Yeah, sure." I pat the sand next to me.

Ronan sits down and I catch a hint of his scent—fresh linen, sun, salty ocean, and something else that is deep, comforting, and just him. It's clean but masculine, and it makes my head a little woozy. I look at him without speaking and I can't help but smile as he cocks his head slightly to the left, an eyebrow raised.

"Is something wrong?" he asks.

"No, sorry," I laugh stupidly. "I'm just awkward, I guess."

At that he chuckles. "You don't strike me as awkward," he says. "So, Cat, is that short for something?"

I can't help but exhale deeply. This is a question I get all the time. "Nope. It's just Cat, with a *C* to boot," I explain with an exasperated eye roll.

"So, like... like the animal?" Ronan checks, and I laugh at his confused expression.

"Just like the animal," I nod, pressing my lips together.

"Interesting." Ronan flashes me a bright smile, causing my heart to flutter in my chest. "Do your parents love cats, then?"

"Not particularly," I say, laughing. "My mom was really into music by Cat Stevens when she was pregnant with me, and my last name is Stevenson, so she just went balls to the wall, I guess." I shrug, and Ronan laughs.

"Got it. Well, it suits you."

I feel my cheeks warm. "Ronan is an interesting name, too," I note, desperately attempting to get control over my face. "I've never heard it before."

"It's Irish. It means 'little seal,'" Ronan laughs.

"Really?"

"Really, really." He nods, then pauses, cocking his head to the side. "Do cats and seals get along?"

"I have no idea," I say with a laugh. "I'm not sure that's ever been tested before, considering they probably live in different climates."

"You're probably right," he chuckles.

I have to admit I enjoy the sound of his laugh.

"Okay, so you moved here from North Carolina? Just you and your mom?"

"Yep, just the two of us. I have a younger brother and sister, but they're with my dad in North Carolina for now. It's kind of... complicated," I say, not wanting to go into detail and, even if I did, I wouldn't really know how to explain.

Ronan studies me for a moment, his green eyes looking directly into my soul, and it's all I can do to meet his intense gaze before he nods almost imperceptibly. "I can understand complicated," he muses, his voice tight.

"So, how come I haven't met you before?" I ask, feeling surprisingly comfortable in his presence, though I know that this feeling can be deceptive, can lead to a false sense of security, and I warn myself to keep my guard up.

He shrugs. "Uh, well, I guess Vada and I haven't really had a chance to hang out lately, or at least when you were there, too. Things have been kind of... hectic," he says with a small frown. "Alright, so you moved from North Carolina to NYC with your mom—complicated, got it. Do you play softball with Vada and Tori?"

I nod. "Yeah, I'm a hitter," I say proudly. "Do you play ice hockey like Shane, Steve, and Drew?"

Now it's Ronan's turn to nod. "First line center forward," he says, and instantly smiles at my look of confusion.

"Sorry, I know absolutely nothing about hockey."

"No need to apologize," Ronan says reassuringly. "What does your mom do?"

"She's a psychiatrist; works mostly in crisis intervention with combat vets. It definitely keeps her busy."

"I bet it does. How about your dad?"

I laugh because the contrast between my parents' careers is so stark. "He's a high school math teacher."

"Wow!" Ronan sighs. "Talk about pressure with a teacher dad and a psychiatrist mom."

He's got a point.

"I never thought of it that way," I wonder out loud. "I don't know, my parents are pretty cool. Sure, does my mom try to psychoanalyze my every mood? Absolutely. Does she regularly sit me down on our couch and ask me about my feelings? One hundred percent. Is my dad dismayed if I get an A^- on a math exam? You bet. But other than that, it's smooth sailing at home," I say, my voice dripping with sarcasm, and Ronan laughs. It's a great laugh, and I smile at him. "No, really—it's not so bad. My dad is pretty strict, or I should say protective, but my mom makes up for it. She's laid-back and pretty easygoing. Honestly, I wonder sometimes how they ended up together because they're so different, but I guess that's the way the world goes 'round, right?" I say to Ronan, who gives me a half smile and a shrug. "What about your parents? What do they do?"

"My dad does some kind of classified work for the military. He's gone most of the time and has been for as long as I can remember. And my mother is an ER nurse at one of the hospitals in the city."

"That's got to be hard having your dad gone so much."

Ronan shrugs again. "I honestly don't know any different."

"But having a nurse as a mom; I bet that comes in handy, especially with you and Steve playing hockey—such a physical sport."

And there it is again—Ronan's expression changes for the briefest moment, and again, I can't decipher the emotion that appears in his eyes. Just as quickly as it appeared, it's gone. He doesn't address my statement though; instead he asks if I'd like another drink, motioning to the empty cup in my hand.

"Thank you, I'm fine." I'm very aware of the effects too much alcohol has on me, and I pull my legs to my chest because, despite the bonfire, I feel a bit chilled in my shorts and thin t-shirt. "I don't know how they can still be in that water." I nod in the direction of our mutual friends still splashing happily in the waves, illuminated only by the moon and the porch lights emanating from the house some feet above us.

"Well, the copious amounts of alcohol everyone has consumed probably help them not feel anything," Ronan chuckles. "Here!"

Before I can stop him, Ronan pulls his hoodie up and over his head, exposing a few inches of bare skin where his shirt pulls up along with the sweater. I see the definition in his lower abdominal muscles, a perfect V-cut that leads down and disappears into the waistband of his boxers, which peek out from his jeans.

I blush and direct my gaze away from his body before he can catch me staring. "No, I'm fine, really! I don't want you to get cold," I protest as Ronan offers me his sweatshirt, though I bet it's still nice and warm with his body heat.

"Cat, you're shivering," he says, amused. "Please."

"Okay," I say in mock defeat. I take Ronan's hoodie from his hands, push my arms through the sleeves, and pull the sweater over my head. As I had suspected, Ronan's body heat still lingers in the fibers of the fabric and I instantly cease to shiver as his warmth envelops me. As my face emerges, I catch Ronan's scent again—that particular something unique to him. It's intoxicating. I decide to leave the hood on my head for extra warmth and smile stupidly at Ronan, thankful for his thoughtfulness. He is so nice. Too nice, maybe.

"Better?" Ronan asks.

"Very much. Thank you! Are you sure you're okay, though?"

"I'm perfectly fine," he says.

I scan him for any sign of chill, but he does indeed seem comfortable. I wonder why he wore the sweater in the first place. Now his upper body is only covered by a perfectly fitted, crisp white t-shirt that hugs his shoulders, upper arms, and chest before the fit becomes slightly looser around his sculpted midsection. Even with the hoodie on, I could tell Ronan very obviously spends a good chunk of time at the gym, but I didn't expect him to be quite this cut, his lean muscles well-defined underneath his shirt, the swell of his pecs and biceps most definitely tempting my eyes to wander like some silly, lustful girl.

"How long have you known Vada?" I ask in an attempt to distract myself from looking at him too much.

"Forever. We went to preschool together. Stevie has obviously known her just as long, but they only hooked up last year. It's funny how that happened; they went from playing tag and hide and seek to, 'Ew, cooties,' to, 'Let me get in your pants.'"

I laugh, and he laughs along with me.

"Seriously," he says, "do you have any idea how weird it was when I realized my brother had a thing for Vada? That took a minute to get used to."

"I bet. Vada said she sleeps over at your house sometimes. That's got to be awkward. And how does that work with your parents and her dad?" My parents would never.

"Easy. My dad's always gone and my mom works nights."

"Wait, so it's just you and Steve at home? Alone? At night?"

"Most nights." Ronan nods. "My mother usually works twelve-hour night shifts; sometimes she'll put in eighteen and twenty-four hours. As far as what Vada tells her dad, I have no idea. You'll need to ask her. I doubt she divulges the fact that she spends the night with Steve."

"What don't I divulge to whom?" Impeccably timed as ever, Vada makes her way toward the bonfire, her movement a weird mixture between a hop and a jog, her forearms pressed against her wet upper body, her hair dripping, lips tinged blue. She's freezing. Just behind her is Steve, equally as soaked, the skin on his arms covered in goosebumps.

Ronan grabs two towels from the stack behind him and throws them at Steve, who deftly catches them and proceeds to wrap the first towel around Vada and the second around his own waist. "You haven't told your dad that you've basically moved in with Steve and me," Ronan says.

"Oh, yeah, no. Definitely not," Vada says.

"So, where does he think you spend the night?" I ask her.

"Tori's," Vada states matter-of-factly, just as Tori and the rest of the group return from the water to the bonfire. Once again Ronan distributes towels, first to the girls, then to the guys.

"It's an understanding in this group," Vada says. "If Tori wants to spend the night at Shane's, she'll tell her parents she's spending the night at my house, and vice versa. Cheyenne and Summer have the same arrangement. Well, Summer has that arrangement; Cheyenne isn't currently in a relationship."

I see Cheyenne's eyes flit to Ronan. "How would you even know, Vada?" she asks, her voice contemptuous.

Vada raises her eyebrows at Cheyenne. "Because I know who you want to hook up with, and I also happen to know that your advances haven't been all that successful. Or am I wrong?"

Cheyenne huffs loudly, collects her clothes, and turns her back toward the group. "I'm going to change." She stalks up the stairs to the house.

"Was that necessary?" Ronan asks Vada, who immediately looks guilty.

"Sorry," she says, her voice small. "I'm right though, aren't I?"

"That's beside the point. You make me feel like shit, too, when you say crap like that," Ronan grumbles, and I wonder if he's the person Cheyenne has been in pursuit of, to no avail.

"You're right, I'm sorry, Ran. She just irks me."

"Okay, let it go, guys!" Shane tries to diffuse the tension.

The girls all make their way upstairs to change back into dry clothes while the guys simply throw on their dry shirts and—keeping their towels wrapped around their hips—exchange their wet clothes for dry pants.

We spend the next hour huddled around the bonfire, which slowly dies down. I sit, appreciating the warmth that Ronan's sweater provides me, listening to the banter of the group. Vada has her head in Steve's lap. Drew passes out on one of the blankets, snoring loudly to the amusement of Zack, who pretends to be sawing wood to Drew's rhythmic grunts. Tori engages me in chatter, but my gaze finds Ronan's over and over again. His eyes more often than not meet mine, causing a weird little tingle to spread through my core.

***

I'm happily surprised at how great a time I'm having, despite my apprehension about going to a party and hanging out with people I would have perceived as exactly the kind of people to stay away from. By the time eleven-thirty rolls around, I'm dismayed to remind Vada that my curfew is in thirty minutes.

"Well, let's get you home," Vada says, equally as disappointed. She and I both stand up and wipe the sand off our clothes.

While Vada gives Steve an elaborate goodnight kiss, I take a few steps over to Ronan. I begin to pull the hem of his hoodie up and over my body, but Ronan's hand on mine stops me. "Keep it on," he says, his voice low and flowing over my skin like a warm ocean breeze. "You can give it back to me the next time we see each other." He gives me a sexy half smile, his green eyes bright despite the low light.

"That sounds like a plan," I say more confidently than I feel, and I reciprocate his smile, which makes his wider.

"Good."

"Good," I reply, blink once, and turn to leave.

***

"Did you have a good time tonight?" Vada asks me as she winds her way through my neighborhood and toward my house. "I honestly think you fit right in."

"I had a fantastic time." The evening really did go better than I had expected, given I haven't been to any sort of party in months and had sworn off gatherings like that in an act of self-preservation. "Everyone is so nice!"

"Especially Ronan, huh?" She grins, wiggling her eyebrows.

I shrug. "I have no idea what you're talking about."

Vada huffs, rolling her eyes hard. "Oh please, don't think I didn't notice you check him out constantly tonight."

The heat rises to my face, and I'm glad that the interior of Vada's car is dark. "I was just looking around."

"Hey, Kitty Cat, it's all good. And, if it makes you feel any better, he was checking you out constantly, too," Vada says, nudging my arm with her elbow.

"Really?" I hadn't noticed except for the few times when our eyes met. I guess I'm not only obvious, but also oblivious.

"Uh-huh! What do you think of him? Pretty hot, huh?"

"He's really nice," I say, acutely aware of the soft fabric of Ronan's warm hoodie caressing my skin.

"Nice? Oh, come on, Cat! Don't hold back on me."

"Fine," I concede. "He's hot! They're all hot," I say, downplaying how attracted I am to Ronan; I cannot allow myself to go there. "But, is there something between Ronan and Cheyenne? I get a weird vibe from her, and then when you made that comment about her not seeing anyone, she kind of looked at Ronan and she got all defensive."

Vada doesn't respond right away; she wrinkles her forehead and presses her lips together. "No, not really," she finally says.

"Not really?" I prod.

Vada is silent for a few seconds before she takes a deep breath. "Alright, from what I know from Summer—and obviously just watching Cheyenne and the way she interacts with Ran—Cheyenne definitely has a thing for him. My understanding is this has been going on basically since Ran and Stevie moved back from Montana almost two years ago. Cheyenne has tried to get closer to Ran, but he always deflects. Ran has never made a move on Cheyenne and always tells me he isn't interested in anything romantic."

"So, it's unreciprocated feelings from Cheyenne. That's rough, especially when you're around that person so much."

"Yeah... sort of."

I raise my eyebrows at her. "What does that mean?"

"Well, I guess like a couple of months ago, Ran and Cheyenne did hook up. I told Ran it was a stupid thing to do knowing how she feels about him, but he was adamant that it didn't mean anything. And Summer told me that Cheyenne told her that Ran said—sorry, I know this gets convoluted—that he wasn't interested in a relationship and that Cheyenne assured him it was 'just sex.' And I guess it was fine and they actually hooked up again a couple of weeks later, but..." Vada shrugs, sighing.

"Now it's not fine?"

"Right. I warned Ran that sleeping with her, regardless of what she said and their intentions at the time, was stupid because—I mean, I'm a girl, and I know I would say it didn't mean anything, too, but then I'd still secretly hope that being intimate would somehow change his mind, you know? Anyway, it didn't work, and now Cheyenne is hurt and it's really awkward. And I know Ran feels like shit about it because he didn't want to hurt her. I know he warned her, but then he still gave in to her for ten minutes of pleasure and, really, he should have known better. *Never sleep with your friends if you don't intend to take it further!*"

I can tell she's frustrated by the situation, and I certainly understand what all the tension was about earlier in the evening.

I nod in agreement with Vada's frustration. "That stinks," I murmur, not really knowing what else to say. "Were they pretty close before all this went down?"

I got the impression that although the group is tight knit, there are still two factions.

"I mean, is Cheyenne as close to Ran as I am? No. He's one of my closest friends. Usually it's Tori, Shane, Zack, Steve, Ran, and me in one huddle, and Drew, Cheyenne, and Summer in another, with Summer sort of buzzing between the two groups because Zack is her boyfriend, but Cheyenne is her best friend. Some of us are closer to each other than we are to the others, you know?"

Again, I nod. This makes sense to me. When I lived in North Carolina I had a large circle of friends—or what I thought were my friends. I was closest to my friend Julie, while others—though they were people I hung out with regularly—weren't those that I actively sought out to spend my time with. It took no time at all for them to turn against me once things fell apart.

Vada pulls up to the curb directly in front of my house. "Sorry to unload on you. I get protective of Ran, and Cheyenne bugs me."

I shake my head. "Don't even worry about it. I really had a great time tonight, and yes, Ronan is cute," I admit to her and myself shyly.

"Right? I actually had a huge crush on him when we were like thirteen. Man, you should see my diary from back then. It's embarrassing," Vada laughs.

I'm surprised by her confession. "Seriously? And now you're dating his brother!"

"I know. Weird, right? Well, they left for Montana, then came back almost two years ago, and last year things just developed between Steve and me. There was never actually anything between me and Ran; I just had butterflies for him for a hot minute there." She laughs again.

"Wow, I have to say I learned a lot tonight," I tease her as I open the passenger door and climb out of Vada's car.

"Hope none of it is too off-putting for you," Vada jokes in response.

I pretend to think about her statement for a minute, then shake my head earnestly. "I've heard worse."

"Whew"—Vada dramatically wipes the back of her hand across her brow—"that's a relief. I'll see you later, Kitty Cat!"

"Good night, Vada!"

I walk up the three steps to my front door, unlock it, and slip into the dark house, knowing that my mom, though not hovering, is still awake in her room, waiting to hear me come home before she turns in for the night.

Ronan

It's just after two-thirty when I manage to drag my drunk-off-his-ass brother back to his car and I begin our drive home. Steve is passed out in the passenger seat, his head tipped against the window. Any attempts to wake him or have a conversation with him are futile, leaving me without any distraction from my thoughts of Cat.

She keeps crossing my mind during the drive home.

I had every intention of just relaxing this evening, maybe having a few drinks to numb my brain, but then I got so caught up in talking with Cat that I really didn't want to drink, didn't want my thoughts to blur, for the world to slow down around me. Even when Cat was sitting down, chatting with Vada and Tori later in the evening, I found myself getting distracted, my eyes wandering to her. I've never met this girl before tonight, but fuck, her energy was so damn familiar and it felt like I had been around her, had talked to her a thousand times before. It's disconcerting how badly I want to see and talk to her again. This can't be fucking happening; I can't catch feelings for some girl. Not now, not ever. It's not what I do. It's not safe.

"Fuck," I mutter under my breath when I finally pull up to the house and my headlights illuminate the white Camry parked in the driveway. My mother is home instead of at work like I thought. I have a 1 a.m. curfew; that's if I'm not working and my parents are home, which they typically aren't. With my dad mostly gone and my mom working nights, Steve and I don't usually pay close attention to when we get in on the weekends, except when we know one of our parents is home. Because Steve is a year older than me, he has a 2 a.m. curfew. Stupid, right? Especially given that we have the same group of friends and hang out so much. It's honestly the dumbest thing when I have to end my night an hour before Steve. He's usually nice enough to cut his night short, too, unless things are getting hot and heavy with Vada, then he just sends me on my way. And now that Steve is officially eighteen, he doesn't have a curfew at all anymore, starting now, I guess. But I still do, which is complete bullshit. But that argument doesn't fly in my house, and seeing as it's now past three in the morning and my mom is unexpectedly home, I'm obviously well past my usual curfew. Fuck.

I shut off the engine and nudge Steve to wake up. He doesn't stir, even when I punch him hard in the shoulder.

"God damn it," I grunt, step out of the car, and move around the front to Steve's door. When I open it, he slumps to the side, and I brace my hand against his right shoulder to prevent him from falling out of the car. I bend over and sling his right arm over my shoulder and around my neck, hoisting him into a standing position. I slam the door shut with my foot and begin to maneuver Steve to the house, briefly contemplating the easiest—and quietest—way to get him inside. I decide to just use the front door, which is the fastest way upstairs, and regardless of which option I choose—the backyard, the garage, or the front door—I'll have to figure out a way to get Steve up a bunch of steps before we're even inside the house.

Steve only weighs a few pounds more than me, but at the moment he's nothing but dead weight and I struggle to get him up the front steps, cursing under my breath as he mumbles incoherently. He really pounded back those shots after Vada left with Cat, and I start to think we should have just stayed at the beach house so Steve could sleep it off. But I wanted to give Shane and Tori some space because they were getting pretty handsy with each other, and besides, Onyx has been in the backyard all day, which makes me feel guilty.

Onyx is my black German Shepherd. Well, technically she's our family dog, but she spends most of her time with me and sleeps in my bed. I'm the one who walks and feeds her, and she gets really upset when I leave her for too long, so really she's my dog.

I finally accomplish the near-Herculean task of getting Steve, whose legs have apparently lost all bones and muscle, up the stairs. I unlock the front door, pushing it open with my right hand while still supporting almost all of Steve's body weight with my left shoulder. I take a deep breath and mentally prepare myself to drag my brother up the stairs to his bedroom. By the time I make it up the twenty-four steps—I have never counted them before tonight—into Steve's room and let him plop onto his bed, I'm sweaty and out of breath. I roll him onto his side in case he needs to throw up and I pull his boots off, letting them fall to the ground. He mutters something I can't understand, and I walk through the bathroom into my own room where I pull off my own shoes and socks. I discard the socks in the hamper and tiptoe out onto the landing and back down the stairs to stash the shoes in the closet.

The living room is dark when I walk to the sliding glass door to let Onyx into the house. As soon as she hears the click of the lock, she comes bounding toward me, her tail wagging as she squeezes past me and into the house.

The light in the living room turns on as I lock the door. My heart sinks, beginning to beat double-time in my chest; I know what's about to happen. I can sense it.

"Where the hell have you guys been?" My mother's words are short, her voice harsh.

I turn to face her. She's dressed in a pair of navy pajama bottoms with a matching button-up top and black slippers. Her arms are crossed in front of her chest, and she looks pissed.

"At Shane's," I say, not moving an inch. "I thought you were working tonight." I keep my voice neutral so as not to come across as having a shitty attitude.

"What does that have to do with anything?"

I know there is absolutely no response to this question that would satisfy her, so I let it stand unanswered.

"And who the fuck do you think you are, getting in at past three in the morning?" she growls, looking at the watch on her wrist. "God, Ronan, you are such a little shit. You just cannot follow the rules around here, can you?" She takes a step toward me. "Where is your brother?" she hisses.

"Upstairs. He's sleeping," I say, willing myself to keep looking her in the eyes.

She continues toward me, stopping a mere two feet away. "Are you drunk?" Her voice is sharp but low so as not to wake Steve. She scans me for signs of intoxication. As an ER nurse she's skilled at detecting the signs of drug and alcohol use—bloodshot, watery eyes; the smell of alcohol; slurred speech; dilated pupils; unsteady gate; and a swaying stance.

"No," I say truthfully, but know it won't matter. Whether I say yes or no, the outcome will be the same tonight.

"Don't fucking lie to me, Ronan! I can smell the alcohol on your breath."

She's shorter than me by almost a foot, and petite—maybe a hundred and twenty pounds—but she packs a punch, and years of conditioning have made me acutely aware—and afraid—of my mother's wrath.

"I had a beer." I swallow hard and I break the eye contact, looking at her feet.

Without a warning or another word, her right fist crashes into my jaw and it knocks me backwards into the glass door. Before I can get my bearings, my mother takes another step toward me and follows her hit up with a punch to my gut, eliciting a grunt from me as nausea and pain threaten to bring me to my knees.

Onyx is at my feet, whimpering as I stand doubled-over, my right arm across my stomach, while I cradle my left hand against my jaw. I try to steady myself, black dots popping in front of my eyes.

"Lie to me again, Ronan!" she dares me, taking another step toward me as she balls her fist.

I raise my hands in front of me, ducking my head. "I'm not lying. I had *a* beer. I'm sorry I broke curfew." The words spill from my mouth. My breathing is hectic, and I feel like a fucking child. Adrenaline pushes forcefully through my veins, fine-tuning my senses, and I try desperately to defy my body's fight-or-flight response. Neither reaction has served me well in the past, and I've gotten good at suppressing my instincts to flee or defend myself.

My mother evaluates me for a few seconds, her brows furrowed, eyes unfeeling, before she finally unclenches her fist and her face softens. "Get to bed," she orders simply, and turns to walk back upstairs.

I don't move until I hear her bedroom door close, then take a shaky breath, flinching as I move my jaw from left to right and crack my neck. The spot where her fist connected with my face throbs painfully, but all in all this could have been a lot worse.

I motion for Onyx to follow me upstairs as I tiptoe my way into my room, then lock the door behind me. Onyx hops onto my bed, makes a couple of circles, and lays down at the foot of my mattress.

I pull my shirt over my head, careful not to bump the fresh bruise, then unbutton my jeans and drop them to the floor. I sneak into the bathroom where I close the door to Steve's room before I turn on the light and position myself in front of the mirror. I turn my head to examine my injury. Already a blue hue is spreading across my jawline, painting it like watercolors, and I try to think of some excuse to tell my friends and Steve when they inevitably ask me what caused this bruise. Frustrated by my goddamn inability to defend myself, I yank my toothbrush from its holder, smear some toothpaste on it, and brush my teeth angrily, making my jaw hurt even more.

Finally I shut off the light to the bathroom and walk back to my bed, where I crawl under my blanket and shut my eyes tightly, willing myself to drift into unconsciousness.

Sunday, May 2nd

Ronan

"What the fuck happened to your jaw?" Shane asks me first thing this morning when I meet him at the gym.

I woke up early this morning after a restless few hours filled with confused dreams. I called Shane, waking him from a deep sleep to convince him to work out with me. It's what I do when I'm restless, overwhelmed, or frustrated—unable to express some shitty fucking emotion trapped inside my worthless head. I go and work out, push my body to its limit in an effort to make it bigger, stronger, better. It's always about being better.

"Man, Stevie was so damn wasted last night I had to drag him into the house and I got knocked around," I lie, keeping my face neutral, completely expressionless.

Shane narrows his eyes at me for a moment but doesn't question the bullshit excuse. Not this time. "He really went for it with that tequila after Vada went home," he agrees with a chuckle.

I nod. "Yeah, he did."

"Good thing you were so mesmerized by Cat that you apparently forgot how to drink and were able to drive," Shane says with a smirk.

I frown. "What the hell are you talking about?" I train my gaze on the barbell in front of me; I know exactly what he's getting at.

"Oh, come the fuck on, Ran," he laughs, and nudges me with his elbow. "I'm not blind, man. I noticed the way you kept looking at her, and I'm pretty sure I saw her wear your sweater."

"She was cold, dude. I'm not a fucking asshole."

Shane grins widely. "Yeah? Maybe you should have offered to warm her up with your body instead. I fully expected you to take her back up to the house and do your thing, man," he chuckles, because that is exactly what I'd usually do.

I would set my sights on a girl for a night and then flirt, charm, and compliment my way into her pants or under her skirt. Though it wasn't unusual for a girl to make the first move, which I rarely turn down.

But a hookup with Cat didn't even cross my mind. She just seems so different from the girls I've been with. I could tell she was uncomfortable last night, her body tensing when Drew stumbled toward her and pressured her into getting in the water. Cat told him "no" a few times, and her body language made it clear she didn't intend to go anywhere with Drew last night—or ever—but he just wouldn't back off, which pissed me off to no end and resulted in an overwhelming need to step in, to protect her, to make her feel at ease. So I told Drew to knock it off and asked for Cat's permission to sit with her. We talked for a while, and though she warmed up a bit—physically and emotionally, I guess, after I gave her my hoodie to shield her from the ocean breeze—I got the impression she's guarded and cautious, analytical and aware. She didn't come on to me, and I didn't come on to her.

She's a beautiful girl—fuck, so damn beautiful—but I sense darkness. I could see it in her eyes—the fractures. Tiny, but there nonetheless. I can tell because I know all about that, and I would be a horrible person if I made a move on Cat, if I let myself feel anything for her, because I would shatter her. I could never be enough. For anyone.

"Whatever." I shrug, which is my way of telling Shane that I'm done talking about a particular subject.

He doesn't bring up Cat again for the rest of our workout.

***

"You want to hang out later, or do you have plans with Tori?" I ask Shane when we finally walk out of the gym and back to our cars.

"Yeah, she's coming over a little later today. Not sure what we're going to do yet, but I'm sure she won't mind you hanging out."

I used to spend most of my time outside of school, work, and hockey with Shane whenever I lived in New York, but that has understandably changed ever since he started dating Tori. He has different priorities now, and I don't blame him, but the unfortunate side effect is that I can no longer count on Shane's place as a sure hideout, as a refuge—not unless I want to encroach on his time and privacy with Tori, which I'd never want to do.

"Yeah, okay. Maybe just text me when you guys have figured out what you're gonna do." I guess my decision will depend on the vibes at home. I don't really want to cockblock Shane, and I also don't want to feel like the odd man out, but anything can be better than being home.

I never really know what I'm about to walk into, but when I get home, my mother is in the hallway, sorting through a stack of unopened mail, quietly singing along to some country song.

She looks up at me, her face soft, posture unthreatening when I shut the front door. "Hey," she greets me, like our last interaction didn't end in violence.

"Hey." I'm already in the process of taking off my shoes so as not to drag any dirt into the house. I feel my mom's eyes on me when I put my shoes in their normal spot and out of the way.

"How was your workout?" She has obviously noted my attire, my sleeveless shirt stuck to my body with sweat.

"It was good," I tell her, itching to get back up to my room, which is about the safest place for me in this house.

"That's great, Ran." Her use of my nickname provides further confirmation that she's in a good mood... for now. "How... How is your jaw?" She's already reaching for me, her hand on my chin, turning my head to the right to grant her a better view of the injury she inflicted last night.

"It's fine," I say simply, but she doesn't release me as the silence between us grows awkward.

"I have some arnica upstairs. Let me get it for you. It helps with the bruising," she says, lets go of me, and walks past me up the stairs to the master bathroom. I hear her rummaging through the medicine cabinet. I just stand there, rooted to the spot, waiting for her to return, which she does a minute later, smiling brightly as she hands me a tube of the medicine. "Put some of this on your jaw a few times a day. It'll take care of the discoloration." She makes to place her hand on my left cheek, but I instinctively move my head out of her reach.

"Thanks, Mom. It'll be fine."

She nods, biting her bottom lip, her eyes flitting between my bruised jaw and my eyes, a pained expression on her face like she's battling with herself.

"I'm sorry for hurting you," she finally says, just like I knew she would. I could practically see the words waiting to tumble out of her mouth. "That wasn't okay," she adds quietly as if she's talking more to herself than me, then locks eyes with me. "But when you're not working, Ronan, your curfew is 1 a.m. Not a minute later, do you understand me? You know how much it bothers me when you disrespect me and my rules."

I nod. "Yeah. Sorry, Mom."

"It's... You need to get this under control. Stop disobeying. Do as you're told, and we won't keep having these issues, okay? Don't make me angry," she says, her tone a mixture between a plea and an order.

"Sorry," I say again, and she nods.

"Okay, well, why don't you go shower and put on some of that arnica. Want something to eat?" she asks, her voice chipper. "I have leftover lasagna. I made it with ground turkey." She walks into the kitchen without waiting for my response. "Oh, maybe wake your brother and see if he feels like eating something," my mom laughs from the kitchen.

I exhale deeply, then walk up the stairs and to my room. I shower, get dressed, then unceremoniously march into Steve's room, grinning. He's still passed out, wearing the same clothes he wore yesterday, lying with his face buried in his pillow, his left arm hanging off the side of his mattress. I'd be worried that he's dead, but the steady rise and fall of his rib cage lets me know he's still very much alive.

I nudge his dangling hand with my foot. "Stevie!"

He doesn't stir. God, he was so trashed last night. I think I counted seven or eight shots of tequila and at least a couple of beers between the time Vada took Cat home at eleven-thirty and when I heaved Steve into the passenger seat of his Challenger to drive him home three hours later.

"Stevie!" I say again, louder, but he still doesn't move. I place my foot against his bed and kick it forcefully enough that my brother startles awake, jerking upright only to apparently regret his quick movement a fraction of a second later; he grips his head tightly with both hands.

"God, fuck you, Ran," Steve groans, making me laugh.

"How are you feeling today, birthday boy?" I ask him with a smirk, convinced he feels like death. He looks and smells like death, that's for sure.

Steve just grunts and forces himself out of bed, standing for a moment while I observe him. I feel a mixture of pity and amusement as what little color he had drains from his face before he bolts past me and into our shared bathroom. I hear him drop to his knees and retch just a few seconds later.

"Mom wanted me to tell you that she has leftover lasagna if you're hungry," I call to him with a mean grin on my face, knowing full well that the last thing on Steve's mind right now is food.

"Fuck you so much," he moans, and I hear him gag again.

I sit on the edge of his bed and wait for him to finish throwing up, not particularly keen on walking back into my room through our shared bathroom. I can handle a lot of things, but seeing, hearing, or smelling people vomit is *not* one of those things, so I wait.

"Jesus Christ," Steve groans when he finally returns to his bedroom. He looks like he already feels a lot better after his little heart-to-heart with our toilet.

"Better?" I say with a chuckle.

"Much." He nods and pulls his shirt over his head, then drops it to the floor by his feet where it joins the boots I pulled off him last night. He unbuttons his jeans, which is my cue to head back into my own room.

I make my bed, take my sweaty gym clothes to toss them in the hamper, and walk back downstairs with a basket full of my dirty clothes. I head through the kitchen and into the garage to start a load of laundry.

Sunday, May 23rd

Cat

Time is a funny thing, isn't it? When you want it to slow down—either because you're living some of your best moments or because you know something dreadful is coming up—it seemingly speeds up, whereas when you want it to pass quickly, it tends to drag on and on.

This past month has flown by, and so this weekend I've found myself holed up in my room, poring over textbooks, class notes, outlines, and little index cards, studying for final exams next week before summer finally kicks off.

I take the occasional break to grab a snack, text Vada, Tori, or my friend Julie, and around three in the afternoon I finally put my stuff away. I feel drained, my brain no longer able to store any additional information about isotopes or the half-life of uranium.

I stand and take a look around my still-bare room. Since moving here almost six weeks ago I've moved my bedroom and desk three times, trying to maximize the small space. There are still boxes I haven't unpacked, and I make a note to spend some time this summer organizing my room and making it cozier.

The ringing of my phone draws my attention away from my plans. I answer Julie's call, spending a good thirty minutes chatting about our current goings-on. I also fill her in on my mom's plan to head home to North Carolina in a couple of weeks to spend some time with my dad and siblings. I'm both excited and nervous to be back there.

"It'll be totally alright," Julie reassures me. "You know Nate and I got your back, right? Screw Adam and his posse."

Anxiety bubbles up in my stomach. "It's not just Adam, it's literally everyone in town."

"Cat, first of all, it's not everyone. And secondly, you did nothing wrong!"

I shake my head with my phone to my ear because I have a hard time believing her. Julie has always been my biggest supporter, but even she couldn't save me from the vitriol that was spewed at me from so many people before my mom finally decided to remove me from the situation.

"Things have simmered down. And it'll be so fun to have you home for a few days. I miss you!"

"I miss you, too." I really do. I miss my friends, I miss my dad, my sister and brother.

The door to my room opens and my mom brings in a basket of clean, folded laundry that she sets down in front of my bed. My eyes immediately find the dark-green sweater—folded neatly atop the rest of my clothes—and my heart gives an unexpected jolt as my thoughts turn away from my conversation with Julie to Ronan. I haven't really spent any time with him since meeting him at his brother's birthday party a few weeks ago, only crossing paths with Ronan at school here and there, but I've inadvertently found myself thinking of him at random times, which always throws me off.

I've run into him at school and we've stopped to chat for a few minutes between classes. Just last week, actually, I stepped out of my French class to use the restroom and bumped into Ronan in the hallway. That strange flutter immediately expanded in my stomach, especially when he looked up at me as I approached him at the water fountain.

"Ditching class again?" Ronan chuckled.

I grinned. "You know it. You?"

"Obviously," Ronan laughed. "What class do you have right now?"

"French. With Ms. Trudeaux."

Ronan made a face. "And all you got yourself was a hall pass? You need to fake sick and just go to the nurse's station."

"It's not so bad," I giggled.

"Whatever you say," he chuckled.

"How about you? What class are you escaping?" I was enjoying our banter way too much, and I knew it.

"History," he told me so dryly that I had to laugh yet again, which made him smile in turn. "My plan is to slowly drink about a gallon of water from this fountain, praying for time to pass so I don't have to go back in there. I'm pretty sure boredom can be a cause of death."

"Sounds terrible," I told him with a grin.

"Take the damn class and find out for yourself. Or, actually, maybe don't take it. I wouldn't want you to die of boredom, or anything, actually." His eyes met mine, the air between us crackling for a moment.

We were interrupted by a girl who approached us and struck up a conversation with Ronan, her tone flirty, suggestive. So I simply waved goodbye and made my way to the restroom.

"Umm... Cat? Hello? Are you still there?" Julie's voice comes from my phone's speaker, and my thoughts snap back to her and our conversation.

"Sorry, brain fart," I say, taking a deep breath to get Ronan out of my head. He should not reside there. I can't let him invade my thoughts. "What did you say?"

Julie's laugh rings through the speaker. "I was just saying that I have to let you go. I'm heading out to meet Nate."

"Oh, okay. Hey, tell him I said hi."

"Will do. I'll talk to you later!"

We hang up, and I turn my attention back to the clothes basket, and more specifically Ronan's sweater. I scoot to the foot of my bed and move the hoodie from the basket and onto my comforter. I should really get this back to him, but have no way of contacting Ronan; I neither have his phone number nor know where he lives. I guess I could call Vada and get that info from her, but I have a thing about seeming too forward, too aggressive, too permissive. It got me in trouble in the past, and it's not about to get me in trouble again.

So I get up from my bed and grab the handles of the laundry basket, walk over to my little closet, and begin putting away the laundry my mom had washed and folded for me, making a mental note to thank her.

I'm used to being self-sufficient. Both my parents work, and my brother and sister are quite a bit younger than me, so it was usually on me to pick them up from school, feed them, and do basic chores before my parents got home every night. To alleviate some of the burdens on everyone, I took it upon myself to wash and fold my own laundry. Since moving to New York, things have been a bit easier, obviously, as my brother and sister stayed with my dad while my parents figure everything out. They both agreed that they didn't want to uproot my siblings in the middle of the school year.

My phone buzzes while I put away the last pieces of clothing and I pick it up off my bed. Vada's name is displayed in large letters across the screen, and I push the button to answer.

"Hey!" I say, chipper.

"Hey Kitty Cat! What are you up to?"

"Not much; putting away laundry. How about you?"

"Just got done cramming whatever crap I can into my brain and now I'm ready to relax. Feel like going to a movie?"

I can picture her lounging on her queen-sized bed. Vada's room is decorated in a beachy, minimalist theme with nude neutral tones, a hanging wicker chair, and a giant majesty palm in the corner by her window. It's the most relaxing room I've ever stepped foot in, and I love hanging out at Vada's and doing my homework there.

"Actually, that sounds fun." I haven't been to the movies in forever.

"Sweet, I'll be there to pick you up in about ten minutes," Vada says, and hangs up the phone before I can get another word in.

I put the last few clothes in my closet, then step in front of my floor-length mirror and make a face. My hair is in a messy bun and I'm still in my black sweatpants and oversized Duke sweater that I may or may not have swiped from my dad's closet before I moved. So I grab a pair of faded blue jeans and a heather-gray crew neck shirt and change outfits. I hastily pull the tie out of my hair, letting it fall loosely across my shoulders and down my back. I give it a rough brush, put some mascara on my lashes, and add a little blush to my cheeks, thinking I really should try to get some more sun; I look ghostly pale for this far into May.

I yank a green plaid flannel off its hanger in case I get cold at the movies, tie it around my waist, and race down the mahogany stairs. I'm taking two steps at a time when I hear a knock on the front door.

My mom beats me to the door, opens it, and smiles as she invites Vada into the house.

"Hi, Mrs. Stevenson," Vada says politely.

"You have stop calling me that," my mom says. "It's Jen, please, just Jen."

"My dad would have a heart attack, but if you insist," Vada laughs.

I've met her dad: he's a short, stout man with tightly cropped hair the same shade of bronze-brown as his son and daughter. He's a professional through and through, ever the lawyer, but he's also really nice. He works crazy hours from what I understand. Makes sense; I know lawyers work a lot.

Zack has told me his father prosecutes violent crimes, homicides and all that. I cannot imagine the things he must see on a daily basis, but putting away bad guys is certainly worth it. Vada and Zack's parents divorced years ago—the demand of their respective careers too much for their marriage—and Zack and Vada live with their dad full-time. Their mom, a flight attendant for one of the major airlines, travels overseas too much to make it feasible for the twins to live with her, but both spend as much time with their mom as possible.

"Are you ready to go?" Vada turns to me as I slip my feet into my black Doc Martens boots.

"Where are you guys headed?" my mom asks.

"We were going to head to a movie," Vada informs her, "and then maybe hang out after, if that's alright with you. I don't know, maybe grab some dinner?" I can't tell if the question is directed at me or my mom.

"How fun!" my mom says and turns to me. "You have exams tomorrow, so curfew is nine. Please have your phone on you," she says, handing me some cash from her purse.

"Thank you, Mom!" I exclaim.

She smiles at me and Vada. "Be safe, girls!"

Vada and I drive for only a few minutes before Vada pulls up to a curb and puts her car in park, then turns off the ignition.

"Where are we?" I say, confused as Vada steps out of the car. We're stopped in front of a brick two-story home. Like my house, some steps lead up to a stoop and a dark-green front door. There isn't much of a front yard, but the solid wood fence to the left of the house and the garage leads me to believe there's a fairly sizeable backyard.

"Steve's," Vada says matter-of-factly.

I follow her up the five or so steps, where she knocks on the front door. I laugh to myself; did I seriously think it was just going to be the two of us going to the movies? Of course not.

"But of course," I say with a laugh. "Who else is joining?" I ask, wondering if she'll say Ronan's name and gauging how I would feel if he joined us at the movies.

"Zack and Summer are meeting us there," she says, just as a young-looking woman opens the front door. I wouldn't peg her as older than late-twenties or early thirties. She has blonde hair that's pulled back into a tight ponytail and familiar-looking green eyes. She's around five foot six and slender. Her light-blue scrubs are perfectly fitted, and the badge clipped to her breast pocket displays the name of a hospital, and below it a picture of her and the name "Rica Soult." This must be Ronan and Steve's mom, and by the looks of it she's either heading to or coming home from her shift as a nurse.

"Oh hi, Vada," she says, standing aside so Vada and I can enter the house. We step into a small hallway with stairs directly in front of us leading to the second story of the home. To the left, the hallway leads to the living room on the right and then straight to the kitchen.

"Steve!" Mrs. Soult calls upstairs. "Vada is here with..." She stops and looks at me, apparently realizing she hasn't met me yet.

"Mrs. Soult, this is my friend Cat," Vada says.

"It's nice to meet you," Mrs. Soult tells me. She studies my face for a moment before she turns toward the stairs again, where Steve has just appeared at the top. "I have to get going. I'm scheduled for an eighteen-hour shift, so I won't be back until tomorrow afternoon," she tells Steve. She grabs her purse and keys, then heads past Vada and me and out the door without saying goodbye.

I give Vada a look conveying how weird this interaction was. "She's kind of gruff," Vada whispers to me.

Steve arrives at the bottom of the stairs and pulls Vada into his arms to give her a kiss on her forehead.

"Are you ready to go? The movie starts in thirty minutes," Vada says, her tone flirty and light as her arms wrap tightly around her boyfriend.

"Yeah, I just need to grab my wallet and keys. Do you think you'll be okay at the movies like this, or do you want me to grab you one of my sweaters?" Steve looks admiringly at Vada, who is wearing cutoff jean shorts and a tank top.

"A sweater might not be a bad idea," Vada muses. "And actually, I'm going to go to the ladies' room before we head out." She follows Steve upstairs, but briefly turns to me. "Be right back!"

Just as Steve and Vada disappear up the stairs, the back door in the kitchen opens. My breath catches when Ronan enters the house from the garage, a black German Shepherd prancing behind him. The dog stops to look at me. Ronan, on the other hand, doesn't notice me right away and startles when I say, "Hi," from the hallway.

"Hey. What... What are you doing here?" He briefly scans his surroundings before he gives me a dazzling smile as he steps out of the kitchen and into the hallway, his dog not missing a beat, following him like a shadow. Ronan must have been working in the garage because his hands are black and greasy, and I spot a smudge of some oily substance under his right eye.

"We're heading to the movies." I crouch and hold my hand out to the dog. It looks up at Ronan as if awaiting his permission to approach me. Ronan smiles, then gives the dog a quick nod. It joyfully tramps over to me, offering me its belly the moment I begin scratching behinds its ears.

"You're much less scary than you look," I giggle at the dog, then look back at Ronan, whose smile makes my heart hammer stupidly in my chest.

"Nah, Onyx isn't scary." Ronan claps his left palm against his leg once and Onyx follows him as he walks to a sliding glass door leading to the backyard. "Come on, girl. It's nice outside," Ronan says to Onyx. I smile at his sweet way of talking to his dog and watch Ronan close the door once Onyx is outside.

"Are you joining us at the movies?" I ask, not totally sure what I want his answer to be.

"I can't," Ronan says, and I'm surprisingly pleased by the disappointment in his voice. "I'm working tonight."

I didn't even know he had a job. "Oh. Where do you work?"

Ronan walks past me and back into the kitchen. "Murphy's." He scans my eyes for recognition. When he doesn't find it, he adds, "It's one of Shane's parents' places."

"Oh wait, that's on Seventeenth, right? I've eaten there before. It's this Irish pub-slash-restaurant? Awesome bangers and mash."

Ronan smiles at me. "That's the one."

"How long will you be working tonight?" I feel myself relax around him just like I did the night I met him and every time I've run into him since. There's something about him that makes me feel comfortable, safe, and I have to once again remind myself to remain vigilant, to keep my guard up. I will not repeat history.

"Only till ten tonight."

I watch in silence as Ronan turns on the kitchen faucet and scrubs his grimy hands. I scan his perfect face, the arch of his nose, the shape of his full lips, his masculine jawline. He must feel my gaze because he turns his head to look at me while working the soapy suds into his skin.

I give him a small smile and put my finger below my right eye. "You have something under your eye," I say. "Right there."

He attempts to remove the spot, and I instinctively move toward him. I wet my hand under the still-running faucet and touch my fingers to his cheek to wipe off the smudge. His eyes stay focused on me, though I don't dare take my gaze off my hand. The warmth of his soft skin spreads from my fingertips all the way down my arm. I once again notice his full lips. I wonder what it would feel like to kiss those lips, what he would taste like.

I'm pulled back into reality when Vada clears her throat behind me, and Ronan's eyes snap from mine to Vada.

"What are you two doing?" Vada's voice is pitchy and excited.

I yank my hand away from Ronan's face, clamping it to my side. Telltale heat rises in my face; I feel caught doing something I shouldn't.

"Cat was helping me get some grease off," Ronan says, not a hint of embarrassment or unease in his voice. He looks back at me. "Did you get it?" His eyes smile at me, and he runs his left thumb over the wet spot I left on his high cheekbone.

My anxiety eases. I nod and take a step back. "Yep, all clean."

"Thank you," he says, taking me in with his eyes for a long moment before he resumes scrubbing his hands.

"Alright, let's head out," Steve orders from behind Vada, who grabs my hand and pulls me down the hallway with her.

“I’ll see you later,” Ronan says, low enough that only I can hear it. I smile at him, giving him a nod.

***

The movie is entertaining enough—lots of action, just a bit of romance—and the two hours pass quickly. I’m not a big fan of popcorn, so I’m positively ravenous by the time the lights come back on and am overjoyed when Zack suggests grabbing a bite to eat.

“You guys feel like Murphy’s? Ran and Shane are working tonight,” Steve says, and there’s a general murmur of assent.

Within twenty minutes Vada pulls into the small parking lot of an old, industrial-looking building. Above the double doors, flanked by two large windows, is a shamrock and the name “Murphy’s” in Gaelic. From the outside Murphy’s doesn’t look like much, but once we step through the doors it’s almost as though we step back in time. The floors are a creaky hardwood, worn and soft with the slightest give when we walk, and the whole place smells of mahogany, teakwood, cedar, as well as the deliciously wafting vapors of food and ale. It’s barely seven-thirty on a Sunday evening, and already this place is packed.

Murphy’s is a great place for people watching if you’re into that kind of stuff, because it really doesn’t cater to just one type of customer. There’s a loud group of five or six guys hanging out by the bar, right next to two older gentlemen in suits. Just a little farther into the restaurant, a family of four has squeezed into a booth; the mom bounces a restless toddler on her knee while the dad peruses the menu next to his older child, who’s playing with her dad’s phone.

We’re standing in the entrance, looking for an open table, when Shane spots us from behind the bar counter. He smiles and strides toward us. He’s wearing a black long-sleeved shirt with “Murphy’s” printed in small letters on his chest. A small green apron is secured around his waist and his undercut strawberry blond hair is pulled back into a small bun. The reddish scruff on his chin and cheeks makes it clear he hasn't bothered to shave in a few days, and even though I know his parents disapprove of this look as "unprofessional," I have to admit that Shane pulls it off nicely. His whole vibe fits Murphy's perfectly.

"Hey guys!" he calls out, his hand raised in a greeting. "I didn't know you were going to show up here tonight."

"We went to a movie and then thought we should grab a bite to eat. Obviously, there's no place better than Murphy's, especially with you and Ran working tonight," Zack explains, his arm draped over Summer's shoulder.

Shane stands with his hands on his hips looking first at us and then around the crowded room. "Well said, mate," he says in a fake Irish accent, then motions for us to follow him to a booth just past the bar area. "It's kind of a tight squeeze; for some reason we're packed tonight. If something else opens up, feel free to grab it."

Shane's right. The only tables available accommodate no more than two people. Vada and Summer slide into the booth, followed by Steve and Zack. At the booth next to ours, Shane seeks permission to grab one of their unused extra chairs, then moves it, offering me a seat.

"Where's my brother?" Steve asks, poking his head around the room.

"Taking his break." Shane nods toward a door behind the bar. "I'll send him your way when he's back. He'll be so stoked to wait on you guys." Shane laughs mischievously, and the guys chuckle. "What do you all want to drink?"

Shane listens as Summer, Vada, Zack, and Steve inform him of their beverage choices.

"How about you?" Shane asks me.

"Uh... I have no idea," I say, because I really don't. It's not that I've never had a drink. In fact, nothing could be further from the truth. It's just that I never really knew exactly what I was drinking. I was always too trusting, too infatuated, too giddy and stupid to say, "No, thank you," even once I learned what I do when the booze takes effect, when I get tipsy, when I lose my inhibitions.

"What do you like?" Shane asks.

I shrug. "I'll just take a water."

Shane chuckles and winks at me. "I'll surprise you."

He returns mere minutes later, a round tray skillfully balanced atop his right hand holding five glasses of water and five more glasses containing liquids of varying shades and hues, as well as a tiny shot glass with some brownish liquor.

"Pale Ale for Zack." Shane slides the pint of beer toward Zack, followed by a glass of water. "Guinness for Steve. Malibu Pineapples with extra cherries for Summer and Vada, and—my favorite—an L.A. water for Cat. Cheers!" He lifts the small shot glass off the tray and drinks whatever liquor was inside it without making even the slightest face.

"So, how does it feel to be officially done with high school?" Zack asks Steve and Shane, both of whom were seniors and took their last finals early last week, then walked at graduation Friday night.

"Pretty fucking great," Steve says with a fervent nod.

Shane laughs. "Feels like freedom," he says, then walks back to the bar.

Ronan's break must be over, because at that moment he appears behind the bar counter. He's also wearing a black shirt, the long sleeves pushed up over his elbows. Shane tells him something, and Ronan's eyes find our group, then me. A smile tugs at his lips as he grabs something from the counter and walks over to our table.

"Hi Ran!" Vada exclaims. She leans over Steve and wraps her left arm awkwardly around Ronan's waist to give him a half squeeze-hug.

Ronan rests his left hand on the back of my chair and his knuckles lightly graze my back. It feels like electricity going down my spine. I can't tell if his physical contact is purposeful or pure accident, but he doesn't pull back his hand and instead glides his thumb an inch up and down my back.

Nobody notices this momentary physical interaction between us.

"Hey guys. How was the movie?" Ronan asks, and Summer and Zack give a quick critique of the film.

"Would have been nice if you had been able to join us." Vada looks at me with a smirk. "And then Cat wouldn't have been so lonely." She now has a full-blown smile on her face.

"You're pretty pushy, you know that?" Ronan says, his brows creasing.

"I sure do!" Vada says and folds her arms.

"Okay, so do you guys need to see menus, or do you want the usual?" Ronan offers us a stack of laminated menus.

"Can't hurt to look." Steve takes the menus from Ronan's hand and distributes them around the table. "How's your day so far? Looks busy!"

"It's insane," Ronan says, a slight frown on his face. "I was hoping it would be slow so I can cram for calculus tomorrow, but it doesn't look like I'll have much luck."

"I bet it's because it's almost summer break and you have the college students," Zack says.

"Probably," Ronan agrees. "College students, and you guys," he teases, that half smile of his flashing again.

"Whatever, you know you love it when you get to serve us." Steve elbows his little brother in the side. "That's sort of the job of a younger sibling. To serve and... well, that's it."

Ronan nods slyly. "You know I'm the one handling your food, right?"

"And I would know if you spit in it."

"Would you, though?" Ronan says, eyebrows raised and his eyes mischievous.

"Do it and I won't give you a birthday present," Steve threatens jokingly.

"When have you *ever* given me a birthday present?"

Everyone is laughing at the brothers' back-and-forth.

"There's a first for everything." Steve shrugs. "Apparently this year is not it." He exaggeratedly props up his menu, pretending to peruse the selection.

"If you guys are done being dicks to each other, can I order the corned beef hash?" Zack says, fake annoyance in his voice.

"Noted," Ronan says, looking expectantly around the table.

"Oh, I'll have the same." Vada hands her menu to Ronan.

Summer orders a club sandwich, while Steve just asks Ronan to bring him "the usual."

"How about you, Cat?" Ronan asks. His voice is sexy as he says my name. "Bangers and mash?"

"How did you know?" I ask, confidently returning his gaze.

"You mentioned it earlier today."

I smile. "You paid attention."

"I try." He flashes me a smile that sends ripples through my body, then collects the rest of our menus. He turns to leave to put in our orders, but not before giving my back another tiny rub with his thumb, once again shooting electricity down my spine. I watch him walk away out of the corner of my eye, paying attention to his dark-washed jeans hugging his hips and the way his black shirt hints at his muscular back and V-shaped torso.

"In all seriousness, babe, what are we going to do for Ran's birthday?"

Vada's question to Steve refocuses my attention away from Ronan, who put our orders in at the bar and then moved to the table with the family of four. The toddler managed to get ahold of his mother's glass of soda and deliberately spilled it, the liquid running all over the table and dripping onto the floor.

"When is his birthday?" I interrupt.

"On the second," Vada says.

"I have no idea," Steve admits. "I'm not even sure if he's working or not. I don't know, let's check with Shane. Maybe we'll just hang out at the beach house?" There's some affirmative nodding by Zack and Summer. Steve puts his thumb and index fingers to his lips and whistles so loudly Vada jumps in her seat.

"What the hell?" Zack looks bewildered at Steve, who's waving for Shane to come to the table.

"What in the world, Steve!" Shane says, laughing. "Are you going to complain about the service to me?" he jokes, nodding his head at Ronan, who's busy cleaning up the spilled soda.

"Nah, he'll do just fine," Steve jokes back. "We were just talking about Ran's birthday coming up. Have you talked to him about it?"

"Oh, shit. Man, that's right. That's in like ten days! We haven't talked about it. I completely spaced. I've been so distracted with my apartment," Shane explains.

"When are you moving in?" I ask.

"Officially on the first. I was actually going to ask if you all are free to help me move. I feel like total shit right now," Shane says, deflated, his eyes full of guilt.

"Okay, well, it's not too late to remedy the situation. Ran's not much for crazy shindigs anyways, so maybe we can just hang out at your new place or the beach house after we move you in?" Vada suggests, ever the optimist.

Shane nods. "That's a great idea. I better check the schedule to make sure we're not working." He makes a face. "But yeah, we can probably hang out at the beach house if you guys help me move all my stuff the day before?" He looks around the table hopefully. "Pretty please?"

"Of course we'll help," I say, and the others nod.

"Awesome. I'll text everyone the details tonight and then we'll figure out Ran's birthday situation," Shane says, then heads back to the bar to grab another tray full of beverages that he delivers to a table of ten wildly giggling girls.

Ten minutes later, Ronan returns to our table balancing a giant tray on his hand and shoulder. He skillfully lifts one plate at a time off the tray and places them in front of their respective recipients. The food looks delicious, and I close my eyes as I breathe in the warm aroma of the Irish fare.

"Do you guys need another round of drinks?" Ronan asks.

"I'd love another beer," Zack mumbles, his mouth already full of corned beef hash. "Shit, this is good."

"I'll have another Malibu Pineapple with extra cherries," Summer says, and points at Vada, who simply nods in agreement.

"Pale Ale and two Malibu Pineapples; no more drinks for Steve because he's a lightweight," Ronan says without looking at his brother, but with a huge grin on his face.

"Hey, watch it, asshole," Steve chimes in, again elbowing Ronan in the side. "But yeah, I'm fine. I still have to drive," Steve says, and Ronan laughs.

"How about you, Cat?" Ronan asks, his gaze trained on me.

I have a mouth full of mashed potatoes and put my hand in front of my lips so as not to spew food all over the table. "I'm fine. I still have this... whatever this is," I say, my speech garbled.

Ronan smiles at me. "Looks like an L.A. water," he says, and I nod. "Shane is trying to test you. Have you tried it yet?" Ronan picks up my glass, takes a sniff, then scrunches his nose and puts the glass back down. "Whew, I'd be careful with that if you're planning on actually *walking* out of here today," he says, his voice light but warning. "Jack makes these really, really strong." He points over his shoulder at the guy tending the bar.

"What's in it?" Vada asks.

"Vodka, tequila, rum, gin, triple sec, Midori, Chambord, Blue Curacao, and sweet and sour. This thing will get you wasted fast."

Vada pulls my glass toward her to sniff. "Can I take a sip?" she asks me, and I wave my hand for her to go ahead. She takes a sip and her lips pucker. "Oh, holy mother of Santa Claus, this will wake a sleeping grizzly." She pushes the glass back toward me.

"Told you this stuff is strong," Ronan says. He watches me intently as, intrigued, I pick up the glass and take a swig of the cold drink. I know I shouldn't; I should have declined the drink to begin with, but here I am, decidedly too close to overstepping my own, newly set boundaries as I leave my better judgment behind.

Vada is right: it's strong, but also delicious. I follow up the first swig with a second, and the liquid goes down my throat easily, warming me from the inside. God, it's like muscle memory. I feel the alcohol wind its way to my head, rounding the edges, slowing the pace.

I can feel the stares of everyone around me.

"What?" I say, taken aback. "It's not so bad!"

We eat our ridiculously good food while chatting, and I'm once again enjoying the company of my new friends, truly feeling content with the people around me.

***

"Okay, so here's the game plan," Shane says about thirty minutes later, leaning back on a chair while Ronan stacks our now-empty plates on top of each other. "Summer kickoff party this Saturday at the beach. It's going to be fucking epic, okay? So, no excuses."

"Bossy much?" Ronan mutters, making everyone laugh.

"You guys are still okay with helping me move Tuesday?" Shane double-checks.

"Yep, and then Wednesday are we partying at your place or are we heading to the beach to celebrate Ran's birthday?" Zack asks.

Shane grins at Ronan. "Honestly, the beach house is probably better because my apartment is crammed and there'll be shit everywhere. Plus, the bar is well-stocked. And there's plenty of space for people to crash if the party gets too wild or... wet."

Everyone agrees to the plan before we finally leave Murphy's in time for me to make my curfew. I say bye to Zack and Summer, and I clamber into the backseat of Vada's car while she takes the passenger seat.

Steve starts the engine. "Do you want to stay with me after Shane's party next weekend?" I hear him ask Vada.

She smiles at him, then places her left elbow on the back of her seat and twists to face me. "Would it be okay if I tell my dad I'm spending the night at your house next weekend?"

"Of course!" I say, and laugh. "Whatever you need, friend."

"You're the best. And feel free to use sleeping over at my place so you can spend the night at a guy's house, too," she says, grinning.

"Okay," I laugh again. "But that won't be necessary."

"We shall see about that," she says, and I roll my eyes at her, shaking my head. "All I'm saying is that you're hot and single and Ran is hot and single, so..." She draws out the last word and shrugs.

"Jeez, babe, you really *are* pushy," Steve says.

Vada turns to him, crossing her arms over her chest and cocking her head to her side. "I'm not pushy. I just want people to be happy!"

"And hook up," Steve says.

There's a momentary silence before Vada nods her head fervently, laughing. "Yes, and hook up."

Vada and Steve drop me off at my house. After talking with my mom for a few minutes, I make my way up to my room and get myself ready for the night, knowing Vada will be back to pick me up early the next morning so we can walk to school together and get finals weeks started and over with.

Saturday, May 29th

Ronan

Yep, I needed this. I needed a night away from home, a night at the beach house, a night with my friends, just letting go of everything for a while.

It's been a hell of a week. Like the rest of my friends—with the exception of Shane and my brother, both of whom are officially done with high school—I spent my week either taking exams or studying. I tried to do the vast majority of the studying either at school or at the public library because things at home have been tense since my dad cancelled his planned trip home at the last minute.

It's not anything new or particularly surprising. My dad changes his plans all the time, calling home the day he was supposed to arrive to inform us that something came up at work or whatever. It's to the point where I don't even believe my dad will actually show until I see him walk through the front door. I'm surprised my mom reacts this strongly to his broken promises, but she's been seriously on edge this week. So I've been feeling on edge in turn and have avoided being home as much as possible.

But right now all of that stuff feels light-years away as I sit in my usual spot on the sectional outdoor sofa on the porch of Shane's mom's beach house. My best friends take up the remaining spots around the fire while Shane's summer kickoff party is in full swing. There are probably a hundred and fifty people hanging out on the deck, inside the house, or down by the beach, drinking, eating, talking.

I can tell Shane is proud of how things turned out; he has a relaxed smile on his face as he leans back on the sofa, Tori in his arms, her body seemingly contouring to his. Shane's parties are mostly like this:

hundreds of people, only a small percentage of whom we actually know, word about the party spreading by word-of-mouth, first through our school, then through schools of neighboring boroughs. Friends telling other friends, inviting girlfriends, boyfriends, hookups, whatever. Shane doesn't mind. He thrives in this environment, enjoys providing a space for people to have a great time. He's going to be perfect at running Murphy's. It's just in his blood.

But all that is just backdrop, background noise. For Shane it's the energy, the vibes, and I know he's most at peace, happiest, when he's surrounded by the six of us—or, I guess, the seven of us now.

My eyes move to Cat, seated across the sofa from me, and linger on her face. I allow myself a moment to drink her in. God, it's like she gets more beautiful each time I see her—which, admittedly, hasn't been too frequently. I didn't see her at all this past week, not even at school, and she's definitely a sight tonight. I mean, she always is, but definitely tonight. She's wearing a pair of low-rise jeans with worn knees, and a light-blue tank top exposes her shoulders, her smooth skin freckled, just like her nose and cheeks. Her blonde hair is in a half-up, half-down style, strands of it falling loosely down her back and over her shoulders.

She doesn't seem to wear a ton of makeup, not like some other girls I see around school and at Shane's parties. I'd guess Cat is probably wearing some mascara, maybe some blush, although the warming temperatures and the setting sun could certainly be the cause of her rosy cheeks. Or maybe Vada, who's chatting with Cat, motioning her hands wildly, might just have said something that caused Cat to blush. That's one thing I noticed about Cat right away—the way her cheeks get all flushed with heat when she gets embarrassed or someone compliments her. I don't think Cat is particularly fond of it, but I really, *really* like it.

There are other things I notice about her, too: the way her hazel eyes change color from green to more of a brown depending on the light and, apparently, the mood she's in; the sound of her laugh; and how she nibbles on her bottom lip when she's deep in thought. All of these things are incredibly attractive, sexy, and they're all things I shouldn't be aware of, shouldn't pay attention to because it can only lead to pain. I'm obviously a glutton for punishment, consistently fucking up in one way or another, but that doesn't mean I can allow myself to drag someone else down with me.

"You alright?" I hear Shane ask me, his voice low, hushed.

"Yeah," I tell him, nodding.

"You seem like you got something on your mind," he says, analyzing my face.

"Actually, just wondering what your plan is as far as working at Murphy's now that you're done with school," I lie.

Shane dives into a conversation with me about his vision for the future—particularly the next few months—our schedules at Murphy's, making time for friends, to hang out and all that.

I try to focus on Shane, on nodding and responding appropriately, but find myself glancing in Cat's direction too often. I take note of the way she plays with a strand of her hair while she pays close attention to something Tori tells her and hear her laugh freely with Vada and Summer. And I watch as she stretches her arms over her head, exposing a slight sliver of skin where her tank top rides up over the waistline of her jeans. I feel my body stir, my blood hot with a longing to touch her.

God damn it, this needs to stop. This is not how the evening was supposed to go. I need to take my mind off Cat, do something to distract myself. So I look past Cat down the deck and spot a group of four or five girls standing in a tight circle. I don't know any of them, but that doesn't matter. It's actually better to hook up with someone I don't have a history with, a girl I've never seen around school before, and it's one of the most effective ways of distracting myself from whatever is going on in my head.

"Sorry, man, but..." I interrupt Shane and nod toward the group of girls, one of whom—a petite brunette in a short, plaid skirt and white cropped top—smiles at me while leaning back against the deck railing.

Shane follows my gaze, then grins. "Alright, well, go do your thing, Ran." He chuckles and nudges me to stand up from the sofa.

"Hey Ran," Shane calls after me just as I pass Cat, and I look back at him, feeling our friends' eyes on me. "Use my room. It's locked, but the key is tucked up on the doorframe."

I nod, then make my way to the brunette. I force myself to keep my eyes trained on her rather than allowing them to look at Cat, because for some weird fucking reason I feel even shittier than I normally do when I'm about to hook up with a girl.

Cat

"Where's Ran going?" Zack inquires from the outdoor sofa at Shane's this evening.

It's been a lovely afternoon and evening so far, and I'm enjoying my time with my new friends, just like I always do—relaxing, mostly talking with Vada, Tori, and Summer. I feel myself unwind after the stress that was last week, filled with finals and studying. I feel safe even with the seemingly hundreds of upperclassmen and recent graduates in attendance, owing in large part to how easily and quickly my new friends have taken me into their fold. It honestly feels like I've known Vada, Tori, Summer, Zack, Steve, Shane, and Ronan forever. God, Ronan....

"Well, Ran apparently set his sights on Sophie, and Sophie on him," Shane laughs. He nods in the direction of Ronan, who has made his way over to a group of girls. He stands with his hands in his jeans pockets, his posture confident, assured as he apparently strikes up a conversation with this Sophie girl.

Something stirs inside my chest, a tightness I've not felt before when I note the smile on Sophie's lips, the way she carefully moves her hair over her shoulder, exposing her neck, looking at Ronan with big, brown doe eyes.

"Oh, for crying out loud," Vada sighs, shaking her head at Shane, her lips pressed together with obvious displeasure at Ronan talking to Sophie.

"Jeez, babe, let him have some fun," Steve says to Vada.

"He has fun for however long he's in that bedroom with whatever girl he's hooking up with, but you guys don't notice how down he gets afterwards?" Vada questions the guys, all of whom shrug. "Yeah, I figured," she huffs. "All you guys worry is about is that your boy gets laid." Vada turns toward me, demonstratively, her back to the guys.

They shake their heads at Vada's strong reaction to Ronan apparently trying to get lucky.

"Does Ran do this a lot?" I ask Vada with a whisper.

Vada frowns. "Yep, all the time. The guys always cheer him on and stuff, but..."

"But what?" I try to ignore that tiny monster in my chest rearing its head at the thought of Ronan being intimate with some girl.

Vada looks at me for a moment, wavering, then smacks her lips loudly. "But I disapprove. I think Ran deserves better than random fucks." She emphasizes the last three words, enunciating them clearly and loudly for the boys to hear.

"Stop being a party-pooping cockblock," Zack scolds his sister.

"Psh, I couldn't cockblock Ran if I tried," Vada huffs. "You guys make damn sure of that."

"Aww, baby, why are you so angry?" Steve asks, pulling Vada into his arms and onto his lap. I see her face soften. "Don't worry about Ran so much; he knows what he's doing," Steve adds in a low voice.

Vada's eyes shut when Steve moves his lips to her, kissing her softly.

"He sure does," Shane chuckles.

Out of my periphery, I see Ronan take Sophie's hand, then lead her into the house as she smiles at him. They disappear in the crowd of people blocking my view of the interior of the home.

I vaguely notice the conversation shifting focus, Vada giggling between kissing Steve, though that feeling in my chest remains, my stomach in knots. God, why am I reacting so strongly to Ronan retreating into the house with some random girl? We're just friends. It shouldn't bother me like this, but for some reason, knowing he might be in a bedroom undressing some girl makes me restless.

There's no way Ronan could already hold this kind of power over me. We haven't even known each other a whole month. We're friends. Good friends, yeah, and even after this short time I would consider him one of my closest friends. I feel safe and comfortable with him, but nothing more than that. He has every right to hook up with whomever he pleases, and I have no business at all judging or being... jealous.

I have the most difficult time focusing on whatever everyone is talking about. I'm unable to sit still and let the minutes tick by without my mind turning to Ronan, thinking about what he's doing in that room just feet away from me.

Is he kissing her? Do his green eyes stare into her soul like they've stared into mine? Is he touching her? Telling her he wants her, or worse, is he already on top of her, feeling her body, filling her?

I stand abruptly, not sure what the hell I'm going to do or where I'm going to go, but I walk into the house without even knowing my destination. I don't know how or why, but I beeline it to that white marble counter tucked into a corner of the living room. I sit on one of the beautiful white-leather upholstered barstools and rest my head in my hands, my elbows on the cool stone surface.

"You look like you need a drink," I hear a guy's voice from behind me.

I lift my head to watch a short but lanky boy with cropped brown hair make his way around the counter and to the shelf that holds various bottles of alcohol. He peruses the selection.

"No, I'm fine. Thank you, though," I tell him with a small smile.

"I'm Corbin." He places a couple of bottles he snatched from the shelf down on the counter in front of him.

"I'm Cat," I say.

Corbin smiles at me as he begins making a drink. "So, what's got you down, Cat?" he asks me, pouring a little bit of this and a little bit of that into a sleek whiskey glass he retrieved from below the counter. "Wait, don't say it," he says quickly, tapping his left index finger against his temple. "Your boyfriend cheated on you," he guesses with an a-ha face.

I shake my head, laughing lightly. "No. I don't have a boyfriend."

"So, your *girlfriend* cheated on you?" Corbin asks, making me laugh again.

"No."

"Okay, so just to clarify then: you *don't* play for the same team?" He stirs whatever drink he's mixed in that whiskey glass.

"No," I tell him with another laugh.

"That's a relief. Would have been such a shame if someone like you was into girls. A real loss to all of *man*-kind." He laughs at his own joke, and I smile.

"Thank you," I tell him.

"But wait, you don't have a boyfriend? How is that even possible?" He pulls another glass out from the shelf beneath the countertop.

I shrug. "Not a priority, I guess." My thoughts immediately turn back to Ronan. I shake my head and squeeze my eyes shut, hoping this will make the image of Ronan dissipate from my mind.

"Shame," Corbin says, bringing the drink he just mixed up to his mouth to take a long draw. "So, you're not here with some guy then?"

"No. Just my friends. They're occupied with each other." I look out to the deck, where Vada is still securely seated on Steve's lap with a smile on her lips. She looks love-struck.

"Are you sure I can't get you something to drink?" Corbin double-checks with a grin.

I inhale, then exhale deeply. Oh, what the hell. "Yeah, okay."

"Awesome. What can I fix you?"

I giggle at his word choice. It seems so old-fashioned. "Uh, how about a rum and coke?"

Corbin nods. "That's what I would have guessed, honestly." He turns his back to me to retrieve some bottles.

"Yeah? How come?" I ask him, making conversation while he tinkers around mixing the drink with his back to me.

"You strike me as a girl who likes something that goes hard, but is soft at the same time," he chuckles. He finally turns back around, swirling the drink with a stir stick for a minute before he finally sets the glass down in front of me.

Corbin raises his glass. "To non-priorities."

I smile, then raise my own glass, clanking it against his. I chug the rum and coke, one half of me scolding myself for being so reckless, the other half telling myself to enjoy my evening. I'm safe here. My friends are outside; Adam isn't around. I'm safe.

Corbin nods appreciatively, his eyes moving from my empty glass to my face. "You just keep on surprising me," he laughs, taking my glass to begin mixing another drink for me.

I wave him off. "I'm good," I say, half-hearted.

"Just one more. This time maybe just sip it," he adds with a laugh. "No need to go so hard."

I nod with a smile, feeling myself relax noticeably. "So, who are you here with?"

Corbin is already in the process of pouring a splash of coke into the generous amount of rum in the glass. "A couple of friends," he tells me vaguely, once again stirring the cocktail before he pushes the glass back toward me and begins making himself one.

"What are you having?"

"Vodka Red Bull." He nods, pouring a little—or, actually a lot—of the bubbly energy drink into the vodka in his glass.

"I always thought it was a weird idea to mix uppers and downers," I say, and am taken aback by how heavy my tongue feels inside my mouth, my words coming out slow and slightly slurred. Weird.

"Yeah, it is kind of a weird concept," Corbin admits with a chuckle. "But it tastes good."

I make a face, scrunching my nose. "I don't like vodka." My speech is drawn out, and I suddenly have the urge to rest my head on the cool marble countertop.

"I don't ever drink it straight, either. It's pretty bitter." He takes a sip from his glass. "But this is nice. Do you want to try?" Corbin offers me his glass.

I shake my head, noting the seeming lag of my vision with the movement of my head from left to right.

Wow, I know I haven't had much alcohol lately, but I can't remember my head ever going so foggy this quickly. This is only my second drink, but my eyelids suddenly feel heavy, almost as heavy as my arms and legs. I probably shouldn't have downed that first rum and coke so quickly.

"Hey, you good?" Corbin asks, and I vaguely notice the smile on his lips.

"Yeah, I'm fine." I feel like I haven't slept in three days straight. I have a desperate desire to go find a soft surface, lie down, and go to sleep.

"You sure? You don't look super steady. Maybe you should lie down," he suggests, walking around the counter and to my side.

"Yeah, I think I may need to," I admit with a nod, which makes my surroundings spin violently.

"Here, I'll help you." He's already moving my left arm over his shoulder and around his neck to help me off my barstool. I don't particularly like the feel of this guy's hands on me, but I can't muster up the energy to protest.

"Cat?" I hear Ronan's voice, which sounds echoey and distanced, like he's talking to me through a metal tube or like he's not real. Maybe I'm just imagining his voice, actually. But no, his face appears next to me, and I'm taken aback by the deep crease on his brow, the stern look on his handsome face. His masculine features are harder for some reason.

"Are you already done?" My question to Ronan comes out slurred, like I've suddenly lost control over my tongue, which feels dry and fuzzy. Ronan's expression changes to confusion. "With that girl," I add, unable to hide the pain in my voice.

He doesn't respond to my question. "Are you alright?" Ronan checks with me instead. His left hand moves under my chin, tipping my head up; he studies my face, my eyes. God, he has gorgeous eyes. They look like the northern lights I saw when my family visited Alaska last summer, with hues of light green and aqua.

"She's good. Just tired. I'm gonna help her find a place to lie down," Corbin says, tugging at my arm to get me to stand up.

Ronan's left hand glides up to my right shoulder, exerting enough downward pressure that my tired legs are unable to lift my body. "The fuck you are," he growls at Corbin.

I'm totally confused about what the heck is going on when Ronan reaches for the glass I was just drinking from and moves it to his nose as if to smell it.

"What is this?" Ronan asks, looking at the nearly empty drink.

"Rum and coke." I shrug. "That's my poison, Ran. Rum and coke," I slur in a deep Southern drawl that only emerges when I'm severely impaired. *But I haven't had that much*, I wonder to myself.

"Cat, did you make this drink yourself?" Ronan asks me, adding to my confusion. Why is he asking me this?

"Corbin did," I say, no longer able to keep my eyes open. I let my eyelids fall shut.

"What the fuck did you put in this?" Ronan growls. Why is he mad at me?

"Nothing," I say, but when I force myself to open my eyes, I realize Ronan isn't talking to me. He's glowering at Corbin, his right hand balled into a fist by his side, his nostrils flaring, lips pressed together like it's taking everything in him not to go ballistic.

"Nothing, man," Corbin says, releasing my arm from his hold.

"Fucking bullshit," Ronan says, his voice a low, threatening rumble. "I can see the fucking residue on the glass, you fucking asshole. What is it? Molly?"

Corbin doesn't answer, taking a couple of steps back from me and Ronan.

"Fucking answer me," Ronan shouts, taking a step toward Corbin. Even in my impaired state, Ronan's stature is impressive. His chest puffs out, muscles flexing so intensely they strain against the fabric of his white shirt. His back flares, testing the resolve of his plaid flannel as he steps around me, shielding me from Corbin.

"It's just Rohypnol, man. It'll be out of her system in the morning. I swear, man," Corbin finally admits, his hands raised. "I swear I didn't touch her."

"What the hell is going on?" I hear Shane ask.

It's the last thing I'm conscious of before I feel myself black out and begin to slump off the barstool in slow motion with nothing to brace my fall.

Sunday, May 30th

Cat

It's a slow ascent into consciousness. The brightness shining through my closed eyelids lets me know it's daytime, though I have no clue what time it is, where I am, or what the hell happened.

I'm obviously lying down, that much I can tell. I have soft cushions underneath me, a light blanket covering me, and I feel warm and safe. Cocooned, almost, with cushions pressed against my back.

I become aware of a warm body in front of me.

I blink my eyes open slowly and grimace. My head pounds and my whole body aches, though my discomfort is eclipsed when I realize I'm cuddled up against Ronan. He's on his back, sleeping soundly next to me. Heat rises in my face when I notice how close he is to me. My body is turned to him, my left leg hitched over his, and my left hand—oh god—is tucked underneath his white shirt, resting on his bare chest, which rises and falls calmly, steadily.

I withdraw my hand and sit up next to Ronan, looking around in an effort to orient myself. We're still at Shane's beach house, on one of the large white sofas in the living room.

I carefully move the blanket off me, noting that while I was completely covered in my sleep, Ronan slept on top of the blanket rather than underneath it with me. I can tell without even looking down at myself that I'm still completely dressed, as is Ronan. Though he must have taken off his flannel because his chest is only covered by his fitted white t-shirt contoured to his pecs, his shoulders, his abs.

I climb over him slowly, careful not to wake him; his face is relaxed in his sleep.

The moment I stand, my stomach churns uncomfortably.

"How are you feeling this morning?" Shane asks, and I turn my head to my left. He's standing in the open kitchen, his shoulder-length, undercut hair loose and swept to the right side of his head this morning rather than held in place by its signature bun. I have to admit that even this hairstyle suits Shane exceptionally well.

I make my way into the kitchen before speaking, trying to keep any noise to a minimum. Shane's eyes reflect unfiltered concern as he watches me. "Horrible," I admit.

Shane nods. "How much of last night do you remember?" He pours a cup of coffee and pushes it across the counter to me.

I take it into my hands gratefully. I rack my brain for a minute, trying to recall last night's events, and am dismayed to find that I have absolutely no memory of what happened after I saw Ronan disappear into the guestroom with Sophie.

"I remember Ran... Ran talking with that girl, and then... then it's blank," I admit to Shane, horrified. "Oh god, Shane. What happened?" I ask him, suddenly panicking. Snippets resurface in my mind's eye: of me sitting at the bar counter with some random boy, taking sips of a drink. Memories of incidents with Adam mix with blurred memories of last night, and anxiety pricks at the soles of my feet. Fear of what I did—of what someone may have done to or with me—bubbles in my chest.

"Nothing," Shane reassures me, his right hand on my arm. "Nothing bad, Cat. Ran stopped it."

"Stopped what?" I ask, my eyes wide.

Shane sighs deeply before filling me in on what took place after I apparently stormed into the house once Ronan and Sophie went into the guestroom.

"Ran was ready to beat Corbin's ass, but you passed out right then. It was like slow motion. Ran caught you just before your head was about to hit the tile," Shane tells me, his already deep voice low, quiet, mindful of a sleeping Ronan in the living room.

"Vada and Tori went to town on Corbin," Shane chuckles, "and Steve and I made sure that motherfucker left knowing not to ever show his face here again. Ran was just really worried about you. You were completely out of it. So Ran took you to the guestroom so you could sleep. He locked the door behind you to make sure nobody could walk in on you, and Vada called your mom to let her know you were already asleep and everyone was spending the night at my place," he tells me.

I feel relief at his words, knowing my mom knew where I was, that I was safe, and she wasn't up all night worried sick.

"But... wait, why did I wake up on the couch?" I ask.

My question must be funny to him, because he laughs. "You wandered back out of the room at like three or three-thirty last night. Ran and I were still up just talking about..." He trails off, clamping his mouth shut for a moment. Then he continues, "You came out to the deck and told Ran you didn't want to be alone."

"What?" I say, mortified.

Shane chuckles again. "Yep. So Ran asked you if you wanted him to sleep with you. You very adamantly said 'yes,' took his hand, and led him back into the living room. He was so confused," Shane tells me with a barely contained laugh. "And then you just decided that the couch was the perfect spot for the two of you. You laid back down, waited for Ran to lie down next to you, and passed out again without another word." Shane's face is alive with amusement.

"Oh god," I sigh and rest my head in my right hand, my elbow on the countertop, feeling embarrassed.

"No, Cat, you're fine. Everything is fine," Shane says again, his tone sincere as he pulls me into a one-armed hug. "This wasn't your fault, okay?"

This is a refrain I've heard over and over in the past. But it *is* my fault. I know better than to drink, especially drinks I didn't make or didn't carefully watch being made. And who knows what I did or said to Corbin to put myself in this situation in the first place? What made him think I was the catch of the night for him?

Tears sting at the back of my eyes. I swallow the lump forming in my throat, blinking furiously to prevent the tears from falling.

"Hey," Shane says, and he wraps his other arm around me, too. "You're okay. Ran got to you in time. Nothing happened. Corbin didn't touch you, and you didn't do anything to deserve this, okay? He's just an asshole who can't get any, so he feels he has to drug girls to make shit happen for him, but you're okay. Ran would never let anything happen to you; none of us would."

My heart gives a weird jolt in my chest at Shane's words. Ronan would never let anything happen to me. He cares about me; he took care of me last night—truly took care of me. He didn't take advantage of me even though I was about as vulnerable as I had ever been in my life. He carried me into a bedroom—didn't touch me, didn't violate me, didn't take inappropriate pictures of me—and made sure to lock the door on his way out to keep me safe. And when I rudely told him I needed him to be able to sleep, he obliged, probably spending some pretty uncomfortable hours on the narrow sofa while I slept contently cuddled up against him, soaking up his comforting scent and body heat.

And in that moment, it dawns on me that I can trust him.

Shane sweetly makes us some egg, cheese, and bacon breakfast burritos that help settle my stomach, and I quickly begin to feel better while we chat. The house remains quiet for a little while longer until Steve and Vada eventually emerge from one of the bedrooms and quietly make their way into the kitchen.

Vada immediately pulls me into her arms and hugs me tightly, apologizing profusely and repeatedly.

I wave her off. "Not your fault," I say. "I should have known better," I add with a shake of my head.

"Nah. It's not your fault either," Steve says, a crease on his brow. "Assholes like Corbin piss me off to no fucking end. It shouldn't be on you to make sure some motherfucker isn't trying to roofie you.

Fucking bullshit," Steve growls again, grabbing the second half of Shane's breakfast burrito and taking a huge bite from it.

"The fuck?" Shane says, a consternated expression on his face as he watches Steve chew.

I laugh, feeling some of the ickiness from last night's experience fall off me.

"Sorry, I get hungry when I'm angry," Steve says with a chuckle.

"Okay, well there's a whole-ass fridge with food inside it you can eat," Shane grumbles.

"Are you about ready to head home, Kitty Cat?" Vada asks me, her normally bubbly spirit slightly subdued this morning.

"Yes. I'm in desperate need of a shower," I admit, running my hands through my knotted hair.

"Yeah, I'm heading out, too," Steve nods, his mouth still full of burrito. "You got Ran or should I wake him?" Steve checks with Shane because Ronan and Steve drove here together last night, whereas I rode with Vada.

"You don't think hitchhiking would be a good option for Ran?" Shane jokes.

"Nah, he's too pretty for hitchhiking. He'd get kidnapped in seconds," Steve says, making Vada giggle.

"Then I guess I got him," Shane nods with a chuckle. "I'll get him home when he wakes up."

Steve and Vada head to the front door, and I give Shane a quick hug, then follow Vada to her car.

Ronan

"Wanna talk about it?" Shane asks out of the blue, eyeing me when I turn my head to face him.

I'm in the passenger seat of Shane's Jeep Wrangler while Shane makes his way to my house to drop me off. I woke up maybe an hour ago—the house quiet, Cat no longer next to me. Shane informed me when I made my way into the kitchen that Cat had left with Vada and my brother. I just nodded without comment. What was there to say?

Last night did not turn out the way I had planned or expected. Things took a complete turn when I spotted Cat sitting by the small bar, looking decidedly out of it while some dude I had never seen before had her arm slung around his shoulder, trying to hoist her up. I instantly knew something wasn't right and got confirmation pretty quickly that this lowlife had slipped a roofie into Cat's drink. It doesn't take a genius to know what this prick's intentions were with Cat, and if Cat hadn't passed out exactly when she did—slumping off the high barstool like a rag doll—I'm not sure I wouldn't have lost my absolute shit on this Corbin kid right then and there. But instinct took over and my body moved seemingly on its own, rushing toward a falling Cat and catching her just before her head would have hit the gray wood tile.

I let my brother and best friend handle Corbin while I cradled Cat in my arms, her body soft and warm against me, and carried her into one of the guest bedrooms, laid her down, then covered her with the blanket. I left her to sleep, locking the door on my way out to make sure she was safe.

It's weird how something so dramatic can take place, yet only a handful of people are aware of what went down. The party continued for several more hours, the vast majority of people blissfully unaware of the bullshit that took place inside the house.

It was maybe two-thirty in the morning when things finally quieted down. Zack left with Summer, my brother and Vada retreated into Shane's sister's usual bedroom, and Tori turned in for the night, leaving only Shane and me on the deck, recapping the night. That was until Cat emerged from the small bedroom and made her way out to us.

I couldn't help but smile at her spacey expression and the way her wavy hair was slightly disheveled. It was obvious she was still completely out of it, her speech gravelly, slightly slower, a mixture of sleep and the lingering effects of the Rohypnol affecting her physical and mental state.

"Hi," I said when her eyes found me. God, even in her impaired state, her grogginess and heavy eyelids on full display, she was still perfect. "You okay?" I got up from my spot next to Shane on the sofa while Shane stayed silent, keeping a watchful eye on Cat as she swayed slightly.

"I don't want to be alone," Cat said, her gaze not moving from mine.

"Uh, do you... Do you want me to stay with you?" I asked. I didn't want to make her uncomfortable, and I knew I was going against my resolve to stay away from Cat. Though I felt a weird sort of elation expand in my chest when Cat—without even the slightest pause—said, "Yes," then took my hand into hers and led me into the house.

I can't even explain the battle raging inside me when Cat made herself comfortable on the sofa instead of going back to the bedroom—which would have afforded us much more space and distance than the couch—and waited for me to lie down next to her. Against my better judgment, I obliged, trying my hardest to maintain some physical separation from her. That went out the window when Cat cuddled up against me, rested her head on my chest, and fell asleep within seconds.

I tried to figure out what to do with my hands, where to put them. I ended up just shoving my right hand underneath me and allowed my left to rest on Cat's shoulder as she slept pressed against me. I just lay there, feeling the rhythmic rise and fall of her rib cage—forcing my thoughts away from the sensation of Cat's small, round breasts pushed against me. I focused instead on my breathing, inhaling her delicate scent—rosewater and lavender. The warmth of her body seeped into my pores and the strangest thing happened: I felt myself relax. The stress of the last few days and the tension in my body melted away, and only minutes later I passed out, too.

I woke up only once, feeling too hot. I took off my flannel and dropped it to the floor, then carefully lay back again. Cat shifted in her deep sleep, and my breathing picked up slightly when she hitched her left leg over mine while gliding her hand underneath my shirt to rest it on my bare chest. Part of me knew I should retrieve her hand, but I admittedly enjoyed her touch, the softness of her fingers on my skin. I fell asleep again before I mustered up the energy—or the willpower—to do anything about Cat's subconscious caress.

I know I'm in trouble. I knew it the moment I laid eyes on Cat, knew it this morning when I woke up without Cat next to me and felt disappointed—and simultaneously relieved—that she had left with Vada and my brother.

What am I going to do?

"Talk about what?" I ask Shane, feigning ignorance.

"Whatever it is that's got you stuck in your head right now," he says matter-of-factly, his eyes moving between me and the road ahead of him. "I've known you pretty much all my life, Ran. I can tell when something is off, even though you never want to talk about it."

I turn my head away from him to look out the passenger window, watching the cityscape fly by. Shane's right; I'm in my head. I'm in my head a lot, but today is different. I'm in my head about Cat. Of course it's about her. I know I should stay away from her. No, not should—*have to*, for her sake. But god, I'm drawn to her. "I have no idea what you're talking about. And we did have a talk that one time," I say, referencing the time Shane figured out what was going on in my house, with my mom. Kind of.

Shane shoves his hand against my shoulder, getting me to look back at him. I frown at the unnecessary force. "You gotta stop bottling everything up, Ran," he says, both anger and concern in his eyes. "And we didn't really talk then; you never gave me the chance!"

I cock my head to the right. Here goes nothing. "I think..." I start but trail off. I'm scared to say the words out loud; that might make them real.

"You think?" Shane's eyebrows rise expectantly.

I take a deep breath and let the words fall out of my mouth. "I think I may be falling for Cat," I say, the weight of the confession slumping into the pit of my stomach like I just swallowed a rock.

Shane looks taken aback, but a smile forms on his lips. "Okay, well that's not what I thought you'd say. Not really that surprising, but still not what I thought you'd say. But I mean, you falling for Cat is good, isn't it?"

I look at him, confounded and exhausted. "No, it's not!"

"Why not?"

"Because I can't, Shay."

"Can't what?"

"I can't be with her. She deserves... someone... not so fucked up. Someone who doesn't get his ass whipped by his mother. Someone ... better... I don't know." I let my head fall back against the headrest.

Shane stays silent for a long moment, looking ahead of him, but there's pity in his eyes. I hate pity.

"She's still hitting you, huh? Your mom?" he asks with a glance at me. I don't answer his question. I don't want to get into it; there's no fucking point. "Ran, I..." he starts, but I hold up my hand, cutting him off before he can give me a lecture about how I need to tell someone or whatever.

"Fine," he exhales. "But let me say this about the whole Cat situation, and I know this is probably way more information than you want to know, but you remember when I lost Liam?"

I look at him and nod. Liam is Shane's little brother. Was. He was the same age as me, though I didn't know him too well. He hung out with a different crowd, did his own thing, got into some bad stuff. And then a couple years ago he overdosed on painkillers. Shane's dad found him in bed the next morning. There wasn't anything anyone could do.

"You remember how screwed up I was?" Shane asks, his voice quiet as he stares ahead.

I do remember. Of course I do. I was with Shane when he got the call from his dad that Liam was dead and, of course, Shane lost it.

"I was a fucking mess," he says, staring at the road. "And I wasn't able to get out of that for months." He looks over, his eyes meeting mine, and I nod again, remembering the many days of school Shane missed, even months after his brother's death; his growing affinity for partying and getting drunk, first only on the weekends, then during the week, and even at school; and the dark thoughts he sometimes shared with me when he was too wasted to stop himself.

"But then I met Tori." His eyebrows lift as he looks at me, his face softening at the thought of her. "She was exactly what I needed. She made all that pain go away just by being around me," he says with a smile on his lips.

Shane really was in a dark place when he met Tori, but only a couple months later he had stopped drinking, with the exception of the occasional drink at his parties. He attended all his classes again and seemed to have gotten out of that hole he was in, managing to catch up and graduate on time.

"What's your point?" I ask, knowing full well what his point is.

He elbows me. "That Cat may be good for you."

"Yeah, but I may not be good for her," I say with a deep sigh.

"I say you let her be the judge of that. It's not like she has to have dinner dates with your parents."

I shake my head at him. "No," I say. "It's better if we're just friends." I'm desperately trying to convince myself, and I know it.

"Better for who?"

I look at him. "For her," I say matter-of-factly. He raises his eyebrows at me. "And for me," I add quickly, less confident in that last part.

"Yeah?"

"Yeah."

Shane exhales, obviously frustrated. "Well, I can't honestly say that I love you standing in your own damn way, but you're my best friend, and whatever the fuck you decide to do or not do, I got your back."

"I appreciate that," I say with a nod.

Shane grins at me. "Can't wait to see you be 'just friends' with Cat." He chuckles and pulls up to the curb in front of my house.

Tuesday, June 1st

Cat

I wake up before my alarm goes off at six-thirty. I stretch my limbs before raising myself up to lean back on my hands. The sun peeks through the sides of my blackout curtains, and I enjoy the stillness of the house. I pull my down comforter off my legs and swing them out of bed, softly placing my bare feet on the carpet. I sit for a moment, looking around my room; the walls are still bare. I make a mental note to finish unpacking and maybe decorate my room a little bit, then head to the bathroom to shower and get ready. Vada should be here in an hour so we can help Shane move into his apartment, just like we promised.

After my shower, I rummage through my unorganized mess of a closet for a couple of minutes before pulling out a pair of jeans and a loose-fitting white shirt that, although it's cropped, skims the top of my jeans. I figure a pair of chucks is probably best for moving boxes and put them on my feet. I tiptoe downstairs into the kitchen, where I quickly toast myself a slice of bread that I eat with some mashed avocado and a sunny-side-up egg. "You were born on the wrong coast," my mom likes to tease when I have avocado toast. "It's such a California thing to do."

My phone dings just as I shove the last piece of toast into my mouth. I pull it out of my back pocket to read the text from Vada, letting me know she's waiting for me outside.

"Hey! How was your *night*?" I ask once I'm in Vada's car, wiggling my eyebrows as I buckle my seatbelt. I knew Vada was going to spend last night at Steve's, taking advantage of the fact that we're officially on summer break, and Steve's mom's regular night shifts, to sleep over at her boyfriend's house as often as possible over these next few months.

Vada sighs deeply, throwing her head against the headrest. "Amazing," she says all happy and glowing.

"Yeah, you look like it was amazing. Where is Steve?"

"He and Ran took separate cars. They figured that way we can take more stuff at once and don't have to make so many trips."

"Smart," I say matter-of-factly.

Vada looks at me briefly before putting her eyes back on the road. "Hey, I'm sorry if I'm being pushy." She's apparently still thinking about the conversation we had on the phone yesterday. The topic had returned to the party on Saturday, how Ronan stopped something potentially really bad from happening, and then Vada repeatedly tried to insinuate that there could be something between Ronan and me.

"You're fine," I say. "I promise. I'm not offended or anything."

Her shoulders relax and a small smile appears on her lips. "Good, because I really do think you and Ran would make a cute couple."

I sigh and shake my head.

"What?" she asks. "Don't you like Ran?"

"I don't even really know him, Vada," I say, unwilling to tell her that a little flutter expands in my chest each time he crosses my mind or I see him, that I've imagined his lips brushing against mine more than once already, that I love his scent and the way his warm skin feels against mine. And I'm also not going to tell her that I'm too afraid of getting hurt and simultaneously ruining his life, because all those things have been true in the past. I'm afraid of being found out, afraid of stepping into the same traps I've stupidly stepped into before. There's no way I'm going to let history repeat itself.

"So get to know him, fall in love, and boom," Vada says, clapping her hands together.

"No, Vada. Just trust me when I tell you I can't. I just... I just can't," I say, leaving her no room to argue.

Vada's head swivels between the road and me a few more times as she searches for a way to get me to open up, but she mercifully changes the subject to tell me that she's narrowing down her choices of colleges to apply to come fall.

She dithers between wanting to be adventurous and move to California with Zack or staying closer to home and Steve, who will be heading to Boston come September. "I don't know; we don't even know what will happen to us after summer," she says, and I detect sadness in her voice. It's obvious to me how much she cares for Steve and how much he cares for her, but the two of them are also painfully aware that long-distance relationships are hard work and the likelihood that one of them will end up getting hurt is great. Both of them have told me they're trying to be realistic, but they're also trying to enjoy the summer with each other and not put too much pressure on their relationship.

Vada and I are the first to arrive at Shane's, and he takes a minute to introduce me to his dad and younger sister, Lauren, before he leads us up to his room. I notice several family portraits lining the wall along the stairs, and I stop to admire a photo that clearly depicts Shane's parents in the middle, flanked by Shane, Lauren, and another boy who looks like a slightly younger version of Shane.

"That's my little brother, Liam." Shane's tone is somber when he stops next to me. "He died almost two years ago."

"Oh, I'm sorry," I say.

Shane gives me a nod. I don't ask any questions about his brother's death and instead follow Shane the remainder of the way to his room, where several boxes are stacked atop each other.

"Where are Ran and Steve?" Shane asks, looking at the heavy boxes that need to be carried all the way down the stairs.

"They should be on their way," Vada says. "Ran seemed really tired when I headed out. He's probably just running behind." She nudges Shane's shoulder. "But why don't we start loading some of this into my car?"

The three of us begin to carry some of the lighter boxes downstairs, where we're met by Zack, Summer, Cheyenne, and Drew, who follow our lead and begin packing boxes into vehicles to make trips to Shane's new apartment.

Ronan

I'm exhausted. After closing Murphy's with Shane last night, I didn't get home and into bed until well after 3 a.m. Not even four hours later my alarm screamed at me to get my ass back out of bed to help Shane move.

I dragged myself out of bed, brushed my teeth, and threw on a pair of jeans and an army-green shirt, not bothering to shower. I knew full well I would be drenched in sweat in no time flat since it promises to be a hot day—perfect for moving heavy shit.

Vada's car was parked in front of the house when I got home, and the closed doors to Steve's room let me know she slept over last night. I ran into her and Steve when I made my way into the kitchen, desperate to find a quick way to wake up my body.

"You look like shit," Steve said as he handed me a full glass of water, knowing exactly what I was looking for.

"Fuck you, too," I grumbled.

He chuckled, passing me the black jar that holds my pre-workout.

I scooped some of the powder into my water and stirred, watching the substance dissolve. I chugged the bitter liquid, rinsed the glass out, and set it back in the cupboard, always careful not to leave a mess and risk a confrontation with my mom.

"I don't understand how you can drink that," Vada said, eyeing me and pulling a face in disgust. "It's so gross." She actually shuddered, which made my lips pull into a smile.

"It gets into my bloodstream quickly and it tastes a lot better than coffee." I shrugged. Coffee has never been attractive to me; in fact, the taste of it makes me gag. I'm weird, I guess.

We split up, with Vada informing us that she was picking up Cat to give her a ride to Shane's house—a fact that made my heart rate increase slightly.

I catch my mind wandering toward Cat sometimes. Okay, that's a lie. It wanders toward her a lot. Way too much, actually. It throws me off because, honestly, this is the last thing I want or need. My first and last serious relationship was when we lived in Montana the last time, and that was because things were okay. Things are mostly okay when we're in Montana, but they're never okay anywhere else. Since coming back to New York, I've hooked up with girls a bunch of times, but I'll be damned if I get myself into a situation where I have to bring someone home with me. I can't let someone really into my life—especially someone like Cat, who's obviously been through some things, has experienced pain, and who deserves someone good. And that someone would definitely not be me.

***

I take my own car and follow Steve the fifteen-minute route to Shane's house. The neighborhood that my parents' house is in is nice, but it's nothing compared to where Shane's dad lives. Shane calls it "yuppie." The homes are modern and the cars parked in the driveways are expensive, including Shane's dad's shiny black BMW and the little silver convertible Shane's sister, Lauren, zips around in. A lot of young, affluent families live in this neighborhood, somehow able to afford this lifestyle.

When we pull up to Shane's house, Zack, Summer, and Cheyenne are already there. Steve and I get out of our respective cars and head toward the open garage where Shane is taping a large cardboard box shut.

"Man, I thought you weren't gonna show." Shane heads toward us, and his eyes momentarily flick to a baseball-sized bruise on my right forearm—the result of a confrontation with my mom yesterday afternoon when Steve was out with Vada and before I left for work.

"Dude, it's ten minutes after eight," Steve says, before Shane can ask me about what happened. "We're not that late!"

"Whatever. Most of the stuff is packed; we just need to get it over to my apartment," Shane instructs us, and we walk after him through the garage into the house.

As I imagined, it gets hot quickly, adding to the suffocating humidity, and I'm drenched in sweat twenty minutes later. I'm schlepping boxes from Shane's room to my car while Steve, Shane, Zack, and Cheyenne make trips to Shane's place to unload. I have two boxes stacked up and I'm carrying them out of Shane's room, unable to see, when I run into someone with enough force that I stumble back and fall on my ass, hitting my head hard on the doorframe.

"Oh shoot, I'm sorry. I didn't see you coming around the corner," Cat says, hurrying toward me with her hand extended to help me up.

It's the first time I've seen her since falling asleep next to her. Her long blonde hair is braided back today, revealing her delicate neck and flawless skin. She's wearing tight jeans and a cropped scoop-neck shirt that slides off her left shoulder. As she moves close to me, I can see little beads of sweat running from her neck over her collarbone and down to her chest, where they disappear under her shirt.

My heart thumps stupidly in my chest and my breathing is amplified as I take in her sexy figure. She bends over toward me and her scoop-neck plunges down, giving me the perfect view of her black lacy bra and the swell of her breasts. I swallow and force myself to look up into her face before I grab her hand and feel her heat against my skin.

She grunts, trying to hoist me up, and I laugh because she has such a small frame. I help her out by pushing myself up with my other hand, and she stumbles backwards. My hands snap forward just in time, and I steady her with my fingers on her hips.

Her eyes are big, and I can't tell if it's because she almost fell or because of my hands on her hips. My thumbs and index fingers touch the bare skin just above the top of her jeans where her cropped shirt doesn't reach.

"Thank you," she says, slightly breathless.

"Thank *you* for helping me up," I say, looking into her eyes, trying to figure out if they're brown or green. A wave of heat washes through me as I take in her eyes, her full lips, her neck, her shirt that's clinging to her damp skin, all the way down to her tight jeans that show off her long legs. God, why does she have to be so perfect?

"Are you alright?" She examines my face, concern in her eyes.

"I'm fine," I say, rubbing the back of my head with my right hand. I'm still holding on to her with my left, unwilling to let go of her just yet.

"How about you? Did I hurt you?" I ask, scanning her face for obvious signs of injury. She shakes her head and peeks into the empty room behind me. "These are the last two boxes." I motion toward the two boxes that were just in my arms and are now on the floor, not taking my eyes off hers.

Looking into her eyes is almost like looking into a mirror. I've noticed it before: despite the brightness in her eyes, there's something dark, something hidden—a hint of defeat that's so damn familiar to me. It stares me in the face every time I see my reflection, and it makes me wonder what happened to her. But what's more unsettling to me is that it makes me want to protect her. From what, exactly, I'm not sure of.

"Do you want to help me get these to my car and then head over to Shane's new place?" I ask, hoping she'll agree to ride with me.

She hesitates for a moment, then smiles and nods her head. "Yeah, okay. I'll text Vada that she doesn't have to come back for me, then."

"Great, I'll meet you downstairs."

I restack the last two boxes and am on my way out when she reaches for me. "Wait, let me take one of these," she says, and I let her grab the box balanced on top of the other. Together we make our way down the stairs and to my car, where we deposit the boxes in the backseat. I stop to open the passenger door of my car for her and watch her slide into the seat before closing the door behind her and making my way around the front.

"I never thanked you for... for the other night," Cat says the moment I start the engine.

"You don't have to thank me," I say. "If anything, I should thank you for passing out when you did. I'd probably be in jail otherwise," I joke, trying to relieve the tension that has visibly seized Cat's freckled shoulders. I don't want her to feel tense around me.

"You're welcome," she giggles, making me smile. "That was totally planned," she adds, and I laugh.

"I figured as much. Trying to keep me out of trouble?"

"Yeah, you know, just your everyday heroine," she says with a bright smile.

I don't exactly know why I say it, but I suddenly feel like Cat needs to know. "I didn't sleep with her." I glance at Cat as I drive.

She creases her brow, obviously not understanding.

"With Sophie. Saturday night," I say. "When... When I saw you sitting by the bar, you asked me if I was already done with her and... I didn't sleep with her."

Cat's eyes widen, her lips parting with comprehension. She looks ashamed.

"I just thought you should know," I add, remembering the pained look in Cat's eyes, the strained tone of her voice when she asked me about Sophie. It was like me disappearing into that room for a one-night stand caused Cat pain, which I never meant to do, if that's the effect it even had on her. I don't know.

To be honest, I had every intention of hooking up with Sophie—at first. But when we got into Shane's room, I couldn't go through with it. An overwhelming feeling of guilt stopped me from kissing Sophie when she leaned in, her hands already unbuckling my jeans. I knew, like I had never truly known before that night, that I was only using Sophie to distract myself. *I* was *using* a girl. If that isn't low, I don't know what is. At first, I tried to push the feeling down. I'd always been good at that, but not Saturday night. I stood there as Sophie, apparently picking up on my strange energy, abandoned my belt and instead pulled off her shirt and bra. But no matter how hard I tried, I just couldn't get into it. My mind was on Cat and my body gave it away. So I apologized, then handed Sophie her bra and shirt, and left her to get dressed again. I felt like complete shit, until I found Cat and immediately focused on the situation at hand rather than the fact that I had just acted like a complete fucking asshole.

"Anyway," I deflect before Cat can say anything at all, "do you mind if I roll down the window?" I ask her while we drive.

"A little bit of a breeze would be nice," she agrees, pulling her shirt away from her sticky skin. I can tell Cat is one of those girls who has absolutely no freaking idea what kind of effect they have on people, and I smile as I crank my window down.

"Sorry, it's an old car," I say. "No automatic anything, except the stereo."

She looks around the interior of my '69 Mustang Boss, taking in the well-worn leather and the black dashboard. "It's a nice car." She runs her hands gently across the conditioned leather of her seat. "Did you put all this work into it?"

"Yep," I say, feeling proud. "This car actually belonged to Shane's dad, but it wasn't operational and was just sitting around their garage. I think he was hoping to restore it eventually, but he's just so busy with his restaurants that he didn't ever get around to it. And then last year, the car was still there so I took a leap of faith and asked him if he'd sell it to me."

"That's so cool!" I love how enthusiastic she is. "My dad has a classic Chevy Chevelle that he loves, but I honestly don't know too much about cars. My dad taught me how to change a tire, change the oil, and make sure I don't get ripped off if my car ever has to go to the shop, but that's about the extent of it," she adds, a little disgruntled.

"That's more than most people know about their cars." I smile at her. "Honestly, some people don't even know which side of their car the gas tank is on," I add, recalling the time Vada attempted to fill up her car and had to pull the pump handle over the roof of her car to get to the tank. Steve would not let her live it down the whole drive home.

"How do you know so much about cars?" she asks.

Talking to her feels light and easy, not forced at all, and I really hope it keeps going because I really enjoy talking to Cat.

"That comes with living on a ranch, I think. My grandparents are pretty cut off from everything, so they do the majority of their own work. My grandfather and dad taught me how to work on cars, do repairs and stuff when I was like eleven; same time they taught me and Steve to drive, actually."

"You drove when you were eleven?" She sounds shocked, and I can't help but laugh.

"Yeah, not like on freeways, but we drove the trucks when we needed to move hay or corral cattle. It's a different life on a ranch. You grow up faster because you're expected to help with the manual labor from a pretty early age."

"Do you like living in the city better than on the ranch?" Her entire body is turned toward me now as she leans her elbows onto the center console.

I worry we may be heading toward a touchy subject. "I don't really know." I finally exhale, then pause. "My best friends are here, but things are good in Montana." I glance at her.

She nods and leans back in her seat, withdrawing her arms from the center console and adjusting her long legs.

We stay quiet for a while, and I enjoy that Cat isn't afraid of the silence. In fact, being silent around her doesn't feel awkward like it does with so many people. It's comforting, and I feel content in her presence. Once in a while the breeze from the open window will make her scent drift over to me and I catch the smell of lavender and rosewater. It's delicate and intoxicating, and I realize yet again that I'm in trouble.

Cat

I remember now. That night I asked Ronan about Sophie, and I remember how much it affected me, even though I didn't want to admit it to myself. And I feel a strange sensation of relief when he tells me he didn't sleep with her—what do I do with that?

Ronan and I have the easiest time talking, and the more we do, the more I want to know about him, discover who he is. And, holy hell, is Ronan gorgeous. It's like I notice his perfection anew each time I see him—how tall he is; his muscular body—lean and cut rather than bulky. Even the way he is dressed today—a pair of blue jeans and an olive-green shirt with sleeves that are just a little too fitted, straining against his biceps. It's enough to make my mouth dry. And Ronan's face... God. But it goes way beyond his looks. He seems so unlike the guys I've hung around in the past, so unlike Adam. Ronan wants to know things about me—truly know them. He asks about softball and my family. I find myself shifting toward him as we talk, leaning on the console and verging on invading his personal space before I retreat, not wanting to appear as though I'm coming on to him. But it's difficult, like trying to resist a magnetic pull.

Ronan's knuckles graze against me as he shifts into a higher gear, and I allow myself a moment to relish the tingling sensation. I look at my knee, half expecting to see an electrical discharge, and notice Ronan looking at me, his green eyes glistening against the sun through the windshield.

"What?" I ask self-consciously.

He gives me that sexy half smile. "Nothing, sorry." He redirects his attention to the road, but the half smile remains, and it makes my heart thump in my chest.

"Your mom looks so young," I say out of the blue, remembering my encounter with her a few weeks ago.

His smile fades, and I can tell he's working to maintain a neutral expression. "When did you meet my mother?" he asks, jaw clenched, not taking his eyes off the road this time.

"When I was at your house with Vada; before we headed to the movies with Steve, Zack, and Summer," I remind him. "She was on her way out to work, and I just thought that she's really beautiful and seems young."

Ronan nods. "That's because she is young. My parents had Steve at sixteen and me exactly thirteen months later at seventeen. She's only thirty-four."

"Wow," I say, shocked. "I can't imagine having a baby right now. That would be really hard."

"I'm sure it was hard for them," he says, his expression unchanged. "It wasn't exactly in their plans. In fact, I don't think that they even planned to be in a relationship at all."

"What do you mean?" I ask him, trying to decipher his demeanor.

He exhales slowly. "So, my dad left Montana when he was sixteen. He just up and left because I guess he was sick of the ranch life, wanted something different, I don't know. He really didn't have anywhere to go; he just sort of scraped by working all kinds of odd jobs. His plan was to enlist in the Air Force as soon as he turned seventeen, but he had a year to go. Anyway, a couple of weeks after he came to New York he met my mother. They hooked up and he got her pregnant, like, that night. I don't really think they intended to see each other again afterwards, but... well. I've only met my grandparents on my mother's side a handful of times. They're really, really strict. Very Catholic. My grandfather is also a general in the Army, so he has that no-bullshit attitude."

He glances at me and I look at him, eager for him to keep telling me the story.

"So, my mother's parents kicked her out, disowned her, or whatever."

"That's awful," I say quietly.

"My dad's parents are equally as Catholic, but much, much kinder." Ronan's expression brightens a smidge. "They told my parents that they would take them in, but they had to get married. They couldn't have a child out of wedlock. So my parents went back to Montana, got married, and had Steve a couple months later. My dad enlisted in the Air Force as soon as he turned seventeen, and just before he left for basic boot camp..."

"Your mom became pregnant again?"

He nods grimly. "Yep, four months after Steve was born. My dad still left for boot camp while my mother stayed in Montana with my grandparents. At some point my mother's parents decided that maybe they did want a relationship with their daughter and grandsons after all. You know, legacy and all that bullshit." Ronan frowns. "They helped my parents buy our house here in New York, but otherwise aren't super involved in our lives."

"Where do your mom's parents live?" I'm fascinated by this backstory.

"White Plains," he says. "In Westchester."

"I don't know where that is," I admit, feeling like a total newcomer.

"It's about an hour or so north of the city," he says, his voice soft after telling me his parents' story.

I push a breath out between my lips, my cheeks puffed out, processing everything Ronan just shared with me.

"And now your mom is a nurse." I find it amazing that after having children as a teenager, she made it all the way through high school and college.

He nods again. "She got her GED and then attended night classes whenever she could. That's why my mother never wanted to move with my dad and we stayed mostly here in New York while my dad was stationed wherever. After she finished school we did move with him a few times over the span of twelve months, but my mother hated it. So we stayed in New York, with the exception of a couple moves back to Montana when I was ten and again three years ago."

"That's incredible. Good for your mom going after it," I say.

Ronan doesn't respond, his expression indifferent. "Tell me something about you," he finally urges.

"Uh, well, my parents also had me pretty young; they were twenty. I have a sister—Samantha—who is nine, and a brother—Benny—who is six. My parents are actually from New York, but they eloped to North Carolina when they graduated from high school. They met their freshman year," I rattle off.

Ronan smiles at me. "They're high school sweethearts?"

I nod. "Cute, right?"

"Can I ask why you and your mom moved to New York and your dad stayed behind in North Carolina?" There's hesitation in his voice, as though he senses that everything may not be as happy-go-lucky as it seems.

I always dread this question. I'm just not ready to talk about what really happened and how I'm at fault for breaking up my whole family and literally ruining people's lives, their futures.

"My mom thought it was time for a change of scenery, but my dad didn't, so my mom decided we'd move as a sort of trial run while my parents figure things out."

"But they're still together?" Ronan asks, perplexed.

"Uh-huh," I nod. "They're just... trying to figure out what's best, I guess." I trail off, not wanting to get into details, and I'm relieved when

Ronan doesn't ask me to explain further. It's like we have this odd understanding of each other, that there may be things we shouldn't press just yet. I'm respectful of him and he of me, and I really like that.

We chit chat for the rest of the drive and I find myself smiling and laughing easily, which hasn't been the case in a long time.

When we arrive at Shane's new place, we get out of the car and each of us grabs a box from the backseat. I notice Ronan's eyes lingering on me and it sends a strange sensation through my body. I pretend not to notice or care, but I can tell that something inside me is changing. The chains around my heart loosen the more time I spend with him.

We make it up the stairs together, and the door to Shane's apartment is wide open. Noise wallows through the entrance as Ronan and I step into the hallway of the apartment.

Shane walks toward us, taking the box from me. "Is this the last of it?"

I nod. "Yes, that's it."

"Perfect, there's pizza in the kitchen." Shane moves his gaze to Ronan. "Let's drop these boxes off in my bedroom and get some food."

Shane and Ronan make their way down the hall and vanish into a room just to the left.

"Did he finally ask you out?" Vada's voice is so close to me that it catches me off guard and I spin around, finding her face only about a foot from mine. She giggles and pokes my arm with her index finger. "I saw you checking him out just now."

"You did not!" But I blush nonetheless because I know it's true. I was watching the way his back flexed as he carried the box down the hallway. And I was wondering what it would feel like to run my hands over his back, for him to touch me in turn. It confuses me; I've never craved anyone's touch before. Any sort of physical intimacy has been uncomfortable, forced on me, even painful, and I swear... *swore* I wouldn't ever want another guy to touch me like that.

I shake my head, hoping it will clear my thoughts, but Vada's giggle doesn't help the situation. I'm about to retort when I sense Ronan next to me.

"How about some food?"

The sound of his husky voice makes my heart skip a beat, and I turn toward him. His eyes meet mine, and there's a smile on his full lips. I can only manage a nod, feeling stupid for acting like such a giddy girl around him when I don't even really know him, when I'm determined to stay on the straight and narrow, to be the good girl everyone expects me to be.

Ronan leads the way into the kitchen as Vada whispers stuff into my ear about him and me. I step on her foot to make her stop, but she only laughs.

In the kitchen, Cheyenne hugs Ronan and gives him a kiss on the cheek. I act as though I'm indifferent, but something weird stirs inside me. Ronan gives her a one-armed hug, then makes her pout when he picks up two plates with a couple of pizza slices and makes his way toward me. I can feel Cheyenne's gaze bore into me when Ronan hands me one of the plates with a smile, but he positions himself in a way that blocks my view of Cheyenne and hers of me.

"Hey, what about me?" Vada gripes jokingly. "No pizza for your favorite of your brother's girlfriends?" she asks, eyes huge as she flutters her lashes at Ronan.

Ronan gives a quick laugh. "Well, first of all you're my brother's *only* girlfriend, or at least I think you're the only one," he says in mock contemplation. "And second, Cat here helped me with the last couple of boxes, so I thought she deserved some pizza."

"You two are pretty cute together." Vada grabs me by the arm and pulls me out of the kitchen and into the living room. We plop down on the dark-gray couch and I look around the small apartment as I eat my pizza. I take note of the little things, like the Xbox by the TV, the boxes randomly strewn around the apartment, the still-bare walls. Tori's sitting on the floor, her legs crossed while she chats with

Zack and Summer, and Vada jumps in on a conversation about college campus tours.

After I finish my pizza, I put my head in Vada's lap and listen to the conversation. When my body becomes heavy, I allow my eyes to shut, and I doze off.

***

"Kitty Cat!" Vada's voice washes into my consciousness, and I blink against the afternoon sun streaming in through the living-room window. I hear a number of people in the background and become instantly self-conscious, tugging on my shirt to cover my stomach where the cropped top has ridden up. I sit up abruptly, smoothing my hair. My braid is a total mess, and I pull the hair tie out, letting my hair unravel. It's wavy and crazy, so I gather it into a messy bun and secure the hair tie around it.

I look down at myself instinctively. My jeans are still buttoned and my bra still in place underneath my shirt, which has only ridden up a few centimeters, hardly exposing anything at all. I relax, looking around at my friends who are conversing with each other easily, clearly not at all caring that I was passed out, unconscious, vulnerable yet again. Nobody took advantage of me, and even Zack's camera is turned away from me. I'm safe.

"I'm sorry for falling asleep," I mumble, rubbing the sleep out of my left eye.

"No worries. You're not the only one." Vada points to the couch opposite us. Ronan is fast asleep, his back turned to us, his chest rising and falling slowly. I can't take my eyes off him. The idea of lying down next to him and feeling the warmth of his body against mine is enticing.

"Alright, babe, I'm going to head home to change. I'll be by your house in an hour." Steve cups the back of Vada's head and gives her a kiss before grabbing his keys from the kitchen counter and heading out the door.

"So, what's the plan for tonight?" I ask Vada, feeling more refreshed after my nap. I stretch my arms over my head and yawn.

"Well, Shane and Ronan are working at Murphy's again tonight and the rest of us were going to hang out there. What do you think?"

I take another glance at Ronan, who seems to be oblivious to the movement around him. He's obviously exhausted. "Yeah, I just need to shower and put on some different clothes."

***

We end up getting to Murphy's around eight, and again the place is packed. A band is playing on the little stage in the back of the bar and a few girls are already dancing. Instead of finding a booth or table to sit at, I follow Vada, Steve, Zack, and Summer to the bar where Tori is chatting with Jack, the bartender.

"Hey!" Shane greets us, setting five small glasses filled with clear liquid in front of us. "This one's on the house. Thanks for helping me out today."

"Sure thing. Thanks, man," Steve says, handing a shot to Vada, sliding one toward me, and picking one up himself.

I eye the glass, and Zack gives me a gentle shove. "It's tequila—the good stuff. Not roofied, probably," he says with a grin. He raises the glass in the air, his GoPro—as always—propped up in his other hand, capturing the goings-on as he waits for us to join him.

"Dude, too fucking soon," Steve scolds Zack, who looks at me sheepishly, but I have to laugh nonetheless because it actually was kind of funny.

Vada, Steve, and Summer join in raising their glasses, but I'm skeptical. I promised myself I'd stay away from alcohol when I left North Carolina, and I've already slipped too many times.

"You don't have to do this if you don't want to," a husky voice says next to me, and goose bumps erupt all the way down my spine. I turn my head; Ronan's standing behind me wearing an all-black ballcap over his tousled hair and another long-sleeved black shirt.

"Why don't you do one with her, Ran? Maybe she'll feel more comfortable then," Shane says loudly from behind the counter, and hands Ronan a shot of tequila.

I look around at Vada, Steve, Zack, and Summer; their heads are tipped back as they gulp down their shots. "Okay," I nod, surprising myself.

Ronan extends his shot glass toward me. "To peer pressure," he grins.

I clink my glass against his. "To peer pressure."

I watch him tip his head back and swallow the alcohol, then slam the glass back onto the counter.

I pinch my nose with my left hand and put the glass to my lips with the right. In one swig, I work the alcohol down my throat and feel the burn spreading into my stomach. "I forgot how bad this stuff tastes," I sputter, scrunching my nose.

"You're kind of a pro at this," Ronan observes, his brows raised in amusement. "I wouldn't have guessed." He reaches for the bottle of tequila and pours everyone another round.

"I was a bit of a party girl back in North Carolina," I confess, and quickly take my second shot.

I can feel everyone staring at me, and Vada busts up laughing.

"My Kitty Cat a party girl! Well, this should be a fun night."

"Oh no, that girl is no longer me," I say vehemently, shaking my head as Vada pushes another shot glass my way.

Ronan

Murphy's is busy again tonight, which means great tips. Jack is mixing and pouring drinks for a bunch of drunk frat guys loitering around the bar counter and shouting shit at each other about their latest hookups. It's mildly amusing. Shane nods in their direction, grinning at me as I pass him with a tray of food and head for a table occupied by six or seven girls. They're all in tight, short dresses, their hair done up. They're celebrating the birthday of one of their friends, a brunette in a blue-sequined dress. She's donned a sash with the phrase, "It's my 21st birthday," printed in gold, glittery letters. She hops up, clapping her hands together as I approach, and before I can set down the food she grabs the plate of hot wings off my tray.

"Jeez, Emily, calm down," a red-haired girl in a dress so tight that it looks like her breasts will pop out the top says to the brunette. Her words are slurred and her voice is louder than it needs to be. "Let him put the food down." She eyes me possessively, letting her eyes roam over my body.

I smile to myself while I pass out the plates of appetizers. When I've finished, she steps toward me and rests her right hand on my chest. "You're really fucking hot." She licks her bottom lip, and I pull away as she moves her face closer to mine. "What time do you get off? You should join us for some drinks later." Her right hand slides down my chest to my stomach, and I grab her wrist just as she reaches the top of my jeans, stopping her from moving farther south.

"Sorry, I already have plans later," I say, trying not to sound like a dick because that would jeopardize my tip. Her bottom lip pops out and she's trying to make puppy eyes, but she's so drunk that her face just contorts, causing her brunette friend to dissolve into a fit of laughter. The redhead turns to scold her friend, and I take the opportunity to retreat from the table of handsy sorority girls.

"You know, I bet that redhead would take you home tonight, if you let her." Shane grins at me suggestively when I return to the bar to pick up a drink order.

I'm about to retort that he really needs to stop being so concerned with my sex life, but I'm distracted when the front doors open and Cat walks in. She looks around the place before she makes her way toward the bar with Vada, my brother, Zack, and Summer, and I can't keep my eyes off her. She is by far the most beautiful girl in this place, and actually the most beautiful girl I've ever laid eyes on.

I quickly deliver the drinks and return to the counter where Shane has poured tequila and everyone is starting to do shots. I'm amazed at how easily Cat takes the first shot, and then the second. She says something about having been a party girl back in North Carolina, which is interesting because she doesn't strike me as that type of person. But an hour and a half, three more tequila shots, and two long island ice teas later, I can see what she means.

Vada and my brother are making out on the dance floor while Cat sits at a table chatting animatedly—and rather loudly—with Tori, Summer, and Zack, her face flushed, cheeks and lips rosy.

Cat changed outfits after the move today; she's wearing tight, faded blue jeans and this red, sleeveless blouse tucked into the band of her jeans. The blouse is a sheer material, and underneath it she's wearing a white, strappy tank top. She looks fucking incredible.

Apparently I'm not the only one who notices her, because a tall frat guy with a scruffy face makes his way toward her table. I eye the guy, keeping a watchful eye on Cat, especially after Saturday.

Shane bumps his elbow into my arm. "God damn it, Ran. You're obviously into her. When are you going to make your move?"

I frown at him. "I can't, Shay. I can't drag her into the shit that is my life," I say against gritted teeth, reiterating my stance from only a few days ago.

Shane knows what happens at my house, sort of. He doesn't have a full grasp of the extent of the violence, but he is aware that my mother occasionally loses her shit on me. He figured it out earlier this year when we were at the gym.

It was the morning after a particularly vicious beating and my ribs were raw and bruised, maybe cracked, I don't know; it's not like I can go to the doctor to figure out the extent of my injuries. I pushed myself hard that morning, and after a solid set of bench presses Shane playfully punched me in the ribs as an attaboy. The pain that shot through my body made my knees buckle, and it freaked Shane out. I tried to compose myself and kept telling him I was fine, but he made me pull up my shirt in the locker room and quickly realized that something wasn't right at home. His dad and mine are close friends and have known each other since Shane and I started playing hockey together when I was only seven, and Shane knew Steve wouldn't ever hit me like that, so he came to the right conclusion about my mother. I didn't even have to say anything; he figured it out all by himself.

I made him swear not to tell anyone, and he begrudgingly agreed after I told him over and over that I was fine and that I could handle it. I definitely downplayed the frequency and seriousness of the violence I endure at home.

"You know you deserve to be happy, Ran. And I think she could make you happy," he says in a serious tone, briefly glancing at the bruise on my forearm like he did this morning. I pull the sleeve of my shirt down to my wrist, covering myself. I have a feeling Shane has a pretty good idea that the bruise didn't happen by accident, though he hasn't bothered asking about it, knowing that it won't change anything.

My eyes wander back to Cat and I nod absentmindedly.

A grin spreads across Shane's face. "And I also think you could make her happy, if you know what I mean," he says with a chuckle, one eyebrow cocked.

"Whatever." I focus my attention on a girl who just moved up to lean on the bar; she's wearing decidedly too much sparkly eyeshadow. I move out of the way so Jack can take her order and make a round through my table section. I check if people need refills or are ready to order before returning to the counter where Shane is wiping down laminated menus with a damp rag. I look back toward Cat's table and realize she's no longer there. Instead, she's standing at the end of the bar some feet away from me, the scruffy-looking frat guy leaning in and saying something into Cat's ear. She's clearly uncomfortable; her whole body is closed off and trying to turn away from this guy who has his hands propped on the counter on either side of her small frame so she's trapped between his arms. Fuck, it seems like Cat is a damn magnet for creeps. Can this girl ever go anywhere without someone trying some shit?

"I'll be right back," I say to Shane, and make my way toward Cat. That overwhelming need to step in, to protect her, has taken over again.

As if she can sense my approach, her eyes find mine and she looks at me pleadingly.

"Hey baby," she says loudly when I reach her, and the guy instantly takes a couple of steps back from Cat. I almost look over my shoulder to see who she's talking to, but then her hands glide up to my chest and around my neck, pulling me in for a kiss.

Shit, this isn't good. *I* am not good. But fuck, it feels amazing.

My eyes close with the softness of Cat's lips, which she parts, allowing my tongue to slip carefully into her mouth. She tastes like tequila and iced tea as I massage her tongue with mine. My hands find her hips and I gently tug her toward me, making a small moan escape from her lips. Her warm body conforms to mine and my heart races. I can feel her heat against every part of me, and I start kissing her more deeply.

I vaguely notice the guy making a face and leaving, but I get lost again when Cat gently bites my lower lip. I can't help the small groan that escapes my mouth. Her hands are still around my neck, her chest pressed to mine. I have no idea what's happening; all I know is that I really don't want it to stop.

I slowly pull away from Cat, and she opens her glossed-over, hooded eyes, swaying slightly as she looks at me with her head tipped back.

"Are you alright?" I ask her, my breathing erratic, blood pulsing in my veins.

A look of confusion spreads across Cat's face. "Why did you stop?" she asks, her speech garbled and slow, her pupils huge.

"Because I don't want to take advantage of you. And I don't want you to do anything you don't really want and aren't going to remember in the morning," I tell her sincerely, omitting the fact that she shouldn't want to kiss me, shouldn't want to get involved with me because she is too damn good for me. For anyone, really, but most definitely for me. I'm fucking worthless. If there's anything I know, it's that.

She presses her lips together, her eyebrows knitting as she studies me like she just discovered a new species. "You're so different," she muses, and turns toward Vada who approaches us hand-in-hand with my brother. "I'm tired," Cat announces, and it makes me laugh.

"Come on, Kitty Cat, we'll get you home," Vada says with a nod to Steve. She hooks her arm under Cat's and leads her out of Murphy's.

Cat turns abruptly to face me, and though she's obviously intoxicated, her eyes nonetheless lock on mine. "Thank you for saving me. Again," she says, her voice slow but steady, sincere. She gives me a heart-stopping smile and then follows Vada out the door.

Wednesday, June 2nd

Cat

Vada dropped me off at my house at a quarter past ten, way before my midnight curfew. My mom took one look at me stumbling into the house and sighed heavily before leading me up to my bedroom.

"Kitty," she sighed as she pulled off my shoes, "I thought we moved on from this?"

I blinked at her, my eyelids heavy. All I wanted was to go to sleep. Well, maybe throw up first, then go to sleep.

"We did, Mom. Nothing happened, I promise. I'm safe, and unlike last time I have some pretty great friends." I tried to keep my voice steady and held her gaze as she searched my eyes.

She pressed her lips together, but finally nodded her head. "You do seem to have some pretty good people around you," she agreed, and gently stroked my hair back over my head. "I'm going to bring you some aspirin and then you should try to get some sleep."

She headed to the bathroom, where I could hear her fill a glass with water before she returned with two small white pills in one hand and the glass in the other. I chased the bitter-tasting medicine with water before falling back on my pillow, where my eyes instantly fell shut.

I wake up a few hours later. My throat is parched, but other than that I feel pretty good. It's quiet in the house with the exception of the nightly sounds of light neighborhood traffic traveling up and through my open window. It's cool in my room, and I sit up to stretch my legs. I'm still in the jeans and red blouse from earlier and, looking down at myself, I replay the events of the evening... and that kiss.

Ronan thought I wouldn't remember it, or that I'd regret it—but neither is true. I remember it. Everything. Vividly.

When we were at Murphy's, this guy came up to talk to me. I tried to lose him. I had too much to drink, yes, but I was sober enough that, somewhere in the back of my head, the alarm bells went off when this guy kept following me, wouldn't leave me alone. I tried to lose him, but he eventually cornered me, trapped me with his large frame, and I froze.

I still remember being a little girl and my parents telling me, repeatedly, to kick and scream if someone ever grabbed me, hurt me, did something I didn't want. But the reality is that whenever I'm in a situation that would call for such a reaction, my body freezes. I don't fight or run away; I freeze. I didn't realize that was an option, but apparently my body did. It happened to me over and over, and it did last night at Murphy's.

But then Ronan was there, and just like he did with Drew and Corbin, he stepped in. He stopped whatever was happening—he protected me. And I want to say that my drunkenness caused me to let down my guard, caused me to do what I did next—move my hands to Ronan's chest, feeling the contours of his sculpted muscles through his shirt and the heat of his rock-hard body against mine as I wrapped my arms around his neck to pull him into me. But it wasn't that. It wasn't the alcohol.

It was me. I wanted him to kiss me. I want it now, even though I know I shouldn't.

God, I can't believe I let my guard down like that, allowed myself to fall back into the same patterns that already cost me everything. Shame washes over me at the realization that I led him on, that I used him, that I lost my inhibitions, which is something that hasn't happened in a long time.

Ugh, all these thoughts make me antsy. I get off my bed and pace my small room before I decide to go outside for a few minutes to enjoy the cool night air. My phone informs me that it's 2:27 in the morning. I don't bother putting on shoes or even slippers as I make my way quietly downstairs, unlock the front door, and slip outside. I sit down on the stoop, lean back on my hands, and close my eyes, enjoying the breeze that gently moves strands of my loose hair.

I let my mind wander, and I remember back to when I last overstepped my personal boundaries and paid for it dearly. A lump forms in my throat as I recall what happened in North Carolina, how my fairy tale turned into a nightmare that continues to haunt my days and nights, all because of my personal choices.

My tears burn hot as they stream quietly down my face. I haven't talked about what happened since leaving North Carolina, except with my friend Julie, who witnessed the whole thing and its aftermath. But I don't care what Julie says—the events that unfolded were my fault. How could they not be? My ex, Adam, didn't ask much of me, honestly. Especially considering how I acted around him when I was drunk, then shut him down each time he tried to do what I was so very obviously hinting at, according to him and a lot of other people. It's no surprise things took the turn they did. I'm still so ashamed, and I swore to myself I'd never again be that girl—the girl who would get drunk, lead a boy on, then ruin his life forever.

I notice the black dog before I notice who's walking behind it. Out of the corner of my eye I see movement and turn my head to spot Onyx prancing along the sidewalk. A short distance behind her is Ronan. He's wearing a white, hooded thermal and jeans that sit low on his hips. His head is lowered, his right hand in his pocket, and he seems lost in a world of his own, not taking his eyes off the sidewalk in front of him. I don't know if Onyx can smell me or otherwise senses my presence, but her tail wags happily. She props up her ears only for a second before she veers off the sidewalk and runs toward me at full throttle.

Ronan's head snaps up and he sprints after his dog. "Jesus, Onyx, get back here."

Onyx reaches me and jumps, her front paws on my shoulders as she excitedly sniffs my face with her wet nose. I pet her, laughing, when

Ronan makes his way up the four steps to my front door and grabs Onyx by the collar, yanking her off me.

"I'm so, so sorry," he pants breathlessly. "She usually doesn't... Cat?" His lips turn into a smile as his eyes fill with comprehension. "I had no idea this is where you live."

"Yep. Welcome to my humble abode." I smile, still petting Onyx as she strains against Ronan's hold on her collar and licks my arm. Luckily Onyx's intense greeting erased any signs of my crying a few minutes ago.

"I swear, Onyx is usually really good when she's off the leash. She's actually pretty shy around people... well, with the exception of you, apparently. I don't know what's gotten into her. I'm sorry if she freaked you out."

"It's all good," I say, smiling and standing up to escape Onyx's wet nose in my face. The moonlight reflects in Ronan's eyes, making them shine like emeralds, and his skin looks like ivory. "What are you doing walking her so late?" I ask, grabbing my phone out of my pocket. It's a quarter till three.

He bends down to secure the leather leash on Onyx's collar. "Vada is staying over at my house," he says, his lips pressed together.

"Yeah, I know," I tell him, aware that Vada was going to spend yet another night pretending to be sleeping over at my place, when, in reality, she's staying with Steve. I'm not sure why that would be the reason for him to be walking his dog at almost three in the morning.

Ronan just looks at me, a slow smile spreading across his face, his eyebrows raised as if he's quizzing me. And then it dawns on me.

"Oh.... Oh," I giggle. "Oh my god." I put my hand over my mouth and laugh. "Does this happen a lot?"

He nods with a grin. "Yep. Let's just say that when Vada is over, I don't get a whole lot of sleep," he says, and I immediately understand.

"And how long do you have to stay out?"

"I don't know; I haven't exactly timed them before," he says, and we both laugh out loud.

"Sometimes, if I'm too tired, I just end up crashing on the couch in the living room, but tonight I thought I'd take Onyx for a little stroll and let those two get the horniness out of their system. Things can get a bit noisy," he says, his eyebrows knitted, but his lips are still smiling. "How about you? Why are you out here?"

"Well, I woke up and thought I'd enjoy the nightly breeze."

"It is a really nice night," he agrees. "Are you feeling okay, though? You had quite a bit to drink earlier." He looks at me with concern.

"Yeah, I'm fine. I drank a bunch of water and took some aspirin. I feel pretty good, actually," I assure him, and drink in his handsome features. His smile is gentle, and the fullness of his lips makes me want to graze mine against them.

"I'm really glad to hear that," he says, and pulls his bottom lip slightly into his mouth, running his tongue over it and wetting it. Our eyes meet and we look at each other so intensely my whole body is covered in goose bumps.

I swallow hard. "Ronan, I'm sorry."

"For what?" he asks, his eyes not leaving mine.

"For kissing you to make that other guy go away." I feel lousy; this is exactly the kind of crap I vowed never to do again.

"Oh, so you were just using me," he says with mock offense, and I can't help but laugh.

"Yeah, I guess so...."

He considers me, his gaze locked on me, burning their way into my soul. His lips are pressed together, brow tense as if he's battling with himself the way I'm battling with myself. Part of me wishes he would step closer to me, would move his hands to my hips, would pull me toward him and kiss me; another part of me is afraid, ashamed, trying desperately to remind myself of my boundaries.

Ronan hesitates for a fraction of a second longer, but then seems to lose the war with himself. He steps toward me and his left hand moves under my chin, gently lifting my head toward him. I know exactly what's coming, and I do nothing to stop him.

The truth is, I want it to happen.

Ronan leans in and brushes his lips against mine, kissing me softly. I part my lips, and his tongue slips inside my mouth. He tastes me while his hand moves from my chin over my shoulder and down to my hip, settling on my lower back. He pulls me into him, and our bodies melt together as our kiss intensifies.

My breath falters, my heart beats erratically against my ribs, and I press my chest against his. He continues caressing my tongue with his, his kisses igniting a fire inside me I didn't know existed. I've never felt this way, not even with Adam, and it feels new, raw, and breathtaking. My senses are in overdrive and my legs become weak as Ronan deepens the kiss, his tongue venturing further into my mouth, devouring me. His hand on my low back is searing hot, and it sends a wave of desire through every fiber of me. I don't want it to stop, ever, but Ronan pulls away, slowly opening his eyes. I can still feel my lips tingling and my breathing is frantic.

"There, now we're even," he says, his voice gravelly. A smile begins to form on his full, soft lips, his green eyes intense when I meet his gaze.

It's subtle, but I can feel my world shift.

I blink at him as he takes a small step back to give me some space, staying close enough that I can still feel the electricity between our bodies.

He pulls out his phone. "I feel like I should ask for your number. I mean, I've saved you a couple of times, and we've officially made out twice now." He flashes me that sexy half-smile.

"Yeah, I guess we're kinda going about this the wrong way, huh?" I say, blushing.

"I'm not sure I'd call it wrong"—he shrugs, still smiling—"but if that's how you feel, then I guess I should do something to make it right."

My eyes flicker back to his lips and I swallow hard before looking in his eyes. "What are you thinking, exactly?" While I'm excited, I also feel a little on edge, like this conversation might be taking a turn I'm not comfortable with.

He senses my apprehension, and his eyes turn serious. "I'm thinking we slow it down a little, and maybe you'll let me take you out?" He looks at me with a mixture of doubt and childlike hopefulness.

My lips tug upward into a smile. "I think I'd like that."

"Me, too." His eyes are soft as he smiles at me. "Thursday? Shane will be pissed if I blow off his party tonight. You'll be there, right?"

It takes me a second to remember which party Ronan is talking about. "Oh shit!" I exclaim, slapping my hand over my mouth. "It's officially your birthday!"

He chuckles. "So, are you going to be at Shane's tonight and then go out me with the next day?"

I lower my hand from my mouth, exposing my huge smile. I nod, blushing. "Yes. I'm really looking forward to it," I say, actually feeling pretty giddy.

"So am I," Ronan agrees earnestly. He tugs on Onyx's leash as he steps backwards off the stoop and turns to leave.

"Ronan," I say loudly.

He turns his head in my direction and nods for me to say whatever it is I'm going to say.

"What do you like?"

He cocks his head to the side, eyebrows furrowed. "What do you mean?"

I laugh. "For your birthday. I want to get you a present."

He smiles widely. "You just did!"

Ronan

Well shit, talk about a coincidence. I had no idea Cat lived within a ten-minute walking distance of my house. And who would have even thought she would not only be awake at well past two in the morning but also outside, sitting on the stoop of her front door?

I was exhausted and so lost in my own damn thoughts that I hardly paid attention to my surroundings. I was on autopilot, biding my time until it was safe to head back home and not interrupt, or accidentally eavesdrop on, Steve and Vada getting busy in Steve's room. And, man, I wouldn't have even noticed Cat if it hadn't been for Onyx abruptly veering off the sidewalk and running toward her. But I can't blame her, because there's something so damn magnetic about Cat.

I have the hardest time staying away from her, and I can't even really put my finger on why. I mean, she's stunning. Holy shit, she's fucking gorgeous. She has these incredible eyes that I swear change color like mood stones—one minute they're a cinnamon brown, and the next they're a deep, dark green. Her high cheekbones and cute nose are specked with light freckles, and she has probably the most enticingly full lips that were so damn soft when we kissed.

But it's not just her looks. She just radiates warmth and light, like she is the sun. And there's something about her energy, like she matches mine. Or maybe "match" isn't the right word; maybe it's more that she complements my own energy, diminishes the darkness hidden inside me. Talking with her is so easy, and I feel so fucking calm around her.

I mostly live my life in a state of anticipation and anxiety, always on edge, expecting the next fight, the next hit, more pain. The tension obviously eases when I'm around my friends, but nothing compares to what it feels like to be around Cat. It makes me want to spend more time with her. I've honestly never felt this drawn to someone, never met a girl I wanted to get to know as badly as I want to get to know Cat. There is something so damn compelling about her; it's familiar yet new, and my thoughts turn to her constantly. What's crazy about this whole thing is that I only met her a month ago, but I swear it was like she flipped a switch when she walked down those stairs to the beach. And even though I really should try a hell of a lot harder to stay away from her, because, really, she doesn't need any of my shit, I can hardly wait to see her in just a few hours.

Once I'm home, I make my way up the stairs, pulling my shirt off as I walk. I shut the door to my room behind me, throw the shirt in the corner, and unbutton my jeans, ready to take them off.

"So, where do you go when you leave in the middle of the damn night?" I hear from behind me.

I jump. "Jesus, Vada, you have a knack for sneaking up on me."

Vada is standing in the doorway between my room and the bathroom connecting Steve's and my bedrooms, wearing a pair of Steve's boxers and a t-shirt. I peek past her through the open door to Steve's room and spot him passed out on his bed.

Vada has an inquisitive look on her face, her arms crossed in front of her chest like she just caught me red-handed.

"I just walk," I whisper, holding on to my kiss with Cat, guarding it like a fragile piece of glass.

"Well, you have an awfully happy look on your face for someone who 'just walks,'" she says, making air quotes.

"What are you getting at?"

"I got a text message from Cat." Vada grins, pushes herself off the doorframe, and walks toward me with a smug look. "So, what are your intentions with her?"

I raise my eyebrows in amusement. "What?"

"What are your intentions with her, Ran?" She takes another step toward me, poking her index finger into my chest. "I mean, you just happened to walk by her house? That's kind of weird, isn't it?"

I laugh. "It was a complete coincidence. I swear I had no idea she lived there. I mean, what kind of guy do you think I am?" I press my lips together, pretending to be offended, but the corners tug into a smile.

"And you two just talked? In the middle of the night?" Vada raises one eyebrow. That means Cat didn't tell her about the kiss, and I appreciate this because it makes me think the kiss was just as precious to Cat as it was to me.

I nod, keeping my face neutral, unwilling to give anything away.

"Okay," Vada finally says, not looking convinced. "Just do me a favor. Don't hurt her, alright? Don't just hook up with her if you're not interested in anything more. I'm not stupid; I can see that she likes you, and if you don't feel the same way then please, please don't lead her on," Vada says, taking on a serious tone.

I nod slowly. "I have no intentions of hurting anyone, Vada. I promise."

She moves in for a quick hug. "Thanks, Ran. I should get back to your brother, although he looks like he wouldn't even know if I just left." She giggles and walks back through the bathroom into Steve's room, shutting the door behind her.

I move to shut the bathroom door, finally get out of my jeans, and then crawl into bed, turning off the light.

My fingers trace a line over an inch-long scar on my left palm. I got this scar when I was nine and my mother swung a kitchen knife at me after I didn't take out the trash before I left for hockey practice. I tried to shield myself and the tip of the knife slashed into my hand, cutting it open. And then I got my ass whipped for daring to bleed onto the kitchen floor. The one thing I always tell myself is that I would never intentionally hurt anyone I love. And although I have no idea what I feel for Cat, I know in my heart and soul that the last thing I will ever do is intentionally inflict pain on her—physical, emotional, or otherwise.

My phone rings, waking me up. I reach for it next to my pillow without opening my eyes. "Hello?" I manage sleepily.

"Hey! Happy fucking birthday, dude! Did I wake you?" Shane's voice says on the other end.

I move the phone away from my ear to get a look at the time. It's nine in the morning. "Kinda. What's up?" I slowly sit up in my bed. I can hear the shower running in the bathroom and giggles coming from behind the still-closed door. I roll my eyes, shaking my head.

"Want to come to the gym with me? I have a shit-ton of pent-up energy and feel like lifting some weights, but I need someone to spot me. Plus, you're getting older; can't let you get rusty," he adds with a chuckle.

I contemplate this, but my mind is made up the second I hear Vada moan in the bathroom. "I'd love to join you," I say, and jump out of bed.

"Sweet. Meet you there in twenty," Shane says, and hangs up without a further response from me.

I grab some gym clothes from my closet and get dressed. Then I take a few steps toward the bathroom door, from behind which I can now hear heavy breathing. I take a deep breath, exhale, and pound my fist against the door.

"Sorry to interrupt, but I need my toothbrush," I say loudly, and the noises stop.

A few seconds elapse before I hear the door lock slide back. The door opens just wide enough for Steve to shove my toothbrush at me before he slams the door shut and the lock clicks back into place.

"Thanks," I say, more to myself. Judging by the renewed giggling, I don't think Steve can even hear me.

When I come down the stairs, my mother is in the kitchen pouring herself hot water for tea; I wonder if she knows Vada spent the night. I pause in the hallway, hesitating, analyzing my mom's posture, her movements. She's humming, which makes me think she's in a good mood, so I risk it and venture into the kitchen to grab a bottle of water from the fridge.

"Happy birthday," she greets me lightly when she notices me.

"Thanks."

"Are you heading to the gym?" She turns toward me and leans against the kitchen counter, taking a sip from her steaming cup.

"Uh-huh," I nod.

"Little birthday workout. Just you?"

"No, I'm meeting Shane."

"Great! How was your night?"

"Fine," I say matter-of-factly, not wanting to get involved in conversation. It's too early, and I'm still too damn tired to be fully on guard. I would much prefer she ignore me like she does most days. Her eyes flicker to the bruise on my forearm—an early birthday present from her and the result of a closed-fist punch that I'm pretty certain was aimed at my stomach, but I shifted and she caught my arm instead. It's been a couple of days since she struck me, but the bruise is still a deep, dark blue.

"That's good," she says awkwardly. "Oh, so it appears your dad is finally coming home this weekend," she tells me joyously.

"Really?" My dad has been saying he'd come home for some time now, but something has always come up at the last minute. His absence doesn't make much of a difference to me anymore. It's his broken promises and the resultant fights he has with my mother that make my life hard.

"So he says." My mom shrugs. "Anyway, I just got home and I'm working a twenty-four-hour shift tonight, so I'm headed to bed. Are you working tonight?"

"No, but Steve and I will be at Shane's tonight."

"Okay. Remember your curfew," she says, then walks out of the kitchen. "And, Ronan," she calls back, stopping just before the stairs. "Clean up this mess of a house before I get back tomorrow night." She points at something out of my sight.

I nod, frustrated. Even though I try to keep the place tidy so as not to provoke a fight, she always finds something to nitpick.

"What the hell is that face for, Ronan?" She turns toward me completely, holding her hot tea in one hand, resting the other on her hip.

I check myself and immediately replace the look with a neutral expression. "Nothing. Sorry, Mom. I'm just still a little tired. I'm gonna head out." I try to release the tension that has seized my shoulders, but I'm only able to relax once I'm safely outside and in my car.

Cat

I'm in my room, listening to my music at full volume while texting Julie about my upcoming trip to see my dad and siblings. It's perfect timing because it's Julie's seventeenth birthday next week and I'll get to celebrate with her. She's giddy about my brief return home, responding to my messages in all caps with lots of exclamation points.

I do look forward to seeing my dad, brother, and sister. And my friend, Julie, and Julie's boyfriend, Nate. But of course, there's always the risk of running into my ex, Adam, or any of the myriad of other people who made my life a living hell. When I talked to Julie last week, I made her give me an update on things. Are people still talking? Is my name still brought up despairingly?

The town I grew up in is so small—everyone knows everyone—so chances are I'll run into Adam or some of his posse. It's a thought that leaves me feeling uneasy and anxious, but I push it aside, not wanting to ruin my anticipation of seeing my family and friends.

I'm singing along loudly when there's a knock on the front door. Not making any effort to see who it is, I wait for my mom to answer the door, which she does just a few moments later. I can't make out who it is and just assume it's the mailman or a neighbor, but then my mom walks into my room with a smile on her face.

"There's a really cute guy waiting in the hall for you," she says, wiggling her eyebrows.

"Who?" I ask, trying hard to make any sense of the situation.

"He said his name is Ronan." Her smile grows even wider.

Heat rises in my face and body. "Oh," is all I'm able to get out, and I stand stupidly in my room, my phone still in my right hand. This is unexpected.

“Well, are you going to come talk to him or do you want me to tell him you’re busy?” my mom asks, still grinning at me, obviously enjoying my stupid reaction.

I fling my phone onto my bed and run to the small mirror hanging above my nightstand to fuss with my hair. I hear my mom giggle in the background and I take a deep breath—a feeble attempt at calming myself down. Why the hell am I reacting this strongly?

“Okay,” I say, more to myself than her, and stalk past my mom, wishing—no, willing—my heart to return to a steady beat. Even though I saw Ronan only twelve hours ago—a fact that my mom is blissfully unaware of—my heart hammers at the prospect of laying eyes on him in just a second or two.

I thought about him after he left last night and again this morning when I woke up, and I keep replaying our interaction: his soft lips on mine, his tongue in my mouth, his gorgeous green eyes, his sexy hair... Ugh, I need to get a grip.

But all my composure melts into a puddle and I smile widely when I step into the hallway where Ronan is standing. He clearly just left the gym because he’s wearing gym shorts, sneakers, and a gray, sleeveless shirt that is damp over his tight abs. I resist the urge to let my gaze roam his body and instead lock eyes with him.

Ronan gives me a small smile, seeming uncomfortable as he says, “Hi.”

“Hi,” I say back, and Ronan starts to laugh. “What?” I say, becoming instinctively self-conscious.

“Sorry, I just feel really stupid stopping by like that. And this definitely wasn’t my smoothest opening line.” He still chuckles, and it’s so contagious that I join in.

“Alright, so what’s up?” I’m giddy, but try hard to appear unfazed by his presence.

“Well, I...” He breaks off as my mom saunters down the stairs, clearly eavesdropping.

“How about we step outside?” I suggest, sounding harsher than I intended, and Ronan looks as though he may be regretting his decision to come here. So I take his warm hand into mine and pull him out the front door. Once the door is closed behind me, I let go of his hand and turn back to him. He looks even more breathtaking in the sunlight. The sun makes his skin look golden and the rays dance in his eyes.

“Alright, you probably already think I’m crazy for just showing up like this… again, looking like a freaking mess, but, well, it’s my birthday, and Shane is ditching me to take care of some stuff for the party tonight, and Stevie and Vada are busy, and I’m hungry, and… I was thinking I really don’t want to wait until tonight to see you again,” he confesses, the words spilling out fast. He takes a deep breath and he looks like he’s fighting a silent battle inside his head as his jaw tenses for a fraction of a second. I wait patiently for him to continue. “So, do you feel like grabbing something to eat in, like, half an hour?” He flashes me a smile that makes me want to throw myself at him.

“Okay,” I say, attempting to be confident, but my voice is off pitch and my heart is doing somersaults.

Ronan flashes me another smile that I can imagine would cause every other girl’s panties to drop. “Great. I’ll be back in thirty minutes.” He gives me a small peck on my cheek that makes my face burn with heat. I stand there nodding as he turns and walks away, just like he did last night after he kissed me on my front stoop.

Of course, my mom is on my case as soon as I step back into the house, wanting to know anything and everything about Ronan. She has been pretty concerned about me ever since what happened with Adam, but I don’t have time to explain now. I race upstairs to my room where I stand in front of the mirror, braiding my long hair into a fishtail and letting some loose strands fall around my face. I have no idea where Ronan plans to take us, so I decide to wear a pair of jean shorts and a white tank top.

***

Ronan's lips curl upward and his eyes sparkle when he picks me up less than half an hour later. The way he scans my body from head to toe makes me blush.

"Are you ready?" he asks, his voice velvety. I nod at him and wave to my mom, who closes the door behind us. Ronan leads the way to the passenger door of his car and opens it for me, waiting for me to get in before closing it behind me and walking around the front. He's wearing a pair of dark-blue jeans that sit low on his hips. He also has on a gray-and-black three-quarter-sleeve baseball shirt and black chucks. It's obvious he took a quick shower before returning to pick me up because his dark-blond hair is still damp and small strands fall onto his forehead. It's the perfect kind of tousled. Judging by his relaxed outfit, whatever it is we're going to be doing will be casual and I'm happy with my choice of attire.

Ronan gets in and smiles at me as he turns the key in the ignition and his car purrs to life.

"So, happy birthday," I singsong at him. "I still need come up with something to give you because it just doesn't seem right that it's your birthday and I don't even have a gift."

"Thanks, but you don't need to get me anything. Seriously, the fact that you haven't called the cops on me yet is a pretty amazing gift in and of itself," he chuckles. "Again, I'm sorry for showing up like a creep last night; I swear it wasn't on purpose."

"I'm not complaining." I smile as he scans my face. "But speaking of being sorry, I'm sorry for kissing you," I apologize again like I apologized last night, though I'm really not *that* sorry about it. Despite the fact that my inebriation almost got me into hot water and ended with me using Ronan to get out of an uncomfortable situation, I can't say I'm not excited about where it's led so far.

"I'm not," Ronan says. "It was a nice kiss."

I nod in agreement.

"And besides, we're even now, remember? Since I stole that kiss back last night," Ronan says with a mischievous smile.

"Were things... okay when you got home last night? Or did you have to crash on the couch again?" I ask cautiously, alluding to Vada staying at his house.

"No, no crashing on the couch," he chuckles. "Actually, Vada confronted me about randomly showing up at your house last night. She said you had texted her." He glances at me before turning his attention back to the road.

"I did," I admit. "Sorry."

"Don't apologize," he says. "She would have found out somehow anyway. Vada has a weird radar for things like that," he adds with a rueful laugh. "She asked me what my intentions are with you."

"She what?"

"Asked me what my intentions are with you," he repeats with a smirk.

"Huh. And what are your intentions with me?" I lean on the center console.

He looks at me again, a smile tugging at his lips. "Right now, my intention is to feed you," he laughs.

"And then?"

"I don't really know. I think... I mean, I like spending time with you," he admits, keeping his eyes focused on the road now.

"I like spending time with you, too," I say, eliciting another smile from him.

"You know, I don't usually do this," he says.

I raise my eyebrows at him. "You don't usually do what?"

"This," he says, and motions around his car, which does nothing to help me understand what he's talking about. "I don't usually go on dates."

"You don't?" I ask, truly surprised. Ronan is exceptionally handsome and I have no doubt at all that he could get any girl to go out with him if he so much as hinted at it.

"No," he says, shaking his head. "In fact, I don't usually even take a girl's number, and I definitely don't give out mine."

"Huh, I must be special," I say, wiping imaginary dust off my shoulder.

"You are," he says with such sincerity that it throws me off.

I blush violently, not knowing how to respond. "So why don't you go on dates?" I ask, studying him and forcing the heat to leave my face. "You're not gay."

Ronan laughs out loud. "No, definitely not gay."

"You're hot, so it can't be that girls don't want to go out with you."

"You think I'm hot?"

"Does that surprise you?" I ask, my tone flirty, but he just laughs again. "Okay, so if you don't go on dates, then you're either a serial killer or you have some weird fetish or something."

"Or maybe it's both," Ronan teases with a shrug.

"Oh god, why didn't Vada warn me?"

"She's scared of me," Ronan says with a knowing nod.

"Yeah, she seems absolutely terrified," I agree, then laugh.

"Actually, I should be scared of her. She has a total thing for sneaking up on me. She scared the crap out of me last night," he tells me. "I have no doubt she would murder me in my sleep."

I laugh out loud but shake my head. "I would say I could see that about Vada, but I'm pretty sure she cares too much about you to kill you."

"Sheesh, I hope you're right," he sighs, making me laugh even more.

We drive for a while, though I don't pay particular attention to where Ronan is taking us. I only realize we're deep in the city when Ronan pulls into a small parking lot in front of a hole-in-the-wall Italian restaurant.

As soon as we step inside, it's obvious that Ronan knows the owner because a short, round man with flour all over his turquoise apron walks around the counter and gives Ronan a bear-hug. He shouts something in Italian that neither I, nor apparently Ronan, understand. "I haven't seen you in ages," the short man says in a thick accent, repeatedly clapping Ronan on the back. "Sit, sit. I have a new creation you must try. Oh," he says after he spots me, "and who is this?" he asks, not taking his eyes off me.

Ronan laughs, shaking his head. "This is Cat." He introduces me to the short man, Benito, and I shake his hand. He has small, crinkly eyes and a strong handshake. His belly shakes when he laughs and he talks as though he's attempting to have a conversation with a heavy metal band playing right next to him, and it makes me laugh.

"Si, Ronan, she's beautiful," he says, clearly attempting to whisper but failing miserably. "Your girlfriend?"

Ronan's eyes meet mine. "No, not my girlfriend, Benito. Just... Just a friend." As if trying to challenge me, Ronan keeps his eyes locked on mine, but I'm forced to break eye contact when Benito turns to me.

"Say, bella señora, you need to have Ronan here as your boyfriend. He will take good care of you."

I blush and look down.

"Alright, Benito. Why don't you whip us up something good? Surprise us," Ronan says, and I'm grateful for the subject change. Benito walks back behind the counter and shouts something in Italian again. Ronan is laughing as he leads me to a table and we sit down. "I'm sorry, I should have warned you about Benito. He's very..."

"Friendly?"

He laughs again, nodding. "Yeah, you could say that." Ronan's eyes sparkle as he laughs, and I join in because it's so contagious.

By the time Benito brings our pizza, Ronan and I are deep in conversation about growing up in a small town. I pick a piece of pizza off the tray and transfer it to my plate, grabbing my knife and fork, ready to start eating.

"What are you doing?" Ronan asks with amusement, scanning the silver utensils in my hands.

"Umm, I'm about to eat some pizza," I reply with a confused look. Ronan bursts out laughing, and I look around for an answer. "Am I doing something wrong?"

"Is this how you always eat pizza?" he asks me, still grinning, eyes sparkling.

"No, but this piece is huge." I poke a piece of artichoke with my fork. "And the crust is so thin."

"You've never had New York-style pizza," he observes as he pushes up the three-quarter sleeves of his shirt. He grabs a slice of pizza, slowly folds it in half, and takes a huge bite. His eyes are smiling at me. "There you go," he says with his mouth full, and it makes me giggle.

"Okay, I got this," I say, flexing my biceps at him, and he chuckles. I pick up a slice of pizza, imitating his way of eating, and take a giant bite. He nods at me proudly and I snort a laugh through my nose. I'm having a great time and I can't believe how much I enjoy my time with Ronan.

We talk about our respective athletic endeavors, and Ronan wholeheartedly admits that he doesn't know the first thing about baseball or, for that matter, softball. "It just seems... really slow," he says, glancing at me as if he's worried that his words have offended me, though I quickly assure him that I don't have the slightest clue about hockey either. I find out that Ronan started playing ice hockey when he was seven, and I delightedly tell him that, coincidentally, I began playing softball at the same age. Then I spend some time explaining the rules of softball, and he enlightens me about hockey, which actually sounds like a really fun sport to play and watch. I make a mental note to try to make it to some games next season.

When we're done eating, Ronan declines my offer to chip in for the pizza.

"But it's your birthday! And you won't even let me give you a gift," I protest, amused.

"No way," he says, shaking his head, "Benito would never let me live this down." He hands me my ten-dollar bill back.

"Fine, but I will find a way to give you a birthday gift, sir. If it's the last thing I do today!" I fold my arms over my chest and sit back in my chair, making Ronan laugh.

"You're feisty. I like it," he says, his voice gravelly, making me blush.

On our way home, my phone rings. "Hey, are you home?" Vada asks the moment I hit the speaker button.

I look at Ronan, at his handsome features and his hand shifting gears as we merge lanes, nearing my house.

"No. Actually, I'm running some errands. What's up?"

I'm not really sure what this is about, but I don't want to tell Vada that Ronan and I went out to eat. I don't want to tell her about our kiss last night, and I don't yet want to tell her that I think I'm falling really, really hard for him. I love Vada, but she gets so enthusiastic, and excited, and... pushy, and I just want to keep this little thing that's developing between Ronan and me to myself for now because... because I just really don't know how to feel about all of this. It feels so new and precious and fragile that I'm afraid if I move too fast it'll disappear on me, that if I talk about it, if I tell Vada about how my heart flutters when I'm around Ronan, things will take a bad turn. As far as I'm concerned, I'm just testing the waters right now, carefully, gently dipping a toe into the dark, scary ocean full of sharks and monsters, to see what awaits me. If I keep this quiet, I can back out of it and nobody will be the wiser. At least it's what I tell myself.

Ronan turns his head toward me, a small smile on his face as he gives me a minuscule nod, understanding.

"Oh, okay. I was just wondering if you think six is good for me and Steve to come get you so we can drive to Shane's for Ran's birthday tonight."

"Yes, six is perfect!" I note, and Vada's voice is chipper when I promise to ask my mom for a 2 a.m. curfew. I'm not completely convinced she'll go for it.

Ronan

I drop Cat off at home and walk her all the way to her door, where she gives me a hug. I have the overwhelming urge to pull her into me and kiss her, and I think she feels the same charged energy—her eyes rest on my lips for a second—but before we can act on it, the front door swings open.

Cat's mom steps outside to take out the trash, smiling at us knowingly, and the moment dissipates.

I remind Cat that I'll see her later, and I leave her with a sort of tingling sensation in my stomach.

The first thing I do when I get home is get busy cleaning up. The house isn't in huge disarray, but that doesn't mean I don't try like hell to make it even tidier. I start a load of laundry, fold and put away the clothes that have been sitting in the dryer for the last couple days, wipe down the kitchen counter, unload and reload the dishwasher, and sweep the kitchen, hallway, and living room. I look around, and though everything looks clean, I have no doubt that my mother will find something to complain about. But hopefully what I've done is enough to keep things civil.

I can't explain what it is between my mother and me. We just don't get along, and I have no idea why. It's been like this for as long as I can remember. The thing is, she doesn't treat Steve the way she treats me, and I'm glad about that. It's enough that she gets pissed at me; I don't want my brother to feel her rage. My mother knows not to lay a hand on me in front of Steve because he will step in. He's done it in the past, so she changed her M.O. Things really only get bad when it's just her and me, when there are no potential witnesses, when there's no one there to stop her. So I've gotten good at avoiding her, but, since we live in the same house I can't always escape her. And the reality is that, try as I might to be the perfect son, get good grades, clean the house, succeed at whatever it is she asks of me, it's never enough.

But I've made it this far. Seventeen years of fear and violence, and I only have to endure one more year before I'm out of here. One more year before I'm free to go wherever, which will be far, far away from my mother. That thought sustains me.

But now there might be something else. Someone else, I should say. And this thing that's happening between Cat and me is scaring the shit out of me. I'm afraid that if I let it go where my heart so badly wants it to go, she's going to get hurt. I know that the longer this goes on, the harder and faster I'm going to fall for her because I can already feel it in every fiber of my being.

I've successfully rebuffed every attempt by any girl to get close to me ever since I moved back to New York, staying removed and closed-off. But it's different with Cat. I'm so completely drawn to her. I think of her constantly, crave being around her, which is crazy because we only met each other mere weeks ago. It's just so damn easy with her, like I can rest around her, which is an insane feeling. I'm never *not* on edge, never *not* on guard, never *not* anticipating, preparing for a battle because my *life* is a battle. I can't drag Cat into this shit; I can't expose her to the darkness; I can't fucking ruin her like I do everything else.

But maybe Shane is right; maybe I need to let Cat be the judge and decide if being with me is something she would want. And maybe, if I try hard enough, I could keep her safe? Ugh, why does this shit have to be so confusing?

The house is quiet. Steve isn't home, and it's only half past one, meaning my mother should be sleeping for a while longer in preparation for her nightshift. I'm careful to be as noiseless as possible, lest I conjure up her wrath by waking her too soon. Honestly, I hate being at home when I know it's just her and me; it puts me on high alert and it's exhausting as hell.

I decide to wander into the small dining area where I open the sideboard and pull out a half-full bottle of Jack from the back, like I have so many times before. I take a second to make sure no sounds are coming from my parents' bedroom upstairs, then unscrew the lid, put the brown bottle to my lips, and tip my head back. The liquid warms my throat and insides as I work it down.

"Happy seventeenth birthday, Ran," I mutter. I don't do this all the time, only when I feel particularly on edge, which for some reason I do today, even though I just got to spend a couple of really nice hours with Cat—or maybe it's because of that.

Shane is right: I'm too fucking stuck in my own head.

My phone buzzes. I pull it out of my back pocket and smile when I recognize the Montana area code.

"Happy birthday, baby boy," my grandma's voice chimes.

"Thank you," I chuckle at her.

It's almost a crime to call her my grandmother. Like my own parents, my grandparents had my dad at a really young age. My grandmother was fifteen and my grandfather seventeen when they emigrated from Ireland and came to the U.S. My grandmother was pregnant with my aunt. They settled in Montana and had my dad a couple of years later. That makes my grandparents fifty-one and fifty-three, respectively. It's strange, I know.

"You know I'm not a baby anymore, right?" I ask her, amused.

"Don't start with me, Ronan Perry Soult. You will always, always be my baby boy," she says in her strong Irish accent. "I miss you. Are you doing okay?" she asks, her tone somber. My grandmother has always had a soft spot for me, I think because she secretly knows that my mother is not good to me.

"I'm fine, Morai," I respond. "How is everyone doing?"

"Fine, fine, everyone is fine. Athair and Tom are branding some new bulls," she says of my grandfather and his wrangler. "So he's not here to wish you a happy birthday himself, but I told him I'd call you, and he asked me to tell you that he loves you."

My grandma's words hit me like a ton of bricks. Maybe it's the whiskey finally making its way through my bloodstream, but I actually feel a little emotional.

"Tell him I love him, too," I say, my voice a little off pitch. I unscrew the whiskey bottle, needing another gulp.

"I will. Is your father home?" She always asks if he's home, but I suspect she knows the answer most of the time.

"Nope, I haven't seen him in about six weeks," I say, starting to feel my body relax as the alcohol makes its way to my head.

There's silence for a moment before my grandma speaks again, her voice sharper than it was before. "He's not home for your birthday? Has he at least called you?"

"No."

I'm seriously contemplating another shot of whiskey, but I hesitate because my mother is still home and I don't want to put myself in a situation where I can't leave on a moment's notice.

"Unbelievable. Well, baby boy, do you have any fun plans for today?"

"Going to hang out with my friends and Steve." I place the Jack back in the sideboard and slide the door shut before wandering over toward the couch, where I plop down and put my feet on the glass coffee table. I hate that thing because it's impossible to keep clean. It's all glass and the second someone touches it it's full of fingerprints and grime, which inevitably results in my mom ordering me to clean it again.

"Lovely." My grandma's voice is clipped. I can tell she's upset about my dad being absent today, though it doesn't bother me. My dad's lack of a physical presence in my life hasn't bothered me in a long time. "I hope you have a nice day and lots of fun with your friends tonight. Don't go overboard, okay? Take care of yourself." I hear the concern in her voice.

I close my eyes, leaning my head back against the sofa as my body relaxes. "I will, Morai. Don't worry about me."

"I always worry about you."

We end the conversation, and I remain on the couch with my eyes shut, head tipped back, feet resting on the coffee table. My body feels heavy—probably due to lack of sleep and alcohol—and I give in to my desire to rest, falling asleep within minutes. But the slumber doesn't last long.

"What the hell is this, Ronan?" My mother's stern voice startles me awake as she kicks my feet off the coffee table. "This isn't a fucking youth hostel."

"I'm sorry," I mumble, and quickly get up off the couch to stand and face her. She's dressed in her scrubs, her dark-blonde hair in a high ponytail.

I brace for whatever she has in store for me, expecting to at least get yelled at, but she turns and heads toward the kitchen, leaving me standing in the living room instead.

"Again, I expect you to clean this pigsty up before I get back tomorrow evening," she calls back over her shoulder.

I furrow my brow. Before I can stop myself, I retort, "I already did." *God fuck, why did I have to do that?*

My mother turns on the spot and comes stalking back toward me, her jaw tense.

"You're kidding, right? This?" She gestures around the living room. "This is supposed to be clean?" She lets out a dry laugh.

"Yeah." I know I'm asking for it at this point. "I don't understand what else you want me to do." I mean, fuck it, right?

"Excuse me?" She steps closer to me, invading my personal space. Her hands are on her hips and her face is contorted in anger. "I don't appreciate the way you're talking to me. You think just because today is your birthday, you can have a shitty fucking attitude with me? You might want to rethink this strategy, Ronan, because I'm going to put you in a world of hurt."

"I'm just saying that I already cleaned today and I don't see what else I can do," I say, adjusting the tone in my voice. Even though the alcohol might have loosened me up a little bit, I'm still sober enough to realize I just got myself into some deep shit.

"I don't really give a shit, Ronan. I don't give a shit if this house is spick and span and sparkly as a fucking Christmas tree. If I tell you to clean, you fucking clean, do you understand me?" Her tone is high and her voice loud as she takes another step toward me. She's so close to me that her toes touch mine. "Do you fucking understand me?" she screams at me.

I back away, nodding my head. My phone buzzes on the couch, and both our eyes flit toward it. My dad's name is displayed on the screen, and my mother's face changes instantaneously as she steps back, finally moving to the kitchen.

I take a couple of shaky breaths, willing my adrenaline to return to normal while I pick up the phone off the couch and answer. "Hello?" My voice is as tense as my body feels.

"Hey bud," my dad greets me, his deep voice warm.

"Hey, what's up, Dad?"

"I'm calling to wish you a happy birthday!" He sounds like he feels really guilty. I bet my grandmother called him to rip him a new one.

"You forgot, huh?" I ask, not even pretending to hide my frustration. The encounter with my mother, coupled with the fact that my father isn't around to protect me, is getting to me right now.

"No, I didn't forget," he says. "I've been tied up in meetings this morning. But hey, I wanted to let you know that I transferred some birthday money into your account. I figured you could finally replace that carburetor in your Mustang."

"Thanks, Dad, I appreciate it. But I already replaced the carburetor a few weeks ago," I say, and I hear him sigh in disappointment. "But look, I still want to change out the brake system, so that's perfect." I hate disappointing him. I hate disappointing my mother, too. I just hate feeling like I'm letting people down. Ugh, this day is turning into a total shit show. The momentary happiness I felt from spending time with Cat has been erased without any trace.

"Okay, well maybe we can work on changing out the brake system together," he says, his voice taking on a happy tone. He's obviously hoping for me to get excited, too.

"What do you mean?"

"I'm coming home Friday. I'll be home for a whole week before I'm shipping out to Germany for two weeks."

"Oh, yeah, Mom said you'll be home this weekend," I remember, still not completely convinced he'll actually show. "What time are you coming in?" I ask, willing my voice to project some semblance of excitement.

"Probably sometime in the evening."

"Cool. I'm working Friday, but I'll definitely see you Saturday morning, then."

"Is your mom home?" he asks, finally.

"Yeah. Do you want to talk to her?" I ask, eager to end our conversation. My dad is a nice guy; he's pretty badass, actually, and I used to love spending time with him when I was younger. But he has no idea what goes on at home, no idea what his absence means for me. I used to cry and beg for him not to leave, but of course he always did, and eventually I built enough of a wall that it really doesn't matter now. He doesn't really know me anymore, and I've found ways to cope and the means to survive.

I walk into the kitchen where my mother is in the midst of making herself a sandwich. She looks up at me, exasperated by my mere presence, that I dare show my face to her after I just talked back to her without repercussion. "Dad wants to talk to you," I state matter-of-factly, and extend the phone toward her. Once she takes it, I back out of the kitchen and hurry upstairs into my room where I stand for a while, rubbing my hands across my face and through my hair, desperate to shed the tension that has taken over my body. I finally sit on the edge of my bed and rest my head in my hands, taking a deep breath in, holding it for a three-count, then slowly exhaling.

I hear my mother's voice downstairs as she talks to my dad, but I can't hear specifics. My mother calls me downstairs to retrieve my phone about twenty minutes later, and her face leaves no doubt that their conversation didn't end on a high note.

I stand in the doorway to the kitchen, the threshold like an invisible boundary, and deftly catch my phone when my mother throws it at me without warning.

"I'm leaving for work," she tells me, her voice brusque.

"Okay," I nod, sliding my phone into the back pocket of my jeans while she walks past me out of the kitchen and down the hallway.

I spend a little more time finding things to tidy up before I finally decide to change and head out to Shane's at around five o'clock. I know Cat should be there by around six-thirty, and even though the afternoon wasn't very pleasant, I find myself smiling at the thought of seeing her in a little while.

When I finally make it to the beach house, Shane grins and hands me a shot of tequila. I throw it back, followed by two more in quick succession, and relax when I finally feel the alcohol dull my thoughts.

Cat

Vada and Steve stop by my house at six to pick me up. I'm euphoric when my mom agrees to a 2 a.m. curfew, which I'm pretty sure has to do with the fact that she met Ronan today and thinks "he's *so* boyfriend material," as she pointed out to me the second I got home from lunch with him this afternoon.

I can tell my mom is relieved and elated at my willingness to put myself out there again after months of withdrawing from just about everyone and everything. My world had been blanketed by fear and sadness, and I didn't know who to trust. My foundation had been rocked—had been getting rocked for a while, but I was too young, too dumb, too blind to realize what I was doing, how my actions were affecting others, how they were affecting me. And then it all came crashing down around me.

Things had slowly been escalating, deteriorating back in North Carolina. I remember the night of the winter formal like it's burned into my memory—the moment when I knew I had gone too far, had put myself in a dangerous and possibly irreversible position. I remember thinking it couldn't possibly get worse than this. But boy, was I wrong. The weeks and months that followed were not only devastating for me, but also my family. The guilt over what my parents went through, what my friends had to endure, what Adam went through, has haunted me since that night almost four months ago.

Throughout it all, my parents never wavered in their love and support. The guilt I feel is completely self-imposed. Neither my family nor my closest friends—namely, Julie—have even once implied that anything that happened was my fault. But I know better. I know what boys want, what they need. I knew what Adam wanted and needed; he told me, he showed me, he made it very, very obvious—and I kept withholding that from him. How long did I expect him to resist the temptation, especially given the way I was acting?

"Ronan is just a friend," I tried to convince my mom earlier today. She studied me for a long moment, her blue eyes filled with love, warmth, and this sort of expression that she knew better.

"Oh yeah, the way you guys looked at each other this morning is exactly how 'just friends' look at each other," she smiled. "They're not all bad, Kitty," she said then. "Not all boys are bad. I promise. You'll learn to trust again."

I texted Julie about forty times after getting home from lunch with Ronan, and she finally called me, wanting to know what the heck was going on with me. I fessed up that there's this boy that I'm really attracted to, but that I'm trying to take things slow, not wanting a repeat of what happened with Adam. I told her about my fears, about what happened at the party last weekend, about Ronan stepping in and protecting me—twice.

Julie encouraged me to follow my heart, but be cautious. "Make sure you set those boundaries and don't let anyone cross them. Remember that every time you let someone cross your boundaries, you're allowing that person to push them further and further back until they're nonexistent."

"You're so wise," I chuckled.

"Must be because I turn seventeen next week."

After my chat with Julie, I decided to do exactly what she had advised, which is to follow my heart but set boundaries. And my heart tells me that I want to see where this thing with Ronan goes. That I want to kiss him again. But I'm also setting my boundaries. Mostly about not going crazy drinking, because that lowers my inhibitions and makes things complicated and dangerous.

I don't tell Vada or Steve about my lunch date with Ronan, and they don't bring it up, either, making me think Ronan hasn't told them yet. That's absolutely fine with me, because I want to keep this new thing between Ronan and me to myself just a little while longer.

***

By the time we get to the beach house, the party is in full swing. There are so many cars parked on the private road to the house that I'm afraid we'll have to track about a quarter mile to the house, but Steve maneuvers his car right behind Ronan's Mustang parked in the driveway that Shane has reserved for his closest friends.

"Looks like Shane spread the word about this party," Steve notes when we walk into the house. There are people everywhere, and it's so crowded that I have to apologize to more than one individual for stepping on their toes as we carve our way to the back of the wraparound deck.

I spot Ronan sitting on the outdoor sofa next to Shane and Zack. My pulse speeds up as Ronan's eyes find me and he gives me a barely noticeable half smile. He doesn't take his eyes off me as I follow Steve and Vada toward him, Zack, and Shane. I feel like the way Ronan and I look at each other is going to tip people off in no time that there's something going on between us.

He stands up, and his eyes lazily roam across my body as goose bumps erupt on my skin.

"Happy, happy, happy birthday, Ran!" Vada screeches and gives him a tight bear-hug.

Steve follows Vada's example and pulls his little brother into a hug, wishing him a happy birthday.

"Thanks guys," Ronan says.

When it's my turn, I step close to Ronan and fold my arms around his shoulders, feeling his fingers on my exposed lower back. I'm acutely aware of the warmth of his hands against my skin, my chest pressed against his as I hug him. His head is tipped forward, and I angle my face up, moving my mouth close to his ear.

"I think I have a birthday present for you," I say, and I feel him chuckle quietly. His warm breath feathers against the skin on my neck, sending shivers down my spine.

"And what's that?" he asks in a low, gravelly voice that only I can hear.

"You'll find out in a little while." My tone is flirty, and I remind myself that my intention is to take it slowly, but also to see where this goes with Ronan. Because I want it to go somewhere.

"Okay, come on. Y'all can't tell me there's no sexual tension between Cat and Ran," Vada says loudly.

Ronan and I immediately, though reluctantly, step back from each other while Ronan shakes his head, smiling. "So damn pushy," he says to Vada as he offers me his spot on the rattan sectional sofa, and I take a seat.

"If that's what it takes for you two to get hot and heavy with each other, then I'll be pushy all day, every day," Vada laughs.

"You assembled quite the crowd," Steve interrupts.

I'm grateful for him taking the attention off Ronan and me because Cheyenne, who's sitting next to Tori and Shane, has been throwing me looks that I swear could kill.

"Wasn't that hard," Shane says, taking a sip from his beer. "A few texts to the hockey team and some of the cheerleaders and boom, it's a rave. Everyone loves Ran, and everyone loves a party." Shane lifts his bottle toward Ronan and cheers him.

"You mean everyone loves free alcohol," Ronan corrects, smirking.

"Yeah, that too," Shane laughs.

"You know, you guys should play later," Tori chimes in. She's immediately next to Shane, who allows her to lean her head on his shoulder while his arm drapes around her. I'm honestly not sure how long I can or want to keep this budding relationship between Ronan and me a secret, because right now I would really, really love to do what Tori is doing. I would love to lean against Ronan, feel his warm body, inhale his comforting scent, have him hold me.

"Oh, that's a great idea," Vada exclaims, clapping Steve on his leg.

"Play what?" I ask.

"Music, of course," Cheyenne says, her voice dripping with disdain. She leans back in her chair, rolling her eyes.

"I didn't know you guys played," I say, choosing to ignore Cheyenne's attitude toward me, and instead focus on Ronan and Shane, making a concerted effort not to make my attraction to Ronan too obvious.

"We don't," Shane huffs. "Not really. We don't have a band or anything. I just take my frustration out on a drum set, to be honest. But this multitalented asshole here has the voice of a fucking angel and plays like 398 instruments." Shane throws Ronan an exaggerated look of fake contempt before laughing.

"Don't be jealous, Shane," Ronan says, leaning forward on the sofa, his elbows resting on his knees. "It's hard work being perfect. Enjoy your mediocrity." Ronan's grin is mischievous.

"Ouch," Zack chuckles while everyone busts up laughing.

But I'm intrigued.

"Okay, really though, do you play and sing?" I ask Ronan.

He chuckles. "Not really. Shay's being stupid," he says, throwing Shane a look before he continues, "My grandfather taught me some chords on the guitar, but I'm really just average at playing. Nothing to write home about. Seriously."

"Ran, you should play and Kitty Cat could sing," Vada says, looking between the two of us, and I blush.

"So, you sing?" Ronan asks, his eyes a liquid green.

"In the shower," I say, not intending to come off as teasing, but by Zack and Steve's wolf whistles, I can tell it nonetheless had that effect. "Get your minds out of the gutter," I scold them, and more laughter erupts.

"Best acoustics for sure," Ronan notes, still smiling. "I'm down to play if you'll sing!"

"In the shower?" Vada calls out, her eyebrows wiggling.

"Oh boy," I sigh, shaking my head. Vada is relentless.

"You have got to let this go, babe." Steve pinches her side, causing Vada to squeal.

"I can't help it," she laughs. "I'm on a mission."

"And I'm going to grab some food." Ronan gets up from his chair. "Anyone need anything?"

Everyone starts throwing out requests for Ronan to bring back food and more drinks and he finally walks into the house.

"We're the worst," Shane points out. "It's his birthday and we're letting him serve us."

"Nah, we're just making sure none of those people"—Steve points toward the house and the gaggle of party attendees none of us know particularly well—"steal the best seats in the house."

"I guess," Shane chuckles.

But I do decide to get up and give Ronan a helping hand. I wander through the giant wall-to-ceiling glass doors and into the open living space where people are mingling, chatting with each other.

I spot a group of girls from my softball team and stop to chat for a few minutes. Out of my periphery I see Cheyenne stride into the kitchen, where I suspect Ronan is. She's wearing a short plaid skirt and black combat boots, the combination showing off her toned legs in the most perfect way. She's also wearing a tight black tank top, and her red-and-black hair, perfectly cropped to her shoulders, is nothing but sexy. She really is a badass, and even though I try not to be, I'm intimidated by her. It doesn't help that I know her history with Ronan, and I know if it were up to her, it would be her kissing him and not me.

After a couple minutes, I'm able to steal away from my teammates and make my way toward the kitchen. Ronan has his back to me while Cheyenne stands directly in front of him, her hand on the back of his neck as she stands on her tippy toes and leans in close. Her eyes find and lock on mine, and a grin spreads across her face as she whispers something into Ronan's ear. I can't see Ronan's reaction, but it's immediately apparent that whatever Cheyenne expected or hoped his reaction would be is not what she gets. Her face sours and her hand retreats from his skin as she steps back from him, turns, grabs some of the bottles lined up on the counter, and walks out of the kitchen.

"Stay away from him if you know what's good for you, Cat. He'll leave you high and dry if you let him," she huffs as she stalks past me and back to the deck. I can't tell if this is meant to be some well-meaning advice or a threat, but I can't say that Cheyenne's prior interactions with me have led me to trust her.

I continue into the kitchen and around the counter where I meet Ronan, who looks frustrated, his forehead creased as he tries to balance food and bottles in his arms. He's still wearing the dark jeans from this afternoon, but he changed into a white shirt, and a black watch adorns his right wrist. Such a simple outfit, yet so effective at rousing something deep in my core. Good god.

"Can I help you?" I ask as I approach him.

The frustration leaves his handsome features. "That would be great." He unloads the goodies back onto the counter. "So, when are you going to tell me about this alleged birthday gift?" he asks, rearranging some jars of salsa in front of him.

"I could show you right now," I say, and my heart begins to hammer in my chest while I take a step toward him.

He eyes me suspiciously up and down, noting my empty hands. He's probably wondering what in the world I have to give him. He turns his body toward me. "Okay?" he says, arms by his sides.

I decide it's now or never because I will overthink this and stop myself. I close the small distance between us, reach my hands around Ronan's neck and tip my head up, pulling him in for a kiss. I can feel his breath hitch as I open my lips to allow him entrance, and his tongue finds mine.

Without hesitation, he reaches for my hips and pulls me in toward him. The feel of his body against mine is becoming more and more familiar each time we kiss. I relax into him and allow his warm hands to rest on my bare lower back, sending electricity up and down my spine.

He pulls away from me too soon, and I open my eyes, blinking back at him. "You are making it extremely difficult for me to take it slow and do this 'the right way,'" he says. "I... God," he groans, running his left hand over his face. "It's so damn confusing, but I'm not sure I can keep kissing you like that for much longer and continue to pretend we're just friends," Ronan tells me, his eyes staring into mine.

I nod at him, feeling torn.

"Cat, I'll move at whatever pace you need me to move, but can you give me a hint of where you see this heading? What are we doing?" he asks, his gaze intense.

I know exactly where I see this heading, what my heart wants out of this. But my head is in a different place. It's an internal battle I'm fighting. I want to be with him; I want him to claim me as his and I want to claim him as mine, but I'm so, so scared that I'll mess this up for him like I did for Adam. I bite my lower lip, wanting to phrase my answer carefully. "Ronan, I... I think..." I trail off, swallowing hard, trying to push through the fear and reach for what my heart wants. "I want to be with you," I say, suddenly aware of how clammy my hands feel and how hard my heart is beating. "But you need to know that, just before I left North Carolina, I got out of a bad relationship. It was not a good ending at all and, actually, it's the reason why my mom moved me to New York. I think I'm still a little messed up, and I don't want to force you to deal with my stuff, so..." I lift my eyes to gauge his reaction.

His expression remains neutral as he contemplates me. "Complicated, huh?" He's referring to our very first conversation, when I told him my move to New York was complicated.

I nod again.

"I can handle complicated." I can tell he's making a statement more profound than what his words relay, but I don't press him right now. "Listen, Cat, I don't want to make you do anything you don't want. And I can't promise you that things will be less... 'complicated' with me," he says, then hesitates. "But, I at least need you to know that I'm really falling for you. Hard."

His tone is serious, but my heart flutters in my chest at his words, spoken so sincerely.

"And... this could be really good or... or really bad, but... I guess... I'd be down to give this a shot if you are?" He lifts his eyes to look at me, his lips slightly parted—kissable, enticing.

Even though my head is putting forth all the reasons why I shouldn't be with Ronan, my heart wins this one. Without needing to speak another word, I close the small gap between us and fling my arms around him.

"So, we're giving this a shot then?" he asks, his arms still by his sides.

A laugh—partially nervous, partially elated—escapes my mouth as I look into his gorgeous face. "Yeah, I guess we are. But don't say I didn't warn you."

He gives me my favorite half smile before encircling me with his arms, pulling me close to him, and kissing me like I've never been kissed before.

Before making our way back to the deck, we agree to play it cool with our friends. "Vada has been so pushy, I kind of want to let her squirm a little bit longer," I say ruthlessly, and I love it when Ronan says he's one hundred percent on board with this plan. So, we grab the food and drinks from the counter, then make our way back out to the deck, where Vada promptly makes a comment about us being gone for a long time while giving us a knowing grin.

Ronan shakes his head, avoiding eye contact with me. We manage not to make our attraction for each other obvious. Although it's tough, especially when one of the cheerleaders, Dani, joins us out on the deck and just about throws herself at Ronan. That tiny monster in my chest rears its head, especially now that I've let my guard down with Ronan, leaving myself open and exposing myself to pain. But Ronan is respectful and gently declines her offer to go somewhere a little more private, to the utter surprise of Zack and Steve, who give Ronan the hardest time.

"Are you feeling alright tonight, Ran?" Zack asks.

Ronan just chuckles, his eyes finding mine.

"No, seriously," Zack continues. "Did you hit your head or something? Dani is smoking hot and she just made it blatantly clear that she would like you to please fuck her. And you're turning her down?"

"I don't have to hook up with every girl who hits on me, do I?" Ronan shrugs.

"No, but you usually do, especially when she's as hot as Dani."

Ronan shifts uncomfortably in his seat, no doubt eager for a subject change. "Okay, well I guess I'm older and wiser now."

"Wait, so your birthday resolution is to fuck less? I think you're doing this wrong, Ran," Steve chimes in, laughing.

"Fuck, guys, I'm glad you're so very concerned for me and my sex life, it's truly touching, but I'm good," Ronan says. "Things change," he adds simply, gets up from his seat, and walks into the house without another word, leaving Zack and Steve to exchange questioning looks.

"I, for one, am glad that he didn't go for it this time," Vada huffs. "I'm not a fan of him constantly hooking up."

"Yeah, we know, babe," Steve chuckles.

"Seriously," Vada continues, rolling her eyes at her boyfriend, "I know you guys always encourage him, but you know that's not fulfilling to Ran, right? There's no meaningful connection or anything. It makes me sad for him," she sighs.

"Maybe he likes it that way?" Zack says with a shrug. "I mean, he's not complaining, and I'm sure if he wanted something different he'd have no problem making it happen."

"Maybe it's just about finding the right girl," Shane suddenly chimes in with a small smile, and I swear I see him glance at me with a knowing look in his eyes before they lock on Vada.

Ronan doesn't come back outside, and after a few minutes I conjure up needing to use the restroom as an excuse to go into the house to try and find him. I meander into the living room, then the kitchen.

"Hey, can I help you find something?" a tall guy with brown hair that flips up at his ears asks me with a warm smile on his face, his gray eyes sparkly.

"Oh, I'm looking for a friend," I say, still looking around for Ronan.

"Who?" he asks, taking a small step toward me.

"Ronan?" I say, not totally sure if the name is going to ring a bell for him.

"Oh, I'm pretty sure I just saw Ran on the deck in the front talking with Connor and Avery," the guy explains, then grins when I raise my eyebrows at him. I have no idea who Connor and Avery are.

The guy chuckles at my confusion. "They all play hockey together."

"Right," I say, my lips tugging into a smile.

"I'm Eli." He holds his hand out for me to shake, and I do so.

"I'm Cat."

"Yeah, I know," he nods. "I've seen you around at school. You're on the softball team."

"Are you on the hockey team, too?"

"Yep. Just got moved up to varsity, so I'll be playing with Ran next season. Do you guys hang out a lot?"

"Yeah. Well, we actually just met a few weeks ago," I say, wavering.

"Right, but you hang out with, like, Shane and Steve?"

"Uh-huh," I confirm, nodding. "I'm good friends with Vada and Tori."

"Oh, yeah, it's a whole package deal," Eli chuckles. "Good group of friends."

"Yes, it is," I agree wholeheartedly.

"There's Ran," Eli says, nodding his head in the direction of the front deck.

I turn my head to see Ronan walk back into the house. He spots me standing in the kitchen and changes course to meet me with a smile on his lips. It sends a rush of heat through me and I return his smile, unable to stop myself.

"Hey." Ronan reaches for me, but then apparently remembers our plan to keep things on the down-low and resolutely shoves his hands into his jeans pocket.

"Hey, I was just coming to check on you," I say, already regretting our decision to play it cool; I want to step closer to him, want him to wrap his arms around me. "Is everything alright?"

"Yeah, I was just catching up with some teammates." He smiles at me, then looks at Eli and raises his right hand in a greeting. "What's up, Eli?"

"Not much. Happy birthday, man," Eli says.

"Thanks," Ronan says, then looks back at me. "I'm going to head back out there. You coming, too?"

"Sure," I say, trying hard to keep my voice steady while Ronan gives me my favorite half smile, then turns to walk back out to Shane and the rest of our friends. "It was nice to meet you, Eli," I say, smiling.

"Hey, Cat," Eli says, looking slightly unsure of himself, his eyes moving from me to Ronan and back again in an apparent attempt to determine what my connection is to Ronan. I notice Ronan stop a few feet behind me, waiting for me. "Could I... Could I ask you for your number?" Eli asks sweetly, one eyebrow raised. "I've been meaning to talk to you for a while, but I never really got the chance at school, so..."

"Oh," I say. "I'm sort of seeing someone," I tell Eli apologetically.

"Right. Yeah, I figured." He smiles and looks at Ronan again. "But I thought I'd put myself out there just in case. No regrets, right?" he says with a chuckle.

"Absolutely." I reciprocate his smile. "I'll see you later," I say, and he nods before I turn and join Ronan to walk back out to the deck.

"I have to admit, I got worried there for a second," Ronan says amusedly, his voice low.

I giggle. "Why?"

"I don't know, maybe because you're incredibly beautiful and I'm actually shocked that some dude hasn't snatched you yet."

"Oh, they tried," I say, feigning swagger.

Ronan grins at me. "Trust me, I'm well aware," he says with a sincere nod. "Thanks for picking me," he adds, his voice husky.

"Likewise," I say, and smile at him.

His green eyes lock on mine, and he takes my hand briefly in his, squeezing it before letting go again just in time for us to walk out onto the deck to join our friends.

Thursday, June 10th

Ronan

It's Thursday afternoon and I just managed to drag myself out of bed after leaving it all at the gym this morning. I didn't get home from work until just before three last night and was up again by seven, when Steve and I went to meet Shane and Zack at our usual gym—a repurposed warehouse uniquely suited for boxing, weightlifting, and CrossFit. Shane has a deep-seated dislike for chain gyms, as he calls them, because he thinks people go there to show off their physique but don't actually put in the work.

It was a brutal workout, and I crashed hard after taking a hot shower that relaxed my tired muscles. When I finally wake up, neither Steve nor my mom are home, but I find my dad in the living room where he's working on his laptop.

As promised, my dad came home last Friday. I was working, so I didn't actually see him until I got back from the gym at noon on Saturday. It's been nice having him around. While I don't spend a ton of time with him, it's mostly the energy at home that's different when he's here. My mother's mood is better, more stable. She doesn't lose control like she does when my dad's gone, doesn't seem so agitated by my mere existence.

My dad looks up from his work when I walk into the living room. "Hey, Ran. You look beat. How was the workout?"

"Rough," I admit, still exhausted. I notice his packed bag by the foot of the stairs. "You're still leaving tomorrow?" I ask, my voice neutral, unaffected by what I know his answer will be.

He nods, giving me an apologetic look. "Yeah. I'm heading to Germany for a couple of weeks and then back to Virginia."

"So, I won't see you for a while, huh?" I ask, already formulating a plot of how to best avoid sticky situations at home. When I was little, I would dread my dad leaving, though some years ago I learned to just accept the fact that when my father was gone, things were bad for me. It's been like this my whole life—my dad being gone for long stretches of time, coming home for brief periods, then leaving again. I'm resigned to the fact he's always gone, numb to what awaits me the moment he steps out the door for weeks or months on end.

But that doesn't change the fact that I have noticed him being gone longer, being home less frequently, and appearing happier as his departure day approaches. It's been so noticeable that I shared my suspicions with Steve a few months ago.

"I think dad is having an affair with some woman in Virginia," I randomly threw at Steve one night after I had a little too much Jack at one of Shane's parties. My dad hadn't been home in over two months, and it was the evening following a more violent confrontation with my mother. The bruises were dark, the cut on my jaw was still raw and deep, and I was sore, and drunk, and pissed off after just having told the same bullshit lie about how the fuck I got so banged up for the ninth time that evening.

I had been observing and analyzing my dad's behavior for a while by then, and the only explanation I could come up with was that he was happier somewhere else. Things had been getting progressively worse at home since we moved back to New York, and my mother's violent outbursts were more frequent and painful.

At first, I thought it was because I was getting bigger, stronger, and maybe she felt she could use more force without breaking me so easily, but then I realized she genuinely seemed angrier at me than ever before. The only correlation I saw was my dad's increasingly prolonged absences.

Steve had waved me off, chalking my talk up to the fact that I was less than sober and obviously in a bad mood.

"I'm sorry, bud," my dad says genuinely. "I know I haven't been spending any time with you. But hey, if you have some time now we could get started on replacing that brake system in your Mustang?"

"Yeah, actually, that would be great," I nod happily. "I already have the conversion kit, so it shouldn't take all that long."

"Awesome."

We change clothes and get to work on my Mustang fifteen minutes later. It should be a quick job, especially with both of us working together, and I have to admit that I enjoy spending time with my dad. It's such a rare occurrence to have him home, and even more seldom that I get to spend time with just him.

"So, tell me how you've been, bud," my dad urges me, working on one side of my car while I install one of the mounting brackets. Onyx lays on the floor next to me, keeping a watchful eye on things. She's always been attached to me.

"Um, fine, I guess," I grunt, tightening a screw.

"Yeah? How's hockey?"

"Hockey's done for now, Dad. Conditioning doesn't start up again until a couple of weeks from now."

"Oh, yeah, right. I knew that," he says sheepishly. "Okay, well how did last season go?"

"It went fine, Dad." I'm semi-annoyed; his questions are a constant reminder of his absence.

"Do you still enjoy being on the defense?"

I stop my work and stare at him, though he doesn't look back at me. "I'm a center forward."

His head finally pops up to look at me. "What? Since when?"

"Umm, for like the last nine years, Dad." I'm trying to figure out if he's pulling my leg or if he seriously has no idea what position I've been playing.

"No, you're a defenseman," he says. "Stevie's a winger, you're on the defense."

"No, Dad. I started as a defenseman when I was seven but was moved into a different position after like two months." I shake my head. "I've pretty much never not been a forward."

My dad falls silent for a moment, studying me, his strong brow furrowed. "I'm sorry, Ran, I..." he starts with a sigh, but is interrupted by his phone ringing in his pocket. He doesn't finish his sentence and instead retrieves his phone. A telling smile brightens his expression when he looks at the screen. It's obviously someone he enjoys talking to and he doesn't hesitate before he answers the call, puts the phone to his ear, and walks back into the house. I'm left standing by my car, the brake system still disassembled.

I don't know if my dad forgets about me or if he's still on the phone talking to whomever, but I finish changing out the brake system on my Mustang alone. It takes a lot longer than it would have had my dad not left me hanging, but I get it done. An hour later I stand in the garage, my hands fucking filthy, admiring my handiwork.

I give a quick, approving nod, then ascend the three steps into the kitchen with Onyx right behind me. I take note of the time on the large clock hanging just above the doorframe. I need to shower, change, and then head to Shane's where I'll be spending the evening, just like I have most nights these past few days.

I quickly wash my hands in the kitchen sink, then let Onyx outside to the backyard before finally walking upstairs. My dad emerges from the master bedroom just as I reach the landing. His face falls, the color draining from his cheeks as he observes me and my stained shirt. He very clearly forgot about me in the garage.

"Shit," he sighs when I pass him on the staircase. "Ran, I was on the phone and..."

"It's fine, Dad. Whatever," I tell him, and disappear in my room. I know I'm blowing him off, not giving him a chance to explain, and I feel bad seeing the look of disappointment on his face. But in the end, he's going to leave like he always does, and I'll be left to deal with the repercussions of his absence. So I try to do what I can to live my life—to survive without him here to protect me.

I grab my phone off my bed and swipe through my notifications, finding some text messages from Shane.

Shane: God damn it, Tori is wearing her short-shorts and that ass of hers is gonna be the fucking death of me... I just straight-up ran into the fucking doorframe because I kept staring at her...

Shane: Also, can you bring some guac? The chunky, spicy kind!

I laugh at the randomness of his messages and scroll up only to notice a missed call from Cat. I smile like a little kid at the prospect of getting to hear her voice in only a few seconds, and my heart rate increases a couple of beats as I sit on my bed, already dialing her number.

Cat left for North Carolina a couple of days after my birthday—after I decided to heed Shane's advice to let Cat decide whether she wanted to be with me and just see where things would go. And even though she's been gone this past week, I've still been happier than I can remember being in a long damn time. She's set to come back tomorrow, and just the thought of seeing her brings an almost giddy excitement.

We spent a few hours together the day before her trip, eating at a small BBQ place where I amusedly watched her devour a full rack of ribs. Then we spent some time sitting by the beach with her leaning back against me, chatting about everything and nothing. It was an incredibly peaceful afternoon that left me feeling content and sad at the prospect of not getting to see her for a week while she spent some time with her family in North Carolina.

But Cat and I have been handling this week pretty well, though that's probably because we're constantly talking or texting each other. I still haven't told anyone what's going on between Cat and me; nothing about the hot make-out sessions we've had more than once;

nothing about the part where, like an idiot, I told her I was falling for her; and nothing about the fact that I was seriously lost to this girl after knowing her for just a little over a month.

Part of the reason I haven't told Shane, my brother, or even Vada—who's actually spending way more time at my house than even I am—is that I feel like if I don't talk about it, I'll be able to keep all this excitement and the rush of being with Cat, even over a temporarily long distance, to myself.

It's the best, hottest, and most incredible secret I've ever had in my life. Most of my other secrets are dark, but not this one. And with all the crap that's locked up inside me, why not add something really amazing to the mix? Something that makes me incredibly happy.

Another reason I'm able to make it through this week without thinking of Cat every waking minute is because Shane not only saw fit to schedule me for the night shift every day this week, but also insists that we work out with Steve and Zack every morning. So between working until two thirty or three every morning, getting back up by 7 a.m., and working out for two or three hours, I'm so wiped out that I end up sleeping away a huge chunk of the day. This is all fine for now, but conditioning for hockey is going to start up again soon, and I keep telling Shane he's going to run me into the ground if he keeps this up.

This next season is going to be strange. Both Steve and Shane have graduated, leaving only Drew and me on the team. Drew is a pain in my ass and I honestly can't stand the guy. He's a mediocre player who doesn't take responsibility for his mistakes and doesn't have any fucking discipline. He also can't stand me, so there's that. The only reason we hang out is because he's good friends with Cheyenne, who happens to be Summer's best friend.

"Hey sleepy head!" Cat answers on the second ring, her voice happy, and a grin spreads across my face as I picture her smiling.

"I've actually been up for a while already," I chuckle. "What are you doing?" I ask, wanting to hear her voice.

"Not much. Just getting ready for Julie's birthday dinner tonight."

Cat has told me about Julie during our hours-long conversations this past week, and I feel like I've known Julie all my life even though I've never exchanged a single word with her.

"Where are you headed for dinner?" I lie back on my bed, staring at the white ceiling.

"Her parents are taking us to this itty-bitty seafood restaurant," she says, then lowers her voice to a whisper. "I actually don't like seafood, but I didn't want to be rude."

I laugh. "I'm sure they have chicken or something for special people like you."

I can just about hear the smile on Cat's face when she says, "Jeez, I hope so. Otherwise I'll have to binge on the biscuits and then I'll be huge and you won't want to go out with me anymore."

I laugh again. "I don't think that's a possibility."

"What, me getting huge? That's definitely a possibility," she says, trying to sound serious.

"No, I mean me not wanting to go out with you anymore. That's not a possibility," I say, realizing just how true my words are.

She sighs. "I miss you!"

Her words hit me like a ton of bricks. I miss her, too. How can it be possible to feel so strongly about someone I've just met?

"I miss you, too," I finally say. "I can't wait to see you."

"Me neither." She exhales loudly, then pauses. "But we only have to make it another twenty-four hours. So, what are you gonna be doing the rest of today?"

"Well, I'm heading to Shane's in a little bit, but first I'm gonna take a quick shower."

"Oh," she says, making her voice sound sad. "That means you'll have to take off all your clothes, right?"

"It would appear so." I love this banter.

"Will you think of me?" she asks, her voice sexy.

"Would you like me to?"

"Yes!" she says.

"Then I will."

She laughs, and I can't help but smile. "I have to go, but can I call you later?" she asks, as she always does.

"Of course. Call me anytime," I say, already dreading hanging up the phone.

"Think of me."

I do think of her under the shower. Not so much in a sexual way, although those thoughts certainly cross my mind more often than I'd ever admit out loud, but more about how much I already care for her. Hearing her voice is the best part of my day, and I can't wait for her to come back so I can see her perfect face.

I make it to Shane's mom's beach house by six. His mother is on a two-week vacation in Europe, apparently with some new boyfriend, and has asked Shane to house-sit, which to Shane means throwing one continuous party.

"By the amount of booze you got, it would seem you invited half of Manhattan," I joke, grabbing a cold beer from the cooler. The chilly water from the ice runs down my arm.

"It's not over the top, is it?" Shane feigns concern, fanning himself with his left hand while propping his other hand on his hip.

"Not at all," I chuckle and take a sip, letting the cool liquid hydrate my throat. I haven't eaten yet, which means I should take it easy, though I probably won't. I tend to get myself into sticky situations when I drink too much. Both times I hooked up with Cheyenne I was less than sober, and I regretted it each time. I also don't want to be one of those people who drink their problems away rather than facing them head-on, but then again, I don't know how much more head-on-facing I can take without my mother finally killing me.

Steve and Vada arrive a little while later, holding hands and smiling. I can tell by the way they're acting that the two of them just hooked up.

"You two have fun?" I ask, not even trying to hide my insinuation.

"Very much!" Steve exclaims, squeezing Vada's ass in front of everyone.

Shane whistles, and Zack makes a face.

"That's my sister, man," Zack whines, disgruntled.

"Oh please, as if you and Summer don't enjoy a good PDA session." Vada lets go of Steve to grab a drink. "Probably the only one here who isn't hooking up regularly is you." Vada spins around and points her index finger squarely at my chest. "Well, at least not with the same girl," she adds disapprovingly.

Here we go again.

"Yeah, we need to change that," Shane chimes in.

I raise my eyebrows. "We do?"

"Oh yeah," Vada says again, moving past me to hand Steve a beer. "And I have the perfect person in mind."

"And who would that be?" I ask, genuinely interested, though I have a suspicion whose name she'll drop.

"Cat," she says matter-of-factly.

Ding, ding, ding. My heart skips a beat at the mention of Cat's name.

"I've seen you look at her, Ran," Vada says. "And I know you'd like her. She's super sweet and really hot, as you know."

I haven't told a soul about Cat and me with the exception of telling Shane that I was starting to develop feelings for her, and this little conversation is getting fun.

"I feel like you're trying to pimp me out, Vada," I say, and the guys bust up laughing.

"Oh please, as if you need any help pimping yourself out, Mr. Hooks-Up-With-a-Different-Chick-Every-Damn-Weekend," she says with an eye roll.

"Hey, it's been like three weekends," I joke.

Vada huffs. "What a world record. How can you possibly manage without nailing some new girl for so long? But come on," Vada continues seriously, "Cat is awesome. All you need to do is ask her out."

"That's what I've been saying," Shane says loudly from behind me. "I think she'd be good for him."

There is a general affirmative tone in the room as the guys, Tori, and Summer nod in agreement. I spot Cheyenne out of the corner of my eye, and she does not look amused by all of this.

"Oh, and I didn't even tell you the best part," Vada interrupts, then hesitates. "I probably shouldn't tell you this, but if it means you'll ask Cat on a date, I have to."

I laugh at her attempt to convince herself to tell me whatever it is that's on her mind. "Now I'm curious. What is it about Cat that makes you think I should go out with her?"

"Well, she's... gosh, I really shouldn't say anything," she wavers.

"Nah, you gotta finish what you started," Zack eggs her on.

Vada hesitates for a second longer. "Cat's... she's a virgin," Vada says, catching me completely off-guard.

My head snaps up. I hadn't really thought about whether Cat had any experience, and quite honestly, it doesn't matter to me, but the fact that she hasn't had sex makes me want to be that much more careful with her. I immediately feel even more protective of her.

"Fucking shit, babe," Steve laughs. "Way to drop a freaking bomb like that," he says while Shane coughs violently after choking on his drink.

"Wait, all guys like virgins, right?" she asks, looking from me to Steve to Shane. "Right?"

"Why do you say that?" Shane asks earnestly.

"Am I wrong? I thought guys like the idea of being, you know, the first and all." Vada seems uncomfortable now.

I laugh at her. "Whatever you say, Vada." I shrug and walk into the kitchen to grab some food.

"So, are you going to ask her out?" she yells after me.

I laugh again, not providing her with an answer. She'll find out soon enough.

Cat

My week in North Carolina has been better than expected. When I'm not hanging out with my family, I've spent my time with Julie. I've known Julie since I was four and she's one of my closest friends. She was also one of the only people who stood by me as the town turned against me when my relationship with Adam imploded. The aftermath was very public and even more dramatic.

"What do you think?" Julie asks, twirling in front of me in a short white skirt she bought today.

I bite my lower lip as I examine her. "I don't like that top with the skirt," I say, and move toward Julie's closet to pull out a different top for her to wear tonight. It's Julie's birthday and my last night in North Carolina, so we decided to spend tonight in style. Julie's parents are taking us to a local seafood restaurant. And after a lot of begging and whining, Julie also convinced me to go to a party at one of her friend's houses.

I don't like the idea of going to a party where I'll surely run into some of the people who made my life miserable before I left for New York, but Julie promised me we would leave if I felt uncomfortable. Julie's boyfriend Nate is also tagging along, and I hope their presence will keep the vultures away.

"Try this," I say, and hand Julie a lilac top that shows off her slender arms and shoulders. Julie takes the shirt from me and I sit down on her bed, taking out my cell phone as she tries on the shirt.

"Are you checking if Ronan texted you?" Julie asks in a teasing tone, looking at me through the mirror.

"Maybe," I say with a smile on my lips as I scroll through my last text messages.

"Didn't you guys just talk on the phone like a couple of hours ago?" she asks, and sits down on the bed next to me.

I shrug while I swipe to lock the screen. "No text," I say, but still smile. I let myself fall backwards onto Julie's bed and continue grinning. Julie follows my lead and, together, we look at the ceiling of her room. She still has those glow-in-the-dark stars she used to have when we were little. I used to spend almost every weekend at Julie's house, mostly to get away from my younger siblings.

"You have such a huge crush on him, don't you," she states rather than asks.

"I do." I'm still incredulous that I find myself willing to open my heart when, only months ago, my heart and soul were crushed. "Do you think I'm moving too fast?"

I trust Julie's opinion. She was one of the only people who told me from the start that she thought Adam was trouble, but I was too naïve to listen. She doesn't respond to my question right away, and I roll onto my stomach to look at her. Again, she mimics my movements and looks at me intently.

"Nope, I don't," she finally says. "Adam was a real ass. Always was, even before he started paying attention to you. And you didn't date for a long time."

She's right: Adam and I only dated for about five months, though the impact our short relationship had on his life and mine goes far beyond that. I still wonder how something that started out so sweet, so innocent, could turn so toxic and end in such devastation.

"I'm glad you decided to trust Ronan," Julie says, and I stay quiet for a long moment. "You deserve to be happy, and he seems to make you happy."

"I *am* happy," I say, and picture Ronan in my head. I've spent a lot of time this past week picturing him, thinking of touching him, of him touching me in turn. And I'm always surprised at my body's reaction to my mere thoughts. This is definitely new territory for me.

Julie interrupts my thoughts with a giggle. "You look like you're thinking dirty thoughts."

I blush. "I guess I kind of was," I say, and join in her laughter.

"So, is he going to be the one then?"

I raise my eyebrows. "The one?"

"You know, the one you'll finally sleep with."

Before I can answer, Nate walks through the door and both Julie and I sit up.

"Hey babe, you ready to go?" he asks, pulling Julie into his arms when she gets up from the bed.

"Yeah, let's go."

Dinner is nice. Julie has a small family, so it's just her and me, Julie's parents, and Nate. I'm glad to see that the restaurant has chicken, and I smile, replaying Ronan's and my conversation in my head. After dinner, Nate, Julie, and I head to the party.

The house is crowded by the time we arrive, and I have to lift my arms above my head to squeeze through the cluster of people in the entrance. Music plays loudly in the background. There are people dancing in what must be the living room, although it's barely recognizable. Nate, Julie, and I make our way through the crowd and into the kitchen, where Nate hands Julie a drink. I recognize a number of faces, and some people even come up to me to chat as though there's no bad history between me and this town. Before I moved away, things had been pretty tough. Adam was the town hero who was going to go off and play pro-football one day, if it hadn't been for me—or at least that's what people told me after Adam was sentenced to six months' probation.

Julie and Nate are in their own little world. His hands rest on her hips, and she giggles into his chest as he whispers something into her ear.

I take my phone out of my bag and send a text to Ronan.

Me: I can't wait to see you tomorrow.

I push the button to make my phone go back to sleep. Only seconds later, I feel it vibrate and a tingle spreads in my stomach when I find a message from Ronan.

Ronan: I wish it was tomorrow already.

I smile to myself.

Me: What are you doing?

Ronan: I'm at the beach house. Shane's got some people over. How about you?

Me: Julie talked me into going to a party with her, but I feel awkward.

Ronan: Try to have some fun. It'll make the time go by faster and before you know it, you and I can have some fun...

I blush. Is he talking dirty to me? Before I can respond, someone snatches my phone out of my hands.

I whirl around to face Adam. I look around for Julie and Nate, but they must have moved to the living room because I can't see them anywhere.

"Can I please have my phone back?" I ask, trying to keep my voice steady. Adam is tall and he's put on some weight since I last saw him. It must be because he stopped playing football.

He doesn't respond and instead reads Ronan's last text message. A mean grin tugs at his lips while he scrolls through the conversation.

I'm agitated and manage to yank my phone away from him before he can further violate my privacy. "What are you doing here?" I ask, anger bubbling inside me.

"I should ask you the same thing. I thought you left town?" His voice is steady, and he seems genuinely curious. I expected a more threatening tone. After all, the last time I saw Adam was at school after he had been given probation.

"I'm here to visit my family," I say, locking my phone and stuffing it into my back pocket to avoid another hijacking by Adam.

"You look good," Adam says sincerely. I'm completely thrown for a loop; I didn't expect him to show me any kindness at all, but then again, this is how he always was while we were together—sweet and complimentary one minute, violent and condescending the next. He could make me feel beautiful and then worthless in a matter of seconds.

"Thanks," is all I can muster, suspicion rising within me.

"Listen, do you have a second to talk?" he asks, his brown eyes big and bloodshot. I can tell he's been drinking.

"I don't know, Adam," I say, again looking around for Julie and Nate, hoping they'll come to my aid and stop me from walking straight into a trap.

"Come on, Cat. What do you think is going to happen?" he asks, his hands stuffed into the pockets of his jeans.

Despite my intuition screaming at me, I give in to Adam's request. He's always held this weird sort of power of me. The way he exerts control is subtle but effective.

"I guess," I say, and Adam turns and walks toward the back door. I follow him, still looking around for Julie, but she's nowhere to be found. I quickly send her a text as I follow Adam out the door and into the backyard, just to make sure to let her know where I am and, more importantly, who I'm with.

Adam holds the door for me as I step out into the dimly lit backyard. My senses immediately heighten, and I take stock of my surroundings. The windows to the house are wide open, and the backyard, though not bright, is lit by little string lights. I noticeably relax when I see a couple making out on the porch swing. Not that the fact that people are around has ever stopped Adam from hurting me, but after everything that's happened, I feel he's less likely to lose it with witnesses around.

"What do you want?" I ask, harsher than I planned.

His brown eyes are huge now, and he towers over me, his shoulders broad. He's wearing a tight red shirt that emphasizes the weight he's put on, and not in a good way. He really let himself go, and part of me feels bad because, ultimately, I was the reason he couldn't continue playing the sport he loved.

"I wanted to apologize," Adam states, his voice soft, surprising me. This was the last thing I expected him to say.

"For what?" I press, although I know what he's getting at.

"For that night when... when I lost control," he says, looking at the ground. Everything about this feels weird.

When I don't respond, Adam lifts his head again, his eyes meeting mine expectantly.

"Thanks," I say simply.

Right on cue, his face contorts. His eyebrows knit together and his eyes narrow as he stares at me.

"Thanks?" he repeats. "Thanks? Is that really all you got?" I hear the anger rise in his voice, and his features become hard. I've seen this version of Adam all too often, and my body begins to tense.

"What do you want me to say?" I whimper. There it is again: my voice has lost all its confidence, just like it used to when Adam and I were dating and he would rip into me.

"Umm, I don't know, how about a fucking apology in return?" His words come out sharp, and the volume of his voice is rising. "You ruined my fucking life, you bitch. And all you got is 'thanks?' The least you could do is apologize for getting me arrested, and even worse, for getting me kicked out of college before I even started. You ruined everything!"

There he is; this is the Adam I knew. All Southern charm one minute, and when that doesn't work he gets nasty and violent.

His eyes have lost all compassion; they're enlarged and cold as he lays into me. "It wasn't my fault you acted the way you did."

I'm too afraid to move and just stand there, my shoulders slumped forward, cowering.

"I was a good boyfriend. Hell, I took you out, I made you popular. And how did you pay me back? You never put out, you fucking tease, and then you got me fucking arrested!"

He starts toward me.

I will my legs to move but stumble over my own feet and fall to the ground.

"But I bet you're putting out now! By the looks of those text messages, you got yourself a new boyfriend, you slut. I bet you have no problem letting him fuck you." The Adam who used to beat on me is back, and I'm consumed by my fear. "I swear to god, Cat, you'll pay for this." He raises his fist at me.

I squeeze my eyes shut, waiting for the blow to my face, just like he's done before. But the blow doesn't come.

I squint and see Adam still hovering over me, but his arm is lowered. He's breathing heavily, though he appears to be coming to his senses. Whenever he used to get like this, he would lose all control of himself. I've never seen him regain his grip like this, and I decide to jump up before he changes his mind again.

I whirl around and away from him, storming back through the kitchen door and into the house where I find Julie and Nate in the kitchen.

"We were just coming to check on you," Julie says, concern in her eyes.

Nate checks me over, looks past me, and spots Adam.

"Are you okay?" Julie asks as she puts both her hands on my shoulders and looks at me intently.

"Yeah. I want to go home," I say, my voice still shaky.

"What happened? Did he touch you?" Nate growls, picking up on my fear.

I quickly shake my head at him. "No. I promise, he didn't touch me. Is it okay if we leave, though?" I feel bad because it's Julie's birthday.

Julie nods and then looks at Nate. "Sure, we'll drop you off at home," she says, turns around, and puts her arm around my shoulder to lead me out to Nate's truck.

Ronan

Shane's party was what he would consider a success. As I expected, the crowd that showed up was huge, and by the time Shane tries to call it a night we've had to make two additional booze runs—thank God for excellent fake IDs and Shane's charm. People are passed out by the beach, and when I try to use the bathroom, I find the door locked and hear a telling moan from inside.

"How do you plan on getting the stragglers out of here?" I ask Shane once I make my way back to the deck where everyone's hanging out. Tori is sitting on Shane's lap, her head resting on his shoulder, and it makes me ache for Cat.

"Easy," Shane says, a slow grin spreading across his face. "All we need to do is yell, 'Cops!' and people will scatter like mice."

We all laugh at the image. I sit down in one of the chairs ringing the fancy table that doubles as a fire pit and retrieve my phone to send Cat a text message for I-don't-know-what-reason, other than to check in on her.

Me: Hey, how is your night?

I text her and stuff my phone back into my pocket just as the glass door slides open and Cheyenne stumbles onto the deck. Her short red-and-black hair is a mess, and it's obvious she's beyond wasted. She's barefoot, her shoes in her hands, and her already-short skirt is hiked up her thighs, barely covering things. Her eyes are glassy and blood red, and she makes her way over to us while holding on to imaginary things to maintain her balance.

"You should sit down, Chey," Tori says with a laugh in her voice.

Cheyenne considers Tori for a second, then moves toward me, swaying her hips. She stops right in front of me and slides her short skirt up her thighs an inch more, almost exposing herself to me before she straddles my legs and sits down too high on my lap, pressing herself against me. "This seems like a nice spot," she says, attempting to sound flirty, but her speech is slurred and slow and she reeks of alcohol and smoke. I can feel her heat against me and try to get up, not wanting to give her any ideas, but she holds on to the arms of the chair, pushing herself closer to me.

"Cheyenne, I have to get up," I say.

"Oh, come on, Ran. It's been like two months since we hooked up," she says, and her left hand snakes under the bottom of my shirt. I cringe when I feel her fingertips caressing the bare skin of my abs just above the waistline of my jeans, but I'm able to avoid her when she leans in to kiss me.

I grab her hips and stand up, then set Cheyenne down in the chair and move away from her. She has a look of disbelief on her face as she gets up from the spot I put her in. She adjusts her skirt, pulling it down to cover herself. She crosses her arms in front of her chest, looking determined, though a bit unsteady on her feet.

"I don't mean to be an ass, Cheyenne, but we should never have hooked up in the first place," I admit, feeling like such a dick.

"Oh, okay. I guess it took you fucking me twice to realize that?" Cheyenne says with pain in her voice.

None of our friends are talking; their eyes are on us as they listen to this unfolding shit show.

I open my mouth to respond but feel my phone vibrating in my pocket with an incoming text message. When I pull it out, I see Cat's name on the screen and my heartbeat quickens.

"You're right, it was a dick move. It should have never happened," I say, but turn away from her and our friends before she can say anything further. I start down the deck stairs and to the beach, where I open Cat's message.

Cat: It was fine.

Even though I don't have the benefit of hearing her voice, I have an immediate gut feeling that something isn't right. It's the way she describes her evening in the past tense and how short her response is. I should probably just ignore that feeling, pretend not to feel the unease making my scalp tingle; but ignoring vibes, words, and their meaning—no matter how subtle—isn't something I do. My life, my circumstances have conditioned me to be alert at all times, consistently living in a state of awareness. So I don't fight myself and simply dial Cat's number.

It rings only once before she answers.

"Hi," Cat answers, and her tone is immediate confirmation that my gut feeling was spot-on. Something's wrong.

"Are you okay?" I hold the phone to my ear with my left hand while my right is stuffed into the pocket of my jeans.

"I'm fine," she says, but she sounds tired and sad. "The party was just really uncomfortable and I'm glad to get out of here tomorrow."

"Did anything happen?" I try not to press too much.

Cat hesitates before answering. "I ran into my ex-boyfriend."

I stop walking. "Okay?" I urge.

"He's kind of a bully, and he wasn't very nice to me. So, I made Julie take me home."

"I'm sorry, baby." The last word slips out before I can stop it, startling me. God, fuck, I hope Cat didn't catch that. "What did he do?" I ask, hoping to keep the focus on the topic of our conversation rather than my inadvertent term of endearment for her. I have no fucking clue where that came from. I've never called anyone "baby," although I have to admit it feels kind of nice.

She doesn't respond right away, and I worry she's as startled by my pet name for her as I am. Shit, I hope I didn't fuck things up somehow. "He was just... being himself, I guess. He's an asshole. I don't really want to talk about it right now," Cat finally says.

I exhale deeply. "Yeah, okay," I agree without hesitation, because I know exactly what it feels like to not want to talk about something, and I know how frustrating it is when you've made your wishes clear and people still try to get you to divulge painful or uncomfortable stuff you're just not in a position to say out loud yet... or ever.

Cat hasn't really talked about her ex-boyfriend before—she just mentioned that things ended badly—but from her brief mention of him tonight, it doesn't sound as though he's a pleasant guy.

"Are you sure you're okay, though?" I double-check, unhappy that I can't be there with her to provide comfort.

"I'm fine. I'm just tired. And I miss you," she says in the sweetest voice that makes my heart beat furiously in my chest. I'm feeling very protective of her right now, and the fact that her ex messed up her night pisses me off to no end. "Will I get to see you tomorrow?"

The tone in her voice makes me want to be there with her right now. "Of course," I say. "I can't wait. What time are you getting in?"

"My flight gets in at noon. Do you have work or anything tomorrow?"

"No. Give me a call when you're home and I'll head right over."

Cat sighs. "That sounds good." Her voice sounds lighter now, and I hope I was able to take some of tonight's stress off her shoulders.

"Try to get some sleep," I urge her. "I'll see you tomorrow."

We hang up, and I make my way back up the stairs and to the deck where Cheyenne is occupying the chair I sat in earlier. She refuses to make eye contact with me. So I sit down on the sofa next to Shane, who gives me a sympathetic shrug, grab the bottle of Jack sitting on the wooden floor boards, and take a gulp right from the bottle. The liquid burns as I work it down my throat.

"Who were you talking to?" Vada fires at me, eyeing me suspiciously.

I cock my head to the side, narrowing my eyes. "Why do you care?" I shoot back.

She presses her lips together before shrugging. "Just curious. Seems like you're hiding something," she says, her eyes narrowing, boring their way into my head.

I laugh. "You're too much, Vada, seriously," I chuckle, and take another big gulp from the bottle. I need to slow it down, so I set the bottle back down on the floor next to me.

"Was it a girl?" she questions.

I swallow the Jack too fast, making myself cough hard.

Shane comes to my rescue. "What are you, his mom?"

"I'm just asking!" Vada leans back in her seat, huffing, then mutters under her breath, "If it's some chick, she better be cool. We don't need some weirdo in our group."

"Wow, babe," Steve chuckles. "What's up with you tonight?"

"Sorry, that was mean. I just really want Ran to get with Cat already," Vada gripes, and I laugh. If only she knew.

"We know, babe. We know," Steve placates her, patting her head with his hand, making all of us laugh.

We spend a couple more hours hanging out on the deck before Shane makes good on his threat and yells, "Cops!" at the top of his lungs. As anticipated, the stragglers quickly disperse, and Drew volunteers to drive Cheyenne, who fell asleep in her chair in a rather unflattering position. Summer covers her with a blanket, then helps Drew get Cheyenne to the car, warning him not to try anything with her.

In the end only Shane, Tori, Zack, Summer, Vada, Steve, and I remain, and it's exactly the way I like it. The six of them are my closest friends, and I'm about as content as I can be. The only missing piece is Cat. My night would be fucking perfect if she was here with me right now, and my thoughts turn to her at every possible chance. It's fucking exciting yet unnerving at the same time. Deep down I know I have no business being with her. I should stay away from her, for her sake.

Unfortunately, I don't slow down with the alcohol, and by the time Zack takes Summer home, I'm way too trashed to drive myself home. So when Vada suggests Steve sleep over at her place, noting that her dad is in California at some week-long legal conference, Shane simply decides that I'll be crashing at his place tonight.

"Hand me your keys, man. You're not driving like this," he says, studying my glassy eyes. "How much did you have?" He takes the bottle of Jack from my hand, noting that it's decidedly more empty than full.

"Who even knows," I say slowly, giving him an exaggerated shrug, then fish my car keys out of my pocket and drop them into Shane's outstretched hand.

"Alright, I'm going to make a quick fast food run; we gotta get some greasy-ass food in you before you fucking pass out on me," he says with a nod to Tori. "Keep an eye on him for me, babe," he says, grabs his keys, then heads out the door behind Steve and Vada.

Tori starts to collect empty plastic cups and bottles of beer, trying to tidy up the house as much as possible. Shane's place is usually trashed after his parties, and though I try to help, Tori insists that I just sit down and drink some water instead.

"So, Shay told me a little secret," she says, sitting down next to me on the white sofa in the living room. She hitches a knee up onto the cushion so she can face my wasted self.

"Oh yeah, what's that?" I say, squeezing my eyes shut, willing the room to stop spinning.

"He said that you have a thing for Cat," she says with a smile.

"Fucking asshole," I groan through clenched teeth.

Tori laughs. "He didn't do it on purpose. I have a way of finding out things," she says with a gleam in her eyes, and winks.

"Using your hot female powers to your advantage again?" I say, looking at her, but immediately regretting opening my eyes when I get dizzy. I lean my head back against the sofa and close my eyes again, fatigue and nausea gnawing at me.

"What can I say? He's dough in my capable hands." She shrugs smugly.

"Yeah, he is." Shane has been head-over-heels for Tori for a year and a half now. I wasn't one to believe in soul mates and all that shit—I'd never been as drawn to a person as Shane was to Tori, and vice versa—but it became obvious pretty quickly that those two were meant to be together.

"So, is it true?" Tori pokes her index finger into my shoulder.

"Is what true?" My head feels foggy and slow from the alcohol.

"That you have a thing for Cat," she says with an eye roll.

"Oh... yeah. I do."

Tori squeals, clapping her hands, and I flinch from the noise. "Sorry," she says quickly, then throws her arms around my neck. "That's so exciting! Vada is going to die when she finds—"

"Don't tell her," I say, sitting up. "Seriously, Tori, this thing... it's so new, and Vada has a way of pushing things too hard." A wave of nausea comes on, probably because I sat up way too quickly. I groan. "God damn it." I stand and walk out of the living room.

"Where are you going?" she asks.

"To the bathroom," I say quickly, and bolt into the small guest bathroom where I barely get the toilet lid up in time to drop to my knees, clutch the cool porcelain bowl, and purge what alcohol remains in my stomach.

"Are you going to make it?" I hear Shane chuckling as he stands in the door to the bathroom a few minutes later.

I manage to get everything out of my stomach but feel drained and fucking exhausted. I rest my head on my forearms draped over the toilet with my eyes shut, seriously just trying to get my bearings.

"Probably," I groan, trying to gather the strength and energy to stand and go back to the living room, where I have every intention of passing out on the sofa. Fuck, I might just pass out right here on the bathroom floor.

"Come on, let's get some food in you," Shane says with a chuckle, and crouches next to me to help me up. "I can't remember the last time I've seen you this fucked up."

"Been a minute," I agree, and let Shane guide me out of the bathroom. "Hey, why the fuck did you tell Tori about me falling for Cat?"

"Fuck," he mutters. "Sorry, man, she was..."

"Using her hot female powers on you?"

"You could say that," he says with a chuckle.

"You need to stop thinking with your dick," I say, and fall back onto the sofa. I tip to the side while I kick off my shoes before pulling my feet up on the couch, ready to pass out.

"That's hard to do when I'm with her."

"No shit," I mutter. I can barely keep my eyes open.

He grabs my hand and pulls me into a sitting position. "Sit up, man. No sleep yet! You need food or you're going to have a hell of a hangover in the morning."

"I have a feeling that will be the case regardless," I say, regretting my earlier lack of judgment. I knew this would end badly, and, voilà, here I am, hating life. "So, what?" I say taking the tacos out of the paper bag Shane hands me. "You just tell Tori all my intimate secrets while you're on top of her?"

"After," Shane says with a chuckle. "I'm pretty sure I told her all your intimate secrets *after* I was on top of her."

"TMI, dude," I say with a chuckle, and take a bite of my food. It immediately settles my stomach. "Fuck, okay, I needed this."

"Told you," he says, biting into a giant burrito. "Sorry for divulging your feelings for Cat to Tori," he adds after a few minutes of silence during which I manage to scarf down two chicken tacos.

"It's all good," I say, my mouth full. "I should have known that whatever I tell you, you'd obviously share with Tori. She's like an extension of you."

He smiles and nods. "Yeah, she kind of is," he says with an admiring glance toward Tori, who's bustling about the kitchen, still trying to clean up the mess. "Babe, stop. Come sit with us," he calls to her.

"Be there in a sec," Tori calls back, and continues to wipe down the marble kitchen counter.

"Just, Shane, please don't ever tell her about my mom," I say intently, and he frowns at me. I know how strongly he feels about this whole thing; anytime he gets wind of another incident, he lays into me about finally telling someone. But he just doesn't fucking understand—doesn't understand that I just can't. "Please," I say again.

"I got you," he finally says, equally as intense. "I haven't said a damn thing to anyone, but—"

"Don't start," I warn him, my jaw tight. I know I don't need to say anything else; my body language and facial expression adequately convey that I need him to keep this one thing absolutely between him and me.

"Fine," he relents through gritted teeth. "Just remember that I have your back. Always."

"I know that," I nod, and crumple the paper bag in my hands before standing up and discarding it in the trash. "Thanks for the food, Shay. I'm going to bed," I inform Shane and Tori, who passes me to sit with Shane.

"'Kay," Shane says.

"See you in the morning," Tori says sweetly. "Dream of Cat," she adds with a giggle.

I shake my head and roll my eyes at her and Shane, then disappear into the first guestroom to the right of the hallway. I climb into bed without bothering to undress and pass out seconds later.

Friday, June 11th

Cat

I didn't tell my parents about what happened with Adam when I got home after the party. It would just result in completely unnecessary drama, given I was flying back to New York in the morning. I have every intention of forgetting about the encounter altogether.

The flight back to NYC is quick, but I get antsy during the cab ride home. My mom is occupied with my younger siblings, and I spend my time staring out the window and checking my phone. My mom seems to know that my heart and mind are somewhere completely different because occasionally she'll catch my eye and grin.

When we finally pull up in front of our home, I jump out of the cab, grab my bag, and hurry up the front steps to unlock the door. Inside, I hurry to my room, where I drop my stuff and pull out my phone from my bag, dialing Ronan's number with eager fingers. It rings and rings, but Ronan doesn't answer.

Disappointed, I hang up and drop my phone onto my bed before I decide to begin unpacking. I throw unworn clothes back into my closet and the dirty stuff into my wicker hamper. I decide to freshen up and change my clothes, and I'm standing in the bathroom when I finally hear my phone ring twenty minutes later. I sprint back into my bedroom, and a huge grin spreads across my lips when I see Ronan's name displayed in bright letters on my phone's screen.

"Hey," I say, unable to hide my relief and excitement.

"Hey, sorry I missed your call. I was out for a run," he says, sounding winded. I imagine his shirt, damp and clinging to his lean muscles. "Are you home?"

"Yeah, we got back half an hour ago," I say, dropping onto my bed, letting my head fall back onto the pillow.

"I want to see you badly, but if you're too tired..." Ronan trails off.

My grin becomes even wider. "Not tired at all," I say. "I want to see you, too."

I hear him chuckle in a low voice. "I'll be over in twenty minutes."

"Okay." My heart is beating hard in my chest and my hands are clammy with nerves and sweat. Jesus Christ, I'm a basket case over this guy. "I can't wait to see you."

"Same here. I'll see you in a few, baby." There it is again. He called me "baby" last night and again now, and it sends a small, pleasant shiver through my body.

We hang up. Instead of calming down, my heart and head go into overdrive. I desperately search through my messy closet and come up with a pair of jeans and a basic black V-neck shirt. Once I'm dressed I fuss with my hair but end up making it worse than it was after the flight. *You're being ridiculous, Cat.* I take a deep breath and decide to let my hair be. No use in messing with it; it's too unruly. Once I'm done, I walk around my room, sit on my bed, stand up and walk around again until finally I hear a knock on the door.

"I got it!" I yell to my mom as I spring down the stairs and toward the front door, yanking it open.

Ronan is tall and gorgeous, his skin sun kissed, as if he's been outside a lot these past few days, and it makes his green eyes look incredible. Some of his dark-blond hair has lighter strands bleached from the sun, and he's wearing dark jeans that caress his hips and a simple white shirt that hugs his shoulders and arms, hinting at his lean, muscular chest and torso before covering the top of his jeans. *Stop staring.*

His smile is breathtaking as he takes me in, his eyes roaming across my body. Finally, he steps toward me and cups the back of my head in his right hand, coaxing me to face him. I don't know what I expected, but when his warm, soft lips find mine, my legs buckle. Ronan's left hand finds my lower back to pull me in even closer. I willingly part my lips and let his tongue explore mine while I reach around him to his shoulders and hold on to him as if my life depends on it.

When our lips finally part I can feel the heat in my face, and Ronan's eyes are glossy, his cheeks flushed.

"Fuck," he mutters in a low voice, and I giggle. "I can't believe how much I missed you."

The happiness I feel at this moment is indescribable.

"I hate to interrupt this obviously joyous reunion," my mom says with a smile in her voice, my siblings—Benny and Samantha—right behind her, "but we need to squeeze by you two lovebirds and run to the store. We're out of groceries."

She stops in front of us and looks at Ronan with a warm smile. "Are you going to be joining us for dinner, Ronan?" I just love how warm my mom is with him.

"Oh, I don't want to impose," Ronan says.

"Not at all. Why don't you stay? Unless you have to go home, of course," she says, and Ronan gives me a questioning look.

"Stay!" I say, almost pleading.

"Alright. I'd love to."

"Perfect. We'll be back in a bit. You two, behave!" my mom says as she shepherds my siblings past us and out the door.

Ronan takes my hand, and I let him lead me into the house. I close the front door behind me before Ronan scoops me up and into his arms. I loop my legs around his waist while he interlaces his fingers under my butt, holding me against him, and I dip my head down to kiss him, appreciating the softness and warmth of his lips on mine. But before things can get too heated, my mom is back in the house, my little brother, Benny, and my little sister, Samantha, just behind her like little ducklings.

"Sorry, guys," she says awkwardly. Ronan is still holding me against his body, and I blush once more. I'm surprised my face isn't permanently beet red at this point. "My car isn't starting; I need to call a tow or something. Last thing I need right now. I really need to replace that piece of junk," my mom mutters.

"I can take a look at it for you," Ronan offers as he slowly lowers me back to the floor.

My mom turns toward him, an eyebrow raised. "Really?"

"Yeah. I know my way around cars," he says, his voice confident, and I smile again. Good-looking and handy. *I wonder what else he's good at*. I'm surprised by my own thoughts; I can't believe I'm even thinking about sex this early in the game. I've never slept with anyone, but after only a little over a month of knowing Ronan, I'm ready to drop my panties. *You need to get ahold of yourself, Cat!*

My siblings make themselves at home in front of the TV while my mom and I watch as Ronan gets to work on my mom's car. My mom giggles and gives me a little shove with her elbow when Ronan leans over the hood, checking whatever it is he's looking at.

"You got yourself a hottie," she whispers at me, and I throw her a shocked look. "What?" she says. "It was a compliment."

I smile to myself and return my eyes to Ronan. His shirt has ridden up, exposing just a sliver of his smooth back and the waistband of his black boxer briefs. It gets me thinking about what it would feel like to run my hands all over his body.

Ronan has my mom attempt to start the car while he's still bent over the hood, but the car only makes a clinking noise.

"I'm pretty sure it's your starter," Ronan says, his head reappearing from under the hood as my mom slams the door shut.

"That doesn't sound good," she says with a frown.

"It's not too difficult to fix, it just needs a new part." Ronan's hands are greasy, and I feel bad that he's over here fixing my mom's car rather than us spending some time together, alone.

"Okay," my mom sighs, putting her hands on her hips and cocking her head to the side. "I'll need to call a tow, get the car in the shop, and then figure out how to efficiently travel between my office and the clinic tomorrow morning."

"Or I can get the part for you and put it in right now," Ronan offers. He's so damn sweet, and my mom is eating it up. This situation is completely different from my parents' interactions with Adam. My dad couldn't stand him from the beginning; my mom really, really tried, and she never said a bad thing about Adam to my face.

"Oh, no, you don't have to do that," my mom responds, but I can tell she likes the idea.

"It's really not a problem. I don't mean to be rude or anything, but you have kind of an old car, so it's actually much easier to fix. It'll take me a couple of hours to get it running again," Ronan assures her.

My mom looks at me apologetically, and I give her a quick smile.

"There you go. Having an old clunker turns out to be a good thing," my mom tells me, nudging me with her elbow after Ronan leaves to get the part for the car.

"Yeah, except if you weren't driving an old clunker, Ran probably wouldn't have to spend the next few hours fixing your car," I retort.

My mom's face falls. "I'm sorry, I didn't mean to hijack your afternoon with your boyfriend." The word "boyfriend" catches me off-guard. Ronan and I haven't put any labels on our relationship yet, but yeah, I guess he is my boyfriend. And I'm his girlfriend. A huge smile erupts on my face, and my mom gives me a quick squeeze, sensing my giddiness. "He seems pretty great, Cat. And he's really, really cute." She winks at me but turns thoughtful.

"What, Mom?" I'm unnerved by the sudden shift in mood.

She looks at me contemplatively. "We should get you on the pill."

It takes me a few seconds to register what she's talking about. "Oh," I finally say as she grins at me. "Uh, I guess?" It's probably a good idea, considering where my mind goes when I so much as think about Ronan; not that I want to rush things, but it's good to be prepared.

"It's absolutely happening. I've seen you guys together more than once now, and I have firsthand knowledge what can happen when boys look at girls the way Ronan looks at you. Why do you think I had you at only twenty?" She winks at me again.

I blush. "Eww, Mom. I don't need to hear about your and Dad's sex life, please," I beg, and she laughs. "And I'm not rushing anything with Ronan," I try to assure her and myself.

She only smiles at me. "Right. We'll see about that," she says, and walks back into the house.

Ronan

I run to the store alone, leaving Cat behind, assuring her that I'll make it quick. I didn't think she'd be interested in going car-part shopping with me. I quickly find what I'm looking for and pay at the counter. The guys at the small family-owned shop know me well; I'm in here all the time.

My phone vibrates on my way out the store. I pull it out of my back pocket; it reads "Mom" on the screen. *Damn it.* "Yeah?" I answer, my voice uneven.

"You didn't put away the laundry," my mom says stiffly, her voice barely containing her anger.

Crap! This is already my second fuck-up today, and it's barely past noon.

I woke up at the crack of dawn this morning, disoriented by my surroundings, until I remembered I was at Shane's. My pounding head rudely reminded me that I'd overdone it last night. And then I had an oh-shit moment when I realized I never let my parents know that I wouldn't be home. I walked out to the living room of Shane's mom's beach house—no sign of Shane and Tori, who were likely still asleep in Shane's bed—and sent Shane a text letting him know that I'd be heading home.

Both my parents were already up when I got home, and the look on my mother's face when I stepped foot in the house, probably looking hungover and disheveled as fuck, spoke volumes.

"Where were you?" she asked me in a clipped tone. I knew she was pissed but was reining in her anger because my dad was standing behind her in the kitchen. She never loses her shit on me outright when my dad is home. She saves that for when it's just her and me.

"Sorry, I passed out at Shane's last night. I'm really sorry for not letting you know," I said in a small voice.

"Why is it possible for Steve to let us know he would be spending the night at Zack's, but you can't manage to do the same?" she asked me, her hands on her hips.

"I'm sorry," I said again. "I was..."

"Drunk?" my mom interrupted with a frown.

"Come on, Rica," my dad stepped in. "Take it easy. I told you Ran probably spent the night at Shane's; it's not a big deal," he said in a calm voice.

"To you, maybe. There are rules, Frank, and one of those rules is that the boys tell me if they're spending the night somewhere else. It's common courtesy."

"I know you were worried about Ran, but he's here now; he's okay," my dad said back, his voice even.

I knew better, though. She wasn't worried about me; she was pissed that I didn't obey, that I broke a rule. Not only did I violate my usual curfew—again—but I didn't bother giving her a heads-up. I was going to pay for this. Maybe not right then and there, but eventually.

"If he was in fact drinking, he made the right call spending the night at Shane's rather than driving," my dad continued.

I wanted him to stop talking and just let my mom lay into me, because the longer he stood there defending me, the more painful it would be for me later when he was gone.

"It's easy for you to say, Frank. You're always gone; you're not the one who has to raise these boys. I work most of the time, and that means the boys have to follow the rules around here. But for some reason Ronan has a tough time with that," she said, glowering at me.

"Hey, babe." My dad's voice was soft as he put his hands on my mom's shoulders and turned her toward him. "I'm sorry you have to handle so much. I appreciate everything you do for this family. I'm sure Ronan didn't do this on purpose. Let's just enjoy our breakfast before I have to head back out, okay?"

I went up to my room then, stepping out of my clothes and under the hot shower to wash off the stickiness and alcohol clinging to my pores.

My dad left after breakfast, and I was careful to avoid my mother the rest of the morning, knowing that my dad's departure would just add to her shitty mood. I only had to hold her off until Steve got home, which he did around eleven, looking relaxed and happy.

"Yeah, I did! I put everything away," I say to my mom as I walk across the parking lot. *Stupid*. I know this will only piss her off more.

"No, you didn't. There are clothes piled up in the garage on top of the dryer, Ronan!" The volume of her voice has risen.

It doesn't matter what I say at this point; my mom is pissed off, capital *P*.

"Sorry, I thought it was just the stuff in the basket in the living room," I say, unlocking my car.

"Well, you thought wrong. God damn it, Ronan, why can't you ever do what I tell you to? Where the hell are you? You better be getting your ass home to finish your chores right now!" She's all-out raging.

"I can't right now; but I'll finish everything when I get home later."

I hate how she makes me feel like a five-year-old. My mother terrifies me, and by the time I hang up the phone I have to take a couple of deep breaths to stop my hands from shaking. *Fuck!* I hope to god she's working tonight, because otherwise I can expect some kind of repercussion when I get home. Steve has already announced his intent to spend another night over at Zack and Vada's, and Shane is working tonight, so I won't be able to crash at his place.

I drive back to Cat's place slowly, giving myself time to get my fucking head straight again. All my mom's crap leaves my mind when I pull up to the house and find Cat bent over the front of her mom's car, looking intently at the engine block. I smile, taking in her perfect body. She is so damn sexy.

I get out of my car, grab the new starter from the passenger seat, and make my way toward Cat. She looks up, startled, when I put my hand on her waist, but then she smiles widely and turns toward me, her hips leaning against the hood.

"I got the part," I say, reciprocating her dazzling smile. I let my eyes roll down Cat's body and she shivers under my gaze, which makes me want to do things to her I don't yet dare say out loud. I vow to take it easy, though. I care about her too much to fuck this up. Every minute I spend with this girl makes me fall harder and harder for her. So, I allow myself a brief moment of weakness, kiss her perfect lips softly, then step back from her with a smile.

"I better get to work," I say, and she nods before sitting, legs crossed, on the concrete driveway. I raise my eyebrows at her, astounded that she wants to watch, and she smiles back at me.

I have to admit, I like that she's sitting with me while I work.

Cat

I watch Ronan work, which is one of the sexiest sights I've had the pleasure of witnessing. I can't believe where my mind is going, but I can't deny how damn gorgeous he is. I'm totally lost to him, and I wonder if he feels the same way.

Finally, Ronan pulls back, letting out a deep breath. "Baby, do me a favor and see if you can get the car started," he says, and my heart gives a jolt at his new nickname for me.

I get up off the ground and slide into my mom's car, then turn the key to the ignition. The engine immediately turns over, and I smile broadly when I get out of the car and go to meet Ronan. "You did it," I exclaim. "Good job."

He gives the hood a shove to lock it into place and turns to me. There's a grease spot on his forearm and his hands are filthy, but his smile is bright and inviting. When I reach him, his smile falters and his gaze is intense as he wets his lips with his tongue.

"If you knew what effect you have on me..." Ronan says as he moves his lips closer to mine. His breath feathers against my skin, and my eyes shut of their own volition. I angle my chin up, wanting Ronan to caress my lips with his.

He meets my need when his soft lips touch mine, beckoning me for more. My lips part and his tongue enters my mouth, gently massaging my tongue. My hands find his chest and grab onto his shirt, pulling myself closer to him. He deepens the kiss, slowly tasting me. Heat flows through my body as I savor him, the tingling sensation pooling deep in my core, pressure beginning to build.

"Woah!" Vada's voice tears through the moment like ice water.

I pull away from Ronan, who's breathing shallowly, his hooded eyes resting on my lips a moment longer.

Vada stalks toward us, her mouth open, eyes wide. Her index finger is pointed at Ronan. "Oh. My. God! You two are totally making out!" she says, her voice pitchy and excited. "What's going on?"

I have a feeling she already knows the answer to her own question.

"Are you guys, like, together?" She stands with hands on hips, eyeing Ronan, then me, a look of incredulity on her face.

I turn toward Ronan, blushing.

"Yeah," Ronan says to Vada, but he's looking at me, his eyes soft.

"Holy shit! How long has this been going on? Why didn't you tell anyone?" she asks, her voice a mixture of excitement and accusation.

Ronan shrugs. "Have you ever had a dream that was so damn good, you wanted to keep it all to yourself?"

A wide smile makes its way across my face.

"Well, yeah, but those were usually dirty dreams." Vada grins, then hops up and down, clapping her hands, obviously happy that her mission has been accomplished. Though I'm not sure really how much she had to do with it, other than that she was why Ronan and I met.

"Ah," Vada squeals as I gently wrap my arms around Ronan's waist and lean into him. His greasy hands are still by his side, not wanting to dirty my clothes. "I'm so excited right now! Does anyone else know? Ran, I'm gonna kill your brother if he knew and didn't tell me."

Ronan shakes his head. "I haven't told anyone."

"Me neither," I say, and he smiles at me. "But I guess the cat is out of the bag now." I shrug against Ronan. "No pun intended."

The three of us make our way into the house, where Ronan disappears in the bathroom to scrub his hands. Vada and I wander into my room, where I lounge on my bed while Vada sits facing me.

"For real, how long has this been going on between you and Ran?"

I feel a little guilty not having shared something so big with her before now. "Since the night I kissed him at Murphy's," I admit sheepishly, and tell her what really happened when Ronan stumbled upon my house in the middle of the night while Vada was spending the night with Steve.

"Oh my god!" she exclaims. "I knew it! I knew he looked happy when he got home that night, but he didn't say shit. And this whole week while you were gone, he didn't give anything away. But I knew something was up." Vada is on her feet now, pacing in my room as she puts two and two together, connects the little dots. "And I asked him yesterday who he was talking to on the phone, if he was talking to a girl, and he was totally evasive. And here I was just laying into him about how I thought he should ask you out. Everyone agreed with me, too!" She smacks her hand against her forehead. "Well, almost everyone. Cheyenne will not be amused, but whatever."

"I know," I say. "When we hung out at Shane's on Ronan's birthday, she told me not to get involved with Ronan because he would leave me high and dry."

Vada lets out a huff while shaking her head. "I told you, she's had a thing for Ran for a while. But don't let that get between you and Ran."

"I'm not. I just don't want things to be weird with her since we hang out so much." And I certainly don't want a repeat of what happened in North Carolina, where people picked sides and I ended up getting the short end of the stick.

"What's weird?" Ronan steps into my room and looks around.

I sit up on my bed, very aware that he hasn't been in my bedroom, and I feel weirdly self-conscious.

"Nothing." Vada stops pacing. "Cheyenne is just being difficult, but I told Kitty Cat not to let it affect"—Vada forms a heart with her hands—"what's going on with you two." She winks and grins at Ronan.

He chuckles as he walks over to my bed and sits down, then finally pulls me toward him.

Vada looks at us for a moment and smiles. "I'm gonna give you two some space. Steve and I are heading to a movie tonight. Oh, and Ran, your brother is staying over at my house again."

"Yeah, he told me," Ronan says, and I notice that brief change in expression again, though I can't decipher it. It looks like a mixture of fear and frustration, but before I can analyze it more, it's gone. Ronan rubs his hand across his face. "When is your dad getting back from California?"

"Next Wednesday," Vada says. "Steve will probably be over at my house every night until then," she adds with a giggle.

"Right," Ronan says stiffly. I can see his wheels turning, though I have no idea what he's thinking about.

"Alright, I'm heading out. I'll see you guys later," Vada says, then leaves.

Ronan and I spend the afternoon together, and it feels like our first real chance to truly get to know each other. With each hour that passes, I fall more for him, learning small details about him, seeing the complexities and multiple facets of the boy sitting across from me.

And I tell him all about my trip to North Carolina, though I leave out the details of my run-in with Adam. I can tell Ronan is curious about it, but I change the subject, and he doesn't press me.

I want to know more about Ronan living in Montana, and he spends hours answering my questions about ranch life. He's so modest about his abilities, but I'm absolutely fascinated when I find out that he rides horses and is skilled at just about every aspect of Montana ranch life. At first glance he comes across as such a city boy, but talking to him, I can tell that Montana owns a huge piece of his heart. He likewise wants to know about my life in North Carolina, asking me about my friends, my family, my love for softball.

My mom peeks her head into my room here and there, but doesn't otherwise interrupt us, even as Ronan lies back on my bed and I lie perpendicular to him, resting my head on his chest, facing him. He softly runs his hand up and down my right arm, leaving a trail of goose bumps while I tell him about my life growing up.

At just past six my mom tells us that dinner is ready, and we join her downstairs. My mom, too, wants to know everything there is to know about Ronan; she peppers him with questions, and he answers politely.

When Ronan leaves just after nine, my mom accosts me as soon as I shut the door behind him.

"Umm, tell me again how you met him? Because I really like him; let's keep him," she giggles at me, and I bite my lip so as not to laugh. "How into him are you?"

"Really, really, *really* into him," I sigh, my heart fluttering in my chest.

Vada calls me a few minutes later, on her way back from the movies with Steve, eager to know how my afternoon with Ronan was.

"I still can't believe he didn't tell me," I hear Steve grumble in the background as I reminisce about my time with Ronan to Vada, who's still bubbling with excitement over the fact that Ronan and I are together, just as she had pushed for these past couple weeks.

"This is just too good," she shouts into the phone. "My best friend dating my other best friend, whose brother is my boyfriend. This is like rom-com material, seriously!" she squeals, and gushes about how ecstatic she is for me for another five minutes before we finally end the call.

After getting ready for bed, I climb under the covers, feeling the exhaustion from today's traveling in my bones. I fall asleep almost instantly.

A buzzing wakes me in the middle of the night. It takes me a minute to realize that my phone is vibrating on my nightstand. I reach for it and mentally note the time—3:19 a.m.—and the fact that the call is coming from an unidentified number. I hit the hang-up button, too sleepy to educate whoever it is that they probably have the wrong number. But just as I'm about to fall back asleep, my phone rings again, and a third time when I let it go to voicemail. When my phone rings for a fourth time, I worry it may be my dad trying to get ahold of me.

I answer the call. "Hello?" My voice comes out scratchy from sleep.

"I was beginning to think you're too damn good to answer my calls now," a deep male voice says on the other side of the phone.

I sit up, recognizing Adam's voice, despite his slow and slurred cadence. He must have been drinking.

"How did you get my number?" I ask. I changed my number while I still lived in North Carolina; the constant barrage of prank calls and threatening messages was overwhelming.

Adam chuckles. "Are you kidding me? You forget that this is a small town? Getting your new number was as easy for me as it was for you to get me arrested," he snarls. "But listen, I didn't call you to fight. I just still think you owe me a talk."

"I don't think I owe you anything, Adam," I respond, feeling braver now that he isn't physically present.

"Fuck, Cat, you seriously have a way with words. Why are you so hellbent on pissing me off? I treated you like a fucking princess and you repaid me by ruining my whole life." I can hear him pacing.

"I'm sorry about that," I say, feeling tiny, because I did ruin his whole life. I'm the reason Adam was kicked off the football team, the reason he couldn't play in the championships, the reason his scholarship to Duke was revoked, the reason he was arrested and put on probation, the reason he now has a criminal record that may impact his life forever.

"There you go. That wasn't so hard, right?" he says, his tone smug. "I tell you what, the next time you're in town, you should seriously consider finishing what you started. Hell, you spent four months just leading me on, getting me hornier than hell, and you never put out. But I'm willing to give you another chance." His voice is low now, and I'm beginning to feel nauseous. "Or maybe I should just come visit you in New York. You could make it up to me then."

"I have to go, Adam. Please don't call me again," I beg, my voice no longer brave but quiet. I hang up the phone without hearing his response.

I'm unable to go back to sleep. I lie in bed, thinking about the four months I spent with Adam, our physical altercations, the abusive words he spewed at me.

My family, my friends—at least, those who were still on my side after everything was said and done—keep telling me I did nothing wrong; that Adam had no right to hurt me; that the consequences to his actions were deserved.

But I can't help but feel responsible. A huge part of me does feel like I led him on and then rebuffed his efforts to be intimate. Honestly, I wasn't ready, and I didn't want to be intimate with him. I just didn't have an emotional connection with him. That's what every single one of our fights was about. Sex. And the fact that I didn't want to have it with him, yet he kept pushing and pushing, and pushing—not only emotionally, but physically, always escalating until he finally went too far. So why do I feel so bad? Why do I have such a hard time accepting that I did nothing wrong?

Saturday, June 12th

Cat

I'm still pondering the past when my phone buzzes again just past eight this morning. The sun is up; its fresh, newborn glow washes in through my windows. I look at my phone apprehensively but relax as soon as I see Vada's name.

"Isn't it a little early?" I ask when I answer the phone.

"Yeah, it's way too early," she yawns. "But I was telling Steve last night that we have softball camp in like two weeks and I haven't really worked out since our season ended, so he talked me into going to the gym with him this morning. I thought I'd pay it forward and convince you to join me. Pretty please?" She sounds desperate.

I laugh. "I don't think I'm up for it; I didn't really sleep well, Vada," I say, about to fall back onto my pillow.

"I have pretty reliable information that your boyfriend will be there as well," she teases, and my heart skips a beat. Weird how just minutes ago my heart felt heavy reliving the memories of my relationship with Adam, but then Ronan is brought up and I feel euphoric. This is already so unlike anything I ever felt with Adam. Even in the beginning of our relationship I was never this giddy to see Adam, never this excited to spend time with him.

"Alright," I giggle, unable to hide my enthusiasm. "How long do I have to get ready?"

"Like five minutes. Steve went home to change and I'm heading out the door now!"

I brush my teeth, pull my hair into a messy bun, and throw on some black workout pants and an olive-green racerback tank top at the speed of light. I rush down the stairs and slip my feet into my running shoes just as I hear Vada honk her horn outside. I only have time to yell at my mom that I'm going to the gym with Vada in response to her questioning look before I'm out the door and in Vada's car.

"Didn't take a lot of convincing." Vada eyes me as I buckle my seatbelt. "Now I know what carrot to dangle in front of your face anytime I want you to do something—Ronan!" She makes flirty eyes, blinking her eyelashes as she says his name.

I smack her shoulder. "Hey, you can't push me to date him and then hold it against me when I'm actually excited to spend time with him."

She laughs. "You're right. Plus, you guys are too cute together. He's gonna be so stoked to see you. He's probably gonna drop the weights," she laughs to herself.

The drive is short, and Vada pulls into a small parking lot outside of a converted warehouse. It's unlike the gyms I usually see. A large rollup door stands open, and I peek inside as Vada pulls her car into a spot right next to Steve's black Challenger. We get out and we walk into the gym.

I spot Ronan right away, like my eyes are drawn to him, and I smile watching him. He finishes a set of pull-ups with his back to me, muscles flexing as he pulls up his bodyweight over and over again with ease before he lets go of the bar and lands effortlessly on his feet.

As if he can sense my presence, he turns around and his eyes find me immediately. He clearly wasn't expecting to see me here; his eyebrows knit together for a second before he beams at me.

There's some kind of black tape strategically placed on his left shoulder and, as he approaches me, I see two dark, menacing bruises stretching from his left bicep all the way around to his shoulder blade.

"What happened?" I ask him, unable to take my eyes off his injury. I didn't really see his shoulders yesterday, but he didn't appear hurt when I saw him last.

"I'm fine," he says without further explanation, and all concern is erased from my mind when he pulls me into his arms as soon as I'm within reach of him. "What are you doing here?"

I shut my eyes for a moment, feeling his warmth radiate off his body. His scent is comforting.

"Steve made Vada work out, and she made me come, too," I complain loudly, but grin at Vada.

"Don't let her fool you, Ran. The second I told her you'd be here she was ready to sweat her little butt off." Vada drops her bag to the floor. "So, what are we doing, boys?"

"Uh, there's some cardio equipment upstairs," Zack chimes in, pointing in the direction of a metal staircase that leads to what appears to be a landing with some treadmills, ellipticals, and stationary bikes. I notice a small tripod set up with Zack's camera mounted on it. Apparently there truly isn't a moment Zack isn't filming.

Vada snorts, shaking her head. "Nah, we're here to do what the boys are doing. So what are we working on today?" She turns her attention to Steve.

He smiles proudly at her. "Back and shoulders. Better go warm up because I won't take it easy on you."

She smiles as she pulls me away with her to warm up.

Ronan

Looking at Cat, you'd never expect such a beast of an athlete. I should have known, though—she's been playing softball as long as I have hockey. She's obviously fit; her legs, arms, and stomach are toned, which I've certainly noticed before. Like, a lot. In fact, it's pretty much impossible for me not to notice with the inordinate amount of time I spend just staring at her like she's some goddess. She's kicking ass working out with us, and I'm having a hell of a time watching her push around weights. She has incredible form, and Zack is dumbfounded when she easily outnumbers his push-ups. And man, those tight black workout pants contour her curves in all the right places, leaving little to the imagination. I have to work to keep a straight head. The need to touch her, to kiss her, is overwhelming. I'm definitely distracted by her presence, something Shane points out to me about a handful of times over the couple of hours we spend at the gym.

As soon as Vada found out about Cat and me yesterday, she spread the word. First to my brother, obviously, then Tori, who in turn told Shane, who literally called me at midnight to find out if the rumor was true. And when I met up with Steve, Shane, and Zack this morning, they immediately requested firsthand confirmation, whooping and high-fiving me like I just won the fucking lottery. And honestly, I feel like I did.

I still feel weird talking about Cat and me. Not because I'm embarrassed or anything, but because she's the one thing in my life that makes me so completely happy that I feel like if I say it out loud, I'm going to jinx it. I feel vulnerable with her, which is a feeling I've spent my life avoiding. Vulnerability is not a good thing where I'm from; it exposes me to pain. Although I can't say that not being vulnerable has spared me before.

I was right: failing to let my parents know I would be sleeping over at Shane's, followed by not putting away *all* the laundry yesterday and the resultant telephone call with my mother didn't go unpunished. Steve wasn't home last night, and my dad had left for Germany just hours earlier, which created the perfect fucking storm.

When I got home from spending the afternoon and evening with Cat, my mother immediately cornered me in the hallway.

I could tell she had spent the last several hours stewing, getting more pissed off by the minute, and she didn't hold back once she was finally face-to-face with me. She laid into me for a good ten minutes, screaming about what a stupid, disrespectful fuck-up I am, and reminding me over and over how worthless and irrelevant my life is. I didn't say anything, didn't defend myself. I could tell she was trying to get a rise out of me, to provoke me into talking back, which would give her a reason to punish me more.

She does that sometimes. She tries to pick a fight with me, to get me to overstep, and it works more often than I want it to, especially when she starts insulting things or people I really care about. It didn't work last night, though, because I'm used to her personal attacks, used to her telling me what a worthless piece of shit I am. I'm so used to her words by now that they hardly make an impact. What did make an impact, though, was when she picked up one of her wooden clogs—shoes she wears to her job as a nurse—and began hammering it into my body again and again while she screamed at me. And, again, I didn't defend myself. I let her beat me, taking the blows and the pain, until she abruptly decided it was enough. She dropped the shoe, told me to get the fuck out of her face, and walked back into the living room.

But all of this doesn't matter. Not here, not now that Cat's by my side, looking absolutely incredible in her tight black workout leggings and a racerback that keeps diverting my attention to her toned shoulders and the soft skin of her back. By the time we're finished with our workout, Cat has worked up enough of a sweat that her skin glistens when the light hits it just right, and little beads of sweat roll down her delicate neck to her collarbone, then disappear under her shirt. She's stunning with her damp shirt clinging to her body, and the primitive, irrational side of me wants nothing more than to pull her into the locker room, undress her slowly, caress her skin until she can't take it anymore, and then thrust my dick inside her so I can feel her soft body.

"Stop drooling!" Shane purposely bumps into me and grins at having caught me checking out Cat for the millionth time.

"I don't think I can," I admit as I watch Cat put away the dumbbells she just finished using.

He nods at me approvingly. "I'm glad you went for it with her. You deserve good things, and judging by that look on your face, she's good for you."

I make a doubtful face. "Yeah, let's just hope I'm good for her, too," I say, picking up my own, heavier dumbbells.

"Stop overthinking and just enjoy this," he scolds me. "Cat is smart; trust that she'll tell you what she needs."

Cat comes walking back toward me, and I swear, I still can't believe I get to call her mine. She undoes her hair and shakes it out just to gather it back up and secure it on her head again. She is so fucking beautiful, both inside and out, and I've been attracted to her like a moth to a flame since the moment I laid eyes on her. If only I could allow myself to feel all of it, to live in the moment and forget about my demons.

But I push it all aside for the moment when Cat stops in front of me, smiling. I take in her face. Her hazel eyes are a deep green in the late-morning light, gold flecks speckling her irises. She has freckles on her nose and cheeks, which are flushed from the physical exertion, and her lips are full and so irresistible that I take her right hand, pull her toward me, and kiss her without regard for who's around us.

Her lips are soft as she kisses me back. She parts them so I can slip my tongue into her mouth and taste her like I've been starving. If it weren't for Zack's wolf whistling, I would be happy kissing her without end.

We break apart slowly, and I smile when I notice Cat's glossed-over eyes. Her lips are still slightly parted, not ready for me to stop tasting her. I stroke her cheek with my left thumb. Her eyes close under my touch, and my heart hammers in my chest as it threatens to break apart over this girl. I know there is no turning back with her.

"So, what now?" Vada asks, sounding decidedly winded.

"We fuel," Shane proclaims, and both Vada and Cat raise their eyebrows. "We go eat," Shane clarifies, then grabs his backpack off the floor and swings it over his shoulder before marching out to the parking lot.

We decide to head to Murphy's for lunch, and Vada throws me a dirty look when Cat asks her if she would be upset if Cat rode with me.

"Already choosing your boytoy over your friend. I see how it is. Apparently sisters before misters means nothing to you," Vada accuses Cat, who immediately looks guilt-stricken. "No, Kitty Cat, I'm totally joking. Of course, I'm cool with you riding with Ran; I honestly didn't expect anything else," Vada assures Cat, whose expression changes to relief.

"Be nice," I scold Vada, and I take Cat's hand in mine to lead her around to the passenger side of my car, where I open the door for her.

"Or what?" Vada challenges me as Cat gets into my car and I close the door behind her.

"Or I'm going to tell your dad where you really spend your nights." I grin at her and get into my car before she can find the right words to protest. She stands with her mouth open, shocked that I would threaten to disclose her secret like that. Of course I would never actually do it, and Vada knows as much, but it's a good threat to keep her from going overboard. Vada tends to speak first and think later—no filter, as Steve likes to say—which can be good, but she can also hurt people with her silver tongue.

As soon as I get into my car I take Cat's hand, no longer worried about being too obvious or coming on too strong. I know our feelings for each other are mutual. I move her hand and rest it on the gear stick, then place my own hand on top of hers, allowing me to feel her skin while I drive. She has a smile on her face the entire drive, which is decidedly too damn short, and I wish I could spend more alone time with Cat right here, right now.

It's eleven-thirty when we walk into Murphy's, and the place is already busy with the usual weekend brunch crowd. I don't usually work the day shifts since Shane typically closes and likes it when I'm around to help him shut the place down. Plus, during the school months working during the day is obviously impossible, so I've been working after class and hockey practice, mostly to get out of the house.

I wouldn't really need to work if I didn't want to. My dad transfers money into Steve's and my bank accounts monthly, but it's another way to avoid being at home and getting into sticky situations. And the extra cash doesn't hurt. I've been saving; I'm dead set on getting far away from here the second I graduate.

My ideal plan would be to get a full-ride scholarship to some college. My parents make good money, but we're not wealthy by any means, and I'm not sure they would be able—or willing—to pay for out-of-state college tuition. My mom has already made it blatantly clear that I'll be on my own once I turn eighteen, and honestly, that's fine with me. I hate that I'm not yet of age, that I don't really have a choice than to stay in that damn house until I graduate in May—not if I want to ensure that my secret stays nice and hidden. No one knows what my mom does to me. Well, with the exception of Shane and my ex-girlfriend, Miranda. But Shane doesn't know the full extent of things, and Miranda lives in Montana—or at least she did when I was there two years ago. I had heard she left the state soon after I moved back to New York, and I haven't had any contact with her since I was fifteen.

If I can't get into a college with a good scholarship, I guess I'll figure out something else, but regardless of what that something else is, I'll move far away from that hellhole the minute I'm able. That's if I survive the next twelve months.

I'm already dreading this next school year. Steve is moving up to Boston at the end of August to attend college, and as I don't see my dad's work assignment changing anytime soon, it means it'll only be my mother and me at home—a perfect recipe for disaster. Just thinking about it makes my chest constrict.

Once we make it to Murphy's, the six of us walk to our table in the back of the pub, and I let go of Cat's hand, allowing her to slide into her chair before I sit down next to her. I stay close enough that her shoulder brushes against mine as she reaches for the menu, and I flinch as pain shoots down my arm. My mother's beating last night left some gnarly bruises on my left side, and my shoulder is pretty banged up. She ended up taping it. She does that all the time, doctors the injuries she inflicts on me.

"I'm so sorry. Are you okay?" Cat asks with a guilty look.

"Yeah, I'm fine," I say quickly.

"What happened?" she asks again, a crease between her eyebrows as she looks me over with concern in her eyes.

"I tripped over Onyx when I got home last night." It's scary how easily I'm able to come up with excuses for injuries, but it's something I have a lot of experience in, and I don't even bat an eye as I do it.

"And what, you fell out of the second-story window?" Zack says. "Those bruises look painful."

I chuckle, plastering a fake smile on my face. "No, but I fell onto the damn stairs. I should have turned on the hallway light, I guess."

"It looks like it hurts," Cat says, and her fingertips caress my arm gently, causing goose bumps to travel all the way down into my hand.

"It's a lot better now," I say, meaning it. "Your touch feels good."

She smiles at me, a pink hue creeping up her cheeks.

Casey, one of the Murphy's waitresses, walks toward our table. "Hi everyone," she says with a smile before she gives me a quick wink and touches my left forearm.

"Hey Casey," Shane says. "How has it been today so far?" he asks, going into work mode.

"Busy as usual for a Saturday morning," she says, wiping her brow with her forearm. "Jenna called out, but Tyler was able to come in, which is good. What time are you coming in today?"

"Five," he says. "Ran, too," Shane adds with a nod in my direction.

Casey turns to me, an even bigger smile on her face. "Awesome. I won't get off until eight. I'm excited to hang out with you guys for a little bit," she adds. "Are you guys ready to order?"

We go around the table ordering our food and drinks, and Casey eyes Cat intensely as Cat wavers between two menu options before deciding on a traditional Irish breakfast.

"How about you, Ran?" Casey touches my forearm yet again as if to get my attention, even though she already has it.

"Just scrambled eggs and some turkey bacon, please," I say.

"Are you sure?" she asks. "That doesn't seem like enough to feed a big boy like you."

"I'm sure."

"Okay." She shrugs. "Food should be out in about fifteen minutes." She turns to walk away, but not before looking Cat up and down again.

"Bitch," Vada mumbles, and all eyes turn to her. "What? Did you see the way she was eyeing Cat?"

Zack laughs. "Uh-huh. She wasn't subtle at all. Girls are so catty. No pun intended."

"Why, though?" Cat asks me.

Zack answer for me. "Probably because she and Ran"—he motions his hands to indicate sex—"and like so many girls Ran hooked up with, she was hoping to take it further. But Ran over here always kept it strictly business... or maybe I should say he kept it strictly pleasure," Zack laughs.

My brother snorts a laugh, and even Shane looks like he has to work hard to keep a straight face.

I throw Zack a death stare, feeling the urge to sucker punch him for telling Cat about my prior promiscuity. He's not wrong: I did hook up with Casey at one of Shane's parties back in February or March. It was stupid. A lot of my hookups were stupid, actually. I don't even really know why I did it other than to fill some void inside me, to numb the pain or whatever.

It started when I was fifteen and we moved back to New York. I quickly found that I had no problems getting girls to hook up with me. One-night stands became a regular occurrence, and I'd have sex with a new girl almost every weekend. I made it a rule never to give out my number, and I didn't take theirs, either, letting them know right from the start that I had no intention of taking this any further than just a casual fuck. And most of the time the girls were fine with it. Occasionally feelings would get hurt, and then I'd have to deal with a week or two of whispering and angry side-glances if the girl happened to go to school with me, but it never really deterred other girls from sleeping with me. In fact, many of them sought me out, and I was usually more than willing to oblige. That all came to a complete halt, of course, the minute I met Cat.

"Huh, that makes sense," Cat says, and I can't tell if she's merely feigning or truly is as confident as she sounds. She takes my hand into hers and, very carefully, leans against my taped-up shoulder. "I'd want more, too. I guess I should consider myself lucky," she says with a smile.

"You should," Steve agrees. "Do you know that you're only one of two girls my little brother has been in a relationship with?"

"Okay, can you guys stop talking about me like I'm not here and switch the damn subject to anything other than my sex life?" I groan.

"But what's the fun in that, Ran?" Steve asks with a malicious grin on his face. "There's so much to talk about."

"Yeah, like how you had sex with Candace Bell under the bleachers *during* the damn homecoming game? Such a ballsy fucking move," Zack says, nodding approvingly.

"Or remember that one time at Shane's party when some asshole spilled his drink all over you and you told us you were going to take a quick shower and some random chick asked if she could join you?" Steve chimes in. "And then she actually did!"

"Seriously, guys, drop it! Please." I'm worried that all of this will be too much for Cat and scare her away, especially given that, according to Vada, Cat doesn't have much experience at all. I don't want her to think I'm only with her for this one thing, because that's as far from reality as can be. "And also, can you stop filming for a fucking second?" I beg Zack with a nod at his damn camera.

He smirks at me. "I'll never stop filming, and I don't really feel like dropping this subject." Zack leans back in his chair.

"Well, then maybe we should start talking about your sex life, too," Shane says. "Or rather the lack thereof."

"What the fuck are you talking about?" Zack asks, his brow creasing now. "I'm with Summer."

"Yeah," Shane says, "but remember when you and Summer first got together and you were whining one night about how nervous you were about your first time with her, and how Ran had to talk you through how to give a girl a manual orgasm?"

Zack turns beet red. "Hey, what the fuck, man? I talked to you guys in confidence about that shit."

"Then maybe we should honor Ran's request and change the subject." Shane shrugs and grins at me.

"Wait, wait, wait," Vada says, and only then do I realize she has tears in her eyes. She's holding her side because she's laughing so hard she can barely breathe. "Ran really had to tell you how to get a girl off manually?"

"Oh, shut the fuck up," Zack huffs, crossing his arms in front of his chest, looking embarrassed and pissed off.

"But, like, really though?" Vada wheezes. "What, did you have trouble finding it?" she adds, barely able to get the words out before dissolving into another fit of laughter.

"You know what..." Zack starts but doesn't finish his sentence when Vada's laugh turns into a shriek and she leans onto Steve, who is very much enjoying this turn in the conversation.

"I need to use the bathroom," Zack says, anger tingeing his voice. He stands abruptly before striding away.

"Hope you find it," Vada calls after her twin brother with a wicked laugh.

Our breakfast comes. We eat and chat about nothing in particular. Once again, I'm content with my company and enjoy having Cat next to me. I can't help but glance at her again and again; I'm distracted by her presence and drawn to her like a magnet.

Saturday, June 26th

Cat

Ronan and I spend almost every day together over the next couple of weeks, and each minute I spend with him makes me yearn for even more. We spend our time together hanging out with our friends, though we both crave alone time, which is hard to come by. Although my mom tries to work from home a few times a week, her obligations to her patients frequently require her to leave the house, saddling me with the responsibility of looking after my siblings. Ronan is nothing but patient and understanding, and he spends time with me and my siblings whenever he can. I actually think my sister, Samantha, has developed a crush on Ronan because she gets almost as excited to see him as I do.

Ronan and I spend time at his house only twice, each time making a pit stop for him to change into his work clothes before we head back to my place to spend a few hours together before he heads into work. I don't think much of it, to be honest. I don't really care where we spend our time; I just enjoy being with him.

Whenever Ronan works, I try to make it to Murphy's for a few hours, and although we don't get to interact a whole lot, it's still comforting—and sexy as hell—to watch him. I notice how frequently Ronan gets hit on while he works. He politely rejects any advances, and I relish that he makes a regular point to steal a kiss from me. And at the end of the day, I'm the one who gets to be with him.

I've also been hitting the gym with Ronan, the guys, and Vada, which, often ends up with Vada and Shane scolding Ronan and me for getting distracted by each other. What can I say? Ronan is nice to look at, and it doesn't help things when he's pumped and sweaty.

Whenever I'm with Ronan—and even when I'm not—my mind tends to wander, and I find myself thinking about what it would be like to be with him all the way. Whenever he touches me, my body immediately responds and I long for more. But we never get too far.

What happened with Adam still haunts me, casting a shadow over my new relationship, and I hesitate to open up completely, to let down my guard, to let Ronan in all the way. And the other reason why we never get further than a hot ten-minute make-out session is that we're never alone long enough to explore each other. We'll get interrupted by a phone call, or someone will walk in on us. Vada, in particular, has a real thing for barging in on Ronan and me, usually just as things are getting hot and heavy. And though Ronan never, ever pushes me or makes me feel bad, I can tell he's frustrated by the constant interruptions. I know it's not about sex for him but our ability to be together, alone, which is further impeded by Ronan's overfull schedule. He's been working a lot, has been working out with Shane almost daily, and on top of that, conditioning for hockey started a few days ago. And I get the impression there's something else going on. I sometimes catch him pensively staring into nothingness, and he startles when I approach. But whenever I mean to ask him about it, he distracts me with a kiss or a joke.

"Here are your cleats, Kitty," my mom says as she walks into my room. I've been packing for the last thirty minutes because Vada, Tori, and I are heading to Buffalo tomorrow for five days for training camp for our varsity softball team. It's apparently something our coach does every year, as Vada told me, and now I'm getting ready to leave for the second time this summer. "Do you need anything else?" my mom asks as she hands me my cleats.

I pack them into my gym bag along with my bat and three fresh uniforms. "No, I think I'm good," I say, my hands on my hips as I contemplate what else I need.

"Okay, then I'm going to take Sam and Benny shopping with me. I promised them ice cream after, so we won't be back for a while," she says and turns to leave, but stops abruptly and turns back to me. "When is Ronan coming over?"

I smile at my mom's mention of his name. "He should be here in a few minutes," I say, grinning from ear to ear as excitement spreads through my body.

"Well, then you better finish packing so you can spend some quality alone time with your boyfriend."

She's right. I finish packing the rest of my stuff while my mom gets my siblings, herds them into the car, and leaves.

There's a knock on the front door just a few minutes later, and I giddily bound down the stairs, taking two at once, and yank the door open, feeling breathless.

"Woah, are you alright?" Ronan chuckles as he steps into the house.

I didn't see him at all yesterday because we were both busy—Ronan with work and conditioning, and me watching my brother and sister while my mom had emergency patients to see.

"I'm fine, just couldn't wait to see you," I say, catching my breath. "You got a haircut!"

Ronan's hair is my favorite kind of effortlessly tousled on top with longer strands falling across his forehead, but his hair fades and is tightly cropped around the back and sides of his head. I run my hand over his neck and the back of his head, loving the feeling of his fresh cut. He must love the feeling, too, because his eyes close as soon as my fingers begin to caress his skin. I can't help it—I kiss his lips softly as I urge my body closer to his.

I've been feeling adventurous, braver, more eager to test my boundaries with him, and for some reason, I feel extra feisty today. Maybe it's because I know I won't get to soak in his presence, his warmth, his energy for a few days, and it makes my heart ache. How is it even possible to have only known someone for a month and already be so lost to them?

Ronan's hands find my hips, and he pulls me against him. My whole body touches his, and I part my lips to allow him entrance. We kiss like this for a few minutes before he reluctantly breaks the contact, then takes a small step back to look into my eyes. I swear he has a way of looking directly into my soul.

"So, training camp tomorrow, huh?" he asks, his voice husky. I can still taste him on my lips.

"Unfortunately." I slide my hand from his neck down his chest to rest it on his side. "So, what should we do with the last few hours we have together?" I ask, forcing my voice to sound innocent as I blink up at him.

A mischievous grin forms on his full lips. "I can think of a few things."

"Oh yeah? Like what?" I ask, raising one eyebrow.

He takes my hand into his. "I'll show you." He leads me out of the hallway, through the living room, and up the stairs to my room.

My heart speeds up with each step, anticipating his touch. My senses are heightened, my nerves under tension as I analyze myself, trying to figure out how far I want this to go.

As soon as we get to my room, Ronan's lips are on mine, searing hot as our tongues explore each other. His hands find my low back, sending ripples of excitement through my core. Goose bumps erupt when Ronan's fingers sneak under the hem of my shirt to gently stroke the bare skin of my back.

I don't think I have control over my body at this point; I follow suit and carefully slide my right hand underneath his shirt. My fingers discover the contours of Ronan's firm stomach, outlining his abs, tracing each ridge. I push his shirt up to gain access to more of him, reveling in the feel of him as his lips leave mine to trace my jawline before he kisses my neck.

"You are so beautiful, Cat," Ronan whispers against my skin, sending shivers down my spine. Ronan slowly glides his hand up my back. The feel of his fingers on my bare skin is intoxicating, and I moan softly while my fingers roam his chest. God, his skin is so warm, so soft. My other hand moves underneath Ronan's shirt, up his side, feeling his ribs as I push up the hem of his shirt even more, exposing him to me.

He hesitates for a second, studying my eyes, then reaches his left hand over his head and tugs his shirt off, dropping it to the floor. It's the first time he's done this, the first time we've gotten to any sort of state of undress, and my heart speeds up, hammering against my chest, testing its resolve. I let my eyes roam his naked torso, marveling at his sun-kissed, smooth skin, his lean, muscular shoulders, arms, and chest, his sexy stomach. But before I can get too distracted, Ronan crashes his lips against mine and I'm immediately lost in the feeling of him touching me again. My hands are everywhere, exploring the landscape of his back and shoulders before sliding across his ribs and coming to rest on his chest. His heart hammers against his ribs, and his breathing is as erratic as mine.

"Cat?" my mom calls from downstairs.

My eyes fly open, meeting Ronan's.

"Of course," he groans quietly, then takes a step back. His hands retreat from my skin as he picks up his shirt off the floor and pulls it back over his head.

"Kitty, are you upstairs?" my mom calls again, making her way up the stairs.

I adjust my shirt, making sure I don't look too disheveled as I try to get my breathing under control. It feels like I just got off an amazing rollercoaster ride that ended too soon. "Yeah, Mom. What's up?" I say, my voice pitchy. I run my hands through my hair. This is beyond frustrating.

"Hey," she says as she reaches my doorway. I didn't close the door when Ronan led me upstairs, expecting to have the house to ourselves for a couple of hours, and both Ronan and I stand awkwardly in the middle of my room. "Hi Ronan," she adds, and smiles warmly at him.

He reciprocates the smile, though I can tell he's working hard to calm himself down, sobering himself up as quickly as humanly possible.

I smile to myself, knowing I turn him on so much. It makes me feel beautiful and, yeah, powerful.

"I'm really sorry, I feel like I always interrupt you two. But I just got a call." She turns her attention to me. "I need to run to the clinic; I have a patient in crisis and need to see him right now. I'm sorry, Kitty," she adds, looking crestfallen.

"It's alright, Mom." I don't want her to feel bad for doing her job, for helping people. "Where are Benny and Sam?" I ask, and move to take Ronan's hand. He interlaces his fingers with mine.

"Downstairs. Benny is really upset because I promised them ice cream," she sighs, shaking her head.

"We'll take them for ice cream," Ronan says, like it's a given thing. My mom beams at him while I stare at his perfect profile and marvel at how selfless this boy is and how I got so damn lucky.

"Oh my gosh, that would be amazing. Thank you!" My mom throws her arms around Ronan's neck, hugging him tightly. He raises his eyebrows at me, one hand still holding mine while his other arm is by his side, unsure of what to do with my mom's affection toward him, and I giggle. My mom releases Ronan from her hug. "I'm going to head out, then. I promise I'll make this up to you guys somehow. Hopefully I didn't interrupt too much." She winks at us with a grin and walks out of my room.

I have a hard time reading Ronan; his face is serious and his jaw tense. "Are you okay?"

His expression softens. "Yeah, I'm fine. Should we go and take Sam and Benny to get ice cream?"

I nod, and we make our way into the living room where, to the absolute jubilation of my little brother and sister, I announce that Ronan is going to take us to get ice cream. We shepherd my siblings into Ronan's car, and he grabs my hand just as I'm about to hop into the passenger seat, pulling me toward him.

"You have no idea how sorry I am that we don't ever seem to have time to ourselves," he whispers, our lips only an inch apart. My eyelids shut, waiting for him to close the last bit of distance and kiss me. He chuckles in a low voice before he gives me what I crave and grazes his lips softly against mine. But it's not enough; my hunger for him is reawakened, and I part my lips, intensifying our kiss, tasting him on my tongue, wanting to continue where we left off.

"Ew," Benny whines from the backseat, and Samantha starts giggling.

Ronan and I break apart, and I see my resignation reflected in his eyes. I give him an apologetic smile and a quick kiss on his cheek before I slide into the passenger seat and he closes the door behind me.

***

We drive fifteen minutes to a small Italian gelateria, where Benny's and Sam's eyes become huge when they see the variety of ice cream flavors. Despite their tiny statures, each picks two giant scoops of ice cream.

"Could I get a scoop of strawberry?" I ask the girl behind the counter, and she places a perfectly round blob of pink ice cream in a cone for me. "How about you?" I ask Ronan, but he shakes his head. "Wait, don't you like ice cream?" I ask, my right hand resting on his forearm; I'll take any chance to have physical contact with him, regardless of how small.

"Not really," he admits.

I cock my head to the side. I don't know that I've ever met someone who didn't like ice cream. "Really?" I question as I take my cone from the girl behind the counter. "Oh no you're not." I stop Ronan as he's in the process of paying for the ice cream.

He laughs. "Why not?"

I shake my head vehemently. "Because I'm an independent woman who can pay for her own things. You're not paying for anyone's ice cream today, sir!" I pronounce with a grin, and pull some cash out of my jeans pocket and hand it to the girl.

"Oh, okay, sorry Miss Independent," Ronan laughs while I take my change and shove it into my pocket. Ronan and I wander to the table Benny and Sam are already occupying. The two of them are absolutely devouring their ice cream and I remind them to slow down, but I might as well be speaking Chinese with a cow. I start eating my scoop of strawberry gelato, and it gets quiet for a minute before I feel Ronan's eyes on me.

"What?" I ask, noting the mischievous grin on his face.

"I have to say, I enjoy watching you eat your ice cream," he says in a suggestive tone.

But two can play that game. "What, like this?" I sensually lick the melting ice cream off the cone before closing my lips over the scoop, then lick the ice cream off my lips.

Ronan narrows his eyes, his gaze flitting between my eyes and my mouth. "Yeah, like that," he says, his voice gravelly.

My heart flutters in my chest. "Are you sure you wouldn't like a small taste?" I ask, and take another lick of my strawberry ice cream before I lean into him and part my lips.

He doesn't need to be asked twice. With his left hand under my chin, he angles my face up before brushing his lips against mine. His tongue carefully enters my mouth as he tastes me, then licks my lips before he pulls back.

"You guys are so gross," Benny exclaims with chocolate ice cream all over his face.

"Dude, come talk to me again in ten years," Ronan chuckles, and I watch him take a napkin and wipe Benny's face clean. I'm so taken aback by Ronan. He is so different from the guys I've known before, and certainly a complete one-eighty from Adam.

***

We finish our ice cream and clamber into Ronan's car. Back at my house, Benny and Sam ransack the kitchen, tear open a bag of chips, and make themselves at home in front of the TV.

"Do you really not like ice cream?" I whisper into Ronan's ear after I crawl onto the couch next to him.

He wraps his arms around me, pulling me toward him. "No," he says, his tone neutral. "It's not something I grew up with."

I look at him, trying to decipher if he's joking. "What do you mean? You didn't eat ice cream as a kid?"

He shakes his head. "No. No ice cream, no candy. It wasn't really available on my grandparents' ranch, and here..."

I scan his face. His green eyes are unfocused. "Here what?"

He swallows hard, then seems to snap out of it. He focuses his attention on me and smiles. "My mom just isn't a fan of junk, so she didn't let me have it growing up." Though that's a perfectly reasonable explanation, I feel like there's more to his story.

"But wait, I've seen Steve eat plenty of junk at Shane's, and at the movies he definitely chowed down on a huge package of red vines." I remember Vada joking to me that Steve has even more of a sweet tooth than she does, which is saying a lot.

Ronan only shrugs, and I get the distinct impression he no longer wishes to talk about this. I put an earmark in this conversation, determined to come back to this; it just doesn't make sense to me.

"What time are you guys heading out tomorrow?" he asks, and I can tell he's eager for a subject change.

I oblige, hoping to relieve the tension that has seized his shoulders. "The bus leaves at seven," I wince. "I'm still not an early bird." I close my eyes as Ronan kisses my head, and I snuggle against him, enjoying his arms around me and the warmth of his body. How does he always manage to make me feel so safe?

"But you've been coming to the gym with me in the mornings," he says.

I nod into his chest. "Yes, but getting to see you first thing in the morning is a much better incentive than getting on some bus for a seven-hour ride to Buffalo."

Ronan chuckles. "Fair enough." He lifts his arm to look at his watch, then sighs. "Baby, I have to get going. I still need to change and then get to Murphy's."

He pulls me in tighter, kissing my head again before he lets go of me and gets to his feet. "Hey, little people," he says to Benny and Sam, who turn their attention from the TV to Ronan. "Be good to your sister; she's pretty awesome. I'll see you guys later," he says, making me smile a stupid happy smile.

I follow Ronan into the hallway, where he turns to me, gently places his hands on my hips and pulls me into him again. "What are you doing to me?" he sighs, and even though I don't think he actually expects an answer from me, I feel the need to provide him with one.

"Hopefully the exact same thing you're doing to me," I say, and for some reason there's a knot in my stomach. I know it's ridiculous; we've only been seeing each other for a little over three weeks, and I'll only be gone for five days, but I can't help the way I feel about him. I just don't want to be away from him.

He searches my eyes, and I detect sadness in his, so I angle my face up and kiss his lips softly.

"I'll miss you," he says against my lips, "but I hope you have fun."

"I'll miss you, too, and I'll try really hard to have fun. I promise."

He smiles at me, then kisses me deeply before letting go of me and heading out the door.

Ronan

I know exactly what Cat is doing to me. She's breaking down every wall I've ever built, my carefully constructed cocoon meant to shield me from vulnerability, and she's making me fall hard and fast in love with her.

Being with her is unlike anything I've ever experienced. Even when I was with Miranda—the only other serious relationship I've ever had—it was nothing like being with Cat. Granted, I was fourteen, and Miranda was my first *everything*. We were together the whole year I lived in Montana. She was forbidden: two years older than me; the daughter of the pastor whose church my grandparents, and by extension I, attended religiously every Sunday; a freaking rebel, hell-bent on defying her father's stiflingly strict rules. So we started sneaking out together, getting high on pills and weed, drinking, having sex in the backseat of her truck or the pew of her father's church after Sunday service when everyone was in the mess hall having lunch. It was exciting and dangerous, but it wasn't a relationship meant to last. It was an escape for both of us, each from our own private hell.

After Miranda, there were only random one-night stands, hookups, and meaningless sex to scratch the itch, but I never allowed it to go further than that. But with Cat it's all different. I feel seen with her—truly, deeply seen—which scares the shit out of me because I worry about what'll happen when she sees all of me and realizes how broken and fucked up my life is. How broken and fucked up I am. So part of me waits for the day she'll recognize that I'm not enough for her, just like I'm not enough for my mom.

Sometimes I get the feeling Cat knows something is off by the questions she asks. Like the ice cream thing today. The truth is that my mother never allowed me to have any of it, but not because she's against junk food per se. She let Steve have it. It was just a way for her to withhold something I wanted, so I learned to just *not* want it.

***

The drive back home from Cat's house takes me less than five minutes, and dread overcomes me the second I spot my mom's car in the driveway but not Steve's. I bet he's spending his evening with Vada, soaking up as much time with her as he can before she leaves for the better part of a week, just like I had wanted to do with Cat.

I park on the curb in front of my house, shut off the engine, and take a few deep breaths. I hope my mom is in a good enough mood and that any interaction I have with her today will be civil. But the moment I step foot in my house, I pick up on the negative vibe and my body tenses.

My mother is in the kitchen, pacing left to right across the tiled floor, her shoes click-clacking. She's holding her phone to her ear, talking loudly, arguing. The second she makes eye contact with me, her eyes livid, I know who she's arguing with—my dad—and that I better get my stuff and get the hell out of here. I contemplate my strategy; all I need to do is get upstairs, change into my work clothes, and leave. Simple.

"No, your responsibility is to your family, Frank," I hear my mother hiss into the phone. "You think it's easy raising two teenage boys alone while you're off living the life you've always wanted, only coming home whenever the fuck you feel like it? You've been coming home less and less, and I'm tired!"

I hurry upstairs, listening intently to my mother's voice, which becomes louder by the second until she's yelling into the phone. In my room, I kick off my shoes and yank open my closet door, desperate to find my shirt. It takes me way too long to retrieve the black long-sleeve with the Murphy's logo, but when I finally do I hastily pull it over my head.

Then I realize that my mother's shouting has stopped.

I stop in my tracks, hoping she's still on the phone, but I don't hear anything else. No voices, no pacing. *Get a move on*. I slip my arms through the sleeves, pull the shirt down over my torso, and put on my black ballcap.

I'm not fast enough, though.

My mother is leaning against the fridge in the kitchen as I step off the staircase and reach for the doorknob, almost tasting the fresh air.

"Ronan." My mother's voice is sharp as she says my name, and my breath gets trapped in my chest. Anxiety claws at me, and I close my eyes, willing my feet to move me forward. Finally, I turn my head toward the kitchen. She's not looking at me, but I can tell by the sound of her voice, her posture, the way her thumb is spinning the simple silver wedding band on her ring finger, that whatever she has to say to me isn't going to be good.

Her voice comes out clipped. "Get over here."

I wish I had it in me to just defy her, take the three steps that separate me from the outside world, and drive away to safety. But that's not what I've been conditioned to do. Instead, my body betrays me. My legs carry me to the right, down the hallway, and to the doorway to the kitchen where I stop. My shoulders hurt with the tension seizing my muscles, anticipating what comes next, bracing for pain.

"I thought I told you to clean out the fridge yesterday, did I not?" my mom says against gritted teeth.

"You did." My voice is feeble, which pisses me off. I'm not small by any means. I'm over six feet tall and weigh maybe 175 pounds. I'm muscular—lean and conditioned. But in my mother's presence I feel tiny, weak, and like I'm five years old. She's the reason I work out as much and as hard as I do. I had the honest belief that if I got stronger, bigger, she would back off a little, but it's almost like the complete opposite has occurred. She just hits me harder now.

"So why did I find moldy bread in here this afternoon?" She points to a loaf of bread on the counter.

"I haven't had a chance to do it yet, Mom. I had practice yesterday and then I worked last night," I try to defend myself, knowing it's useless. I could be running a fortune one-hundred company, and all she would see is the fact I didn't do what she told me to do.

She pushes off the fridge, facing me. Her face is contorted with anger. "So did I, Ronan. I work every god damn day to make sure that you—spoiled, ungrateful little brat—have a roof over your head, food on the table, and gas in that fucking car of yours. And you repay me by dodging your responsibilities, not doing your chores, giving me lip, and not following the rules. And I'm really fucking tired of your shit and your weak excuses, Ronan. You're not the only one who lives in this house!" Her voice is pitchy as she yells at me. "You are such a fucking failure, Ronan. All I ask is for you to contribute at home, but you can't fucking do that because either you're too fucking lazy or too fucking stupid. Which one is it, Ronan?" She puts her palms against my chest and pushes me backwards. "Which one, Ronan? I asked you a god damn question. Are you stupid or are you lazy?"

She shoves me again when I don't answer.

"Or is it both? Answer me!"

What am I supposed to say? Her words aren't meant to elicit a response; they're meant to injure. And they hit the mark, slowly eroding my self-worth, wiping out any trace of confidence and self-respect left after years of being told I'll never be good enough.

She walks back into the kitchen where she grabs the broom off its hook, and I know without a shadow of doubt what's going to happen next. This has been her go-to form of punishment lately.

"Come here!"

I don't move.

"Come. Here!" Her tone is authoritative, militant.

I blink, calculating my options and the odds of getting out of this unharmed. Absolutely zero. I've learned not to beg, not to ask her not to hurt me; it makes her angrier and draws out the punishment.

"I'm only going to tell you one more time, Ronan. Come. Here. Now!"

I walk into the kitchen, stopping in front of her, and she points to the counter across from her.

"Turn around and put your hands on the counter!"

I do as she says, closing my eyes as I brace my hands on the edge of the counter. I hold my breath, waiting for the first impact.

It comes a fraction of a second later. The pain is blinding when the metal handle of the broom connects with the right side of my back. I inhale sharply through my teeth but make no other sound. If I just shut up, it'll be over faster.

The first hit is followed by another, and then another in short succession. Each time she pulls back and then lands another blow to my back, just below my right shoulder blade. A groan involuntarily escapes my mouth on the ninth hit, and I grip the counter like it's my lifeline, knuckles white, keeping my knees from buckling under the pain.

After the fourteenth and final strike I slowly open my eyes, my head lowered, my breathing ragged. Yet I don't dare retrieve my hands from the counter. I wait for more pain, never knowing when it's over, when I'm safe.

It's quiet with the exception of my heart hammering in my chest and my blood rushing through my head, drowning out any outside noise.

"Get out of my sight," my mother says, sounding drained, like it was me hitting her.

I straighten up slowly, loosen my death grip on the countertop, and walk out of the kitchen. I'm deliberate in my movements so as not to show weakness, so she doesn't see how much pain she inflicted. I don't look at her as I pass.

Outside, I ease myself into my car, flinching when I make contact with the seat back.

***

"You're early," Shane states when I show up at Murphy's fifteen minutes later, but his face falls when he sees my expression. "What's wrong, man?"

I nod for him to follow me to the office, and he looks at me expectantly as I close the door behind us.

"I had a run-in with my mother. I just need you to tell me how bad it is," I say, feeling so damn sore. It's the first time I've been this forthcoming with him—or anyone, for that matter—about what my mother does to me. I'm not totally sure why I feel the need to share with him today of all times that my mother has hit me, but without further warning, I turn around and pull up my shirt.

"God, what the fuck?" Shane steps closer to me, carefully touching the throbbing area on my back. I flinch and take a sharp breath in through my teeth. Even the slightest touch elicits a sharp pain.

"This looks terrible, Ran," he says as I lower my shirt and turn toward him. "What the fuck happened?"

"She was mad because I forgot to clean out the fridge." I shrug.

"You need to get this checked out, dude. Does it feel like she cracked a rib?"

I shake my head with a frown. "You're joking, right? I can't walk into a doctor's office like this; what am I supposed to say?"

"The fucking truth!" Shane says, as if his answer is the obvious choice.

I shake my head. "No. I just need some ice." I sit down in the creaky chair, feeling stiff and exhausted. The adrenaline coursing through my body just minutes ago is finally wearing off, and all I want to do is sleep off the pain. "And a shot. Ice and a shot. Can you do that for me?" I ask, lifting my eyes toward my best friend.

I can tell he's not happy with my refusal to rat on my mother, but he leaves nonetheless, only to return a minute later with a bag of ice and a double shot of tequila.

I take the shot, then gingerly hold the ice against the bruise. "Thanks." My voice is raspy, and I close my eyes as my raw skin becomes numb from the ice.

"Why don't you just hang out in here a bit? Come out when you're ready. There are some painkillers in the top right drawer of the desk," Shane says.

I don't tell him this enough, but he's an amazing friend.

"Okay. I'll be out in a few." I lean back, careful not to put any more pressure on the sore.

"Take your time. Seriously, take some pain meds, it'll help." Shane looks at me a second longer—his eyes a mixture of pity, worry, and anger—before he leaves, closing the door behind him.

I sit, letting the ice numb me for a few more minutes before I retrieve the painkillers from the desk drawer and swallow a couple of pills dry. Finally, I get up and leave the office, joining Shane and Jack behind the bar, where I get a lay of the land. It's already crowded in here; it'll be a full house tonight.

"Are you gonna be alright?" Shane checks with me, his voice low, eyes worried. "I can take over your section if you need the night off."

"I'll be okay." I adjust my ballcap. "And besides, I'd rather be here than home."

Shane makes a face like he gets the point, and I start my shift.

The painkillers take the edge off, but I have to stop every thirty minutes or so and put more ice on my back. It's almost half past eight and I'm standing by the bar, waiting for Jack to mix a drink order for me, when Shane flags me down and motions for me to follow him into the office.

"You still doing okay?" he asks, searching my eyes.

"Yeah, I'm alright." The pain has subsided somewhat, and work is keeping me sufficiently distracted from thinking about what a fucking hell my life at home is.

"Okay," he says, skepticism in his voice. "I want you to take your break. Grab some food, I'll cover your section."

We head back out and I move to the bar, pulling a stool around so I can sit for a minute to gulp down a glass of water.

"Hey, did Steve tell you about our plans for July Fourth?" Shane asks me, leaning onto the bar counter as he waits for Jack to mix some drinks.

"I thought we were going to hang out at your place?" I say.

"Yeah, well, turns out my mom is planning her own party, and I really don't want to stick around for that," Shane says with a grunt. "And I sure as fuck don't want to be in the city. So Tori thought it might be fun to go camping in the Hamptons. Right on the beach. We could head out Friday and come back on Monday. What do you think?" Shane tells me, and I can tell he likes the idea.

"Uh, yeah, that sounds good." I love the idea of getting away for a few days, especially if Cat can come along. A long weekend with her and my best friends, away from home? Fuck, sign me up!

"Sweet. Should be a good weekend," Shane chuckles and gets back to work.

I scarf down a bowl of Irish stew and spend another twenty minutes chatting with Jack before I, too, get back to work until Shane finally locks the doors at just before 2:30.

"Hey, Shay," I call to him on our way to our cars.

"What's up?"

"Do you mind if I come work with you every night until Cat gets back into town? I need the distraction."

He nods. "You got it, man."

***

I pull up to my house fifteen minutes later and see the living-room lights on through the window. I send up a silent prayer that Steve is watching TV, but I'm not that lucky. I walk into the living room and see my mother on the couch, reading and drinking some tea. Her sleep rhythm is even more screwed up than mine. She's in her pajamas, her legs kicked up on the sofa, her feet covered by a blanket.

She puts her book down when she sees me and observes me while I slide the backyard door open. Onyx immediately rushes past me, tail wagging as usual. "Hey," she says, her voice soft.

"Hey," I reply, sliding the door shut.

"How was work?" She moves off the couch and gets to her feet.

"Fine."

She begins to walk toward me, and I watch her move, internally analyzing the threat level, like I always do. Her movements and expression are soft, almost kind, and I relax my shoulders as she stops a few feet away from me, giving me space.

"How is your back?" I recognize concern in her voice. I never know what to expect with her, whether I'm safe or about to get hurt. It's a constant mind fuck.

"It's fine," I lie, feeling the slight throbbing below my right shoulder blade. It's just about time for another couple of pain pills.

"Let me see." She moves around me, pulling up the hem of my shirt without waiting for my consent. I don't fight her as she exposes my bruise, examining it like the skilled nurse she is. She gingerly touches the injury, her fingers soft and cool against my hot skin. Slowly, she pulls my shirt back down. "Were you able to ice it?" she asks with honest compassion, and it's pissing me off how concerned she is.

"Yeah, every thirty minutes."

She nods approvingly. Then it's quiet for what seems like an eternity.

"I'm sorry, Ran. I don't want to hurt you. It's just... you have a way of getting under my skin. I get so angry at you, and then... I just lose it." Her forehead creases, teeth gritted. "If you would just do as I tell you, we wouldn't keep having this problem."

"I'm sorry, Mom." I know I brought this on myself. I didn't do what she asked me to do. I fucked up. Yet again. "Is it okay if I go to bed? I'm tired," I say, my face expressionless.

She considers me, scanning my face with her green eyes that are the exact same color as mine. Finally, she nods.

I turn to head upstairs.

"Your report card came in today," she announces, and I stop in my tracks. "It's really good. Straight As, just as I'd expect."

She picks up a piece of paper from the coffee table and peruses it. It's obviously my report card. "I just wish you had fewer absences. Thirteen days last semester," she notes, and looks up at me. She doesn't realize that all but three of those were because I was too hurt to make it to class and hockey practice. I'm pretty sure that after a particularly mean confrontation in February—during which she slammed my head against the wall, leaving a good-sized dent in the drywall—I had a pretty nasty concussion. I felt nauseated and dizzy for days, and the near-constant headache was soul crushing. But I sucked it up, knowing I couldn't afford to lose too much time at school or practice without arousing suspicion.

"I'll do better next semester."

She seems satisfied and places the report card back on the coffee table before she returns to the couch to continue reading. My mom nods at me, a small smile on her lips. "Okay. Get some sleep."

I finally drag myself upstairs, the day crashing in on me, and I suddenly feel drained of all energy. In my room I manage to pull off my shirt and kick off my shoes and jeans before collapsing onto my bed. I vaguely register Steve asleep in his bed in the other room before my eyes fall shut.

Wednesday, June 30th

Cat

"Go, go, go, Cat!" I hear my teammates yelling as I sprint toward home plate. It's the end of the last inning and we're about to win the game after Vada just hit a fly ball. I take a dive, sliding into home, ending the game with a score of two to one.

We shake hands with the other team and make our way back to the locker room, where I follow Tori and Vada's lead and plop down on one of the benches.

"Nice work, ladies," Coach Keaton exclaims. It's been a great few days filled with some friendly competition and worthwhile practices, but I'm ready to head home tomorrow, ready to sleep in my own bed, and above all, ready to see Ronan—a fact that both Vada and Tori have teased me about on several occasions.

"Oh girl, you're in deep with him, huh?" Vada smirked at me Monday evening after I hung up with Ronan, my cheeks still heated, a mushy smile on my lips only he can elicit.

"You have no idea," I sighed before falling back onto my pillow, pulling out my phone, and scrolling through my pictures of Ronan and me together, and those of just Ronan. My favorite picture is one I took of him while he was working. He was standing at the bar at Murphy's, waiting for a drink order. He was looking down, his face kind of serious like he was thinking about something important, and I got the perfect shot of his perfect profile. I love the way his head dips down in the picture, the light reflecting off the soft skin of his neck. His taut muscles, those strong shoulders—I can't get enough of looking at this picture.

"Cat," Coach Keaton redirects my attention to the present and away from my thoughts of Ronan. "That was a risky move there, running two bases on Vada's fly ball, but good call!"

Tori claps me on the back, and Vada grins at me before Coach Keaton finally herds us to the bus for the short drive back to our hotel. Vada, Tori, and I make plans to get cleaned up and then head to get some dinner together.

"Ladies, seeing as you're all seniors, you're free to spend your evening exploring, but don't go anywhere alone. No drinking, no clubs, no drugs, no boys! Curfew is ten o'clock. I'll be making rounds. Our bus leaves at seven tomorrow morning, so I expect everyone to be in the hotel lobby by six-thirty. Have fun, make good choices, and I'll see you later," Coach Keaton announces before the team disperses and we head to our individual hotel rooms. Tori, Vada, and I are sharing a room, and we head up the elevator together.

Back in our room, I take a quick shower before switching off with Vada, then I blow-dry my hair, put on some mascara and blush, and rummage through my bag for a fresh pair of jeans and a shirt. Vada and Tori are still in the bathroom getting ready, so I snatch my phone off the nightstand, sit cross-legged on one of the two queen beds, and unlock my phone. I have a missed call from Ronan, and I smile as I dial his number.

"Hey baby," he answers on the first ring. He sounds tired, though happy to hear my voice.

"You have no idea how much I miss you," I greet him, and my heart thumps in my chest when he chuckles in a husky voice.

"Oh, I think I may have an idea. What time are you coming home tomorrow?"

"Our bus leaves at seven and it'll probably take eight hours to get home, so three-ish?" I say, and bite my bottom lip.

Ronan sighs. "I can't believe I won't get to see you tomorrow."

"Why?" I ask, my voice tinged with disappointment.

"I have practice at two and then I work at five."

"I'm going to kill Shane," I grumble.

Ronan laughs. "Shane actually has nothing to do with this. In fact, he's not even working tomorrow. Shane's dad asked me to come in for some reason. I'm obviously not going to tell him no, but I'd be lying if I said I'm happy about it because, well, I'm kind of dying to get my hands on you," he says, his voice low, and I shiver. "But hey, did you check with your mom about camping in the Hamptons?"

"Oh, yeah, I talked to her yesterday," I say. "She made me promise that I'd be sleeping in a tent with Vada, but other than that she was fine with it."

"She doesn't trust me?" Ronan asks, his voice still gravelly, flirty.

I let my eyelids fall shut, pretending he's right next to me. "It's me she doesn't trust around you," I confess, and even though I'm all alone, I blush.

"Oh yeah?" His voice is driving me crazy. "And why is that?"

I exhale shakily. "Because she can tell I have a hard time keeping a straight head when I'm around you."

"That makes two of us, then." His voice is so low now he might as well be next to me, whispering in my ear, and I can all but feel his breath feathering against my neck, his hands leaving scorching-hot trails on my bare skin.

"Good thing I have to share my tent with Vada then, right?" I whimper.

"Probably," he laughs quietly. "Cat, I meant it when I said I would take this relationship at whatever pace you need me to." His voice, still low, is serious now.

I open my eyes. "I know. And you don't know how much that means to me." It's something I'm beginning to understand about my relationship with Ronan—that he truly *will* move at my speed, refusing to pressure me into having sex or otherwise doing anything I don't want or am not ready for. By this point in my relationship with Adam, I had already been victim to a handful of Adam's outbursts when I didn't do what he wanted. I'd already been called names, and it was about this far into our relationship that Adam started to get physical with me. Things only escalated from there.

Just then I can hear Ronan's mom in the background, his name way too sharp on her tongue.

"Shit," he mutters. "Baby, I gotta let you go. Text me when you're home and I'll call you on my break, okay? I can't wait to see you Friday."

"Me, too."

"Hey," he adds, sounding rushed, "you're the best thing in my life. Seriously." His voice is heavy, and I hear his mother call his name again. Ronan hangs up the phone before I can respond.

I sit, emotions flooding my body, my head spinning. The tone of his voice just now—there was something else. There's something I don't yet know beneath the still water, underneath the surface of this boy I'm falling in love with.

***

Tori, Vada, and I leave the hotel ten minutes later and head to a little Italian place two blocks from the hotel, where we eat the most amazing pasta and make plans for the camping trip this weekend. We decide that Ronan and I will drive with Tori and Shane because Shane's Jeep Wrangler Rubicon is roomier than either Ronan's Mustang, Steve's Challenger, or Vada's Focus.

After dinner, Vada insists on walking around, focused on finding a present for Steve. She ends up pulling us into a little gift shop that sells touristy Niagara Falls mementos. She and Tori peruse the selection while I wander down to a corner of the store that's arranged like a candy shop. The shelves are stacked with glass jars of varying sizes containing different types of candies—sweet, sour, all the colors of the rainbow, chocolate, gummi bears, taffies, local specialties, and foreign imports—and I decide to bring Ronan a little bag of sweet treats.

"What did you get?" Vada asks after she leaves the store empty-handed, unable to find a present she found suitable. I hold up the clear bag filled halfway with an assortment of sweets. "Candy?" Vada cocks her head to the side and looks at me like I lost my mind. So, I recap Ronan's and my ice cream date last Saturday.

"You know, that doesn't totally surprise me," Vada says when I tell her about Ronan's mom not letting him have candy growing up. "I told you, their mom is kind of gruff, especially with Ran." Vada shrugs. "She's really not like the warmest person I've ever met." She eyes the bag of candy and smiles. "He's going to love it." She nudges me, and I blush.

***

We get back to our hotel well before our ten o'clock curfew. I wash my face and change into pajama shorts and a tank top, then climb into bed. Because there are only two beds in our room, we've been playing musical chairs; each night one of us gets one bed while the remaining two share the other. Tonight, it's my turn to enjoy a queen bed all to myself. Vada and Tori have their backs turned toward each other, each holding their phones to their ears talking with Steve and Shane respectively. It's kind of comical, actually.

My phone chirps at me with a new text message, and I feel a rush of excitement as I grab it, fully expecting to see a text message from Ronan. My giddiness turns to dread, however, the moment I see the unknown number, and I instantly know the message is from Adam. He's been sending me random text messages, calling me at the oddest hours—only sometimes leaving me messages—ever since I came back from North Carolina.

Unknown: Hello Sexy!

That's all Adam's message says. His messages are mostly like this: short and somewhat alarming. I don't know what this is about, whether he just texts me because he's drunk or because he wants to remind me, again and again, of what happened between us, holding me hostage to the past, preventing me from fully moving on.

I delete his message, like I do each time, without responding. I haven't told my parents about these messages, haven't shared with them that I ran into Adam while I was in North Carolina. Nobody knows. Not Julie, not my parents, not Ronan. My intention is to just keep ignoring him, to delete all the messages and hope he'll get tired of his game and stop contacting me altogether.

But tonight is not my lucky night, because I receive yet another message only minutes later. I open it, intending to delete it like I did the last.

Unknown: I need a picture of you.

Delete.

Five more minutes pass before my phone buzzes for a third time, but this time my breath hitches when I see the picture Adam attached to his latest text. It's a photo of me passed out at a party, half-undressed, my chest bare and exposed. I swallow hard, my heart racing as my fingers fumble around on my phone, desperate to erase the picture, when a new message pops up underneath the incriminating photo.

Unknown: You still owe me! You don't want to ignore me, Cat. Not unless you want me to post a little sneak peak of slutty Cat on the Internet. Send me a picture!

I delete this text message, too. Maybe if I don't respond at all, he'll think I'm asleep and will leave me alone tonight.

Unknown: DON'T IGNORE ME, YOU SLUT. You have exactly two minutes to send me a picture of your perfect, perky tits or I'm posting you for all to see. Countdown starts now.

I quickly climb out of bed, ignoring the startled expressions from Vada and Tori, and disappear into the bathroom, locking the door behind me.

My fingers shake when I slide first one, then the other spaghetti strap off my shoulders and push my tank top down, exposing my breasts, before I hold my phone up, covering my face in the mirror, and take a picture of myself—my bare breasts—feeling so ashamed, so used, so dirty.

As soon as the shutter clicks, I lower my camera and quickly pull my tank top back up, covering myself, only to sit on the edge of the bathtub and compose a text message to Adam, attaching the photo. I choke back a sob when I press "send." The realization that I'm sending a topless picture to some guy who isn't actually my boyfriend makes me feel sick. I haven't even sent Ronan a topless picture of me; in fact, Ronan hasn't even seen me without a shirt on, and here I am sending such an intimate, vulnerable photo of myself to another guy.

Tears stream hotly down my face as I go back into my photo gallery and delete the photo I just took, feeling disgusted with myself.

I knew Adam had pictures of me, most taken without my express consent when I had once again overdone it and found myself impaired, my inhibitions lowered, my judgment affected. I trusted Adam; I trusted my "friends," ignoring the red flags, the signs, the increasing volatility of my relationship, even though I should have known better.

The vile feeling in my stomach compounds when yet another text message pops up.

Unknown: Fuck, yes. Not so damn, difficult, right? We could have been great if you hadn't been such a little cunt.

I delete it like I did the others, along with my message to him with the picture, desperate to erase any trace of my betrayal of Ronan tonight.

I sit in the bathroom for a while longer, letting my tears dry, pretending to use the toilet. Adam doesn't text me again, and I eventually emerge from the bathroom, only to crawl into my bed without a word to Tori or Vada, dead set on pretending I didn't just send a nude picture to my ex-boyfriend, that I didn't just betray Ronan, that I didn't bring this on myself.

Friday, July 2nd

Ronan

It's finally Friday, the beginning of a long weekend very much needed after an even longer week. I'm at home, packing the rest of my stuff into my backpack. We're heading out to the Hamptons in thirty minutes. The plan is for Steve and me to share a tent, and both our sleeping bags are stacked next to the door downstairs.

Camping brings back memories of when I was younger and my dad would take Steve and me out into the Montana wilderness when he was home for more than a couple days during the summer months. I used to love spending time with him; I always sought his presence. I was his little shadow when he was home, until I was about seven or eight and I began stacking the bricks, cementing the figurative wall meant to protect me from the pain.

When I finish packing my stuff I take a quick shower, knowing the next time I'll have a real, hot shower is when I get back on Monday. I smile at the idea of spending a few uninterrupted days with Cat. The thought of possibly sharing a tent with her when Vada invades my space to hook up with my brother causes a rush of want and need. I know I need to take it slow, but the way she feels when I kiss her makes restraint really fucking difficult.

On top of that, Cat's smart and funny. We spend hours talking about every possible topic and I've learned so much about her over the past weeks. And more importantly, I've shared so much with her, more than I've ever shared with anyone. Well, except for the one huge elephant in my own private prison cell. But I wouldn't even know how to broach the subject with her. "Oh, hi baby. Guess what, my mom beat the shit out of me last night."

I tried to be out of the house as much as possible this past week, but I can't seem to escape my mom. She's been more on edge these past six months, and it just keeps getting worse. Lately it seems every time we're in the house alone together, we have a run-in.

Two days ago, while I was on the phone with Cat, she hunted me down in my room, which she doesn't usually invade, but it turns out she had a shit day and was looking for a fight. Well, she found the perfect fucking excuse when she went to make herself a drink and found the almost-empty bottle of Jack neatly placed in the back of the sideboard. She obviously figured I was the one sneaking drinks—and for once she came to the right conclusion—and came storming into my room. I took one look at her face and the bottle of whiskey in her hand and knew my night would end in pain. And so it did. My right side, just above my hip bone, is adorned with two bruised streaks where she hit me with the whiskey bottle seventeen times. I always count her hits. Always. I started doing it when I was maybe twelve as a way to distract myself, to withstand her terror in an effort not to show weakness.

I take my time under the shower, washing myself thoroughly, brushing my teeth. By the time I get out of the shower twenty minutes later, the small space is steamed up. I grab a towel and tie it around my waist. Just in time, too, because just as I tug the end into the towel, the door to Steve's room flies open and Vada is standing in front of me, ogling my naked chest, grinning.

"Jesus, Vada! A little privacy?" I growl.

"Cat is going to go nuts when she sees you naked for the first time," Vada says, grinning.

I grab the doorknob and force the door shut.

I walk into my bedroom, knowing that if Vada is here, Cat must be, too. Vada was going to drop Cat off here so she could ride with me, Shane, and Tori while Steve and Vada drive in Vada's Ford. Cat's mom made Cat leave her car in North Carolina when they moved to New York because she didn't think more than one car was feasible in the city. She's not wrong, but Cat isn't too pleased that she has to rely on other people for rides. I rather enjoy it because it means I get to drive Cat and therefore have more time to spend with her. And knowing she's in my house now makes me smile.

Oh crap! The smile is wiped off my stupid face when I realize that Cat being here, but not with Vada in Steve's room or mine, must mean that Vada left Cat to fend for herself with my mother. *Shit, shit, FUCK!* I hastily throw on a fresh pair of pants and pull a navy shirt over my head. Yanking my bedroom door open, I hurl myself barefoot down the flight of stairs, whip around the corner to the hallway and into the kitchen, where I find Cat leaning against the kitchen counter, chatting with my dad.

She's a sight for sore eyes, and I suddenly realize how much her fairly short absence actually wore on me.

"Hi," she says as she turns toward me, the wide smile on her full lips, her sweet voice immediately relieving the anxiety clawing in my chest. She takes three steps toward me, and I close the distance between us to pull her into my arms, burying my face in the crook of her neck, inhaling her as she wraps her arms around me. Although we talked for a little while last night after she returned home from Buffalo and while I was on break at work, it's the first time I've seen her in almost a week. Contentment washes through me as I bask in her physical presence.

"Hey," I breathe against her, relieved, forcing the breath trapped in my chest out through my mouth. "God, I'm glad you're back," I tell her, meaning every single word. I feel my shoulders relax and I lift my head. Her hands unravel from my neck, allowing me to take one and interlace my fingers with hers. I stare into her eyes, the gold specks pronounced in the light streaming in through the kitchen window, before turning my attention to my dad.

"I didn't know you were coming home today," I say to him, unable to hide my surprise.

"Just over July Fourth," my dad says. "I'm flying to D.C. on Monday. But I'm glad I'm home and get to meet Cat." He smiles at Cat, who's fucking stunning in a tight white t-shirt, a pair of distressed cutoff shorts that show off her long, smooth legs, and a pair of strappy black sandals.

"I didn't know you had a girlfriend," my dad says to me, smiling, clearly pleased with my relationship status.

"You're not really home enough for me to tell you these things," I say.

The door to the garage opens behind my dad, and my mom steps through carrying two bags filled with groceries. My dad turns around and moves toward her, taking the bags out of her hands. My mom is all smiles, relaxed and happy, as always when my dad is home. She spots Cat next to me, and her eyes narrow as she looks from me to Cat and back again, pausing on our interlaced hands.

"Mom, this is Cat. I think you met her a few weeks ago," I say, then look at Cat. "Baby, this is my mom."

Cat's sweet, innocent smile tears me apart, and my heart feels like it's in a vise as both the very best and the very worst parts of my life collide—standing, facing each other in my house. Cat extends her hand toward my mom and shakes it, introducing herself again. Perfect Southern manners.

"You and Ronan are together?" my mom asks, her voice kind. I tense, but Cat nods, smiling as she leans her head against my shoulder. "How long has this been going on? Ronan never said he was seeing anyone."

Cat turns her head to look at me and I can see the confusion and disappointment in her eyes. She must think I'm embarrassed of her, when in reality I just want to protect her.

"Just haven't had a chance yet, Mom," I say through clenched teeth.

Cat, picking up on my strained tone, squints her eyes at me, trying to read me.

"Well, Rica, you aren't the only one who didn't know," my dad chimes in as he unloads the grocery bags and begins putting things into the refrigerator. "But hey"—he stops and gives my mother a quick kiss on the cheek—"from what I can tell, our son has excellent taste in girls."

At this comment, Cat's cheeks take on my favorite rosy hue. I smile, brushing my thumb across her cheek, gaining me an approving grunt from my dad, who observes us with pride in his eyes.

"Cat was telling me you're heading to the Hamptons for beach camping over the Fourth," my dad says, bustling about the kitchen, putting away the last purchases while my mom busies herself brewing some fresh coffee.

"Yeah." I'm unwilling to let go of Cat's hand; she's my anchor, and I feel immense calm with her by my side. "Shane and Steve are coming, too."

"Great," my dad says, then presses his lips together, obviously hesitant. "I know I don't need to say this to you, Ran"—his eyes dart briefly to Cat—"but, you know, please use protection."

"Oh, for fuck's sake, Dad," I sigh, rubbing my hand across my face.

Cat blushes violently, tightening her hold on my hand, embarrassed.

"Ronan!" my mother warns me, as if she doesn't constantly cuss at me.

"It's okay, Rica," my dad assuages her with a laugh, waving her off.

She glowers at me a second longer, and I hold her gaze, knowing full well she isn't going to do shit to me with my dad home and Cat next to me. That doesn't mean I won't pay for this later, of course.

"So Cat, what do your parents do?" my dad asks.

I exhale quietly, dropping my head. I really don't want to stand here chatting with my parents. I want to take Cat up to my room where it's safe, where she's not exposed to my mother, where I don't run the risk of her finding out about the shit that haunts my life. And yeah, I want to kiss her in peace for five minutes before we head out and I won't get to enjoy her undivided attention.

"My dad teaches high school math and my mom is a psychiatrist," Cat says. I lift my head to look at her while she speaks, memorizing her beautiful features. "My mom mostly works with combat veterans, primarily in the crisis setting."

"That's great," my dad says in his deep voice, fully invested in his conversation with Cat. "I don't know if Ran told you"—he glances at me quickly—"I work intelligence in the Air Force."

Cat nods. I never actually told her exactly what my dad does in the Air Force because I honestly have no clue other than it's classified and he's always gone.

"I see our guys come back from deployment all the time completely messed up. Good for your mom specializing in that area. It's very much needed and appreciated," my dad says, smiling, his hands on his hips, standing up straight. I would be able to tell he's military even if he wasn't my dad, just by the way he stands: straight-backed, his legs slightly spread—the power stance, as he calls it—hands usually on his hips or behind his back. He's 6'4" and all muscle, and I remember thinking my dad was Superman when I was three or four years old because I could have sworn he looked just like him with his brown hair and tall, muscular frame. But I quickly realized he was anything but Superman, because Superman would surely have saved me from my mother's abuse.

"Dad, if you don't mind," I interrupt, "I still have to finish packing, and Tori and Shane should be here any minute." I look at the watch on my right wrist while gripping Cat's hand tightly in mine.

"Oh, yeah, of course," he says, and disappointment crosses his face. I know I'm not giving him an opportunity to be part of my life, and maybe that makes me a shitty son, but somewhere along the way I closed that door in an act of self-preservation.

I turn around and lead Cat out of the kitchen and up the stairs to my room, where I close the door behind us. I slip my hand out of Cat's, but only to take her face into both of my hands before pressing my lips to hers. Her fingers slide under the bottom of my shirt and up my naked back when I slip my tongue into her mouth, tasting her. I give myself a good minute to kiss her, allowing her to kiss me back, to lose myself in her, feel her hands on my skin and forget everything around me.

I pull back slowly, and Cat blinks her eyes at me. I chuckle at her spacey expression. She looks high as hell, and I understand the feeling. Being with her, kissing her, feeling her has the exact same effect on me.

"I'm glad you're home," I say, still holding her face in my hands.

"Why haven't you told your parents about us?" she asks out of left field.

My face falls and I let go of her. She studies me, expecting an answer. I take her hands into mine, and my eyes lock on hers because I need her to understand that she's not the reason for my secrecy.

"Baby, please don't think this has anything to do with how I feel about you. You are the absolute best part of my life. I hadn't told my dad about us yet because since I met you, I've seen my dad once, and that was in the beginning when we were keeping things quiet. And I haven't told my mom because"—I sigh heavily, trying to choose my next words wisely—"because she and I aren't really that close." I clench my teeth, hoping that's enough to put Cat at ease.

She studies me a few seconds more, and I begin to tense at her lack of a reaction. Then she steps closer to me, lifts her head, and kisses me softly. "I've missed you," she says against my lips, then steps back. I'm relieved to see a smile on her face.

There's a knock on the front door, and I hear my dad boisterously greet Shane and Tori just moments later.

"Let's go," I say, excitement bubbling up inside me at the prospect of being around her for the next few days. I pick up my backpack before taking Cat's hand to lead her down the stairs.

Steve and Vada saunter down the stairs behind us; Vada giggles while Steve whispers something into her ear. My dad chats animatedly with Shane and Tori while I grab the tent and my sleeping bag and stow it in Shane's Jeep.

"We're heading out," I announce once Steve and I have everything packed in the cars. I take Cat's hand, ready to leave out the front door behind Shane and Tori. "Glad you're home, Dad. Too bad you can't stay longer," I ramble, and follow Cat out the door. He'll never know how much I mean those last few words.

I follow Cat out to the car, unable to stop my wandering eyes as they follow the swaying motion of her firm ass. I open the door to Shane's Jeep, and Cat slides in behind Tori, buckling her seatbelt while I walk around the back of the car and slip in next to Cat.

Cat's hand finds mine, and our fingers intertwine.

We hit the road, and it's quiet in the car as Tori connects her phone with the car's Bluetooth. Some indie band starts playing in the background while she and Shane chat it up in the front, but I have no interest in their conversation and instead face Cat.

"How was softball camp?" I ask and notice her face fall, though she quickly composes herself.

"Really good," she nods.

"Yeah?" I study her, trying to get to the bottom of the momentary look of anguish in her eyes.

"Yeah, really good," she tells me, more cheerful now. "We won both scrimmages and I ran two bases on a fly ball from Vada."

I chuckle at her. "Okay, I have no idea what that means, but it's obviously good, so good job, baby," I say, and she grins. "But did anything bad happen? You had a look on your face."

Her hazel eyes are wide for a moment as she wavers, but then she shakes her head. "I just... I really missed you," she tells me, and I have a hard time analyzing her. I note the obvious sadness in her eyes, although there seems to be something else. Shame?

"I missed you, too," I tell her, meeting her gaze. I want her closer to me, so I push the button of her seatbelt and unlatch it.

Cat gives me a quizzical look. "What are you doing?"

I only pat the middle seat. She smiles, then slides over willingly. She buckles herself in, but all I notice is her leg pressed against mine, and I move my right hand to her bare knee, resting it there, stroking my thumb back and forth an inch, cautious not to push any of her boundaries. She turns to face me and kisses me, softly at first, but she deepens the kiss as her hand finds my left arm. My breath catches when she hitches her left leg over my right.

Feeling encouraged, I move my hand further up her leg and toward her inner thigh, softly grazing her warm skin and causing goose bumps to erupt all over her leg. Her breathing is rapid while we make out in the backseat of Shane's car, and I slide my hand even farther up her leg until I reach the hem of her shorts. It's driving me insane, knowing how short her cutoffs are, especially in the position she's in. It's arousing as hell, my body stirring in ways that are impossible for me to control with the blood pulsing hotly through my veins. I badly want to explore further, want to caress her silky skin, taste her, make her mine in the most absolute way. And I want to protect her, give her the damn world. A small moan escapes Cat's lips when I stroke the sensitive part of her inner thigh. My tongue tastes her while she grips my arm.

"You guys should try to cool it until we get to the beach and you have more privacy," Shane says, grinning at us through his rearview mirror.

Tori promptly turns around whooping.

To my dismay, Cat withdraws her leg from mine and blushes so violently that I give in to the urge to place my hand on her cheek and turn her head to look at me. I gently press my lips to hers before I drape my arm over her shoulder. She rests against me, her head on my chest.

Cat dozes off eventually, cuddled up against me, and I relish the peace and calm that envelops me for the first time this week. It's a feeling I know only when I'm with Cat. My anxious mind finally shuts off and I lean my head back, listening to the soft music playing and Shane flirting with Tori.

***

The ride to our spot on the beach only takes a couple of hours. After rousing Cat, who has an adorable look in her eyes as she blinks away the sleep, we unload and I join Steve, Zack, and Shane in setting up the tents. Drew and Cheyenne set up a fire pit while Cat, Summer, Vada, and Tori move around some logs, set up the camping chairs, and strategically set out some beach towels.

Once everything is set up, the girls disappear into their respective tents, and I watch as Cat crawls into hers behind Vada. When she finally emerges, she's wearing nothing but a light-blue, stringy two-piece. *Holy. Fucking. Shit.* I've never seen her in this state of undress, and seeing her skin, soft and smooth, covered only in the most important places, I have the urge to grab her, pull her into my tent, and do things to her I would never say out loud. I can't even begin to explain how badly I want to kiss every single centimeter of her body. Fuck.

Honestly, Cat has no idea what an impact she has on guys—hell, even girls. My eyes follow her every move as she walks toward the beach with Tori, Vada, Summer, and Cheyenne, all dressed in their bikinis. As attractive as all the girls are, none of them come even close to Cat's raw beauty and sex appeal. I imagine her endless legs wrapped around my waist while I feel her soft curves under my hands, her breasts pressed against me, her heat seeping into my skin. *Shit.* That was a dumb idea. I have a hard-on and need to get it under control immediately.

I close my eyes and breathe deeply, redirecting my thoughts and letting things... calm down. Once my body no longer gives me away—probably the hardest part of being a guy—I walk back to the Jeep and take the cooler out of the trunk. I bring it to the fire pit, setting it next to a big log that's angled toward the pit where, later this evening, a fire will be lit.

"Hand me a water, Ran?" Shane says, watching Tori intently, who's splashing in the water along with Cat. I grab two bottles of water from the cooler, the cold condensation feeling nice against my heated skin. "Damn, I never get over how fucking amazing my girl looks," Shane says, twisting the cap off his water and taking a long sip.

I smile to myself, because I have a feeling I'll never get over how amazing *my* girl looks.

"I know what you mean," I say, taking a swig myself. My eyes never leave Cat, whose wet skin shimmers like a thousand diamonds when the sunlight hits it.

"You'll need to watch out, man," Shane says, his eyebrows knit. "I spot vultures." His gaze moves, and he nods his head in Drew's direction.

Drew is sitting in the sand a few yards closer to the shoreline, and it's obvious he's checking out Cat.

"Fucking ass," I mutter. Drew has been vying for Cat's attention from the beginning, and it pisses me off to no end that he doesn't even pretend to back off knowing she's with me. I'm usually not the possessive type, but I can feel Drew moving closer and closer to an invisible boundary line, and if he crosses it, I will fucking flip.

"Try to ignore him," Shane says, and I frown. "Here, help me move this log closer to the pit."

Shane and I heave the log into place, and Steve and Zack join us. Together, we start pulling all the coolers closer and throwing the firewood into the pit.

Once we're done, I sit in the sand and lean against one of the logs. I suck in a sharp breath through my teeth when the bruises on my side make contact with the wood, reminding me of the ever-present undercurrent of pain and darkness in my life.

Shane throws me a knowing look, his eyebrows raised. "You okay?"

"Yeah," I lie, knowing it's completely useless.

Cat and Tori wade out of the water and toward us. Cat's arms are crossed over her chest, her shoulders are raised, and I can tell she's cold. So I get up, grab a towel from behind me, then wrap it around her. I pull her against me, silently cursing the fact that this extra piece of fabric is keeping me from feeling more of her. I want to touch her so badly, want to make her feel things she's never felt before. But I just stand there, rubbing my hands up and down her back over the towel, warming her with the heat of my body and the friction of my hands.

She leans gratefully into me, sighing contently, and I smile.

Cat

I let Ronan hold me for about five minutes, taking in his body heat, his scent, his touch. His hand rubs circles on my back in an attempt to create heat. It's working, but not so much because of the rubbing—more because he's holding me like that. I can't help but wonder what his hands would feel like on my naked skin.

I'm so glad to be home, to be in Ronan's arms, and I can almost make myself believe that what happened in Buffalo, when Adam blackmailed me and I sent him a topless photo of me, didn't actually happen. I want to forget it so badly, but the memory keeps forcing itself back to the front of my brain, and the guilt I feel over my betrayal nauseates me.

There was a moment when I almost told Ronan, when I wanted to open up to him. He deserves to know the truth about everything. He's so good to me, was so obviously happy to see me, and god, he's so soft with me, so gentle, so caring. It's not something I ever knew with Adam. I don't want to lose it. I don't want to lose Ronan, and I know that if he knew what I did—not only two days ago, but during my relationship with Adam—there's not a chance Ronan would be able to see past that and choose to stay with me. God, I hope he never finds out.

After I change out of my wet swimsuit and into a fresh shirt and jean shorts, I join Ronan and the rest of the group. I situate myself between his legs and lean back against his chest while his arms encircle me. Shane animatedly discusses hockey strategy with Ronan, Steve, and Drew while I chat with Tori and Vada about our last softball game and the upcoming season. Every few minutes I get distracted when Ronan randomly kisses my neck or earlobe; he sends shivers down my spine each time before his attention turns back to the guys.

At some point Steve gets a pretty nice fire started, and we all watch the sun set over the horizon. It's an incredible sight and I'm happier right now than I've ever been before, surrounded by friends and in Ronan's arms. I want to grab this moment and put it in a mason jar so I can relive it every single day.

When the sun has set completely, the guys start barbequing steak, hot dogs, and chicken, and we don't move from our spots while we eat and bottles of tequila and Jack get passed around.

"Who's up for a game?" Vada finally asks, her mouth full of bread.

"What kind of game are we talking?" Drew asks, rubbing his full stomach.

"I call it five hundred questions," Vada explains, swallowing her food. "Basically, we go around asking each other questions and we have to answer truthfully. The person who answers gets to ask a question to another person, but it can't be the same question posed immediately prior, and the question can't be directed at the person who just asked the last question."

"And what's the goal?" Tori chimes in.

"No goal, just for fun. Let's see how many embarrassing details we can get out of the boys." Vada grins and takes another swig from the bottle of whiskey that's making its round.

There's a general murmur of consent, but I'm once again distracted as Ronan's hand glides down my cheek before he gently runs his tongue along the skin on my neck.

"I'll start!" Summer volunteers, her brown eyes bright. She sits up straight and looks around the group, ultimately resting her eyes on Vada. "Alright, what's your favorite thing to do in bed?" Summer asks with a giggle.

Oh. My. God. I didn't think it was going to turn into that kind of game so quickly. Heat rises in my cheeks, and the question wasn't even directed at me. I'm such a freaking prude.

Ronan eyes me, and a smile tugs at his full lips.

"Oral sex, by far," Vada explains, taking another shot of Jack before Steve takes the bottle from her, putting it to his own mouth. The girls laugh while the guys hoot and whistle.

"Giving or receiving?" Summer follows up, almost making Steve choke on the Jack.

Vada shakes her head at her, grinning and shaking her finger exaggeratedly. "One question at a time!" Vada lets her gaze roam. "Tori," she says.

Tori stops giggling abruptly, causing everyone else to erupt into laughter. "Be nice!" Tori warns with both panic and laughter in her voice.

Vada clears her throat loudly. "How often a week do you and Shane get it on?"

"Not often enough," Shane hollers, which is followed by more laughter.

Tori swats his arm before sitting up straight and looking proud. "Plenty," is all she says with a smile, and her eyes focus on Ronan. "Ran."

I feel Ronan tense behind me as I lean against him, resting my head on his shoulder, and I can tell he's anticipating the question. "Uh-huh?" His voice is a low growl, warning Tori to be careful, and everyone is in absolute stitches.

"How old were you when you lost your virginity?" Tori inquires.

I lift my head up and look at Ronan expectantly, unable to hide my curiosity.

Ronan takes a second to answer before saying, matter-of-factly, "Fourteen." He yanks the bottle of Jack out of Steve's hand and gulps back a huge shot.

"Shut up!" Vada blurts out, her eyes wide. "Really?"

"Really," Ronan says, his voice light, and the tension in his shoulders eases. Jesus, I obviously knew he had experience, but man, fourteen is really young.

It's Ronan's turn to ask a question, and he eyes Shane mischievously. "Oral sex," Ronan starts, "better to give or to receive?"

Tori turns to Shane, puckering her lips and raising her eyebrows. "Yeah, babe, better to *give* or better to receive?" she asks, and everyone laughs again.

I take the bottle of Jack from Ronan's hands and take two shots, then a third while he watches me intently.

"Gotta call it a tie, man," Shane finally says, and Tori seems pleased and proud at the same time.

More questions get thrown around, all equally as intimate, and I learn things about my friends I'm not sure I ever wanted to know but find fascinating nonetheless. I haven't been hit with a question yet, but just as I'm beginning to feel tipsy from the whiskey and have been lulled into a false sense of security, it's Cheyenne's turn to ask a question.

"Cat! When did you have your last orgasm?" she asks, a derisive grin on her face, and there's more giggling and wolf whistling from the group.

"You don't need to answer that," Ronan chimes in, his words directed at me, but his eyes lock on Cheyenne, throwing her a tense look. I love how protective he is.

I don't know if it's the alcohol sloshing in my head or just the fact that I think he should know, but I rest my hand on Ronan's chest and lean forward to face Cheyenne. "I have never had an orgasm, Cheyenne," I say, feeling brave.

There's a collective gasp from my friends.

"Yikes, Ronan, I'd always heard you're so fucking good in bed," Drew laughs obnoxiously, and Ronan flips him the bird.

"Are you for real?" Summer asks me, her voice high, incredulous.

"Hey, remember the one-question-at-a-time rule," Vada repeats, and I smile as everyone laughs. "Alright, Kitty Cat, your turn."

I don't think for too long. I lean away from Ronan and turn to face him. He narrows his eyes at me, amused, and his smile makes my heart speed up and makes me crave my very first orgasm. *Damn alcohol.*

"Ran," I say, "when was the last time *you* had an orgasm?" A little hiccup escapes my mouth, and I swear he must think I'm more intoxicated than I really am. But I have to admit, I do feel really comfortable, and I genuinely want to know. I figure it couldn't have been that long ago.

Ronan chuckles. "You're breaking the rules, baby. You can't ask the same question that was just asked of you," he reminds me, smiling. I pout, and Ronan takes my face into both his hands, pulling me toward him and placing a soft kiss on my lips. As he pulls back I hear the guys hooting at us, but my eyes stay shut.

"But I really want to know," I whine, knowing I sound like a little kid begging for candy. He places another kiss on my lips, this one more intense than the last, and my hand moves down his firm chest to his hard abs. My index finger slides under the hem of his shirt, feeling his warm skin.

"Get a room!" someone yells while everyone else chuckles, and Ronan stops kissing me.

"Well, I guess the game's over," Vada says, grabbing the bottle of whiskey and tipping her head back to take another gulp. Chatter erupts among the group, and I feel Ronan get up. He extends his hand out to me, and when I grab it he pulls me up and intertwines his fingers with mine.

"Let's go for a walk," he says.

We walk to the shoreline and away from the group. The stars are bright tonight, and I love being out here with only him. My hand is warm in his and we walk silently for a few minutes, out of earshot and sight of the group.

Ronan stops, and I turn to face him, angling my chin up to look into his gorgeous eyes. “Last night,” he says out of the blue.

I’m confused. “What happened last night?”

“My last orgasm. It was last night,” he says, and I immediately blush, clamping my mouth shut.

“Does that make you uncomfortable?” Ronan puts one hand under my chin and moves his face closer to mine, our lips only about an inch apart as his intense eyes search mine. “Because I was thinking of you,” he says in a low tone that sends a wave of heat through my body and between my legs.

“Really?” The word comes out breathy.

“Uh-huh.” He kisses me softly, and I stand on my tippy toes, eager to have more of him. “Have you honestly never had an orgasm?” he mumbles against my lips.

I lower myself onto my feet and look to the ground. “Never,” I say, a little embarrassed.

Ronan’s hand under my chin urges me to look back at him. “I would be more than willing to change that,” he says with a low chuckle.

“Are orgasms really that big of a deal?”

“Oh, baby, you have no idea,” he says, and I shiver against him.

Ronan

Vada had divulged that Cat was a virgin, but the no-orgasm thing still surprises me.

After our little walk on the beach, Cat and I head back to the group. We hang out for a couple more hours until people start either turning in or passing out from the crazy amount of alcohol we’ve all been drinking. Cat and Vada duck into their tent around one in the morning, and the rest of us go to our respective tents soon thereafter.

Though I fall asleep quickly, I wake up just a short while later, feeling movement next to me.

"Oh, fuck. Really, guys?" I mumble, my voice thick with sleep.

Vada has made her way into the tent, and she's looking at me apologetically as she straddles Steve, who has both his hands under her shirt.

"Sorry, little brother, but could you give us some privacy?" Steve asks.

I shake my head, annoyed. "Yeah, yeah, whatever," I say, rolling out of my sleeping bag. I fully anticipated this, but haven't really thought about what I would do next. I get out of the tent, zipping it shut behind me, then go to sit on one of the logs by the now-extinguished fire pit. My feet are bare, and although it was nice and toasty throughout the day, it's cooled down. My white shirt and black sweatpants don't keep me nearly as warm as I had hoped.

"Ran?" I hear Cat's voice from behind me, and I turn my head to see her emerge from her small tent. She crosses her arms over her chest as she stands, dressed in only a pair of light-blue drawstring shorts and a tank top, which would provide even less warmth than my clothes.

"Hey," I say, watching as she approaches me.

She sits on the log next to me, and the light ocean breeze causes her intoxicating scent to drift into my nostrils. God, she smells so good. "Did Vada invade your tent?" Cat giggles when I drape my arm around her, then pull her against me to share what body heat I have left.

I chuckle, nodding my head. "She sure did. It's stupid because I knew this would happen, but then it did and now I'm not really sure what to do with myself."

"Well, I mean... my tent is small, but... if you want..."

I turn my head to look at her, to analyze her, study her. Is she inviting me into her tent? To sleep with her?

"It's a lot cozier in there than it is out here," she adds sweetly, motioning around our dark surroundings.

"I bet it is," I agree with another chuckle. "But are you sure you'd be okay with me... with me sleeping with you?" I don't want to push her into anything she isn't ready for.

"It wouldn't be the first time we shared a small space and slept next to each other, right?" She shrugs with the cutest fucking smile I've ever seen.

"True," I admit, remembering the night we spent sleeping on Shane's couch just a few weeks ago after some fucking asshole decided to slip Cat some roofies in an effort to... I can't even think about it without getting absolutely pissed off.

"Okay, then," she says, getting to her bare feet, silently beckoning me to follow her into her tent.

I stand, wiping the sand off my pants, valiantly attempting to stop my eyes from rolling up her long, sexy legs to her tight ass. But I fail. Of course I do. She's so damn hot. I can't even count the number of times my thoughts of Cat have resulted in me needing to... release some tension—under the shower or first thing in the morning after waking up from a vivid dream of her.... Ugh, I'm so fucking drawn to her and have been from the moment I met her. Though I remind myself not to overstep any fucking boundaries. I don't want to hurt her. Ever.

It's quiet as we move to the tent. The only sound disrupting the night is the waves gently rolling in and crashing against the shore. I duck to enter Cat's tent behind her, noting that she apparently wasn't sleeping in a sleeping bag like I was, but instead has a thick blanket cushioning the tent floor, some pillows, and another thick blanket to cover her. I have to get on all fours to move around in her small tent and wait for Cat to take her spot. Once she does, she pats the spot next to her, smiling sweetly, a quiet ask for me to lie down with her.

I won't make her ask twice. I scoot in next to her, still trying to maintain a little distance between our bodies, to give her space while I pull her blanket over the both of us, though my senses are in overdrive, heightened and very aware of her nearness, the heat radiating off her barely dressed body. Her scent in the air gives me a head-high.

Then Cat closes what little distance remains between us and conforms her body to mine. Man, how many times I've already wished to be alone with her like this. *Cat is smart. Let her decide*, I remind myself, then reach for her hips and pull her closely toward me, paying attention to her body language, feeling the tension build between us.

Holy shit, don't lose your head, Ran.

Cat

I face Ronan as he pulls me closely toward him, his arms reaching around me. I can smell his scent—a mixture of sun, and ocean air, fresh linens, and something that's just him. It's delicious. I nuzzle my face against the crook of his neck, and Ronan releases a deep breath, his hands sliding to my hips. I can feel the tension between us rising, and I'm craving his touch.

It appears Ronan is thinking the same thing. "I'm going to kiss you, baby," he says, and in one swift motion he rolls over and onto me, holding up his weight with his elbows, one leg between both of mine. My stupid heart beats ridiculously against my ribs and my chest heaves in anticipation of his kiss. And he doesn't disappoint. So unlike the soft kisses from earlier today, Ronan's kiss is strong and passionate, his lips scorching hot against mine. He parts my lips with his tongue before slipping it into my mouth, exploring it, tasting my lips. I may not have much experience, but I do consider myself a pretty good kisser. Soon, our tongues engage in a sexy back-and-forth and it makes my body yearn for more.

My arms make their way around Ronan. I bury one hand in his hair while the other runs down the side of his ribs, then finally finds its way under his shirt. His skin is soft, and his muscles tense under my touch. A moan escapes my mouth as Ronan's lips leave mine, but only to trace kisses down my jawline to my neck and collarbone. *I want his shirt off right now*. I tug and pull until Ronan sits up on his knees and takes his shirt off. I take in his lean muscles, his firm abs and sculpted chest. Ronan leans toward me again, kissing my collarbone.

I run my hands across his naked back, needing something to hold on to, and I dig my hands into his sides. Ronan's breath hitches for a second as though I hurt him, and I pull back. But he only looks at me, his eyes glossy, breathing rapid, before he crashes his lips against mine again.

Ronan

Cat's hands on my bare back are addictive. She leaves a heated path wherever her fingers make contact with my skin. She glides her hands down and digs them into my sides, finding my bruises when I kiss her collarbone. It reminds me momentarily of the constant hell at home, but none of it matters right now. I'm too lost in her, too turned on to care. Her hands roam across my hot skin, and I can't get enough.

I kiss her collarbone, glide my tongue back up to her neck, then trail kisses back to her lips. I slip my tongue into her mouth and savor her long enough to make her breathless before I leave her lips again to kiss her delicate neck, then her earlobe, sucking it into my mouth. Cat's breathing is rapid and, God, I'm harder than I've ever been. My rational brain works overtime to keep me in line, knowing I can't push too hard, but also wanting to push the boundary just a little. The little tidbit about her never having had an orgasm has me determined.

I find the bottom of her thin tank top and slowly move my left hand underneath it, gliding gently across her tight stomach, causing her breathing to pick up, until I reach the bottom of her breast. I let my fingers trace it, her soft curves, outlining each breast, gently grazing my fingers around her nipples without touching them, and I can tell it's turning her on. God, I've been wanting to touch her like this for weeks, feel her soft body, taste her. I cup her breast. It fits perfectly in my hand. Cat's legs snake around my waist, pulling me closer toward her, pressing me against her. She must feel how my body responds to her, how worked up I am, but rather than pull away, Cat begins moving her hips, pushing herself even closer to me. *Fuck*. I don't know where to draw the line. Cat's breathing is erratic as my hand lingers on her breast and my mouth finds hers once again. She continues to grind her hips against me, her heat penetrating the thin cotton of her shorts and my sweats, and, shit, it's getting me harder than rock. I keep teasing her, then carefully glide my thumb over Cat's hard nipple. She moans loudly and it almost causes me to become unglued. I want her so badly.

"Shh," I moan into her ear as she continues to thrust her hips against me. Still bracing myself with one hand so as not to crush her under my weight, my other hand moves from her breast down her side, over her hips. I feel the hot skin of her leg and glide my hand to her inner thigh, pushing her shorts up an inch. My fingertips linger on her inner thigh, wanting to feel the warm, sweet spot between her legs to fucking badly, wanting to give her that first orgasm.

"Ran, I..." Cat's voice seeps through the fog of sex that clouds my mind.

"Yeah, baby?" I whisper softly against her neck.

"I've never..."

I pull my head up, looking into her huge, glossy eyes. She looks at me, shyness and embarrassment causing small creases to form on her brow, and realization spreads through me. She's not ready for me to take this any further tonight.

"It's okay," I breathe, my heart still hammering against my ribs. "I won't make you do anything you don't want."

I feel her relax underneath me, but I slide my hand back up her thigh and across the side of her body, just to feel her shiver against me one more time before I roll off her. I position myself to face her, adjusting my hard-on in the process. I can't even begin to describe how angry my dick is, how pent-up I am right now—the need to get relief, to reach climax almost overwhelming—but Cat is more than worth it.

"You are so different," she muses without looking at me. It makes me think that there have been some guys who were obvious about wanting only the one thing, and it makes me want to go hunt them down and teach them a lesson. "I've never done anything," she says, apparently in a confessional spirit.

I look at her intently, not sure what exactly she's getting at. Never done *anything*? "What do you mean?"

Cat sits up, adjusting her tank top to cover her exposed stomach. I can't help but pout a little bit. She notices, and her giggle rings like silver bells, making a smile appear on my face. "I mean I haven't done anything but kiss a guy."

"Okay, so no sex. Nothing wrong with that," I say, completely honest, sitting up.

"No, no sex," she says, looking down now. "And no oral sex, or anything like that."

I don't understand why she looks so embarrassed. Whether she has or hasn't had sex is of no concern to me. It's her body, and she should get to choose whether to be intimate with someone without judgment.

I put my hands on her cheeks, pulling her closer toward me, looking directly into her gorgeous hazel eyes that have taken on more of a green hue right now. "I can wait for you. No matter how long it takes. And even if you decide you never want to, or never want to with *me*..."—my heart stings at this last thought, but I shake it off for her sake—"then I'll be okay with that."

I mean every fucking word, no matter how painful it would be if I could never feel all of her.

Cat

Only six months ago, me shutting down the boy I was making out with would have ended in me getting hurt. Adam would have been angry, he would have screamed at me, called me names. But not Ronan. He stopped the second I expressed hesitation, and he didn't make me feel guilty, didn't accuse me of leading him on or being a tease. Instead, he told me that I set the pace at which we move, and I cannot even begin to express how safe I feel with him.

We lie facing each other, his fingers drawing patterns on my shoulder and arm, and he places soft kisses on my forehead.

"What are these?" I ask, lightly touching the thin gold necklace around Ronan's neck that holds two small gold pendants.

He stops kissing me and pulls back slightly, his hand reaching for the necklace. "This one"—he taps on the oval pendant that appears to have an angel with a large sword on it—"is Saint Michael. And this one"—he traces the other pendant, a woven-looking cross—"is Saint Brigid's cross. She was an Irish saint. Both of these are supposed to protect against evil. My grandmother gave them to me when I turned fourteen."

"She really wanted to make sure you're protected, huh?" I say somewhat jokingly, and Ronan nods.

"I guess so," he says, his voice soft. "She always worries about me," he adds, and kisses my forehead again.

"Why?" I ask, my eyes falling shut under the tenderness of his touch.

He doesn't respond, and instead dips his head down and kisses my lips. I let him distract me like that, and we end up tasting each other for what seems like hours. My hands forge paths across his still-bare torso while his fingers glide under my tank top again, softly touching my feverish skin. His caress of my breasts, my pebbled nipples, is sensual and unspeakably arousing. I feel the want growing deep within me, warm moisture pooling between my thighs, though Ronan refrains from venturing farther down again.

We drive each other to the near brink before we finally stop, breathless and exhausted. I end up falling asleep in Ronan's arms, my head resting on his bare chest while his steady breathing and beating heart quickly pull me under.

Saturday, July 3rd

Cat

When I wake up, Ronan is still next to me, his front to mine, his arm resting on my waist while my arms are tucked against his chest. I can feel the warmth of his body, and his slow breathing is peaceful and content. His features are relaxed, his eyelids shut, and I don't move out of fear of waking him. But the scent of him arouses my senses, and I can't help but wiggle against him a little, spreading my fingers over his chest and drawing small patterns on his warm smooth skin.

A low growl alerts me that Ronan is awake, and I giggle as he pulls me into him tighter.

"This might be my new favorite way of waking up," Ronan whispers into my ear.

I angle up my head to look into his face. His hair is sexy as hell messy like that, and his green eyes are brighter than usual. "Good morning," I whisper back.

He kisses my forehead and I feel his rib cage expand with a deep breath in.

"Did you... did you just smell me?" I ask.

"Uh-huh," he says, and inhales again deeply. I tip my head up to look at him.

"Do I smell bad?" I feel a little self-conscious because I haven't taken a shower yet or brushed my teeth. I probably look like a total mess, too—my hair, especially, likes to give me a hard time in the morning.

"Far from it," he groans as if it takes him a lot of effort to get the words out. "You smell too damn good. It's really addicting."

"Really?" I feel all tingly at his words.

"Uh-huh."

"You smell really good, too," I say, closing my eyes for a moment. "Like fresh laundry that was hung up to dry in the warm summer sun. It's so clean..." I trail off.

I open my eyes when I hear him chuckle quietly. "That sounds nice," he says with an appreciative nod and a mischievous grin.

I smile at him. "It is. I love your smell. It's really comforting and... manly," I say, blushing. I wonder if there will ever come a time when I'll be able to control my face.

"Manly, huh?"

"So manly," I nod, then close my eyes when Ronan begins to kiss my shoulder and glides his hand under my tank top to sensually stroke my back.

"Rise and shine, sexy people!" Vada's voice becomes increasingly louder before the door to the tent is zipped open.

"You've got to be fucking kidding me," Ronan mumbles under his breath, and even I'm slightly annoyed.

"Hey there. Have a good night?" Vada sing-songs, wiggling her eyebrows.

Ronan sits up, grabbing his shirt and pulling it over his head. "I swear, Vada, your timing is impeccable." Ronan's voice is tinged with irritation.

I don't want him to leave; if it were up to me, we'd spend the whole day in this tent just making out, but it seems Vada has other plans for us.

"Aww, so angry, Ran. Didn't you have a fantastic night?" Vada asks, a naughty gleam in her eyes.

Ronan doesn't answer and instead turns to me, his face softening as he takes me in. "I'm going to go change and brush my teeth. Care to take a dip in the ocean with me in ten minutes?"

I nod and smile as he plants another kiss on my forehead. I watch him move out of the tent past Vada, who sticks her tongue out at him and he shakes his head at her, chuckling.

Vada zips the tent shut as soon as Ronan is out of sight. "So? Tell me *everything*!" She sits down quickly. "What happened last night?" she continues like a waterfall, but her voice lowers when she asks, "Did you two... you know?"

I blush and shake my head. "No, we didn't. Ran was a perfect gentleman."

Vada gasps as if I had thrown away a winning lottery ticket. "Is everything okay?"

"Yeah, everything is great. Really great, actually," I blush. "It's just..." I trail off.

I expect Vada to chime in, but she sits silently, waiting for me to continue.

"I want to. Really badly. Really, really badly. Oh Vada, he's so perfect, so damn sexy, and the way he touches me...."

"So, what's the problem?"

I shrug, shaking my head. "I think I'm just scared."

"That's okay, Kitty Cat," Vada says in a soothing voice. "It's kind of a big step. I remember being scared as hell before Steve and I finally did it."

"When did you realize you were ready?" I ask, needing some girl talk.

"Actually, I didn't. It just kind of happened. Steve and I were hanging out together a couple of weeks after we started dating, and one thing led to another. But it was perfect that way, you know? I was afraid I'd overthink it, wanting everything to be perfect, putting too much pressure on us. I promise, you'll know when the time is right. And in the meantime, just enjoy a really, really lengthy foreplay." Vada smirks, then grabs her toothbrush and her swimsuit before ducking back out of the tent and zipping it closed behind her.

***

I change into my still-damp swimsuit before grabbing my toothbrush and crawling out of my tent to run off to the public bathroom, where I quickly scrub my teeth clean. When I reemerge, I make my way back to our cluster of tents and immediately spot Ronan, who's talking with Shane, Tori, and Zack. He's wearing only black board shorts that sit so low on his hips I can make out every single one of his abdominal muscles and that V-cut, which, like an arrow, leads downward. I know it wouldn't take much for me to pull his shorts off him, exposing him to me completely. I wonder what he looks like naked? I felt him last night, felt his hardness when I pressed myself against him, and from what I can tell, he's... well-endowed.

The sun kisses his skin, reflecting off his toned shoulders and arms. He notices me staring as I make my way toward him and he smiles. When I reach him, I run my hand up his bare chest, not caring that we're not alone. He eyes my entire body, lingering on the exposed parts, and goose bumps erupt on my skin when he interlaces his fingers with mine.

"Zack thinks we underestimated the amount of food we'd need for the weekend, because apparently, we 'scarfed like hungry wolves' last night," Ronan says, making air quotes. "So we may need to make a run into town a little bit later," he says, giving my hand a squeeze, and I nod.

"Anyway, ready for a swim?" Ronan asks, nodding toward the ocean.

"Yes," I say, and wave at Shane, Tori, and Zack as Ronan leads me to the water. He stops in his tracks just as we reach the shore, forcing me to turn around, and, without warning, he scoops me up, cupping my butt with his hands, and carries me into the ocean. I laugh loudly until the cold water licks at my feet. He keeps going, only stopping briefly to take in a sharp breath when the frigid liquid reaches his groin, then he dips down with me still in his arms. I squeal as he submerges us under the salty ocean water.

Still holding on to me, Ronan pulls me toward him, kissing me softly under water before letting go. We break the surface, our heads reemerging, and we both take a deep breath.

"God, you have no idea how perfect you are, Cat," Ronan says, his eyes hooded. He reaches for me again, pulling me toward him effortlessly with one hand while he paddles with the other.

"I can say the same about you, Ran," I say, and wrap my arms around his neck while winding my legs around his waist and crossing my ankles behind him.

He only shakes his head. "I'm waiting for the day you figure out I'm not good enough for you," he says seriously before kissing me so deeply that I think my heart might give out.

I honestly have no idea where that just came from, why he said what he said, because I've never been happier in my life than I have this past month with him. "Ran," I say when we finally break apart, "I don't think you understand how happy you make me."

I'm relieved to see some of the sadness that had temporarily resided in his eyes subside. "I seriously don't deserve you, baby," he says, and I wish he would stop talking to himself like that.

I put my finger to his lips. "You are so good to me," I urge him, needing him to understand how safe I feel with him, how cared for, how loved, even though we haven't actually uttered those words yet. "What you did last night, when you stopped—that meant so much to me," I admit, memories of Adam's violent outbursts running through my head. "Ran," I say again, my voice steady, "I don't know why you would think that you're not good enough for me, but you are."

I stare into his eyes and put my hand under his chin, forcing him to continue looking at me when he's about to break eye contact.

"Whatever you say." He smiles, apparently having decided not to go further down this dark path, and I exhale, relaxing into him. "But you do know that this position right here"—he motions his hand up and down our bodies—"makes things really hard. Literally."

"Well, yeah, that's sort of the point, isn't it?" I ask, then laugh when his mouth drops open. I kiss his bottom lip before taking it between my teeth, eliciting a small moan from him. I love that I have that effect on him.

"Jesus, Cat. We're going to have to take a break from this," he groans. "I don't trust myself right now." He cups my butt again and trudges out of the water with me in his arms, our lips still tasting each other until he finally sets me down on the warm sand. "How about some breakfast?" he asks, and I nod. I didn't realize how hungry I am, but now that he's mentioned food, my stomach is positively growling.

Holding hands, we walk back to the cluster of tents. Ronan turns to take a towel, and my eyebrows knit together when I see two large, streaked bruises on his right side, just above his hip bone. Those are what I must have touched last night when I held on to his sides.

I take a step toward him as he turns back around, ready to wrap the towel around me.

"What's wrong?" he asks at the look on my face.

"What happened to your back?" I ask him, my eyes wide, and it takes him a second to understand what I'm talking about.

"Oh, I tripped and fell backwards against the desk in my room the night before you came home," he says, then drapes the towel over my shoulders.

"Those are some painful-looking bruises," I say, craning my head to the side to look around him, eager to assess his injury more properly.

"Yeah, well, it was a pretty gnarly fall," he responds, not looking me in the eyes. He takes my hand and leads me back to the logs surrounding the fire pit.

"You must be one of the clumsiest people I've ever met," I opine, remembering his bruised and taped shoulder only a few weeks ago when he said he tripped over his dog. It's odd, because he doesn't appear clumsy at all. I've never seen him so much as stumble.

He only shrugs, but I can't help but stare at his injury. The bruises are a deep, dark blue; they look almost like two rungs of a ladder: about four inches wide, an inch tall, and a couple of inches apart from one another. I make a mental note of their precise location so as not to dig my fingers into them again when he's back in my tent tonight. At least, I hope he'll be in my tent again tonight, and maybe even the night after that.

We walk the thirty feet to the fire pit and sit with our friends. Shane, too, asks about the bruises on Ronan's back, and Ronan gives him the same response he gave me—that he tripped and fell backwards against his desk in his room.

"Huh," Shane says, narrowing his eyes at Ronan, giving him this look that definitely has more meaning to it than I understand.

Ronan presses his lips together, but they don't talk about it more, and we all turn our attention to breakfast. Zack and Drew cook bacon and eggs, and we devour our food, downing bottle after bottle of water.

"I'm so hungover," Summer laments, pressing her right palm to her temple.

"Me, too," Tori agrees, looking less pallid after having eaten her breakfast. "But last night was worth it." She winks at Shane, who smiles broadly at her.

"And tonight will be equally fun," Vada grins. "We should play another round of five hundred questions. What do you guys think?"

"Or maybe something else," Cheyenne says. "Personally, I'm a big fan of truth or dare," she says, looking around at us.

"How about strip poker?" Steve throws out, to the collective approval of the guys.

I look at Ronan, who grins at me.

"No way," Vada protests. "I'm not stripping for all you horny perverts."

"Okay, maybe just for me, then," Steve says with a smirk.

Everyone laughs, and the mood is light.

After breakfast Ronan and I get back in the water, where we spend a good part of the day, splashing each other, making out, talking, making out again. The rest of the group joins us and we only exit the ocean to play a game of beach volleyball. Tori and Shane each pick their teams, and Ronan and I end up on opposite sides. Watching Ronan play, his muscles flexing, a light sheen of sweat making his lean body glisten in the sun, is a thing of beauty, and I try hard not to get distracted by him. He, on the other hand, is not as successful.

"Will you come to my tent again tonight?" I whisper to him when we take our positions at the net. I give him my most seductive smile. "Because I would really like a repeat of last night," I say just as Steve jumps up next to me and spikes the ball clear past Ronan, scoring.

"What the fuck are you doing, Ran?" Shane yells. "You're supposed to block, not stare at your girlfriend."

"Sorry man, she's not playing fair," Ronan complains, and I grin at him mischievously. I turn around, watching Tori serve the ball when Ronan pinches my butt, making me jump. He laughs a beautiful, lighthearted laugh that rings in my ears. My team ends up winning the game, a fact that Shane blames squarely on Ronan.

"You're too distracted by Cat," Shane concludes.

Ronan shrugs but doesn't argue. "What can I say? I have a hard time concentrating when I'm around her," I overhear him say, and I smile. My heart is full with Ronan, our friends, and the fun we're all having.

By the time the afternoon sun lowers on the horizon, I'm exhausted. After changing out of my swimsuit and into some jean shorts and a t-shirt, I go to sit by the fire pit next to Tori. Drew is passed out on a beach towel, snoring, and I spot Cheyenne, Summer, and Vada in the water.

"Ran wanted me to let you know he went with Zack and Steve to make another food-and-booze run," Shane informs me. "They left when you were changing."

He hands Tori a wine cooler, but I decline when he offers one to me, too. I'm too sleepy and hungry, and alcohol would just amplify my exhaustion.

"Oh, okay. Thanks, Shane," I say, and lean back against the log.

Shane smiles at me for a second. "You know Ran's in deep with you, right?" he asks, amused, and sits in one of the foldout chairs.

I blush. "What makes you say that?" I ask shyly.

Tori laughs. "It's sort of really obvious," she says, and Shane nods.

I enjoy hearing this, but then remember that Ronan hadn't shared that we were together with his mom and dad. "He didn't tell his parents about us," I say, looking from the ground to Shane. "They only found out about Ran and me yesterday."

Shane studies my face before he nods and leans forward in his chair, resting his elbows on his knees. "I've known Ran more than half my life. He's my best friend, and I feel like I can say I know him really well," he says, his tone somber. "But even I'm still learning things about him." Shane takes a deep breath in, then exhales. "Ran is kind of a hard nut to crack, and man, he doesn't let a lot of people in." He chuckles, then his face becomes serious as he locks eyes with me. "I've seen Ran with a bunch of girls," he says, and I frown at the thought of Ronan with other girls, "but I have never, ever seen him like he is with you."

I release the breath trapped in my chest.

"He already cares about you more than he cares about anything or anyone else in his life," Shane says. "Cat, you can't take Ran not telling his parents about you as a reflection of how he feels about you and your relationship." He leans back in his chair, his expression contemplative. "He's just being protective of what you guys have."

Shane's words and sincerity ease my mind, but I'm also understanding more and more that I have some serious work to do in getting to know the boy I'm falling for head over heels.

I tap my index finger against my lips. "Tell me something about him that I don't know—that not a lot of people would know."

Shane looks at me, then at the crashing waves. It takes him a good thirty seconds before he replies, "Ran doesn't actually like playing ice hockey," he says matter-of-factly, and a smile tugs at his lips as I gape at him. "Well, I guess he likes it okay now. I mean, he's good at it—really fucking good—but if it were up to him, he wouldn't be playing like he does now; he wouldn't play club and varsity; he wouldn't be training like this. Maybe he wouldn't play at all."

"Why not?"

Shane leans forward in his chair again, grabs the half-full bottle of beer from the sand, and takes a sip. "I don't think he likes the physicality of it. Hockey is a full-contact sport and it's easy to get hurt, like really bad, especially in Ran's position as center forward. You're always getting checked or tripped, and audiences love a good fight, so there's that."

"But then why does he play it?"

Shane opens his mouth as if to respond, then closes it again. "I think he does it mostly to please his parents," he finally says somewhat hesitantly.

I contemplate this. "His dad seems nice." I recall my brief interaction with him yesterday morning, how warm and welcoming he was and how genuinely excited he became when he figured out that I'm his youngest son's girlfriend. "But his mom..." I trail off.

"Is a bitch," Shane finishes for me.

I blink at him, taken aback by his harsh words. "I mean, I don't know, I've only met her a couple of times, but she seems kind of... cold with Ran."

Shane nods. "That's the understatement of the century." He takes another long sip of his beer and I cock my head at him, waiting for further explanation that doesn't come. "The point is that I think Ran trains so hard, works so hard, studies so hard to keep the peace at home, and that includes killing himself playing hockey."

"What do you think he would like to be doing instead?" Curiosity ignites my mind as I learn these tidbits about Ronan. Why haven't I ever asked him these things myself?

"Books and music," Shane states, not a hint of doubt in his tone. "He loves to read, and we used to hang out and just play music. And he'd probably be getting a lot more sleep than he is nowadays."

"I didn't know he loves to read. And I've never actually seen him play," I frown, feeling like maybe I don't know Ronan at all.

"Because he doesn't ever really get the chance," Shane says. "He's constantly doing other shit, like hockey, then school, and he works, too. Now he has you, so he's obviously preoccupied. Don't get down on your relationship with him."

I smile at him. "I'm not," I promise, and mean it. "But, why do you work him so much?" I ask, fake accusation in my voice.

"Because he asks to work this much, especially when you're out of town."

"But why?"

I wonder if I'm starting to annoy Shane, but he grins at me. "For the distraction, obviously. He was so restless this last week that you were gone."

Shane gets up off his chair, stretching his legs before taking the few steps to me. He squeezes my shoulder as I look up at him. "You're really fucking important to him, Cat; it's like when he's around you he comes to rest."

He takes a seat next to Tori, pulling her into his arms.

Shane's white Jeep Wrangler pulls up a few minutes later, and my heart rate elevates when Ronan gets out of the driver's side. He walks around the back of the car to the trunk where he's met by Steve and Zack. Together, the three of them retrieve their grocery haul and make their way back over to us, where they drop the bags and bottles of booze in the sand before storing everything in the coolers.

"You guys good?" Shane asks Ronan.

Ronan tosses Shane his car keys and then leans down to place a soft kiss on my lips. "Yeah, all good." He moves his forearm across his forehead, wiping off small beads of sweat. He looks at me for a split second, then apparently decides that it's too hot and pulls his gray shirt over his head. I let my eyes roam his body, trying to be inconspicuous as I drink him in: his lean muscles, the light sheen on his skin where it's heated and damp. He must not be wearing anything underneath his jeans because I don't see his boxer briefs peeking out, and my cheeks flush.

Tori stands up and meanders to the coolers to inspect the goods. "So, what's for dinner?"

"Burgers," Zack says. "And your man is cooking tonight," he adds slyly, then wanders off to his tent.

"Well, I guess I better get started then." Shane sighs and throws Ronan a look. "You wanna help?"

Ronan sits down next to me, draping his arm over my shoulder and pulling me toward his bare chest. "How about no? But I'd be happy to sit here and provide you with emotional support while you flip the burgers."

Shane chuckles. "Alright, whatever. Extra-burned beef for Ran comin' right up."

Ronan shakes his head, "No beef, dude. Turkey, please," he says, then places a soft kiss on my temple.

"Oh right, how did I suddenly forget about your aversion to beef?" Shane chuckles and pours some lighter fluid over the charcoal in the small barbeque grill he brought with him.

"You don't eat beef?" I ask Ronan, interested in these small details, especially after having that little talk with Shane.

"He doesn't," Steve chimes in before Ronan can answer. "Ever since he witnessed our grandpa slaughter Ran's favorite cow."

My eyes are wide as I stare at Ronan. "You saw your granddad kill a cow?"

Ronan shakes his head, a slight smile on his face. "It wasn't quite that dramatic," he says, rolling his eyes at Steve. "My grandfather doesn't actually do any of that himself; he just selects the cattle and hauls it off to be..." He trails off. "But yeah, he did take one of the cows that I, as a ten-year-old, felt was, for some reason, more like my pet. And then he explained to me that the meat we eat is actually from the animals on the ranch, and, yeah. So I don't eat beef. I can handle turkey and chicken, but no beef and no pork."

"Oh," I say, finally comprehending. "That's why you didn't want to try my ribs when you took me to that barbeque place!"

He chuckles. "I can't believe you noticed that."

"Of course I noticed," I say. "I notice everything about you." I think about how Ronan probably isn't wearing boxers right now, and I blush.

"That's a super-touching story," Shane says, "but seriously, Ran, can you help me out really quick?"

Ronan sighs deeply and kisses my temple again before he gets up to help Shane cook the burgers.

Ronan

By the time food is ready, the sun has completely set and Steve has started another fire in the pit. Cat is still sitting on one of the huge logs by the fire pit, chatting with Tori about god-knows-what. My eyes keep wandering toward her and I get distracted admiring her. She's such a reprieve from my life, the constant anxiety, and the perpetual exhaustion.

"Alright, food's ready," Shane yells loud enough for everyone to hear, and we gather around the fire pit. Shane and I carry the food and place the plates on a beach towel for everyone to serve themselves.

"Man, I wish I was a guy and could walk around without a shirt on all day," Vada says to me as she wraps a towel around herself and eyes my bare chest. I haven't bothered putting my shirt back on since getting back from the store a while ago. I tend to run hot, even without clothes on.

"Who's stopping you?" Steve asks, amused. "I would have absolutely no problem with you walking around without a shirt on all day." He finds the edges of the towel Vada just wrapped around her shoulders and opens it up, letting his gaze roam her upper body, lingering on her breasts.

She giggles and swats his hands away, then wraps the towel tightly around herself. "Yeah, I bet you wouldn't, you horny pervert." She gives him a peck on his lips, and her hands snake around his backside before she squeezes his butt, making him jump. "But hey"—she turns her attention to me—"I'm thinking we should just say it how it is. I'm for sure going to sneak into your tent tonight, so should we just cut out the waking-up-in-the-middle-of-the-night stuff and agree that I'll sleep in your tent with Steve and you stay with Cat?" Vada grins, her eyes moving between me and Cat.

I lock eyes with Cat, and I can see her blush in the firelight. "It's your call."

She nods, apparently in agreement with the plan, and I smile.

We all sit and eat our burgers. After a little while, a couple of bottles of tequila start getting passed around, and it takes no time at all before the mood around the fireplace becomes livelier as people get tipsy and verge on being drunk.

"Game time," Vada calls out as she takes another swig of tequila.

"What's it gonna be tonight?" Summer asks. By her glassy eyes and slow speech, it's clear she's had more than her fair share of tequila already.

"Never have I ever," Vada exclaims, looking around at us. "We go around and each of us says something they've never done. If you have done it, you have to take a shot; if you haven't, well, then you don't have to take a shot." Vada places red plastic cups in everyone's hands and tips the bottle of tequila to pour a very generous amount of liquor into each cup.

"Okay, easy," Summer hiccups. "I'll go first." She clears her throat. "Never have I ever..." She thinks, then makes an a-ha face. "Never have I ever used a fake ID." She looks around with a grin.

"Uh, Summer, I think you misunderstood the rules," Shane laughs. "You're supposed to say something you haven't done, not something you do at least three times a week."

"Oh, shit," Summer says, giggling. "Guess I have to take a shot then." She tips her cup against her lips. Everyone, except for Cat, follows suit. The tequila heats my throat as it goes down, stinging slightly. I lock eyes with Cat, who watches me intently. I'm not usually a fan of these games because they're designed to embarrass each other, but I look at them as an opportunity to learn more about Cat. After all, last night's game of five hundred questions disclosed some really insightful information.

"Tori, your turn," Vada says.

Tori sits up a little straighter. "Never have I ever gotten a tattoo," she says, and Shane and Cheyenne both take a sip from their cups.

"What's your tattoo of?" Cat asks Shane and Cheyenne.

"I have my little brother's name tattooed on my ribs," Shane says and takes another shot of tequila, even though he already took one. I don't think Cat knows what happened to Liam, but she picks up on Shane's sudden mood shift and doesn't press him. I love that about her; she is so empathic that she picks up on the subtlest shifts in energy.

"How about you?" she asks Cheyenne, who throws Cat a contemptuous look. It's agitating how much of a bitch Cheyenne is to Cat, though I obviously know what the origin of her dislike is.

"I have a few," Cheyenne finally says.

I shake my head at Cheyenne, who frowns at me as Cat scoots a little closer to me and I wrap my arm around her waist, holding her.

"Alright, alright, my turn," Vada says, and by the way she's looking at Steve, I know hers is going to be a zinger. "Never have I ever cried after sex," she says, grinning from ear to ear.

"What the fuck, Vada? That was one time, and I was drunk. Way to call me out," Steve says, and takes a big gulp while everyone is dying of laughter.

I watch Cat, who has both her arms crossed over her stomach while she's folded over, laughing. When she comes up for air she has tears in her eyes, and I love how alive her face is.

"So, why exactly did you cry?" Shane wants to know, a wide grin on his face.

Steve gives him a look meant to kill. "Because I was fucking wasted, and Vada is beautiful, and that's when I realized I may be in love with her."

Vada swoons. "Is that really why?" she asks, her voice giddy and three octaves higher than usual. "Because that's when you realized you loved me?"

The annoyance leaves Steve's face, and he smiles at her. "Yep, but thanks for embarrassing me anyways." He squeezes her side, and she squeals. "Payback time," he says, and raises his voice. "Never have I ever thrown up on my teacher."

Vada's eyes go wide. "I can't even believe you would go there," she says before putting her red cup to her lips and taking a swallow while more laughter surrounds us.

"Shit, I remember that," I laugh, and Vada gives me a warning look, but I'm not about to let her off the hook so easily. "That was right after you decided it would be a great idea to down a water bottle full of tequila because you wanted to celebrate Cinco de Mayo." I recount the incident from just a couple of months ago, when Vada snuck some booze into school and chugged it all during lunch time, then threw up violently on our history teacher who was going around passing out graded tests.

"And then Megan threw up, too, because she couldn't handle Vada throwing up. Do you remember?" Tori gasps, unable to catch her breath laughing.

"Oh my god," Cat laughs, and I watch the tears streak down her face while she tries to compose herself. "Why didn't I know about this? We were already hanging out."

"I had known you for like two weeks. I wasn't about to tell you something that freaking embarrassing," Vada says, looking pissed while we laugh at her expense. It takes a moment for the laughter to die down and people to focus back on the game, but we keep going around.

Nobody drinks when Summer says she's never been to California or when Zack boasts that he's never been in a car accident. To my amusement, Cat ends up having to take two sips in a row when Tori says she's never played hooky from school, and when Shane says he's never stolen anything.

When Drew says he's never been in love, Shane, Tori, Zack, Summer, Vada, and Steve immediately put their cups to their lips and drink.

Cat's eyes find mine, and she hesitantly lifts her cup to her lips and takes a small sip, not breaking eye contact.

It's scary as hell; I don't know if I should be drinking or not. I've never felt the way I do with Cat, and I know I'm falling in love with her. It's terrifying admitting it to myself, but it's even scarier admitting it to someone else, especially when my life is such a shit show.

I finally bring my cup to my mouth and drink, though I'm unable to keep looking into Cat's eyes as I do it because I know, deep down, that I should be stopping what's happening between us. She's too good for me. I'm too much of a fucked-up, worthless piece of shit who's too damn selfish to cut her loose because it feels too good when I'm with her. And that fact makes me even more worthless and fucked up.

I swallow another shot of tequila to drown out my thoughts, then I wrap my arms around Cat and pull her toward me because I'm a selfish asshole who knows better but won't do the right thing.

Cat

The evening is turning out to be as much fun as last night. Though it takes no time at all for people to get drunk, especially because after just a few minutes, the statements get targeted at individual people, like Vada's "never have I ever" about crying after sex. We throw around things like never having had sex in a car—Ronan drank on that one, as well as the one about never having a one-night stand. And I end up having to drink when Shane says he never stole anything and when Zack says he's never been on a cruise ship.

"I think I'm going to leave the game," Ronan says, his left hand resting on my hip while he sets his red cup in the sand. Vada has had to refill his cup a couple of times, and he's just taken three shots in a row when people said they had never done drugs, had never fallen asleep in class, and had never broken a bone.

I lean forward and turn around to face him. "Are you okay?" I whisper, my face close to his.

He nods. "I'm fine," he says, and strokes his thumb across my cheek. I let my eyes shut under his small touch and feel him lean in to brush his lips softly against mine. "Just need to slow it down. I'm going to go cool off really quick," he mutters.

I open my eyes as Ronan shifts behind me, then gets to his feet. He holds out his hand to me. "Care to join me?" he asks with a gleam in his eyes.

He still hasn't put on his shirt, and even though it's cooled down quite a bit since the sun set, I agree to go for a dip in the ocean with him.

I take Ronan's hand and he walks me to my tent before changing into his board shorts in his own tent. He's back, waiting outside my tent, only two minutes later.

"You're fast," I say to him through the paper-thin tent walls, and I can hear him chuckle.

"It's a lot easier for me to change into shorts than it is for you to change into that little blue number you were wearing earlier," he says, and for some odd reason I blush.

"Were you... You weren't wearing boxers under your jeans, huh?" I ask, trying to sound blasé about the whole thing even though my heart speeds up in my chest.

"What makes you think that?" he asks, and there's something in his voice that makes me think he's flirting, but I can't see his face, so I'm not totally sure.

"Well, usually I can see the waistband of your boxers over the top of your jeans, like, when your shirt rides up or... like when you weren't wearing one last night..." I say, taking a deep breath. "But not today. Just your jeans... hugging your hips... and..." I trail off.

"And what?" His voice is low now.

I unzip the tent, ducking out of it before standing straight up only a foot away from Ronan. "And nothing," I say breathily.

I blush violently when he puts his index finger under my chin and tips my head up to face him. "I don't know how I feel about you noticing these things," he admits, and there's something in his eyes I can't quite decipher. There is want, definitely, but there's something sad in them, too, and I don't know why.

"I can't really help it," I say.

He scoops me up, interlacing his hands under my butt, while I wrap my legs around his waist. And just like this morning, he carries me off into the waves, though he doesn't submerge us when he's waist-deep in the ocean. Instead, he keeps holding on to me and begins kissing my collarbone so softly it sends goose bumps down my arms and back.

He makes his way slowly up the side of my neck and to my jawline before I tip my head down to meet his lips. His tongue slips inside my mouth, tasting me the instant I part my lips. And even though we're standing in the cool water, my body is scorching hot from the heat radiating off Ronan's perfect body and the want coursing through my veins.

Ronan slowly lowers me into the water, his lips never leaving mine as my hands greedily explore his back, his neck, his chest, finding their way into his dark-blond hair before gliding back down his neck, too eager to rest. His hands roam my body, equally restless, and my breath hitches when Ronan suddenly undoes the string to my bikini top.

"Is this okay?" he groans against my lips.

I push against him in response, deepening our kiss, wanting him to feel more of me as my heart beats in my chest like hummingbird wings. His left hand glides from my back to my ribs, then gently outlines the curve of my breast before he slides the fabric of my top up and cups my breast in his hand. He runs his thumb over my already-hard nipple, eliciting a moan.

"Please just tell me when to stop," he begs, his breathing erratic as his right hand glides up my back to my neck and unties the other string before he pulls the offending piece of clothing off my body.

My chest heaves under his touch. "Okay," is all I manage to whimper as Ronan's mouth leaves my lips.

He begins kissing a path down my neck to my shoulder, then my chest, kissing my breast before circling my nipple with his tongue, then sucking it gently into his mouth. The sensations tearing through my body are intoxicating, and pure, unfiltered need erupts in me as I get more and more aroused by his hands, his mouth, his body.

He continues to kiss my breasts, and nips and sucks on my nipples. The feeling is indescribable as my mind goes to a place where only Ronan's touch exists, my world shrinking to include only him and me. Heat pools between my aching thighs, an overwhelming desire to be consumed by him, to have him fill me building deep inside my core, but my body stiffens and my eyes open as I hear splashing and voices approaching us.

"Ran," I breathe, "we're not alone."

He stops tasting my skin to look over his shoulder. "Crap," he mutters.

Everyone has apparently decided to go for an evening swim, and a mere thirty or so feet separate Ronan and me from our friends. There's no time for me to refasten my bikini top, and I start to panic because I'm about to give everyone a show when they reach us.

"Are you two having fun?" Steve calls in our direction.

I look at Ronan, eyes wide, my arms crossed over my chest.

"I got you," Ronan says. "Come here."

He pulls me into his arms and picks me back up, guiding my legs around his waist. Jesus, I can feel how hard he is where he presses between my thighs. It sends electricity through my core. But now is not the time to get more worked up, and I suppress my need to grind against him. Instead, I wrap my arms around his shoulders, pressing my upper body to his, letting him blanket me as he carries me toward the shore.

"Wait, where are you guys going?" Vada calls out to us.

I can hear the guys whistle.

Ronan doesn't let go of me until we're back in front of my tent, where he slowly lowers me back to the ground. His eyes travel from mine down to my exposed chest, and I can see the want in his eyes before he raises them back up.

"God, you're beautiful, Cat," he says, his voice husky, before he exhales deeply. "I'm going to go change."

"You're coming back though, right?"

He nods at me, smiling. "If that's what you want?"

"It's what I want," I say, and stand on my tippy toes to give him a soft kiss on the lips.

The inside of my tent is nice and warm, and I'm out of my wet bikini bottoms in no time. I dry off quickly and slip on my cotton shorts and a fresh white shirt before pulling my blanket over me and resting my head on my pillow.

***

"Are you falling asleep on me?" I hear Ronan whisper softly in my ear.

My eyes flutter open. "Oh my gosh, I didn't even realize I was falling asleep. I'm sorry," I say groggily. I didn't hear or feel Ronan get into my tent, but I'm enjoying the feel of him next to me under the blanket. He cuddles up next to me, and I move closer to rest my head on his chest. He's wearing a shirt and sweatpants, his hair still damp from when I ran my wet hands through it.

"Don't apologize," he says, pulling me close to him. He nuzzles his face into my hair and inhales deeply. "You're seriously intoxicating," he exhales, and I giggle. "So, what did you steal?" he asks, catching me off guard.

"What?"

"What did you steal? You took a shot when Shane said he had never stolen anything."

I grin against him. "Stickers. I stole stickers when I was like seven or eight. My mom wouldn't buy them for me, so I nicked them. My mom found them and I got into so much trouble," I laugh. "She grounded me for a whole week." I lift my head, my hand on his clothed chest. "Did you really lose your virginity when you were fourteen?" He searches my eyes, then nods. "That's really young," I remark, and lower my head back onto him. I can hear his heart beating in his chest, solid and steady. It's an exceptionally comforting sound. "Can I ask who she was?"

"She was my girlfriend. Well, she became my girlfriend afterwards," he says, his voice thoughtful. "She was sixteen. Her name was Miranda."

"How long were you together?" I honestly don't even know why I'm asking him all these questions about his ex-girlfriend other than to learn more about him.

"About a year, while I lived in Montana this last time. But we broke it off when I moved back to New York."

"I'm sorry," I say. "That must have been hard."

I kiss his chest and feel him tighten his hold on me. "Don't be. I didn't have hopes of being with Miranda forever, and if you'd ask her, she'd tell you the same thing," Ronan assures me. "She was with me because she was bored and because she wanted to stick it to her dad, and I was with her because I needed an escape."

I lift my head again, eyebrows creased as I search his face. "Escape from what?"

He looks at me as though he just realized he was talking out loud. "Just stuff," he says, and I know he's evading my question, but whatever that "stuff" is, he's obviously not ready to talk about it. I'd be a hypocrite if I pressed him to pour his heart out about his "stuff" and why he thinks he's not good enough for me when I still haven't found the courage to tell him about Adam. So, I let it go.

It becomes quiet for a few minutes while neither of us speak.

"Can I ask you something?" I ask into the silence.

"You can ask me anything," he says in a low voice.

"Okay, you don't have to tell me if you don't want to, but... so..." This is weird to talk about, and it kind of feels like it's none of my business. "Shane said something today about having seen you with a bunch of girls, and I get the impression, you know, just from what I hear, like, from Vada, and I obviously see how girls react to you," I mutter incoherently. Ronan studies me as I talk. "I just, you know, Vada told me about Cheyenne and you, and then Zack said something about homecoming, and just..."

"Are you asking me if I've slept around?"

"I think so, yeah," I admit sheepishly. "Sorry, I know it's none of my business."

"It kind of *is* your business," he says, then exhales deeply.

"Oh, okay," I say, somewhat taken aback by how forthcoming he is.

"I don't really know how to say this without sounding like a complete dick," he groans. "But, yeah, I've had my share of random hookups. That's what I meant when I told you I don't usually go on dates, because before you, I didn't," he says, causing me to lift my head and look up at him. "I just had casual sex and then I'd never see the girl again."

"How many?" I'm not sure why I feel the need to know this, because it actually stings a little bit imagining Ronan being intimate with other girls.

"I'm not sure, but... a lot," he sighs, then falls silent. "Do you think I'm a horrible person?"

"No," I respond truthfully. "But, isn't it risky to sleep with so many random people?"

"What do you mean?"

"I mean, like, you know, STDs and stuff."

"Oh, yeah. No, baby, I've never done it without a condom. I couldn't even tell you what that feels like," he says earnestly, his hand gliding up and down my arm.

"Really?"

Ronan nods. "Really."

"Yeah, me neither," I say for some levity.

Ronan chuckles. "So, I heard," he says, his voice gravelly.

"I don't think you ever told me why you never went on dates," I say, recalling our prior conversation and realizing I never actually did find out why he didn't take girls out or even exchange numbers with them.

"I was holding out, waiting for you," he says with a shrug, and it seriously makes my heart speed up in my chest.

"You're so full of it," I say despite loving his statement.

"I'm serious, Cat," he says, pushing himself up into a sitting position, looking at me with intense eyes. "I've never felt like this; I've never been this drawn to someone."

I study him. His eyes are serious, conveying the depth of his words. I didn't think boys like him existed, yet here we are.

"Oh my gosh." I jerk up, and Ronan looks at me, eyebrows raised. "I completely forgot to give this to you." I begin rummaging through my bag as Ronan leans back on his elbows. Finally, I find the small, clear bag filled with candy I bought in Buffalo. I turn around and hold it out to him.

He furrows his brow as he analyzes what's in the bag, then a smile breaks across his face as he beams at me. "You got me candy?" he asks, laughter in his voice.

"Yep. It made me so sad when you told me your mom wouldn't let you have any, so I thought I'd try to make up for you missing out."

For a second, Ronan's face takes on a pained expression. He shakes his head before reaching for me and kissing me so fiercely it takes my breath away. I drop the bag with candy as my hands wind around the back of his neck and hold on to him for dear life.

"Why are you so good to me?" he breathes against me while his hands sear scorching-hot paths under my shirt and across my skin. It takes only seconds before both our shirts come off and I'm in his lap, my legs wrapped around and my hips grinding against him while he kisses my right breast, cupping the other with his left hand. "I don't deserve you," he breathes again just as a moan escapes my lips.

My hands come up to his face and I force him to look at me. His eyes are glossy and hooded but intense. "You keep saying that," I say breathlessly, "but you're wrong."

He responds by crashing his lips against mine, once more stealing every breath and thought from my body.

Sunday, July 4th

Ronan

I don't deserve Cat, not in the least. And I don't understand her, don't understand why she's so damn good to me.

When she held u the bag of candy and told me she wanted to make up for me missing out, it felt like she was breaking me into pieces. I don't know what to do with all of that. I know I should stay away from her because of all the reasons in the world. I'm not worthy of her; I'm not good enough. It's a fact that has been pounded and beaten into me all of my life, no matter what I do to prove my worth. And if this keeps going, Cat is going to get hurt somehow, and it will have been my fault.

The problem is, I don't know how to stay away from her. I'm drawn to her like a ship out on the dark sea sailing toward a lighthouse, because that's what my life feels like—an endless, dark ocean, ready to drown me any second. And Cat is the light in the dark. When I'm with her all the heaviness momentarily lifts. It's such a welcome respite for my anxious mind and tired body—until I realize that I'm setting her up for pain that is surely going to come for her, because that's what I do: I fuck things up—always have, always will. And if I were less selfish, I would have never let it get this far. I'd have put a stop to this before it had a chance to get started, or I would at least stop it now. But I can't find the strength or the willpower. She's like medicine for my aching mind. And, fuck, I want to make her happy. I want to be with her. I want it more than I want anything else in my life. I'm at war with myself—the need to keep her safe and protected clashing with my desperate desire to be with her because the two cannot coexist. Not in my world. They're mutually exclusive.

I woke up startled after a nightmare. It happens sometimes—indistinct darkness pressing on my chest, causing me to wake up, making it impossible to fall asleep again. And so I've been lying next to Cat, feeling her body against mine, breathing her in, allowing myself to feel this moment. Being with her feels unbelievably good, and it's so damn scary because I feel so much with her when I've been shutting it all down for the past seventeen years. Everything has always been muted—even the good times, the fun, the laughter, because no matter how good a day was, I know that at the end of it all I have to come home. I have to step back into the darkness where monsters wait, where life is unpredictable, where I'm always on guard, always on edge, always anticipating the pain that inevitably comes.

I'm such an asshole for doing what I'm doing—dragging her into my bullshit. She's not like Miranda. Miranda had her very own demons to battle, just like I have mine. Miranda knew what my mother was doing to me just like I knew what Miranda's father was doing to her. We bonded over the fact that we were both occupying our own versions of hell. But I can't share that shit with Cat; I want to protect her from it, so fucking badly.

"How do I keep you safe?" I whisper, grazing her arm softly. We both fell asleep without putting our shirts back on and I kiss her shoulder softly, moving her long hair from her neck before kissing her warm skin there, then her earlobe. The darkness in the tent is diminishing with the slow rise of the sun over the horizon.

"This might be my new favorite way of waking up," Cat says sleepily, repeating my own words, and just like that my racing mind stills.

I smile. "Hey," I say, nuzzling the space between her shoulder and her neck. Her skin is warm and soft as I kiss her. Her left arm reaches up and around my neck and I let my hand slide up her side and to her breast, caressing it. I allow myself a minute to feel and taste her before urging her to face me.

"You're up early," she says, her hand resting against my chest, right over my heart. I wonder if she can feel it beating against my ribs, if she has any idea at all what she does to me, how much I care about her. "You should try to get a little more sleep," she says, and I can tell she's beginning to doze off again. Her nearness, her breathing, and her scent begin to pull me under, and I gladly drift off to sleep with her.

The next time I wake up the sun is high in the sky. I can hear voices outside, people splashing in the water. The smell of food is in the air, but no Cat next to me. I maneuver out of the small tent and spot Cat in the water with everyone else, so I quickly brush my teeth, then change into my board shorts and join her.

We spend the day much like we did the last, with lots of time in the water, and we squeeze in another round of volleyball. This time, though, I make sure Cat is on my team. It's still distracting as hell seeing her get after a ball or spike it, but at least I'm not giving away points, to Shane's absolute delight. Nonetheless, I have the hardest time keeping my hands off Cat, who stays in her blue bikini the majority of the day, and even though she eventually pulls on a pair of short jean cutoffs, it really doesn't help my situation. I take every opportunity to touch her exposed skin, every chance to kiss her. She does the same, running her hand up my stomach and chest, touching my back, kissing me whenever she has the chance. And I fucking love it. I love everything about this weekend: the uninterrupted time I have with Cat, having her near me around the clock, spending the days with the people I care about most, and, fuck, just not being at home and in a constant state of alertness.

I help Zack prep dinner by the time the sun gets low on the horizon. I throw aluminum foil-wrapped potatoes into the embers of the fire pit and cut up whatever food Zack instructs me to chop while he mans the barbeque.

"You sure you want to go to L.A. and direct movies? You should be a chef instead," I tell Zack while I poke the potatoes with a stick to roast them evenly.

"Dude, once I'm a director I'll *hire* someone to cook for me," he says.

I laugh. "Fair enough."

"Food!" I yell loudly once everything is prepped and ready to be devoured, and everyone gathers around the crackling fire pit. Cat is still wearing her blue bikini top and short cutoffs when I sit down next to her in the sand. We eat, not to mention drink—god, there's so much drinking—while Shane tells us all about his less-than-successful search for a roommate for his apartment in Queens.

"I'm pretty sure the guy who showed up on Thursday was just released from prison," Shane says, "because he was wearing a gray sweat suit and only had a plastic bag with him."

"Oh, an ex-felon. How exciting!" Summer snorts a laugh.

"Just make sure you lock your bathroom door," I say. "And whatever you do, don't drop your soap when he's around."

"Knowing Shane, he'll drop the soap on purpose," Drew laughs.

"Come on, dude. Don't project your feelings on me, okay?" Shane retorts, garnering a "burn" comment from Steve and a flip of the middle finger from Drew.

Once the sun has completely set, Shane and Zack bring out some fireworks that, we all agree, couldn't possibly have been obtained legally. They're loud as hell when we set them off, but they're pretty sweet and certainly beat lighting those outrageously priced rinky-dink fireworks they sell at the stands. We all sit in the sand, facing the ocean while Zack lights one rocket after another. Cat sits between my legs, her back against my chest while she gazes at the sparkly lights in the sky. She smells like lavender shampoo, but there's something sweet that's just her. If there was a way to bottle it up, I would.

We all stay up well past three in the morning and, after going for a middle-of-the-night dip in the ocean, head to our tents. Vada made it clear that she intended to spend the night with Steve again, so I follow Cat into her tent. The make-out session that ensues is so hot, getting me so damn worked up, that I have to sneak out of her tent once she falls asleep and relieve the pent-up sexual tension. As much as I want to take it all the way with her, I'm not about to pressure her into anything. I promised her I would move at her pace, and that's exactly what I intend to do.

Monday, July 5th

Ronan

We all leave the beach at around one the next day. Shane stops at Cat's first, and I walk her to the door, carrying her stuff inside for her. Shane already warned me that I would be working with him that night, so I know I won't see Cat again until tomorrow.

"This was one of the best weekends of my life," Cat says sweetly when I head back out the door after depositing her things in the house.

"I couldn't agree more." I draw her toward me and kiss her. "I'll call you when I'm on break?"

"Yes, please," she says, and kisses me softly again.

I get back into Shane's car a few seconds later. The closer we get to my house, the more anxious I feel. It's always been like this. Anytime I come home, my muscles tense as soon as I turn the corner to our street, and the tension only increases the closer I get to the house. It usually either peaks or dissolves once I see the driveway and whether my mom's car is parked there. It's only four, so I expect my mother to be home, and sure enough her car is pulled into the driveway. Steve went to hang out with Vada after dropping off her stuff at her house, so my brother being gone, coupled with my dad leaving this morning, pretty much guarantees I'm about to walk into fire.

"I'll see you in a couple of hours," Shane says before he pulls away to drive Tori home and then head into Murphy's.

I stand at the entrance to the short walkway leading to the dark-green front door, bracing myself for what awaits me inside. Then I take a couple deeps breaths, grab my crap, and walk into the house.

I'm pleasantly surprised to run into my dad of all people. It's interesting, because when I think about it, it's almost like I'm prey that's aware it's being stalked, and I swear my muscles ache with the anticipation. It's my go-to response when I know only my mom is home; I don't even wait to see what kind of mood she's in anymore. I stopped doing that when we moved back to New York a couple years ago, when I was old enough to realize that nothing I did would be good enough. So, I just assume it's going to be bad unless and until her movements, her facial expression, or the tone of her voice tell me otherwise. I'm constantly analyzing the threat level, and to say that this shit gets old quickly would be a real fucking understatement. Honestly, I just avoid her at all cost now, at least to the extent that's possible.

"Hey, Ran!" my dad says when he steps out of the kitchen and into the hallway. I'm in the process of taking off my shoes and storing them neatly in the shoe closet, always careful not to leave a mess or do anything to provoke my mother.

"Hey, Dad!" I say, unable to hide my surprise yet again. "I thought you were already gone?"

"Heading out in a few minutes, actually," he says in his deep voice, and nods toward his packed camo-green duffel bag on the floor of the living room.

"Oh, right," I say just as my mom descends the stairs. I step back to make room for her to pass me and she does so without so much as a "hello" to me. "When do you think you'll be back?" I ask my dad, hoping he'll check in a little more frequently, especially once Steve leaves for Boston.

"Uh, I'm not sure. Probably not for a while. Your mom's not very happy with me right now," he admits sheepishly.

I nod, pressing my lips together. *Fucking great.*

"How was camping?" my dad inquires, eagerly changing the subject. He leans back against the doorframe, watching me.

"Great," I say with a smile. It really was an incredible weekend and I already miss Cat.

"Yeah? You look like it was a great weekend," my dad grins at me. "Cat seems pretty great, too."

I notice my mother behind him in the kitchen, analyzing me. "She is," I agree with him and grab my stuff off the floor to take it up to my room.

"When were you going to tell us about the fact that you have a girlfriend?" My mom already has a small frown on her face.

Never. I was never going to fucking tell you about Cat, I think as I turn around to face her. I only shrug.

"How long has this been going on, Ronan?" she asks, her arms crossed in front of her chest.

"Cat told me they've been dating a month now," my dad says, still smiling, completely unaware of the rising tension. "I like her. You had already met her?" my dad asks my mom.

"Once, I guess," she says, her tone dismissive. "But she didn't say anything about seeing Ronan then."

"Because she wasn't at that point," I say against gritted teeth.

My mom narrows her eyes at me but doesn't say anything else as she walks past my dad and into the living room.

"Don't mind her. She's a little grumpy today," my dad whispers, chuckling.

I only shake my head. He has no fucking idea what goes on around here. I start up the stairs to finally take my stuff to my room, take a shower, and get ready for work.

"Ran," my dad says, drawing my attention back to him, and I stop, backtracking a couple of steps. "I know I already said it on Friday—and I'm sorry. I know it made you uncomfortable."

I know where he's going with this. So I exhale deeply, waiting for him to just get it over with.

"You're seventeen," he says. "Cat is a beautiful girl; I obviously don't expect you and your brother to be abstinent."

I can tell he's trying hard not to make this conversation awkward. "Are you seriously having 'the talk' with me right now?" I chuckle, making him laugh.

"I guess so." He shrugs.

"Dad, I promise I'm safe. I'm pretty sure Steve is being safe, too. I mean, I haven't, like, checked or anything, but seeing as Vada isn't pregnant yet, I assume they're taking precautions," I say like a smartass.

My dad laughs. "Okay, I'm glad to hear that," he says. "By the way, I had lunch with Seamus on Saturday." Seamus is Shane's dad, and he and my dad have been pretty close friends ever since Shane and I started playing hockey together.

"Oh, yeah?"

"Yeah, he said you and Shane are basically running Murphy's at night now, that you both work all the time."

"Yeah, I mean, Shane plans on taking over the restaurant, and he likes it when I close with him, so...." I give a small shrug.

"That's what Seamus said. He was impressed by you, said something about giving you more responsibility once you're up for it. I reminded him that you have another year of high school ahead of you," my dad laughs. "He told me he asked you to come in last week so he could watch you work and thought you kicked ass."

"Huh," I say, finally comprehending why Shane's dad had asked me to come in and work last Thursday when Shane wasn't scheduled to work. I had really wanted to see Cat after she was gone for five days, but of course, I didn't argue with Shane's dad. He's always been good to me, letting me work at Murphy's when I got back to New York exactly two years ago, then quickly making me a waiter even though I'm technically still not old enough to serve alcohol, but recognizing that I could really use the extra money from the tips. He lets me close with Shane, even though I'm really not supposed to work this late. And he always allowed me to crash at Shane's when—unbeknownst to his family—I desperately needed to escape my house for a night or two. I've spent many weekends and even holidays with Shane and his family, who've always treated me like one of their own; and there were many times when I wished I didn't have to go back home at all.

And then, when I asked him last year if he would sell me his Mustang, he agreed without a second thought. I know for a fact that I got the car for a freaking bargain. I mean, it wasn't in great shape, but it's still a classic, and I'm pretty sure he could have sold it for a hell of a lot more money than he sold it to me for. At sixteen, I didn't really have any money saved up—a few thousand, maybe—but I emptied my savings and then agreed to work two months for free, which, still, likely didn't come close to what the car was worth even in its run-down state. But Shane's dad still let me take it off his hands. Fuck, I still remember how excited I was. I spent a ton of time on my weekends fixing it up. I even dropped a couple of grand on a sweet satin-black paint job once I had scrounged up enough money.

"Anyways, I just thought I'd tell you that I'm proud of you. You're doing great, Ran. Working so hard; and I saw your report card, too, so you're obviously doing really well in school. I… just… good work."

"Thanks, Dad," I say, my voice a little unsteady. He's not usually around long enough to notice these things, or, if he does, he never says anything. And my mom sure as fuck never has anything good to say, so this is unexpected, and honestly, a little uncomfortable. I don't really know how to react, so I just stand there for a few seconds.

"Alright, bud, I have to head out." My dad moves to the living room to grab his duffel bag off the floor before walking over to my mom to give her a quick hug and a kiss on her cheek.

"Have a good trip, Dad," I say, already feeling the tension rise in my body again as I finally head up the stairs and into my room. I hear my dad leave just a few minutes later. I still have a couple of hours before I have to head to Murphy's, and the prospect of spending this time in the house with only my mother is anything but calming.

I wish I could hole myself up in my room until it's time for me to head to work, but Onyx is in the backyard—and likely has been there all damn day, maybe even all weekend while I was gone—and I really need to take her on a quick walk. So I take a shower, relishing the hot water against my skin, then get dressed in jeans and a white t-shirt and make my way back down the stairs and to the sliding glass door in the living room to get Onyx.

"Don't think I don't know what's happening," my mom says from the couch. There's already an edge to her voice, and my shoulders slump. Why can't we ever just go about our lives pretending the other doesn't exist and just leave it at that?

"What do you mean?" I ask, and turn to face her.

"Your little girlfriend." She stands up. "I don't appreciate that you're keeping secrets, Ronan, but it would certainly explain why you've been slacking so much," she says sharply.

My eyebrows knit together. I know for a fact that I haven't been slacking. The only thing that's changed around here is that I've been working more hours while her list of chores for me keeps growing longer and longer.

"What? Cat's got your tongue?" my mother says, and laughs about her own fucking joke.

"Very funny," I mutter. God damn it, she's getting a rise out of me, and I can't stop myself. "I don't think I've been slacking." I'm becoming defensive, even though I know I need to just back off, need to shut up and take her fucking shit if I want even the slightest shot at getting out of here unharmed today, but I can already feel myself reacting to her.

"No? Then you're not only stupid, but you're apparently also blind, Ronan," she says, her voice getting louder. "You've been breaking your curfew, you can't manage to do the things I ask of you, and you have a shitty fucking attitude to boot. Don't think I forgot the way you were talking to your dad on Friday when he told you to use protection when you're fucking around."

"I'm pretty sure you're talking exactly the same way to me right now," I say, adding fuel to the damn fire. I swear it's like I have two versions of me sitting on my shoulders right now. One's telling me to back the fuck off and the other is telling me to double down. And it's obvious which one is winning right now.

It's a stupid game I'm playing, and I'm about to win a stupid fucking prize.

"I don't appreciate the tone with which you're talking to me, Ronan," she hisses back at me.

"God, fuck, Mom," I say against gritted teeth, my jaw tight as I run my left hand through my hair. "What do you want from me?" I say, my voice louder now.

"You better knock it off, Ronan." She steps closer toward me. "This is a war you don't want to start."

"I'm pretty sure this war has been going on for a long time already," I argue with her, unable to control myself. I'm honestly surprised at myself for talking back like this, though I'm perfectly aware this will not end well.

"Ronan, I'm warning you. You will lose." Her hands are already balled into fists, ready to strike.

"Go the fuck ahead, Mom. This shit means nothing to me; I have nothing to lose," I growl, and brace myself for her first hit. I've obviously lost my damn mind.

"Are you sure about that, Ronan?" She hammers her fist into my stomach, causing me to double over. "You think you're so brave talking back to me, you worthless piece of crap. Did your little girlfriend suddenly make you lose your god damn mind that you think you can talk to me like that?" She shoves me, and I stumble backwards as I straighten myself up. "You know she's going to see straight through you, right? You know that sooner or later she's going to figure out that you're useless. Or maybe she won't; maybe that little blonde bitch has even less of a brain than you do."

She takes another step toward me. She has her fist clenched, about to slam it into my stomach again, but I'm ready for her this time. I flex my abs as tightly as I can as her arm darts forward and she punches me. It still hurts, but not nearly as badly as the last time, and this time I can tell it caused her pain, too. She briefly looks at me in disbelief as she steps back, breathing heavily as she flexes her right hand. "Are you fucking serious, Ronan?" she asks in a tone that lets me know I'm in deep fucking shit now. And sure enough, her fist comes flying forward again, sucker-punching me in my stomach for a third time. I wasn't expecting it this time, didn't flex to dampen the blow, and I hunch over again, only for her to crash her fist into my nose, which immediately begins to gush blood.

I drop to my knees in front of my mother.

"Get up, Ronan!" she orders, but I don't. What's the fucking point? "Get the fuck up!" She kicks me in the stomach, forcing me onto all fours. The blood is positively dripping from my nose, a little puddle forming on the hardwood floor. "Ronan, I will fucking kill you if you don't get up right this fucking second."

I gather whatever strength I have and slowly push myself up off the ground. I wipe my bloody nose with my forearm. It doesn't feel like it's broken, which is a fucking relief. I wouldn't even know how to explain that one to my friends and Cat.

My mother studies me for a moment, looking me up and down like I'm a pest, like she can't believe she had to give birth to me. "You better knock off your shit or I will make your life a living hell, Ronan." She takes a step back, signaling she's done beating my ass for now. "Clean that up"—she points to the blood stain on the floor—"and get out of my sight."

She turns and goes upstairs, leaving me standing in the living room, feeling punch-drunk.

I do as I was told, grab some paper towels from the kitchen, and clean my blood off the floor while trying to stop the bleeding with a cold washcloth to my nose. As soon as I'm done, I walk into the kitchen—all plans of walking Onyx gone—to wash the blood off my face, hands, and forearm, ensuring there are no visible signs of injury. Then I head into the garage, and I'm relieved to find a clean, long-sleeved Murphy's shirt in the dryer. I change out of my bloodstained white t-shirt and discard it in the trash can. I decide to just leave the house now, eager to get away from this fucking hell hole, but quickly go back inside and grab an unopened bottle of Jack from the sideboard in the dining room. I just need something to take the edge off.

I make it out to my car seconds later and chug two large gulps of the whiskey. Then I sit for a second, eyes closed as I lean my forehead against my steering wheel, letting the alcohol hit my stomach.

Just hours ago I was happy, surrounded by my friends, kissing the most incredible girl in this world, but all that is so rapidly overshadowed and drowned out by my mom and her apparent desire to wipe out anything good in my life. I hate the effect she has on me, hate what she does to me. I fucking hate her. And I fucking hate myself for letting her get to me, for not being strong enough to withstand her, for not fighting back.

"Um, you're early again," Shane says when he spots me walking into Murphy's fifteen minutes later, and his eyebrows immediately crease.

I have no intention of telling him what just went down at home and instead plaster on a fake smile. "Yeah, you know, after that long weekend with you I just started having immediate withdrawals and I needed a quick Shane fix."

He grins at me. "I guess I can't blame you. I'm surprised everyone else isn't here also."

"Me, too," I laugh. "Guess we know now who loves you the most."

"Just don't tell Tori or she'll kick your ass," Shane says with a nod.

"I can take her," I joke back.

"I don't know, she fights dirty," he laughs.

"Are you speaking from experience?" I make my way behind the bar counter to drop off my keys and wallet.

"I'd rather not say," he says sheepishly, now making me laugh for real.

"Fair enough. Is Tori coming in today to make eyes at you while you work?"

"That's the plan," he says with a smile.

"Tell her to bring Cat." I give him a grin, wanting to see her more than anything. I guess I could call or text her and let her know, but I don't want to overwhelm her. We just spent seventy-two hours together, and I want her to decide what she wants to do tonight without feeling pressured by me.

"Oh, for sure. Wouldn't want you to be jealous that nobody is making eyes at you," Shane says, then adds, "Although, that's never really been an issue. In fact, I'm pretty sure that chick over there is making eyes at you right now." He nods in the direction of a table occupied by three girls.

"Nah, I only want Cat making eyes at me," I say, then get to work.

Thursday, August 12th

Cat

July was an insanely hot month, and August hasn't been much better. I'm used to humidity and heat, but that's in a small town in North Carolina, and man, heat and humidity in the city are a whole different ball game. My days are spent either indoors or at Shane's mom's beach house. I even end up dragging Sam and Benny with me a few times when my mom has an emergency patient. Vada, Tori, Summer, and even Cheyenne completely dote on my younger siblings, which is really nice because they don't get bored while we hang out with my friends, and my little sister Sam still appears to have a huge crush on Ronan. I can't blame her; every day I spend with him my feelings for him grow more intense.

Ronan has been extremely busy with work and hockey practice for both his club and varsity teams, spending hours every day at conditioning, which throws off his daytime schedule a bit, but we still see each other just about every day. At some point I started sending him text messages every night before I go to bed. It's usually something short, just meant to let him know that he's my last thought before I drift off to sleep. And then I usually wake up in the morning to find a text from him—typically sent in the middle of the night—telling me he got home and that he misses me.

But it's not just Ronan's sweet messages I get to read in the morning. Adam has been calling and texting me randomly, too, always from an unknown number, which makes it impossible to block him. I've made the mistake of picking up his calls a handful of times when my fingers were faster than my brain, and I hit the answer button before I could remember that the unknown number most likely meant Adam was about to terrorize me again.

It's always the same with him—he's usually drunk when he calls, the phone ringing at the most random hours of the day and night. His tone is always accusatory, even when he texts me. A couple of times he said he should just come and take what he deserved all along. I know he doesn't know where I live, but it still makes me uneasy. The fact that he somehow got my number is concerning enough, and I wouldn't put it past him to get ahold of my address.

And then there are the pictures; the evidence; the proof of my promiscuity, my missteps. Adam wasn't satisfied with the one photo I sent him when I was in Buffalo, and has forced me to send him new ones. I feel sick to my stomach each time I stand in front of my bathroom mirror, exposing my breasts to the camera, my hands shaking as I take a picture only to delete it the second I hit "send."

And then, two weeks ago, things went from bad to worse when Ronan was at my house, spending the rare evening with me when he didn't work.

I was cuddled up against Ronan on the couch, watching a movie I already can't remember, when my phone notified me of a new text message. My stomach dropped when I read Adam's words.

Unknown: Your tits are nice and all, but I think it's about time I get to see the rest of your tight little body. You strung me along for almost five months, Cat, and I don't think I need to remind you of what you did to me...

"What's wrong?" Ronan asked, immediately alarmed when I clambered out of his arms, feeling pallid, my heart racing in my chest. "You don't look so good," he added, looking me over.

"I don't feel good," I said, my throat dry. "I feel really sick. I think... I think maybe I should go to bed." I felt awful about ending our night so suddenly, about asking him to leave when all I wanted was to stay on the couch with him, to feel his body against mine and spend time with him.

"Okay," Ronan said, obviously taken aback, but he got up off the couch nonetheless. God, he is always so considerate of me, so respectful, which made this entire thing even worse. "Are you going to be alright?" he asked, a crease on his handsome brow. His concern for me—my fake reason for cutting our evening short—tore at me. The building tears made the back of my eyes sting, but I nodded nonetheless.

I felt my phone vibrate again. I knew it was going to be another message from Adam and ushered Ronan out of my house, not daring to look at the text until I had closed the front door.

Unknown: Do I need to remind you of what will happen if I don't get a picture of you right now? Don't try me, Cat! Picture. Full frontal. Now.

I hurried up into my bedroom, locking the door behind me before I undressed and positioned myself in front of my floor-length mirror, feeling so, so ashamed. I always feel like that when I comply with Adam's demands, when I send intimate pictures of myself to him, when I betray Ronan. But I felt even worse that night, felt even more violated than before.

All I kept thinking while I snapped the picture of my fully nude body, then quickly attached it to my wordless response to Adam, was that Ronan had never even seen me like this—completely naked—even after more than two months together, and I was sending pictures like that to some other boy after lying to Ronan. Granted, I don't think I really had a choice but to obey Adam's orders—not unless I was prepared for Adam to make good on his threat and post my body on the internet for all to see—but that didn't take away from the avalanche of guilt crushing me in that moment.

It took only seconds for Adam to respond.

Unknown: Shit, that's even better than I could have hoped for. If only you hadn't held back on me.

I began to sob then, overwhelmed by guilt and shame. I pulled on my pajamas and climbed into bed, where I cried myself to sleep. I didn't pick up when Ronan tried to call me a little while later, didn't respond to his text messages checking in on me, and I didn't visit him at Murphy's while he worked the next day. I just couldn't talk to him, couldn't see his face; I was too afraid that he would hear the betrayal in my voice, see it in my eyes.

I haven't told anyone about Adam's phone calls or text messages; nor have I told anyone about the photos he took of me while we were together, the ones I sent to him, the ones he's now using to blackmail me into providing him with new pictures. Nobody knows—not my parents, not Julie, and definitely not Ronan. In fact, I haven't shared anything about what happened between Adam and me with Ronan. And all of this is beginning to weigh heavily on my chest as our relationship grows. Ronan and I spend so much time together talking about everything under the sun, but I hold back every time he asks me anything remotely related to my relationship with my ex. I'm so terrified of what Ronan would think of me if he found out that not only did I lead on my ex, but I reported him to the police when he lost control and I ruined his future. And I'm convinced that my relationship will end the moment Ronan learns about the photos I sent Adam.

Like I did in the past, I erased any trace of my interaction with Adam, once again ignoring the glaring red flags, and I resolved to go about my days pretending none of this had happened. I hope Adam will tire of his game soon, will finally forget about me, will move on. What else can I do? Nothing at all. Defying Adam is too risky. God, I would die if Adam posted the pictures on the internet, if my friends founds out about them, if Ronan saw what I've done.

***

It's another scorcher of a day; the temperature outside is a blistering 108 degrees Fahrenheit, and while the A/C is running around the clock, I still have a fan going in my room. I've been hanging out at Vada's house the majority of the day, hiding away from the heat. Zack has been in and out of the house all day. I know he went to work out with Shane, Steve, and Ronan this morning, and although I love joining them and ogling Ronan while he gets all pumped and sweaty, today is not the day for physical exertion.

It's around four when Zack walks into Vada's room with Summer in tow.

"Hey, hey," Summer chirps. She joins Vada and me on Vada's bed, where I lie, stomach down and feet up, thumbing through a glossy sports magazine.

"What are you guys up to?" Zack asks, stepping into Vada's room; as always, his camera is balanced in his left hand. It's seriously impressive how the constant filming seems second-nature.

"Not much." I smile at Zack, who stands there looking a little lost without the guys as his backup to all the estrogen in the room. "Just trying to stay cool. Is it still miserable outside?"

"It's hotter than hell," Summer answers for Zack, who nods wholeheartedly.

"We're trying to figure out what to do tonight," Zack says. "Shane's working, so the beach house isn't an option. But I talked to Steve and he thought maybe we should catch a movie."

"Oh, I like that idea." Vada screws her bottle of candy apple-red nail polish closed. All ten of her toes are beautifully painted, as are mine thanks to Vada's polishing skills.

"Awesome," Zack says. "Steve was out and about somewhere, but we checked and there's a seven o'clock showing of some movie Steve said he wanted to see. Maybe we could grab some food beforehand."

We're all on board with that idea. Vada calls Steve and confirms the plan.

"Okay, so we'll meet you at Javier's in an hour," she tells Steve, then reminds him she loves him before hanging up the phone.

I try to call Ronan to see if he's up for a movie, but he doesn't pick up. My text goes unanswered as well.

"Do you guys mind if we stop by Ran's house really quick? I can't get ahold of him," I ask into the room, and am met with unanimous head-nodding.

***

We pull up to Ronan's house fifteen minutes later. His car is here, so he must be as well. Zack, Summer, Vada, and I clamber out of Zack's car and, walking up to the front door, I can spot Ronan in the kitchen through the window. My heart speeds up at seeing his face and I increase my pace as I step up to the front door to knock.

"Hey," Ronan says, surprise in his voice and a smile on his lips when he opens the front door for us. "What are you guys doing here?" He steps back, holding the door open, and allows us into the hallway.

"Well, we're checking on you because you're apparently not answering your phone," Vada says, poking her index finger into Ronan's chest.

He gives her a quizzical look.

"I was trying to call you," I say. "We thought we'd head to a movie and I wanted to check if you can come."

He pulls me into a gentle hug and kisses my lips softly. "Sorry, baby, I..." he starts, but is interrupted.

"Well, hello everyone," Ronan's mom says. She walks down the stairs dressed in her light-blue scrubs, her hair in a long braid. She really is a beautiful woman, and her green eyes are exactly the same color as Ronan's.

Vada, Zack, Summer, and I greet her politely.

She turns her attention to Ronan. "I'm heading out," she says, her tone noticeably cooler. "I'm working a twenty-four-hour shift, and I expect everything to be done by the time I get back tomorrow evening."

Ronan just nods.

She raises her hand as a quick see-you-later to us, then heads out the door.

Ronan sighs, and his eyes return to mine. "I can't go to the movies tonight," he says, and there's defeat in his voice.

"Oh, come on, Ran," Zack says, his tone teasing. "You can finish whatever she wants you to do later, can't you?"

"No, really, I have to get it done now. You guys go ahead," he says, and strokes his thumb across my cheek.

"Jeez, Ran, I didn't take you for such a momma's boy," Zack jokes, and Ronan's body tenses.

"How about I stay here with you?" I say.

Ronan's eyes soften. "No, you should go and have fun."

I search his eyes. There's sadness and frustration reflected in them. I put my hands on his chest. "If it's okay with you, I'd like to stay here with you. Please?"

He nods. "Okay."

"Are you guys sure?" Vada asks, and I assure her that I would actually prefer to stay with Ronan than be the fifth wheel at dinner and a movie. So, the three of them head out to meet up with Steve at this little Mexican restaurant not too far from the theater.

"I feel terrible," Ronan says once Vada, Zack, and Summer are gone. His hands rest on my hips while mine are laced around his neck.

"Don't! I promise, I want to be here with you. I'll choose being with you over going to a movie with friends anytime. Plus, maybe I can help you get whatever you need to get done sooner?"

For a moment he looks like he doesn't know how to respond. He shakes his head slightly. "Why are you so good to me?" He brushes his lips against mine.

"Because I care about you," I mumble against him. "A lot."

He deepens the kiss, and we stay like that for a minute before I pull away, giggling at his disappointed expression. "So, what do we need to get done before we can enjoy the fact that we're alone in this house?" I ask.

His eyes instantly brighten, a mischievous grin spreading across his full lips. "Laundry. A shit-ton of laundry. And then the dishes."

"Okay, how about I do the dishes and you start on the laundry?" I suggest, and saunter into the kitchen, purposely swaying my hips.

I feel his eyes on me, and he chuckles, his voice low. He follows me into the kitchen and stands behind me, his hands on my hips. "Thank you for staying and helping me," he whispers against my neck, then kisses it softly. My eyes fall shut as goose bumps erupt on my skin. "You being here makes everything better."

We go to work. Ronan folds and puts away mounds of laundry while I wash and dry the dishes and try to figure out what goes where. I'm done half an hour later and jump in to help Ronan finish what laundry he has left.

"Is that it?" I ask after Ronan and I take the last bit of folded laundry upstairs and deposit it in his closet.

"Yeah," he says with an enticing smile on his face. "Thanks, baby. This would have taken me hours without you. You're seriously amazing," he says and scoops me into his arms.

"Anytime," I giggle, my arms around his neck, head dipped down to look into his gorgeous eyes. He kisses me softly while taking the few steps that separate us from his bed and somehow maneuvers us onto it without our lips separating. He hovers over me, his lips tenderly caressing mine; his left hand touches me softly, brushing over my shoulder then down my arm while his other supports his body weight. He kisses me so slowly and sensually that my eyes shut on their own. Seemingly on their own accord, my hands snake under Ronan's shirt where my cool fingertips meet his hot skin. He's always so warm. I run my fingers up and along the curve of his spine before moving to his sides, tracing his ribs, and coming to rest on his shoulder blades. My touch must feel good to him because he intensifies his kiss, urging me to part my lips before his tongue slips into my mouth, tasting me.

Heat rises inside me and pools between my legs when Ronan pushes up the hem of my shirt over my stomach. His lips leave mine as he moves down to kiss the newly exposed skin above my jeans while his hand glides up my waist. My breathing is ragged and I focus on Ronan's touch, waiting for his fingers to reach my breast, to graze over my nipple, which is already hard in anticipation of his touch. I can feel his breath against my skin as he continues to lick and kiss my stomach, my belly button, before moving north and toward my chest.

"Ronan," I breathe, urging him on without really knowing what exactly it is I want him to do. I just know I want more of him. I'm too eager for my own good as I retrieve my hands from under his shirt and push it up impatiently.

Barely even leaving my skin, Ronan reaches behind his head and pulls his shirt off before his tongue resumes its exploration of my skin, slowly but steadily moving toward my chest. When he reaches the bottom of my shirt still covering my bra, Ronan inclines just enough to push my shirt up over my breasts, then leans toward me and pulls the fabric of my bra down, exposing my pebbled nipple. I want him to touch me so badly. I push against him when his thumb gives me what I crave and brushes across my nipple while he kisses the spot between my shoulder and neck, nipping at my skin. I bury my hands in his hair, tugging at the roots while I inhale his scent that is just so perfectly him, I'd know it anywhere.

His lips move from my neck to my jaw, then to my mouth. He kisses me fiercely, pushing against me, and I grind my hips in rhythm. I can feel him hard between my thighs and wrap my legs around his waist. His mouth leaves my lips, which feel swollen and sensitive from kissing Ronan so greedily, and seeks out my nipple instead. I inhale sharply, wet heat coursing through my body to that needy flesh between my thighs as he begins licking and sucking on my sensitive skin. I feel his hand glide down the side of my body, hyperaware of his every touch, focused only on the sensation of his hands and mouth on my skin. I moan when his fingers glide down the outside of my left leg before moving to the inside and slowly sliding back up my sensitive inner thigh. I feel an almost overwhelming ache for him, for his body on mine, for relief from the pleasure swirling and the pressure building deep in my core. It's like nothing else exists and I want to stay lost in this moment forever.

I feel my phone vibrate in my back pocket and quickly move to retrieve it, to get it away from me so as not to let it distract me from Ronan's touch.

I don't know why I do it, but as I go to place my phone to the side, I glance at the screen and see *Unknown*, along with the beginning of the text message Adam just sent me.

Unknown: Can't stop looking at those pictures of your tight body. I'm thinking I should pay you a vis...

That's all it takes for the bubble around me to implode and for me to come crashing back down to earth. And suddenly, everything feels wrong: Ronan's hands on my body while memories of Adam's violence flash through my mind, the guilt of what I did to Adam, of what I've done to Ronan. It's too much. Tears begin to fall, and just like that I've lost control over myself and the situation.

Ronan

God, Cat is perfect. In every way imaginable. Soft and warm and so damn gentle with me, and I love nothing more than getting to spend time alone with her like I am right now.

I feel high with her hands tugging at my hair while I caress her soft breast, licking her hard nipple, sucking it into my mouth over and over again while I allow my left hand to inch down the heated skin of her stomach. I reach the waistband of her jeans and let my hand slide down her leg before moving to her inner thigh. I never get tired of exploring her perfect body, of feeling her react to my touch, hearing the sounds she makes, watching her facial expressions when she gets turned on. I swear it gets me higher than any drug.

My heart pounds in my chest and heat thrashes through my body as she grinds her hips against me. I'm so hard, and her heat penetrating our clothes only makes it worse. I'm consumed by the way she feels underneath me, and I'm desperate to finally touch that sweet spot between her thighs, to feel her, to make her come apart. I've been thinking about it, envisioning it, fantasizing about feeling all of Cat way too often for way too long. But I will not pressure her; I will not go back on my promise of moving at her pace. Even if that means having to stroke myself to climax in private every single day until she's ready. And, yeah, at this point, it's every day because, man, I'm pent-up.

"Ran," her voice cracks, and it has an immediately sobering effect.

I pull back and feel like shit when I see tears running down Cat's face. "Baby, what's wrong?"

My breathing is still ragged as I move to give her space to sit up. She doesn't answer right away; she furiously wipes her eyes, trying to stop the tears that keep coming.

I take her face in my hands, searching her eyes. "Cat, I'm sorry if I'm moving too fast. You can tell me to stop any time; I'll never make you do anything you don't want."

She still doesn't speak and I'm starting to freak out a little bit, wondering if I missed some cue that she wanted me to stop, scared that I got too carried away. But then she leans into me, and I wrap my arms tightly around her as she begins to sob in earnest. She cries for what seems like a long time, her shoulders heaving while tears run hot down her cheeks and onto my chest. I have no idea what to say, no clue what triggered her, and I decide to just let her cry, waiting for the moment she's ready to open up to me.

When the moment finally comes, though, I'm not prepared for what she has to tell me.

"My ex, Adam, just texted me," she finally starts, her eyes red and puffy, her voice still shaky, cracking here and there. "He's been calling and texting me since I ran into him when I was in North Carolina a couple months ago, and, Ran"—she moves out of my arms and looks me in the eyes—"you're going to hate me."

My eyebrows crease. "I doubt that," I reassure her, but I worry about what she's going to tell me that would make her think I'd hate her.

She takes a deep, shaky breath as if to brace herself as she talks about what I'm beginning to understand is a traumatic part of her life. "Adam and I started dating last fall. He is... was... the star quarterback of my high school's football team. He got a full-ride scholarship to play for Duke this fall. His team was going to play in the state championship. Big deal, you know?" She looks at me, and I nod for her to continue. "Anyway, he asked me out—I was so flattered," she says, rolling her watery eyes like she was stupid for enjoying the attention. "So, we started going out. He took me to all these parties and stuff. He's really popular; everyone loves him because, you know, football and all that. But pretty much right away he started pressuring me to have sex with him."

Her voice becomes thinner as she continues to tell her story, and I'm suddenly acutely, uncomfortably aware that I'm not wearing a shirt. So I reach for it off the floor and put it back on, needing to provide her some comfort that I'm not like this Adam guy.

"I've never had sex," she continues without looking at me, her attention directed at her hands as she picks at her nails. "Before Adam, I had never even kissed a guy, and he was just pushing me. It was always about that. But I didn't want to." She stops picking at her nails and looks at me again. "I didn't want to with *Adam*."

There's a brief moment of silence as the meaning of her words fills up the space between us.

"A couple weeks into our relationship, we started to have fights about it; he would accuse me of leading him on. We'd go to parties; I'd have too much to drink," she says, ashamed, "and we'd make out. But then he would inevitably do something that I didn't want, touch me where I didn't want to be touched, or whatever, and when I asked him to stop he would get mad at me."

More tears roll down her cheeks, and I can feel my body reacting to her story, feel my shoulders tense as anger starts to build in my chest.

"He would end up yelling at me, calling me names, and accusing me of purposely leading him on. He would call me a slut and say that I'm sleeping with other guys. He was so mean." A heart-wrenching sob breaks from her chest.

I reach for her hand and am relieved when she allows me to hold it. Her eyes close as the steady stream of tears flows down her rosy cheeks.

"The fights got worse and worse the more often we had them, and then, a few weeks into our relationship"—I know what she's going to tell me even before the words escape her mouth—"he became physical."

It takes everything in me to keep my composure, to stay neutral as animalistic rage twists my insides. "What happened?" I urge as gently as I can, still holding her hand in my right while my left is balled into a tight fist by my side.

"At first it was just a push or a kick, maybe a slap, and only when we were by ourselves. But then he became more violent and he would do it front of his friends, especially when he had been drinking, which was pretty much every weekend."

I squeeze her hand to remind her I'm here, still listening.

"Then he took me to the winter formal last February and afterwards we were at his friend's house. Adam was wasted, and, honestly, so was I." She looks at me, her tears falling hard and fast, and I detect more unwarranted shame in her eyes. I brush my thumb over her cheek, trying to convey that she has nothing to be ashamed of. "I thought, okay, maybe this is the night, maybe I can just suck it up and have sex with him. Everyone does it after these dances, right?"

She looks as if she's waiting for me to answer the question, but when I don't, she continues.

"Adam and I were in a room, making out, and..." She trails off for a moment, and I think she's purposely skipping over some information, but continues, "He just... He started to push up my dress, grabbing at my legs. He was so drunk and it all felt so wrong. He was on top of me and it felt like I couldn't breathe, so I asked him to stop. He didn't; he just kept going and I kept telling him to stop and then it was like instinct took over and I tried to get away from him, kicking him and hitting him to get off me, and he finally did, but he was so, so angry." Her voice chokes as fresh tears spill from her eyes. "He screamed at me that I was a bitch and a slut. He said he should just take what he deserved, and I tried to get around him. He grabbed me by my throat and started to squeeze and then he punched me with his other fist." She sobs loudly.

I let go of her hand and pull her toward me, encircling her with my arms, holding her tightly against me. She grabs on to me like a lifeline, burying her face against my chest, and it's honestly a good thing because a murderous desire to find this guy and beat the living shit out of him is boiling in my chest. But I know that, for Cat's sake, I need to stay calm or I risk her shutting down on me. So I hold her, forcing myself to take deep, steadying breaths.

"How did you get away?" I ask after several minutes, when Cat's breathing has normalized a little.

She loosens her grip on me but doesn't move her head away from my chest while she continues her story. "Adam had pushed me against a dresser in the room while he was choking me, and the commotion got people's attention. Someone burst into the room and then Adam finally let go. Julie took me home. I was such a mess. My parents of course saw the bruises on my throat and in my face; I couldn't hide it anymore. So, I told them everything and my dad called the cops. Adam got arrested that night. He ended up getting like six months of probation. He was kicked off the football team and lost his scholarship to Duke."

There's guilt in her voice. I pull back, forcing her to lift her head and look at me. "Baby, you know that none of this was your fault, right? You did the right thing here."

She shakes her head. "But why doesn't it feel like I did the right thing?" She searches my eyes for an answer to the question that I now understand has been haunting her for way too long.

"Because this asshole made you believe this whole time that you were the problem. Because he kept telling you that you were wrong for setting boundaries, that you were wrong for telling him no," I explain to her. She nods, but I can tell she's unconvinced, that there's more to her story, though she's obviously not ready to tell me *everything*. And who am I to press her when she still has no idea about what happens in this house when she's not around?

"Basically, the whole town turned against me," she finally says, her voice small. "I kept getting prank calls and threatening messages; school was horrible. My parents pulled me out and started to homeschool me in March, but that didn't help. My car got trashed; the calls kept becoming worse and more frequent. So, my mom made the decision to move me to New York," she finishes with a sigh. "When I went to visit a few weeks ago, I ran into Adam at that party I told you I was going to. He grabbed my phone and read your messages to me. But he seemed okay and said he just wanted to talk, so we talked, but then things ended up being the way they always were."

"Did he hurt you?" I ask, trying to keep a steady voice, but I swear to god if he touched her I'm going to find this guy and beat him to a pulp.

To my relief, she shakes her head. "No. I mean, he started yelling and then I thought he was going to hit me, but he didn't. He just calmed down and I ended up walking away. And then Adam started calling and texting me."

"What does he want?" I ask, trying to figure out what to do about this guy, pissed that he fucked with her when I was already in her life, sorry that Cat didn't feel ready to tell me about him earlier.

Cat hesitates for a long moment as if she's battling with herself, and I hope she trusts me enough to open up to me. "I don't know," she finally says, and I squint at her because I'm pretty convinced she's holding back. "The first time he called, he said he wanted an apology for me ruining his life. He kept calling, though. It's an unknown number, so I just don't answer, and he doesn't leave messages. But sometimes he sends a text message. I delete it every time, but I can't block him..." she says, her voice tight, uneven. "I had changed my phone number before I came to New York, but he got it somehow..." she trails off, defeated.

I nod at her, frustrated that I don't have a way of tracking this guy down, but vowing to try to let it go for Cat's sake unless an opportunity somehow presents itself.

"Do you hate me?"

Her question forces my attention away from my urge to hurt this guy, and I once again take Cat's tear-streaked face into my hands, making sure she understands the full force of my words.

"Of course I don't. Baby, you did nothing wrong. The only one who fucked up is this Adam guy." I search her eyes for acceptance of what I'm telling her before I move my hands from her heated cheeks and pull her in toward me again. "Can you promise me something, though?" I ask as she conforms her body to mine, allowing me to hold her. "Can you promise me that you will let me know if I'm ever doing anything that makes you uncomfortable, or that you don't want me to do? Because I don't want to hurt you; I don't want to make you do anything you don't want. But I have to be honest here, I can get carried away when I start touching you and you're touching me. So I'll need you to let me know when to stop, okay?" I make her promise because I don't ever want to be like Cat's asshole ex. I know what it's like to have shit done to me, to have somebody hurt me, and I'll be damned if I ever hurt Cat, even unintentionally.

I feel her nod against me, and she inhales deeply. "I can do that," she says, her voice tired but serious. "But, you should know that I love it when you touch me." There's a change in her voice now; it's determined, more present, and warm. "And everything that we've done, I wanted... I want. I want you, Ran."

There's finality in her voice, and she sits up to look at me. Her cheeks are flushed, but not because of her crying. I feel a shift in the air, a sudden electricity crackling between us that causes my heart rate to pick up.

My eyes are fixed to her mouth as she wets her lips with her tongue, and I struggle to read Cat's body language. Luckily I don't have to analyze her too much, because without another moment's notice she leans forward and brushes her lips against mine. I kiss her back, softly at first, letting her set the tempo but deepening the kiss when she parts her lips, allowing me to taste her again. I move my left hand to her low back and glide my thumb over her bare skin; it's still hot from the emotional upheaval of reliving her relationship with Adam. I can feel her breathing accelerate and I carefully urge her backwards until her back rests on my bed and I'm next to her, my lips still on hers. She reaches around and slides both her hands underneath my shirt and up my back, leaving hot trails where her fingers touch my skin. It's incredible how easily and quickly her touch makes me forget everything around me.

My lips leave her mouth and I kiss her jawline, her delicate neck, breathing her in, tasting her soft skin. She moans softly and I feel her tug on my shirt, sliding it up, exposing my torso, and I finally just yank my shirt over my head and off again while her hands explore my back, tracing each rib, softly gliding down my sides and back up to my neck before running her fingers through my hair.

I kiss her lips again briefly, then travel back down to her neck and collarbone, allowing my left hand to slowly travel underneath her shirt, discovering the silky skin of her toned stomach. I make sure to give her time to stop me as I move my hand upwards and outline her bra as I continue to nip at her skin. Her hands forge searing-hot paths on my back, and her quick breathing and closed eyes make it clear she doesn't want me to stop.

I withdraw my hand from under her shirt and push up the fabric, exposing her stomach and bra before my lips break contact with her skin. I sit up and reposition myself. Cat makes a face as though about to protest the sudden pause of our physical contact, but before she can say anything I lower myself and begin to kiss her stomach, licking and kissing a path upward as my left hand traces the edge of her black lacy bra. As my mouth is about to reach her right breast, I graze my left thumb over the thin fabric covering her left nipple, and Cat's hands find my shoulder blades as she moans my name. I fight hard not to lose my head knowing how turned on she is, and with my left hand I pull down the lace, exposing her nipple before running my tongue over it and drawing it deep into my mouth while teasing her other nipple with my hand.

I want to be right here in this moment forever, exploring Cat's body, tasting her, hearing her moan quietly as she runs her hands over my back, pushing her further and further toward the edge, but my phone rings. Of course it does. This shit never fails. I ignore it at first, too lost in Cat to care, but when it rings for a third time in a row, I groan, frustrated, before sitting up and grabbing the offending piece of technology. It's Shane. I swear, the universe is conspiring against me.

"What's up," I ask, attempting to control my ragged breathing without much success.

"Oh shit, dude, did I interrupt something?" he asks, his voice tinged with both guilt and insinuation.

"Yeah, kind of." I let my eyes roam Cat's exposed body as she lies on my bed, looking at me expectantly, her eyes still glossed over with need, and I shiver with want. Jesus fuck, she's so damn perfect.

"Sorry. It's just, I need you to come in, if you can. Trace, Cory, and Amy all called out today and we're seriously short-staffed tonight."

I sigh. "Fuck, Shay, I really want to spend some time with Cat."

"I'm sorry, man. I really hate to do this to you, but is there any way you can be here in like thirty minutes and close with me tonight?"

Cat props herself up on her elbows and adjusts her bra before pulling down her shirt, making me pout like a little kid. She giggles, then mouths at me, "You should go in."

I sigh again. "Okay, I'll be there in half an hour."

"Man, thank you! You're a freaking lifesaver. Tell Cat I'll make it up to you guys."

"I'm sorry," I apologize to Cat after I hang up the phone. "I don't want to leave you after you just poured your heart out to me."

"Ran, I feel so much better now that you know. Like a huge weight is off my chest. I was so afraid of what you would think of me." I pull her back into my arms. "I'm so glad I found you," she mumbles against my chest. She has no idea how much her words reflect how I feel about her. She is the best part of my life.

When we finally break apart, I walk to my closet and pull out a black, long-sleeve Murphy's shirt. I feel Cat's eyes on me the entire time, and I smile to myself, though I wish I could keep exploring her perfect body right now rather than getting ready for work.

There's nothing like being with Cat, nothing that stills my restless soul like she does.

The last month and a half have been more of the same bullshit at home, except that my mother's volatility is at an all-time high. I've been trying extra hard to keep things civil, to not let her provoke a reaction when she's looking for a fight or a reason to punish me—she has a way of getting a rise out of me, even though I know better—and I mostly am able to avoid a complete collision course. Though there are still the almost-daily shoves, the nasty words, the backhands, and the broom hits.

But honestly, whenever I'm with Cat everything around me just kind of recedes into the background. All the other shit suddenly doesn't seem as heavy. It's hard to explain what she does to me; I'm not totally sure I can even wrap my head around it. All I know is I feel a million times better when I'm with her, so I give in to my need more often than not.

I wasn't sure if I was going to see her today, but then she showed up, surprising me in the best way. My mom had just finished laying into me about some chores I hadn't gotten around to yet. It's not like I skirt my responsibilities; I keep this fucking house clean essentially on my own. Never mind the fact that her to-do list for me is never-ending and that, aside from almost-daily hockey practice, I also work basically a full-time job. But that's not what ended up getting me in trouble. No, it was the fact that I got pissed off when my mom said some derogatory shit about Cat. More specifically, she said it was clear that I was thinking with my dick and that getting into "that little blonde bitch's pants" was more important to me than fulfilling my responsibilities at home. And then she reminded me that I'm worthless, and sooner or later Cat would dump me because that's all I'm good for: being used up. I didn't say a damn thing, but my body apparently gave my reaction away because, not seconds later, I got backhanded so hard it made little black dots pop before my eyes.

And then Cat showed up with Zack, Vada, and Summer, and instead of heading to the movies with them, she chose to stay with me and help me take care of shit. She chose spending time with me doing some boring chores over doing something fun with her friends. I swear, this girl is an angel, or a saint, or, I don't know, but whatever she is, one thing is for certain: she is too good for me.

She helped me finish up my chores way faster than I would have been able to accomplish myself, making some comment about us being able to enjoy having the house to ourselves. I had to keep drowning out the urge to touch her the entire time she was helping me, but all bets were off as soon as we put away the last of the laundry. I just wish she could stay with me a while longer, that I wouldn't need to part with her just yet, but I'm not about to leave Shane hanging.

I drop Cat off at home and get to Murphy's fifteen minutes later, immediately understanding why Shane called me in a panic. The place is packed. I jump right in, getting to work as soon as I check in with Shane. The crowds don't let up all evening, and I'm so busy I don't even have a chance to take a break, only stopping here and there to exchange a quick word with Shane or gulp down a glass of water.

***

By the time Shane finally locks the doors, it's just him and me.

"Alright, let's clean this place up and go home," Shane exhales, clearly exhausted.

We start moving around, putting up chairs, sweeping, and wiping down tables.

"How is Cat?" Shane asks me as we work.

"Good, I think. I haven't seen her in"—I stop to look at my watch—"about eight hours now."

Shane chuckles. "I hope I didn't interrupt you guys, like, right in the middle of something when I called."

"Yeah, actually, you did," I admit.

Shane takes on a guilty expression. "I figured as much. You sounded... breathless," he says, and chuckles again. "Sorry about that."

"Don't feel bad. We get interrupted all the time. Story of our lives. We never get anywhere; it's like the universe is against us," I muse, thinking about all the times when it felt like Cat and I finally had the chance to explore each other, just to be interrupted by her mom, or Vada, or a phone. "But then again, maybe it's the universe telling me to slow down. I don't think Cat's ready," I say more to myself than Shane.

He stops in his tracks. "What do you mean she's not ready? Are you telling me you guys haven't had sex yet?" Shane asks, his eyebrows raised in surprise. I shake my head at him. Shane is the only person I talk about these things with, and only because he has a way of getting them out of me or already knows. For example, he always had a knack for figuring out if I hooked up with a girl and he would ask me about it, and I could never figure out where he got the info in the first place. "Oh," he says, concern edged into his face. "Why not?"

I start sweeping the floor. "You mean aside from everybody and their mother interrupting us?" I say sarcastically, trying to lighten the mood, and he nods. I take a moment to answer before I stop to face him, deciding to confide in my best friend. "I know she's never had sex before, so I just want to take it slow, you know. I want to make sure it's what she wants. I'm in deep with her, Shay," I confess, the weight of my feelings for Cat sinking into my chest.

"Do you love her?" he asks, searching my face.

I nod slowly as the realization of it threatens to crush me. What did Shakespeare write? *These violent delights have violent ends*, or something like that? "Yeah, I do."

"But that's a good thing, right?" I can tell he's trying to understand the sudden shift in my mood.

"I'm scared of fucking it up. I'm scared of not being good enough for her. I don't want to hurt her, Shay." The words come out of my mouth before I can stop myself. "She told me about her ex today and it made me want to hunt this asshole down," I growl.

"What happened with her ex?"

I give Shane a brief summary without disclosing details, not wanting to divulge Cat's secret when she only just trusted me enough to tell me today. But I need to unburden myself and relieve the anger that courses through my body when I think about some random guy laying a hand on Cat.

Shane pats my back. "You're a good guy, Ran, which is exactly why I know you won't hurt her; you're not going to fuck this up. I've said it before, and I'll say it again: trust that Cat will tell you what she needs. Stop overthinking your relationship with her and just feel it. You deserve this. You deserve to be in love with her and you deserve to be loved."

"Okay, I wasn't aware that you were my personal therapist." I have a hard time believing anything he just told me, especially this last part about deserving to be loved. I've grown up believing the complete opposite, being shown over and over that I don't deserve good things, that I'm not good enough.

"I just think you need to hear these things sometimes," Shane says matter-of-factly before he walks away.

I continue sweeping the floor, replaying Cat's story in my head and feeling the urge to be with her right now, even just to hold her and be in her presence.

"Alright, man. Looks like this was the last of it," Shane finally announces half an hour later, slapping a dirty rag into the sink, wiping his hands on the apron securely tied around his waist, and looking around the deserted restaurant. "Thanks for jumping in today. I know you had plans to spend the evening with Cat. You're a good friend."

I shrug. "No worries. I know you would have done the same for me."

I set the stack of menus neatly on top of the bar, take off my ballcap, and comb my fingers through my hair. I check the clock over the large mirror by the bar. It's 2:50 a.m. and my body aches with fatigue. I stretch my arms over my head, and my neck and back crack gratefully.

"Are you up for heading to the gym in the morning?" Shane asks, grabbing his keys and locking the door to the little office located just to the right of the counter.

"I don't know. I think I need a rest day or something." I grab my own car keys and wallet and shove them back in my pockets, then put my ball cap back on my head. "How about Saturday?" I ask, hoping he'll agree to skip the gym tomorrow because, man, I really need some sleep. "I'm not sure I can handle another four-hour night, honestly."

He nods. "Yeah, me neither. Okay, Saturday sounds good."

He turns off the lights while I head to the front door and hold it open for him. He shuts it tightly behind us and locks the deadbolt in place before we head to our cars. We say good night and drive off in different directions.

***

It only takes me ten minutes to get home, and I notice Vada's little Ford Focus parked on the curb in front of my house. She's obviously spending the night with Steve and probably told her dad she's actually over at Cat's. My thoughts immediately wander to Cat, and I yearn for her—to be near her, to kiss her, feel her body against mine. I'm a little frustrated at how abruptly our afternoon ended. What I wouldn't give to get to spend the night with her again. I would suggest she tell her mom that she's spending the night at Vada's when, really, she'd be spending it with me, but I don't want to pressure her into something she's not ready for, and I would feel fucking shitty if I made her lie for me.

I back up into the driveway next to Steve's Challenger and get out of the car, locking it manually. I decide to trudge up the front steps rather than make my way through the garage so as not make too much noise. Inside the house, I kick off my shoes and stash them neatly in the shoe closet just to the left of the staircase. I make a pit stop in the kitchen where I fill up a glass with cold water and chug the cool liquid while listening to the quiet of the house before deciding if it's safe to head upstairs. It's a habit I formed when Vada started randomly sleeping over toward the end of last year—I listen hard to make sure I don't interrupt anything. If I hear Steve and Vada upstairs, I either leave the house and walk Onyx—who is always down for a nighttime stroll—or I end up passing out on the couch downstairs. But it's quiet tonight—probably because it's past 3 a.m.—and I decide it's safe to go upstairs. I'm relieved because I can feel my energy waning quickly and I want nothing more than to lie down and pass the fuck out. I'm not even sure I have enough left in me to get undressed as I drag myself up the stairs.

When I round the corner, I notice that my bedroom door is closed but don't think much of it. Turning the knob, I open the door enough to slip into my room and close it quietly behind me. It's pitch-black in my room. The shades are drawn and the bathroom door is closed—another sign that Vada is sleeping over; privacy reasons. I toss my ballcap in the corner and sit down on the edge of my bed to take off my socks—I hate sleeping with socks on.

"Hi!" Cat's soft, sleepy voice startles me, and I turn my head toward where her voice is coming from. I can sense her on my bed behind me but not see her; the darkness has rendered me momentarily blind. I feel her sit up and scoot closer to me, so I close my useless eyes, letting my other senses take over as she glides her hand up my back and around my shoulder to my chest before her soft lips graze my neck. I let my head fall to the side, enjoying her nearness as she trails kisses down onto my shoulder.

"What are you doing here?" I ask, my voice low as my breathing increases under her soft lips. My heartbeat kicks in my chest. Her touch feels incredible, and my senses are heightened in the pitch-blackness surrounding me.

Her hair falls over my shoulder and caresses my skin as she moves to the other side of my neck, her lips never breaking contact. It's driving me fucking crazy. "I told Vada you got called in to work at the last minute and how disappointed I was, so she suggested I tell my mom I would spend the night at her house," she giggles quietly, her warm breath tickling my skin. It sends shivers down my spine. "And since we didn't get to spend our evening together like I had hoped, I thought I'd take her up on the suggestion. Are you okay with me being here?" she asks, abruptly pulling back.

I hitch my knee onto the bed and finally turn to face her. "Are you kidding? Of course I'm okay with you being here," I say. "In fact, when I saw Vada's car outside I was thinking about how badly I wanted to spend another night with you," I say, my voice gravelly. God damn, I want to touch her so badly. In one swift move, I pull my other leg onto the bed and position myself on either side of her hips so I'm straddling her. She falls back onto my pillow.

My eyes have finally adjusted to the darkness and I can see her perfectly. Her long blonde hair is splayed across my pillow, her eyes dark in the dim light. Her lips are slightly parted and begging to be kissed. I take my time, though, letting my eyes roam her body, taking in her delicate neck, the curves of her breasts under the thin white tank top. I can tell her nipples are hard and I want so desperately to run my tongue over them. My body stirs with arousal, blood pumping hotly. I can't believe this is all it takes for me to go rock-hard. *Seriously, Ran*. I mentally warn myself to take it slow and not push her, but, *fuck*, the want is almost unbearable.

She squirms under my gaze and bites her bottom lip. That's it. I drop my upper body, lean on my hands on either side of her head, and crash my lips to hers, positively starving for her. They part willingly, allowing my tongue entrance. She tastes like minty toothpaste and her breathing is rapid, matching mine. She nips my lip, and a groan escapes my mouth when her hands snake around my neck, pulling me closer. I deepen the kiss, our tongues entwining. Still holding myself up with my right hand so as not to crush her under my weight, I move my left hand under the blanket covering the lower half of her body. I groan and my dick gives a little jerk when I realize she's only wearing panties. I begin touching the sliver of bare skin between the waistband of her panties and her tank top, then slide my hand upward slowly, savoring the heat of her skin, her softness, trailing up her side and feeling every one of her ribs before I allow my hand to travel to her front just under her left breast. I outline it with my hand before cupping it, once again marveling at how perfectly it fits in the palm of my hand. It's like she was made for me. Her breath hitches as my thumb glides over her cloth-covered nipple and a breathy moan escapes from her lips.

I move my lips from her mouth toward her jawline, her neck, her collarbone, savoring every inch of her soft skin, and she turns her head to allow me full access. I lick and suck on her skin, driving us both further and further toward the edge. With my left hand, I slide the strap of her tank top off her shoulder and kiss her searing-hot skin, breathing her in, unable to get enough of her as my heart pounds in my chest. Her breathing quickens even more when I pull her tank top down, revealing her breast and hard nipple.

Gliding my tongue down her shoulder, I make my way toward her chest and kiss the velvety skin of her breast. Then, finally, I lick her nipple before gently sucking it into my mouth. Underneath me, Cat's hips thrust upward and grind against me as I keep teasing her with my mouth. God, fuck, I'm already so damn turned on.

"Ran," she moans, moving one of her hands to my shoulder while the other finds my hair, her fingers frantic to hold on to something. "I need this blanket off," she begs, desperation in her voice.

Giving her what she needs, I sit up on my knees, pulling the blanket off her and from underneath me before I gently situate one of my legs between hers. Her legs fall open of their own volition, making her vulnerable to me. I bring my other leg in, then reach behind me and pull my shirt off, needing badly to feel more of her. Her breathing is erratic, but her eyes, though glossy, fixate on my every move. I allow my gaze to once again roam her body, this time taking in her long legs, the curve of her hips, the way her thighs travel up. Her black panties hint at the sweet spot hidden underneath the thin fabric, outlining that soft, feminine *V* of her most sensitive flesh. I want to touch her, smell her, taste her.

Fuck, it's almost too much to take and I have a hard time keeping my head straight, but I nonetheless lower myself onto her slowly. I want nothing more than to make her feel safe in my arms, to let her know I would never do anything she isn't ready for. I love the feel of her, of my bare chest grazing her hard nipples as she kisses me fiercely. Her hands find my shoulder blades, and she digs her fingers in when I return my mouth to her exposed nipple. I suck harder this time, grazing my teeth against her sensitive skin. Her legs come up and around my hips, gripping me tightly while she grinds against me. Her heat penetrates my jeans and it makes my body ache with primal need. It takes everything in me not to rip off the rest of our clothes and feel her all the way.

"Ran, please," she whimpers under my touch. "I need..." She trails off with a moan.

"I got you," I whisper against her. "Do you trust me?" I ask, seeking her consent, and I can feel her nod. Without moving my lips from her breast, I allow my left hand to glide down and over the bare skin of her tight stomach before halting at the waistband of her panties. When she doesn't protest, I slowly inch my hand underneath the fabric and find what I've been craving for weeks now.

Gently, carefully, I begin to caress her most sensitive skin, savoring the feel of her as I glide my hand over that soft, female mound and down between her thighs. God, she is so warm, so soft, so damn turned on. It doesn't take me long to find the right spot with my middle finger, and her body responds immediately, thrusting rhythmically while I carefully sweep my fingers back and forth over that soft but hypersensitive bundle of nerves between her heated thighs. I feel it swell, her wetness clinging to my skin. Fuck, I love doing this to her, love getting her turned on, and I want nothing more than to keep caressing her until she reaches the edge and finally has her first orgasm.

My mouth leaves her nipple and I pull back, scanning her face for any sign that she wants me to stop, but there's only ecstasy sketched into her features. Her eyes are closed, her lips parted, and heat radiates off every inch of her skin.

It takes only a few soft strokes, the slightest bit of pressure, before her breathing becomes erratic and I know she's there. I know it by the way her face contorts with pleasure, her breathing—shallow just a fraction of a second ago—becomes deeper, and her back arches before she seemingly steps into the void of ecstasy. She breathes my name once, twice. Her hips buck against my hand while I continue to caress her, easing up the slightest bit in an effort to draw out the high, to prolong her climax without overstimulating her. I want this to be fucking world-shattering for her.

I watch her as she comes undone underneath me. She lets out the sexiest moan, which I'm sure can be heard by Steve and Vada, but I couldn't care less. Her face, the way her body moves, and the sounds she makes while she rides the waves of pleasure are everything. Shit, I can't even put into words how worked up I am just doing this to her. My cock is rock-hard and straining against the fabric of my jeans. I seriously feel high just watching her.

I bring my lips to hers while she works to regain control. My chest presses against hers, and I feel the warmth of her skin on mine. Her climax recedes, but I don't yet withdraw my hand from between her thighs, relishing the feeling of her aftershocks against my fingers. I want so badly to slip them inside her, to feel her like that for a moment, but I don't. Not tonight. I move at her pace. Always.

When I feel her body relax underneath me and her breathing slows, I pull back. She blinks her hazel eyes at me, a shy smile on her face.

"Hi," I say quietly, placing another kiss on her lips. Even in the dark I can tell her cheeks are flushed. "Are you okay?"

"Yes," she says, breathless. "More than okay. I'm really glad I decided to sleep over at Vada's," she giggles underneath me.

I laugh quietly. "Me, too." I look into her eyes, still hooded from the high a few seconds ago. "You are perfect."

She gives me a wide smile, places her hands on my neck, and pulls me in for another deep kiss.

Cat

I'm absolutely lost to this boy, that much is clear to me. I finally felt brave enough to open up to him, to share at least part my story with him, to tell him what happened between Adam and me. Ronan didn't judge, he didn't run. He chose to stay, and although I still haven't worked up the courage to tell him about the photos—I desperately hope I'll never have to come clean about my ex having nudes of me—I realized in that moment that I'm head over heels in love with him.

I feel so safe with him, physically and emotionally, and I let him touch me in ways no one ever has. I felt like I was flying. He was gentle and respectful, seeking my permission before touching me in the most intimate way imaginable. And it felt so, so good.

I've never felt anything like it. Even when I was by myself, exploring my body, I never managed to take myself all the way. But I could tell things were different with Ronan. I could feel it the first time he ever touched me. Even just the way he kisses me ignites something I didn't know could exist. I don't know what it is or what exactly he does; maybe it's how patient he is with me both physically and emotionally, never putting any pressure on me to take our intimacy further than what I'm absolutely ready for. Or maybe it's how committed he is to making sure that whatever he does to me feels incredibly good. I truly don't know. I just know that when I finally let down my guard and trusted him enough to take it further than I had ever gone before, it was more than I could have ever hoped for: his warm hands caressing my skin; his mouth kissing, licking, nipping, sucking; the weight and heat of his body on mine. It was everything, and when he asked if I trusted him, I gave him my answer without hesitation. Yes, I trust him.

It took Ronan no time at all to find the right spot, the perfect pressure and speed. He touched me so softly, so sensually as he varied the patterns his fingers were drawing, and all I could focus on was the way it felt against my most sensitive flesh. Good god, I never anticipated how incredible it would feel, how all-consuming, how intoxicating, until Ronan skillfully got me there.

I can't stop kissing him, relishing the feel of his body on mine, running my hands up his back and through his dark-blond hair. After another deep kiss, Ronan rolls off me and sits up on the edge of his bed. His eyes are happy, although I can see the exhaustion in them.

"I'm going to take a quick shower," he says quietly when he stands up.

"But it's late and you look so tired," I protest, wanting him to lie down next to me again. "Can't it wait until the morning?" I give him my best puppy-dog face.

He chuckles, then leans down to give me a soft kiss on my lips. "I'm sorry, baby, but you got me all worked up and I really need to go take care of this before I can even think about getting some sleep," he mutters against my lips, then straightens himself up.

I blush in the dark when my eyes flit to his jeans, noting his hardness still straining against the fabric. I realize he obviously didn't get his needs met while I'm lying here, relaxed and satisfied, my body feeling like butter after the amazing high.

"Oh, okay. Is there... Is there anything I can do?" I ask, slightly nervous despite what I just let him do to me.

Again, he chuckles in a low voice. "Don't worry about me. I'll be quick; trust me. This won't take long."

He glides his thumb down my cheek, and I watch him walk into the bathroom before he gives me a wink and closes the door behind him.

I listen to the shower running, feeling like I'm spying on him. I try not to listen too hard for any sounds he might be making, but at the same time straining my ears because part of me wishes I could be in there with him. I'm seriously conflicted. I want him—all of him—so badly, but I'm so scared at the same time. How do I know if I'm ready?

"Ugh!" I turn onto my stomach and bury my face in Ronan's pillow, breathing in his familiar scent—a mix of sun and salty ocean air, detergent and something that is so uniquely him—and I relax again. The hour of the night and the deep relaxation in my bones has caught up with me.

Friday, August 13th

Cat

The next thing I know, my eyes flutter open. Rays of sunlight streak in through the cracks of the window shades, painting lined patterns on the hardwood floor. I hear movement down below, but it's quiet in the room with the exception of Ronan's calm breathing next to me.

His left arm is draped over my waist and his face is nuzzled against my hair. I scoot back a tiny bit, careful not to wake him while I press my back against his front, conforming my body to his. I could lie like this forever, feeling his bare chest against my back, the weight of his arm making me feel safe, his quiet and calm breathing relaxing.

I didn't feel him crawl back into bed with me after his shower last night. It's like I fell into a deep, restful sleep—the best sleep I can remember getting in a very, very long time. My body tingles as my memories return to last night, his hands and mouth caressing my skin until I had my first orgasm. I understand what the big deal is now, and a grin spreads across my face as I attempt to move even closer to Ronan's warm body, wanting and needing to feel as much of him as I can without waking him. My movement causes him to shift in his sleep and his arm moves to tighten his hold on me. If I could, I would melt into him completely.

The door to Ronan's room opens slowly, and Vada peeks at me through the crack in the doorway. She smiles when she sees I'm awake and opens the door a little wider, allowing Onyx to rush past her legs and into the room. The dog promptly jumps on the foot of Ronan's bed and curls up to lay with us.

"Sorry," Vada mouths, and I hold back a snort when she makes hilarious hand motions, obviously trying to ask me if I want to come downstairs with her. I nod and hold up my hand to indicate that I'll be down in five minutes. Vada nods and quietly closes the door behind her.

I stay cuddled up against Ronan a few moments longer before I carefully wiggle my way out from under his arm, slowly getting out of bed without waking him. I stand for a second, watching him sleep, memorizing his perfect face, his tousled hair, his lean, muscular back. For the first time this morning, I notice a large, dark bruise on his shoulder blade that I hadn't seen yesterday. I crease my eyebrows, making a mental note to ask him what happened. It seems like an odd spot for a bruise.

I collect my jeans off the floor and slip them on before taking off my tank top and replacing it with my bra and t-shirt, then tiptoe into the small Jack-and-Jill bathroom Ronan and Steve share. I comb my fingers through my hair and pull it into a ponytail, then quickly brush my teeth.

***

I decide to leave through Steve's bedroom rather than risk waking Ronan. I make my way downstairs, where I find Vada hanging out in the living room.

"Good morning," she sing-songs at me, grinning. "You had a great night, I take it?"

I can tell her question is completely rhetorical, but I answer it nonetheless. "The *best* night," I admit, and fall back onto the couch beside her, sighing deeply.

"I figured. Stevie and I could tell by the sounds you were making," she giggles.

Of course, I turn red immediately. I hadn't realized I was noisy and I make an embarrassed face. "Oh my god, Vada. I'm sorry."

She laughs at me and scoots to hug me. "Don't apologize! Go have fun with Ran! You both deserve to feel good. I'm still so excited that you two got together."

"Me, too," I admit, and hesitate for a second. "I had my first orgasm last night."

Vada leans back, her eyes wide, mouth open. "Are you serious?" I nod, my face burning. "And?" She draws out the word. "How was it?"

"Let's just say I know now what the big deal is," I giggle, and Vada joins in.

"Yeah, it's a pretty great feeling, huh? Kind of addictive, actually," Vada says.

"I always heard people saying it feels like fireworks, but it was more like these waves of, just, incredible pleasure pulsing through me. I didn't want it to stop. And we didn't even have sex."

"Just wait until you experience the full thing," she says. "You're going to wish you hadn't waited this long to feel him like that. It's just a whole different level of intimacy; you're both completely vulnerable to each other."

"Really?" I wonder out loud. After last night I feel even more connected to Ronan. The physical intimacy of his touch required so much of my trust, and I was able to open up to him without any hesitation on my part.

"Yeah," Vada confirms. "After Steve and I had sex for the first time, it was like our relationship was on a whole new, higher level."

I can see that. With Adam, I never felt the emotional connection; I didn't trust him. But that's different with Ronan. I haven't trusted anyone like I trust him. "I feel kind of bad," I confess to Vada.

She cocks her head at me. "Why?"

"Because Ran took his time, he was so perfect, it felt unbelievable, and he gave me my first orgasm," I explain. "And I didn't do anything for him. He had to go shower and 'take care of himself' afterwards, and I feel guilty."

Vada laughs. "Kitty Cat, I wouldn't worry about it. They 'take care of themselves' probably like three times a day. And I bet if you asked him if last night was enjoyable for him, even though he didn't get off with you, he would tell you yes, it was the best night ever. But if you're really worried about it, but you're not ready to have sex yet, there are obviously things you can do to... help him."

Of course, I blush again. "I know I'm overthinking this, but, I haven't even seen a guy naked. Well, a guy that I wanted to see naked, at least," I add. "What if I touch him wrong? Ugh..." I trail off.

"Okay, you need to get out of your head. First of all, I'm not sure you can actually touch him wrong, but even if you do, he'll let you know what feels good and what doesn't. And you can usually gauge their reaction pretty well. Guys aren't hard to read when it comes to sex. And second of all, just try things out, see what feels good to you. I promise, you'll know when you're ready. It'll just happen one day; you guys will be making out or whatever and suddenly you're not going to want to stop. Your body will scream for more, you will want to feel him—and I mean *all* of him—inside you, and then you're never going to want to go back," she laughs, and I join in.

"What's funny?" Steve walks into the living room wearing black jeans and a navy-blue t-shirt. He has a mug of a hot liquid in each hand and places them in front of Vada and me on the coffee table.

"Sex," Vada exclaims, and reaches for her cup.

"Oh yeah? What about it?" Steve asks, his hands in his jeans pockets as he stands, facing us, eyebrows raised.

Vada shrugs and takes a slow sip of her coffee. "Cat is worried about not knowing what she's doing, and I told her guys are pretty easy to read when it comes to sex."

I blush for the hundredth time today and bump Vada's shoulder, embarrassed that she so readily discloses my concerns to Steve.

Steve's attention turns to me, his face kind. "Honestly, Cat, just do what feels good to you. Odds are it will feel good to Ran, too." Then he creases his eyebrows. "Well, unless you're into, like S&M. Maybe go easy on that. I don't know; I honestly don't know what Ran's kinks are, so... yeah, I don't know, just, don't overthink it. Have fun," he says, and turns to head back to the kitchen for another cup of coffee.

"Told you." Vada leans back on the couch, sipping her coffee. "So, what's on the agenda for today?"

I shrug and take the second cup of coffee from the table before leaning back against the couch. "I don't know; Ran and I didn't exactly get a chance to talk last night," I grin. "Do you have any ideas?"

"Not really."

"I have an idea," Steve calls out from the kitchen, then appears from around the corner with another mug in hand.

"Well, enlighten us then," Vada says.

Steve takes a leisurely sip from his steaming coffee. "Why don't we go skating?" he finally says. "I probably won't get a lot of opportunity to once I'm away," he adds, and Vada turns her attention to me.

"Wait, like, *ice* skating?" I ask her and Steve, both of whom nod. "Oh, I don't know. I've never been."

"You've never been ice skating?" Steve asks, squinting at me as if trying to detect a lie.

"Never in my entire life," I say, making an *X* across my heart.

"What in the world? That's just sad, Kitty Cat." Vada pats my shoulder.

"So, skating it is, then," Steve decides. "Your boyfriend will be delighted, since it's kind of his thing, you know." Steve grins at me.

"So I heard," I grin back at him.

***

Ronan doesn't wake up for another two hours while Steve, Vada, and I eat cereal and hang out. I hear him trudge down the stairs at just before eleven, and when he finally steps into the living room, I can't help but smile. He's wearing light-gray sweats, sitting low enough on his hips that the waistband of his black boxer briefs peeks out, but that's all. I follow the ridges of his abdominal muscles up to his chest before finally finding his gorgeous face and locking on his eyes. The grin on his face tells me my staring did not go unnoticed.

"Good morning, princess," Steve says while Ronan saunters toward me. "Did you get sufficient beauty sleep last night?" Steve winks at Ronan.

"Sure did," Ronan says, and pulls me against his bare chest after he sits down next to me. "You on the other hand look like you could use a lot more beauty sleep," he teases his older brother, who flips him off.

"Fuck off," Steve says with a chuckle.

"We decided to go skating today." Vada brings Ronan up to speed on our plans for the day.

Ronan leans back a smidge to look at me.

"I've never been," I tell him. "So, you'll need to teach me."

"Oh, I'll teach you, baby," he says suggestively, his voice low, and I swat his shoulder playfully, rolling my eyes.

"Jesus," Steve says with a huff. "Maybe you two should stay home and only Vada and I go skating."

Ronan shrugs. "Works for me." He plants a kiss on my temple while I inhale him. "But if you really want to go, let's do it!"

It takes us an hour before we're finally ready to head out the door. Ronan scarfs down a hastily made turkey sandwich as he and I sit, squeezed in the back of Steve's Challenger while Steve drives us to the ice rink.

It's freezing when we step into the ice center. I'm not sure what I expected, it being an *ice* rink and all, but I didn't think I would be shivering within the first three minutes of arrival. I certainly understand now why Ronan grabbed not one, but two of his hoodies before we left, and I gratefully accept a navy-blue sweater Ronan hands to me with a knowing grin.

"What size shoes do you wear?" Steve asks me while Ronan, his fingers interlaced with mine, leads me down a narrow walkway adjacent to the icy rink where people, young and old, are already exhibiting varying levels of skating prowess.

"Eight and a half," I say.

Steve gives me a quick nod. "Perfect. We'll be right back." He pulls Vada with him to the counter where people can rent ice skates. "Oh, wait," Steve calls out to me, "what kind of skates do you want? Hockey or figure skating?"

I shrug and look at Ronan. "What's the difference?"

He smiles that sexy half-smile at me that always makes my head go all mushy. "Go with hockey skates," he says, then quickly pulls my hand toward him, and with it my whole body, stepping around a burly guy who didn't look like he had any intention of avoiding a collision with us. He's tall and wide, his stature familiar, and for a second I think it's Adam. My body tenses, the hairs on my neck standing up when I look back at the guy who's walking away from us, head ducked, hands shoved into his pockets.

"Okay," I say, still craning my neck, but the guy's head is covered by a hood. Before I can make out details, he disappears from my view, and I quickly shake off the eerie tension in my body. There's no way Adam could be here in New York, let alone at the same ice rink I'm at right now.

"Get her hockey skates," Ronan yells at his brother, who gives me a quick salute. "Hockey skates are easier to learn with," Ronan explains to me, not picking up on the momentary change in my demeanor as he continues leading me down the walkway. "Figure skates have toe picks in the front," he says as he holds open a glass door and I step into a small room.

"Oh, it's warm in here," I remark gratefully.

Ronan chuckles. "That's probably because this is the warm room," he says, and I give him an incredulous look. "I swear," he says, amused by my expression, "it's called the warm room." He laughs now, and it's infectious.

"Got it," I say, sniggering at him. "The warm room. I'm learning," I say proudly, and he plants a kiss against my temple. "Teach me more," I urge while I touch the spot where his lips just met my skin. "What are toe picks?"

"Toe picks are those little zigzag things on the front of the figure skate blade. They allow figure skaters to dig their toes into the ice and then do their fancy jumps and stuff," he says, and motions for me to sit down in a chair.

I sit and begin to untie my shoes, slipping them off one by one.

Steve and Vada join Ronan and me in the warm room. "Here you go," Vada says, and drops a pair of black hockey skates in front of me.

I give her a smile but turn my attention back to Ronan. "And hockey skates don't have those," I observe, scanning the blade of one of the skates Vada just dropped in front of me.

"No. Hockey skates are shorter and more rounded, making them ideal for speed and quick maneuvering," Ronan says, sitting down next to me. A tingling sensation moves up my leg when his knee touches mine while he takes off his chucks.

"Do you think I should be using skates that are made for speed and 'quick maneuvering?'" I ask, eyeing the skates with a concerned look on my face.

He laughs again. "The toe picks on figure skates tend to trip people up, so yeah, I think you'll be more comfortable with hockey skates." He puts on his skates, tying them quickly and skillfully while I fumble around with the seemingly yards-long laces on my own pair.

"Can I help you?" he asks, his eyes a liquid green. I could get lost in those eyes, swim in them like an ocean. Ronan takes a knee in front of me, then helps me slide first one foot, then the other into the skates before he laces them for me.

"You never lace my skates sexy like that for me," I hear Vada complain to Steve, who snorts a laugh.

"I'll tie your laces for you next time," Steve laughs.

"Ready?" Ronan asks, taking my hand and pulling me to my feet.

"Ready as I'll ever be," I say hesitantly, and follow Vada, Steve, and Ronan out of the little room and to the ice rink. I feel wobbly on the thin blades, but nothing prepares me for my first time on the ice. Ronan steps on before me and immediately spins around to face me. He looks absolutely comfortable on the ice as he holds out his hands to me, and I take them. I step onto the ice and immediately lose my footing.

"Holy shit," I squeak as Ronan tightens his hold on me.

"You're doing great," Ronan smiles at me. "Try to keep your feet straight. Yeah, like that. Just try and get a feel for the ice." He skates backwards, holding my hands and pulling me along with him. We make two full rounds in the rink like that while Vada and Steve keep passing us up and cheering me on, which makes me laugh.

"Focus, baby," Ronan says, smiling when I look over his shoulder at Vada and Steve, who are skating hand-in-hand. Steve is definitely the better skater, his motions fluid and confident, but Vada can hold her own.

And then I spot him again, the burly guy from earlier. He's standing by the boards, apparently looking on, his hood pulled low over his head, making it impossible for me to make out a face. But his size, his wide shoulders, it all reminds me of Adam. Am I going crazy?

"I'm going to let go of your hands, okay?" Ronan says, drawing my attention back to him and away from the guy.

I want to protest, but Ronan gently slides his hands out of mine, spins around, and joins me to my left. "You're looking great," he says, his eyes on my feet as I glide the blades across the ice like we've been practicing. Surprisingly, I feel pretty steady.

I allow myself to briefly glance back at the guy, noting that he's gone again.

"You're a natural at this," Ronan says, making me smile now.

"I have a good coach," I say in a flirty tone, and his eyes lift toward mine. He smiles at me and, right on cue, I lose my footing and fall, landing straight on my butt.

Ronan's blades scrape to a sudden halt. "Are you okay?" he asks, grabbing my hands, helping me back up.

"Fine," I respond, and wipe my wet bottom. "I just got distracted by you."

"I have to admit, it's a nice change. Usually I'm the one getting distracted by you," he says, grinning. Then he pulls me toward him and kisses me softly.

"Hmm, well, I think I need a little break," I say against his lips, and carefully slide toward the dasher board. "Go ahead, let me see what you got," I tell Ronan as Vada and Steve pass us for the umpteenth time.

"Yeah, little brother, let her see what you *got*," Steve yells at Ronan as he passes him, smacking him hard on the back.

Ronan takes off after his brother at neck-breaking speeds. Steve speeds up, breaking from Vada, who skates over to me and gets off the ice.

"Is this what they do?" I ask her, watching Ronan's every move, how he zips around Steve and the other people. It's thrilling as hell, and I decide right then and there that I'm going to go watch him play actual games.

"Yep," Vada says, her eyes glued to Steve. "I wish you had been here when Steve was still on the team, because the two of them together were pretty incredible. I don't know if it's some brother thing or whatever, but Steve had more assists to Ronan's scores than anyone else, and vice versa. It was pretty hot," she adds, and bumps me playfully.

Finally, Ronan makes his way back over to us. He brakes, scraping his blades against the ice, and it looks like he made snow.

"Do you feel like trying a little more, or do you want to call it a day?" he asks me as he steps effortlessly off the ice. I swear, I can't tell which comes easier to him, walking or skating.

"Honestly, I think I'm good for my first time," I admit. "My butt is wet."

There's a naughty little gleam in Ronan's eyes, though he doesn't say anything. Instead he takes my hand and leads me back to the warm room where we're met, minutes later, by Vada and Steve. I put on my shoes while Ronan takes my skates back to the rental window, and I meet him there on the way back to Steve's car.

The four of us decide to grab some burgers at a small burger joint in our neighborhood before we make our way back to Ronan and Steve's house.

***

"What time are you heading to work?" I ask Ronan when we're up in his room a little while later. I'm lounging on his comfortable bed, facing Ronan who's next to me, his hand grazing up and down my arm softly.

"In about an hour," he says, his eyes on my lips.

I smile. "You want to kiss me, don't you?" I whisper.

His eyes briefly flicker to mine before settling on my lips again. "Very much."

"What's stopping you?" I ask, and scoot closer to him.

His hand slides off my arm and to my hip before he pulls me in toward him. "Honestly?" he starts, and laughs. "This. It's always this." He pulls his phone out of his back pocket. I didn't realize his phone was buzzing. He takes a quick glance at the screen, his smile widening even more. "Sorry, baby, I'm going to take this really quick."

He sits up next to me on his bed. "Hi, Morai," he answers, his voice light. I have no idea who he's talking to, but he doesn't appear too concerned with privacy because he doesn't move from my side. His right hand still rests on my hip, or more like my butt cheek. I try not to eavesdrop, but it's unavoidable.

"I'm fine," Ronan continues, and looks at me, smiling. "But it's not a great time, actually."

He pauses for a moment while the person on the other end says something, and Ronan chuckles. "I sort of have company." He moves his hand to my cheek, continuing to smile at me. He doesn't break eye contact with me even while talking to this Morai person.

He chuckles in a low tone. "Yes, a girl. Her name is Cat. No, not Catherine. Just Cat. With a *C*. Yep, like the pet," he says and rolls his eyes at me, which makes me giggle. "Uh-huh," he continues, his voice taking on a gravelly tone. "She's my girlfriend, Morai."

Ronan is full-on laughing now, and I cock my head to the side, analyzing him. "What? You want me to describe her to you?" His smile becomes even wider. "She's perfect, Morai. She has beautiful hazel eyes with these amazing gold specks in them. Really long eyelashes and the most gorgeous face—full lips and high cheekbones. She has long legs and delicate features and long, soft blonde hair. She's the most beautiful girl I've ever met, Morai. And she is so incredibly good to me." Ronan's voice is so soft as he describes me, his eyes never leaving mine. I can't tell if he's describing me to me or to the person on the other line on the phone, but I lean in and kiss his lips softly. I pull back and notice that Ronan's eyes are closed while he continues to talk. "Okay," Ronan sighs. "Yeah, I promise. Love you, too."

He opens his eyes, then hangs up the phone.

I look at Ronan expectantly, hoping he'll finally enlighten me as to the identity of this mysterious caller.

"That was my grandmother," he says, grinning from ear to ear, and my face breaks into a smile. "She calls me about once a month to check up on me."

"I love that," I say, meaning it. "Is her name Morai?"

"No, that's the Irish nickname for 'grandma,'" he explains. "She was really interested to hear about you," he chuckles.

I blush a little. "Thank you for describing me the way you did," I say, leaning against Ronan.

"I didn't say anything that wasn't true." He studies my face, his eyes intense like he's deep in thought, like he has something he wants to get off his chest. But he seems to reconsider and kisses me deeply instead, making all thoughts vanish from my head as I lose track of time and my surroundings during the ensuing make-out session.

"Did you enjoy skating today?" Ronan asks after we get our fill of each other about thirty minutes later.

"I did," I say, and watch Ronan roll out of his bed reluctantly. He slips on his signature black Murphy's long-sleeve, covering his bare torso, while I sit up and pull my shirt back down. "I'm going to need some practice, though, if I want to keep up with you."

He smiles, then leans onto his bed and over me, brushing his lips softly against mine. "I'll be happy to practice with you any time," he says. "Are you stopping by Murphy's tonight?"

"That was my plan," I say, and kiss him back, not ready to let him go. I could really get used to sleeping in the same bed as Ronan, waking up next to him, and spending the day with him.

***

Ronan leaves for Murphy's about twenty minutes later, and after hanging out with Steve a while longer and making plans to meet the rest of our friends at Murphy's as well, Vada takes me home. She hangs out in the living room, ensuring a proper alibi for last night—after all, I told my mom I'd be spending the night at Vada's—while I change. I pull on my favorite pair of faded blue jeans—the ones with the worn knees—and a well-fitting vintage Johnny Cash shirt, then slip my feet into my red chucks and skip down the stairs.

"Let's go," I say to Vada, who walks out the door ahead of me while I wave to my mom.

Vada and I get back into her car and make it to Murphy's fifteen minutes later.

"I'm going to run to the restroom really quick," I say, and Vada nods before heading off to find our friends. I glance around as I walk, trying to find the one boy who always makes my heart rate increase, and I spot him standing at a table about twenty feet away, talking with some customers. As if he can sense me, Ronan looks up and over, his lips tugging into a smile the second his eyes lock on mine before he turns his attention back to the three people sitting at the table.

I walk into the bathroom. It's completely empty when I stand in front of the sink, washing my hands, then drying them and discarding the paper towels in the trash. I feel my phone vibrating in my back pocket and pull it out to see a text from Vada.

Vada: we're at the large table right by the bar... you'll have the perfect view of Ran from here. Just try not to get all swoony ;)

I smile to myself, thinking about Ronan, and begin to text her back as I pull open the bathroom door and walk out just to crash right into someone. I look up from my phone, an apology on my lips, when a hand encircles my wrist and recognition floods my brain.

"Adam!" I say, stunned, my eyes wide. I swallow hard as my whole body tenses. He really is here, in New York. I wasn't mistaken earlier—it was him at the rink. I knew I recognized him, even with the hood obscuring his face. My body knew. It remembered.

"Surprise!" he says, eyeing me from head to toe. I pull my hand back. He towers over me, his shadow eclipsing the light around me.

"What are you doing here?" I say meekly. I'm scared of him, and he knows it.

"I don't know why, but I can't get you out of my head. Probably has something to do with those tasty pictures you've been sending me," he adds with a chuckle. "So, I thought I'd make good on my promise of a visit," he says, smiling ominously.

"How did you even find me?" I ask as I try to step around him.

He blocks my path with his large body, moving close to me, the space between us diminishing.

My body stiffens with fear.

He chuckles quietly, though his tone reflects no humor at all. "I swear, Cat," he says, sliding a finger under my chin, and I recoil from his touch, "you seem to keep forgetting how small our town is. It's really not hard at all to get information from people. I had no problem finding you. I got your number, then I got your address. I've actually been here a couple of days already; just kind of wanted to see what you've been up to, you know. You're a busy little bee," he chuckles, and I get a strong whiff of alcohol. He must be drunk. "And then I just happened to get to your house right as you were leaving, so I figured I'd follow you here and see if you wanted to catch up," he says, his voice low, threatening, and I don't think he understands how fucking insane he sounds.

"You need to leave," I say, gathering as much courage as I can muster. I look over Adam's shoulder, but there's nobody there; the hallway to the bathrooms is around a corner and out of sight of everyone, including my friends... and Ronan.

"What? No, I just got here, and you owe me. You owe me a lot more than pictures of your tight little body," Adam says, familiar anger flashing in his eyes. "You can't just fuck up my life and then blow me off, you fucking little cock tease," he spits, moving even closer toward me.

I back away, but there's nowhere to go and my back hits the wall. Adam slams the palms of his hands against the wall on either side of my head, trapping me like an animal, his face only inches from mine. I'm acutely aware that we're alone, that I have nowhere to go, and that it wouldn't take much for Adam to overpower me and just take what he thinks he deserves. I'm scared. I know I should scream or kick him or something, but it's like I'm frozen, just like I was every time he towered over me before he hit me.

"What do you want from me?" I ask, tears stinging in my eyes. But I refuse to cry, to give him any kind of power or control.

"I want you to make up for what you did to me," he snarls, his words slurred but his nostrils flared. His eyes are hard yet bloodshot. "I was good to you; all I asked was that you be good to me in return, and you never were. Instead you led me on for five months, you bitch, and you never put out. But you can make up for it right now," he says with a vicious grin, moving one of his hands to stroke my cheek.

I take the smallest of opportunities and squeeze under his arm and around him, walking as quickly as my feet will move down the hallway and into the open restaurant area. I can feel Adam on my heels, and just as I make it into the seating area he reaches for me, grabbing my wrist again, squeezing it tightly and pulling me roughly toward him.

"Adam, please stop!" I say as loudly as I can.

Suddenly it's like time slows down, yet speeds up all at once, and Ronan is there, yanking Adam away from me.

"Get the fuck away from her," Ronan growls as he steps between me and Adam, shielding me with his body. His muscles are so tightly wound they strain against the fabric of his shirt.

"This is none of your damn business, man," Adam hisses at Ronan, who doesn't move an inch, one hand reached back and resting on my hip. Realization suddenly seems to hit Adam, and a malicious grin spreads across his face as he looks at Ronan. "Oh shit, I recognize you," Adam says before his eyes find me cowering behind Ronan. "I saw you with him earlier, holding hands and shit. Is this the guy you're putting out for? You're fucking him, aren't you? You wouldn't ever put out for me, you little slut, but..."

He doesn't get the chance to finish his sentence because Ronan's left fist crashes into Adam's face with the sound of bones crushing. Adam stumbles back, swaying precariously. But Ronan doesn't let up, his fist colliding with Adam's face again and again.

There are chairs scraping and shocked shouts from restaurant patrons while Shane, Steve, Zack, Vada, Summer, and Tori run toward us.

Vada pulls me out of the way as the guys try to wrestle Ronan away from Adam, whose nose is bleeding profusely. Blood is spattering onto Adam's shirt and the floor, and his right eye is already swelling shut. Steve and Shane pull Ronan backwards while Zack tries to block Adam, but Adam is able to get in two vicious punches—one right below Ronan's left eye, the other on his lip, causing it to split open. It only seems to inflame Ronan, who tears himself away from his brother and best friend and punches Adam so hard in the stomach that Adam drops to his knees with a loud grunt before Ronan follows it up with a knee to Adam's already beat-up face.

Shane and Steve manage to get ahold of Ronan's arms again, yanking him back and away from the heaving pile that is Adam. Ronan's eyes are filled with undiluted rage as he strains against Shane and Steve's hold on him. I've never seen Ronan like this before, consumed by anger, and I don't even think he realizes he's hurt and bleeding. I hate that I'm the reason for all of this.

I run over to Ronan and fling my arms around his neck. It takes only a heartbeat before I feel him relax against me.

"Are you okay, baby?" he asks, his breathing still erratic. Shane and Steve let go of Ronan, and he pulls me into him, his chest heaving. I feel his heart kicking in his chest, adrenaline pumping in his veins.

"I'm okay," I nod against him.

"What the hell happened?" Steve asks, his eyes on Adam, who remains on the floor.

I briefly recount what happened while Shane and Zack grab Adam and pull him off the floor rather unceremoniously.

Adam looks unsteady on his feet, and his face resembles a blackberry, all bruised and lumpy. As he wipes the blood from his mouth and obviously broken nose, he gives me a contemptuous look.

Ronan's lip is still bleeding as he unravels his arms from around me and takes a step toward Adam. I reach for him, grabbing his biceps—a futile attempt at holding him back—and Steve and Shane immediately take on protective postures. Shane's hand presses against Ronan's chest, trying to prevent a flare-up of the situation, and ready to jump in and provide Ronan with backup if he needs it.

"Stay the fuck away from Cat," Ronan growls again at Adam.

"Or what?" Adam slurs, trying to sound intimidating, but he fails in his inebriated state and after getting his ass kicked.

"Or I'm going to hunt you down, and I'm going to fucking kill you," Ronan says with so much hate in his voice that it almost scares me.

Adam considers Ronan for a second. The two of them are the same height, and though Adam has a larger frame, Ronan is leaner, more muscular, harder—his solid chest well-defined under his black shirt. Ronan's solid stature and the fact that Adam is woefully outnumbered—Ronan, Steve, Shane, and Zack create an intimidating front—seems to bring Adam to his senses, at least momentarily.

"Don't think we're done," Adam says, pointing his index finger at me.

I feel Ronan coil again. "No, you're fucking done," he says, his voice a low, threatening rumble.

Finally, Adam relents. He walks slowly to the front doors, pushing them open before he leaves.

I exhale the breath that has been trapped in my chest.

"What the fuck?" Shane says, his brow furrowed. "Cat, are you alright?" I nod, aware of the looks and whispers from customers around us, but Shane doesn't seem to care. "How about you, Ran? You okay?" he asks, eyeing Ronan's left cheekbone where a bruise is already blooming.

"I've had worse," Ronan says absentmindedly as he looks me over, so much worry in his eyes.

"Maybe you should take Cat home," Shane says, "and put some ice on that bruise. I'm going to clean up this mess," he adds, motioning toward the blood spatter on the floor.

Ronan nods at him, and I interlace my fingers with Ronan's. He leads me over to the bar where he reaches over the counter and picks up his wallet and keys.

"Ready?" he asks me, his voice soft, and I nod. Giving my hand a quick squeeze, he leads me past our friends, out of the restaurant, and to his car where he holds the door open for me while I slip into the passenger seat. I watch Ronan as he quickly takes stock of our surroundings, making sure Adam truly has left. Then he maneuvers around the front of his car, wipes the blood from his lip, and gets into the driver's seat.

"I'm sorry," I say quietly, looking at him.

His eyebrows crease and he looks at me, his eyes soft, as he turns his whole body toward me and takes my hand into both of his. "You don't have anything to be sorry about," he says forcefully. "You did nothing wrong." He doesn't break eye contact with me, his gaze intense, and finally I lift my hand to carefully touch his lip with my index finger.

"I didn't mean for you to get hurt," I whisper.

"I'm fine, Cat. I promise." He takes my hand, pulls it to his lips, and kisses it softly. "This isn't anything I can't handle. What I wouldn't be able to handle is if this guy put his hands on you," he adds stiffly. He begins to drive toward my house.

"But I hate that you had to protect me, and that you got hurt. I hate that Adam was there; I hate how he made me feel." I start to cry as the adrenaline leaves my body and the reality of what just happened crashes in on me. "I hate it all."

Ronan's hand tightens around mine. "I'm sorry," he says quietly. "I'm sorry that assholes like him exist. He has no right to do this shit to you; I'm sorry I didn't prevent him from... God, I want to kill him," Ronan says, his jaw tight, and I can feel him tense again.

"You stopped him, though; you protected me," I whisper.

Ronan's eyes leave the road to look over at me briefly, his expression softening. "I wish I could keep you safe always."

"That's impossible," I sigh, feeling defeated. Even though Ronan may have stopped Adam from hurting me today, he still doesn't know about the pictures I sent to Adam, still doesn't know what kind of hold Adam has on me, what kind of power Adam could exert if he wished to do so.

"I know," Ronan says. "But that doesn't mean I won't try."

Ronan

I stay with Cat for about twenty minutes after dropping her back off at her house. I sit with her, my arm wrapped around her, while she tells her mom what happened—not only tonight, but over the past couple months. By the looks on Cat's mom's face, Cat hadn't told her about Adam's late-night phone calls and creepy texts. Her mom is furious and insists on calling the police. Cat tries to talk her out of it, but when she looks to me for support, I agree with her mom.

"I'm no cop, but I'm pretty sure that if he got six months' probation, then he probably isn't supposed to have even left North Carolina, let alone make contact with you," I urge Cat.

She just shakes her head as tears silently roll down her face. God damn, I just want to make it all go away for her. I want her to feel safe, and I know that calling the cops on this asshole is the best chance to keep him away from her. Hopefully he'll be in violation of his probation and he'll have to pay the consequences, meaning he'll stay as far away from Cat as possible.

"This isn't up for discussion, Cat," her mom says sternly, and ends up calling the police. I wait around, holding Cat, letting her cry in my arms, until two uniformed officers show up. Then her mom, over Cat's vehement objection, suggests I leave.

"Your cheek looks like it needs some ice on it," Cat's mom says warmly, and hands me a small bag filled with ice. I nod gratefully, putting the bag against my cheek and allowing it to numb my skin.

"And Ronan," she calls after me as I'm about to walk out of the front door. She closes the little distance between us with a couple of steps. "Thank you for protecting her." Then she encircles me with her arms and gives me a tight hug.

I don't really know what to do and awkwardly pat her on the back.

The whole drive home I replay what happened in my mind. I only saw Cat briefly when she walked into Murphy's and headed to the bathroom. I was busy getting orders out. When I was at the bar getting ready to grab a drink order from Jack, I noticed her rush out of the bathroom, some asshole right behind her. I saw him grab her and was already making my way toward them, my hands clenched into fists, when I heard her say his name: Adam. And it's like everything went blank.

My body went on autopilot. I remember telling him to stay the fuck away from her, and when he started insulting her, calling her a slut, I fucking lost my shit on him. And I couldn't stop—didn't want to stop. Shane and Steve pulled me off him, and this asshole got a couple good licks in, but that just pissed me off more. Every cell in my body wanted to kill this guy for everything he had ever done to Cat and for having the fucking nerve to show up here and threaten her, touch her, call her names. Not on my fucking watch.

The rage I felt was blinding, but then Cat threw herself at me, slinging her arms around my neck, and my whole body relaxed against her. It was the craziest thing. It's like she's the antidote to the fear, the pain, the anger, the hurt, and all that's messed up in my life, at least momentarily.

***

I pull up to my house, knowing full well that my mom is home—she's not working tonight—and I briefly contemplate just heading back to work right now. But I have blood stains on my shirt and jeans; no idea whether they're from Adam or me. Honestly, I didn't even realize I was bleeding until I was about to get in my car. It's worrisome because I didn't even recognize myself; it's like I just lost it, and I wonder if that's what happens to my mother when I'm around her. Like I just set her off and she loses all control, just like I did with Adam. If it hadn't been for Shane and Steve, I'm honestly not sure I would have stopped beating the shit out of him. What the fuck does that mean for me?

"Fuck," I mutter to myself, running my hands roughly over my face, wincing when I graze the fresh bruise on my cheekbone. I get out of my car, walk into the house through the open garage, and head up the three steps into the kitchen.

My mother stands at the sink. "I thought you're working," she says, and her eyes flit first to my cheek, then my lip. "What happened to your face, Ronan?" She takes a step toward me, looking me over. "Did you get in a fight?" She's getting agitated; I can hear it in her voice. "God damn it, Ronan."

"So what if I did?" I say, trying to move around her. I seriously wonder about myself sometimes; it's not like I don't know that these last five words are going to piss her off. But I don't really give a shit right now. I'm still too on edge, my body still under tension with restless energy pricking my skin.

"Excuse me?" she says, taking another step toward me, her hands on her hips. "I'm not raising you to be a god damn hooligan, Ronan. You're making this family look bad walking around looking like you got into a bar fight."

I don't know if it's some remnant of the adrenaline that was thrashing through my body not even an hour ago or the utter hypocrisy my mom is throwing in my face, but I shut up the voice in my head that tells me to back off and instead decide to double down on my already disrespectful comment. "I don't get you. You beat the shit out of me all the damn time and you don't care what I look like."

Yep, that did it. Her face darkens and she shoves her hands against my chest, pushing me back. "So, are you telling me you enjoy getting the shit beat out of you? Because that's what I'm hearing right now, Ronan," she yells, shoving me again. "That you're asking for it."

"Why do you hate me so much?" I yell back, matching her volume.

"Because you're a fucking piece of shit, Ronan. Because you're a waste of space, a fucking worthless, no-good screw up who should never have been born," she screams at the exact moment that she smashes her fist into my cheekbone, exactly where Adam caught me earlier, catching me off guard. She shoves me a third time—hard—toward the open garage door. I fall backwards down the three steps, trying desperately to get a grip on the doorframe to prevent the fall, but I'm unsuccessful and crash into the steel utility shelf, pulling it down with me.

Pain shoots down my arm the moment I land on the concrete floor, and I grab my right shoulder as I try to find my footing.

"Fuck," I groan. I can tell I'm hurt. I shut my eyes tightly, gritting my teeth as the pain rips through my body. I attempt to breathe through it, to maintain my composure. I refuse to show weakness when she's around.

"Ronan!" My mother's voice is sharp as she calls my name.

"I need a second, Mom. Please," I breathe, not ready for more of her bullshit. *Why the hell did I have to provoke her? Was I really asking for it? What the hell is wrong with me? I'm so screwed up.* I take a sharp breath, push myself up off the floor, and climb the three steps back into the house and to the kitchen.

My mother's expression—full of anger just seconds ago—has changed to one of concern. She finally lets me pass as I continue to cradle my hurt shoulder against my body.

"Let me see," she urges, following me into the living room.

"No, please don't touch me!" I whimper with another wave of pain. I'm pleading, I know, and I know how much she hates that, but right now I don't have the willpower to play her games. I can feel myself crashing.

"Ronan!" Her voice is all authority again. I stop in my tracks, obeying, and lower my left hand from my right shoulder to allow her to examine me. "Your shoulder is dislocated," she diagnoses me, alive in her role as a nurse.

"Yeah, no shit," I mutter.

She gives me an angry look. "I'm going to set it." She extends her hand toward my shoulder, but I flinch back.

"What? No!" I protest, my voice panicky. No way am I going to allow her the sadistic pleasure of hurting me even more.

"Ronan, I need to put your shoulder back in its socket." Her arms are crossed in front of her chest, and I just about fucking lose it. "It will feel a lot better once it's set, I promise," she urges now, her voice soft, and I get whiplash from her constantly changing emotions. It's nothing I'm not used to, but it's particularly exhausting and unpredictable when I'm in pain and have a hard time processing the threat level.

I analyze her face for a few seconds, unsure of the right move, unsure of whether I should allow her to help me or if I'm setting myself up for more pain. But my shoulder throbs painfully and I'm desperate for relief.

I take a deep breath. "Fine."

My mother's body relaxes as she takes a couple steps toward me, then places her left hand on my shoulder and her right under my elbow. I dip my head down and close my eyes, bracing for the inevitable. "I'm going to count to three," she says, her voice steady. "One..."

She pushes my arm up forcefully and relocates my shoulder with a loud pop.

I squeeze my eyes shut tightly, taking a sharp breath in. "What happened to the three count?" I ask through gritted teeth, breathing hard.

"I find that nothing is worse than the anticipation of pain." She takes a step back, admiring her handiwork before she turns and walks into the kitchen, where I hear her open the freezer. I stand there, eyes closed, wondering how the hell I got to this place, what the hell I did to deserve all this. Well, I know what I did, what it is that I'm doing—I keep fucking up. I keep not being good enough, *ever*. I open my stupid mouth when I just need to shut the fuck up. God damn it. I can't do anything right. I can't keep Cat safe; fuck, I can't even keep myself safe. I'm worthless.

My mom returns to the living room with a bag of ice. "Here, you'll need to ice your shoulder and take some ibuprofen. Your ligaments are overstretched right now. And put some ice on that," she adds, motioning toward my cheek.

"Okay," I say, feeling unsteady on my feet. I take the ice from her and place it against my shoulder, then walk out of the living room.

"Where are you going?"

"Upstairs so I can change. I still need to get back to work," I say, and I don't wait for a response as I make my way to my room. I change as quickly as I can, my shoulder sore, my face throbbing, and get back downstairs in less than five minutes.

My mother is back in the kitchen when I walk in. "Please take the trash out with you," she says like nothing happened. Her voice is even, normal, just like I'd expect any mother to sound. It's such a god damn mind fuck.

I grab the trash bag, ready to walk back into the garage to deposit the trash in the can and get into my car.

"I'm sorry for hurting you." My mother's voice is quiet as I pass by her, and I almost miss what she just said. She sighs, puts down the coffee mug she was just rinsing, and turns to me. "I don't want to hurt you all the time." Her eyes search mine for acceptance of what she's telling me.

"I have to go, Mom," I say simply. I've heard her say this a million times; I can't count the number of times she's said that she's sorry, that she doesn't want to hurt me, that she didn't mean to hit me. It's a constant back-and-forth of bullshit. Her words never back her fucking actions.

Once I get to my car, I sit for a minute, gripping my steering wheel so tightly that my knuckles turn white. I think about the hug Cat's mom gave me just before I left her house, how she thanked me for protecting Cat. My mom has never hugged me. The contrast between Cat's mom and mine is so stark, I don't even understand how these things can coexist in this world. It feels like my head might explode, and I can't tell if it's from all the shitty emotions pumping through me right now or the fact that I received some pretty nasty hits to the head, but I feel like I'm going to need something to shut this all off soon.

***

I get back to Murphy's a little while later and walk to the bar, where I deposit my keys and wallet behind the counter, then grab a shot glass and fill it to the brim with tequila—the cheap kind. It tastes like shit, but it makes my brain nice and fuzzy in no time at all.

Shane and Steve walk up to me, standing on either side of me just as I'm about to bring the glass to my lips.

"You okay?" Shane asks, eyeing the glass in my hands, then my face, lingering for a moment on my swollen, bruised cheekbone.

"Sure," I lie, then take the shot, letting the liquid burn its way down my throat.

"If you need the evening off, I get it," Shane says as I slam the shot glass down on the counter.

I shake my head. "No, I want to be here. I need the distraction."

"Okay, well we're closing at nine anyways. My dad just called me to tell me the air vents are being cleaned out tonight. It's going to take all evening."

"Oh, okay," I say, not happy about the prospect of going back home when my mom's not working tonight.

"Should we hang out at the beach, then?" Steve chimes in, and I welcome the idea.

"I'll check if it's cool with my mom, but I can't see why it wouldn't be," Shane says, and pulls out his phone. I take the opportunity to start making my rounds through my section, noting that Shane was able to wipe the floor clean of the blood—either mine or Adam's, who the fuck knows—and get busy with work in no time.

The rest of the evening flies by, and Shane and I close up shop while Steve, Zack, Tori, Summer, and Vada hang out, waiting for us to finish cleaning and locking up. My head is still in a weird place when we head to our cars, agreeing to meet at the beach house.

"You're picking up Cat, or do you want us to?" Vada asks me as I'm about to get into my car. I cock my eyebrows at her. I haven't even talked to Cat since this afternoon and was planning on giving her a call as soon as I got in my car. "I called her earlier and told her we'd be heading to Shane's after you guys got off work," Vada says in answer to my confused expression.

"Is she even up for hanging out after..." I trail off. I sort of assumed she wasn't in the mood for more outings today after her ex stalked her here.

"Duh. I'm pretty sure she's always game for hanging out with you." Vada winks at me.

For the first time in the last few hours, my lips tug into a smile. "I'll get her," I say, my heart squirming in my chest. Weird how even just the thought of Cat makes life infinitely more bearable.

***

I knock on her door half an hour later after making a quick pitstop, and her little sister Samantha opens the door. A huge grin spread across her face.

"Shouldn't you be in bed?" I ask her, amused, as I step into the house.

Her eyebrows crease as she crosses her arms in front of her. "I'm nine, not two. I don't have to be in bed for another half hour," she says stoically, making me laugh. "What happened to your eye?" she asks, pointing at my face.

"It's rude to point," I note with a cock of my eyebrow and a chuckle.

"You look like you were in a fight," she doubles down. This kid cracks me up.

"Your sister did that," I tease.

Sam's mouth drops open, but closes almost immediately as she eyes me suspiciously. "No, she didn't," she says, trying to sound convinced, but I hear her wavering. There's a brief moment of silence between us before Sam calls out, "Cat, did you hit Ronan?"

"What? No! Why would you say that?" I hear Cat say, her voice getting louder as she moves toward us. She rounds the corner into the hallway and stops dead in her tracks when she spots me. She has the most stunning smile on her face.

"Hi," she says, and her voice comes out breathy.

"Hi," I respond, returning her dazzling smile because she makes me feel almost delirious when I'm with her, regardless of all the other shit going on in the background. "Are you sure you're up for going somewhere tonight?"

"Yes, please," she says. "My mom's been hovering all afternoon and it's suffocating me."

I nod, even though I have no idea what it feels like to have a mom or, hell, even a dad who are so deeply concerned for my well-being.

Cat's mom joins us in that moment and, again, she hugs me tightly. It still startles me and feels awkward as hell. "You guys heading out?" she asks, looking from me to Cat.

"Yes. Mom. Would it be okay if I spend the night at Vada's again?" Cat asks, and my heart begins to beat double-time in my chest. I know enough to know that this is Vada's and Cat's code for when they're actually planning to stay over at Steve's and my house. Cat obviously only took advantage of it for the first time last night, and it was one of the best nights of my life. Having her in my bed next to me, feeling her body, touching her like I had never touched her before, then falling asleep next to her was happiness like I had never felt before. There was finally peace.

"Sure," Cat's mom responds in a warm, caring tone, and she hugs her daughter tightly. All this physical affection is something I'm not used to at all. Really, the only physical affection I ever got was when I hooked up with random girls prior to meeting Cat, and even then, it was just sex. There was no hugging, only making out, sex, and then goodbye. I was just filling a void, never really understanding how big that void was until I met Cat. "You guys be safe," she adds, her face serious, and I can see the worry in her eyes as she looks at Cat.

"We will, Mom," Cat says, and interlaces her fingers with mine. The warmth of her touch immediately travels up the length of my arm, easing the tension in my shoulders I didn't realize was there until it began subsiding.

"How are you doing?" I ask Cat as we drive down the freeway, the lights of the other cars and streetlamps reflected in Cat's eyes.

"I'm fine," she says.

Unable to take my eyes off the road, I try to analyze her tone for any hint of apprehension, but she sounds like she really is fine. "What did the cops say?"

Cat tells me that the officers told her mom that Adam was in violation of both his probation and the restraining order, which is enforceable across state lines. It was just a matter of finding Adam, who apparently had failed to check in with his probation officer.

"You know what the worst part is?" She looks at me, and her hazel eyes are sad. I don't respond, letting her finish her thought. "That even though I know I shouldn't, and even though he did all these things to me, and even though he found me here—"

"Stalked you," I interrupt.

"Fine, stalked me... I feel so terribly guilty. Like this is all my fault. I mean, I got him arrested; he lost his spot on the football team, his scholarship to Duke. His whole life was upended. And now he might have to go back to jail or pay additional consequences, and it just makes me feel even worse. He would have been better off never meeting me."

The sadness emanating from her crashes against me like waves, and I veer across three lanes of traffic, take the next off-ramp, and pull my car over on some dirt strip next to the freeway.

"What are you doing?" she asks as I turn off the ignition and get out of my car.

I walk around to her door and yank it open, then crouch down next to her and take both her hands into mine. She looks at me with utter confusion on her face. "Listen to me," I say sternly, my eyes locked on hers. "You have nothing, *nothing* to feel bad about. This guy took advantage of you. He called you names. He hurt you, emotionally and physically. For crying out loud, he choked and punched you, Cat, and I bet there are things he did to you that you haven't told me about. Baby, he *abused* you." I can see her flinch. "He abused you," I say again, really wanting the words to sink in. "This is not your fault. None of it is. He had a choice; he had control over his actions, and he chose to do this shit to you, over and over again. He chose to hurt you, he chose to stalk you even after you made it abundantly clear that you wouldn't put up with his shit any longer. And if he hadn't done it to you, he would have done it someone else, baby. You're a badass for calling him out on his shit." I'm probably being way too intense with her right now, because I can see her eyes swimming with tears. "Baby," I breathe, softening my voice, "please, *please* believe me when I say that you have nothing to feel bad about. He deserves everything that's coming his way."

She nods, her head tilted down, and even though I can't see her eyes, I know she's crying; tears drip onto my hands. My heart aches for her, wishes for the ability to take her pain away, to undo the past for her. We stay like this for a while, neither of us speaking as Cat cries quietly.

"Please tell me what I can do," I finally whisper, feeling helpless at my inability to make her pain stop. I hate that she's hurting.

She doesn't respond right away, but her tears seem to dry up and her breathing slows just a little. "Can you just drive us to Shane's, and then can you just hold me?" she says, her voice small, her eyes watery and blood-red from crying as she looks at me with her tear-streaked face.

"I can do that," I nod, and bring her hands to my lips, kissing them softly over and over again. Finally I stand and reluctantly let go of her to close her door and get back into the car to take us to Shane's.

The moment I'm back in the car, she reaches for my right hand, leaning across the center console and resting her head against me as I drive. It doesn't matter that my injured shoulder throbs painfully under the weight of her head against it—I will give Cat whatever she needs right now.

We get to Shane's a short while later and, without speaking, I scoop Cat up. Her legs lace around my waist as I walk her into the house. Everyone's eyes are on us when I stride through the door and turn down the wide hallway to take us to one of the smaller bedrooms without so much as acknowledging our friends. Still holding Cat, whose head is buried against my neck, I kick the bedroom door shut and take the four steps toward the large bed that forms the centerpiece of the room. I climb onto the mattress on my knees and softly lay Cat back against the pillows, then lie down right next to her, our bodies facing each other. I pull her toward me as closely as possible, her arms tucked against my chest. My right arm is wrapped around her waist, holding on to her as I kiss her forehead again and again, inhaling her scent. I'm perfectly content lying with her like this all night if that's what she needs. I would do anything for her. *Anything*.

Cat

I don't really know what came over me. I was upset by the whole Adam incident, sure, but I thought I was handling it alright after the cops came to my house and took my statement. They assured me that this situation would be handled, but when they said there's a good chance Adam's probation may be extended or that he may even go to jail for violating his terms, I felt overwhelming guilt. And, god, what if he finally makes good on his threat to post those pictures? What if he shares them for the whole world to see, for Ronan to find out what I've done? It ate at me all afternoon, and saying it out loud to Ronan suddenly amplified the feeling and I just bawled my eyes out.

Ronan pulled off the freeway, just came to a dead stop on the side of the road somewhere, and got out of the driver's seat to come around to my side. The way he talked to me, the way he held my hands and wouldn't break eye contact—it meant more to me than anything. I could see my pain reflected in his eyes, something that I've never experienced with anyone. When he used the word *abuse* to describe what Adam did to me, I think I realized for the first time that, yes, that is what Adam was doing to me. And it's crazy because Ronan recognized it and he gave it a word when I never could.

There was so much meaning to Ronan's words as his eyes were locked on mine. In the end he asked me what I needed, what he could do for me, and honestly, I just needed him. So, I told him, and we drove to Shane's in near complete silence before he carried me into the house and into one of the spare bedrooms, where he went to lie down with me. It's really not a huge thing, but this small gesture of just being with me, his physical touch—so gentle and comforting—means the world to me.

I lie facing Ronan, my hands on his chest, feeling the rise and fall of his breath as he kisses my forehead, making my eyes fall shut.

"Thank you," I whisper, breaking the silence for the first time since we arrived, "for... just... for today."

I realize the day turned into a complete crapshoot. I raise my head to look at Ronan. It's dark in the room because Ronan didn't turn on any lights before laying us down, but I can see the reflection of the moon in his eyes.

"You don't have to thank me," he says quietly. "I'd do it over again in a heartbeat."

"Does it hurt a lot?" I ask, moving my hand from his chest and touching his bruised cheek gently. It looks painful.

He shakes his head. "Not really. And even if it did, it's completely worth it."

I glide my fingers down his cheek to his lip. It's still a little swollen where Adam hit him and split Ronan's skin open. Seeing the physical sacrifice Ronan made to keep me safe from Adam sends a rush of longing through me, and I crash my lips against Ronan's without warning. I feel his hand tightening on my hip, his fingers digging into my skin, and he pulls me even closer against him. We're both so pent up with tension from today, and right now all I need is for him to touch me, to make me forget, and I want to do the same for him.

I part my lips and his tongue delves into my mouth, exploring, tasting me, licking my lips. He pushes me back against the bed, positioning himself to hover over me, his forearms on either side of me. His hand moves down my waist and over the apple of my hip to my thigh, then he slides it over my jeans and between my legs. I can feel the warmth of his hand through the fabric, and it's enough to make me moan.

"Ran, can you touch me like you did last night?" I whimper.

"Are you sure?" he breathes against my mouth, his chest rising and falling fitfully.

"Uh-huh," I moan again.

He moves his hand and pulls my thighs apart, then situates one leg between them, pushing it against me. I gratefully grind against him while his left hand pushes my shirt up over my bra, leaving a scorching-hot path where his fingers touch my hyper-sensitive skin.

I run my hands under his shirt and up his back, eager to memorize his taut muscles. I pull his shirt over his head and his hands momentarily leave my body so I can pull his shirt off him. I incline onto my elbows, my mouth leaving his lips, hungry to taste him as I kiss his jaw, then neck. He groans when I reach his shoulder, my hand in his hair, tugging at the roots as I pull him down to me. He rubs his leg against me while his left hand slides up my bare stomach and to my breast and I thrust against him again, wanting his hands all over me. He cups my breast while I kiss his shoulder, then his hand moves up and he pulls the lacy fabric of my bra down, exposing my nipple. He grazes his thumb across it again and again, my nipple pebbling with arousal. I fall back against the pillows, completely lost in him and in the way his hands feel on my skin.

Ronan kisses the sensitive skin on my neck, nipping and licking a path to my chest, then circles my hard nipple with his tongue. He keeps pushing me toward the edge with his mouth while I grind against his leg slowly, sending delicious waves of electricity straight to my core where the pleasure builds like it did last night. I can't contain my moaning; I'm close. Just as the mounting wave of pleasure is about to crest, Ronan moves his leg, and the pressure between my aching thighs ebbs.

"Please don't stop," I whimper under him, and he chuckles in a husky voice. He glides his hand between my legs, but he doesn't linger there and instead undoes the button of my jeans, pulling the zipper down. He begins to kiss a trail from my breast down my stomach, licking my belly button, then the spot below it. It tickles, but in the best possible way as his soft lips caress my hot skin. I angle my knees and lift my hips, allowing Ronan to pull my jeans down to my knees and off me, revealing my black lacy panties.

"This is as far as I'll go until you tell me you want more," Ronan says, his voice gravelly as he repositions himself between my legs.

His mouth seeks and finds my nipple for a second time, eclipsing any thought in my head, and I'm once again lost to him, his touch consuming me. I grind into him while he licks, kisses, and sucks my nipples, alternating between my breasts, his left hand softly stroking my inner thigh while his leg rubs against me. The pleasure begins to swirl anew, stronger still, hotter, and I feel my arousal soaking into my panties.

"God, Ran," I moan loudly, my breathing out of control, eyes shut when he grates his teeth carefully against my sensitive nipple, and the pleasure builds in my core. I'm almost there when he moves his leg away again, resulting in a frustrated groan at being denied climax for a second time in a row. This must be what edging feels like, and while I want nothing more than to reach that blissful high, I can't deny that each time Ronan pushes me to the brink only to let off again, the pleasure that rebuilds just moments later is even more powerful, more intense than before.

"Fuck, I love how badly you want this," Ronan says, his gravelly voice low, quiet, filled with need of his own. He glides his hand up my thigh, pushes my panties aside, then begins to stroke me. I moan gratefully at the feeling of his fingers on my bare needy flesh. It only takes him a few soft sweeps to find the perfect spot, the perfect pressure, and I'm pulled under the waves of pleasure, ecstasy pulsing exquisitely through my body.

I thrust my hips against Ronan's hand, arching my body into him, his mouth still tasting my nipple while he continues to stroke me. It's all-consuming, addictive, and I wish it would go on forever. When I finally regain control, his breathing is as erratic as mine.

My eyes settle on his, still hovering over me. He looks high, his pupils blown wide with need, almost completely swallowing the green of his irises. I wonder how that's even possible since I did nothing for him while I'm here once again, my body feeling like it dissolved under his touch.

"I keep doing this to you," I whisper, and gently glide my hands up the curve of his back. His skin is so soft, so smooth, yet his back is strong and hard as his muscles flex to hold himself up.

"What do you mean?" he asks, his eyes bright like they get when he's really turned on. I can still feel his hardness pressing against my leg.

"This." I wag a finger between his chest and mine. "We get all worked up, and in the end only I find relief," I explain, feeling guilty.

He chuckles, then places a soft kiss against my lips. "Don't worry, I'll get relief," he says, his voice teasing. He rolls my nipple between his fingers, causing electricity to shoot straight to my core. "I'll just have to do it myself," he adds, a smile on his perfect lips.

"How long... how long did you take under the shower last night?" I ask, blinking at him shyly. I can't believe I'm prying into something this private.

There's a mischievous little gleam in Ronan's eyes as he grins at me. "Are you asking about the actual shower or just..." he trails off.

"Just... just the... you know." I bite my bottom lip, feeling the telltale heat creep up my neck.

Ronan chuckles. "Probably thirty to sixty—"

"Minutes?" I interrupt him, my eyes wide.

"Seconds," he corrects me with a husky laugh.

I raise my eyebrows at him. "That fast?" I feel both surprised and kind of proud at the same time.

Ronan nods. "Yeah. I mean, I was under the shower longer than that, obviously, but yeah." He shrugs and I think I note some slight embarrassment in his eyes. "I told you it wouldn't take me long to take care of... the issue. Baby, I don't want to put any pressure on you, so please don't take it as that, but... I'm really pent-up," he says with a low groan. "And when we do things like we did last night... when I touch you like that, when I hear you make those little sounds and watch you... come...." He exhales noisily, shaking his head slightly as if trying to clear it of the titillating memories. "Let's just say I was locked and loaded," he adds with another chuckle.

I contemplate him.

"Is this even enjoyable to you? You know, last night and... just now?" I ask. With Adam, it was always about what he could get out of the situation, never about what I wanted... or didn't.

Ronan pushes up off his elbows, supporting himself with his hands now, creating more space between our bodies. I want to pull him back down toward me. "Fuck, yes I'm enjoying this," he says, his face sincere as he locks eyes with me.

"But how can you when you don't... when we don't..." I trail off, feeling embarrassed.

"Have sex?" he finishes for me, and I nod. "Because it's really not about that," he says, and moves out from between my legs. His eyes lazily roll over my body. "Sex isn't everything. I mean, do I want to feel you all the way? I'd be a lying piece of shit if I said 'no.' Fuck, Cat, just the way you sound, your facial expression when you get turned on, when you lose control, fuck, it gets me so worked up. It's seriously the biggest turn-on to know I can make you feel like that," he says, his breathing picking up again. "But I told you I'm not going to push you, and I won't. It's more important to me that you feel safe and that when you say you're ready, it's really what you want," he finishes resolutely.

I do feel safe with him. I feel completely protected, and not just physically—my soul as well.

A mischievous grin spreads across my face. "So, you'd be okay just doing this for the next year? Never going all the way?"

His face takes on a pained expression before he nods, swallowing hard. "Yep," he says, then tries to plaster a smile on his gorgeous face.

"Really?" I say, then slowly slide my fingers down his bare chest, tracing his abs to the spot just above his jeans, grazing his skin. "You'll wait forever and ever?" I glide one finger underneath the waistband of his boxer briefs.

His breath hitches, but still he nods. "Forever and ever," he stammers, his bright-green eyes threatening to shut under my touch.

"Are you sure?" I breathe against him, inclining my mouth only an inch from his. I know I'm teasing him, and I know I shouldn't. It's such a shitty thing to do when I don't have any intention of taking it further tonight. It's exactly what got me in trouble with Adam, but I trust Ronan more than I've ever trusted anyone. I trust that I can be playful and flirty with him without him going nuclear on me.

"Uh-huh," he groans when I begin to kiss his jawline down to his neck, and his eyes fall shut. I'm inching my hand further down his jeans, but never quite reaching all the way down to touch him. I can feel his body tense with anticipation, wanting to feel my touch on him.

"Are you two okay in there?" Tori's dampened voice seeps through the door, and I instantly withdraw my hand.

"Why does the universe hate me?" Ronan grumbles under his breath, making me laugh.

"We're fine," I say loudly. "We'll be out in a minute."

"Okay, no worries. They all just bugged me to check on you guys. Vada and Shane said they already have bad track records. Not sure what that means, but... see you in a minute," Tori says, and I listen as her footsteps recede on the tiled floor.

"We should get out there, huh?" I turn my attention back to Ronan. His eyes are still bright and hooded with want, and I trace my index finger over his heated lips.

"No. In fact, we should never leave this room," he sighs and leans in to kiss me softly.

"But we'd get all gross from not showering, and we'd starve, and then they'd find us dead in here together."

Ronan shrugs his shoulders. "Dying in your arms actually sounds pretty peaceful," he says, his voice taking on a different tone. I'm taken aback by the sudden sadness in his eyes.

"What's wrong?" I wonder, searching his eyes for a reason of the sudden shift in mood.

"Nothing," he says, and I raise my eyebrows at him. "It's just kind of been an exhausting day, don't you think?" I nod because, yes, it has been a draining day. "Alright, enough of this depressing shit. Let's go," he says and takes my hand, pulling me up to stand.

I pull my shirt and underwear back into place and slide back into my jeans while Ronan picks up his shirt and slips it over his head. I watch him the whole time, and he grins when he catches me staring.

"Like what you see?" he asks with a wicked grin, and to my surprise I don't blush.

"Can't say that I don't," I admit, smiling.

"Good. It's all yours whenever you want it," he says, and a by-now-familiar tingle forms in my stomach as he interlaces his fingers with mine and leads me out of the bedroom and onto the deck where our friends are hanging out.

***

We join our friends outside, taking our seats on the rattan sofa. Shane lights the fire pit and we roast smores while we chat about the craziness that was today. I haven't told anyone about my history with Adam—well, except Ronan, of course—and I can tell they're curious, though kind enough not to pry.

I decide to just come clean. Well, as much as I did with Ronan, I guess. I'm still not ready to disclose my transgression, my betrayals. I'm too ashamed to admit my complete lack of better judgment while I was in my short-lived relationship with Adam and not only allowed a guy to take compromising and vulnerable pictures of me, but continued to do so under threat of being found out. But I do tell them about the escalating physical violence Adam inflicted on me. I owe my friends at least that much. After all, they all witnessed what went down. Ronan threw himself in harm's way to protect me, and so did Shane, Steve, and Zack.

Nobody speaks while I share with my friends. Ronan holds my hand the entire time, and when I get to the part where Adam started to choke me and tears begin to fall again, he pulls me onto his lap. I can feel his body tense with each additional detail that I haven't previously shared with him. I really lay out the things Adam did to me during the five months we dated, the increasingly violent confrontations and arguments we had.

"Jesus, I get why Ran was on the brink of beating this guy to death," Steve says when I finish, and Shane and Zack nod in unison.

"I don't think I would have been able to stop if it hadn't been for you and Shay pulling me away from this guy," Ronan admits, and by the sound of his voice I know he means it. I look into his eyes, a mix of emotions rushing through my body: pain that I was the reason he was hurt today, but also so much gratitude that he was there to protect me.

"This Adam guy sounds like a real fucking douche," Vada huffs. "Honestly, he looks like a douche, too," she adds. "How ever did you end up with him, Kitty Cat?"

I shrug. "I don't know. He didn't seem like a bad guy in the beginning. He was really nice, actually. But I guess I enjoyed the attention. It's stupid, right?" I ask, feeling embarrassed that I fell for Adam's crap, and that I didn't leave him after the first time he became violent. Heck, I should have left the first time he called me a slut, the first time he made me feel less than, way before he ever put his hands on me.

The longer I'm with Ronan, the more I understand that what I went through with Adam wasn't normal. And, of course, I always knew that. I always knew it wasn't okay for someone to belittle their girlfriend, to call her names, and to hit her, but it's so different being in that situation because I didn't recognize it as abuse. It started off so innocent, so sporadic, and I looked past it because when things were good they were *really* good. But once I allowed Adam to overstep my boundaries, he knew he could keep pushing them just a little bit more each time until they were essentially nonexistent, until it became really, really dangerous.

It was similar with the photos. It started out innocently enough, Adam telling me I looked beautiful before snapping a picture of me. Soon he began asking me for more and more compromising pictures, requesting I show more skin, wear less clothing. I was reluctant at first but acquiesced because he was my boyfriend, after all. It wasn't until a couple months into our relationship that I learned about Adam taking photos of me at parties. Some of them were taken while I was passed out, drunk off my ass after overstepping my boundaries. Others appeared to depict me willingly exposing myself to Adam, though I can't remember any of it. Even then he threatened to make the pictures public. He held them over my head to make me fall in line when I was being "difficult" because I tried to set a personal boundary. He'd egg me on, tease me, joke about sharing the pictures with his buddies or teammates. Come to think of it, I'm not sure he didn't actually make good on that last part.

"It's not stupid," Summer chimes in. "I'm pretty sure I'm only with Zack because I enjoy the attention he gives me," she says with a grin on her face, then winks at Zack.

He looks offended. "Uh, pretty sure you were the one who asked *me* out."

Summer puts her finger to her chin in mock contemplation. "Oh, shoot, I think you're right," she says, and everyone laughs.

"Well, I didn't ask Shane out," Tori pipes up. "He pursued me for *weeks*." She drags out the last word, and Shane rolls his eyes. "And I for sure, one hundred percent, enjoyed the attention, so don't feel bad, Cat. How could you have known that things would get so messed up? You can't and shouldn't ever blame yourself for being hurt by one of the people who are pretty much obligated to treat you well."

"I'm going to sound all mushy right now, but I don't know what I would do without all of you," I say, tearing up again. "After Adam was arrested, the whole town pretty much turned against me, so this is a nice change."

"We got your back, Kitty Cat, always and forever," Vada assures me to the general consent of the group, and Ronan places a soft kiss on my arm.

"Oh, that reminds me, Vada. My mom said I could sleep over at your place," I say, my mouth expanding into a smile.

"What a coincidence, my dad said I could spend the night at yours!" Vada laughs.

"So, both of you will be at our house tonight?" Steve observes in a flirty tone.

I smile at the prospect of sleeping next to Ronan again, but my face falls when I see Ronan shake his head.

"Mom's home," Ronan says to his brother, whose smile turns into a frown.

"Seriously? Aw, man," Steve grumbles.

"Hmm, looks like you'll actually need to stay at my place," Vada muses. "Or maybe I'll stay at yours?"

"Why don't you stay with me?" I suggest. "My mom's kind of been on edge ever since this whole Adam fiasco. I'm sure she'd love it if I were home tonight. And she loves you, so I don't think that'll be an issue."

"Uh, yeah she loves me," Vada says, whipping her hair over her shoulder, causing more laughter to erupt. "What's not to love?"

"I love how fucking full of yourself you are," Steve says, then presses his lips onto hers.

"Seriously," I laugh. "Can I have some of your self-confidence?"

Vada eyes me from head to toe. "Kitty Cat, you have absolutely *no* reason not to be full of yourself, too. Have you looked in the mirror lately? God damn, girl. The freaking face and body of a lingerie model," she adds, and I blush violently.

"I wouldn't mind seeing that," Ronan says in a husky voice, so quietly that only I can hear it, and it sends shivers down my neck. "You in lingerie." His hand on my leg slides just a little further up my thigh, unnoticed by everyone around us. "Or better yet, no clothes at all."

Oh jeez. This boy is so pent-up.

"What happened to no pushing, sweet boy?" I ask him quietly, laughter in my voice.

"I move at your pace, baby, I promise. But I can fantasize, right?" His gravelly voice is almost too much, and my heartbeat speeds up.

"I'll allow it," I say, and playfully push my shoulder into him. His lips find mine, kissing me deeply, eliciting wolf whistling from our friends.

"Do you guys need to go back into that room?" Shane motions toward the house and chuckles.

"We do, but there's no chance you guys would leave us alone. I'm starting to understand this now," Ronan laughs, and we all join in.

The rest of the evening is nice as we huddle around the fire. I remain on Ronan's lap, leaning back against him, and his left arm rests on my leg. It's peaceful and comforting and allows my mind and soul to settle. It's so easy with my friends, and it's especially easy with Ronan, and despite the emotional and physical day I feel relaxed and content by the time it's midnight and Ronan lets me know he has to head home. Vada and I ride with him, Vada smooshed into the small backseat of Ronan's Mustang.

Vada takes the opportunity to jabber about my birthday, which is coming up in a couple of weeks, and I remind her that my mom will be taking my brother and sister back to North Carolina. Vada suggests I spend that week at her house.

"No, honestly," she reiterates, "this isn't code for spend the week at Ran's house. I really mean it. Come stay with me so you're not all alone," she says, and laughs when I give her a doubtful look. "Okay, well, maybe if the opportunity arises we can sneak into the boys' house a couple of times," she relents, giggling.

Thursday, August 26th

Cat

I don't hear from Adam again over the next couple of weeks. The radio silence from the police allows me to push any thoughts of Adam, the photographic evidence of my own wrongdoings, and the incident earlier this month out of my mind. Only occasionally do I think of Adam, causing me brief bouts of anxiety—mostly at night or when my phone rings unexpectedly—but the fact that I'm rarely by myself, consistently surrounded by my friends, and of course Ronan, keeps those thoughts at bay.

Instead, I spend the next two weeks—which also happen to be the last two weeks of summer break—soaking up as much time with Ronan as I can between him working, training, and going to hockey practice. I even go watch him at conditioning a handful of times, still in awe of the way he moves on the ice. He moves around at such speeds and so comfortably that it almost seems like he's walking—well, make that running—on the slippery surface of the rink. It's fun learning some of the hockey lingo, which honestly is like a whole new language. Most of the time, I have no idea what the coaches mean when they yell at Ronan or the other forwards to "create a lane," or "build layers on entry," but it doesn't matter because it's still thrilling to watch Ronan play.

We spend most of our time either at my house or at Shane's, which is fine because about a week and a half ago, Ronan's mom walked in on Ronan and me and it was awkward beyond words. It really wasn't anything outrageous; we were just at his place for a few minutes so he could change for work. He had his shirt off and was about to put on his black long-sleeved Murphy's shirt. We were kissing, my hands on his bare chest, when his mom came up the stairs. Granted, seeing her son without his shirt on, making out with his girlfriend was probably as awkward for her as it was for us, but she stared us down with this icy look, never saying a single word. Ronan pulled his shirt on and then grabbed my hand, leading me out of the house without saying a thing to either me or his mom.

From the few interactions I've had with his mom, I can tell they aren't particularly close. I'd even call the relationship strained, though Ronan doesn't talk to me about it. He rarely mentions his mom or dad in conversation. It makes me sad for him because I'm so close to my parents. In fact, sometimes my mom is a little overbearing, and Ronan recently made a comment about my mom always hugging me, my siblings, and even him.

"Oh yeah, she's a hugger," I laughed. "And a kisser if you let her. My parents are super affectionate," I explained to him after my mom once again gave Ronan the biggest squeeze. He just stood there awkwardly, his hands by his sides like he didn't know what to do with this outpouring of love.

My mom left for North Carolina with my siblings on Monday, and I did take Vada up on her offer to spend a few nights at her house.

"I think Steve and I have decided to try this long-distance college thing," Vada says to me Thursday evening as we relax in her bedroom watching a movie on her laptop.

Tomorrow is my birthday, and Vada insisted it would be a crime if I woke up to a completely empty house with no one to wish me a happy birthday the moment I blinked my eyes open in the morning.

"Really? That's great!" I know the two of them had put off the decision on what to do about their relationship once Steve leaves for Boston, but I guess with time running out—Steve leaves for Boston next week—they finally had that conversation.

"Yeah. I mean, we'll see how it goes. I'm really trying to be realistic here. Boston isn't too far away. It's only like a three-and-a-half-hour drive, but still, with school and stuff. Anyway, we both agreed we'd try this and see how it goes. We'll both be so busy and I don't know how often we'll be able to see each other. It's going to be hard," Vada says, exhaling deeply.

I pull her in for a one-armed hug. "You guys will figure it out," I say encouragingly, and my mind briefly wanders to Ronan and me. We're both entering our senior year, so we haven't had to face this whole going-away-to-college talk yet. In fact, I don't even know what his plans are, but I guess we'll have to cross that bridge sooner or later. Maybe I should ask him about it.

I don't have a clue what I want to do, where I want to go, or what I want to study. I love New York, and I love my friends here, so I'm not sure I'd want to be anywhere else, especially if Ronan stays here. *God, I hope he stays here.* We haven't even been together a whole three months, but already I can't imagine being without him, and there are definitely moments where I envision us together forever—getting married, having kids, growing old together. I haven't said any of this out loud to anyone because, one, I don't want to scare the shit out of Ronan, and two, I know people would tell us we're too young to make such a huge decision at our age. Then again, I keep thinking about my parents, who got married at nineteen, and Ronan's parents, who had Steve and Ronan at sixteen and seventeen respectively, and were married when Steve was born. Not that this is something I strive for—oh god, having kids now would be so hard—but the thought of being with Ronan forever is definitely something that makes my heart flutter.

My phone pings and I reach for it, noting that it's just after midnight. I find myself on edge each time my phone notifies me of a text message, never knowing whether it's a reminder from Adam that he's still out there, still lurking in the shadows. But I smile when I find a text from Ronan instead.

Ronan: it's officially August 27. Happy birthday, baby. Too bad I can't return the favor and kiss you in front of your house

right now like we did on my birthday, but I promise to make it up to you later today.

Me: Looking forward to it. How is your night so far? Busy?

Ronan: On a quick break right now. It's not too bad tonight. Miss you though.

Me: Someone once told me to try to have some fun, it makes the time go by faster.

Ronan: Huh, that someone sounds pretty smart...

Me: He is. And really cute, too.

Ronan: Seems like the whole package?!

Me: He sure is. What time will I get to see you tomorrow?

Ronan: I have practice from 11 to 2 and I'll come see you right after.

Me: Can't wait.

Ronan: Same. Get some sleep!

Me: I'll dream of you.

Ronan: You better! And make it spicy...

"Judging by that swoony, mushy look on your face, I'm thinking that wasn't your mom texting you," Vada sniggers at me. "You and Ran are seriously too much. I'm so glad my genius plan came to fruition. I swear I knew right when I first met you that you two would be great together."

"Did you now," I chuckle. "I'd say something snarky, but honestly, I can't argue with you."

I get comfortable on my pillow before I drift off to sleep. The last thought on my mind is Ronan.

Friday, August 27th

Cat

I wake up bright and early the next morning to Vada singing happy birthday to me—loudly and very much off-pitch. I blink my eyes open, laughing at her rendition as she holds a plate of pancakes in her hands, a lit candle adorning the stack of flapjacks.

"You are even more embarrassing than my mom," I laugh once she finishes singing, and I sit up to blow out the candle. "But I love it," I say, then close my eyes and make my birthday wish.

"What in the fucking world, Vada?" Zack grumbles as he shuffles into Vada's bedroom wearing navy pajama bottoms and a black t-shirt. "It's way too fucking early for this," he says, and plops down on her bed next to me. "But hey, happy birthday, Cat." He starts to reach for the plate of pancakes Vada is still balancing in her hands.

"Hands off!" Vada says, and smacks Zack's hand away.

He gives her a scathing look while I laugh.

"Oh, come on Vada, let him have some. I can't possibly eat all of these," I say, and take the plate off her hands.

"I like you," Zack says to me with a grin. He starts picking at the top pancake, tossing pieces into his mouth. "So, what's the plan for today?" he asks and lets himself fall back onto the blanket. "Party at Shane's?"

"Duh," Vada responds, rolling her eyes at her twin brother. "But first, we're going shopping."

"Nuh-uh, I'm not going shopping," Zack says, his mouth full of pancake.

Vada rolls her eyes at him again. "Yeah, no shit, Sherlock. It's a girls' thing, anyways. You're not invited," she says. "Now, if you could please leave my room so Cat and I can get ready, that would be great."

Zack gets up and stretches his arms above his head. "Whatever. You guys have fun," he says, takes the top pancake from the stack, and walks out of the room, shutting the door behind him.

Vada and I get ready, then head out to Murphy's for an early brunch. We meet Tori, who's sitting in a small booth.

She waves us over. "Happy Birthday, Cat!" she says sweetly, and gives me a hug.

"Thanks." I sit across from her and take one of the menus. I'm surprised to see Shane walk toward us. "Don't you usually work evenings?" I ask him when he reaches our table and stands next to Tori, who immediately reaches her arm around him and leans against his hip.

"Yeah, unless I have plans for the evening. My dad's gonna close for me tonight since we'll be celebrating your birthday." He winks at me. "What are your plans for today?" Shane asks me, Tori, and Vada.

"A little bit of shopping, maybe some lunch, then we'll head over to your place," Tori says.

Shane nods as he winds a strand of Tori's gorgeous dark hair around his finger. "Nice. It's just the three of you?"

"Summer is going to meet us a bit later," Vada says.

"Cool. Alright, what do you guys want to eat?" Shane takes our orders and then joins us at our table for about fifteen minutes before he starts hollering orders at some delivery people who marched into Murphy's with a cart full of booze.

Vada, Tori, and I meet Summer in the city, and we spend the next few hours strolling through stores and enjoying each other's company before we grab a late lunch. Somehow we end up on the subject of sex, and Tori chitchats about how glad she is that Shane has his own place now, especially after his sister, Lauren, walked in on them in the middle of a very steamy, R-rated scene.

"Lauren got the full view," Tori laughs, though her cheeks take on a rosy hue. "She's probably traumatized for life."

"I'm glad to hear it's not just Ran and me who keep getting interrupted," I say.

Vada laughs. "I'm really good at barging in on you guys, huh?"

"You and everyone else. But, yes, you definitely seem to have a real talent for it," I agree. My phone vibrates in my pocket and heat rushes through me when Ronan's smile flashes across my screen. I love this picture of him. I took it at the beach one afternoon. The sun was setting and it reflected in his green eyes so beautifully that they looked turquoise and complemented his tanned skin and dark-blond hair perfectly.

I take a few steps away from the girls and answer. "I'm sorry if this freaks you out, but my heart gets all fluttery when you call me," I answer the phone with a sigh.

Ronan chuckles. "Why would that freak me out?"

"I don't know; I'm sure some guys would be weirded out by that, I guess."

"Yeah, well, I'm not some guy," he says. "I'm your guy."

A mushy grin spreads across my face. "Yes, you are," I say, my voice an octave higher with giddiness. "How was practice?"

"Pretty good, actually," he chuckles, and then adds, "Guess who made team captain!"

"Seriously? Ran, that's so awesome!" I shout into the phone, making him laugh. "Do you get to have the letter *C* on your jersey?"

"Yea," he says. I can tell he's pleased, as he should be. I've seen him move about the ice, his sheer speed, the ease and quickness with which he moves the puck, and the force behind his slaps as he drives the black disk into the goal.

"I can't wait to see you play this season," I say.

"I can't wait for you to come watch," he says. "What are you up to?"

I tell him that I'm out and about with Vada, Tori, and Summer.

"Do you want to just meet me at Shane's, then?" he asks. I can tell he's driving because it sounds like I'm on speaker.

"That would probably make sense. We should be there probably around four," I say, looking at my watch. "Best part is, I don't have a curfew tonight since my mom's gone," I add. "I can stay out and with you all night if I want to."

"Oh, okay, Miss Gonna-Pull-An-All-Nighter," he laughs, and I love the freaking sound of it. "I'll see you at Shane's then."

"I can't wait," I sigh, meaning every single one of the three words. "I'll see you in a little bit."

"Hey Cat," he says quickly before I hang up.

"Yeah?"

"My heart gets all fluttery, too, when you call me," he says, and I swear I could melt into a puddle right then and there.

"Really?"

"Uh-huh," he admits. "And it's even worse when I lay eyes on you. It's like my body can't wait to be near you."

"Okay, Romeo, I'm going to let you go before I dissolve into mush and Vada has to scrape me off the sidewalk," I giggle, but my insides are all knotty and tingly.

"I'll see you soon, baby," he says, his voice like velvet before we hang up.

I rejoin Vada, Tori, and Summer. Apparently my face gives me away, because all three immediately begin teasing me about my conversation with Ronan.

"You look like either Ran talked dirty to you or he just said something that made you fall deeply in love with him," Tori observes.

"So which one is it, Kitty Cat?" Vada asks, batting her eyelashes at me.

"It's definitely the second one," Summer chimes in, "otherwise Cat's cheeks would be all flushed with heat," she sniggers, and Tori and Vada join in.

"I'm just glad I provide you with so much amusement," I huff in mock offense.

Vada hooks her arm under mine as we begin our way back to her car. "Aw, Kitty Cat, you know we love you. And we know that Ran loves you, too." She winks, and now I blush for real.

"Yep, and you him," Tori says, and I shake my head.

"Wait, you doubt our words?" Vada asks, her eyes wide. "Have you seen Ran when he's around you?" She pulls me to a stop with a hand on my arm.

"Well, obviously," I say, giggling. "But, okay, we're coming up on three months and he hasn't said anything about loving me yet," I say with a tinge of disappointment. Ronan is more than amazing to me in every aspect of our relationship, and if he uttered those three words to me I would reciprocate without hesitation.

"Yeah, guys are dumb like that," Summer says, puckering her mouth and rolling her eyes. "Zack didn't tell me he loved me until we had been dating for like five months."

"Huh, it only took Steve two weeks." Vada shrugs.

"Shane told me he was going to marry me on our third date, so he's not a good measuring stick," Tori laughs out loud. "But in all honesty, Cat, and I know we've all told you this, I've never seen Ran as happy as he's been since you two got together. He's just not super expressive and open," she says, and it does make me feel better.

Summer nods. "Ran never really shares, especially when it comes to feelings. I mean, boys are stupid that way anyways, you know. Everyone always tells them feelings are bad—unless it's anger. That's apparently fine for them to express. I seriously think they believe anger isn't an emotion," she says, rolling her eyes again. "But anyways, he'll come around. His face and body already say that he loves you—it's super obvious. His mouth is just lagging behind a little bit," Summer says, proud of her characterization of the state of things.

"Hmm, I never considered his mouth as lagging," I say sheepishly, thinking about the way his mouth feels on my lips and on my body.

"Woohoo," Vada howls, and pushes against me.

***

Traffic is terrible, and it takes us way longer to get out of the city than anticipated. By the time we make it to Shane's, it's just before five and I spot Ronan's black Mustang parked next to Shane's white Jeep in the large driveway. I hop out of the passenger side of Vada's car and she, Tori, and I walk into the house followed by Summer, who pulled her car in behind Vada's.

We find the boys down by the beach, all four of them sitting in the sand right on the shore, and we stop for a moment, admiring our guys before they notice us. My eyes are glued to Ronan, who's wearing a pair of faded blue jeans and a white, long-sleeved Henley, the sleeves pushed up to his elbows. His arms rest on his knees as he leans forward, his head turned to the left, and he's laughing at something Shane said. I love watching him and I love being with him.

My feet carry me forward, and he turns toward me, sensing my approach. He gets up off the sand, wiping the light grains from his pants, and meets me in four large strides.

"Hi," I begin, but Ronan silences me with his mouth, his soft lips on mine, urging me to part them. I do, and his tongue slips into my mouth, tasting me with so much passion that I can feel my knees weaken. His hands sneak under my shirt, his fingers stroking my low back, heating my skin.

"Happy birthday, baby," he says when he finally pulls back, leaving me breathless.

"Jesus, you two need to do something about all that pent-up sexual energy already," Vada gripes as she walks past us. "Do us all a favor, go have sex, and get it over with already, would ya?"

Of course, I blush and pull back from Ronan, who takes my hand instead.

"Come with me," he requests. Still holding his hand, I follow him up the narrow flight of stairs—the whistling and catcalls from our friends following us all the way to the deck—and into the house where he leads me over to the large white sectional sofa.

Every time I'm in this house, I'm struck by how beautifully decorated it is. Shane's mom really does have nice taste.

I sit on the sofa, looking at Ronan expectantly. He reaches behind the couch and retrieves a fairly large box wrapped in light-blue paper and decorated with a large silver bow. I face him, my left knee hitched onto the sofa cushion, and Ronan extends the present toward me.

"I hope you like it," he says, suddenly not so sure of himself. I can see hesitation in his eyes and meet him with a smile.

"You shouldn't have," I say. "I didn't get you anything for your birthday!"

Ronan shakes his head. "Yeah you did; you gave me *you*, remember?" he says so sweetly and sincerely that, for the second time today, I wonder if it's humanly possible for me to melt into a gooey puddle of love. I stare into his eyes for a few seconds before he raises his eyebrows and nods for me to open my present.

I remove the silver bow slowly, then carefully remove each piece of tape holding the wrapping together.

"Is this seriously how you open presents?" Ronan asks, and I can hear the impatience in his voice.

"Not usually, but this feels different," I giggle.

"Don't say that," he begs. "I can't handle the pressure."

He chuckles, but I can tell he means it, so I hurry up and pull the paper wrapping apart, revealing a nondescript cardboard box. I open the lid and move the tissue paper to reveal a pair of shiny black-and-gold hockey skates.

"Ran," I breathe, my eyes huge as I run my fingers over the embossed brand name on the side of one of the skates.

"I wanted to get you something that would mean I could have you around me more often. I know that's selfish, but..."

I don't let him finish. I drop the box with the skates to the floor, lunging forward and into Ronan's arms. I push him back onto the couch, crashing my chest against his as I basically attack his mouth with my lips. I'm on top of him, my legs straddling his hips, my hands on either side of his head as I lean forward, kissing him, tasting him, absolutely devouring him. His hands glide under my tank top and run up the curve of my back before he presses on my spine, pushing me closer to him, even though I wasn't sure that's possible.

His present may not seem like a big deal to some people, but it means the world to me. He just told me that he wants to spend even more time with me, wants me to be involved in something that is a huge part of his life. And even though he thinks it's selfish, I love the idea of sharing this with him.

We keep kissing like this for a few moments longer until, finally, he has to break our contact to come up for air, panting.

"So, do you like your present?" he asks, smiling, his hands still hot on my skin.

"I thought my attacking you was a clear indication of how much I love it," I say, returning his smile.

"I guess I'm kind of slow when it comes to these things. Maybe you need to kiss me like that a little while longer to really get the message across?" he says, his smile turning into a playful grin.

"Hmm, you don't strike me as slow at all, sweet boy," I tease him, but give in to him and kiss him again. I finally sit up, and his hands slide down my back before coming to rest on my hips. I can feel him hard, pressing between my legs.

"So, what are we doing today?" I ask Ronan, enjoying the feeling of him underneath me, and the tiny jolts of electricity that zap through my body whenever his hardness presses against my sensitive flesh.

"How about we stay right here and keep doing what we're doing?"

"Sounds enticing," I say, making a face like I'm contemplating this option. "But I'm sure someone is going to walk in on us because, let's face it, we don't have the best luck when it comes to these things. Best reserve these moments for when we're alone, don't you think?"

"Yeah, except we don't have any luck then, either. How many times has a phone call interrupted us?"

I make a face because he has a point. "True. But still, we should get back out there, don't you think?"

"If that's what you want," he sighs, but his voice is light, and he sits up and scoops me into his arms unexpectedly, making me squeal with laughter when he throws me over his shoulder like I weigh nothing at all. I can feel him adjust himself in his jeans before he marches out to the deck and back down to the beach, giving my butt a smack while he carries me down the flights of stairs, and I laugh.

"Okay, so when are you taking me skating again?" I ask as he trudges through the soft sand with me over his shoulder.

"Whenever you want," he says.

"How about next weekend?"

"It's a date," he says, and carefully sets me back down, my feet touching the sand and sinking into the soft surface.

"I love dates with you," I say, and tip my head up to plant a soft kiss on his cheek.

"Me, too."

The guys start a small fire in the fire pit, we eat, and eventually the booze comes out. It doesn't take long for Vada and Tori to start doing tequila shots, and Vada takes Steve's hand, licks the back of it, and sprinkles some salt on his skin. Then she licks it, takes her shot of tequila, and chases it with a lime. Steve doesn't seem to mind at all, and he grabs her and pulls her onto his lap before the two start a make-out session so steamy that Shane orders them to either go up to the house and take care of business or rein it in. Steve and Vada opt for option number one, and I don't know why, but I blush violently when Steve scoops Vada up, her legs lacing around his waist, and then takes her up to the house.

Ronan stands up from his spot in the sand, grabs my hand, and pulls me to a stand. "You look all hot and bothered by them," he says with a grin. "I think you need to cool off."

I give him a confused look, but before I can say anything, Ronan picks me up and jogs toward the ocean with me.

"Don't you dare, Ran! Don't you dare!" I scream, wiggling in his arms, trying to get him to drop me.

But he does dare, and he walks us both into the ocean, fully dressed. My jeans and tank top cling to my body, my shoes are soaked, and my wet hair hangs over my back.

"I can't believe you did that!" I say, deciding if I want to be mad or not. But with one look at his shirt perfectly stuck to him, showing every ridge of his muscular chest and stomach, drops of water beading down his face where I splashed him, I decide that, actually, I'm not mad at him. "What am I supposed to wear for the rest of the evening?" I lament as he pulls me into his arms.

"How about nothing?" he says, his voice a mix of playfulness and need.

"You'd like that, wouldn't you?"

"I would absolutely like that," he says, and kisses me softly. I can taste the salt on his lips. "You don't understand how fucking hot you look right now, wet like that," he mutters against my lips before his tongue dives into my mouth and his hands slide under my wet shirt, heating my chilled skin.

"If the way you look right now is any hint, then it must be pretty damn hot," I say.

He chuckles. "Maybe getting you wet wasn't such a great way to cool down after all," he breathes. "Because I'm getting all hot and bothered right now. We better put a stop to this."

"My sister Lauren's room is the third door to the right of the bathroom," Shane says to me, laughing when he sees us trudge up the shore soaking wet. "Just grab something from her closet. The dryer is in the laundry room. You guys can just throw your stuff in there really quick. Ran, you already know where all my stuff is."

After Ronan and I make our way up to the house, I make a beeline for the bathroom, where I grab us a couple of towels, then walk into Lauren's room. I lock the door behind me before I strip down, discarding my dripping clothes on the tiled floor. I dry off thoroughly, then wrap the towel around my head and open Lauren's closet. I pull out a cute black t-shirt and a pair of workout leggings. I'm not about to borrow some of Lauren's underwear, so I decide to slip on the pants and shirt without anything underneath. I'll just have to go commando, I guess.

Ronan is waiting for me outside Lauren's room. We match perfectly, with Ronan having changed into a pair of black workout shorts and a black t-shirt he borrowed from Shane. His eyes roam my body, lingering on my chest, and I'm sure he can tell I'm not wearing anything underneath because a wicked grin spreads across his face before he takes my wet clothes out of my hands. I follow him to the laundry room where he places our soaked garments into the dryer.

"You look good," he says, smiling at me.

"You, too," I grin.

He starts the dryer and we make our way back to the beach.

Vada and Steve rejoin us fifteen minutes later, to the absolute entertainment of the group.

"Okay, can we please not talk about my sister having sex with my best friend anymore?" Zack pleads, causing laughter to erupt from everyone. "No, seriously, it's weird," he laments.

"Fine," Shane relents. "What's the plan for tomorrow?"

"No-brainer," Steve says. "Let's come here and just chill at the beach again. I'm leaving for Boston next week; you'll be busy with Murphy's," he says to Shane, "and you guys start school on Monday, so we should just take tomorrow and relax before shit gets real again, don't you think?" Steve looks around at Ronan, Zack, Vada, Summer, Tori, and me.

"Sounds like a plan," Shane says. "But Ran and I are working tomorrow evening, so it has to be a day thing. Maybe we'll meet here early."

"Sure! What time are you two working?" Steve asks.

"Five to two," Shane answers. "I'm staying here tonight, so you guys can be here as early as nine tomorrow morning."

"I love that idea," Summer says. "We could bring bagels and stuff and then just enjoy the day."

"Oh, but Vada, Tori, and I have team tryouts tomorrow morning," I note, looking at Vada, who may not actually be in any condition to play softball first thing tomorrow morning. "It's from nine to eleven."

"No problem, we'll just get here when we can," Tori says, and we all agree to the plan and enjoy the rest of the evening with each other.

***

By the time midnight rolls around, Vada and Tori are absolutely wasted, having taken more tequila shots and whatever else they could get their hands on throughout the evening. They've sung happy birthday to me about fifteen times, all in various renditions, some more off-key than others. Summer conjured up a little birthday cake from somewhere, and that was devoured hours ago.

"I think I'm going to take this one home before she throws up all over my car," Steve says, and coaxes Vada to take his hand so he can lead her carefully up the narrow stairway. She trips a bunch of times, and Steve keeps looking over his shoulder to us, shaking his head in disbelief at Vada's drunken state.

"Come on, babe, I'll get you to bed. No way you're going home tonight," Shane says to Tori, who is equally trashed.

"Don't try anything, O'Connor," Tori slurs before she stumbles ahead of him, clearly trying to be seductive but failing miserably.

Ronan offers me his hand and I take it. We stop inside the house where Ronan retrieves our clothes from the dryer and we go to change back into our original outfits. I grab my box with the beautiful hockey skates Ronan got me and then we head out to the car, followed by Summer and Zack. I hug them, thanking them for the fun evening and the birthday cake before they get into Zack's Honda.

I slide into the passenger seat of Ronan's car, and he closes my door he had held open for me. As soon as he's in the car, Ronan takes my hand and places it underneath his on the shifter. It's my favorite way of driving with him, and he smiles at me as we drive down the road and onto the interstate, music playing softly in the background. I enjoy his presence, feeling content and happy.

"I cannot believe how drunk Vada and Tori got," I laugh.

"Oh god, that was nothing," Ronan says. "At Shane's birthday party in April, Vada completely passed out in the sand. It freaked Steve out so bad, they had a huge fight about it the next day when Vada came to our house, hungover as hell. Steve was yelling at her because he ended up having to take care of her for most of the evening, and she did actually throw up in his car," Ronan laughs.

"Wow," I say, giggling. "So, what happened?"

"Nothing, really. He started feeling bad for her because she felt like crap, had a splitting headache, and she was super apologetic. They made up pretty quickly. Vada can get crazy sometimes. I'm not sure she knows what her limits are."

"I can see that," I say. "She's so fun to be with, though, and she's an amazing friend. Plus, she kept pushing us to be together, remember?"

"As if she'd let us forget it," he says, rolling his eyes. "But honestly, I didn't need Vada to know that I wanted to get to know you better," he says, his voice velvety and smooth.

Here I go melting again.

"Can I ask you something?" I say, and turn toward him.

He looks at me briefly, then back at the road. "You can ask me anything."

"What do you want to do after school? Like college and stuff...." I trail off.

"I don't really know," he admits, and looks at me again. "I thought I had a plan, but now I'm not so sure."

"What was your plan?"

"To get as far away from New York as I can," he says matter-of-factly.

My heart squeezes uncomfortably in my chest. "Oh," is all I can say, and I turn back toward the front of the car.

Ronan tightens his hold on my hand, then moves it to rest his and mine on my leg. "But I'm not so sure about that now," he says, and I dare to look at him again. I swear, he gets more handsome each time I lay eyes on him. He smiles at me, his face soft. "I don't really want to be anywhere you're not."

I exhale in relief, a small smile tugging at my lips. "I don't want to be anywhere you aren't either," I confess.

"So, tell me what *your* plans are."

I shrug. "Not really sure, to be honest. I mean, college, definitely—god, my parents would disown me if I didn't go to college—but I don't really know where. I like New York. My friends are here and... *you* are here," I say hastily, then glance at Ronan, who's smiling at the road in front of him. "So maybe NYU, or Cornell, or Columbia, though I doubt I'd get into Cornell or Columbia. My grades are good, but I'm no valedictorian." I nudge Ronan's arm, and he grins at me. "I guess I should apply to Duke; it's where my parents went, but that's in North Carolina and definitely *not* where you are."

"You really shouldn't base your decision on where you go to college or what you want to do with your life on me," he says. "Do what makes you happy!"

"*You* make me happy," I say, awkwardly.

"You make me happy, too."

He looks at me again, and if we weren't driving on the freeway right now, I'd crawl across that damn center console, climb onto his lap, and kiss him until he was out of breath. "Just apply wherever you think you might want to go, and then you can make a decision later; we still have a lot of time," he says wisely.

I nod in agreement. "Do you know where you want to apply?" I ask, needing to know so I can possibly add those places to my own list.

"I thought I'd apply to a couple schools in California," he says. At this my heart squeezes in my chest again. "The University of Montana," he adds, and I nod because that would make sense; his grandparents are in Montana and he really seems to like it there. "Maybe NYU and Brown," he continues, then pauses. "But I actually just submitted my application for early admission to Columbia."

I look at him in surprise. "You did? Why didn't you tell me?"

"I don't know. It didn't seem like a big deal, I guess. The chances of me getting in are pretty slim," he says. "It's an Ivy League school and everyone and their mother is trying to get in," he adds, then looks at me apologetically. "I'm sorry, I should have told you. I really just didn't think it was anything worth getting excited about."

"No, it's okay," I say. "I just didn't realize you were working on that. When did you take your SATs?" How did I miss this?

"Last spring, before I knew you were about to step into my life and make me second-guess all my plans," he says with a twinkle in his eyes and the sexiest smile on his lips. It's a good thing we're pulling up to my house in that moment, because I really want to kiss him.

"Do you have to go home right away?" I ask him, hoping we can hang out a little bit together.

"No. My mom's working, so I'm all yours," he says, pulls my hand to his mouth, and places a soft kiss onto my palm before we get out of his car.

***

It's dark inside the house, so I quickly turn on the light before walking into the kitchen, dehydrated from the little alcohol I had. I open the fridge and grab a bottle of water. "Do you want anything?" I call out to Ronan, my head still in the fridge.

"Only to kiss you," he says, his voice coming from right behind me.

I spin around, slamming the refrigerator shut. "Jeez, I didn't even hear you walk into the kitchen. You scared the shit out of me," I say, my hand over my pounding heart.

Ronan chuckles in a low voice that makes my heart speed up even more. "Sorry, baby," he says, and my eyes flutter shut when Ronan leans in and brushes his lips softly against mine. I can feel the heat radiating off his body and his scent is driving me crazy. He begins to pull away, so I move my hands under his shirt and up his chest, intensifying the kiss as I part my lips and allow his tongue to slip into my mouth.

Ronan nips my bottom lip, and a moan escapes me as my fingers trace Ronan's firm chest and stomach. He backs us up, pressing me against the fridge and trapping my head between his arms on either side of me. He moves his mouth away from mine and leaves a path of kisses down my jawline and the side of my neck.

"God, your skin is delicious," he groans, his lips not leaving my neck, and I shiver as his breath caresses my ear and Ronan lightly bites my earlobe. Heat and want spread through my core as Ronan pushes off the fridge and his left hand finds its way under my shirt. Moving upward, Ronan's thumb traces along the edge of my bra and my breathing becomes increasingly ragged.

"Cat," he whispers into my ear, and I suck in a sharp breath when his thumb outlines my hard nipple, and suddenly it clicks. I think I'm ready to move our relationship to a different plane. I don't think I can resist him any longer; I don't think I *want* to resist him any longer. He and I have waited long enough. He has earned my trust. He has shown me, again and again, that my well-being, comfort, and needs take priority for him. And I love him. I want to share myself with him; I want all of him. So I open my eyes and pull away from him.

He immediately stops tasting me, moving back with a concerned look on his face. "Are you okay?" he asks, his chest still rising and falling erratically, his concerned eyes searching mine.

"Yeah," I say quietly, nodding. Collecting all my courage and letting my desire and feelings for him quiet all my fears, I move my lips to his ear. "I'm ready," I whisper, letting the weight of the words and my decision sit out in the open. Ronan just looks at me for a moment, unspeaking, swallowing hard. "I'm ready," I whisper again.

His eyes bore their way into my soul, searching for doubt. "Cat, if... if this is really what you want, I'll need to go to my car. I don't have any protection on me," he says, still analyzing my face, his gorgeous eyes intense.

"Oh, it's—that's okay," I stammer, feeling awkward, even though I know it's great that we're having this conversation, and even greater that he's so concerned about being safe. "I got on the pill when you and I, you know, became *us*," I say with a small smile.

He scans my face. "Oh," he says, and I can see his wheels turning, trying to figure out exactly what I'm trying to say. "I've never done it without... without a condom," he says, and I smile at his nervousness. I know he's far more experienced than I am, and the fact that this is new territory for him, that this is something he hasn't shared with anyone else, makes me happier than it probably should.

"So, it's sort of the first time for both of us, then," I say.

His lips tug into a smile. "I guess so," he says. "Cat, are you sure?" he asks, his hand still under my shirt, the other resting on my lower back.

"Yeah," I say, not taking my eyes off his, wanting to show him that I'm sincere and that this is what I want more than anything else in this world.

Ronan nods, moves his hand out from under my shirt, and takes my hand. Without speaking, he leads me out of the kitchen, up the stairs, and to my bedroom.

I stand there awkwardly, my skin tingly in anticipation as Ronan closes the door behind him and moves back toward me. His eyes are still searching mine. I give him a shaky smile, wanting to assure him, but I'm so nervous, and it shows.

Ronan moves slowly as he steps toward me.

"You can tell me to stop any time and I will," Ronan promises, his voice soft but serious, before he kisses me gently. As soon as his lips meet mine again, the fire inside me burns brightly and the want rips through me like an avalanche. His tongue explores my mouth, tracing my lips, while his hands carefully push up the hem of my shirt. I remove my hands from his back and lift my arms, allowing him to pull my shirt up over my head. Ronan's lips are back on mine the split second he discards my shirt on the floor. I want to feel his skin on mine so badly it hurts, and I push myself against him, my hard nipples pressing through the fabric of my bra and against his chest. I push his shirt up, wanting it off, and he finally reaches back and pulls it off all the way.

I can feel the sexual tension, the want, the need surge between us as his hands touch me frantically yet so gently and carefully that my skin feels electrically charged. He stops kissing me long enough to unhook my bra, sliding the straps off my shoulders and letting it drop to the floor. He takes me in deliberately, letting his eyes roam my exposed skin.

"You are so beautiful," he moans, then crushes his lips back against mine. He pushes me back gently, sitting me down on the bed. I lean back, letting my head hit the pillow as Ronan puts his hands on either side of my body and moves his legs between mine. He kisses my collarbone, and my heart beats hard in my chest. My hands desperately hold on to Ronan's shoulders as his mouth finds my nipple. His tongue traces it before he nips and sucks on it, driving my body absolutely wild. I begin pushing myself against his legs, and a deep, feral moan escapes Ronan, making me want him even more.

His tongue leaves my breast, and my legs vise-grip around him in protest. His breath feathers against my skin, and I swear I'm going to come apart any second now. He begins traveling downward, kissing and licking the bare skin of my stomach down to the waistband of my jeans, where he undoes the button and zipper. With both hands, Ronan pulls down my jeans, all the while continuing to trail kisses down the newly exposed skin of my legs and thighs. My skin is hypersensitive, and I shut my eyes tightly, focusing on the sensation of his lips and tongue tasting my body.

When Ronan pushes my pants to my knees, he quickly moves off the bed and pulls my jeans off the rest of the way before dropping them on the floor where they join my shirt and his, along with my bra. In one swift motion, he places himself between my legs again and his lips resume their caress of my neck as he lowers his hips against mine.

All I can do is let my hands run across Ronan's back, feeling his soft, heated skin and taut muscles while his lips trail across my neck, my collarbone, my chest, my breasts. He alternates between them, kissing, licking, and sucking my pebbled nipples. He grates his teeth over my right nipple, nipping at it. I never imagined that the slight pain would result in such unspeakable arousal, and I grind my hips roughly against him in a desperate yet fruitless, attempt to quell that hot, needy ache growing between my thighs. The rough fabric of his jeans against my panties only gets me more worked up, and I moan with want.

I can feel him pressing between my thighs, needing to be freed. I don't imagine that his jeans grant him much room to... expand. So, I reach for him, fumbling with the button of his pants, which he finally undoes for me, allowing me to push his jeans down before he kicks them off, his mouth never breaking contact with my skin. He's certainly skilled at multitasking.

I rake my hands through his dark-blond hair when he starts to move his lips across my stomach, kissing every inch as he travels downward. I gasp with pleasure when his mouth finds the right spot, still covered by the thin fabric of my panties. This is all completely new to me, and his warm breath against my most sensitive skin sends raw, wild need through my body. I whimper when Ronan mercifully pulls my panties off me, leaving me completely exposed to him.

"You have no idea how perfect you are," Ronan says, his voice low and gravelly. I watch him as he takes in my naked body, his eyes glossy but filled with what I can only describe as hunger as they linger a heartbeat longer on my most intimate part, and I squirm under his intense gaze.

I always thought I would feel embarrassed or shy when this moment came, but all I want is to feel all of him. My legs fall open willingly, making me vulnerable to him as he carefully places himself between my legs, lowering himself so that his arms support his weight but our chests touch. He kisses me—his soft tongue slow and deep—while his left hand finds my hip and gently glides to my inner thigh where his fingers leave a tingling sensation and cause moist heat to pool between my legs.

I need him to touch me; it feels necessary to my existence. Slowly, almost painfully so, Ronan moves his hand between my thighs and to my most sensitive skin. He circles a finger slowly around that tiny spot that causes the most powerful sensations, then dips lower for a moment, lingering at my entrance without slipping his finger inside me.

"Fuck," Ronan groans against my lips desperately, drawing out the word. God, even his voice—the need reflected in it—turns me on. He glides his hand back up, his fingers sweeping softly over my hypersensitive flesh, stroking me so softly that the want is almost unbearable as he pushes me further and further toward the edge. My body aches with need and my breath is erratic as my heart beats hard in my chest. His lips leave mine and, without warning, his mouth finds my nipple, sucking hard while he continues to stroke me with his left hand, increasing the pressure and speed.

The ecstasy that has been building in my body comes to a peak and finally causes me to come undone beneath Ronan's warm body. My eyes are shut, but lights burst before my mind's eye as waves of undiluted ecstasy crash over me and course through my body. I arch my back, my body moving on its own accord, my hips bucking against Ronan's hand as he continues to pleasure my body and skillfully draws out the high. *Oh god.*

I need to feel him inside me. Now.

I open my eyes, my vision hazy, and my hands frantically find the waistband of Ronan's black boxer briefs. I scramble to get them off, to push them down his hips, to eliminate the last barrier between our naked bodies. Ronan pushes himself up and off me and takes off the last bit of clothing separating his body from mine.

I take him in, my gaze rolling from his handsome face down his body, my eyes intentional as I see all of him for the first time: his lean, muscular chest and stomach, taut in anticipation; sun-kissed skin; his breathing erratic; green eyes bright—hooded and glossy with need that has been building for months; that V-cut I've only ever seen disappear in the waistband of his boxers; and finally, his manhood—long and thick, hard as a rock. It's so arousing to see him like that, to see with my own eyes what effect I have on him, how much I turn him on instead of just the other way around. God, his body is perfect; *Ronan* is perfect.

He lowers himself back onto me, supporting his upper body on his forearms as he kisses me gently. "Are you sure about this?" he asks for what seems like the hundredth time while his eyes search mine for any doubt. My heart is frantic in my chest, my breathing shallow, shuddering with anticipation, with want and, admittedly, nervousness. I'm kind of scared. I've obviously heard that the first time hurts, and Ronan's size is not insubstantial. But I want this. I've never been surer of anything than the fact that I want to give all of me to Ronan right now.

"Yeah," I breathe, because I am sure. I'm ready. I want to feel him—all of him. Despite my nervousness, my inexperience, my body positively aches for him, my thighs tingling where they connect with Ronan's skin.

A jolt of electricity surges through me when I feel him lower his hips, feel his hardness against my hypersensitive flesh. I stare into his eyes, his gaze soft, reassuring, as he reaches down between us, gently strokes my needy skin for a moment, then takes himself in his hand. He guides himself to the right spot and finally begins to push into me.

Ronan

I can tell Cat is scared. I can tell by the way her hazel eyes are wide as I search them, her breath shudders slightly, and her fingers hold on to me tightly as if anticipating pain. So I move cautiously, wanting to give her the chance to back out of her decision. She really has no idea how fucking perfect she is, and I know that tonight is going to change me irrevocably.

I let my eyes roll down her soft curves—her delicate neck, her breasts, her hips, then her thighs and that soft *V* of her most sensitive flesh—taking my time, drinking her in as she does me. I can practically feel her eyes on my body, studying me while I let my eyes travel over her completely naked body for the first time. God, she is stunning—every damn part of her.

She looks at me expectantly as I lower myself onto her. Warmth radiates off her like she's the sun. My mind moves at a million miles an hour, and even though I'm so hungry for her, wanting nothing more than to finally feel all of her, I move deliberately as I gently lower my hips. I carefully begin to edge into her, moving slowly, fighting to keep a straight head while my body yearns to be buried deep inside her. My eyelids want to close with the sensation of my body entering Cat's, but I train my gaze on Cat's instead. She needs to know I'm right here with her—not only physically, but emotionally, too.

And holy fucking shit, the way she feels is unlike anything I've ever felt before; it's beyond anything I could have ever imagined—her unfiltered softness, her pure warmth, the way she's already so damn worked up, wet and ready for me. It's almost too much to handle, and I remind myself to stay in the moment with Cat, because as fucking perfect as she feels, I want to make sure it feels just as good to her.

So I push into her slowly—millimeter by millimeter—watching her intently, hoping to minimize any pain. But her eyes shut tightly and her eyebrows knit together as she takes a sharp breath in through her teeth, her body tightening around me, squeezing me. Holy fuck. Her fingers find and dig into my shoulder blades, her nails piercing my skin as she works through the initial discomfort. I stop moving, giving her time to let the pain pass, taking the smallest opportunity to regulate my breathing and my heart rate as I let my eyes fall shut and breathe her in. Her soft body underneath me feels so damn perfect. I hate the thought of causing her pain when Cat feels so unspeakably good to me.

I feel her fingers relax on my back and hope this means the discomfort is subsiding somewhat, though I'm aware that the first time isn't usually very pleasant for girls. It's one of the most unfair things in my opinion. Sex has never been anything but pleasurable to me, and it bothers me to know that I'm hurting her.

"It's okay. Don't stop," Cat whispers as if she can read my thoughts, can hear my internal struggles. I begin pushing in deeper, carefully moving back and forth, paying attention to her sounds, her body language, while getting lost in the feeling of her.

God, I've been craving her like this for so long, have dreamed about and envisioned this moment, never truly knowing just how incredible it would feel when I finally got to feel all of her like this—unfiltered, raw, without anything between Cat's perfect body and mine. There are no words to describe the ecstasy rushing through my veins, and it's like time stands still. Only the sounds of our labored breathing disrupt the silence, and I could swear I exist in a void with only Cat. Nothing else matters right now.

Finally, I feel the rest of her body relax, feel her melt into me, her face softening.

"Are you okay?" I breathe against her. I'm at war with myself—my need to be gentle with Cat fighting my body's urge to plunge into her hard, to possess her, to claim her.

"Yeah," she whimpers, her eyes shut. "This... you feel so good, Ran."

Her words provide me with reassurance and I allow myself to sink deeper, to thrust into her, slowly at first, letting her test the boundaries, giving her time to stop me. But she doesn't and instead intertwines her legs with mine as her hands hold on to my shoulders. I get lost in the feeling of her, the rational side of me gone with her soft skin underneath me, her warmth enveloping me completely. It's like she's all around me and everywhere at once. Her quiet, breathy moans are driving me crazy, getting me more and more worked up by the second. My breathing becomes more ragged and labored when Cat snakes her legs around my waist and pulls me closer, deeper.

This way of being with her—the way she trusts me, holds on to me, and the way my heart is cracked wide open for the first time in my life... I've never experienced anything like this before and, honestly, I may not ever recover from this.

I kiss her lips, her neck, and her breasts, listening to her whimper and savoring the feel of her body underneath me, my strokes long, slow, and deep. I'm trying to be deliberate in my movements, to be as gentle as I can, but the way she feels is completely consuming. I'm not at all sure I'll be able to last much longer. I increase my pace, thrusting deeper still, harder, but holding back. It's her first time, after all, and I want to take it easy, allow her to test her boundaries. I move my left hand between us, circling my thumb over that swollen sensitive bud of nerves between her thighs, and her reaction is immediate. Her nails dig into my skin, dragging her fingers down my back, the pain of it pushing me further toward the edge. Her breathing picks up, her face contorts with pleasure, and she arches her back, losing herself to me once more.

"Ran," she whimpers and moans out her orgasm. Hearing her say my name as she comes apart underneath me is the last push I need. I join her, the physical high ripping through my body, seizing my muscles for what feels like an eternity, yet not long enough before I still inside her.

I let my head fall forward, eyes shut, inhaling her scent while I regain control, trying to steady my breathing and slow my heart rate. Her legs are still wrapped around my waist, trapping me against her in the best way, her chest touching mine as she breathes in and out.

Finally, I lift my head and my eyes find hers, searching, scanning her face. "Are you okay?" I ask again, still breathless.

I'm relieved when she smiles at me, her eyes half shut and still glazed over, the gold specks amplified and dancing in the low light.

"Uh-huh," she breathes with a nod, and shivers with the aftershock of her last orgasm. I run my right hand over her cheek, down her neck, between her breasts, and to her stomach before moving forward to kiss her again. I look into her eyes, and it feels like the whole world has stopped. There is just Cat and me, and I'd be okay with it being like that forever. I'm in all the way with her.

"What are you thinking?" she asks, her eyes searching mine, forehead creased as she analyzes my expression.

I smile. "How damn lucky I am that I get to be with you," I say, and the smile on Cat's face is heart-stopping. She props herself up on her elbows, her lips only an inch from mine, and I let my eyes fall shut again, feeling her breath on my skin.

"I'm really lucky to be with you, too," she says, and kisses me so softly that goose bumps erupt down my back and arms. "You make me feel so safe," she adds, her voice quiet.

I open my eyes to look at her. "I don't ever want you to feel anything but safe." The thought of doing something, *anything* to hurt her in any way, be it physical or emotional, to lay a hand on her like her ex has done, like my mother does to me, makes me feel physically ill.

"You know what would make me feel really safe right now?" she asks, her voice playful now.

I cock an eyebrow. "What's that?"

"If you stayed with me for a while," she says, brushing her lips against mine again. It doesn't take much convincing for me to slip out of her and, after she heads to the bathroom, to lie down beside her and pull her into my arms. I press my body against her soft skin, kissing her shoulder, her neck, her head while her fingers gently glide up and down my arm until I can hear her breathing become deeper, more rhythmic, and I know she's asleep. I join her, drifting off to sleep while breathing in her scent and feeling her soft, warm skin.

I wake up hours later when Cat sighs contently in her sleep. She's lying next to me, her head resting on my arm, one leg over mine, and I listen to her slow, deep breathing for a while. Her naked body is soft and warm against me, and I've never been as happy as I am right now, in this moment, with Cat by my side. I wish it would never have to end.

It's dark in the room. The only source of light is the moon shining in through the window and the indicator light on Cat's phone, glowing green, noting a full charge. I reach over to the nightstand and grab her phone, which shows me that it's past four in the morning. I should really get home to avoid my mother realizing I've been out all night yet again. I move out from under Cat slowly so as not to disturb her peaceful sleep and get up quietly, feeling the floor with my feet for my boxers and jeans. When I find them, I put them on and reach for my shirt.

Cat begins to stir when I put on my shoes, and her hand glides up my back. "Don't leave," she says sweetly, her voice thick with sleep.

I lean toward her and kiss her forehead. "I have to," I whisper, taking in her scent. "But I promise I'll see you in just a few hours."

She lets out a soft, approving groan and her eyes shut. My heart constricts when I walk out of the room. I don't want to leave her here all by herself, I want to be here and make sure she's safe and warm. As I take in her body, covered only by a thin blanket, her face, her long hair, I realize just how much I care about her—more than I ever thought possible. I love her. *God, I love her.* And I've probably been in love with her since the very beginning of us.

I drive the few miles from her house to mine thinking about Cat, music playing in the background, but it's drowned out by my thoughts of her. I don't want to wait anymore; I'm going to tell her how I feel when I see her later today. I just can't hold it in anymore. I need to let her know what she means to me, that I'm in love with her.

I notice Steve's Challenger parked in the driveway when I get home, and I walk noiselessly into the house and up the stairs to my room where I collapse onto my bed without undressing, passing out immediately and falling into a deep, restful sleep.

Saturday, August 28th

Ronan

"Ran! Are you coming or not?"

My brother's voice pulls me out of my sleep, and I squint against the sun streaming into my room, momentarily blinding me.

"What time is it?" I mumble, covering my face with a pillow.

"Uh, it's like eight-thirty," he says, banging around in the bathroom, the door to my room wide open. "If you want to ride with me, you better get your ass up now!"

"Go ahead, I need a couple more hours of sleep," I mutter as the sleep threatens to pull me under again.

"Okay. Cat and Vada won't be done with practice until eleven anyways." I hear him spray some cologne. "What time did you get in last night?"

"I don't know, like four-thirty," I respond groggily.

Steve laughs. "Nice! Alright, I'm gonna head out. What time do you think you'll be at Shane's?"

"I'll be there by eleven-thirty," I say, and pass out again as Steve heads down the stairs.

It seems like just minutes later when my phone rings and I jerk awake. My eyes are still shut when I answer. "Hello?"

"Hey, are you on your way?" Steve says on the other end of the line.

I open my eyes and squint at the screen. It's 11:27. *Shit.* "No, I overslept, I'm getting up right now," I tell him sleepily, clearing my throat.

"Okay, cool. The girls are here, but Zack needs to pick up the charger for his camera, so we can just swing by and get you if you want. We should be there in about half an hour."

"That sounds good, actually. I'll just take a quick shower. See you in thirty."

I roll out of bed and stretch, cracking my back in the process. Despite the interruptions, I haven't slept this well in a long time. My unconscious hours were filled with dreams of Cat, her face reappearing in my mind again and again, filling me with a kind of happiness and contentment I don't recall ever feeling before. Is this what love does? Is this what it's going to be like now that I've admitted to myself the depth of my feelings for Cat? I wouldn't complain one bit if it was.

I leave a trail of clothes on my bedroom floor, discarding my shirt, jeans, and boxers as I make my way to the bathroom, where I turn on the shower and step under the hot water, letting it bead down my neck and back.

Memories of last night flood my mind. Cat trusted me completely, and I smile as I recall her soft body, her sexy moans, her expression when she came undone, what it felt like when I was inside her. God, it was perfect. It was unlike anything I've ever felt. Cat was right, it was sort of like the first time for both of us. I get hard thinking about her and decide a cold shower might be a better idea than a hot one. She doesn't leave my mind, though, resulting in a near-constant smile on my lips, and I'm determined—obsessed, actually—with telling her how I feel about her as soon as I see her. She needs to know.

When I'm done with my shower, I dry off and get dressed in a fresh pair of jeans and a heather-gray t-shirt before putting on my shoes. A quick look at my watch tells me it's ten minutes until noon, so I grab my wallet and phone and make my way out of my room and down the stairs, checking my phone as I go. I should send Cat a text, letting her know I'm on my way, that I'll be there soon. *I wonder if she is as anxious to see me as I am to see her.*

"Fuck!" I exclaim, startled, when I reach the last step and my mother appears in front of me. She's so close to me that I almost run into her. The expression on her face—which is contorted in anger, her pupils large—is one I recognize, and I instantly know this isn't good.

"Where the fuck were you last night?" she asks, her voice sharp and pitchy. How she even knows I was gone is beyond me. For a split second I wonder if I was mistaken and that she wasn't actually working last night, but she's still wearing her signature light-blue scrubs as well as her wooden clogs, her hair braided as if she just got back from work.

I don't answer. I know better than to try to talk myself out of these situations. Instead, I decide to slip past her, inching my way toward the front door, planning to bolt as soon as I can. I'll deal with the consequences later.

But she blocks my path, mimicking my steps, my movements, and shoves me back hard. It catches me off guard and, unable to brace against her force, I hit the back of my head against the wall with a deafening thump. Instant pain spreads through my skull.

My mother is in my face. "You are such a screw up, Ronan. Just like your father," she yells at me as I step to the side and slowly start backing up into the hallway, hoping to make it to the living room, to the sliding glass door, and to the back porch. I just need to make it outside. My hand reaches for the back of my head where I just hit the wall, and pulling it away, I realize I'm bleeding. *Fuck*. I must have hit the corner.

"You were with your little girlfriend last night, weren't you? Weren't you?" she hisses, her voice getting louder. "I know you fucked her, Ronan. Just like your father is fucking that woman. He's on his way now to get his shit and leave me. For another woman," she adds with a short, maniacal laugh.

I have a hard time following my mom's stream of consciousness. Her words spill out fast, and she's getting more worked up by the second. The pain in my head is spreading, and I feel dizzy as I stumble backwards into the living room, my mother stalking my every step like I'm prey to be hunted.

She's just feet away from me, and, to my horror, I see her grab my hockey stick. It's a brand-new stick, barely broken-in. After practice yesterday and before heading out to celebrate Cat's birthday, I spent some time taping it, then applying wax to make the stick sturdier, harder, less likely to break during hard drives. My mistake was leaving my hockey stick downstairs instead of taking it back up to my room with my other equipment.

I forged the perfect fucking weapon for my mother, who's about to use it against me.

Fuck, this isn't good. I desperately try to make my way out of the house, hoping I'll be able to make it out through the sliding glass door to the backyard.

"Ronan, stop moving and turn the fuck around," my mother orders me, and there's something in her eyes that scares me more than ever. Or maybe it's the blankness, the way her gaze is devoid of any compassion. Unlike in the past, I don't obey her order; I don't stop, my eyes moving between her face and the hockey stick she's obviously intent on beating me with. Fuck that.

"I'm warning you, Ronan," she yells. "Don't fucking try me!"

I just shake my head at her, continuing to tread backwards. I don't know where this resolve to defy her suddenly comes from—does love do that, too? Give you strength and courage you didn't know you had? Part of me is very, *very* aware that I'm playing with fucking fire. I'm internally screaming at myself to stop moving and take whatever punishment she's intent on dishing out, but something is different today. Her rage, her hate seemingly radiate off her, crashing against me, and I know without a shadow of doubt that I'm in real fucking danger. My *life* is in danger.

"Mom, no," I urge, holding my hands up in front of me when she raises my hockey stick over her shoulder, winding it up, ready to swing like a baseball bat. But her pupils are huge, swallowing the green of her eyes, and her face is filled with pure rage.

"I'm so god damn tired of you doing whatever you fucking want. You're just like your father. You don't give a shit about anyone but yourself," she screams, and begins swinging the hockey stick, aiming for my face over and over again, but I manage to duck and avoid it every time.

"You're a worthless piece of shit, Ronan," she shouts, increasing her pace, diminishing the distance between us even more. "All the fucking sacrifices I've made," she screams, taking another swing at me, but she misses. "Me. *I* did it all. And you just take and take."

Another swing; another miss.

I don't understand what she's saying; I don't know what set her off. I don't know why she's so vicious today. Though I don't try to figure it out as I continue to back up into the living room, keeping an eye on her and the weapon in her hands. My adrenaline is in overdrive, shutting down all thoughts, all emotions, everything but the most primal survival instinct as I try to figure out a way to escape her. I attempt to calculate my odds of getting out of here unharmed, or at least alive.

But I'm not lucky enough to get away from her. As my mother pulls the hockey stick back yet again, my heel catches on the small area rug on the living-room floor. I trip and stumble, and I desperately try to regain my balance.

The stick swings forward and crashes into my face right below my left eye, splitting my skin open. The pain is blinding. The force of my mother's hit causes me to fall backwards into the glass coffee table, which shatters under my weight.

A million tiny shards of glass surround me, digging into my flesh, cutting my back, my arms, my hands as I lie on the floor. I struggle to get up quickly, knowing that the longer I'm on the ground, the more vulnerable I am.

I feel like a wounded animal backed into a corner, and while I would have just relinquished myself to my mother in the past, everything feels different today. And not just her anger, but my need to defend myself, to get the hell out of here, to escape her unjust punishment, to fight back.

My mother steps toward me, my hockey stick raised over her head, ready to swing it at me again. I can't say it happens voluntarily or is in any way planned or premeditated, but I kick my leg out and into her knee, hard.

She's thrown off-balance and falls down.

The split second my mother hits the ground, I scramble to push myself off the floor, the shards of glass piercing the palms of my hands, cutting them open. I barely even feel the pain. I just need to get out of this house, need to get to the backyard.

I get half upright, finally regaining my footing. I take two hurried steps—the broken glass making a crunchy sound under the soles of my shoes—my left hand reaching for the glass door only a few feet away from me, when I see my mother move out my periphery.

"You've lost your god damn mind, Ronan!" she shrieks, somehow swinging my hockey stick into my leg. She hooks my ankle and yanks it back, and I slam face-first back to the floor. The pain shooting through my left shoulder knocks the wind out of me, and I groan with the effort to roll onto my right side. I'm still desperate to evade my mother, who's back on her feet now, her eyes wide with hatred.

"You think you can kick me, you piece of shit?" she screams, and brings my hockey stick down on me with as much force as she can muster. "You think you just get to defy me? To disrespect me in my own damn house? I will fucking teach you, Ronan!"

I'm utterly unprotected while she beats me. My face, my head, my shoulders, my back, my stomach, my knees—none of it is off limits, and she keeps hitting me with no relief in sight, hacking and slashing away at me as I try to protect my body against the blows.

I hear bones cracking, and pain pools in the areas where the hard wood of the hockey stick connects with my body. It spreads through every muscle, into every nerve. I keep trying to find a way to get up and off the ground, but the blows, the hits, the pain keep forcing me back to the floor.

Finally, my mother slams her heeled foot down on my left hand so violently that it breaks.

It's not enough. Her rage is unyielding, blinding as she takes it all out on my bruised, bleeding body, all the while screaming at me, reminding me that I'm nothing—unwanted, unworthy, unloved. When she swings the hockey stick over her head and brings it down on my right knee cap, it fractures it into what feels like a million pieces. The pain that tears through my body makes my vision go black for a moment.

I cry out, begging—for the first time—for her to stop. "Mom... please... no more," I plead with a groan, my voice constricted with pain, barely able to get the words out.

"You know how I hate it when you beg, you piece of shit. If you beg me for anything, beg for me to put you out of your misery. Come on, Ronan! Beg! Beg for me to kill you!" she screams, and crashes my hockey stick into my body again.

The wood splinters with a loud crack, and my mother throws the now-useless weapon to the floor with a thud. But it's still not over, and I know it won't be over until I'm dead. Until she has beaten the life out of me. Instead, she begins kicking me in the face and stomach, unforgiving, relentless. I can feel warm blood streaming down my forehead and cheek where my skin is split open and raw from the impact of her tireless blows.

Everything hurts and I'm nauseated. My body is weak, no longer able to guard against my mother's violence. She continues to kick me, taking advantage of my inability to protect all of me at once, finding the vulnerable areas that remain uncovered while my arms attempt to shield my head and face from more kicks and more injuries.

I'm pretty sure my nose is broken, my left eye is already swollen shut, and my ears ring as I beg her to stop—beg for my life, without avail. My mother is the embodiment of wrath, and it dawns on me that I probably won't make it out of this alive. This time, she may finally step over the edge. But this time I have something to lose, and the thought of not being able to see Cat again is as painful as my mother's unyielding blows.

I need to get up somehow; I need to get out of here. So I gather every last bit of strength left in my battered, bleeding body, relying on sheer adrenaline—because I truly have nothing else left—and I move my unbroken hand to push myself off the ground. The sharp edges of the glass scattered on the floor violently embed themselves in the palm of my hand. Big mistake.

My mother's right foot slams into my mouth, knocking me back to the ground. I feel my skin tear open as I start to black out from the pain consuming my body. Every inch of me is on fire, my insides burning.

I take several more brutal kicks to the stomach and am semi-conscious when I hear voices. My brother is screaming at my mother, and there are hurried footsteps on the hardwood floor. But just as I begin to hope for relief, my mother stomps violently on my unprotected rib cage, fracturing my ribs and ripping all the air from my lungs at once.

Finally the beating stops, and at that moment I know only pain as I desperately fight to breathe. In a fraction of a second, Steve is on his knees next to me, yelling at someone who's not my mother, but I don't know who it is. I'm unable to lift my head, and panic pulses through me along with what feels like endless agony whenever I try to move or get air into my lungs. Steve's face is close to mine, his lips moving, but I don't comprehend. My vision is blurred and my heart is beating so frantically in my chest that it drowns out any sound. My struggle for air is desperate; my breaths are short and ragged, irregular and interrupted by violent coughs. I can taste the blood in my mouth, feel it running down my face.

I'm weak and tired. *So fucking tired*. Maybe if I close my eyes, the pain will go away.

"Ran! Look at me, please!"

I hear my brother's voice and I fight hard to open my eyes, to look at him, but his outline is blurred. I begin to cough again, unable to catch my breath, to get oxygen into my burning lungs.

"Just keep looking at me, okay? They're almost here, I promise. Just look at me. Stay with me!" he begs, his voice panicky.

I struggle to take another breath. It's futile; my lungs refuse to expand and I feel as though I'm drowning from the inside. Mercifully, just then all the pain subsides and I let my eyelids fall shut, a vision of Cat flashing before my mind's eye. But I can't hold on to it. I'm just too damn tired. So I give in to the darkness that drags me under, swallowing me whole while silence drowns out the noise around me.

I don't have to fight anymore. It's finally over.

Cat

I had the best morning. Admittedly, I was a little sad waking up this morning without Ronan by my side. I understand, of course, that he couldn't spend all night with me, that he needed to go home. But that doesn't mean I wouldn't have loved waking up in his arms again, my body conforming perfectly to his, feeling his warm skin on mine, maybe feel all of him again before we got the day started.

I lay there for a while, my head on the pillow he slept on for a few hours, his scent still lingering in the fibers of the soft fabric. I recalled last night, how I trusted him, how I gave myself to him completely. Ronan was so careful, so gentle. I anticipated some discomfort in the beginning, and when he first entered me, I felt too tight, overly full. For a moment, the burning pain made me doubt that I'd be able to accommodate Ronan's size. But then I forced myself to breathe, to relax, and I was pleasantly surprised to find it was much less painful than I had thought. He stopped as soon as he felt my body tense, giving me time to adjust to him, allowing me to set the pace. And, god, once I did and he began to push deeper into me, his body so close to mine, the feel of him was all-consuming. I swear I felt like I was flying.

Vada was right when she said I would feel even closer to Ronan after this. It was an act that required complete trust, complete vulnerability—not only on my part, but his as well. Ronan did not disappoint. It was everything; *Ronan* is everything.

Oh, and I can't even describe what it was like to see all of him for the first time. I truly thought it would be more awkward, but it was anything but. He's incredibly gorgeous. I mean, I knew that, obviously, but I had never seen him without at least shorts on. But last night, when he stood in front of me, naked and hard, I had never seen anything more arousing, anything more perfect. His muscles were wound so tightly, flexing, his skin so soft to touch.

I can't wait to venture further, to learn his body and mine, to discover what feels good to him. After all, so far Ronan has usually taken the initiative, has helped me explore my boundaries, my body. He's taken me to the highest of highs, but I have yet to really reciprocate. After last night, I'm ready to experience it all with him.

I'm giddy when I finally climb out of bed and get under the shower, knowing I'll see him in just a few short hours.

The sun is shining beautifully today and tryouts were amazing. The prospect of being with Ronan again in just a few short hours gave me wings, prompting even my coach to comment on my great form this morning.

"Sheesh, girl, you were on fire today!" Vada exclaims when we make our way back to her car after showering and changing. "I'm so hungover today, I could hardly get out of bed," she laughs, but her face looks pained. "How the heck do you have all this energy today?"

I hesitate for a moment while we get in her car and then turn to Vada. "I have to tell you something," I say, my heart hammering in my chest.

A knowing smile spreads across Vada's freckled face. "You and Ran had sex last night, didn't you?"

My mouth falls open. "Wait, how do you know?"

But then it's her turn to look surprised. "Are you for real? I was just joking! You guys had sex?" Her voice becomes higher and more excited with every word. "Tell me everything! How was it?"

I laugh but oblige, needing to share with someone. "Oh, Vada, it was everything. It felt so, so good, and Ran was so... perfect. He was gentle, and he took his time. He kept checking to make sure it's really what I wanted." I swoon, my mind wandering back to last night. "I honestly thought it would hurt more, or I would feel super self-conscious, but I felt so safe with him, and..." I trail off.

Vada smiles broadly at me, her eyes bright. "Kitty Cat, I'm so excited for you! Oh my gosh, I can't believe you guys finally did it. How did this even happen?"

"I don't know. I was finally ready to be with him like that, and then one thing led to another. And it was perfect. God, it felt so incredible," I say, letting my head fall against the headrest, closing my eyes as I picture Ronan in my mind. "Vada, I love him."

I let the last sentence sit in the space, big, and loud and clear.

I didn't think it was possible, but Vada's smile gets even bigger. "Did you tell him that?" she asks, trying to focus on the road but unable to stop herself from grinning at me.

I shake my head. "Not yet, but I don't think I'll be able to hold it in much longer," I admit, feeling my nerves. I don't know why I'm so nervous about telling Ronan how I feel about him. I don't think he would cut and run because I told him I loved him. But it still feels like a big thing to me. I've never told anyone that I loved them, except for my family, of course. Then again, I haven't loved anyone who wasn't part of my family. I was infatuated with Adam, sure, but the relationship never blossomed into love for obvious reasons, and also because we never did have the connection I have with Ronan. It's like our souls found each other.

"Then don't hold it in. He obviously loves you, Kitty Cat," she says. "I mean, he hasn't told me this, but I can just tell. That boy would do anything for you. I bet he's thinking the exact same thing right now, that he loves you and that he needs to tell you already."

I smile at that thought. "You really think so?" I ask, needing to assure myself.

"Definitely. I've never seen him like this. The way he looks at you, the way he acts around you, I've never seen him so happy," she says. "Even when you're not around, he's just different. More content, not so restless. Like he's finally stopped searching."

"I feel the same way," I say out loud, but more to myself than Vada. "It feels like I've finally arrived."

***

I'm giddy when we pull up to Shane's at just before 11:30 a.m., though I don't see Ronan's car. Steve explains that Ronan was inexplicably tired this morning, then winks at me. When Zack announces that he needs to run home to grab a charger for his camera to be able to fully capture this last Saturday of summer, Steve suggests driving him and picking up Ronan on the way back here.

"We should be back in like an hour," Steve promises, and he and Zack walk to the car.

Vada and I join our friends on the deck, where I lounge on the large rattan outdoor sofa overlooking the ocean. Summer excitedly tells us that there's a rumor going around that the hockey coach has a thing with the softball coach, and we all dive into a conversation about how we've all been noticing signs that there might be something going on between the two of them.

It's about half an hour later when Summer's phone starts buzzing. I don't pay too much attention when she gets up off her spot on the sofa and takes a few steps away from the group, which is still chatting excitedly, the conversation having evolved to include other teacher-teacher or even teacher-student affair rumors. But then Summer hangs up the phone and returns to us, her eyes huge. All color has drained from her face.

Everyone falls quiet at once.

"What's wrong?" Tori is the first to ask.

"Zack is driving Steve to the hospital," Summer says, her voice shaky.

Vada jumps up, eyes wide, her voice frantic. "What happened? Is Stevie okay?" Vada half yells as everyone else stands up, too, ready to leave the house and go wherever it is we need to go.

But Summer's eyes lock on mine as she shakes her head. "It's not Steve. It's Ran. I don't know what happened; Zack just said it's really bad and they took him by ambulance to the hospital. Zack and Steve are heading there now."

The silence that follows is deafening, interrupted only by my heart beating hard in my chest and my frantic breathing. My mind begins to race, trying to come up with an idea of what could have happened to Ronan. Did he get into an accident?

Shane is the first one to break the silence. "What the fuck are we standing around here for? Let's go!" He herds everyone through the house and out the front door. On our way down the stairs and out to the driveway, Shane provides directions. "Let's just take my Jeep. We can figure out everything else later," Shane instructs, and we hurry toward his car. Tori slides into the passenger seat of Shane's spacious Wrangler, while Summer, Vada, and I hop into the backseat.

"Breathe, Kitty Cat, I'm sure Ran is going to be fine," Vada says, willing her voice to be soothing, although I can tell she's worried.

I only manage a meager nod, but I focus to slow my breathing down. It's threatening to turn into hyperventilation.

"What exactly did Zack say?" Shane asks, glancing at Summer through the rearview mirror while navigating the freeway at a brisk speed.

"Not much," Summer says. "He just said that Ran is hurt really badly and was taken to the hospital by ambulance. He said we should get there quickly. He didn't say anything else."

"But he didn't say how Ran got hurt?" Shane asks, an edge to his voice and a strange look on his face as he voices the exact question I keep asking myself.

"I swear, Shane. He didn't say a damn thing more," Summer snaps, but immediately apologizes for being on edge.

Shane stays silent while Vada, Tori, and Summer start throwing out theories about what could have happened to Ronan.

"Maybe he fell or something," Vada suggests, her brows creased. "I mean, that would make sense, right? Seems like he's kind of prone to that with the random bruises and stuff?"

"I don't know," Shane says, unconvinced.

I just cradle my head in my hands, hoping to wake up from this terrible nightmare. The fact that whatever happened to Ronan was obviously bad enough to require him to go to the hospital and for Zack to tell us to get to the hospital quickly scares me. Couple that with Shane's weird expression, the tension in his jaw and shoulders visible, and I feel positively anxious.

After what seems like an eternity, Shane pulls up to the ER, most definitely parking in a handicap parking spot but obviously not caring about the risk of getting towed. I will my feet to follow the others when they walk through the automatic doors of the ER. My senses are instantly bombarded with the sounds, sights, and smells of a hospital. Phones ring and a baby cries in the background as a doctor is paged over the intercom system. I close my eyes and swallow hard, my knees shaking. Vada takes my hand, gently tugging me onward.

Shane, ever the leader of the group, makes his way to the reception desk where a sturdy-looking brunette and an older, graying woman are thumbing through paperwork, answering questions and phone calls, too busy to acknowledge us.

A set of glass doors slides open to the left of the reception desk and Zack walks toward us, his phone glued to his ear. He looks terrible. He spots us and starts toward us, motioning for us to follow him back through the glass doors toward a private waiting area away from the chaos of the ER waiting room.

"What happened?" Shane asks after Zack hangs up the phone.

"I have no idea, man," Zack says, looking bewildered, shaking his head. "It's so fucking surreal. Steve and I stopped by my house, grabbed the charger, and then headed to Steve's to pick up Ran. We could hear Onyx in the backyard going absolutely crazy, barking like mad, and when we walked in the house we heard weird sounds coming from the living room, like these relentless thuds, like someone was kicking something, and when we turned the corner..." He pauses, his eyebrows knitted, his lips pressed together.

We all wait for him to finish.

"It was his mom," Zack finally says. But this makes no sense. Apparently, I'm not the only one confused.

"What?" Tori says, her voice shrill. "What do you mean it was his mom?"

"Ran was lying on the ground and his mom was kicking him... hard... over and over and over." His teeth clench as he describes the scene, and I can feel the bile rise in the back of my throat, threatening to bring me to my knees.

"And then she stomped on Ran's rib cage. Steve pushed her away. God, there was so much blood. And..." Zack trails off.

"God, fuck, FUCK!" Shane groans, raking his hand through his strawberry blond hair, and the look on his face, the way his features contort with agony, makes me think things are worse than I can even comprehend right now.

"What about Ran?" I finally manage weakly.

Everyone turns to look at me as if surprised I'm still here.

"Cat," Zack says, almost apologetically, as if it's all his fault, "Ran was coughing up blood. He couldn't breathe. Steve tried to move him, but that made it worse. I called the ambulance. It was all in slow motion. I just stood there, waiting for the medics to get there. Steve was on the floor next to Ran, screaming at him to keep breathing, but... he couldn't. He just kept coughing and there was so much blood." Zack diverts his eyes. "He stopped breathing," Zack says, finality in his tone.

A feral sound of pain escapes my throat and my knees buckle. It's official; I'm hyperventilating, my surroundings fading in and out as my vision blurs and my head spins.

Shane is by my side in an instant, his arms supporting me. "Come on, let's find a place to sit," he says stoically, holding me tightly against him.

We follow Zack into a private waiting room. Shane supports my weight with every step I take, and Vada hovers on the other side, talking softly to me. Everything around me is hazy. How can this be? Confusion, pain, fear, anger—everything clashes in me at once and I don't know what to say or do.

When we enter the small, brightly lit room, Steve is sitting in one of the black plastic-and-metal chairs. His face is buried in his hands. I notice the bloody stains—Ronan's blood—on his shirt and rush to his side and hug him. To my surprise, Frank—Steve and Ronan's dad—is standing there, facing a doctor dressed in navy-blue scrubs. Ronan didn't mention his dad was home.

The doctor stops talking when we enter.

"They're all friends, Doctor Roberts. You can continue," Frank says, his jaw tense. He sounds anxious and on edge, his arms crossed in front of his solid chest. I wonder how much he knows about what happened.

I look around the sparsely furnished waiting area. There are a few chairs, a couch, and a small TV mounted in the corner by the ceiling. It's off and there are no sounds except for the doctor speaking and a buzzing coming from a light board on the wall to the left of me.

"We're prepping him for surgery right now," Doctor Roberts says calmly. "Once we get in we should get an even better idea of how much damage we're dealing with. CTs and X-rays can only tell us so much, especially in regard to internal bleeding."

Internal bleeding? I sit, feeling as though I'm having an out-of-body experience. This can't be real, it just can't. This must be a bad dream, and I want nothing more than to wake up right now.

Everyone's eyes are on Doctor Roberts, the air tense as we begin to understand the extent of Ronan's injuries. Doctor Roberts pins a number of X-rays to the light board, and although I'm obviously not a doctor, I can immediately tell it's bad.

Doctor Roberts inhales deeply. "Okay, so I'll just take you top to bottom," she starts, tapping on an X-ray that clearly shows Ronan's head. "Ronan has an orbital fracture right here." Doctor Roberts points to an area right under Ronan's left eye.

My hands are clammy and cold, and I try to pay attention to my breathing, to control my inhales and exhales and not hyperventilate again. I'm no good to anyone if I pass out now.

"The craniofacial surgeon is going to determine whether this will require surgical repair once we have Ronan cleaned up in the OR. Right now, the lacerations and swelling are making it hard to see the extent of the damage and if there's displacement of the bone, but we'll get that figured out. He'll need stitches for his left eyebrow laceration and the one below his left eye and the one on the back of his head. His broken nose will heal on its own."

I have a hard time imagining Ronan with these injuries, only able to picture him the way he looked last night, when I last saw him: his full lips; his intense, green eyes; his lean body perfect, conforming to mine, uninjured, whole.

"Okay, so that's the head." Doctor Roberts removes the X-ray of Ronan's skull and pins a new image to the light board.

I hadn't realized an image could create such horror until now. My heart squeezes painfully at the sight of the image of the obviously fractured ribs. At first glance, it seems Ronan's entire rib cage is shattered. All I can do is clamp my hands tightly over my lips, stifling the sound of pain that wants to escape my mouth, and I am eternally grateful for Shane as he moves his arm up and around my shoulder, pulling me against him again. His body feels as tense as mine as we sit and listen and begin to understand just how badly hurt Ronan really is.

Doctor Roberts dives right in, confirming what I had already known—that the injuries to Ronan's chest are horrendous. "This is what concerns me the most. There are twenty-four ribs in the human body; from what we're able to tell, seventeen of Ronan's are broken in thirty-two places. Also, do you see that here?" she asks, circling an opaque area on the left side of Ronan's chest. "That's his left lung. It shouldn't look like that—this is an indication of a large pneumothorax; his lung has collapsed. There's some damage to his right lung as well, but it appears to be less severe than his left. He has some internal abdominal bleeding, but we're not sure yet where it originates; it's hard to see sources of bleeding on X-rays and CTs, but his chest and the internal bleeding will be the first order of business because these injuries put a lot of stress on Ronan's heart."

Everyone remains silent as Doctor Roberts looks around the room, waiting for questions before she changes out the X-rays again.

"Ronan's left shoulder is separated, and his left hand is broken; but when I consulted with Doctor Naveen—the orthopedic surgeon who's scrubbing in with me—he didn't think that the hand would require surgical repair. But"—Doctor Roberts pins up a new X-ray—"Ronan's right kneecap is a different story. There was obviously significant blunt-force trauma to his knee, because the patella is completely shattered. Doctor Naveen is going to do an open reduction-internal fixation—he'll go in and put the kneecap back together with some hardware. This injury is likely going to take the longest to heal—we're talking months here—and usually comes with some fairly significant physical limitations. If Ronan was a professional athlete, this would be career-ending."

"Is he going to be okay, though? Like, he's gonna make it, right?" Shane breaks the silence, his voice strained, grating against gritted teeth, and we all look at him. His face is full of fear, pain, and worry for his best friend.

Doctor Roberts' face is warm and full of empathy as she presses her lips together before speaking. "I can't lie, Ronan is pretty sick right now. But we're going to do absolutely everything we can to get him through this," she says compassionately, though her response doesn't really ease my anxiety.

"How long do you anticipate the surgery to take?" Frank asks. He's dressed in jeans and a fitted, dark-gray long-sleeved Henley, emphasizing his broad, muscular frame, which honestly looks like it's weighed down by a million pounds of lead. His handsome, masculine face is grief-stricken.

"I'm not sure exactly how long it'll take, but judging by what we know so far, probably in excess of eight hours. I'll send in a nurse to give you periodic updates."

Frank nods. "Thank you."

Doctor Roberts flashes a little smile, making sure to make eye contact with each of us before leaving the room in her clean scrubs.

***

The next hours seem endless.

Frank paces the room, too restless to sit, making several phone calls, his voice clipped, tense. He makes Steve and Zack retell the story multiple times. Steve makes it through the first part of the story, but his voice constricts and he's unable to continue every time he gets to the part where he sees his mother standing over Ronan's broken body curled up on the floor, desperate to shield himself from her relentless violence. The way Steve describes his mom, it doesn't sound like she's human. According to Steve, all compassion was gone from her eyes when he rushed over and shoved her away from Ronan.

"Steve pushed her down and she just sat there, not moving a damn muscle," Zack explains, his voice strained and cracking here and there. "He yelled at me to call an ambulance, and I did. Ran was coughing up blood and he was having a hard time taking a breath. Steve kept talking to Ran, telling him to keep breathing, to look at him. And Ronan tried so hard, he fucking fought for his life, but I could tell he was losing, and then he stopped breathing. And the 911 operator told Steve to do CPR, and she walked him through it and he fucking did it until the EMTs got there and shocked Ran's heart.... This is all so fucking surreal," Zack says as my chest tightens around my already-aching heart.

Frank wants to know whether we had any knowledge of issues between Ronan and his mom, and even though a couple of us mention that the relationship seemed strained, we all deny knowledge of any physical altercations. Everyone except Steve and Shane, who admit they knew that Ronan had been hit before.

Steve explains that when he was a lot younger, he had witnessed a few altercations between Ronan and his mother, but that had been years ago. Shane, though, seemingly collapses into himself, utterly devastated as he tells Frank of the times over just the last few months when Ronan confided in him, told him that his mom had hurt him, showed him his bruises.

"I kept telling him he needed to tell someone, but he always fought me on it. God, *I* should have told someone," Shane says, running his hands roughly across his face.

It hits me then that I was already with Ronan when his mother was hurting him, and I rack my brain for clues, hints, and signs of the abuse he was enduring while we were together. Moments flash before my mind when I noticed a bruise here, a cut there, and suddenly everything falls into place—the way he looked when someone brought up his mother, the random injuries for which he always seemed to have an explanation, his reluctance to bring me home with him, the sharp tone in which his mom spoke to him.

She had been hurting him all along, and I had no idea.

I'm angry at myself for not checking in with him. I'm also angry at Ronan. Angry that he never told me. Why didn't he say something? Why didn't he trust me? There's anger at Steve for not knowing, anger at Shane for knowing something was wrong and not saying anything, anger at Frank for not protecting his son, and so, so much overwhelming anger at Ronan's mother for doing what she did. But what's more potent than the anger is the fear, the worry, the sadness, the pain residing in my head and heart as the seconds, the minutes, and hours tick by. God, I need him to be okay; please just let him be okay.

A nurse comes in periodically to give us updates, scaring the shit out of us when she informs us that Ronan's heart stopped beating, but they were able to resuscitate him. She says he's stable—for now.

Shane calls his dad, letting him know what happened. Then he hands the phone to Frank, who speaks with Shane's dad for a long time while Shane tells me that his dad and Frank are close friends. Even Vada and Zack's dad, Jay, stops by to see if Frank needs anything. He tells Steve to stay at their house for a while so he doesn't have to go home and Frank can stay with Ronan at the hospital for as long as he needs. Vada immediately informs her dad that I'll be staying with them, too, since my mom won't return from North Carolina until tomorrow morning.

I'm beyond grateful for my friends right now. I don't want to be alone tonight.

I call my mom and break the news to her. She is devastated, and of course wants to drive back home immediately. I assure her that I'll be with Vada tonight and that she should drive home, safely, tomorrow.

At around four o'clock, two police officers show up and talk to Frank, Zack, and Steve in private. When Frank returns to the waiting area, he briefly informs us, matter-of-factly, that Steve and Ronan's mother has been arrested. The mood in the waiting area shifts as the time passes, anxious energy turning to somberness and eventually restlessness.

***

By the time Doctor Roberts finally comes back to give us a status update, it's almost midnight. Ronan has been in surgery for close to eleven hours and everyone's nerves are frayed. The past twelve hours have felt surreal and I feel very on edge, my body under tension, my muscles wound like guitar strings. Every time someone dressed in scrubs passed by the glass door to the waiting area, everyone's heads snapped up just to be disappointed that we still hadn't had any news.

Doctor Roberts looks tired when she enters the waiting room, dressed in fresh scrubs. I grab and squeeze Shane's hand, jumping up from my chair at the sight of the doctor, my heart beating more rapidly, my hands tingly and clammy with nerves. *Oh god, please let it be good news.*

"How is he?" Frank asks, ceasing his back-and-forth pacing. His shoulders and jaw are tight, and there's a look on his face only a parent in this type of situation can have.

"He's doing okay," Doctor Roberts says intently, pulling out a new set of X-rays and pinning them to the light board.

"He made it through?" Shane asks, apparently in need of plain-language confirmation that Ronan is still alive, still breathing.

Doctor Roberts nods, and the smallest of smiles appears on her lips. "He made it through."

Shane exhales audibly. His hand is still in mine and probably drained of all blood by now because I'm squeezing it so tightly.

My throat is painfully dry when Doctor Roberts flips the switch of the light board and the LED lights illuminate the pictures of Ronan's bones. I scan them with hectic, untrained eyes, feeling the pressure in my chest decrease a little when I notice that the fractures no longer appear ragged and displaced. Instead, what appear to be metal plates and screws adorn Ronan's ribs and his right knee.

"We were able to internally fix a good number of his ribs. A few of them will have to heal on their own. Luckily only two ribs splintered, which greatly decreases the chance of any additional internal bleeding," she explains, pointing at Ronan's rib cage.

Okay, one concern down; a million more to go.

"His lungs are both functioning again, although he gave us a bit of a scare during the surgery."

What kind of scare? Did he stop breathing again like Zack said Ronan did after his mom broke his ribs? Was this the moment the nurse informed us about—the moment Ronan's heart stopped beating?

"We have him intubated right now and will keep him that way for a couple of days, just to make sure his body is recovering okay."

I listen intently, as does everyone else, not wanting to interrupt Doctor Roberts' summation of the repairs they performed on Ronan's body.

"He has a large number of cuts on his body, especially on his back and on his right side. We had to pull embedded shards of glass out of his skin, but none of the cuts required stitches," Doctor Roberts adds.

I'm trying to picture it all in my mind's eye: Ronan's injuries, his broken and bleeding body, but it's apparently too shocking, because I cannot for the life of me envision Ronan so hurt, so injured, on the brink of death. I don't even understand where these cuts Doctor Roberts is speaking about are from. Surreal, dreamlike, nightmarish—none of these words come close to describing how this afternoon and evening have felt, how this exact moment feels.

"The bleeding we saw on the imaging came from his spleen, which we removed; it was ruptured and his blood pressure tanked. We couldn't save it. The risk of toxicity was too great at this stage. He'll be fine without it. We'll put him on broad-spectrum antibiotics for a few days to lower the risk of infection. The spleen is an organ that helps our immune system fight bacteria. Ronan's system received quite a shock, and with surgeries and then long-term recovery, there's always a greater chance of infection.

"As far as Ronan's left arm is concerned, his shoulder and hand did not require surgery. With regard to his right knee, we inserted a titanium plate that will stay in place for the rest of his life. His facial injuries are basically surface-only, with the exception of the orbital fracture under his left eye and his broken nose. We did end up inserting a small plate to repair his orbital fracture. We didn't see a traumatic brain injury on the CTs, but it's safe to say that, given the extent of his head and facial injuries, he probably suffered a pretty nasty concussion, so once he wakes up he'll have headaches for some time. He's stable now."

Frank lets out an audible sigh, his shoulders tense as he examines the black-and-white images on the light board, comparing the now-repaired fractures to the violently splintered bones on the X-rays taken only hours earlier.

"Can we see him?" I finally ask, my voice cracking and raw like I haven't spoken in days. Shane gives my hand a little squeeze.

"Yes. He was moved to the ICU ten minutes ago. We typically only allow a maximum of three people in the rooms, but we'll make an exception for you. I know you're all anxious to see him."

We follow Doctor Roberts out of the waiting area and toward the elevators.

"Is Ran awake?" Shane asks, holding Tori's hand tightly while I walk beside her through the wide, brightly lit hospital corridor.

"No." Doctor Roberts shakes her head. "His body went through a lot of trauma. There's no telling when he'll wake up. That's completely up to him."

But he will wake up, right? He has to.

No one speaks while we take the elevator to the intensive care unit on the seventh floor, and Doctor Roberts leads us through a set of double doors secured via an intercom and down another brightly lit corridor. We pass a number of rooms, all walled off by glass, curtains drawn. We finally arrive at Ronan's room, where a young nurse greets us with a smile.

"I'm Jessica. I'll be Ronan's night nurse. Let me know if you need anything at all," she says warmly, and the tension in everyone's shoulders eases just a little.

Doctor Roberts slides the glass door open and enters the room, followed by Frank and the rest of us. I'm so anxious to see Ronan, but when I finally lay eyes on him, my heart stops. I cover my mouth with both hands, suffocating the cry of shock and pain forming in the back of my throat.

Ronan looks nothing less than broken. His bare chest is beaten and battered; hues of scarlet red and the darkest blue spread across his ribs, punctuated by various-sized cuts and abrasions all over his arms, shoulders, and torso. A large bandage covers the fresh incision on his left ribs, while a smaller bandage covers a surgical incision by his abdominal muscles. He's hooked up to a number of machines that monitor his heart rate, blood pressure, oxygen levels, and other vitals. His face is unrecognizably swollen and bruised, and there's a large cut on both his upper and lower lips. The entire left eye, brow, and cheekbone of Ronan's handsome face are concealed by a white bandage. His cheek and forehead are violently bruised. His left hand has been wrapped tightly. A white sheet covers his lower body, but it's obvious that his right knee and leg are immobilized by some kind of brace. An IV is connected to his right hand, and Ronan's body is completely still with the exception of his chest rising and falling mechanically, unnaturally, aided by yet another machine that pumps air into his lungs. If I didn't know it was Ronan lying in that hospital bed, I wouldn't be able to say for certain that it was him. His handsome, masculine features are so distorted by the dark bruising, the cuts, the swelling, and the bandages.

"God, fuck," Shane whispers against gritted teeth, his voice cracking, face white as a ghost.

Vada cries as Steve holds her, looking pale and worn out.

I want to move, want to hold Ronan's hand, but I'm frozen, unable to will my feet forward. The pain in my heart constricts my chest, making it hard to breathe.

Frank moves around the bed to Ronan's right hand and takes it into his own. "Hey buddy," he whispers to his youngest son. "I'm here." Frank addresses Doctor Roberts. "Can he hear us?"

Doctor Roberts smiles. "We're not sure. Some people strongly believe that individuals in a comatose state can hear and perceive their loved ones; others argue there's no science to back it up. Personally, I think people heal better and faster when they're surrounded by people they love. So, talk to him as much as you want."

It's going to be a shock every time I see him like this, and I silently beg for him to wake up soon so I can hear his voice again. It doesn't feel as though we were together only yesterday, that we made love for the first time only twenty-four hours ago. He was perfect, happy, and so full of life.

Frank gently asks us to leave the hospital only a few minutes later, urging us to get rest, to let Ronan rest. Everyone takes their turn taking Ronan's hand, whispering to him, telling him to be strong, to fight, to wake up.

"I'm so sorry, Ran. I'm so sorry," I hear Shane whisper to Ronan, choking on his words when it's my turn.

I take my time, holding Ronan's hand—which is cool to the touch, but just as soft as it was yesterday when it caressed my body—studying his injured, deformed features.

"Please come back to me," I plead quietly. "Please. I have to tell you something important," I say, wishing his eyes would open, eager for me to tell him that I'm in love with him. That I've been in the love with him since the moment I met him. But this isn't a movie, and Ronan's eyes don't open. His body remains still, almost lifeless, with the exception of the rise and fall of his chest. I gently kiss the palm of his hand before resting it on the bed.

Vada takes my hand in hers. "Come on, Kitty Cat. Let's try to get some rest."

Frank settles on the small loveseat across from Ronan's bed and we agree that Steve and I will be back at the hospital first thing in the morning.

***

On our way to Zack and Vada's, we stop first by my house so I can grab a few things. I give my mom another call, even though it's late, to tell her I'm alright and that I'll be at the hospital tomorrow. She's worried about me—I can hear it in her voice—and I have a hard time reassuring her that I'm feeling okay because, quite honestly, I'm not. My whole world has been turned upside down from one minute to the next.

In my room I walk over to my bed, still unmade from last night, and spot the pillow Ronan's head lay on before he left me not twenty-four hours ago. I grab it as I sit down on the edge of my bed and bury my face in it, inhaling his scent—sun, ocean air, fresh linens, and that special something that belongs only to him. It's so masculine, so warm, and so, so comforting.

Images from last night reappear in my mind and, finally, uncontrollably, I begin to sob, my cries like wails echoing through the night. Even when someone's warm arms pull me in toward a warm body, holding me against a strong shoulder, my sobs don't let up until a good fifteen minutes later. My body shakes and I breathe erratically as hot tears spill from my eyes and down my cheeks where they soak into the soft fabric of the pillow. I'm drowning in sorrow, the emotional pain making my body ache, threatening to rip me apart.

Eventually I'm able to rein it in and finally realize that it's Steve who has been holding me, letting me cry on his shoulder. His face carries an expression of the pain I've been feeling, and I hug him tightly while Zack and Vada look on.

"He's going to be okay," Steve whispers, his voice strained.

I nod, even though I don't know if it's true. I don't move, letting Steve hold me while Vada silently gathers a few of my things and stuffs them in a bag.

"Ready?" Zack asks, his voice heavy and thick with the stress of today's events. He must be exhausted.

Together, the four of us make our way to the car as Steve continues to hold on to me, and I to him. I'm really not sure who's supporting whom, but I draw on his strength to keep me moving. My mind and my body are heavy, and they only get heavier when I notice us pulling up to Steve's house.

"I'll be right back," Steve says, sounding hesitant as he opens the car door.

"I'll go with you," Zack volunteers, and Steve gives him a grateful nod.

"I'm coming, too," Vada says resolutely, unbuckling her seatbelt. She turns to me and puts her hand gently on mine. "Are you okay waiting here?" she asks, her eyes full of concern.

I contemplate this question. "Yeah," I say briefly.

She nods and gets out of the car, taking Steve's hand. Together, the three of them enter the house and I'm left sitting in the car. The silence is smothering, and in the solitude all my thoughts come crashing down on me, threatening to suffocate me as they weigh on my chest. Without thinking, I unbuckle my own seatbelt, open the car door, and move out of the car and toward the house.

The scene that awaits me inside when I stupidly round the corner to the living room is almost too much to bear. I can only imagine the struggle that took place here. There's broken glass all over the floor among the splintered remnants of the coffee table. Dark-red—almost black—blood is soaked into the rug. It's dried into the fibers and staining the wooden floor. My eyes find the fractured wood of Ronan's hockey stick, and I immediately understand that his mom must have beaten him with it. I'm sick to my stomach.

It looks as though a war was fought here, and picturing Ronan lying in his own blood, not breathing, hurts more than I could have imagined. I'm frozen to the spot, taking in the gruesome scene, imagining Ronan all alone, fighting for his life while I was sitting by the beach with our friends, laughing about some stupid rumors.

I flinch when I feel a hand on my shoulder. "You shouldn't have come in here," Steve says heavily. I don't move, too shocked by what has taken place here.

"I had no idea," I finally say, my voice cracking as my eyes roam the living room floor, the glass and fractured wood, noting a blue latex glove the EMTs must have left behind along with other evidence of them stabilizing Ronan enough to get him to the hospital. "He never said anything." I choke back the bile that burns hot in my throat. "Why didn't he ever say anything?" I ask, searching Steve's eyes for answers.

Steve only shakes his head, his eyes lost, sad, and tired. "I don't know," he says wearily, and takes my hand in his. "Let's go, Cat. There's nothing more we can do tonight. Let's get some sleep so we can see Ran first thing in the morning."

I nod and turn around, leaving the scene behind, knowing my life will be forever changed.

***

I barely sleep that night, and I sneak out of Vada's room and down to the kitchen around 3 a.m. Apparently Steve's mind is as heavy as mine because I find him sitting on the kitchen counter with his head in his hands. There's an open bottle of whiskey on the counter next to him, which he must have snuck from Zack and Vada's dad's liquor cabinet. Steve is wearing a white shirt and sweatpants. His hair is disheveled, and I'm struck by just how much he looks like his little brother. Steve doesn't have Ronan's green eyes or his dark-blond hair, but they have the same nose and strong jawline, and their eyes have the same shape, just like their dad's. Still, no one will ever come close to the perfection that is Ronan.

Steve looks up when he hears me walk barefoot into the kitchen. "Can't sleep either, huh?" He gives me a tired smile. His eyes are red, and I wonder if he was crying.

"No," I say quietly, hoisting myself up on to the kitchen counter next to Steve. He immediately puts his arm around me and pulls me close. He doesn't share Ronan's scent, either. Where Ronan smells like a warm, sunny afternoon at the beach, Steve's scent is reminiscent of a woodsy mountain hike. But the warmth of Steve's body is comforting.

"How are you doing?" he asks, still holding me.

"I feel like I'm trapped in a bad dream."

He lets out a quiet chuckle. "That's a great description, and I completely agree with you. I mean, one minute he's good and then I get home and he's on the floor, struggling to breathe, lying in a pool of blood with my mother standing over him like she's the devil's bride."

I feel him shaking his head in disbelief. "I should have insisted he get up and leave with me in the morning," he says, and I gently push my shoulder against him, wanting him to stop blaming himself. "He said he needed a couple more hours of sleep...." Steve trails off as a grin tugs at his lips, and he turns his head toward me. "Ran got in really late last night. I take it you two had your very own little birthday celebration?" The grin has now turned into a full-fledged smile.

I blush in the dark. "I guess so." My cheeks feel hot as I remember last night—Ronan's hands on my body, how it felt when he was inside me.

Steve observes me for a long moment. "Listen, I think you should know that Ran has never cared for anyone the way he cares about you. I've never seen him as happy as I have these past few months. It's like you've made him come alive. And I can guarantee you that if... *when* Ran comes out of this, it will be because of you. You gave him a reason, Cat."

I tilt my head to the side, looking Steve in the eyes as the lump in my throat grows. I want to say something, thank him, but instead I begin to cry once more. Steve pulls me tighter toward him, his arms encircling me, his chin resting on my head while he lets me sob.

"I didn't get to tell him that I love him," I finally choke out. "I wanted him to say it first, and now I may never know," I say between sobs, which are becoming heavier as I think about Ronan and what he means to me.

Steve rubs his hands up and down my back. "You can't talk like that; he's going to be okay," he chokes, and I realize now that Steve is crying, too.

I wrap my arms around him, hoping to be able to comfort him as he comforts me. We hold each other a while longer, and when I've cried my last tear for the moment, I pull back, my eyes puffy and tired.

"Let's try to get a little more sleep," Steve suggests, his face tear-stained, and I nod, hopping off the counter. Steve holds my hand all the way back up to Vada's room, and I'm so glad he's here with me, sharing the pain.

"Wake me as soon as you're awake," I make Steve promise. Then I sneak back into Vada's room, and Steve back into Zack's.

Sunday, August 29th

Cat

Steve doesn't have to wake me this morning. We emerge simultaneously from our respective bedrooms—already dressed and ready to go—by the time the sun rises. We get to the hospital at seven, leaving the house before either Vada or Zack are awake.

I didn't think it was possible, but in the daylight that streams in through the large window to the right of Ronan's hospital bed, Ronan's injuries look a thousand times worse than they did just hours ago. His bruises are darker, his face even more swollen. His chest is blue and purple, making it obvious that a majority of his ribs are broken. It takes me a few seconds to jumpstart my breathing and fully enter the room.

It's obvious that Frank spent the entire night with Ronan; he's still wearing the same clothes he came to the hospital in yesterday. His hair is messy, dark circles sit under his eyes, and his chin is scruffy.

He tells Steve and me that he got only a couple hours of sleep on the small loveseat against the wall. "I was terrified that if I closed my eyes, Ran would slip away for good," Frank says, his eyes heavy, gaze hollow. "So, I just sat next to him, held his hand, talked to him," he sighs.

Steve tries to convince his dad to go home for a few hours, take a shower, maybe get some sleep. It's as though Steve is the adult right now, responsible beyond his years. While the two talk, I pull a chair to Ronan's bedside and carefully take his unbandaged but IV-riddled right hand into mine. His skin is startlingly cold, a stark contrast to the warmth that usually radiates off him.

I cover his hand with both of mine, wanting to share my body heat with him, hoping that, just like in fairy tales, this will make him open his gorgeous green eyes.

"I miss you," I whisper, and place a small kiss on his palm, the one place that doesn't have needles sticking into his skin or is covered by bandages. Even so, his palm is bruised and cut up, which I imagine is from all the broken glass he must have been lying in. I force the images of Ronan being beaten out of my mind and instead lay my head onto his bed, right next to his hand. He doesn't smell the way he did when I fell asleep next to him the last time. The smell of disinfectant and hospital clings to his skin and, once again, I wish for him to wake up.

Only when Shane—who looks like he was up all night—walks into the room is Steve able to convince his dad to go home for a little bit. Both boys promise they'll call Frank if anything changes with Ronan.

"Fuck, is it me, or does Ran look even worse today?" Shane asks quietly as he stands behind me, looking down at his best friend.

"He looks worse," Steve agrees matter-of-factly from across the room, and I nod in agreement with the both of them.

"How long have you known?" Steve asks Shane, his eyes on him. "How long have you known about my mom hurting Ran?"

Shane hesitates for a moment, his shoulders heavy. "I found out in February," he says, his voice low and full of guilt.

"You've known for six months that my mom was doing this shit to Ran?" Steve asks with an edge to his voice as he stands.

"Yeah... No... I mean..." Shane stammers. He looks absolutely devastated.

"And you didn't fucking tell anyone?" Steve growls.

"Dude, I had no idea how fucking bad it was. Ran didn't talk about any of this; I only found out by accident, and—"

"That doesn't fucking matter, Shane," Steve shouts.

"Whoa, man, you lived with him! Instead of laying into me, why don't you ask yourself how it was possible for you to *not* know what Ran was going through?" Shane snarls.

Steve looks like Shane shoved a dagger straight into his heart. "I don't fucking know, okay? And it's eating me up. But, fuck, you did know! And you didn't say a fucking thing to anyone. How could you let this happen?"

"Guys!" I say loudly, without letting go of Ronan's hand. "Stop it. Shane didn't let anything happen."

"How can you say that, Cat?" Steve snaps at me. "Shane knew my mom was hurting Ran and he didn't say anything to anyone."

"Man, I wanted to. I told Ran he needed to say something, but he just fought me on it," Shane shouts at Steve.

"And you listened to him? You should have told me at least. He's my little brother!"

"Steve!" I hiss at him. "This isn't Shane's fault, okay? It's nobody's fault. I know you're angry and sad and all that, but this isn't helping. We all feel helpless; we all want Ran to wake up and be okay. Shane did nothing wrong; nobody did, except for your mom. Do you think Ran would want you guys fighting? I can guarantee you that the answer is no, so please stop it!" I plead with them, my voice cracking.

"Man, you don't think I'm beating myself up over this?" Shane says, defeated. "I wish I had done things differently, trust me. I feel like total shit. Ran is my best friend. Fuck, he's like my little brother, too, and I didn't..." Shane trails off, his face anguished.

I can feel the pain emanating from him, and I finally stand to hug him. "Don't do this to each other," I beg them. "We can't fall apart now. Please!"

"Sorry, man," Steve chokes after several long moments of silence. He runs his hands roughly across his face. "I just don't know what to do. I can't believe I didn't know.... How could I miss this?" Steve asks us, his voice tight. The look on his face resembles a lost child calling out for help, but we don't have the answers either. I let go of Shane and walk over to Steve, giving him a hug now, trying to provide as much comfort as possible in the midst of my own pain. "I just don't understand," Steve says, his face buried in his hands.

Shane joins us on the loveseat, patting Steve's back while I hug him. There's nothing any of us can say or do to make sense of the situation, to change the past, to make Ronan wake up. So the three of us just sit in silence, drowning in our own and each other's pain.

***

Frank returns to the hospital only a few hours later. Though he obviously took a shower and changed his clothes, he doesn't look like he slept or got any rest at all. The dark circles under his eyes are pronounced. With him is one of the police officers who came to the hospital to take Steve's and Zack's statements the day before.

"I want to make sure to document your son's injuries. One of the nurses took photographs for us yesterday, but days two, three, and four are always best because injuries tend to show more clearly then. Bruising takes a while to set in," the officer explains, and we watch in silence as he carefully takes pictures of Ronan's injuries, meticulously capturing each bruise, each cut, each laceration.

"I'll probably be back to take more pictures in a couple of days," the officer explains when he's finished photographing Ronan's broken body. "That reminds me," he says. "The nurse handed me a bag with your son's clothes. They're stained and pretty destroyed since they had to cut them off his body, but in the bag was also this." He pulls Ronan's necklace with the two gold pendants out of his pocket, holding it up. "I thought you might want this back."

He hands the necklace to Frank.

"Thanks." Frank carefully holds Ronan's necklace in his right hand, studying it while his left hand traces the pendants. He seems lost in thought for a moment, his eyes soft, reflecting a variety of emotions—sadness, pain, love—before he looks up at me as though he just had an idea. "Cat," Frank starts, "why don't you hold on to this for Ran until he wakes up?" He moves toward me.

I take the necklace from him and, like Frank, study it for a moment before I put it around my neck and fasten the clasp in the back. I run my index finger carefully over the cool metal now resting lightly against my skin and think of that night in my tent almost two months ago, when I had asked Ronan about the meaning of the pendants, and he had explained to me that his grandmother gave them to him to protect him.

I wish it had worked; I wish all it took for Ronan to be safe and healthy was this necklace.

I spend the majority of the day sitting by Ronan's side, sometimes dozing off with my head on the mattress, feeling his skin against my cheek. I only get up to trade spots with Frank, or Steve, or Shane here and there. Sometime in the afternoon, Vada, Tori, Zack, and Summer stop by with Chinese takeout, of which I'm only able to eat a couple of bites.

That afternoon my mom returns from North Carolina, and when I get home from the hospital in the evening, I cry on her shoulder for what seems like an eternity. She sits there, running her hand up and down my back like she used to when I was a little girl, comforting me. She asks me if I feel strong enough to start school the next day and, after some deliberation, we agree that the distraction might be good for me. Steve promises to send me updates throughout the day until I can get to the hospital in the afternoon, and I fall asleep holding on to Ronan's necklace around my neck.

Monday, August 30th

Cat

When Monday morning rolls around it becomes immediately clear that maybe my choice to go to school wasn't the wisest. Despite the size of my high school and the huge number of students, news that something terrible happened to Ronan spreads like wildfire, and whoever broke that news apparently also made our relationship public knowledge. People come up to me all day long, providing pats on the back and sympathetic looks and words. Some girls seem pissed, jealous that I apparently managed to land the notoriously unavailable and sinfully hot—*god, so damn hot*—varsity hockey center forward. They give me dismissive side-glances and whisper as I pass by, though I'm too preoccupied to care. I end up leaving at lunch, unable to concentrate on anything at all.

I call Steve on my way home, and he's waiting for me in his car when I turn the corner to my house.

"Have you seen him yet? How is he?" I blurt out as soon as I get into the passenger seat of his Challenger, leaning over the center console to hug Steve tightly. I can feel the tension in his shoulders as he hugs me back. He looks exhausted.

"No change," he says, his voice strained. "How was school?" Steve finally asks, his eyes on the road, both hands gripping the steering wheel as he drives us to the hospital.

"Awful," I say, and am shocked by the defeat in my voice. I feel like I've aged ten years over the past forty-eight hours. Steve turns his head toward me briefly, raising his eyebrows, beckoning me to explain. "Everyone already knew that Ran got hurt; I don't know how."

Steve huffs out a chuckle. "Figures. People love drama; I bet everyone's eating this shit up." There's anger in his tone.

"Everyone but those involved, I guess," I say, and it becomes quiet again. I turn and look out the window, watching as we fly by other cars on the freeway, pass buildings, and the scene changes. Finally, we pull up to the hospital, walk into the now-familiar building, and take the elevator up to the seventh floor, where we walk down the hallway and through the doors secured by an intercom.

"Two for Soult," Steve says unemotionally as the voice on the other end of the intercom inquires as to our visit. The door buzzes and Steve pushes it open, holding it for me to enter first. I walk past the floor-to-ceiling glass walls that create the barriers to the different rooms. Some of the curtains are drawn, others are open. Nurses bustle about, checking on patients, chatting, others poring over charts and notes. When we reach Ronan's room, the curtain is half drawn.

I spot Frank through the glass, his back to us while he looks out the hospital window, his phone to his ear.

Steve quietly slides the door open. Frank doesn't notice us.

"God, I wish I had done things differently, baby. I wish I had waited to tell Rica about us until I was home, then maybe none of this would have happened," Frank tells whoever is on the other end of his phone call, his voice strained with pain. Steve stops dead in his tracks, his brow creasing as we eavesdrop on his dad's conversation. "This is all my fault, baby," he sighs, and it dawns on me that he must be talking to another woman. A woman he calls "baby," just like Ronan calls me. *Oh no. Is Ronan's dad having an affair? Did Ronan's mom know? Is that why she was so angry? Did she take it all out on her son?*

"Dad?" Steve finally says.

Frank turns to us, startled. "Babe, I have to call you back," he says into the phone. He ends the call, his eyes on Steve, who hasn't moved so much as an inch from his spot.

"Who were you talking to?" Steve asks, his voice as tight as his jaw.

I feel uncomfortable witnessing this, like I'm intruding on a very private family conversation, and I decide to move to Ronan's bedside to give Steve and his dad at least a semblance of space while I sit with the boy I love.

Steve was right: nothing has changed. Ronan is as still as he has been these past two days; the only indication of life is displayed on the monitor. His heartbeat is steady but low. The machine is still doing the breathing for him, his chest rising and falling automatically, unemotionally. I sit in the chair by his bed and take his hand into mine, once again struggling to warm his skin. His features are still almost unrecognizable. Though the swelling seems to have decreased the tiniest bit, the bruises are as dark, as menacing as ever.

"Stevie..." Frank starts after a deep exhale, and I watch as he seemingly deflates, his face pained. "I'm so sorry. I wish it didn't have to be this way. It's all wrong and I know that," he continues, cautiously approaching his son.

Steve doesn't move. "Dad!" he interrupts. "Just say it."

Frank takes a deep breath, looks from Steve to Ronan, then back to Steve. "I've been having an affair."

The confession is profound, and a long moment of silence follows it while I look on. My gaze moves between Steve—whose brow remains creased, his eyes narrowed—and Frank, whose relative youth is obvious. He looks not a lick over thirty. His face is scruffy and more rugged than Ronan's or Steve's, but just as handsome. Like his sons, Frank is tall, lean, and muscular. That masculine build obviously runs in the family.

Steve sighs loudly, shaking his head the slightest bit. "Shit, Ran was right," he says, surprising me and obviously Frank.

"What?" Frank asks, perplexed.

"Yeah, Ran actually said something to me about how he thought you were seeing someone else. He talked about you being gone more often and for longer periods of time, how you were so much happier leaving lately. I didn't really believe him then, until I started to think about it more, and then I thought, hmm, maybe he's on to something." Steve's voice changes at the last few words, and his eyes flicker to his little brother lying still in the hospital bed.

"Oh my god," Frank whispers, rubbing his face with both hands.

"How long have you been seeing her?" Steve asks, his shoulders relaxing a little.

"About two and a half years now," Frank admits sheepishly.

"Are you fucking serious?" Steve asks, anger tingeing his tone.

"Yeah, I... God, Stevie, I'm—"

"So, like, is it just sex? Or do you love her?" Steve's eyes are glued to his dad.

I listen, Ronan's hand still in mine, my index finger gently grazing over his knuckles. I shouldn't be here, shouldn't be overhearing all of this; I wish I had the power to become invisible.

Frank inhales, then exhales deeply. "I love her," he says, nodding. "It started out as... as just sex, but..."

"But then you fell in love?"

Frank nods again. "Yeah. It... I know it shouldn't have happened, but I just.... This is all my fault," Frank says, his voice cracking. His eyes move to Ronan. "I should have been home. I should have known this was going on. I should have protected him from her."

The pain in Frank's voice is too much to bear, and I sit and face the boy I love as hot tears stream silently down my cheeks.

"I don't know what to say," Steve says, shaking his head again in disbelief. "I have so many questions, like... what's her name? Where does she live?"

"Her name is Penelope... Penny," Frank says, with a tiny smile tugging at his lips, his eyes softening at the mention of her, though I can tell he feels guilty for having lived this double life for so long. "She lives in Virginia. I met her about three years ago, and things just... happened."

"When we lived in Montana?" Steve says, his eyebrows raised.

Frank nods. "Yeah. It just... It just happened. I know it's awful; I tried to fight it, but... I just fell in love with her."

"What was your plan, Dad?" Steve asks, studying him.

I remain silent, unobtrusive, still continuing to caress Ronan's hand, though neither Steve nor Frank seem to mind my presence.

Frank sighs. "Honestly, in the beginning I just thought it was a fling, you know. I didn't plan on anything, but after a while, I realized I wanted to be with Penny. On Saturday, when Ran..." He trails off, raking his hand through his dark hair. "I had called Rica at four on Saturday morning to let her know I was coming home; that I was packing my stuff; that I was going to file for divorce. I didn't mean to disrupt her night, but I just couldn't hold it in any longer. I felt so bad; I just needed to get it off my chest. I needed to pull the trigger, you know. I just got in my car and started driving. She was so upset. She left work while I was still on the phone with her," Frank adds, shaking his head. "Never in a million years did I think she would... And then when I turned on to our street, I saw the cop cars and the ambulance in front of the house, and I just threw the car into park and ran up the stairs... I'm so sorry, Stevie," Frank says, trying hard to maintain his composure.

"Holy shit," Steve sighs, combing his hands through his light-brown hair. He sounds tired; actually, everyone does.

"Your grandmother ripped me a new one," Frank confesses. "When I talked to her yesterday, she absolutely laid into me. I felt like I was fifteen again," he adds with a quiet chuckle. "I know I screwed up, but I couldn't help it. Penny is just..."

"I get it, Dad," Steve says. "Sometimes you meet a person you just can't stay away from. I bet if you asked Ran, he'd agree with you wholeheartedly," he adds with a small smile at me.

"I can definitely agree," I say, and Frank looks at me, his eyes soft.

Steve finally walks to the small loveseat and sits down with his elbows on his knees while he studies his dad. "I want to meet her," he says.

Frank looks slightly taken aback as he studies his son. "Really?"

Steve nods. "Yeah. I mean, it sounds like she's important to you. Like, you called her 'baby,' and... I mean... I'd like to meet her. I think that's only fair, right?" he adds, his eyebrows raised.

Frank analyzes his son for a long moment before he nods hesitantly. "Yeah, I think it is only fair."

"Okay. Have her come visit," Steve says.

"Okay," Frank acquiesces.

Steve pushes up off the sofa, then finally moves to join me by Ronan's bedside. "I can't believe you were right," Steve tells Ronan, chuckling quietly. "I don't know how you always figure these things out, man," he adds, stroking his hand over Ronan's hair. He glances at me. "He told me months ago that he thought my dad was having an affair, but I just waved him off. I thought Ran was full of shit, but..." He gives another rueful chuckle.

"But he was right," I say.

He nods. "Yeah. I wish I was as discerning as Ran. Maybe then I would have realized something was wrong at home," Steve chokes, looking down.

I reach over Ronan and take Steve's hand, giving it a squeeze. "Not your fault," I remind him once again.

***

I spend my afternoon like the last, sitting by Ronan's bedside, holding his hand, talking to him. I trade off with Steve, Frank, and then Shane when he arrives at the hospital a little while later, looking as exhausted as the rest of us.

"Listen, guys, I have to head out for a couple of hours. I have an appointment with a lawyer," Frank says as he gets up from the chair next to Ronan's bed, which he's been occupying for the last thirty minutes. I've been sitting on the small loveseat, leaning against Steve, who's been watching a hockey game with Shane.

Steve raises his eyebrows at his dad. "A divorce lawyer?" he asks, voicing my own suspicions.

Frank nods. "Yeah. I made the appointment last week, not knowing that... that we would be here today, but I want to see what I can do to expedite this whole thing," Frank explains. "I'm so sorry, Steve."

Steve just shrugs, too exhausted to dive further into it.

So, after Frank heads out, Steve, Shane, and I just sit, trading off holding vigil next to Ronan's bed until Vada and Tori arrive with food. Steve and I eat while Shane sits with Ronan, telling him—and probably mostly us—a funny story about something that happened at Murphy's earlier today and how Ronan would have had a great time.

Ronan's nurse comes in every hour to check his vitals, to administer medication, or to hook him up to more saline. Frank returns, and at just after ten Shane and Tori drive me home after Steve falls asleep on the loveseat.

Tuesday, August 31st

Cat

School is nothing but draining, and the hoped-for distraction is elusive because no matter where I turn, someone is always whispering, pointing, asking questions. I'm standing in the hallway with Vada and Tori between classes when two girls approach and stop right in front of us.

"Is it true that you're with Ran?" one of them asks me while the other looks me up and down, eyebrows raised.

"She sure is," Vada snaps back, her right hip popped out, hands on her waist. "You got an issue with that?"

The girl glowers at Vada for a moment before she returns her attention to me. "I heard he got his ass kicked and is in the hospital because of you," she says. "Maybe stay away from him so, you know, he can live." The girl shrugs, then pulls her friend with her as she walks away.

"What?" I mutter, totally confused by this nonsense the girl was spewing. I look to Vada and Tori for an explanation.

"Fucking bitch," Vada huffs. "Spreading all these bullshit rumors. It pisses me off."

"I've heard various iterations of this rumor already," Tori sighs. "One version is that Ran got into a fight at a party. Another is that he got jumped after work. I even heard one where he got in a car accident because he was drunk after you two got into a fight," she tells me. "The common thread in these stories is always that whatever happened to Ran happened because of you—because you two got in a fight or he was defending you or whatever."

"Who's starting these rumors?" I ask, feeling tense. These past few days have been draining enough, and the last thing I want or need is to have to defend against some gossip. I've been the target of whispering and talking before, and it's as uncomfortable now as it was then.

"I don't know," Tori says, shaking her head.

"Kitty Cat, these chicks are just jealous that you did the one thing they never could: you got Ran to fall in love with you," Vada says, and hooks her arm under mine. "Try to ignore them. We got your back, and I'm definitely not beyond kicking someone's ass."

"Okay, I believe you," I laugh.

***

I dutifully attend my classes, relishing the periods I get to spend with Vada, Zack, and Tori, as well as our lunch break, during which I sneak my phone out of my backpack and turn it on to check for an update from Steve. He sent me a quick text around eleven, only saying, "Still no change."

I manage to make it through most of the day but skip my last two periods, feeling tired and anxious to see Ronan. I call my mom, who's nothing but understanding, and Steve sweetly picks me up at home, then drives us to the hospital like he has these past few days.

"My dad should be here soon," Steve notes when he slides open the door to Ronan's room. "He's at the airport picking up my grandparents. They just flew in from Montana today," he explains, and it warms my heart.

"Is he bringing them to the hospital?" I ask. I would love to meet Ronan's grandparents—he's told me so much about them, and I always had the impression that Montana and his grandparents are a good part of his life.

"Yep," Steve assures me. "My grandma was hysterical when my dad told her what had happened. She wanted to come out Sunday, but they had to make arrangements with the ranch and stuff. I mean, my aunt can handle it, but cattle ranches don't really lend themselves to just up and leaving. She's been calling my dad every day to get an update on Ran, though."

Just as Steve predicted, Frank returns to the hospital a couple hours later with both of his parents in tow, and I'm shocked at their obvious youth. Ronan had told me there was a generational cycle of having children young, but the fact that his grandmother—who sweetly introduces herself as Saoirse, an Irish name which she explains to me is pronounced like "sir-shu"—is only fifty-one and looks as though she's only in her forties still throws me off. Steve and Frank are almost carbon copies of Perry, Steve and Ronan's grandfather. But Ronan, with his green eyes and lighter hair, seems to take more after his mother's side.

Saoirse and Perry's reaction to seeing Ronan, his face still almost-unrecognizably bruised and swollen, is the same as everyone else's: utter shock. Though they quickly compose themselves and check on Steve; his grandmother hugs him tightly for a long while before she turns her attention to me.

"So, you're the beautiful girl who stole my baby boy's heart," Saoirse says with a sweet smile when I offer her the chair so she can sit with Ronan. "He told me about you a few weeks ago, and I could tell by the way he spoke about you that he's obviously lost his heart to you," she tells me as she appreciatively takes a seat by Ronan's bedside. "You know, he doesn't open up to a lot of people," she continues as she strokes Ronan's right hand, studying his face, so much worry in her brown eyes. "You must be a very special girl." She turns her head toward me and smiles.

"I don't know," I say, unconvinced. "He didn't say anything about his mom hurting him."

But Saoirse only shakes her head. "Sweetheart, that doesn't mean you aren't special. That just means that the evil witch did a good job brainwashing him. Victims of abuse don't tell anyone because, well, they're being abused, aren't they?"

I can hear the unfiltered contempt toward Ronan's mother in Saoirse's voice, and I wonder if the two women ever had a good relationship.

I sit down at the foot of Ronan's bed, careful not to bump his injured right leg. "Ronan told me you gave him his necklace with the two pendants—Saint Michael and that cross."

Saoirse smiles at me, then at Ronan, gently stroking her hand over his head. "Yes, to protect him against evil. Heck of a lot of good it did," she says with defeat in her voice. "Oh, baby boy," she sighs, her eyes filled with worry.

"He told me a lot about you and the ranch, and..." I say, wishing to comfort her a little. "I could always tell that Montana and you are such an important part of him."

Saoirse looks at me, her eyes brimming with tears before they spill over. She lets them fall unabashedly. "You know, I gave Ronan his name," Saoirse says, now studying Ronan's bruised features. "He's named after my dad who died in a shipwreck when I was twelve. I loved my father very much," she continues, then pauses. "Ronan came into this world with a vengeance. I remember it like it was yesterday. We were having these terrible summer storms and the roads to town were flooded; we were completely cut off. And then Rica's water broke and she had Ronan a couple hours after that—no chance at a doctor making it to the ranch or us getting her to the hospital, no pain medication, just Rica and me. And I helped her deliver this tiny, scrawny little baby boy. He weighed just over five pounds. I always said it was because she became pregnant too soon after having Steve and didn't nourish her body and the baby growing inside her well enough," she says with tears running down her cheeks.

"And she had such a hard time bonding with him. She was so young and so overwhelmed. Only seventeen, two babies. Her parents wanted nothing to do with her or the boys. So, we tried. Perry and

I tried to take some of the burden off her shoulders, especially after Frank left for the Air Force, but it became obvious to me over time that she just didn't have a bond with Ronan."

She wipes the tears from her cheeks, then returns her attention to Ronan. She gazes at him warmly as she carefully runs her thumb over his unbandaged right cheek. "I caught her beating on him once when Ronan was only two and I put a stop to that, but I fear all I did was make her hide it. I always suspected she wasn't good to him. Always. But he never confided in me, and I never saw her hit him again."

Her voice is so full of regret, worry, and self-hatred for her inability to protect Ronan. "Every time they moved away and then came back to Montana, I saw Ronan more and more changed, more guarded. Oh goodness, he was such a feisty kid," she laughs through her tears. "So quick-witted and smart as a whip. But he was so different when his mother was around; he couldn't be himself with her because she would punish him. She always used harsh words with him. But boy, when Rica wasn't around, he shone brighter than the sun. He was always such a good child, though; so helpful and polite. And he cares so, so deeply for the people he loves. But, as Perry always says, still waters run deep, and that is Ronan. He may not be very expressive or easy to read, but he has the heart and soul of a warrior."

I reach out to her and place my hand on her forearm. "He still shines like the sun," I say, looking at Ronan. "By the way he talks about Montana, I think he always felt safe there."

She smiles at me and pats my hand with hers. "You're special indeed," she says, smiling at me despite the tears still staining her cheeks. "And really beautiful," she adds with a nod. "My baby boy did well."

Saoirse and I continue sitting with Ronan while she tells me that she and her husband were married very young and, much like Frank, had children at a young age. She dropped everything in Montana to catch the earliest flight to New York when she heard what happened to Ronan.

I watch as she takes care of Frank and Steve, and when she sits by Ronan's bedside, holding his right hand, talking to him softly. She reminds him of all the reasons he has to fight, to make it through this, to live. And I listen when she sings him an Irish lullaby. But still, Ronan doesn't move.

Saoirse gets Frank to tell her about Penny, who, I learn, is a first-grade teacher in Virginia, though she's originally from New York. Saoirse is stern with Frank while she peppers him with questions about his affair. It's clear she doesn't approve of her son's deception, even though Saoirse has nothing good to say about Ronan's mom, but the guilt Frank feels is equally obvious.

"Is she married?" Steve asks.

Frank looks ashamed as he nods. "Going through a divorce right now. You must think so terribly of me," he says, and runs his hand through his dark hair.

"I don't really know what to think," Steve admits, his voice strained.

"What's the plan, Frankie?" Ronan's grandfather, Perry, chimes in. From what I can gather, he's a man of few words, though when he does speak it's with authority and conviction. It's clear Saoirse is the more expressive of the two, whereas Perry is more observant.

"You obviously can't keep being gone. The boys need their father. They've needed you for a long time, but now more than ever," Perry says.

He makes a great point, one I hadn't even thought about before. What will happen when Ronan wakes up? What will happen with his mother? No way she would be allowed around him again, right?

"I'm in the process of working all that out right now, Dad," Frank tells his parents and Steve. "I'm not going anywhere; no more being away from you guys," he adds, looking at Steve. "I'm already talking with my superiors about a transfer. I'm on leave now until Ran..." He trails off momentarily. "I'm not leaving you guys again," Frank says, and I can see relief and a small smile cross Steve's face.

A while later, Frank takes his parents to the house to allow them to get some rest, but returns to the hospital as soon as he's able with the intent to spend another night by Ronan's bedside.

Shane, Tori, Zack, Summer, and Vada stop by in the late afternoon, bringing bread and pasta. They hang out for a couple of hours but leave when Jessica, the night nurse, comes in to change Ronan's IV.

"I'm sorry guys, but they're pretty strict with the number of people. We just want to make sure Ronan gets plenty of rest," she says sympathetically, and our friends scurry out with promises to visit again tomorrow.

***

It's almost 10:30 and I stretch my arms overhead, accidentally hitting Steve in the head. Frank took my seat by Ronan's side about an hour ago, and has been reading to him like he does every evening. I finished my English homework a few minutes ago and took my spot on the small sofa, leaning against Steve, who lets me rest my head on his chest while he watches TV. I closed my eyes at first and listened to Steve's heartbeat, pretending it was Ronan's warmth, his heartbeat. God, although I've been in the same room with Ronan the majority of the past few days, I miss him terribly. Even though his body is just a few feet away from me, it's as though his mind, his soul, his energy are somewhere else entirely, and I can't wait for him to find his way back to us, to me.

"Shit!" Frank says, his voice constricted.

"What's wrong, Dad?" Steve asks.

My eyes instantly find Ronan's face, then move to the monitors and machines. His oxygen saturation is normal, but his pulse has increased. And then I notice the number in the lower right-hand corner of the monitor: 103.6. Ronan has spiked a fever. "He's burning up!" I say.

Frank is already pushing the red button, calling the nurse.

She instantly appears at the door. "Is everything okay?" Jessica asks as she steps into the room.

"He's running a fever," Frank says, his voice tight.

Jessica looks at the monitor, and apparently unable to believe her eyes, touches her hand to Ronan's forehead and cheek. "Yes, he is. I'm going to page the doctor on call right now. I'll be right back."

"What the hell?" Steve asks, stepping closer to his little brother.

"I was done reading and went to take his hand, and I noticed how damn hot he was. It startled me because he's been feeling so cool. I looked on the monitor and... Jesus!"

It's obvious how frantic Frank is, and anxiety claws at my throat. I feel completely out of control, and the fear of losing Ronan threatens to take over again, like it has at night when I'm alone in my room, taking in Ronan's scent lingering on the pillow.

Jessica and a young doctor dressed in navy-blue scrubs and a white coat with an ID attached to it walk hastily into the room. The doctor doesn't introduce himself as he examines the monitor, then touches Ronan's forehead and cheek like Jessica did.

"What's going on, Doctor?" Frank asks.

The nameless doctor pauses briefly to look at Frank. "I'm Doctor Casteen," the young doctor says, his face unmoved. He turns to Jessica, asking her questions about Ronan's vitals and her regular checks on him. "Okay," he finally says, returning his gaze to Frank.

It's clear that this doctor, experienced as he may be, hasn't learned much about bedside manners. My mom always tells me how important good bedside manners are; that sometimes they can be the difference between a patient going home earlier and staying longer. This doctor's face is serious, void of any compassion as he rattles off information.

"Fevers are indicators of infection. We'll take a quick blood sample and have the lab check Ronan's white count. A high count will tell us if there's anything going on. In the meantime, I'm going to check the incision sites to rule out anything external."

Blood is drawn and sent to the lab, and Doctor Casteen uncovers Ronan's lower body that had been concealed by a blanket. Ronan is wearing what look like sweatpants but in reality are blue hospital pants. The right pant leg is cut open, and for the first time I see the contraption that holds Ronan's right leg and knee in place. It's not a cast, and I take in his knee; it's bandaged with white cloth and ice has been packed around it, presumably to decrease the swelling. My eyes pass over Ronan's entire body, head to toe. Bruises, dark and menacing, stain his sun-kissed skin and I want so badly to touch him, to make it all go away.

"The incisions look fine," the doctor says, uncovering each surgical site and inspecting the wounds for obvious signs of infection. "This has to be internal," he says again, more to himself than anyone else. He takes the stethoscope hanging leisurely around his neck and places it against Ronan's chest. It becomes still in the room as Doctor Casteen listens intently. He takes his time, moving the instrument to various parts of Ronan's battered chest, his ribs.

Finally, Doctor Casteen removes the stethoscope from his ears. "I'm going to take X-rays just to confirm, but this is pneumonia we're talking about," he says, and Frank takes a sharp breath in. "This is not uncommon," Doctor Casteen continues quickly. "Ronan has been intubated for a few days, both his lungs were damaged, his spleen has been removed, and he's not moving. This is the perfect storm as far as pneumonia goes. He's completely unable to clear his lungs of any fluids, so they build up, and his body is too weak to fight the infection right now. I'm going to put him on some targeted antibiotics. But more importantly"—Doctor Casteen waves Jessica over—"let's take the tube out and give him a breathing trial. I would much prefer if we can assist Ronan with a mask. Hopefully he's strong enough to breathe for us; that would really allow his lungs to get some rest."

Jessica nods and heads out through the sliding glass doors. I watch as she heads around a long counter and picks up the phone. Her mouth moves briefly before she hangs up and returns to the room. "Davis will be up to remove the ventilator."

Doctor Casteen nods and checks the monitors again.

A few moments later, a short man with a receding hairline walks in. He's dressed in a white coat and gives us all a warm smile. "Evening y'all," he says in a thick Southern accent that makes me smile and takes some pressure off my heart.

Frank and Steve nod, and I give him a quick wave.

"Alright, let's get this gnarly little contraption out of this young man's chiseled chest," Davis says, and he moves close to Ronan's bedside. He directs Jessica to stand on the other side of the bed. "Alright Jess, I need you to tip his head back."

Jessica moves Ronan's head with both hands, exposing his throat. I realize I'm holding my breath and my heart is pounding audibly in my chest, while Frank wrings his hands and Steve's jaw is tense as we all look on.

"A little further, Jess. That's good. Hold it like that." Davis removes the tape around the ventilator and hands it to Doctor Casteen. "Alright, Jess. I need you to hold real still while I pull this out so we don't injure the trachea."

Davis slowly pulls a clear tube out of Ronan's throat. It's thicker than I had imagined, and much longer.

"Jesus fucking Christ," Steve whispers next to me. Finally, the tube is all the way out.

"'Kay, Jess, you can move his head back to its normal position."

The nurse follows the instructions.

"Good. Now breathe for us," Davis says to Ronan.

I stare intently at Ronan's chest, willing it to rise and fall, but nothing happens. *Please, please, PLEASE!* Tears threaten to blur my vision again.

Davis places his hands on Ronan's chest, right on the sternum. Less carefully than would seem appropriate given Ronan's injured ribs, Davis rubs Ronan's chest, mumbling to himself and maybe Ronan. "Come on, son. In and out, in and out. There we go," Davis says, delight in his voice.

I see the long-awaited rise of Ronan's chest. He's breathing on his own.

Frank laughs out loud, relieved, and Steve pulls me into a bear-hug while I laugh and cry both at the same time.

Jessica and Doctor Casteen take Ronan for X-rays, which confirm Doctor Casteen's diagnosis of pneumonia. Jessica starts Ronan on IV antibiotics. His breathing is steady, but Jessica nonetheless puts him on oxygen. "We just want to make sure he isn't working too hard just yet," she says as she carefully places the clear mask over Ronan's mouth and broken nose.

Before leaving, she takes Ronan's right hand in hers, like she always does when she checks on him. "Ronan, if you can hear me, squeeze my hand," she says, but nothing happens. "Squeeze my hand, Ronan." Again, nothing. She discontinues her efforts and leaves the room, shutting the glass door behind her.

"Buddy, you should take Cat home now," Frank says, his voice depleted of all energy.

The clock shows that it's close to midnight, and although my mom hasn't called, I know she's probably worried. I usually try to be home around eleven.

"Okay." Steve gives his father a hug, making him promise again to call if anything changes with Ronan. "I'll see you in the morning, Dad."

Steve slides the door open for me and waits while I hug Frank and finally move to kiss Ronan's right cheek. It's still hot, but the fact that he's breathing on his own makes me more hopeful. I gently let my hand rest on his chest, eager to feel that natural rise and fall. A little flutter expands in my heart with each breath Ronan takes. It's as if he's breathing for me.

Wednesday, September 1st

Cat

I feel slightly more energized on Wednesday. Ronan's feat of breathing on his own has me feeling more hopeful, almost chipper, as I flip through my chemistry homework. Vada is helping me with it here at the hospital this afternoon. Shane, Tori, Zack, and Summer tagged along and have been watching mindless TV for the past half hour while we're all crammed into the small room. Frank sits by Ronan's bedside, sending text messages and emails from his cell phone.

"So, I've been looking through all my footage I have from the summer," Zack says, breaking the silence in the room.

Shane looks up from the car magazine he's read at least five times already, and Tori blinks against the setting sun shining in through the window.

"And?" Summer urges.

"Well, I put together some footage with music and stuff, and I was thinking we could all get together, like tomorrow, and watch it. It's pretty fun, and it's kind of nice to see Ran, you know, like talking, and walking, and laughing," Zack says. His eyes meet each of ours.

"That sounds like a fantastic idea," Frank says, his voice sounding a little less strained than it has these past few days. "We'll order pizza and watch what you got."

At that, Zack smiles, obviously proud of himself. "We could do it at my house if..." Zack trails off, biting his lip. He's clearly concerned that the Soult house might still be in disarray.

"Not necessary," Frank says lightly. "Everything's been cleaned up," he assures us. "But I think you should bring all the footage, not just what you put together. I've missed so much of my boys, I would like to know what they've been up to."

Zack thinks about this for a moment, and his face drops slightly, his eyebrows knitting together. "Umm... yeah, sure."

"Only if you promise not to get mad, Dad," Steve says, amused. "Because there's probably going to be some stuff you don't want to see." A chuckle escapes Steve's mouth, and it's a nice sound amidst all the tension and stress we've all been under.

"Yeah? Like what?" Frank asks.

"I don't know, but I'm sure there'll be some stuff," Steve says. "Like, probably a lot of Ran checking out Cat and vice versa, a lot of touchy-smoochy stuff. They're pretty handsy with each other," he says with a mischievous grin at me, and I laugh. The sound throws me off, but it feels nice.

"Got it," Frank laughs. "I'm confident I can handle it."

We agree to all meet at the Soult house the next evening at seven, and the rest of the afternoon is spent the same as the past few days. I doze off with my cheek touching Ronan's hand, just like I have so many times now. I want nothing more than to feel his hand move, for his thumb to brush my cheek, for his palm to cup my face as he pulls me toward him and kisses me with those soft lips of his.

Thursday, September 2nd

Cat

Ronan doesn't move on Thursday, either, and even though he's breathing on his own, the fact that he's still not awake is testing my hope. Steve picks me up after school to take me to the hospital, and Frank smiles when he sees us.

"There's only so much one-sided conversation I can have with Ran before I begin repeating myself," Frank says. "I can't even count the number of times I've asked him to please wake up. He's stubborn, though. Must be those Irish genes." He sighs with a tired chuckle. He looks exhausted and his expression is worn. It appears we all feel the same way. These past few days have been an emotional rollercoaster; we've been hanging on to every bit of positivity, only to get crushed by the fact that Ronan is still in a coma.

We spend the afternoon by Ronan's bedside, and then, reluctantly, leave him to head out. This will be the first time Ronan is all alone in the hospital with no one there, and it feels wrong, like we're abandoning him when he's at his most vulnerable. But the nurse promises to call Frank should anything change, and Frank likewise assures me that he intends to return to the hospital in a few hours to spend another night there.

When we arrive at the Soult house, I'm surprised at how neat it looks. I wasn't sure what I had expected; images of the shattered coffee table, the fractured hockey stick, the blood stains soaked into the rug and drying on the hardwood floor are still prominent in my mind. But today, there's no sign of a struggle in the living room, not a trace of the violence that took place here. The bloodstained rug has been removed, as have the pieces of the coffee table and any evidence of what happened. A new, larger rug now adorns the hardwood floor, covering any stains that may have been left over.

Saoirse bustles about the house, a laundry basket balanced on her hip. The moment I step into the house, she puts the basket down and pulls me into her arms as though I'm part of her family.

"Can I just say that my grandbaby has excellent taste in girls?" Saoirse says to Frank before looking back at me. "You are stunning," she adds, giving me a warm smile, which I happily reciprocate.

"How long are you staying in New York?" I ask her.

"Until that grandson of mine decides to wake up," she says matter-of-factly, and stoops to pick up the laundry basket again.

I notice Perry is in the kitchen doing the dishes, and I wave hello before following Steve and Shane into the living room.

Frank orders a couple of pizzas for us all to share. My appetite has been essentially nonexistent these past few days, but I decide to try and eat something. I get up and walk to the small dining room, grab a piece, and make my way to the living room where I sit cross-legged on the floor.

We all watch Zack's home movie for the next hour, and I love everything about it. It's obvious how much time he's put into it. The cuts between footage are flawless, and he even picked out background music. I can't take my eyes off Ronan whenever he's on screen, and my heart aches with how much I miss him.

"It looks like you were everywhere. You have all these incredible shots," Tori says, expressing exactly what I'm thinking.

It looks as though Zack put extra time into finding these perfect, intimate shots of Ronan and me. There are moments of Ronan and me at the beach this past July when he picked me up and carried me into the water. There are shots of us holding hands, hugging, even kissing. One of my favorites is a scene in which Ronan and I had fallen asleep together on Shane's couch one afternoon this last summer. I'm lying with Ronan right behind me, his body protecting me from falling off the narrow sofa, and his arm is draped over me, holding on to me.

Most of the scenes depict everyday life over these past few months, but they hold so many warm memories. Zack's captured so many subtleties, like the way Ronan's lips would break into a smile when he saw me, or the way I would melt into him whenever he held me—which, admittedly, he did a lot. I never realized how physical we are with each other, seeking each other's touch—no matter how small—constantly.

"Told you there's a lot of touchy-smoochy stuff," Steve says slyly, and I have to laugh through the silent tears that stain my face as I take in and remember each moment, recalling the feel of Ronan, his smell. I miss him so unbearably much. The movie ends all too soon.

"What other footage do you have?" Frank asks when Zack's movie is over.

"I have a bunch of stuff," Zack says. "Most of it is pretty boring."

We watch more raw footage from the summer, and footage that's older, filmed before Ronan and I stepped into each other's lives, before I even moved to New York. Ronan looks sexy playing hockey and working out—shirt off, his chest damp with sweat—making Saoirse comment that she feels indecent seeing her grandson this way. It causes everyone to laugh hysterically.

There are scenes from parties, the boys drinking heavily, even smoking weed here and there, and Steve apologizes profusely to his grandmother while the rest of us laugh. I know now what Steve meant when he warned his father. But Frank doesn't react when he sees his youngest son drinking straight from a bottle of whiskey and flirting with random girls, or his oldest son making out with Vada before noticing the camera in his face and angrily shooing Zack away with a flick of his middle finger. The emotions that fill the room are endless—happy and painful—as we watch our lives over the past year or so played out on the screen.

Zack again sifts through his footage and suddenly pauses. "Cat," he says giddily, "I have something for you." I look at Zack, my eyebrows raised.

Zack selects a new recording. The shots must have been filmed before I met Ronan because none of it looks familiar. But then the scene transitions and I see Ronan standing with Shane and Tori, and I can hear Zack's voice in the background; he's obviously holding his camera and filming. The four of them are talking and Shane says something to Ronan about hooking up with Cheyenne and how she probably wouldn't mind. My eyebrows knit at the statement and I'm irritated that Zack felt the need to show me this.

He senses my annoyance. "No, wait," Zack says, "just give it a second."

I keep watching and hear Shane saying Ronan's name. "Ran? Ran! Ronan!"

Ronan seems lost, his eyes fixed on something still out of the camera's view. It looks as though he just saw something profound, life-changing, and Vada gives me the answer I'm looking for.

"He just laid eyes on you for the first time," Vada says to me, tears in her eyes. And I realize that what I'm looking at is the moment right before I met Ronan. I recognize the jeans that sit low on his hips, his dark-green hoodie.

"You're staring," Shane says in the footage.

"Who is that?" Ronan asks, his voice tender, his eyes still fixed on who I now know to be me.

"That's Cat, Vada's friend. She moved here a little while ago. She's been hanging out with Vada and Tori a bunch and they invited her tonight, so... She's cute, huh?"

This is too much; I can't take it. The past six days suddenly crash into me and threaten to suffocate me. I try desperately to breathe, but the room spins around me. *Is this what it was like for Ronan?* I feel eyes on me, hands on my shoulders, and I look up into Shane's face. I realize I'm crying. No, not crying, sobbing. Everyone is staring; Ronan's grandmother's eyes are sad.

"Cat, it's okay. He's going to be alright," Shane says, his voice soft, reassuring.

I shake my head violently, unable to speak through the sobs. I need to get away for just a moment to collect myself, to breathe, and am able to shake Shane's hands loose. I storm out of the living room and up the stairs, tripping and falling to my knees, but I don't let that stop me. I get up, pushing myself forward, still sobbing violently as the tears, the pain, and the fear of losing Ronan finally force their way out of me.

Once up the stairs, I turn to my left and into Ronan's room, shutting the door behind me. I stop dead in my tracks with tears streaming down my hot cheeks.

Everything is untouched. Ronan's bed is unmade from when he got up the morning after we made love for the first time—my first time. A navy-blue hoody is draped over the chair by his desk; a towel lies on the floor along with the jeans and shirt he wore when I last saw him; his black ball cap is tossed in the corner; and Onyx, sweet Onyx, is curled into a ball on Ronan's bunched-up blanket.

"Hi Onyx," I whisper, my voice still shaking. I move toward the bed carefully so as not to startle her. I realize I haven't seen her downstairs at all, and she's usually such a friendly dog.

She raises her head toward me, propping her ears up, wagging her tail just a smidge.

"You miss him too, don't you?" I move to lie next to her. She doesn't leave, instead sighing a dog's sigh and leaning herself into me. I place my tear-stained cheek on Ronan's pillow, closing my eyes. With one deep breath I inhale his scent, and fresh tears spill from my tired eyes, seeping into the fabric.

"I miss him so much, Onyx," I whisper, stroking the dog's fur. "I need him to wake up. I can't be without him. I love him more than words can say. Why doesn't he wake up?"

I lie with Onyx, petting her, breathing in Ronan's comforting scent, taking in the silence of his room and allowing my tears to flow freely for a few minutes longer. Nobody comes to check on me while I seek comfort in the space that belongs only to Ronan. They all respect my need for privacy.

Eventually, my tears dry and I sit up, letting my eyes sweep the four walls of the room. I don't think I ever paid much attention to it because Ronan and I haven't spent all that much time here and, when we did, I was usually preoccupied by Ronan's presence. But I soak it all in now, purposefully paying attention to the little details. I notice the bag that holds his hockey equipment leaning against the wall next to the window by his bed and the small shelf that's positively overflowing with books like the *Iliad* and the *Odyssey*, *The Fountainhead*, *The Trial*, and *Antigone*.

I move over to his desk, running my hands over a couple of graded exams on which Ronan received full marks each time. I feel the indentations of his handwriting on the paper, closing my eyes and imagining Ronan's left hand moving across the pages. I know it sounds dark, but the last few days have been so devoid of his life force, it's as though he's temporarily left this Earth. His handwriting makes it feel as though he's real, like he's still with me, that he wasn't just a dream.

A knock on the door forces me to open my eyes, and I turn to see Ronan's grandmother standing in the doorframe, her expression warm as she smiles at me.

"That was a bit much to take in, wasn't it? That little movie?" she asks, alluding to that last footage where Ronan saw me for the very first time.

I nod, my hand still resting on the papers on Ronan's desk.

She moves to sit down on the bed. "You know, I never truly thought that love at first sight was real, but your friend Zack's movie, Ronan's face... If that isn't evidence that it exists, then I don't know what is," she says. "Are you alright, sweetheart?"

"I'm fine," I say, and go to sit next to her. "It just feels like so long ago that I got to hear his voice, feel him next to me, and be with him. I know it's only been six days, but it feels like a lifetime. I wish he would wake up." I lower my head, feeling drained, and the longing for Ronan overwhelms me.

"He will," she says confidently. "I can feel it in my bones. And I *know* my grandson—Ronan is a force of nature that can't be stopped, try as you might. You might subdue him for a little while, but he'll come back stronger every time. Come on, let's go back downstairs."

We leave the comfort of Ronan's queen-size bed and make our way back downstairs. Shane offers to drive me home while Frank heads back to the hospital, where he will once again spend the night. I accept, realizing how drained I really feel, and seek the warmth and comfort of my own bed the moment I arrive at home.

Friday, September 3rd

Cat

The next morning I'm up before sunrise, just like I have been for the past six days. I can't find any rest even while I sleep. I toss and turn all night, feeling exhausted when I wake up. I have a hard time falling asleep, a hard time staying asleep, and feel drained throughout the day. My dreams are confused. They feel clammy and uncomfortable, though I never remember what I dream about. It's a jumble of fear and chaos, darkness and pain.

Last night when I came home, my mom could see the emotional strain of the past days in my face and she suggested I take something to help me sleep, but I declined. I want to be alert, want to be able to receive any news—good or bad—as soon as I can. But there hasn't been any news. Nothing has changed. Ronan is still not awake.

It's Friday, one week exactly since my birthday. One week since Ronan and I made love. One week since my heart broke open completely, since I gave myself to the boy I love. And it's been a week since I last saw his beautiful eyes, heard his voice, felt his touch, his warmth, smelled his scent. Every fiber of him was alive and happy when we were together the last time. The world shifted right under our feet, under our bodies. And then it all stopped.

But the world keeps turning, moving forward. Except, I don't. It's Groundhog Day for me. Every day is the same routine that feels like it's been going on for infinity. I wake up and I check to see if I missed any calls or messages, if there's anything new. Each day I hope that today is the day he wakes up, that I know for sure he's going to be okay, that he'll be with me like I yearn for him to be.

I get up, shower, make myself presentable. No breakfast for me. Eating is forced right now; it's simply a life-sustaining measure. My mom keeps reminding me that I won't be any good to Ronan if I don't stay healthy, and she's right, of course, but the overwhelming sadness and worry leave me without an appetite.

I couldn't fall asleep for the longest time last night, even though I was exhausted. Snippets of Zack's films kept flashing in my mind and they mostly made me smile. It was unbelievably comforting to see Ronan so full of life, even though I was looking for moments caught on camera that may have provided a hint of what he was hiding from all of us for so long. But, with the exception of the occasional sadness in his eyes when he didn't realize Zack was pointing the camera straight at him or the random bruise on his face or body, Ronan appeared happy and healthy.

I can't wait for this first week of school to be over. Even though it's a distraction, the hours spent on campus are wasted because I can't concentrate. I know Vada, Tori, Summer, and Zack have the same problem because I see them in class with me—see them mindlessly doodling and, more often than not, startled when the instructor calls on them. We're unable to answer the questions posed because none of us are paying attention. We merely bide our time, waiting for the bell letting us know we no longer need to pretend. I always bolt out those doors as fast as my feet can carry me so I can get to the hospital, get to Ronan.

I decide to wash my hair this morning; it's long overdue, but I hadn't been able to muster the strength. I take my time in the shower, washing and conditioning my tresses. I dry off, brush my teeth, get dressed. I let my hair dry, allowing it to do what it wants.

My mom pokes her head into my room at a quarter to eight, checking on me like she has all week. "Were you able to sleep?" she asks, and comes to sit on my bed with me while I tie my red chucks.

"Not really," I confess.

She puts her left arm around my shoulder and pulls me in for the kind of hug only a mother can give while she strokes my hair with her other hand. We stay silent for a few minutes as she holds me against her. Her steady heartbeat and rhythmic breathing are soothing, and I close my eyes as I relax against her, feeling so overwhelmingly grateful to have my mom.

My heart constricts when I think that Ronan never had that, never had a mother who would drop everything to be there for him, comfort him, hold him. He had a mother who abused him, made him feel unwanted, who hurt him. And I know that even when—not if—he wakes up and his physical wounds heal, it's going to take a lot longer to claw his way back from the emotional damage. But I plan to be there every step of the way.

My phone notifies me of an incoming text message and my mom releases me from her arms. Vada is waiting for me outside, ready to make the fifteen-minute walk to school. We've been walking every morning, rather than driving the short way, most often in silence because what is there to talk about? Only banalities, because talking about Ronan gets us both too upset.

I grab my bag, sling it over my shoulder, and wave to my mom, who remains seated on my bed. She's worried about me—I can see it in her face—so I give her a small smile. "I'm going to the hospital after class, okay?" I ask. Of course it's okay; she would never deny me that request.

Outside, Vada is checking her phone as I make my way toward her. She looks up and I see the dark circles under her eyes. She's been sleeping about as poorly as I have. Ronan is one of her best friends and I know she's worried sick. She hooks her arm under mine and we walk, silently, until my phone buzzes in my back pocket.

"Have you heard anything yet this morning?" Shane asks as soon as I answer his call. He sounds tired. The collective stress we're all under is palpable.

"No, you?"

"Nothing," he sighs. "I just tried Steve a few minutes ago, but he didn't answer his phone. I think I'm going to head to the hospital in a little while; I can't sit around at home. You guys coming after class?"

He asks this every day, and my answer is always the same—that I'll be there as soon as I can get out of school.

At school, Vada and I split up. I have Advanced Placement History, which always makes me think of Ronan because he told me the secret to acing this class. "If you have time, stay a few minutes after class lets out and ask Ms. Jennison some random questions about whatever it is you guys are studying. She'll think you're super interested. And make sure to pretend to really listen to her, like you've never heard anything more riveting in your life. You'll get an A, no questions asked," he told me with a chuckle a couple of weeks ago.

"Is that how you aced the class?" I asked him with a giggle.

"One hundred percent," he said with a mischievous grin.

But I have a hard time paying attention to Ms. Jennison's ramblings about the War of 1812 today. Pre-calculus passes equally slowly, as does my English class. By lunchtime I'm already ready for the school day to be over, and I seriously contemplate asking my mom to let me leave early so I can get Steve or Shane to come and take me to the hospital with them.

I wander out to the courtyard where I see Vada sitting in our usual spot under the large shady tree with Zack, Summer, Tori, and Cheyenne, all eating their lunches in silence. I join them, dropping my bag into the grass and sitting cross-legged next to Vada. I'm still not hungry but figure I should at least eat my apple, lest I collapse from lack of nutrition. I pull out the apple and my phone, turning it on. My heart stops when I see that I have five missed calls from Steve and two missed calls from Shane.

"Have you heard anything?" I ask the group as I frantically check to see if I have a text message or voicemail. We're not supposed to use our phones on campus and my hands are sweating as I swipe around on my screen. There's no message from either Shane or Steve.

"No, why? What's wrong?" Tori asks as the others stare.

"I don't know. I have a bunch of missed calls from Steve and Shane." I look at Vada, who shakes her head. "Screw it," I mutter and dial Steve's number, looking around to make sure no teachers are around to confiscate my phone.

"Put it on speaker," Vada practically begs.

I comply. Everyone is silent as the phone rings.

Steve picks up on the third ring. "Hey! Hold on a second." His voice is quiet, almost a whisper. I hear his shoes scuff against linoleum floor and a door slide open, then shut.

"What happened?" I ask, staring at the grass in front of me, feeling my friends' eyes on me as they listen intently, too.

Steve lets out a quiet chuckle, sounding elated. "He woke up. Ran woke up."

My eyes snap to Vada's as I drop my phone into my lap. I'm overwhelmed with relief, and judging by the looks on everyone's faces, they feel the same way.

"When?" Vada says loudly so Steve can hear her through my phone.

"Last night, around two. My dad said the nurse came in to place a new IV line and she asked Ran to squeeze her hand, like she usually does. And this time, he finally did." Steve's voice is giddy as I hear him pace back and forth in the hospital corridor. "And then my dad kept talking to him, asking him to open his eyes. It took him a while to come out of it, but he did. He's back." Steve chokes back a sob as he tries hard to rein in his emotions.

"How is he?" I ask, desperately.

"He's asleep right now; they have him doped up on painkillers, keeping him pretty sedated, but I did talk to him for a few minutes earlier this morning. He's sort of in and out of it; you can tell he doesn't have a lot of strength right now. He'll be awake for a few minutes, but then he drifts off again pretty quickly." There's a pause before Steve continues. "He asked about you, Cat."

My heart skips a beat, and I smile as my eyes water. "I want to come see him right now," I say, my voice thick. I look at Vada, who nods eagerly, ready to skip out on our afternoon classes.

"Take your time; they just gave him some pain meds thirty minutes ago. He's out cold right now and probably will be for a few hours, so no rush. Shane, my dad, and I are here with him."

We agree that we'll be heading to the hospital as soon as classes let out, and Steve hangs up to head back into Ronan's room.

***

The next few hours pass with excruciating slowness, and by the time the final bell rings I have my bag packed and am the first one out of the room. I speed walk down the corridor, out the front doors, and to the parking lot. Tori had agreed to drive since Vada and I walked to school this morning, and I meet her and Vada by her Corolla three minutes later. Zack and Summer are going to meet us at the hospital.

Cheyenne declined to tag along, telling me, privately, that she was sorry for how she had acted toward me, that she could tell how much I cared about Ronan and him for me, and that she wanted to give us some space, but that she would visit him once he was released from the hospital. We ended up hugging before we headed to our classes.

"Is there always this much traffic?" I ask, tapping my foot on the floorboard of the passenger seat of Tori's car. It's slow moving, and I keep checking the clock on my phone every thirty seconds.

"We should be there in fifteen minutes, Kitty Cat." Vada rests her hands on my shoulders from the backseat, giving them a painful rub. She's obviously anxious, too.

It feels a lot longer than fifteen minutes, but we finally reach the hospital where Tori manages to find a parking spot close to the main entrance. We basically sprint through the automatic doors until the security guard gives us a disapproving look and we slow down to a quick walk. Knowing the drill well by now, we beeline it to the registrar's desk, give our names and who we're here to see, stick the visitor badges to our shirts, and quickly walk to the elevators that take us up to the ICU.

I rub my clammy hands on my jeans. "Why am I so freaking nervous?" I mutter more to myself than Tori or Vada.

"Probably because you're not sure what Ran is going to be like when you see him again," Vada says knowingly. "I mean, he's had something really bad happen to him, right? Something so bad that it changes people. And, I think, maybe you're worried about which version of him you're going to get. I know I am..." She trails off, her brown eyes wide.

I stare at her. This was not what I had expected, but I think she's spot-on.

She takes my hands into hers, stopping my fidgeting. "Don't worry, Kitty Cat. It'll be alright!"

I nod at her and take a deep breath. The elevator doors open and we march to the double doors, requesting entrance to the ICU through the com system.

My heart is absolutely pounding when we reach Ronan's room. The curtains are drawn, limiting our ability to see in through the floor-to-ceiling glass walls and door. Ronan's usual day nurse, Krista, is at the nurse's station, and when she spots us she motions for us to go into the room.

Tori quietly slides the door open and pulls back the curtain, holding it for Vada and me to slip past her into the room. The shades of the window to the outside are partially drawn, dimming the brightness in the room. I'm vaguely aware of Steve and Shane, who are both sitting on the small sofa by the window and Ronan's dad sitting in a chair in the corner of the room. The three of them are chatting quietly, their voices subdued.

As we enter, the conversation abruptly comes to an end.

"Hey guys," Frank greets us quietly while Steve and Shane get up and move toward Vada and Tori.

I, on the other hand, immediately move to Ronan's bedside, where I sit down in the empty chair and take his right hand into both of mine.

His hand radiates warmth as opposed to the coolness from the last week, but he no longer feels feverish. He feels... like Ronan. I search his face and immediately notice a difference. Aside from the bruises, which have finally begun to fade, Ronan isn't as pale; some color has returned to his cheeks. He looks like he's sleeping now—his face turned slightly to his right, less injured side—whereas before he looked lifeless, like his body was only a shell.

The nurse must have taken off the bandages last night because Ronan's left eye is no longer covered by the sterile white gauze and tape. If I leaned in close enough, I would probably be able to count the stitches it took to sew up the laceration that stretches across Ronan's left eyebrow and continues under his left eye. I wonder if this wound was inflicted with the hockey stick I saw, fractured and broken—like Ronan's body—on the living room floor. For a second, images of Ronan's mother crashing Ronan's hockey stick into his face flicker across my mind's eye, but I push the thoughts out of my head.

He's still hooked up to an IV that slowly drips a clear liquid into his veins, and machines monitor his heartbeat, oxygen levels, and blood pressure, all of which have increased since I saw him yesterday evening. His chest rises and falls steadily, calmly as he breathes in and out, and it's so comforting to watch. His left hand is still bandaged; his right knee, covered by the blanket along with the rest of the lower part of his body, remains immobile. His chest is exposed, and I notice that the bandages that previously covered the surgical incisions on his ribs and stomach were also removed. I can now see the inches-long incision on his left rib cage where they pieced his ribs back together and the smaller one on his stomach where they removed his spleen. His ribs are still severely bruised, and there are still cuts all over his body, but they're healing well.

"How long has he been asleep?" Vada asks into the room, watching me watch Ronan.

"He's been sleeping since I talked to you guys," Steve replies, and kisses Vada's forehead. Steve looks happy, as do Shane and Frank. All three have more color in their faces and their eyes are bright. I realize how much the last seven days—the uncertainty and worry for Ronan—have worn on everyone.

Franks stands up, stretches his legs, then moves to the other side of Ronan's bed. He smiles at me before his eyes move to the monitors flashing Ronan's vital signs. "The doctor came in about twenty minutes ago and she's really pleased with Ran's stats. If we can successfully manage his pain here over the next twenty-four to forty-eight hours, they'll move him out of the ICU," Frank says, sounding less tired than he has the past few days. It's obvious that his youngest son's health improvement has had an invigorating effect on him. He looks younger, too, his face shaved and no longer scruffy; he's wearing fresh clothes and his brown hair is kempt.

"When do they think he'll be able to go home?" I gaze at Ronan and those bruises, especially the one that basically took over the left side of his face. Though it's beginning to change color a little from deep, dark blue to more of a green, it's still prominent and startling. But his left eye is no longer completely swollen shut, and the cuts on his upper and lower lips are healing. I can finally recognize his handsome features again, and his full lips are enticing and as kissable as ever. I find myself yearning for him to wake up and kiss me.

"Not sure. I think he still has a long way to go before we can bring him home. His knee alone makes it almost impossible for him to move around. He's going to be non-weightbearing for a while," Frank says with a heavy sigh. "Listen guys, I'm going to go run out for a couple of hours to take care of some things. I'll bring back some food for everyone. Will you guys stick around until I get back? Shouldn't be later than maybe five-thirty or six."

We all nod, and Frank gives us the thumbs-up before he quietly leaves the room. I turn my attention back to Ronan while the others chat.

"Man, I had no idea Ran had woken up until I got to the hospital with Shane this morning. If I had known, I would have called you guys immediately," Steve tells us.

"We could tell something was different when we walked in," Shane says. "Obviously, he's not all bandaged up anymore, and for a second I thought that was it, but it's also just the way he looks versus yesterday, you know. He's in a slightly different position. He looks... more alive."

"And then my dad just went, 'Ran woke up.' I thought he was trying to be funny for a second. Fuck, when Ran opened his eyes a little while later..." Steve trails off.

"Steve started to cry," Shane continues, patting Steve's back.

"I'm so fucking relieved," Steve says, his voice cracking.

I nod because I completely share the sentiment. We all do.

***

I'm still holding Ronan's right hand, tracing the lines on his knuckles, when his hand suddenly moves in mine, startling me. My eyes flit to his face and my heart leaps when I find him looking at me. The white of his left eye is blood-red, and although it's alarming, the sheer fact that he's finally awake floods me with relief.

"Hi," I choke, tears spilling unhindered from my eyes.

Ronan lifts his right hand, and my eyes flutter shut as his thumb gently glides across my left cheek, wiping away my tears. I have missed his touch so incredibly much.

"Hey baby," he says, his tired voice barely audible. It's raspy and hoarse, I assume from the strain the intubation put on his vocal cords and from not speaking for almost a week. But that doesn't matter. None of it does. He's awake and talking to me right now, and it's everything.

"Are you okay?" he asks, his eyes searching mine, and I laugh through my tears. He's the one in the ICU, but he's asking me if I'm okay.

"I'm a lot better now. I've been so worried about you," I say, holding his hand against my cheek, relishing his warmth against my skin. "Are you in a lot of pain?"

He considers my question for a few seconds and then gives me a minuscule shake of his head. "Not too bad right now. Just don't make me cough or take a deep breath, because that shit hurts," he says, and I lower both of our hands, letting his rest on the bed.

Vada and Tori join us on the other side of the bed. Ronan slowly turns his head to face them, wincing when he tries to shift his weight, hugging his broken hand to his battered chest.

"Easy!" Steve says, approaching from behind Vada and Tori, and Shane joins a moment later. Together, the two guys help Ronan adjust, slowly, allowing him to sit up more. He needs a minute to breathe through the pain that came with the change in positions. His eyes are shut tightly, brows furrowed and teeth gritted as he tries to manage the pain. Finally, he's able to release the tension and he opens his eyes, trying to smile.

My heart breaks seeing him like this; I wish I could take all the pain away.

Ronan

I heard my dad's voice. It was distant, like listening to someone when you're under water. He was telling me to open my eyes, over and over again. And man, I had to fight like hell to come out of it. It felt like I was stuck in quicksand or mud; I don't even know. But finally, I opened my eyes to near-total darkness and a ton of pain.

I had no idea where I was, no idea how I got here, no idea what was going on. I felt completely out of it. Thoughts of Cat and our night together clung to my consciousness, and at first I couldn't for the life of me figure out what happened after I left her warm bed to head home. But then I became aware of the beeping and clicking of machines around me, the IV stuck in my right hand dripping some clear liquid into my veins, and then my dad, who was sitting next to me, holding my hand, talking to me. It confused me because I didn't remember him being home. There was a nurse by the foot of my bed, and slowly it dawned on me that I was in the hospital—and why.

The memories came rushing back as though a fucking dam broke, and for a second I wished to be pulled into unconsciousness again. But then the doctor came and told me I had been out for six days. He rattled off my injuries, which certainly explained all the pain and why it felt like an elephant was sitting on my chest. He kept talking to my dad, then asked me some questions, like whether I knew what had happened—of course I did—and what level my pain was on a scale of one to ten.

I tried to pay attention, but my brain felt foggy, and even though I had been out for close to a week I had never felt more exhausted in my entire life. Honestly, my body felt like I got hit by a freight train. Only a few minutes later the nurse gave me a pretty good cocktail of what I assume were pain meds, because I passed out pretty quickly again.

They've continued giving me strong pain meds through the IV in my right hand and I've been in and out of it for the past twelve hours, my brain foggy and slow. I'm barely able to keep my eyes open for more than about ten minutes before drowsiness overtakes me. I wake up here and there, wishing to shift my position, but the pain quickly reminds me that I'm completely immobile. I try to take advantage of the few, short awake phases and ask my dad questions, but he treads lightly in his answers. I can tell he doesn't want to upset me, but I need to know.

"Where's Mom?" I asked my dad at some point before sunrise. I wasn't sure if he knew why I was in the hospital, why I was so damn hurt, why I had been unconscious for six days. In case he didn't, I better watched what I disclosed.

"She was arrested," he said, his eyes locked on me, his face soft while the nurse prepared my IV meds.

I didn't know what to say; I was overwhelmed by conflicting emotions. She was arrested? Fuck, so someone knows what she did to me. The full extent of it or just the last time she beat me? Does that mean it's over? Is there a chance she'll be released, a chance she'll punish me?

My dad must have sensed the anxiety rising within me. "Buddy, you're safe now. I promise," he said. "She can't hurt you anymore."

I want to believe him, I really do, but I'm not so sure I can.

***

I fell asleep and woke up again only to find that Steve and Shane got to the hospital at some point in the morning. Steve actually cried when he saw me, lowering his head.

"God, Ran," Steve choked out, furiously wiping his face, trying to remain composed but failing miserably. "I thought I lost you." He sank onto the chair next to my bed.

I had a flashback to being on the ground, struggling to breathe, and I remembered Steve kneeling next to me, how frantic his voice was while I was struggling for air. "Thanks, Stevie," I said, my voice raspy. I sounded like I had been chain-smoking since I was a toddler. The doctor said it was because of the intubation, and it should get better as my vocal cords recover.

Steve analyzed my face. "For what?" he asked, his voice still thick.

"I know I wouldn't be here if you hadn't... hadn't walked in..." I started, but trailed off. I couldn't get myself to say what happened out loud.

"Why didn't you tell me what she was doing to you?" he asked.

I couldn't get into it with him right then. I couldn't unpack this—not there, not then, maybe never.

"Fuck, I'm glad you're back," Shane finally said from behind Steve, his voice tight, emotional. He moved to my side and squeezed my right hand, apparently the only part on my body people aren't afraid to touch. "You scared the shit out of us," he continued, and I could tell by the expression on his face that he meant every word.

We chatted for a few minutes before my body started to feel too heavy again and I needed to close my eyes. Sleep started dragging me under again.

"Hey, is Cat okay?" I asked groggily, looking from Steve to Shane and back again.

"Let's just say she's hanging on," Shane said.

I knitted my brows, becoming exceptionally aware of how much everyone must have been through these past few days. I feel like shit about it. I never meant for this to happen, for everyone to have to find out what was going on behind closed doors.

"Can you guys call her and let her know I'm awake? I need to see her. I need to tell her something..." I managed to say before my eyes fell shut of their own volition and I instantly fell asleep.

***

I woke up to soft, warm hands grazing my knuckles. Cat sat by my bed, her long, wavy hair falling over her shoulders and onto my forearm while she studied my hand in hers. She really is the best thing that's ever happened to me, and, fuck, even in my completely doped-up state she's the most beautiful girl I've ever seen. She's honestly like a dream.

I moved my hand and she looked up at me, her hazel eyes wide, and her tears immediately began to fall. I hate that I've been causing her pain.

I managed to stay awake for a little while, savoring the minutes I got to spend with my friends, but mostly with Cat. She didn't move from my side, resting her head on my right upper arm while Vada chatted at me about nothing in particular. Nobody addressed the giant elephant in the room, and I was grateful for it.

Steve and Shane helped me sit up—a huge feat that took a lot out of me—but I started to drift off to Vada and Tori telling me how they've all been visiting me every day. Cat's soft hair smelled like lavender shampoo, and before I knew it I was asleep with Cat by my side.

***

When I wake up again I'm dismayed to find that Cat has moved from my side, replaced by a nurse who's messing with my IV—hooking me up to more saline, I think. I turn my head to see that my dad is back and that Zack and Summer have joined the party. Everyone is eating takeout.

Shane notices I'm awake. "Hey dude. You feel like eating something?"

I shake my head slowly. "Not hungry," I groan. The pain medication takes the edge off, but there is nonetheless a constant discomfort, amplified by any careless movements or shifts in position. My mother obviously did a number on my body and, honestly, I'm surprised I made it out of that beating alive.

"You should eat something, sweet boy," Cat says, grabs her paper plate, and retakes her spot in the chair next to my bed. I watch her eat, her feet propped up on my bed as she leans back in her chair, smiling at me. What I really want, though, is to pull her into my arms, to kiss her. I want to feel her so badly.

Eventually, my dad decides it would be best if everyone left for the evening and allowed me to get some rest. I don't protest too much, even though I want nothing more than for Cat to stay with me. But I don't want to burden her. She looks tired, and I tell her so as she stretches her long legs.

"I haven't been sleeping great," she admits, and I feel guilty again knowing that my being here is the reason she's so exhausted. "But hey, you're with me now. You're awake. I bet I'm going to sleep like a baby tonight," she says with a heart-stopping smile.

"Cat," I croak, willing my voice to be louder when everyone begins to file out of my room. She turns to me, and I could drink her in. "I should've told you this a long time ago, and I'm sorry I didn't do it sooner, but I'm telling you now."

My voice cracks, and Cat looks at me expectantly.

"I love you," I finally say.

And there it is, the three words I've been holding on to for some time now. Words I should have told her weeks ago, but at least on her birthday, the night she trusted me completely. I've been head over heels for her from the moment I met her but too damn afraid to admit it out loud. I've been scared shitless by what it means for her, for me, scared of allowing myself to feel something this big with how fucked up my life is... was... is; I don't know.

But without a pause, Cat takes the five steps to my bed, leans down, and kisses me softly, gently.

My whole body aches—the powerful pain medication is beginning to wear off—but in this moment, I feel only the softness of her lips. It's not a deep kiss—I can tell she's afraid she might hurt me—but it conveys so much. When she slowly pulls back, her eyes are soft, shimmering, and it looks like she might cry again.

"I love you, too, Ran," she says.

I swear, if I wasn't lying down, my knees would buckle right then and there. Hearing her tell me she loves me is happiness like I've never known, like I had never thought was possible for me.

If only it would last....

Friday, October 8th

Ronan

I spent two more days in the ICU, where I continued to be in and out of sleep. The heavy pain medication kept me pretty sedated and groggy, even during my short awake phases. I did appreciate the way the meds took the edge off the constant pain, but I didn't like not being completely present when Cat, Shane, my brother, or my other friends came to visit. It was similar to getting so wasted at a party that you don't really have control over yourself anymore, which is something I had always avoided.

I did love seeing my grandparents, who showed up to the hospital with my dad the morning after I woke up. But that feeling of happiness at seeing them was quickly replaced by more guilt when I thought about the sacrifices everyone has had to make for me. My grandparents had to drop everything in Montana to somehow get to New York, which added more stress onto my aunt's plate, who was now saddled with running my grandparents' ranch. I also got an idea of how much school Cat missed, how little she was able to sleep and eat while I was out, how Shane wasn't able to focus on work and his dad had to step in, how Steve wasn't able to move up to Boston like he had originally planned, and on and on it went.

On Monday, I was moved to a step-down unit for observation and pain management. A respiratory therapist came twice a day to exercise my lungs. It was the most painful part of my day because I was forced to do deep-breathing exercises, which obviously forced the expansion of my broken ribs. It hurt like hell every single time and I usually slept for two or three hours after each session. It didn't take long for me to comprehend the extent of my injuries, especially to my chest and knee.

Any time a wrong move or deep breath caused a sharp pain to shoot through my body, I was taken back to that Saturday, to my mother standing over me and absolutely obliterating my body.

But my stamina was slowly improving day by day. I was steadily able to stay awake for longer periods of time, and the doctors began to space out the pain meds a little, which wasn't always successful. I'd end up with excruciating pain if they waited too long.

The best part, though, was when I finally got the okay to get out of bed. I was confined to a wheelchair because I was, and still am, non-weightbearing on my right knee, and my broken hand and fucked-up shoulder and ribs didn't allow me to move around on crutches at that point. But hey, anything was better than lying in that uncomfortable bed all day, every day, staring at the same shitty walls and ceiling. Sure, there was the TV and I had my phone, but still, being in the hospital was fucking mind-numbing. I was itching for a real shower, for my own damn clothes, for my own bed, and for uninterrupted time with Cat. I was tired of nurses and doctors bustling in and out of my room, poking me, waking me a thousand times at night to check my vitals or whatever. And I was tired of everyone tiptoeing around me.

I can tell they're all supremely careful with what they talk about and how they phrase things. There's a beast of an elephant in the room, and nobody talks about it. It's fine—I don't want to talk about it. Really, I don't. I just wish I could go back to how things were. I mean, okay, not really. I obviously don't want to get my ass beat again, but I want things to be normal.

My dad hardly left my side. Here and there he went home to shower, eat, or run errands while I rested. It's weird having him around all the time, and at first we didn't have much to talk about. Hell, we hardly knew each other. Strange that you can have a father but not really know him at all.

Once I was out of the ICU, I told my dad to sleep at home. He was staying with me at night, which couldn't have been very comfortable, but I didn't argue with him; he looked like it was something he needed to do for himself. But once I got moved I told him he should get rest at home, that I'd be fine. I still got a pretty good cocktail for pain. It knocked me out for most of the night and I woke up only when the nurse checked my vitals every few hours, placed a new IV line, or took blood.

Steve and Shane hung out with me the Monday morning after I left the ICU, and Steve informed me that our dad went to court to attend my mother's arraignment, which is where everyone found out the charges. I still can't believe this is all happening. Is this really it? Is it over? Am I safe?

My dad made it to the hospital by noon. He was dressed in slacks and a white button-down shirt.

"So?" Steve asked.

My dad looked from him to me and back to Steve, then sighed deeply. "They arraigned her, rattled off a bunch of charges like battery, assault, and child endangerment. They even threw in an attempted murder charge." He glanced at me as my breath caught. "The D.A. doesn't think it'll stick, but he said they're throwing the book at her. She pleaded not guilty."

The silence in the room was deafening. Of course she would plead not guilty to any of it.

I closed my eyes as my dad continued. "The judge set her bail at seventy-five thousand, and the D.A. just called me to tell me she already posted bail. She's out."

I had a hard time breathing and squeezed my eyes shut tighter, trying to focus on each breath, but it felt like the room was spinning. *Fuck, she's out.*

In two large strides, my dad was by my side. "Hey, look at me," he said with authority in his voice.

I opened my eyes, my breathing ragged. I was hot and cold all at the same time.

"You're safe, okay? Nothing is going to happen to you. I promise you. She's not allowed to be anywhere near you or me or Steve. The judge ordered her to stay away. And she doesn't know where you are."

"But can't she find out?" Steve asked. "She's a nurse, after all. Couldn't she just check in her system or whatever?"

My dad shook his head vehemently. "No, the D.A. assured me that Ran cannot be found in the system because he's a victim of abuse. The information is somehow made confidential, only accessible by his treating doctors and nurses and otherwise with his permission."

"Where is she?" I had to know.

"The D.A. said he thought she might stay with her parents. I don't know. She hasn't seen them in forever, but that's probably the best option for her right now. She was suspended from her job."

He proceeded to tell us that the preliminary hearing—the hearing where the judge decides if there's enough evidence that my mother did what the D.A. is saying she did and to hold a trial—was set for October.

I felt my stomach burn. My breathing was off, I was sweaty, and I felt like my heart was going to explode in my chest. I had just enough time to tell Steve to grab the trash can before I got violently sick.

I threw up what little food I had forced down in the morning. It took everything out of me. My whole body ached when the nurse stepped into the room, alarmed, to check my vitals. She ended up giving me a sedative along with my pain medication and I passed out for the rest of the afternoon. By the time I woke up, it was dark and Cat had been sitting next to my bed for the past couple of hours, reading a book in silence.

***

I can't say that the next two weeks helped me get into a better mental place.

Tuesday morning two detectives showed up to ask me all kinds of questions about what happened. They wanted to know about other times my mother became violent, and they took pictures of my injuries. I provided them only the bare minimum information, unable—or unwilling—to talk about the excruciating details of the stuff my mom had done to hurt me over the years. The detectives left after about three hours, but not because they got all the information; I was just too exhausted to keep talking about it.

I was overcome by another panic attack, which ended in more sedatives followed by more sleep, waking up only to find Cat by my side again. Honestly, it was the best and only worthwhile part of my day—when Cat showed up after school. On the weekends she would spend all day sitting with me while I healed. During the week she'd do her homework or study, read to me or just talk to me about her day and what everyone was up to. I missed it all so much.

Shane and Steve visited me every day, too. Steve told me he postponed attending Boston University in-person for one semester and requested to take his classes virtually. His request was apparently granted, given the exceptional circumstances. So he was taking classes online in an effort not to fall behind too much, but he lost his dorm room and obviously doesn't get the full college experience. I added that to my list of shit to feel guilty about.

***

The Saturday after I was moved out of the ICU, my dad seemed off when he got to the hospital in the late morning. It was only after Steve's continued hinting and prodding that my dad finally confessed to me what I had suspected for a while now—that he had been having an affair. It explains so much: the fact that he'd been gone for longer periods of time and seemed more eager to leave when he was home with us. He explained that he met her about three years ago. She lives in Virginia, and at first, he told me, it was just sex, but it quickly evolved and he realized he wanted to be with her. Finally, things came to a head and he made the call to end it with my mother.

"Ran, I think I set Rica off that morning. I had called her and told her I was coming home and that I was moving out, that I wanted a divorce," he said, his voice heavy with guilt. "I pulled up to the house and saw the ambulance and the cop cars outside. And when I walked in, you were on the floor. It looked like a battlefield, and they were working on you, trying to restart your heart..." he choked before he trailed off.

"She's in New York right now. Dad's girlfriend. She's here," Steve told me matter-of-factly.

I creased my eyebrows. "Seriously?"

"Yeah." Steve chuckled dryly, skillfully ignoring the stern look my dad was giving him. "I met her last night. And so did Morai and Athair." He had a grin on his face that made me think my grandmother—usually one of the kindest, most welcoming people in this world—probably gave my dad the hardest time about this whole thing.

I'm not totally sure how I feel about all of this. I mean, I'm not really surprised about my dad's affair, but it still feels strange to finally have confirmation of something I subconsciously knew for a long time.

"You should meet her, too," Steve told me earnestly.

My dad shifted in his spot. "No, bud. There's no rush to any of this." His gaze moved from Steve to me. "What's most important is your recovery right now," he said, his voice serious but warm.

I exhaled deeply. "It doesn't matter, Dad. Whether you bring her around now, next week, or in two months, it doesn't change anything. You're not planning on dumping her, right?" I checked unemotionally.

My dad studied me for a moment, his eyes full of regret, before he finally shook his head no.

I shrugged. "Yeah, well, might as well just get it over with, then," I said, feeling numb. God, was all so fucking surreal. My mother was charged with trying to kill me, and my dad was talking about me meeting his girlfriend.

What we hadn't talked about was what was going to happen once I was out of the hospital. I didn't know if he'd continue being gone so much. I had no idea what was going to happen with my mother. I didn't know anything—how long I'd be in the hospital or how long it would take me to recover from this shit. I had a hard time thinking clearly. My head felt foggy most of the time, probably from the medications, and when I had moments of clarity, everything around me seemed to crash in on me. Panic would constrict my chest, which lead to more medication, more fog. It was a vicious cycle.

***

I met my dad's girlfriend, Penny, when she joined my dad at the hospital on Sunday. The respiratory therapist had just left and I was exhausted and in pain when they showed up. Penny seemed nice, though, and it was clear as day how much my dad likes her, his face positively alight with happiness. He acts so differently with her than he did with my mother—always making small physical contact with her, his hand on her low back as he introduces her to me. It reminds me so much of how I am with Cat—my inability to keep my hands off her, and how I have to quell the need to touch her all the damn time.

I wanted to be happy for my dad, but I couldn't help but feel that if only he had made more of an effort at home, maybe I wouldn't have been in the place where I was at that moment, feeling like my lungs were on fire, lying in a fucking hospital bed while my shattered bones healed.

Mercifully, Penny didn't overstay her welcome. Picking up on my exhaustion and rising pain level, my dad informed me that Penny was heading back to Virginia. She said her goodbyes a few minutes later and left just before sleep pulled me under again.

***

That following Monday I woke up from one of my medication-induced naps only to find my dad sitting with some woman dressed in black trousers and a lilac cardigan. Her light-brown hair was pulled into a bun and she took notes on a clipboard as she chatted quietly with my dad. Her name turned out to be Doctor Liz Seivert and she was a therapist. My therapist, to be exact, as she informed me in a way that made me feel like I was a feral animal to be approached with caution.

She spent some time asking me questions—nothing invasive, nothing about my mother or anything that would trigger a panic attack. She wanted to know about school, work, hockey, my friends, and Cat. She had a comforting way of communicating, urging me to continue talking without pushing when I declined to go into detail about certain things. We talked for a while, my dad listening carefully without uttering so much as a word the whole time.

"With your permission, Ronan, I'd like to come see you twice a week for a while." She stood up, sliding her pen and clipboard into a black purse that she slung over her shoulder.

"That seems like a lot," I said, looking at my dad. "Is this really necessary?"

"It is," he said matter-of-factly, and it kind of rubbed me the wrong way. Who the hell was he to make decisions for me when he hadn't done anything for me for the last seventeen years of my life?

"Fine, whatever," I muttered. I was too fucking drained to argue.

"Okay, I'll stop by on Wednesday," she said to me before turning to my dad. "Call my office if he's released prior to that and I'll come to your home."

My dad nodded, and she left.

***

I didn't get discharged before Wednesday, and not even on Thursday. But on Friday morning, after the respiratory therapist again tortured me for an hour and a half, one of the surgeons who operated on me told my dad that they'd release me that afternoon. A few days prior, the doctor and my dad had talked about sending me to a rehab facility to regain some strength, but all I wanted was to go home. My dad and I fought about it. A lot.

"Ran, our house isn't equipped with what you need right now. I don't think we can even get you up to your room with that knee," he tried to reason with me, pointing at the contraption that had been completely immobilizing my knee for three weeks by then. Even getting into a wheelchair so I could actually use the bathroom and take a hot shower—best shower of my life, by the way—took every ounce of my strength.

"I don't care," I argued. I knew I was being unreasonable and stubborn, but all I wanted was normalcy. "I'll sleep on the couch; I'll use the bathroom downstairs. I'll claw my way up the stairs. I don't care. Please, Dad!"

But in the end the doctors and my dad prevailed, and I was sent to another hospital for rehab purposes. I spent three more weeks there trying to get back some mobility. I didn't think it was possible, but the rehab hospital sucked even more than the other one because I spent so much of my time in physical therapy for my hand, my shoulder, my lungs, my knee, and the visiting hours were much more limited. The unpleasant result was, of course, that I got to see much less of Cat and my friends. I spent way too much time stuck in my own head, and slowly but surely everything began to catch up with me... and not in a good way.

***

By the time I'm finally, *finally* released, it's October. My left hand and shoulder are healed enough that I'm no longer reliant on a wheelchair. I'm able to use crutches to get around, though it's still hard work and requires a lot of energy—energy I really don't have yet—and I typically have to rest every ten feet or so, needing to catch my breath or just sit the fuck down. I'm not used to being so damn dependent on people, and I hate how weak I feel. It's pissing me off.

My lungs are slowly healing, as are my ribs. Really deep breathing still hurts, as does coughing, which I don't do so much now that I've recovered from the pneumonia I apparently contracted while I was in a coma. Who even knew that was a possibility?

Most of the bruising on my body is pretty much gone by now, though the one around my left eye is taking a bit to resolve. The lack of movement and even greater lack of appetite have resulted in some steep loss of muscle mass and weight. I'm down almost twenty pounds from my previous weight and my clothes feel baggy when my dad and Steve pick me up to take me home on Friday afternoon.

It feels weird to drive up to the house. My car is still parked exactly where I left it the night I came home from Cat's and instantly my head is flooded with memories. I'm suddenly not so sure I can go into that house. As much as I wanted to just go home, I don't know that I can actually do it now that I'm here. I feel paralyzed, panic filling my chest, making it hard to breathe.

"You ready?" Steve asks, holding the passenger door of my dad's Tahoe open for me, my crutches in his hands. He must see the panic in my face because he squats down next to me, looking at me intently. "What's wrong?"

"I don't know if I can go in there," I admit, trying to focus on my breathing.

"Yeah you can. You know why? Because Cat and Shane are in there waiting for you. And because this is your home. And Onyx will be so excited to see you. And because I'll be with you, and so will Dad."

He's right—all of those are good reasons. I close my eyes, taking deep breaths in, holding them for a three-count, and letting them out slowly.

I let Steve help me out of the car, carefully positioning my still-immobilized right leg so as not to put any weight on it before grabbing my crutches and carefully hobbling up the stairs and through the front doors.

Cat

I've been a bundle of nerves all day, feeling like a child on Christmas Eve, because Ronan is finally getting released from the hospital today. I just can't wait. It's been six weeks to the day since I was with him outside of the hospital setting, five weeks since he woke up from his coma. Everyone is really happy with how fast he's healing from his physical injuries. His knee and ribs are taking the longest to heal, but that was to be expected. It's the emotional trauma we're most worried about.

Ronan hasn't talked about what happened to him that Saturday; he hasn't opened up to me, his brother, his dad, or even Shane. We don't push him or prod in any way. Despite Ronan's reluctance or refusal to discuss even anything remotely related to the abuse he endured, the impact it has had on him is obvious to everyone who's close to him. Ronan is quieter, more subdued than I've ever known him to be. His appetite is lackluster, especially given his stature; he rarely eats, and when he does, he never finishes his plate. Sure, the hospital food probably isn't really anything to be desired, but Ronan also doesn't eat the food any of us smuggle into the hospital for him. And he's fatigued; everything seems to cost him an incredible amount of energy. The worst part is that even with the passage of time and his physical recovery, his mental and emotional health seem to be declining day by day.

I'm aware that he's been seeing a therapist a few times a week. My mom mentioned early on to me, after Ronan had woken up, that she thought he would need some therapy quickly. She was delighted when I told her that he was getting help already, though she was honest with me when she sat me down one afternoon couple of weeks ago.

"Kitty, I know you really care about Ronan," she told me warmly.

"I love him, Mom," I told her, making her smile.

"I know. And I know he loves you, too. That's been obvious to me for a while now," she said with an earnest nod. "But, sweet pea, I just want you to be aware that the next few weeks and months are probably going to be really difficult. Severe trauma like the kind Ronan has suffered is hard to overcome, and everyone responds to it differently, you know?"

"Yeah, I know," I nodded.

My mom shook her head and sighed. "There will be triggers for Ronan, especially once he comes home, back to the place where really bad things happened to him. It's like a soldier returning to the battlefield," she continued, and I creased my eyebrows. "And it won't always be predictable what will set him off and what his reaction will be."

"What are you trying to tell me, Mom?"

She exhaled deeply again. "You're so young, Kitty. I just want you to be prepared; I want you to think about if you're ready to weather something this tough at your age."

I finally understood what she was trying to relay. "Are you telling me I should break up with Ran?" I asked, a noticeable edge to my voice.

"No, but I want you to at least think about whether you're ready to make such a commitment right now, or whether it might be better for you to take a step back and give Ronan and yourself a little distance while he tries to work through his trauma," she said, her voice warm but resolute.

"He needs me, Mom. I can't just abandon him now," I argued with her, still in disbelief.

"And I need you to be safe, Kitty. You've been through terrible things yourself very recently," she said, reminding me of the abusive relationship with Adam I escaped mere months ago. "I think you still have your very own healing to do. And I don't know that you can or should set your own well-being aside right now."

I nodded at her, letting her words sink in. I really thought about what she was telling me. I knew she was worried for me and wanted to keep me safe. And I knew she wasn't telling me to leave Ronan because she thought he wasn't good enough for me; she was telling me to consider creating a protective barrier, to not get too involved in Ronan's struggles.

"Ran put his own well-being aside when he protected me from Adam," I finally said. "He kept me safe from Adam to his own detriment."

"I know, Kitty, but that's—"

"Ran has helped me heal, Mom. You yourself told me that not all boys are bad, that I would learn to trust again. Do you remember?" I asked her, and she nodded, her eyes soft. "And Ran did that for me. He is... Ran is so perfect to me, Mom. He's kind and respectful. He's never put a hand on me, has never even made me think he would or could do that to me. Mom, Ran has never even raised his voice at me. And he's been nothing but amazing to me even though... even though it looks like his mom was probably hurting him this entire time. I wouldn't be where I am—so happy—if it weren't for Ran. He's helping me heal—has helped me heal for the past four months, Mom. And I'm going to do the same for him," I told her with finality in my voice.

She smiled at me then, though her eyes reflected some sadness. "Okay. Just be mindful, Kitty. Ronan has a long road ahead of him. You are an incredible, wonderful, selfless young woman for wanting to be by his side through this. I honestly didn't expect anything different from you. But, just know that I'm here, okay? Come talk to me about things. And, be patient with yourself and with Ronan. Things will probably be really different while he... while he finds his way back to himself."

Over the next two weeks, my mom has continued to talk to me about what to expect, what Ronan's state of mind might be. She continued to tell me about triggers, anxiety, and post-traumatic stress disorder—all the things she talked to me about after the violent ending to my relationship with Adam. And I've been talking things through with her, taking note of any tips that might be helpful to me because, just like Ronan has been an instrumental part in my own healing, I want to be that for him in return.

***

I've been hanging out at Ronan's house since getting out of school this afternoon, yet again skipping softball practice, which has been a regular occurrence these past few weeks. I missed the entirety of the first week, and my coach has been really understanding. I have made a pretty regular showing at practice over the past three weeks, though, mostly because seeing Ronan wasn't really in the cards while he was in rehab. Visitations at the rehabilitation facility were much, much more limited because he was in therapy so much and their visiting hours weren't as generous. If I was lucky, I had an hour with him every day.

I'm desperate for alone time with him. We haven't been alone together since my birthday. His dad or Steve or one of our friends are always around, and it's wearing on me. I'm obviously aware that we couldn't have done anything intimate even if we had been alone, but I just want to be able to give him my undivided attention, and I want his. And yeah, I want to be physically close to him again, a fact that I mentioned to Vada just a couple of days ago, resulting in her listing all the ways Ronan and I could be intimate without actually having sex. I kept blushing at her suggestions, but I have to admit, I'm intrigued to try some of them.

I'm sitting in the living room of the Soult house with Shane, watching a hockey game. Shane has been pointing out the different shots and maneuvers the players use to score, and explaining penalties and the various positions to me. I have to say, I'm learning a lot, although I'm really just biding my time before Ronan is finally home.

The glass table that somehow shattered when Ronan was assaulted has been replaced with a gray driftwood table. There's a new, light-blue rug on the floor; the old one was thrown out immediately because it was stained with Ronan's blood. Onyx is asleep on the other end of the couch and Shane is telling me all about slap shots when the front door opens. Shane and I exchange a quick glance and stand up. We hurry into the hallway where Frank has his back to us while Ronan makes his way through the front door, followed by Steve.

When Ronan's eyes meet mine, he gives me a dazzling smile. I forget about everyone around me and rush toward him, flinging myself into his arms. I'm probably a little too forceful because Ronan lets out a painful grunt as I collide with him and his still-not-fully-healed chest. But he nonetheless drops his crutches and wraps his arms around me, leaning against the wall for stability as he holds me tightly against him.

It's really the first time I've been able to hug him in six weeks. I inhale him, closing my eyes as I feel his warmth and, for a moment, the weight of the last month and a half feels like it might crash in on me. Now that I'm finally back in his arms and feel the rise and fall of his chest against mine, his pounding heart, I realize just how close I came to actually losing him.

Before I can go further down that road, Frank clears his throat, bringing me back to the now. I pull back a little from Ronan, blushing when I become aware of the presence of Steve, Shane, and Ronan's dad.

"Way to ruin the moment, Dad," Ronan chuckles, and the tension breaks.

"Welcome home, dude," Shane says, giving Ronan a gentle hug. "How are you feeling?"

"I'm okay," Ronan nods.

"Alright, bud, why don't you go sit and rest a little? Shane, what are your thoughts on dinner?" Frank asks, and Frank and Shane start talking about grabbing food for dinner since Zack, Summer, Vada, and Tori should be here soon.

Steve takes Ronan's bag upstairs while I pick up the crutches Ronan dropped and hand them to him so he can follow me into the living room.

When we round the corner from the hallway to the living room, Ronan stops, his eyes darkening. I recognize the look; I've seen it these past weeks whenever he's on the brink of an anxiety attack. He's getting triggered right now. His shoulders tense, his jaw tightens, and his breathing speeds up. He can't seem to make himself move into the living room. He stands there, his eyes on the spot where his mother almost beat him to death.

"Ran?" I say, and cautiously move toward him. I expected some kind of reaction to him actually coming home, back to the place where his life almost ended. Luckily, my mom's professional insight and the wisdom she's shared with me over the last few weeks has prepared me for this moment. "Ronan," I whisper again, trying to snap his attention back to me and away from the building panic.

He looks at me, his brows furrowed, body still tense.

"Come sit with me," I urge softly, and I touch his forearm. My mom told me physical touch is a good way to help ground someone who might be having an anxiety attack, and she was right. Ronan seems to relax a little and he walks with me to the couch.

Onyx, not having realized her person had come home, freaks out, jumping off the couch with her tail wagging. She whimpers at Ronan, who carefully lowers himself onto the sofa before propping up his injured leg on the new coffee table. He pats the spot next to him for Onyx to jump up on. She doesn't need to be asked twice and goes crazy sniffing Ronan, stepping all over him. He gets her to settle down next to him and then reaches his hand out to me. When I take it, he pulls me toward him, urging me onto the sofa, and I gladly comply. But he isn't satisfied with me just sitting next to him and he pulls me onto his lap. I straddle him, my knees on either side of him, and I settle on his upper legs, careful not to add any weight anywhere near his knee. His left hand comes up under my chin, and he gently pulls me toward him until his soft lips meet mine.

I sigh deeply, feeling like I'm finally coming up for air after weeks and weeks under water. I part my lips to allow his tongue access, which he immediately takes advantage of and deepens the kiss. I've waited so long for this, and my pulse quickens as I push myself against him, feeling his heart hammer in his chest. His hands find my waist and he slowly glides them downward, first to my hips, then to my butt as he urges me even closer. I can already feel him swell, pressing between my legs, so I slowly grind my hips against him, causing him to groan against my lips.

"God, Cat, I've missed you so much," Ronan says, his voice quiet and husky.

Heat and need rush to my core and my hands wander to the bottom of his hoodie, pushing it up so my fingers can feel the bare skin of his stomach just above his jeans. He follows my lead, his hands sliding underneath my shirt and up my back, leaving a tingly trail where his fingers touch my skin. His right hand rests on my back while his left moves around my ribs to my front. His thumb first outlines the bottom of my bra, then glides over the lacy fabric, grazing my nipple.

A delicious jolt of electricity zaps from my nipple all the way down to my core and between my legs. "Ran," I moan. "I don't think..." I trail off as his mouth leaves mine, kissing my jawline and then my neck. My head falls to the side, exposing myself to him, wanting more of him as my hips grind against him again. I can feel him rock-hard underneath me, his manhood straining against his jeans.

God, we're both getting way too worked up right now and there are people in the house. I just know we're going to get walked in on any second now, so I force myself to stop and push back a little.

Ronan blinks at me, his eyes hooded and glossy with want, his breathing shallow. My hands are still on his stomach, touching his exposed skin.

"I don't think this is a good time. Shane and your dad are just right over there," I say, trying to catch my breath. There's a mix of disappointment and frustration in my voice, and I know he feels the same.

"You're probably right." With a mischievous glint in his eyes, he glides his thumb slowly across my hard nipple once more before retrieving his hands from under my shirt. I giggle, kissing him softly. "Just hold on a second before you get off my lap," he says. "I need a minute."

I giggle again; I can still very much feel his erection between my legs and I wish we were alone, wish I could feel all of him right now.

"I love you," I say between kisses.

He hugs me against him tightly. "I love you, too."

The happiness that surges through me whenever Ronan says he loves me is indescribable. I had been so afraid that I would never get the chance to tell him how I really felt about him, would never hear him say he loved me. But not only did he wake up, he also made sure to tell me he loves me and has felt that way for a while. It didn't require much of me to reply with the same three words because, much like him, I knew I had loved him for weeks by then. I was only ever waiting for the right moment to tell him.

"Here," I say, and move my hands around the back of my neck, undoing the clasp of his necklace. "I think you should have this back." I place the thin chain in his left hand.

"Thank you for keeping this safe for me," he says, his voice low, contemplative as he puts his necklace around his neck.

Frank, Shane, and Steve walk into the living room then, and I slide off Ronan's lap, but not without purposely grinding my hips against his groin one more time as payback. Everyone is oblivious, but Ronan grins at me. God, I hope we get the chance to be alone very soon.

But we don't, at least not tonight. A few minutes later, Zack, Vada, Summer, and Tori show up, laden with food and drinks, and we end up hanging out in the living room, spread out across the couches, armchair, and the floor while we watch some random movie. We eat, with the exception of Ronan, whose appetite has still not returned. Even though he's wearing that dark-green hoodie today, I can tell his clothes are looser than they were six weeks ago. I'm snuggled up against him on the couch, his right arm draped over my shoulder as I lean against his chest, always aware of his injuries, always careful not to hurt him. I feel him fall asleep after a while, and I don't move, not wanting to wake him.

Shane puts on another movie, and we all enjoy each other's company, relishing the fact that we're all together, all in one piece. Sort of.

Saturday, October 9th

Cat

My phone rings at ten the next morning, and I smile when I see Ronan's name on my screen.

"Good morning, sweet boy," I say, stretching in bed. I had been lounging around, scrolling through my phone for a few minutes and hadn't actually gotten out of bed yet.

"Hey baby." He sounds tired, like he didn't sleep well.

"How are you feeling?" I ask, sitting up in bed.

"Fine," he says, though I don't believe him.

I knit my brows together. "You sound really tired. Bad night?"

"Yeah, kind of. It's just a little weird being home. But I'm fine," he adds quickly.

I get up and walk out of my room and into the bathroom, where I turn on the shower.

"What are you doing?" he asks. I bet he can hear the water running in the background.

I decide to play along. "I'm about to get out of these itchy clothes of mine and stand naked under the shower, getting all wet and soapy."

"Is that so?" he asks, his voice low, husky.

"Uh-huh," I say. "What are you going to do about it?"

"Nothing I can do at the moment, but I will get to see you later today, right?"

"That's the plan," I say, excitement bubbling in my chest with the knowledge that I will get to spend some quality time with him. "Did Steve talk to you? We were thinking about heading to the beach, but I'm not sure you'll be able to get around."

"I'll be fine as long as I stay out of the sand. Just hang out on the deck with me," he says, then adds, "or maybe in one of the bedrooms. I'm desperate to get you alone."

Heat rushes through me as I imagine his hands all over me. "I like that idea," I say. "I'm so glad you're home." A deep sigh escapes me.

He doesn't respond right away. "Baby, I'm so sorry for all the shit you and everyone had to go through these last few weeks. I didn't want any of you to be pulled into this darkness. I know it's been hard on everyone. I'm sorry."

I can't believe he's actually apologizing to us for what his mother did to him. That's how brainwashed he was by his mother; she managed to make him believe that everything that happened was his fault.

"Listen to me, sweet boy: none of this is your fault. Of course we worried about you, because we love you. *I* love you," I say with as much sincerity in my voice as I can possibly muster. I need him to hear it, need him to understand that he's not to blame for what happened to him, just like he needed me to understand that the wounds Adam inflicted on me weren't my fault. It's funny how Ronan recognized the abuse and the fault fallacy in my situation, but he's unable to see it through his own trauma.

There's silence on his end, and I really don't want him to go down a dark path right now.

"Alright, well if you don't mind I'm going to get naked now, so I'll need to let you go," I say, my voice teasing again.

He chuckles. "Or you could also just give me a video call and let me watch you take a shower. I wouldn't mind seeing you... soap yourself up."

For a second, I consider this option. "I didn't take you for a Peeping Tom," I say, stripping off my pajama bottoms.

"Only when it comes to you," he says, his voice gravelly. "I can't keep my eyes off you."

I blush. I'm so in love with him, it's overwhelming sometimes. "Well, I might just need another shower this evening. You know, that beach sand gets *everywhere*."

"You're killing me, baby," he chuckles.

"That's not good. I want you to stay very much alive for a very, very long time," I laugh.

"Then you're going to have to stop teasing me so much."

"As if you don't tease me."

He laughs again. "Good point. Let's just agree to not tease each other. At least not until we see each other in a few hours and I can actually do something about it."

"And what are you going to do about it then, Ran?" I keep edging him on because I'm getting worked up thinking about spending some alone time with him later today.

"Oh, I can think of a few things." I can hear the need in his voice now.

"Even with your knee?"

He lets out a raspy chuckle that sends electricity straight between my legs. "I'll figure it out. Where there's a will, there's a way."

Well, I have no doubt now that the next few hours are going to feel way too long.

Luckily, Vada drops by an hour later and convinces me to go on a quick shopping trip to pick up some warmer clothes now that it's fall and steadily getting colder outside. We talk about Halloween, and Vada throws out the idea of planning a Halloween party at Shane's beach house, of course. I like the idea, especially since this will be my first Halloween here in New York, with my friends, with Ronan. I feel so light having him home, like the opportunities are endless, and I tell her so while we're standing in line to pay for a pair of jeans for Vada and two sweaters for me.

"That reminds me," she says, and her tone takes on a serious note. "When I talked to Stevie this morning he said Ran had a horrible night."

I raise my eyebrows at her. "He sounded tired when he called me, and he told me he didn't sleep well, but said he was fine."

She pulls a face. "Stevie said Ran had some horrible nightmares last night that he couldn't wake up from. It happened like three or four times. Think drenched in sweat, tossing and turning, like night terrors that you can't wake up from."

"Ran didn't say anything like that," I say, my good mood wiped away, replaced by concern and a little bit of hurt that he didn't feel he could tell me about his dreams. But I remember what my mom has been telling me about trauma and people's ability to work through it or talk about it. I know Ronan will need time, and I can't push him into anything. All I can do is be patient and be there for him. I'll just be present, tell him I love him, show him he's safe with me.

"He hasn't talked about it with Stevie this morning, either. Stevie said Ran refused to engage with his dad about it, too, and only said that he's been having these nightmares for weeks now. His dad is apparently really worried about the whole thing. Stevie said his dad called Ran's therapist and, I guess, they're going to keep an eye on it," she continues as we pay and walk out of the store.

"I wish there was something I could do to help him," I say. "It just feels like he's all alone in this."

"I know what you mean, but we're doing what we can, Kitty Cat. All you can do is be there for him. You can't undo the past, but we can all help him get through this."

When she drops me back at home, Vada and I agree that she'll pick me up a little while later to head to the beach.

"Bring your swimsuit, Kitty Cat," Vada says.

"It's October! I'm not going in the ocean," I protest, incredulous that she would even suggest this nonsense.

She laughs. "For the hot tub, silly!"

***

Vada picks me up in the afternoon to head to Shane's. It's cold today, and everyone is hanging out inside the house. I spot Ronan immediately when I walk in. He's standing by the kitchen counter, resting on his crutches. He's wearing black jeans and a black hoodie, and he looks hot as hell in all black. I admire him for a few seconds, relishing the fact that he is mine and I am his, while he chats with Shane with a smile on his face. I'm so relieved to have him home. There was a huge, gaping hole in our midst with him gone. There's still a slight bruise under his left eye, and the scars haven't begun to fade yet, but all that doesn't take away from his perfect features. If anything, it makes him even more gorgeous.

I wave to the others as I leave Vada's side and make my way over to Ronan, whose eyes meet mine.

"Hey baby," he says, moving his left crutch to the other side so he can wrap his arm around my waist and pull me in for a deep kiss.

I taste the tequila on his tongue and pull back, eyeing him. "You're drinking?" I ask, a bit surprised. I'm not totally sure he's recovered enough to drink, and I wonder how the alcohol might interact with the pain medication he still takes.

He just shrugs.

"He's had a few already," Shane chimes in, giving me an apologetic look.

I turn my attention back to Ronan. He doesn't look intoxicated, but I decide to keep a close eye on him nonetheless.

"Don't worry so much about me, baby. I'm fine," Ronan assures me. "And I figured since I'm not really supposed to be here right now, I might as well make the most of it."

I don't really understand what he means by that, but I don't have a chance to ask him about it. My concerns evaporate when Ronan's hand on my low back pulls me close to his body and he kisses me again, urging me to part my lips. When I do, he slips his tongue deep into my mouth. My breath hitches, and a moan involuntarily escapes me as my knees buckle. Ronan's right hand snaps to the counter, steadying himself as his left hand on my back holds me up. I loop my arms tightly around his neck and pull myself closer to him, crashing my chest against his, eliciting a groan from Ronan. I need to be better about being gentle while he recovers from his injuries.

I vaguely notice Shane mumbling something under his breath as he leaves the kitchen to give us some privacy and joins the others in the living room.

Ronan's lips are hot on mine, and I feel as though my whole body is on fire. He continues to devour me, our tongues entwined, his hand on my back, while I hold onto him tightly, not ever wanting to let him go. His lips leave my mouth, kissing my jawline, my neck, before his head dips down and he kisses my collarbone as I let my head fall back. That sensitive spot between my thighs is already beginning to pulse, aching with need for him.

"I want you so badly," Ronan groans against my skin, inhaling sharply, and a shiver travels through my whole body. I can feel the sexual tension between us, the need pooling deep in my core. I want him just as badly; the memories of our one night together are fresh in my mind as if it happened only yesterday.

Just then, Vada comes bounding into the kitchen. "Oh, hey lovebirds," she chirps.

Ronan groans, lifting his head. "I'm starting to think you've made it your personal mission to find the worst possible timing for joining us."

Vada laughs. "Gotta keep you kids innocent, right?" She pokes Ronan's biceps as she passes him on her way to the fridge, where she grabs a can of soda. "We're hopping into the hot tub. You guys coming?" she asks, opening the can with a click and a hiss.

"Umm..." I look at Ronan, and he raises his eyebrows, leaving the decision up to me. "I guess so." I can tell Ronan was hoping for a different answer, but I smile at him. "I'm going to go put on my swimsuit," I say, and wink at him.

"Yay!" Vada exclaims. "I'll see you in the hot tub." She leaves the kitchen and walks out onto the deck where the others are already in their swimsuits, ready to take a dip in the warm, bubbling water.

"Are you coming, too?" I ask Ronan, who has replaced his crutches and is getting ready to limp out of the kitchen.

"I'm not sure I should yet," he says. "But don't worry, I'll still enjoy myself admiring you in your swimsuit." And now it's his turn to wink at me as I grin at him.

I walk into one of the spare bedrooms and lock the door behind me. I take my light-blue two-piece swimsuit out of my bag and strip down, replacing my bra and panties with the simple bikini bottoms and top, which I tie in the back. I stuff my clothes into my bag, leaving it at the foot of the bed, and unlock the door to walk to the deck and get in the hot tub.

I open the door and jump backwards. Ronan's standing right in front of me, his hand up like he was about to knock.

He chuckles when he sees me. "Sorry, I didn't mean to scare the shit out of you," he says, but then his eyes darken as he takes in my barely dressed body. "God, baby," he says, his voice ragged. "You are absolutely perfect."

He takes a step toward me, reaches his left hand around my lower back, and pulls me in toward him with his crutches still supporting him. He crashes his lips against mine. My arms encircle him and I open my mouth eagerly, letting him taste me, tasting him in return.

He urges me backwards until the back of my knees bump against the soft bed.

"Hold on," Ronan breathes, and breaks the contact with me to lean back, push the door shut, and lock it. My heart is kicking in my chest in anticipation of his body on mine, and he doesn't disappoint. His hands are back on me in less than a second, as are his lips. There's a desperate urgency in the way he touches me, like it's this or death for him. He kisses me, nipping my bottom lip, then leaving hot trails on my jawline. He kisses and licks as he works his way down to my neck, then my collarbone, where he grazes his teeth against my sensitive skin. It's instinctive, animalistic maybe, and so arousing. I feel my desire for him between my thighs, feel it soaking into my bikini bottoms as my body readies itself to receive him.

My fingers hook the belt loops of Ronan's jeans, and I eagerly pull him toward me so I can feel his hips against mine. I slide both my hands underneath his hoodie, under his shirt, and hungrily feel his bare skin. His abs are taut under my fingers and I take my time touching him, outlining his muscles, feeling him, traveling up to his chest as Ronan continues to tease my skin. He drops his crutches, taking all weight off his injured leg, to let his warm hands roam my naked back until, finally, with two quick pulls, he undoes the strings on my swimsuit top, which falls off me and to the floor.

Needing to feel his skin against me, I push up the hem of his hoodie and shirt, which he hastily pulls over his head. I allow my hands to run all over his chest and back down to his stomach, purposely tracing his prominent scars, wishing my touch would erase them. My hands slide down farther and I fumble with the button on his jeans, undoing it. I hesitate for a moment, then simply slide my hand down inside his boxer briefs. I encircle him and stroke his hardness, surprising us both with my forwardness. He is thick and rock-hard in my hand, though his skin is silky as I stroke his length from the base to the tip. His hips buck slightly when my fist bumps against the ridge just under the head.

"Fuck, Cat," Ronan groans, and his lips momentarily leave my skin. His eyes close, his breathing heavy while I caress him.

I enjoy the fact that I can make him feel like this, that my touch gets him high. I slightly increase the pressure, tightening my fist as I rub him a few seconds longer, pumping him. My eyes are glued to his face, which looks almost pained with pleasure—his lips slightly parted, brows furrowed, eyes shut tightly as he focuses on my touch. I feel powerful at the realization that I can make him lose control, can make him surrender himself to me like this even after all he's been through.

But I become impatient, needing more of him, and I tug on his pants, wanting them off.

He pushes me back gently, and I sit first on the bed before pulling up my knees and scooting back to lie down all the way. Ronan stands over me, his glossy eyes roaming my body appreciatively, and I shiver under his gaze before he lowers his body carefully onto mine. His lips crash against me as he pulls my swimsuit bottoms to my knees, and I kick them off the rest of the way. I'm completely exposed to him, and his hands and mouth suddenly seem to be everywhere at the same time, his hunger for me seemingly insatiable. He kisses my neck and my collarbone, licking and nipping his way steadily downward. I moan loudly when Ronan's tongue glides over my nipple, making it hard only to suck it into his mouth. His hand cups my other breast, his thumb teasing me, driving me absolutely wild. Heat and voracious want pulse between my legs, and they fall open.

"Ran, I need you," I whisper, and Ronan pulls back, his hands on either side of me as he scans my face. Then he kisses me fiercely. He tries to adjust his position but winces, and his right hand snaps to his knee. "Are you okay?" I breathe, concerned.

Ronan doesn't answer me. Instead, he kisses me deeply before pushing himself up and undoing the brace on his knee.

Although he moves more gingerly, his eyes are ablaze with want. He turns to his side to lie next to me, pulling me with him, facing me. I push his jeans down, and he manages to get them off the rest of the way, always gentle, always careful with his knee. Then his right hand moves around my thigh and pulls my leg over his hip, making me vulnerable to him. I'm beyond ready to feel him, aching for his touch there. My eyes flutter shut and my head falls back when Ronan's hand moves from my back to my stomach, down between my thighs, then gently glides over that throbbing flesh that makes me pant out his name. He pushes me closer and closer to the edge as he strokes me softly, his fingers circling, sweeping, playing with the pressure until he finds one that makes me arch my back into him.

"God, Ran," I whimper.

I moan, my breathing shallow, and I feel the pleasure build, threatening to overtake my thoughts and senses any second now. Just as I'm about to go over the edge, Ronan slips a finger inside me, feeling me like that while he continues to stroke me gently with his thumb. It's all I need and I come undone, whimpering a moan with each orgasmic wave seizing my body.

"Fuck, baby," Ronan groans quietly.

The ecstasy pulses through my veins and my hips grind against his hand. I never want him to stop touching me exactly the way he's touching me right now; the ripples of pleasure rolling through me leave no space for thought or breath. It's all-consuming.

But too soon, the waves let up, my climax waning, and I regain control long enough for Ronan to pull off his boxer briefs and roll onto his back. With both his hands, he grabs my hips and pulls me up and over him. I straddle his lap and, carefully, he pulls my hips down as he pushes up and into me. He watches me the entire time, making sure he isn't causing me any pain as this is only the second time we've been together like this.

But there is no pain, only pleasure as he enters me. His eyes shut when I lower myself onto him all the way.

My body is primed and ready for him. I hold my breath at the sensation of him stretching and filling me, taking up all available space, and I marvel at the feeling that we were made just for one another, like two pieces of a puzzle fitting perfectly.

"I love you, Cat. I've always loved you," Ronan breathes as he begins to thrust up and into me over and over again. He moves slowly at first, giving me time to adjust to him again. The way he feels—his fingers delving into the apples of my hips, his delicious thrusts—and the sound of his husky voice swirling all around me flood me with overwhelming love for him.

I don't know what to do with my hands; all I know is I need to hold on to something. As if he can read my mind, Ronan guides my hands to his shoulders and I grip them tightly, digging my nails into his muscles while he cups my butt with his hands, splaying his palms over my cheeks, and continues to drive us on, his movements becoming faster and harder, matching our breathing, edging us to nirvana. I let my head fall back, eyes shut, feeling only him. God, I've missed him so much.

Unexpectedly, with one quick movement, Ronan holds on to me and flips us so I'm on my back and he's between my legs, supporting himself on his forearms, our chests touching. I look at him, his eyes bright, glossy, fiery, his body burning as he thrusts, hard, and I'm no longer able to contain my moaning. I say his name over and over again before, finally, I'm pulled beneath the waves of pleasure again. I'm vaguely aware of the way Ronan's breathing changes, how his muscles coil and his thrusts become less refined—more desperate—as he, too, seeks those few moments of blissful oblivion. I know he's there, is on the cusp of climaxing, and I move my hips to collide with his. Ronan's face momentarily takes on a pained expression before he seemingly falls into the void and comes. His head dips down as he breathes fitfully against my neck, his body tensing and releasing with each orgasmic shockwave rocking his body until he stills inside me with a deep, quiet exhale.

Tuesday, October 26th

Ronan

"I'm not okay."

I've been home for just under three weeks now, trying to settle into a new routine. I finally went back to school last week, but I have a hard time focusing. I can feel my grades slipping; I'm way too behind from missing almost two months' worth of classes. Plus, I keep having to leave early because it's still too exhausting for me to sit in a chair for more than a couple of hours. My body gets stiff, every bone starts to ache, and I end up calling Steve or my dad to come get me and take me home.

I haven't been able to keep up with the work because my mind is still so damn foggy from the meds I've been prescribed. It's not the pain pills now—my doctors have been weaning me off those—but the anti-anxiety medication Doctor Seivert prescribed when she found out about the nightmares.

I've been having night terrors every night since I was in the rehab hospital. Some nights are better than others and I'm able to wake up by myself. But most nights I can't, and the terror goes on and on until either my dad or Steve shake me into consciousness. I always startle awake, drenched in sweat, my breathing out of control, and my entire body aching. It's to a point now where I'm afraid to go to sleep and I fight it for as long as I can until the exhaustion overtakes me, pulling me under and into darkness.

Each night leads me through the same hallway, into the same living room, facing the same person, feeling the same pain, the same fear. It's relentless, and I'm fucking exhausted from the fractured sleep; the short, interrupted nights. So exhausted that I find myself zoning out or falling asleep in class, unable to focus or form a coherent thought. I doze off when I'm with my friends and Cat. She never says anything, but I know she's worried; they all are. I keep feeling their eyes on me, especially Shane's, who I think can sense my downward spiral.

I'm burdening them with my shit. I know everyone is ready to get back to normal, move on with life, and I'm keeping them stuck in this hole. They've all had to adjust their lives for me and it makes me feel guilty.

My dad is in New York full-time now, traveling only occasionally for work and to see Penny in Virginia. She comes to visit my dad on the weekends. Even this stranger had to adjust her life around me. Penny has stayed with us twice now and it's still awkward as hell having her in the house. It startled the shit out of me when I got up that first morning she was here after I came home from the hospital. I slowly figured out a way to get down those damn stairs by myself with my crutches just to round the corner and see a woman standing in the damn kitchen. For a second, I thought it was my mother—even though she and Penny look nothing alike—and it took me a good minute to get my heart rate under control.

Steve has been taking online classes to stay on top of his credits before eventually moving to Boston, though he told me the other day that he wasn't sure when that was going to happen. He feels obligated to stay and make sure I'm okay. Pile that on top of everything else.

And then there is Cat; beautiful, smart, kind, perfect Cat. Always by my side, loving me through everything, sacrificing her time with her friends to stay with me when I'm too exhausted to hang out with everyone, which has been happening more and more lately.

I haven't been to Shane's in over two weeks now, turning down most opportunities to hang out, and when they come over to spend time at my house, I end up getting fatigued so quickly that I either fall asleep on the couch or need to hobble up the stairs and to my room.

We were all supposed to hang out at Shane's last weekend to celebrate Tori's birthday, but I couldn't muster up the energy. Fuck, I couldn't even get out of bed, feeling the need to just sleep all day after almost no rest the night before, which was riddled by one nightmare after another. I ended up completely bowing out, urging Cat to go have fun, and, in the end, Steve and Vada picked her up and took her to Shane's with them.

When Cat came over on Sunday, after I again declined to hang out with everyone, Cat told me she felt like I was withdrawing, and maybe I am. I don't know. I just know that being around Zack, and Vada, and Shane, and Tori, and everyone else has been draining rather than invigorating. I don't want them to worry about me, so I put on a face when I'd rather be alone. Really all I want is to sleep a dreamless sleep and not fucking wake up.

I have thought about ending it with Cat, for her sake. It would hurt more than hell, more than the physical pain my mother inflicted on me, to let her go, but maybe it's best for her. She would have a chance to move on from this. I'm a burning, sinking ship, and she doesn't need to be dragged down to the depths of darkness with me. She is too good, too perfect to be with someone as broken as me, and I don't know how I can give all of myself to her when I'm half of who I used to be, and even that past version of me was nowhere near good enough for Cat.

It's late Tuesday afternoon and I'm sitting in Doctor Seivert's office. It's a change from before when we would have sessions at my house, but she thought the change of scenery would be good for me, so my dad has been dragging me to her office twice a week for the past week or so, since my right knee still is not nearly well enough for me to drive myself. The doctor says it'll take six to nine months to be fully healed, and even then I'll likely have pretty significant limitations. It's depressing to think that I might not be able to play hockey again or workout and run the way I used to.

Last week I found out that Drew was named captain of the varsity hockey team, purely based on seniority, since it's pretty clear I'll no longer be able to play. I anticipated this, but I'd be lying if I said it didn't affect me. I put so much damn effort into being good enough, into living up to my mom's expectations of me—getting good grades, excelling at whatever she asked of me—and in the end, none of it mattered. It was never good enough, and in just minutes she managed to destroy everything I had ever worked for.

Yesterday was the preliminary hearing, the day when some random judge would decide whether there was enough evidence that my mother beat the living shit out of me, tried to end me, and should stand trial for what she did. Luckily, I didn't have to testify, didn't have to face her. There was enough evidence even without me present. The prosecutor came to our house on Friday and it was really the first time I heard about what some of the evidence would be. Although I was vaguely aware of Steve's presence while I was on the ground, struggling to breathe, I hadn't known that Zack was there too, that he had caught part of what happened on his camera. I haven't seen the footage; I don't think I'm ready, that I will ever be ready, although I have a feeling sooner or later I'll have to watch it and relive everything.

In the end, the judge ruled that my mother should have to stand trial, which is preliminarily set for spring, though the D.A. told my dad that these things sometimes resolve beforehand, which would be the case if my mother changed her plea to guilty. God, I wish she would; I wish I wouldn't have to testify, wouldn't have to relive everything she has ever done to me, talk about it to strangers.

Yesterday was a hell of a day, and the night that followed was one of the worst yet. Every time I closed my eyes, I was right back on that god damn floor, feeling like I was drowning from the inside as my mother's face, contorted in anger, loomed over me while she beat and kicked the life out me. My dad woke me up five or six times and then ended up just sleeping on the floor next to my bed because the dreams were nonstop and I couldn't wake up from them by myself. Eventually, at around four in the morning, I just dragged my ass out of bed instead of going back to sleep, and when my dad joined me in the living room a couple hours later, he looked as sleep-deprived as I've been feeling for the past month.

I actually fell asleep during my math class today, just passed right out with my head on my desk and only woke up when Vada roused me after class had ended. My instructor stood next to her, a sympathetic look on his face, and told me to go to the office and have my dad or Steve come and take me home so I could get some rest.

My teachers have been cutting me a ton of slack, but that doesn't mean my grades aren't suffering. I just can't keep up with classwork, never mind homework, papers, and projects. It's a lost cause at this point.

"I'm not okay," I say again, more to myself than to Doctor Seivert. We've been sitting here for the last half hour, talking about the preliminary hearing and, for some reason, I suddenly felt the urge to let her know what's really going on inside me.

Seeing her for the past month and a half has felt like a delicate balance. Open up just enough to make these hour-long sessions pass, but not enough that I break open completely because I constantly feel like I'm toeing the line of losing myself forever if I open the door too far. Things have been bubbling under the surface, and I feel like I'm getting worse rather than better, which is something I've been realizing for a while now. The dark thoughts have been encroaching on my days and nights, but it really hit me last night while I was sitting in the living room in the dark with Onyx by my feet. It was quiet in the house; Steve and my dad were finally getting some rest now that I was awake and not interrupting their night with my near-constant nightmares.

My mind wandered to the bathroom upstairs—like it has so many times these past couple weeks—and the unlocked medicine cabinet that holds my painkillers and anti-anxiety medication. There's enough that, if I took it all at once, I would be asleep within half an hour—quickly enough that neither Steve nor my dad would know what I had done until it was too late. And the idea that I could just do it—end it all—that I had control of at least that aspect of my life, that I could just finally go to sleep without being afraid, excited me and scared the shit out of me at the same time. And what scared me even more was that I knew exactly how I'd do it, how to increase my chances of keeping a significant number of the pills down long enough to do what I so desperately wanted them to do.

I can't describe the stillness, the peace, and the calm that came over me when I realized I had that power—that I could just end it. And they would all be free—Cat, my friends, Steve, my dad, hell, even my mother would finally get what she's been wanting since the moment she found out she was pregnant with me.

"Can you elaborate on that for me, Ronan?" Doctor Seivert asks, and puts her notepad down on the little glass table beside her black leather chair to rest her hands on her lap. I fucking hate glass tables.

Doctor Seivert is wearing a beige knit sweater—it looks soft, like cashmere or something fancy—and she has on black trousers that only reach her high-heeled, boot-clad calves.

"I'm so damn tired. All the time," I say without looking at my therapist. I keep bouncing my left leg and I can feel how tense my shoulders are. My eyes are burning from the lack of sleep and I shut them tightly while pinching the bridge of my nose between my left index finger and thumb.

Doctor Seivert doesn't say anything, which is her way of urging me to continue talking.

"All I want... is to go to sleep." I raise my eyes now, looking at her, and even though I don't want to say the words that are burning in my chest, I hope to god she can read my face and understand what I'm trying to convey to her. I need help before I do something really fucking stupid.

She nods slowly, her lips parted as she leans forward slightly, lessening the distance between us. "Ronan, are you having thoughts of suicide?"

Her forward question is a shock to the system, and I feel shame wash through me when I nod my head yes.

"Tell me about those thoughts," she urges, her voice soft as she interlaces her hands and scoots her chair toward me a little bit more.

I tell her about last night; the relentless, vivid nightmares I've been having; the near-constant thoughts of not wanting to burden anyone any longer, of not being good enough. I tell her about the physical pain I'm still in, despite my injuries healing; and I tell her about how exhausted I am—the bone-deep fatigue I feel from the moment I wake up to the moment I close my eyes at night, no matter how much I rest; my desperation for sleep, a sleep without dreams, a sleep without the possibility of waking up.

"I wish she had finished it," I finally admit, my voice almost a whisper, expressing my darkest thoughts out loud for the first time ever. "I wish she had actually killed me. Then nobody would have to deal with this. It would just be done."

"What about your family?" Doctor Seivert asks. "What about your friends? What about Cat?"

"What about them?"

"Don't you think they would be sad if you were gone?" she asks, and I know what she's trying to do. She's trying to remind me that there are people who love me. But I know that. That's exactly the problem. They love me too much, are too invested, which means they're weighed down by what's going on with me. I can see it in their faces, feel the tense energy, hear it in their voices when they talk while I'm around.

"I'm sure they would be," I say. "But they'd move on. They'd grieve and then they'd keep living their lives. That's what Shane did after his little brother died. He was a mess for a while, but he was able to move on from it," I tell Doctor Seivert and myself, definitely leaving out the part about Shane going down a dark path of partying and drinking.

"Shane no longer misses his little brother? Doesn't get sad anymore?" she inquires, prodding me on to think logically, rationally, to see the fallacy in my argument.

"Yeah, he does, but he still has a good life," I say stubbornly.

She nods, not pushing me further because she can tell I'm about to shut down on her, just like I have so many times before.

"Ronan, can you do something important for me?" she asks finally, and I shrug. "I want to see you tomorrow morning, if that's possible. I know you have school, but I'll work it out with your dad."

My face falls. "You're going to tell him what I just told you, aren't you?" I bury my face in my hands. This is going to kill him.

"I'm going to have to. Ronan, there are a lot of people who love you. I need you to hang on just a little bit longer, okay? We will get you out of this, I promise. Will you give me a chance to help you?" she asks.

I consider her for what feels like an eternity before I nod.

"Good. Here's what I want you to do before you go to sleep tonight: picture something that feels good to you. Focus on just that, nothing else. Hold that feeling inside you tightly, let it consume you, let it get you to tomorrow when I see you again."

I nod again before she walks me into the waiting room where my dad is on the phone, I assume, with Penny. He ends the conversation when I limp out on my crutches and Doctor Seivert requests him into her office while I take a seat in one of the chairs, knowing she's about to shatter his world by telling him that his son has expressed suicidal ideations.

I close my eyes, listening to water trickling in the little tabletop fountain in the reception area, and I picture the one good thing that will allow me to make it through tonight and into the next day. The one thing that has come into my life at exactly the time I needed her the most and arguably the worst time for her—Cat. I picture her beautiful hazel eyes, her perfect face, her smile that stops a room full of people, and her gorgeous body. I recollect the way her lips feel on mine, her warm hands, her soft skin when I caress her. And I know I need to see her again, that today will not be the end for me.

My dad steps into the waiting room half an hour later. He's pale and there is so much concern in his eyes. I feel like shit for putting him through this, adding more weight onto his shoulders, and the guilt inside me grows. But he strides toward me as I get up off the chair and, with one swift motion, he pulls me into his arms, holding me tightly against him.

"I love you, Ran," he says, his voice thick and full of emotion. "I love you so much."

At first, I want to push away, to escape his hold on me. I'm not really used to any physical affection from my parents. My mom never hugged me and my dad wasn't around enough to do it. And it's always confusing as hell when Cat's mom hugs me. Really, the only person who ever holds me like that is Cat. But then my body relaxes and I let my dad hold me, allow him to be my dad, permit myself to feel his love. It's surprisingly comforting.

We don't talk on our way home, and when we finally arrive, my dad immediately makes his way upstairs to the bathroom where I know he's removing any medication from the cabinet, probably hiding it somewhere I can't find it. He's taking precautions, as he should.

I skip dinner and head to my room, switching my jeans for black sweats and my hoodie for a white t-shirt before I get into bed. My body is sapped of what little energy keeps me moving during the day. My mind and body hurt, my knee is sore, and I'm tired of using crutches, of being handicapped, of having to depend on everyone for almost everything. I grab my phone, swiping to unlock it. I text Cat before my eyes shut, despite me fighting it, and sleep overcomes me.

Me: I love you. You are everything.

***

I jerk awake, my heart pounding in my chest as beads of sweat cool my forehead and neck. My damp shirt clings to my heaving chest and I attempt furiously to catch my breath, to orient myself, to make sense of my surroundings, all the while assessing the threat level like I have all of my life.

It's pitch-black in my room, but I can sense my dad sitting on the edge of my bed, his hand on my arm. He's talking to me, but I can't make out what he's saying. The sound of my blood rushing through my head drowns out everything around me. I had another nightmare and my dad obviously woke me from it. I close my eyes and swallow hard, willing my heart rate to come down.

"You're okay, buddy. You're safe," my dad keeps repeating to me in a soothing voice, like he does every night. Steve stands in the doorway to our shared bathroom, his expression weary, and I can tell he was in a deep sleep before my night terror woke him up, too. I wonder what I say or do that is so noisy that my dad and brother—both in their separate rooms—wake up. Do I cry out? Do I scream? Neither of them has ever told me and I haven't asked.

"What time is it?" I finally mumble.

"It's two-thirty," my dad answers.

I fall back onto my pillow and roll to my side, my back to my dad.

"Do you need anything?" he asks, his hand on my shoulder now.

I shake my head. "I'm okay, Dad. Sorry about that. You should go back to sleep."

He sighs, then squeezes my shoulder before he gets up and walks back to his bedroom just down the hall.

"I love you, little brother," I hear Steve say before he gets back into his own bed, too.

I grab my phone from under my pillow. Cat responded to my message from earlier in the evening.

Cat: I love you more than words could ever say. Can't wait to see you tomorrow!

My racing mind calms as I picture her again. I hold on to that feeling that consumes me whenever I so much as think of Cat and I let myself drift back to sleep.

Wednesday, October 27th

Ronan

I get up at four after another nightmare, which thankfully didn't disturb Steve or my dad for once. My sleep has been fractured for weeks now, riddled with nightmares so vivid that even once I open my eyes, I could swear I see my mother's outline and feel the blood running down my face. I still need a couple of minutes to regulate my breathing and calm my frantic heart. Even the anti-anxiety medication does nothing to combat the dreams; it just makes me drowsier.

I shower and get dressed as quietly as possible with these stupid crutches before slowly making my way downstairs. But my dad must have heard me move around because he's in the kitchen, making coffee, when I finally arrive downstairs.

"You're not going to let me out of your sight, are you?" I say, an edge to my voice as I open the kitchen cabinet to retrieve a glass to fill it with water.

"Not a chance," he says matter-of-factly. His voice sounds tired.

To my surprise, Steve joins us in the kitchen not much later. I'm even more surprised when, at half past seven, my dad lets me know that Steve is coming with us to see Doctor Seivert.

When we arrive at her office, I settle in my usual spot while Steve and my dad sit in chairs on either side of me.

"What the hell is going on?" I ask when the therapist takes her seat across from me. "This feels like a full-on intervention."

"I just thought you could use a little more support here today," Doctor Seivert says. She doesn't have her notepad on her lap, which confirms this isn't a regular session. I'm starting to think she's going to have me committed.

Instead, she nods for my dad to speak.

He clears his throat. "Ran, you're going to Montana," he says matter-of-factly.

I knit my eyebrows together. "What?"

His eyes flit to Doctor Seivert for help.

"Ronan, do you remember the beginning of our first session, when I told you that anything you tell me during therapy will remain confidential, that I wouldn't share anything we talked about with anyone, with a couple of important exceptions?" Doctor Seivert asks.

I nod.

"One exception is when I think you're a serious threat to yourself. When we talked yesterday, I became very concerned. You obviously know that I talked to your dad about what you shared with me."

I look at my dad and then Steve, both of whom are looking at me with concern.

"I think that the fact that you're at home, in the place where the trauma was inflicted on you for so long, constitutes a barrier to your healing. You being in that place triggers a constant fight-or-flight response. You have no control over it; it's your nervous system hijacking you. Your mind and body don't have a chance to come to rest, to process the trauma like we've been trying to do. And while immersion therapy works sometimes, it usually requires very controlled circumstances. So, I think it's best if we remove you from the situation for a while. Allow you to learn some coping and grounding techniques before we expose you again to the thing that, in your mind, threatens your safety. You've never felt safe at home, so we need to get you to a place where you do feel safe, and my understanding is, from talking to you, that Montana is that place."

She pauses, waiting for a response from me.

When I don't provide one, Steve shifts in his chair, sighing deeply. "Is it okay if I say something?"

Doctor Seivert motions eagerly for him to go on.

"Ran, I don't pretend to know what it is that you've been through or that you're going through right fucking now. I feel like total shit that I couldn't protect you, that I didn't even know what was going on...." He swallows hard. "You have to go," Steve says with authority. "I thought I lost you. I walked in on Mom, I saw you on the floor, I was on the phone with 911, you stopped breathing, and I had to do CPR. It felt like forever before the ambulance got there. I just kept pumping your heart. I thought I lost you," he chokes again, looking at the floor. I can see his hands shaking. "I love you, little brother, and I can't lose you. Dad can't lose you, Shane can't lose you. Zack, Vada, Tori can't lose you. *Cat can't lose you!* You have to go. Please."

I know I have to go. I know I need to get better, for my sake and for theirs.

"How long?" I ask Doctor Seivert.

"However long it takes," she says, maddeningly. She can sense my frustration at her vague response. "I'm sorry I don't have a better answer for you right now. We'll have to keep assessing the situation, but at least a few months."

A few months? "And when am I going?" This time I pose the question to my dad.

"Tomorrow morning," he says, finality in his voice. "I booked your flight yesterday evening, and I've been on the phone with your grandparents to get the logistics figured out. Your flight leaves at eight."

"Are you fucking kidding me?" I say, more aggressively than I meant to. I stand up, beginning to pace the room as much as pacing is possible when you have a busted knee and crutches. "What about school, what about my life?" By which I mean, of course, Cat.

"You're going to go back to homeschooling while you're there. I think that will be better for you; provide you more flexibility to get rest. You won't have to be on such a rigid schedule if you can't sleep," my dad explains.

Doctor Seivert chimes in. "We'll continue to have our regular sessions twice a week remotely," she says. "Ronan, I know you don't want to leave your friends and your family, but I believe this is the absolute best thing if we're serious about helping you get better."

And again, I know they're right, but what ultimately convinces me is that this will give my friends, my family, and Cat a chance to heal, to create some distance between my crap and their lives. Out of sight, out of mind, right?

"Okay," I exhale, falling back onto my chair, my face in my hands. "I guess we'll do this."

Cat

Ronan isn't at school today, which immediately has me concerned. I text him to check on him during lunch. I don't mean to be overbearing, but he's been really withdrawn these past few weeks. It's almost like his light is flickering, and I fear it'll extinguish completely.

"I'm worried about him," Shane said last weekend while we were hanging out at the beach, celebrating Tori's eighteenth birthday. Ronan had had a rough few days between therapy, physical therapy, and keeping up with school, and he was exhausted, both emotionally and physically. I wanted to stay with him, but he urged me to spend time with our friends instead, saying he really needed some time alone.

He's been withdrawing, spending less and less time with his friends and me, and sometimes I feel as though he's pushing me away. I have to constantly remind myself that this isn't about me; it's not something that will be fixed overnight or even in a few months like his bones.

We still have no real idea of the extent of the abuse he suffered at his mom's hands—how frequent it was, or when it started—but we're starting to get an idea. I'm slowly realizing that it was a lot more pervasive than it appeared at first glance, and it was probably always a part of Ronan's life.

On Saturday, Shane told us in more detail about the handful of times Ronan confided in him, showed him the bruises, and that was just over the summer. We got into a long discussion about the signs that, in retrospect, were there all along. Signs we didn't recognize as pointing to the reality that Ronan's mother was hurting him. And thinking about it is excruciating. Picturing him being hurt by the one person who, above all, was supposed to love and protect him threatens to break my heart into a million little pieces.

"I recognize what he's doing from what my little brother, Liam did right before... right before he died," Shane added, his lips pressed together.

"Jesus, Shane, could you paint a bleaker picture?" Zack winced.

Steve looked to the ground, swallowing hard. "No, he's right," Steve said. "I'm worried, too. He doesn't sleep, he doesn't eat; it's like he can't remember who he is. He's not Ran right now. He's like a ghost of himself and it's fucking terrifying. I've never seen him like this. Guys, those fucking nightmares he has..." Steve trailed off, rubbing his hands over his face.

This whole conversation put me on edge, like I shouldn't have left Ronan that evening, should have insisted on staying with him.

I ended up calling Ronan a few minutes later to check in on him. He sounded tired but promised he was doing alright, that he had just taken some pain medication because his ribs and knee were bothering him and he was starting to get drowsy. I told him I loved him, and we hung up without him saying it back. And that's okay, because all that matters right now is that he hears from us that he's loved, over and over again. I don't expect him to have room for anything but trying to heal right now.

But it doesn't feel like he's able to get out of that dark place he's in. And although his physical injuries continue to heal, his emotional trauma is as raw as it was when he woke up from the coma, if not worse now that he's home—in the place where he was abused for so long.

I give Ronan space when he needs it, not pushing it when he doesn't want to spend time with anyone. I know he doesn't sleep well, although he doesn't really talk about it. He doesn't really talk to anyone about any of it. My mom keeps reminding me to trust the therapist, trust the process, trust that we're doing the right thing by being present for him. But I can't help but worry about him, especially when it feels like he's pulling away from me.

Me: Are you okay? I didn't see you at school this morning.

Ronan: I'm okay, but I need to talk to you. Can you come by my house after class?

Me: Are you breaking up with me? Because if so, then I'm not coming over.

Ronan: Not unless you break up with me first!

I smile to myself. Sometimes I see glimpses of the real Ronan shining through the darkness, and it gives me so much hope to know he's still in there somewhere.

Vada gives me a ride to Ronan's house after school, and I promise to update her when I get home later. Steve opens the door for me when I knock. He gives me a sympathetic smile, which alarms me a little.

"Ran is upstairs," he says, nodding toward the stairs. I see Frank in the kitchen. He waves at me as I make my way up the stairs and to Ronan's room, his door wide open.

I walk in. Ronan is sitting on his bed, putting some clothes in a navy duffel bag. "Hey," I say, looking from the half-packed bag to Ronan.

He turns around and smiles at me. "Hey, baby. Sit with me," he says, and pats the spot next to him.

I take a seat, my knee touching his, sending little sparks through my body. It's been weeks since the night at Shane's, since we've been intimate. Ronan has been in such a bad place and there has hardly been a time when we were alone long enough to talk, let alone be with each other like that.

"Why are you packing?" I ask, coming straight to the point. I know that whatever his response is, it will be painful.

He takes my hand in his, his jaw tense. "I have to go away for a while," he says, his voice low.

"What do you mean?" I say, confused. "Where are you going?"

"Montana. I have... I'm not okay, Cat." His green eyes meet mine, his brows furrowed. "And if I don't go, I might do something really stupid, something I won't be able to undo."

I immediately understand what he's saying, and his words hit me like an avalanche, making my head spin. I had an idea he was in a bad place, but I didn't realize just how bad. "Please don't hurt yourself," I beg, tears falling hard and fast from my eyes. "I love you."

He takes my face into both of his hands and, to my surprise, he kisses me softly. "You're too good for me," he murmurs against my lips.

I shake my head in protest. "No, I'm just right for you, and you know it," I say, my voice thick.

He chuckles a little but turns serious as he lets go of my face. "I'm not strong enough right now; I feel like I'm barely hanging on, like nothing is within my control. And my thoughts really scare me. Leaving might give me a chance to get better. And I want *you* to have a chance to get better!"

His gaze is so intense, conveying so many emotions where words fall short, and I understand what he's saying. He's leaving not only to give himself a chance to heal, but to give me, his friends, his family a chance to breathe and heal without having to worry about him.

"When are you leaving? How long will you be gone?" I ask, my voice feeble as my heart aches in my chest.

"Tomorrow morning. I have no idea when I'll be back, but it sounds like it'll be a few months at least." He shakes his head. "Cat, if you want out, I understand. I won't hold it against you if you don't want to wait around for me. You deserve to be happy." He makes his voice sound strong and confident, but his eyes give away what he really feels: that it would break him if I said I didn't want to wait for him.

"If you're trying to get rid of me, this isn't the way, Ran. I love you. I have no intention of going anywhere. Although I really wouldn't mind if you hurried up and got better already so I can have you, *all of you*—physically, emotionally—back here with me as soon as humanly possible, okay?" I smile through my tears.

He wipes a tear from my cheek with his thumb. "Okay," he nods, and kisses me again, softly at first, but he intensifies the kiss when need surges through our bodies.

I hitch my leg over him and sit on his lap, straddling him as I tip my head down to kiss him back, deeply. Our tongues intertwine, and I run my hands through his dark-blond hair while both his hands slide under my shirt and up my back, feeling my bare skin. I lift my arms and Ronan pulls my shirt up, then off me, and drops it to the floor before returning his hands to my heated skin. He unhooks my bra just as I become vaguely aware of Steve shutting the door to Ronan's room, and I'm grateful for the privacy he affords us because, right now, I want to feel Ronan all the way one last time.

And Ronan gives me exactly that—kissing me, touching, caressing every inch of my skin, making love to me until my body seemingly dissolves under his very touch. He tells me, over and over again, that he loves me.

***

The sun has set by the time I lie, breathless and content, in Ronan's arms, my back pressed against his front while he strokes my arm gently.

"I'm here for you, you know," I finally whisper into the dark when Ronan kisses my shoulder. "I want you to be able to talk to me."

"I know that," he says, his voice low. "But I don't want to burden you."

I turn over to face him, my bare chest touching his, feeling his hot skin on mine. "It's kind of unfair that we laugh together, but you won't share the bad times with me. I can handle it; you should try me some time," I say. "Let me in."

He only nods. I know I'm probably asking too much of him at the moment, that he's not in a place where he can talk about everything that was done to him, but I need him to know how I feel before he leaves in the morning.

There's a knock on the door.

"Guys, sorry to interrupt, but Dad asked me to let you know that dinner is ready," Steve says, his voice dampened through the door.

"We'll be right down," Ronan replies. His left hand cups my butt and he pulls me against him, kissing me deeply before sitting up to put on his boxer briefs.

We get dressed and make our way to the kitchen, Ronan hobbling down the steps behind me. We have dinner with Steve and Frank, and then it's time for me to go home.

Ronan walks me the ten minutes to my house, and by the time we arrive at my front door, I have a huge lump in my chest. Judging by the look on Ronan's face, I know he feels the same way. Tears spill from my eyes for the second time today, and he hugs me tightly.

"I'll be back," he says, his voice muffled as he buries his face against my neck, breathing me in. "God, I'm going to miss you so much."

I can't speak. Instead, I let him hold me for a long time before we finally part. I watch as he reaches behind his neck and undoes his gold necklace, only to put it around my neck.

"No, you should wear this," I say, my voice thick. "I need you to be safe."

"I will be," he promises. "And I'd feel a lot better knowing that you're safe while I'm away. Just hang on to this for me, okay? You can give it back to me the next time we see each other," he says, repeating the same words he said when he gave me his green hoodie the night the met.

"Okay," I relent, feeling overwhelmingly sad.

"I love you, Cat."

"I love you, too, Ran."

Our lips meet, and we kiss on my front stoop just like we did the night of his birthday—the beginning of "us."

Then I watch him walk away from me, into the dark. I hope he'll be back soon, that he'll step back into the light safe and whole, and still in love with me.

Finally, I turn to walk into the house. I open the front door, and my phone chimes with an incoming text message. I stop, pull my phone out of my pocket, and am immediately thrown into a spiral of panic. I didn't think the state of things could get any worse, but I was wrong.

Unknown: I told you we weren't done...

Cat & Ronan's story will continue.

Acknowledgements

Where to begin? Ronan and Cat have resided in my head since I was fourteen years old. Then, one day, when I was a second-year law student, they very suddenly and urgently needed me to get them out of my head and onto paper. And so I began writing. I wrote when I could between studying, exams, law review editor duties, externships, the bar exam, caring for my husband after brain surgery, and then being a baby lawyer. Then I got pregnant with my first child and my writing had to take a hiatus.

Eight years and three beautiful babies later, I double-clicked on my little word document and opened the roughest of rough drafts that contained the first eighty pages or so, of Ran and Cat's story. And I began to write again, the words, the characters, and the emotions, pouring out of me like a waterfall.

I didn't tell anyone about my writing for a long time until, one day, I told my husband (aka my ride-or-die, my best friend, my lover, my soulmate, my favorite person) about Ronan and Cat and he. was. hooked. I still remember exactly where we were, what we were doing when I "came clean" about my "habit" (it was raining; we were in the drive-through at John's Burgers picking up some food). If it hadn't been for my husband, I wouldn't be at this point today. So, my biggest, most heartfelt acknowledgement goes to the man who has sacrificed many date nights and has spent many hours-long car rides listening to me go on and on about Ran, and Cat, and Shane, and Tori, and Vada, and... you get the point. Baby: thank you for your input, your ideas and suggestions, your (sometimes not so well-taken but mostly warranted) criticism that somehow always made my story better. Thank you for staying up into all hours of the night listening to me read, for being there to provide comfort when I felt overwhelmed or doubted myself. In the words of Ronan: I don't deserve you.

To the whole SelfPublishing.com team, thank you for showing me the way to getting to this point right here right now. I am so lucky to be a part of such a supportive community of indie authors.

To my editing team at MotifEdits, thank you for your incredible attention to detail. Your feedback is invaluable.

To my dad who, just recently, showed me a story I wrote when I was about seven years old, who reminds me how much I have always loved to write, and who tells me how proud he is of me so much it's almost annoying: ich liebe dich unendlich.

To my mom who has instilled in me a fierce discipline, who wasn't always the warmest of individuals, but who (I'm convinced) sends me the most beautiful sunsets: growing up with you was hard, but you shaped me into a relentless, ambitious, take-no-shit woman. And for that: Thank you. I miss you more than words could possibly relay.

To my brother and sister-in-law: you live decidedly too far away from me. I miss you.

To my ARC readers: I have no words. I'm not a cryer, but you've managed to make me exceptionally emotional more than once. You absolutely rock! Your time, your feedback, your reviews... I so appreciate and value everything you do. Thank you for taking a chance on me and my book "baby."

To everyone who has ever encouraged my writing, has ever had to listen to me talk about this book (or any of the other stories residing partially on paper and partially still in my head), or who has in any way, shape, or form, been involved in any aspect of this process: Thank you, thank you, thank you! You know who you are.

And lastly, but certainly not least: my babies (who aren't actually really babies anymore) Emi, Fena, Poldi: you are tiny little energy vampires, but man, I couldn't imagine life without you. You three are my greatest accomplishment. I hope that even as human and very fallible as I am and with all the mistakes I inevitably make, you know, without a shadow of doubt, how much I love you.

Author Bio

Julia lives in a very sunny and very hot part of California (think Death Valley, except less "deathy") where she escapes the demands of everyday life by lifting heavy things, going on little getaways with her favorite people, and writing stories.

Want more of Cat and Ronan?

Sign up for my newsletter and receive an **exclusive epilogue** to *Tiny Fractures*, as well as updates on future releases and giveaways.

www.subscribepage.io/jvreese

I would also love to connect on social media. You can find me on

Instagram – jvreeseauthor
Facebook – J. V. Recse Author

Made in the USA
Monee, IL
19 April 2025